THE FARMER'S DAUGHTER ROMANCE COLLECTION

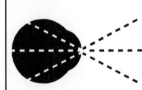

This Large Print Book carries the
Seal of Approval of N.A.V.H.

THE FARMER'S DAUGHTER ROMANCE COLLECTION

TRACIE PETERSON
MARY DAVIS
KELLY EILEEN HAKE
JILL STENGL
SUSAN MAY WARREN

THORNDIKE PRESS
A part of Gale, a Cengage Company

GALE
A Cengage Company

GALE
A Cengage Company

**LIBRARY OF CONGRESS CIP DATA ON FILE.
CATALOGUING IN PUBLICATION FOR THIS BOOK
IS AVAILABLE FROM THE LIBRARY OF CONGRESS**

ISBN-13: 978-1-4328-7593-0 (hardcover alk. paper)

Published in 2020 by arrangement with Barbour Publishing, Inc.

Printed in Mexico
Print Number: 01   Print Year: 2020

CONTENTS

CONTENTS

■ ■ ■ ■

MARTY'S RIDE

BY MARY DAVIS

■ ■ ■ ■

To Abby Stephans, who unknowingly inspired me to keep writing.

CHAPTER 1

Montana Territory, 1887

"I ain't no sissy!" Marty Rawlings yelled to Tommy Jensen, spinning around to face him. She tried to ignore him, but he just wouldn't let up.

The brown-haired boy gazed up and down Marty's calico dress. "Sure look like a sissy to me." He smirked.

"Shut up, Tommy, if you know what's good for you." Tommy was two years younger than she and had obviously forgotten who wupped whom the last time.

Tommy crossed his arms and planted his feet a shoulder width apart. "Who's going to make me?"

"I am, that's who." Marty shoved him.

Tommy stepped backward and unlocked his arms.

"You ain't gonna take that from a girl, are you?" one of his friends goaded.

Stepping forward, he pushed Marty. "Wimpy." The other two boys snickered.

Marty pulled back her arm to punch him but found herself staring Cinda in the face. She had to catch herself from hitting her sister-in-law. Cinda looked mad. She didn't say a word but her eyes spoke an abundance, none of which was good.

"Ladies do not fight," Cinda's prim Aunt Ginny scolded.

"She ain't no lady," Tommy retorted.

"That's enough, Tommy." Cinda whirled around and glared at him. He sobered quickly.

"And don't you forget it," Marty said. She reached around Cinda to poke Tommy, but she couldn't quite reach.

"You, too, Marty. Back to the wagon." Cinda pointed.

Marty stormed back to the wagon and plopped in the back, as unladylike as possible. She might not be allowed to fight, but that didn't mean she had to act like a sissy.

She fussed with her dress as the wagon bounced down the dirt road toward home. Sitting in the back of the double seat wagon on what was normally the luggage compartment, she tried to look as ungraceful as possible. Just because she was forced to wear a dress didn't make her a lady.

Frustration, anger, and humiliation all battled for control. Since her sister-in-law wouldn't let her fight on the outside, Marty would settle for the internal battle. Tommy would be worse than ever now. Why'd Cinda have to go and interfere? Every Sunday Tommy teased Marty when she wore a dress to church. She only put on a stupid dress to get Aunt Ginny off her back. But a person could only take so much. Her brothers wouldn't let her fight with the boys anymore, but her brothers were away on a cattle drive. It was about time someone shut up Tommy Jensen once and for all.

They were almost home, and she could get out of these ridiculous clothes, put on her Levi's and Stetson, and race off on Flash, her horse and companion.

Whether hauling heavy sacks of grain, plowing fields, mending fences, chopping wood, or roping and riding, Marty did it. Whatever the work, she was right alongside her brothers. Sometimes she even did more than her share or took a shorter break to prove she was as good as the men. Lucas, her oldest brother, tried to temper her, but Travis and Trevor let her do as much as she wanted. It meant less work for them. She didn't mind; the physical work felt good to her body.

At eighteen, she knew she should be thinking about marriage and settling down. She also knew her rough, tomboy ways kept the decent boys away. Most of the time, it didn't bother her. She wasn't about to change for any of them. There weren't any boys or men around these parts that interested her anyway.

Before the wagon came to a complete stop, she jumped off and rounded the side, heading for the house. She was in no mood to hear any comments from Cinda or Aunt Ginny about her "unladylike" behavior.

Marty's gaze caught on a tall stranger leaning on the hitching rail. Her heart skipped a beat, but her stride hesitated for only an instant. She tucked a stray strand of her short, dark hair behind her ear. She kept her hair cut just below her ears and loose around the neck. She liked her no-fuss hair.

Determined but cautious, she studied the stranger up and down as she strode to the house. She couldn't see the color of his trimmed hair because of his hat. As she got closer, though, she could see his eyes were brown. Who was this stranger, and why was he lounging on their hitching rail as if he belonged there?

He gave her a smile and raised his eyebrows at her as she boldly assessed him. "Howdy," he said cheerfully, tipping his hat.

Marty narrowed her eyes as she turned her head away, saying nothing. Even though she didn't look directly at him, her attention was all his as she marched up the steps and into the house.

She took stock of his assets. *Colt at his side, rifle's out of reach on his horse, warm brown eyes, and a devilish smile.* What was she thinking? She shook her head to clear it of such foolishness.

Once inside the large farmhouse and out of sight, Marty ducked behind the door and watched the man through the crack at the door hinge. His easy nature and casual smile made her nervous. He was up to something. What did he want? Why was he here? Did he know the menfolk were gone? Was that why he was here? She wished she knew the answers. She could ask him, but she wouldn't believe a word he said.

He helped pregnant Cinda off the wagon. How gentlemanly of him. Then he helped Aunt Ginny with Cinda's three-year-old son, Logan. Davey and Dani jumped down on their own and clung to Cinda's sides. These twin girls had red hair like their father, but everything else reminded Marty of her sister Lynnette. Davey's hair was French-braided down the back, while Dani wore hers in two braids, one over each ear.

Marty heard Cinda and the stranger exchange how-do-you-dos. It made Marty's blood boil, his being so nice. What was he up to?

He introduced himself as Reece Keegan, attorney-at-law.

He's a wolf trying to pass himself off as a sheep.

He handed a piece of paper to Cinda and was explaining it but not loud enough for Marty to hear. She got the gist of it when

Cinda flung the paper back at him.

"You can't have them!" Cinda pushed the girls behind her. She took a step toward the house, but he moved between her and the porch.

"I'm a court-appointed official, ma'am. I have a legal right to the girls." He stepped on the document to keep it from blowing away.

Legal right my eye. He wasn't going to lay a hand on them if Marty had anything to do with it.

She knew how to talk to his kind. She walked lightly over to the gun rack above the fireplace and lowered the Winchester. After checking the chamber, she tiptoed over to the door and across the porch.

Aunt Ginny was scolding the scoundrel. He stood stiff as a board, undaunted as she wagged a finger in his face, telling him why he was *not* taking the girls.

Marty had never much cared for Cinda's Aunt Ginny, especially when she made Marty wear a dress, but right now Marty kind of liked the old biddy.

Marty sneaked up behind the intruder and rammed the barrel into his back. "Keep your hands where I can see them."

He sucked in a quick gasp and slowly raised his hands. "You know how to use that thing, miss?"

Marty mouthed his words mockingly. Dani and Davey giggled. They knew she could shoot the hind leg off a barn rat from across the farmyard. She *never* missed her mark.

Marty cocked the rifle and pushed it harder into his back. "Try me."

Part of her wanted this creep to try something. It would give her a reason to put a hole in him. The other part of her prayed he would leave quietly. She had never shot a person before, though she had thought about shooting Tommy Jensen several times for teasing her. She had shot her share of coyotes, deer, and jackrabbits, but a man? That was different. She didn't know if she could actually shoot a human. Her brother had taught her to cherish human life.

"You ever shot a man before, miss?"

Marty ignored his casual question. If she answered honestly, he might try something, and then she would be forced to shoot. If she lied, he might hear the uncertainty in her answer. She would let him ponder his own question.

"Take the children inside and bolt the door," she said to Cinda and Aunt Ginny.

As Cinda and the others scooted around him, the stranger tried to speak. "I have a legal claim —"

Marty jabbed him with the barrel again. "Quiet."

Cinda and Aunt Ginny moved the children to the house. Cinda stopped next to Marty. "What about you?"

"I'll be fine. Now git."

Once the others were safely inside, Marty said, "Slowly remove your gun and throw it to the ground. No sudden moves. I've got an itchy trigger finger."

He obeyed. He lowered one hand to slip his six-shooter out of the holster and tossed it aside. "I'm going to turn around now," he said cautiously with both hands back in the air.

He turned slowly. She kept the rifle aimed at his chest. He studied her face, then her hands. His scrutiny made her uncomfortable. The swine was trying to read her, to see if she really would shoot or not.

He stared her in the eyes. What did he see there? He was trying to rattle her and make her lose her nerve, but it wouldn't work. She was stronger than that to melt under the powerful gaze of a handsome man.

"You mind if I reach down and get my paper?" he asked, as if they had run into each other at the general store, and he was asking if the apples were good this year.

Marty nodded. "Slowly and don't try nothin'."

He picked up the document. "This gives me the right to take those girls back to Seattle to Mr. McRae."

How could he be so casual and relaxed looking with a gun pointed at him? Unless he believed her to be no threat. Marty raised the rifle and looked down the barrel through the sight. "And Mr. Winchester gives me the right to stop you."

"Now, now, there's no need to be shooting." He looked a little nervous.

Good.

"I'll ride into town and get the sheriff. Maybe you'll be more reasonable with someone you're familiar with. The sheriff can explain my rights."

Reasonable? She was being quite reasonable. After all, she hadn't shot him . . . yet. "Your reasoning has two major flaws." A smirk twisted up the corners of her mouth.

"The sheriff is legally bound to take my side."

He was trying to convince her, but his words were a waste of good Montana air. "Flaw number one, two months ago our sheriff was thrown from his horse and broke his neck."

"Your town has no sheriff?" He raised his brows. "I can wire for a marshal to be sent up to settle this matter."

"We got a sheriff. A temporary sheriff."

"Then I'll talk to him. Is he in town at the sheriff's office?"

"Nope. On a cattle drive."

Mr. Reece Keegan, attorney-at-law, took a deep breath. "I can wait for him to return. When do you expect him back?"

"Flaw number two." Marty was getting real

19

tired of his easy manner and polite conversation like they were sitting in a fancy parlor having a cup of tea. "The temporary sheriff is the girls' uncle, my big brother, and I do mean *big.*" Her oldest brother was six and a half feet tall and quiet broad across the chest — a formidable sight. And her other two brothers were right near close to that. This half-sized lawyer wouldn't stand a chance.

"If your brother wears the sheriff's star, he is honor-bound to uphold the law," he said.

She could tell his confidence was wavering. When would he realize he was defeated?

He waved the paper as he continued. "And this is the law. It's signed by Judge Raymond Vance."

"I don't care who signed it. I ain't letting you take them and neither will Lucas."

"But if he's wearing the sher—"

"Then he won't be wearing it." Her voice lowered to an ominous tone. "I can guarantee it."

His jaw hung open a moment longer still wanting to finish his last word. He sort of reminded her of a stupid cow they once had. It seemed to have no idea of danger, sort of like this lawyer, and injured itself beyond repair. Lucas finally had to shoot it and put it out of its misery. Maybe she would be doing this Reece Keegan a favor by putting him down before he really got hurt.

He appeared to be trying to think of something to say to persuade her to simply hand over her nieces. He had to be a special kind of stupid. It was time for this worm to crawl away.

CHAPTER 2

"I think you should be going, Mr. Keegan, attorney-at-law." The words felt distasteful and dirty in her mouth. "Now!" Let him run off to town and wire a marshal. By the time he got back, she would be long gone with the twins until Lucas returned and settled this.

"Marty?" Cinda's voice was quivering.

They would all be fine if she would just let Marty handle things. She wasn't about to let anything happen to any of them. "I told you to go in the house and bolt the door," Marty said over her shoulder, keeping her eyes glued to the stranger.

The man looked behind her. Rolling his eyes, he shook his head. He looked genuinely displeased. But then shysters could do that, make you think things were that weren't. It was an old trick, and she wasn't about to fall for it and turn around, giving him the opportunity to try to take her rifle.

She heard a little whimper.

"A calico with a gun. That's a might scary sight."

Marty's eyes grew wide, and she stiffened at the sound of the mocking, gruff male voice behind her. She spun around to see a brave Cinda standing next to a scraggly man with Dani in front of him. The man leaned over her sobbing niece with his forearms resting on her shoulders and a six-shooter held loosely in his right hand. A smug, gloating grin plastered across his ugly face.

"You think she can shoot me and miss you?" the second man whispered to Dani but loud enough for everyone to hear.

Dani whimpered and nodded.

"Wylie, don't do this," the lawyer warned.

"Ain't you quakin' in your boots, being at the wrong end of a rifle held by a feeble female?" the ugly man said to the lawyer now standing behind Marty.

Feeble! If he weren't hiding behind her niece, she would show him feeble.

She raised the rifle. If he didn't get his filthy hands off Dani, he would be an ugly, *dead* man. This close she couldn't miss. His smug smile spurred her on. She had him in her sights. He stared squint-eyed down her barrel, trying to gauge if she would shoot or not. She would, if she could be sure he wouldn't move Dani in the line of fire.

Mr. Keegan came around her and took hold of the rifle barrel, lifting it so no one was in the line of fire. "There won't be any shooting here today." He pulled on the gun, but Marty held tight. What could she do? She would be helpless without the rifle. He gently pried her fingers loose. All she could do was relinquish it.

The ugly one, the one the lawyer called Wylie, stood up straight behind the crying nine-year-old, pleased with himself. He shoved the girl toward the door. "Everyone inside."

Cinda followed behind Dani trying to comfort the terrified girl. "Everything will be all right."

Wylie motioned with his gun for Marty to get moving.

She marched up the steps begrudgingly. As she passed Wylie, she socked him in the gut as hard as she could. That ought to teach him to hold a gun to her niece.

Wylie let out a gust of air and dropped his gun as he clutched his stomach. Though caught off guard, he recovered quickly, swinging out wildly at her.

She ducked out of his reach. She expected the counter blow. He came at her again; she was ready. Most of the boys she had fought were bigger than she. She could take him, if the other guy would stay out of it.

Mr. Keegan stepped between them with Marty's rifle resting on his shoulder. "That's enough, Wylie."

"But she started it," Wylie whined.

"And I'm finishing it. Now back off," Mr. Keegan said sternly. "There are better ways to do this. Legal ways."

"You tried your way, now I'm doin' it mine." Wylie snatched up his gun and stormed into the house.

Marty smiled at him smugly, knowing she got the better of him.

"After you, miss," Mr. Keegan said, unfolding his hand toward the doorway.

Marty stood straight and marched into the house.

Davey was sitting on the floor holding Logan on her lap while he sucked his thumb. Dani stood beside her with a hand resting on her twin sister's shoulder for moral support. Aunt Ginny was already tied to a chair, and Wylie was tying Cinda to another chair.

"Leave her alone! She's with child!" Marty stepped toward him but halted when he pointed his gun at her.

"I ain't hurtin' her none." Wylie sneered.

"I'm fine," Cinda said. Her sad eyes said what Marty was trying to deny herself. *We're going to lose them.*

No! Marty wouldn't let that happen. She couldn't.

"Is this really necessary?" Mr. Keegan ground out between his teeth.

"Yes." Wylie pushed Marty down in a third chair and tied her to it. "You don't want them sending a posse after us before we reach the first ridge."

Mr. Keegan clenched his fist, then raked his hand tensely through his hair, knocking his hat to the floor. He looked frustrated, like her brother did when things were out of his control. "If you had let me do this my way, there would be no posse."

Marty's mind raced. What could she do? She had to do something or they would take Dani and Davey.

"Is this all you can do, pick on women and children?" Marty asked. Wylie tied the ropes tighter in answer. "I'll fight you for them. A duel. Unless you are afraid a *feeble* female can wup you."

"I ain't scared of no calico, and I ain't never kilt a woman before. It don't sit right with a man to be killing women and children. But if you like, you can be the first."

He was no man. He was a varmint. "I ain't scared of the likes of you." Marty struggled against the ropes.

Wylie let out a boisterous laugh at her paltry attempt at freedom.

"You're just a yellow-bellied coward," Marty said.

His outburst stopped abruptly, and anger flashed across his face. He didn't like being called a coward.

"Coward," Marty taunted. She hoped she could goad him into the duel and untying

26

her. "Coward, coward, coward."

Wylie grabbed a dish towel and gagged her with it. He secured it tightly, then grabbed her chin firmly in his strong hand and said through gritted teeth, "I ain't no coward."

Marty growled in response.

"That's enough!" Mr. Keegan anchored his hand on Wylie's shoulder. "Leave her alone."

Marty was taken aback and not sure how she felt about a *man* sticking up for her. It had never happened before. Any man around here knew they would get twice what was being given if they did.

"You two better leave, and fast, before the menfolk return. Leave those little girls with us, or you will be sorry," Aunt Ginny said in a moment of bravery. She had backbone, Marty had to give her that.

"Would that be the honorable sheriff and his brothers on the cattle drive?" Mr. Keegan looked sorrowfully at Marty. "I don't think they will be getting here any time soon."

Marty closed her eyes and dropped her head. They were at the mercy of these rats. All she could do at this point was hope they would change their minds and leave without her nieces. Since that wasn't likely to happen, she started planning how to get loose as soon as they left. Then she would go after them and make them sorry for tangling with the Rawlings family.

■ ■ ■

"I don't want to go with you," the girl with the one braid yelled, holding fast to the little boy who looked to be about three. The only way Reece could tell the two girls apart was that one had a single red braid down her back and the other had two, one on each side of her head.

Wylie was trying to get the child free from the girl with one braid, and the other was helping her. "You're a bad man, and I don't like you."

Reece didn't much care for him, either, but was unfortunately stuck with him.

"You don't have to like me, kid, you just have to shut up and do as you're told," Wylie snarled.

"I won't. I won't."

Wylie reached to pry the squalling child from the girl's grasp. The girl screamed. Logan cried louder.

Wylie covered his ears, moving away from the piercing noise, and shouted, "Stop it!"

Enough was enough! Reece pushed past him and knelt next to the frightened girl. "What's his name?" He pointed at the child she held.

She stopped screaming and stared at him. "Logan." Her voice was small and frail.

"Logan, that's a mighty fine name," he said

tenderly. "Logan is pretty scared by all this screaming and noise, don't you think?" When she nodded, Reece continued, "Logan's going to stay here with his mama, and you and your sister are coming with me."

"Why do we have to go? I want to stay here, too." Her lower lip quivered, and Reece wanted to grant her request, but he was honor-bound by the law.

"Because Judge Vance said it's time for you to live with your other relatives. They get a turn to see you." He slowly took the crying child from her lap and set him aside. Logan ran over to his mama and climbed on her lap. "Do you remember your Uncle William?" Reece went on, trying to recapture the girl's attention.

She shook her head.

"He remembers you, and he really wants to see you. Judge Vance said he could see you, and you and your sister would live with him."

"Why can't the judge say we can stay here?"

"Because it's your other uncle's turn to see you." Reece held out his hand to her. "He can't wait to see you."

Tears pooled in her young, terrified eyes as she reached for his hand. "After we see him, then can we come back home?"

His heart ached for her. "Maybe." Reece led her toward the door.

Marty managed a muffled moan. He looked at her as her chair thumped back and forth in protest. Her wild eyes nailed him. If she were a man, he would be afraid of the murderous intent he read in her eyes.

The other girl started crying. "I don't want to go." She rushed over to Cinda and fell to her knees, burying her face in the woman's side. "Please don't let them take us."

Wylie grabbed her by the arm, yanking her toward the door.

"Ease up," Reece warned Wylie. "Things are bad enough. Don't make it worse." Things were happening too fast and way out of control. How could he be caught up in a kidnapping? That was what they were doing after all. He could think his way out of this, if he had a little time. But legally he had a right to take the girls . . . by force if necessary. And Wylie had made it necessary.

"Please don't hurt them. They're just little girls," Cinda begged with tears running down her cheeks.

"Don't worry, ma'am. We won't hurt them," Reece said. Before he followed Wylie out the door, he gave Marty one last look as he picked up his hat. He wished he had met this courageous young woman under different circumstances. She intrigued him.

CHAPTER 3

Before the lawyer could get to the door, the ugly one staggered back in with a shotgun aimed at his chest.

"Keep your hands where I can see them," said the old man holding the gun. "You, too, mister," he said to Mr. Keegan.

Dewight! All was not lost after all. Relief swept through Marty. He wasn't much in the way of help, but he was help nonetheless. Although he wasn't related, he was treated like one of the family. He was in his sixties and wore tattered but clean clothes.

Marty's oldest brother, Lucas, had rescued Dewight from freezing to death one winter. Like a cold lost puppy, he hung around after that. They weren't even sure if Dewight was his real name. But right now he was the only help they had, and Marty would take advantage of it if she could.

"We don't want no trouble here, old man." Wylie kept Dani as a shield. He was such a weaseling coward. Given the chance, she

31

could take him easy.

Dewight looked over at the women. "It looks like there's already been trouble. Now, leave my family alone and get off my land."

"Your family? Your land?" Mr. Keegan narrowed his eyes at Dewight, sizing him up. "Mr. Rawlings?"

"I'm not Rawlings." Dewight turned to Mr. Keegan and cocked his head as if trying to figure out a puzzling riddle. "Rawlings died. His children need looking after. I be doing the looking. My place in the hills is where I watch from. I gotta look after them young'uns."

Oh no, Dewight was losing it. Marty could see it in his incoherent gaze. He had that far-off look when he slipped from reality to reality. If she weren't gagged, she could talk to him and keep him in this reality.

"If you're not Mr. Rawlings, then who are you?" The snake Keegan could sense Dewight's disorientation.

"I'm S . . . I'm . . . D . . ." Bewildered, Dewight looked at Mr. Keegan. "I'm . . . I'm . . ."

Dewight was muddled and unsure of who he was, let alone where he was. And that jerk Keegan wasn't helping. He was purposely trying to confuse him. Marty made some noise to try to get Dani to come untie her. Dani understood but couldn't free herself from the weasel's grip. Davey struggled to free herself as well.

"You let my Essie go," Dewight said to Mr. Keegan.

Davey freed herself from Mr. Keegan and ran over to untie Marty. "The knots are too tight. I can't undo them."

Marty tried to talk, but all that came out was muffled grumbling. Frustration and anger raged inside her at being so defenseless. If she were a man, they never would have gotten the better of her.

Davey loosened the knot on Marty's gag and pulled it from her mouth.

"Get a knife from the kitchen and cut the ropes," Marty said hastily.

Davey raced to the kitchen. Dewight's eyes followed her movement. Wylie pushed Dani aside and rushed Dewight. Quickly, Wylie grabbed the shotgun. They struggled for possession. Dani ran to Cinda and worked at her ropes.

Davey came back into the room. "Hurry," Marty called to her.

Buckshot sprayed the ceiling and debris rained down on everyone. Dewight fell and hit his head. Davey and Dani screamed.

"Stop it," Marty scolded. "Just cut me loose."

With hands shaking, Davey started cutting.

Wylie grabbed the two girls by the arm. He glared down at Davey. "Drop the knife."

Davey immediately released it. It hit the

floor with a silencing thud.

"Leave 'em alone," Marty warned, "or I'll —"

"Or you'll what?" Wylie glared at her.

Marty growled at him and rocked her chair back and forth so hard she tipped over.

He laughed at her with a black-toothed grin.

"Wylie, take the girls outside," Reece said.

"What about the old man?" Wylie asked.

"I'll take care of it. Now go." Wylie had caused enough trouble. Reece took off his hat and raked a hand through his hair. The situation was completely out of control. Reece went over to the old man on the floor leaning against the wall and checked out the lump forming on his head. Wylie scooted the whimpering girls out the door.

The old man looked up into Reece's eyes. "Is the baby gonna die, Doc?"

The poor old fool. "No. The baby's fine."

Satisfied, Dewight smiled. He held out his hands with his wrists together. Reece took a dish towel and tore it down the middle. He gently bound the old man's hands and feet.

"You comin', Keegan?" Wylie shouted from outside.

"Yeah, I'm coming." He wished this had all gone according to his plan.

He came over to where Marty lay toppled over on the floor. She had almost reached the

34

knife. He put the knife on the mantle. "So the little one doesn't get hurt on it." He set a disgruntled Marty upright. "I'm sorry it has to be this way. I wanted to do this legally, but it's a little late for that now." He hoped she understood how truly sorry he was for the way things ended up here. He turned and left.

"You won't get away with this," Marty yelled at the closing door.

Wylie stood next to two horses, holding each of the girls by an arm. "They keep trying to run away. I can't git either one on the horses."

Reece felt for the frightened pair. He knew it didn't have to be this way. He could have done this legally, and the girls would have been much happier. He glanced back at the house. Everyone would have been happier. He knelt down by one of the girls. "Which one are you, Daniella? Or are you Daphne?"

She crossed her arms defiantly and stuck her nose in the air.

"So that's how it's going to be." She got her grit and tenacity from the one inside they called Marty. "Then I'll call you Two Tails." He lifted her up onto the back of Wylie's horse. "And you are One Tail," he said as he put the other one on his horse. The two men mounted and headed west. Reece looked back at the farmhouse behind them before it was completely out of sight. He hoped the women would be all right and that it wouldn't take too long before they got themselves freed. He'd given them a fighting chance.

He thought of the young woman Marty. She would probably go after her brother, the sheriff, for help. It would take at least a week for her to find him on the range, even if she knew where to look. Reece would be in Seattle by then. It would take another week or so for Marty's brother to get to Seattle. By then the twins would be in the custody of their uncle, and Reece would no longer be involved.

He wondered if he were doing the right thing and thought about turning around and returning the girls. If he did, he would surely be arrested and never practice law again. The law was his life. He had studied hard in law school and finished top of his class. He won nearly all his cases. That's what he did, kept people from going to jail or being hanged. He was good at what he did and proud of his achievements.

They plodded along with Wylie and Two Tails in the lead. As Reece stared at Wylie's back, mile after mile, he wondered what kind of a man would hire a bully like Wylie to retrieve a pair of little girls. Why hadn't the *honorable* Mr. McRae sent his own lawyer or gone himself to collect the nieces he was so concerned about?

Why hadn't Reece thought to ask these

36

questions before accepting this job? He was in too big of a hurry to get out of town for a little while, to get away from Gina Sadder, one of the few eligible women in town. She had set her sights on Reece and wouldn't give up until she had him at the altar. Hopefully, in his absence, Miss Sadder would turn her affections toward a gentleman who would gratefully return them.

He had felt like a fugitive leaving Seattle so abruptly. Reece chuckled. He supposed he was now more of a fugitive, and he had a woman angrier at him than a stirred-up hornets' nest. He hoped she would come to Seattle with her brother, and he could explain the situation and smooth things over with her.

Marty's glaring blue eyes flashed in Reece's mind. She would more likely try to kill him again. But a man had to hope for something. Her brother would keep her in check, unless his temper was worse than hers. She had alluded to her brother's determination to keep the girls. And she did say he was a good deal taller and broader than Reece.

Maybe he had better just keep his distance . . . if he could.

CHAPTER 4

Marty struggled against her ropes. It was no use. Wylie made sure she wouldn't get free. After a half hour of trying, she finally gave up. She needed to rest and think.

Logan looked up into Cinda's face. "Mama, I hungry."

"I know, sweety." Cinda and Aunt Ginny hadn't had any luck getting loose, either. They all had red, sore wrists.

"Logan?" Marty said sweetly. "Do you want some of the chocolate cake Aunt Ginny made yesterday?"

Logan nodded his head eagerly.

"I'll give you some, if you go into the kitchen and get me a knife."

"Marty!" Cinda exclaimed. "Logan, don't you dare touch any of the knives."

"But I want cake. I hungry," Logan whined.

"Marty, how could you? He's just a baby. He could get hurt," Cinda scolded, appalled at the thought of her little boy carrying around a knife.

"He's the only one not tied up. If we can't get him to help us, we could starve to death. Have you thought of that?" She could tell Cinda could feel the bite in her words.

A painful expression passed across Cinda's face as she contemplated their possible fate. "Okay, Logan, go get a knife for Aunt Marty." Logan jumped from her lap and ran to the kitchen. "But get a little one and be careful."

The three could hear noises from the kitchen but couldn't see the three-year-old. They heard a crash.

"Logan!" Cinda screamed.

Marty held her breath. She could never forgive herself if Logan got hurt. She could picture him lying on the floor, bleeding, with a knife stuck in his chest.

"Logan?" Marty called cautiously. "Are you okay?"

Logan came out of the kitchen with a big chocolate grin and two handfuls of chocolate cake. "I doed it myself," he said proudly through a mouthful of cake, spraying crumbs on the floor.

Marty let out a sigh of relief.

"Good job, sweety," Cinda complimented through her tears. "Come sit on Mommy's lap." After finishing his cake, Logan laid his head on his mother's protruding tummy and went to sleep. Cinda and Aunt Ginny also fell asleep.

Marty kept working at her ropes to no avail.

After an hour Logan woke up. Marty watched him wander around the room. Finally, he settled in the corner where Cinda kept his blocks. He stacked them and knocked them down. The crash woke Cinda and Ginny.

Logan ran off into the kitchen. He reappeared a moment later with the biggest kitchen knife they had. He walked slowly, staring wide-eyed at the large shiny blade.

"Careful, sweety." The tension in Cinda's voice sent shivers crawling up Marty's back.

Marty held her breath. *Please don't get hurt.* Logan walked up to her and laid the knife gingerly across her lap and ran off to play with his blocks. Marty let out a sigh of relief only a moment before Cinda and Ginny did.

"We got the knife. Now what do we do with it?" Aunt Ginny asked.

Cinda scooted her chair around to Marty's lap, but she couldn't reach the knife with the way she was tied. Marty tried to wiggle it off her lap into Cinda's waiting hands.

"Here it comes," Marty said.

The knife slid off her lap and hit its target. Cinda fumbled with it before it toppled out of her grasp and landed on the floor with a devastating thump.

Marty vigorously rocked her chair back and forth until she toppled over again. She hit the floor hard. It seemed much harder than the first time she did it. She would have a dandy bruise. Cinda guided her verbally until she had the knife within reach. She worked on the ropes that bound her. Her hands ached and cramped, but she kept at it until she was free. Then she cut loose Cinda and finally Aunt Ginny.

Cinda rushed over to Dewight, who was leaning against the wall asleep. Cinda's sudden appearance startled him.

"I wasn't much help, Miranda," he said to Cinda.

"You did your best," Cinda said. Marty joined her.

A single tear rolled down Dewight's cheek. "I'm sorry, Miranda."

Cinda brushed back his hair. "It's okay."

Marty was about to cut Dewight free but noticed the dish cloth wrapped around his wrist and ankles. They weren't even knotted, just loosely tied. He could have gotten free anytime. He was bound in mind more than physically. Why hadn't the man named Keegan tied him securely? She took off the bindings and went upstairs to change.

She returned a few minutes later in her layered riding attire, complete with chaps for protection and warmth.

"Where do you think you are going?" The trill in Aunt Ginny's accusation grated on Marty's nerves.

She strapped on her Colt and ammunition belt, then donned her calf-length canvas duster. "I'm going after Dani and Davey."

"You can't be serious. Those are dangerous men. We'll send word to your brothers, and they will get them back," persuaded Aunt Ginny.

"They will be long gone by then. The best chance we have is for me to go, and go now." Marty would leave with or without Aunt Ginny's approval.

"Cinda, tell her she can't do this. It's dangerous," Aunt Ginny demanded.

Marty looked at Cinda. Would she support her or try to stop her? Not that it would do any good.

"What is it you think I can say to change her mind?"

"I don't know," Ginny snapped. "Say something. It's not right for a lady to go gallivanting across the countryside by herself."

Marty kept her eyes locked on Cinda's. Marty had never acted like a lady. She wasn't about to start now. She wondered what her sister-in-law would say. It didn't really matter; Marty was going anyway. No one could stop her from getting her nieces back. No one.

Cinda reached out a hand and clasped Marty's forearm. "Bring them back safely." There were tears in her eyes.

"What?" Ginny exclaimed. "You can't be serious."

Cinda caressed her plump belly with her

42

other hand and said, "If I could, I'd go with you."

Marty knew she meant it. Cinda loved the girls as much as Marty did. Marty also knew her delicate sister-in-law wouldn't survive the trip. Cinda would be a liability, and Marty would have to look after her as well. She put her hand over Cinda's and squeezed. "I won't come back without them."

"It just isn't right, I tell you." Ginny shook her head.

"I'll pack you some food," Cinda said and headed for the kitchen.

CHAPTER 5

Marty took the loaded Winchester and filled her pocket with additional bullets. She plopped on her Stetson and headed out to the barn to saddle Flash. Marty had raised him from a colt; he had lived up to his name. After saddling him, she tied on saddlebags, a bedroll, and a canvas for extra warmth. In the saddlebags were a compact cook kit and a hunting knife. She had to be prepared in case it took longer than she expected to find these slippery men.

Marty led her brown stallion out of the barn, across the farmyard. Cinda and Ginny waited on the porch for her.

Cinda handed her an old flour sack. "There's some dried meat, hardtack, and beans," she said. "Oh, and coffee. I put in some coffee, and . . ." Cinda paused, trying to think.

"It's all right. I'll make do with whatever you packed. I won't be gone long." Her reassurance was as much for herself as for her apprehensive sister-in-law. She hoped to be back tomorrow or the next day at the latest. "I'll be fine." She stuffed the sack of food into her saddlebag.

Aunt Ginny stepped forward and handed her a lady's reticule.

Marty took it cautiously. It hung between her thumb and index finger like a dead rat. What was she supposed to do with it? "I don't think I'll be needing this on the trail."

"Open it," Aunt Ginny said, her lips pulled back in a straight line.

The bag did have weight to it. Marty opened it and pulled out a neatly folded cloth with something in it. She unwrapped it. A pearl-handled derringer lay in her hand. She never would have guessed proper Virginia Crawford would be packing a gun.

"It's a parlor gun," Ginny offered. "In case you run into trouble."

That's what she had the Colt and Winchester for . . . trouble. "Thank you." She rewrapped the gun, put it in the reticule, and in her saddlebag. Aunt Ginny wanted to do her part to help. She, too, cared for the girls. "I'll get 'em back," Marty said as she mounted Flash. "I won't bring them back here. I'll hide them. Tell Lucas, 'Stone Face.' He'll know where to find us."

"Be careful," Cinda said earnestly. "I'll pray for you and the girls."

Marty nodded and rode away. She didn't

need Cinda's prayers. Marty was more than capable of doing this on her own. And with the way she got along with God, He'd probably just get in her way.

She headed due west. They said Seattle. If that was the truth, which Marty believed it was because her sister had lived with her husband's family there, then this would be the way they would go.

She picked up their tracks before she had even left Rawlings' land. West, straight as an arrow. She got off Flash and studied the imprints. They obviously weren't concerned about hiding their path. They didn't expect anyone to be following them so quickly.

There were two sets of hoof marks, one behind the other. That meant that Davey and Dani were riding on the horses with the men; therefore, they wouldn't be traveling very fast. Good.

It was going to be a clear night. The full moon would light the way. Marty could catch up to them after dark.

The advantages to being raised by three brothers were being an expert tracker and having survival skills. She would put them both to good use now.

At age four, when her parents died, Marty's three older brothers didn't know the first thing about raising a little girl. To them Marty was just another brother. She filled the role well and with pride.

Since she was too young to stay home alone, they took her along and told her to keep quiet. She stalked them like a shadow, not making a peep. It was a game to her, seeing how quiet she could be. Soon they started explaining what they were doing and how they were able to follow an unseen animal. She learned well and put her share of food on the family table.

She swung up into the saddle and took off. She slowed her pace every once in a while to make sure the men hadn't changed direction. The fools were so easy to follow. Tracking was a thrilling challenge for Marty, second-guessing where the prey was headed. These guys were heading west by the straightest means possible. She could follow them blindfolded.

As the sun set, the temperature dropped. She figured they couldn't be much farther ahead. She slowed her pace.

Marty stopped completely when she heard the rush of a stream. If the men had half a brain between them, they would camp by water. She got off Flash and tethered him to a tree.

Marty moved silently through the underbrush until she had the stream in sight. She found the spot where the men had crossed. She studied upstream and down, trying to determine which way they made camp after crossing. When she heard a rustling noise upstream, she ducked behind a fallen tree. It was Wylie collecting water.

She chose a place farther downstream to wade across and made her way back upstream. Finding a good spot below their camp, she watched them. Dani and Davey were huddled together. They seemed well enough, although a little frightened. Reece gave them a blanket. Marty was glad Cinda had insisted on everyone wearing their coats to church this cool fall morning, even though they didn't really need them. They needed them now.

The best time to rescue the girls would be after everyone was asleep. She could sneak in, wake the girls, and sneak out. In the morning, the two men wouldn't know what happened. Even if they guessed someone had come and taken them, it wouldn't matter because she and her nieces would be halfway home by then.

Marty returned to where she tied Flash and moved him across the stream to a prime location for her getaway. She put some dried meat and hardtack in her pocket, then rested the rifle over her shoulder.

When she returned to her lookout spot, Dani and Davey were crying. Wylie was glaring at them, speaking harshly.

Marty's insides knotted. She wanted to go after him with both fists flying.

"Stop crying or I'll give you something to

cry about," Wylie ground out in a growl, raising an opened hand above his head.

Marty lurched forward but stopped herself. Now wasn't the right time. She had to wait. The sound of her nieces sobbing from his cruel words was unbearable. She closed her eyes, trying to block out the sound. She couldn't. Their weeping bit into her soul. She would just charge in there and put an end to her nieces' misery. She opened her eyes and started to stand but stopped.

"Wylie, leave them alone." Reece stood between him and her nieces.

"I cain't stand their whimpering," Wylie said with fire and frustration in his eyes.

"Then go see if you can find a town. There should be one south of here. Get some more food and a couple more blankets." Reece backed Wylie away from the girls.

Good. With Wylie gone, Marty would have only one man to mess with, if it came to that. She was relieved the nicer of the two was staying with the girls for their sake. But she had hoped for it to be the other way around. She knew she could tangle with Wylie and win. She knew his type — predictable. Reece, on the other hand, was a mystery to her. The cunning way he fought with words made him harder to figure. She wasn't sure what to expect from him.

CHAPTER 6

Marty chewed on a piece of jerky while she waited, her eyes fixed on Reece, watching his every move. Every once in a while he would look around the perimeter of camp. He could sense the danger, feel the watchful eyes on him, but didn't know by what.

Reece spread his bedroll out for Dani and Davey. The girls snuggled together. Reece pulled out a harmonica from his coat pocket. A soothing melody soon lulled the girls to sleep.

He settled down by the fire to sleep as well, his rifle cradled in his arms, his hat pulled down, covering his eyes.

Wylie wasn't back. He could stay away all night; that would suit Marty just fine.

Marty hunkered down and waited. Although anxious to free her nieces, she knew she needed to ensure the man was sleeping. It would be easier that way. She waited for two hours past the time she figured he was asleep before she made her move. He hadn't moved a muscle during those two hours.

She circled the camp so she could sneak up behind her nieces and wake them quietly. She hid behind a tree a few feet from the girls. She could almost reach out and touch them. She studied the sleeping man. His breathing was regular, his arms relaxed.

With her rifle in one hand, Marty crawled out from behind the tree, then froze when the man stirred. One arm tightened around the rifle like a child holding a toy, and the other flopped straight out to the side. She held her breath and stared at him. Her heart thumped hard, beating like running horse hooves. Would he awaken? Would she have to face him? That thought gave her a funny feeling inside, and her racing heart beat a little faster. He moved no more.

She crept a little closer with her eyes glued to the kidnapper. He remained still. Once at the twins' side, she shook the closest one.

"Shh, it's me." She put her fingers over the girl's open mouth. "Get on his horse with your sister and meet me across the river."

Marty saw Reece's hand easing down his rifle toward the trigger. She jumped over the twins. He moved more quickly to gain control of his weapon. Marty reached his side before he could and shoved her rifle barrel into his chest. He stayed his hands.

She knew he couldn't see her from this angle. It would be to her advantage if he

51

thought she was a man. "Don't move," she said in a deep, husky voice. "Throw the rifle away with one hand. Gently."

Reece clenched his jaw as he reluctantly tossed his rifle out of reach.

"Go!" Marty called over her shoulder to her nieces.

They scrambled out from under the blanket and to their feet. Dani led Reece's horse over to a fallen log, and the two girls climbed aboard the bareback horse. They did as they were told and headed for the river.

"Those girls are my responsibility," Reece said, trying to talk her out of her own nieces.

"Not anymore," she ground out, keeping her voice low.

When she thought Davey and Dani were across the stream and waiting for her, she ordered him to roll onto his stomach and put his hands behind his back.

Let's see how he likes being tied up.

"Slowly," Marty barked in her deep, disguised voice, as she stepped back from him.

She kept her eyes on his hands. When he started to roll over he brought his legs up and knocked her off her feet. She lost her grip on her rifle and toppled over, landing on her backside with a whoomph. She reached out for her rifle, but Reece jumped her, struggling for control. She fought him with all her might. She had to break free. He was too strong and just as determined as she was.

He finally got both her hands in one of his and pulled them away from her face. He drew back his other hand, fisted, ready to deliver a knockout blow. She saw the realization of her being a girl and the recognition of who she was on his face. His fist hung in the air above his right ear.

Seeing his surprise, she took advantage of the opportunity. She yanked one of her hands free and struck him across the side of the head. Dazed, he tumbled off her. Marty rolled away and scrambled to her feet. She didn't know where either rifle was, hers or his. It didn't matter. Her best chance was to get on horseback. She whistled for Flash to come and took off in his direction.

She heard him scramble to his feet and give chase. His footsteps were heavy and gaining. Marty knew if she could get to Flash, he would have no way to follow her until his partner returned. Marty and her nieces would be long gone by then. Reece knew it, too, and closed the gap between them. Just ahead, Flash trotted toward her. She would make it. She grabbed the saddle horn at the same time she slipped her foot into the stirrup. As she swung her other leg up, she nudged Flash into motion.

Reece grabbed Marty's foot as it flew through the air. He yanked her back, pulling her to the ground.

Flash stopped and neighed.

Marty tried to scramble away on her hands and knees, but he stopped her. She struggled with all her might. She had to get away. She couldn't let him get the better of her. But Reece was bigger and stronger.

He pushed her flat to the ground and twisted one hand behind her back. "Just settle down." He rested one knee on her back. He didn't want to harm her. He twisted her arm further until it hurt enough for her to quit fighting him, amazed at her tolerance for pain, then he backed off.

Not used to running like that, he struggled to catch his breath. "Now, where are the girls?"

Miss Marty Rawlings lay still, panting. She said nothing.

Apparently she wasn't about to help him without a little persuasion. Reece reluctantly twisted her arm a little more. "Where are they?"

"Go ahead and break my arm," she said through gritted teeth. "I don't care."

This was one tough little lady who wasn't going to knowingly betray her nieces for anything. "I believe you don't." He sighed. He took the handkerchief from around his neck and bound her hands behind her back. He winced when he saw in the moonlight her red wrists from the rope Wylie tied her with earlier that day.

He pulled her to her feet. Opening her coat, he relieved her of her Colt .45 and tucked it in the waist of his pants. "For safekeeping." He patted the gun.

Marty glared at him. He reached for Flash's bridle. The horse stepped backward and threw his head around, neighing.

"Flash doesn't know you. You ain't gonna touch him."

Reece didn't have time to mess with a finicky horse. He had to get those girls. He figured they wouldn't go far without Marty guiding them. He took Marty by the arm and headed back to camp but didn't get far when she sat back on the ground.

"Get up," Reece ordered. He had neither the time nor the patience for this.

"Make me." She scowled at him.

Reece frowned at her for a moment, trying to decide how to deal with her. *Make her?* He didn't want to make her. He just wanted a little cooperation from her.

Words were always his best weapon. There was no way she would be talked into anything, so words were useless. He could put a gun to her head and threaten her. That gave him an uneasy feeling. There was only one option left to him. He bent down and flung her over his shoulder like a sack of flour.

"Put me down!" She squirmed and kicked her feet.

"Are you going to cooperate?"

Marty just growled.

"I didn't think so." He adjusted her on his shoulder and marched on.

Once back at camp, he set her down by a tree. He took the rope from his saddle that lay by the fire and tied her to the tree.

He admired her courage. "You have a lot of tenacity and spunk, little lady. I like that," he said with half a smile.

She gave him a warning look like she wanted to strangle him with her bare hands. She struggled against the rope.

He broadened his smile at her puny effort to get free. "I'll be right back. I have a couple of girls to locate." He collected both rifles before he left camp.

"Run, Dani and Davey. RUN!" she yelled as he left after them.

She thought they were close enough to hear her yelling. That told Reece a lot. He shook his head. If the twins were anywhere near the stream, the rushing water would gobble up her warning. He suspected they were waiting on the other side.

He crossed the water on some stepping stones. He stopped and looked around. Which direction? "You can come out now, girls." He closed his eyes and listened for rustling sounds. Nothing. He called in another direction and listened. There. He heard it. Movement. He turned toward the approaching sound.

Daphne and Daniella on top of his horse came out from hiding. He heaved a sigh of relief. They were safe, and he didn't have to go chasing after them, worrying. He approached the girls cautiously. The last thing he needed tonight was for them to get scared and take flight. He reached out and took hold of the bridle.

"Where's Aunt Marty?" the one in the front asked.

Aunt? Interesting. "She's waiting for you two back at camp." He knew it sounded like she was there willingly but couldn't risk telling them the whole truth. He climbed up behind them and headed back.

When they got back to camp, he helped the two girls off the horse. They ran over to Marty. "She's tied up," one said angrily to him.

"Let her go." The other immediately worked on the knots.

They sounded a lot like their aunt when they growled at him. He pulled them away from his hostage. "Let's not bother your aunt."

"But she's tied up," One Tail said.

"It's for her safety." *And mine.* "This way she won't hurt herself." He sat Two Tails down across the fire from Marty, then spoke to One Tail. "Could you go over and get your aunt's horse?" He pointed in the direction of Flash.

One Tail's eyes grew big. She shook her head, looking into the night beyond the campfire.

"I'll get Flash," Two Tails said, marching into the darkness at the edge of camp to spare her sister from the misery. She tethered Flash to a nearby tree.

"Can you bring me the bedroll?" Reece hoped his luck with the girl being compliant would hold.

After he settled the girls back down, he unrolled Marty's bedroll and covered her with it. He tucked it in behind her shoulder so it would stay. When he looked her in the face, she closed her eyes and turned away. He had won . . . for now.

"You aren't going to cry now, are you?" he asked her. He detested it when women used false tears to gain sympathy and manipulate.

Marty snapped her head. "I don't cry."

He raised his eyebrows in surprise, but he believed her. She was too tough of a lady to ever show weakness.

Just the thought of crying appalled Marty. It was true, she didn't cry anymore. She had cried at age four when her parents died. She cried so hard she thought she would never stop. Less than a year later, when her sister married and left for what seemed like the end of the world to her, a world she was now headed for, she had cried and begged her to stay. Her sister left without a care for her baby sister, and Marty cried for a week. On the eighth day, she didn't cry anymore. Her five-year-old reasoning determined she had used up all the tears she had for her life. She hadn't shed a tear since. Not even when she broke her arm falling out of a tree. Nor did she cry when her sister returned, only to die. Marty didn't cry, ever.

CHAPTER 7

Marty sat awake the remainder of the night, a vigilant eye on her nieces. She drifted off near dawn, but movement in the camp woke her. Reece was up. Dani and Davey were still sound asleep. Marty pretended to be asleep as well. He stirred the fire and put on a few pieces of wood. Then he took the coffeepot and headed for the river.

Fool! She would take every chance he gave her.

"Dani. Davey," she called in a loud whisper. Neither one moved. "Dani!" she said louder. Still nothing. "Davey!" When she still got no response from the exhausted pair, she yelled, "DANI!"

Finally, Dani rolled over, forced one eye open, and looked over at her sleepily, trying to figure out where she was.

"Dani, come here and untie me," Marty demanded of the confused girl.

Dani yawned as she made her way over.

"Where's Mr. Keegan?" Dani tugged at the knot.

"He went to the river to fetch some water. Hurry. We don't have much time." Marty's words were curt. "He'll be back any minute. Hurry."

"I'm trying. The knot won't come loose," Dani said.

"In my boot I have a knife. Hurry!"

Dani found the knife. Before she put it to the rope, Reece returned.

"I see you ladies are awake." His light tone was like a bawling cow in pain.

Dani dropped the knife between Marty and the tree, then stood. Biting the inside of her cheek, she couldn't have looked more guilty if she had fallen down on her face and confessed.

He looked sideways at Dani. "I think I'd better check the rope." He set the coffeepot on the side of the fire and walked over.

Marty pushed the knife against herself and tried to cover it with fall leaves. She would find out soon enough if she missed any part of it.

Reece inspected his knots. He seemed satisfied, but as he started to look away, his head snapped back. "It looks like I got back just in time." He pulled the knife from behind her back.

Marty dropped her head. She couldn't get a break. *Just one break, God, and we could be*

61

on our way home. Not even Reece Keegan would be able to follow the path she would take. God Himself wouldn't be able to trail her.

Reece made some coffee and rustled up some grub for everyone. He had One Tail feed Marty. He didn't trust Marty, so he was forced to keep her tied up.

After they had eaten, Wylie came strolling into camp, drunk and singing saucy saloon songs.

"Wylie, that's enough singing." Reece cut him off before the song got too descriptive.

"But I like to sing, partner."

Partner? Reece didn't like being associated with this man and certainly not as his partner. They were nothing more than accomplices in a questionable deed.

"Singing makes me happy." Wylie waved a bottle of whiskey in the air. "I hope those little mites weren't too much trouble for you." His words slurred. His gaze settled on Marty as he tried to focus. He staggered over to her. "I guess you did have trouble." He spun around to Reece. "What's she doin' here?"

Reece raised his eyebrows and rubbed the back of his neck. "She wandered into camp last night." He knew Wylie would be irritated by her presence. He had mentioned several times during the ride about Marty punching him. His pride had been wounded more than his stomach. He seemed to be the type to have a long memory about things like that.

"Wandered into camp? I suppose she just happened to tie herself to that tree." He waved his bottle in her direction. "Whatcha gonna do with her?"

"I guess we take her with us."

"Nope!"

"We can't leave her," Reece said.

"Sure we can. That rope will hold her," Wylie said.

Reece could see Wylie wasn't going to be reasonable in his state of mind. He poured Wylie the last of the coffee and handed it to him.

Wylie grimaced as he swallowed the first gulp. "You call this coffin varnish coffee?" He spiked it with whiskey.

A drunk man was an unreasonable man. If he could get the bottle from Wylie, he would have a chance to sober up on the trail. "Put that down and go cool off. Splash some cold water on your face or something. We leave as soon as we are packed up."

Wylie shook the bottle in front of Reece and stomped off toward the stream.

Reece took the twins to a different part of the stream, so they wouldn't run into Wylie, to wash out the coffeepot. They didn't want to go. He figured they would be easier to handle than Marty. They had wanted to stay with their aunt. Reece knew why. Given the chance, they would have her untied in no time and disappear, probably for good. He was no tracker. Once out of his sight, he would have no hope of finding them. With no alternative, they went with him, though reluctantly.

Soon after Reece and her nieces left, Wylie staggered back into camp. His sour mood had not improved. He looked around camp and saw Marty was the only one there. He leered at her, then turned his back to her.

"If it were up to me, I'd leave you tied to that tree for the wolves to feed on," he said after a moment of contemplation. "You're trouble. Nothing but trouble."

"And you're a coward." Marty immediately regretted her words. Wylie spun around with a crazed look on his face.

He stalked over and crouched down in front of her. "I figure I'm gonna have to kill ya anyway. I can save myself future trouble by gittin' rid of you now." He pulled out a ten-inch hunting knife. "I could jist slit your throat soes you wouldn't have to suffer." He twisted the knife in front of her face. "Then when them wolves come, you won't feel them rippin' at your flesh."

Genuinely scared for the first time in her life, Marty felt helpless and vulnerable at the hands of this madman. She stifled the urge to call him any number of fitting names. Lashing out would only aggravate him more. There was no reasoning with a drunk. She struggled at the ropes and wished Reece would return. He seemed decent enough . . . for a kidnapper.

"The most humane way would be the jugular, right here." He put the cold blade against her throat.

She pressed back against the rough tree trunk.

"That would be the quickest. And it's pert near painless, so I hear. Do you reckon you deserve humane?"

Marty swallowed hard, unsure if his threat was serious or just a game. Her mind raced, trying to think of a way out. If she tried to talk him out of it, it might provoke him into doing something. If she screamed for help, he could use the knife, and she would be dead before Reece ever got here. So she remained quiet, silently pleading for her life. *God, help me.* Beads of nervous perspiration formed on her nose and upper lip.

"Just one quick, easy stroke." Wylie sadistically moved the knife.

Marty heard the click of a gun cock. "Put the knife down."

"Maybe next time," Wylie whispered to Marty. He raised his hands slowly and stood up with the knife still in his hand. He turned around with a sinister smile on his face. "I

65

was jist funnin' with her."

"Well, fun time is over," Reece said with his gun still aimed at Wylie.

Wylie put away his knife and sauntered over to his horse.

Relief swept through Marty as she let out her captive breath. She hadn't seen Reece approach but was glad he did at just the right time. She had never seen him so threatening. The fire in his eyes smoldered still.

Davey and Dani rushed over to her. "Are you okay?" they asked in unison.

Marty nodded. "I'm fine." *Just a little shaken.*

Reece holstered his gun. "Keep your hands away from those ropes, girls."

Reece took several slow breaths to calm his frayed nerves. His insides contorted when he walked back into camp and saw Wylie with a knife to Marty's throat. Reece had never wanted to kill a man before; but if Wylie had hurt Marty in any way, his life would have been in serious jeopardy.

Reece didn't know why he cared about Miss Marty Rawlings, but he did. There was something special about this young woman. She was unconventional, a little bit wild, and a complete mystery to him. He figured this attire of Levi's suited her personality more than the dress she wore back on the farm. He longed to get to know this determined young lady. Anyone that devoted and selfless was worth knowing.

It wasn't going to be easy to keep an eye on two little girls, keep Wylie from killing Marty, or Marty from killing Wylie, and keep Marty and the girls from trying to escape, all at the same time. It would have been easier to evade Miss Sadder.

He looked over at Wylie by his horse. Who was this William McRae he was working for? What kind of a man would hire the likes of Wylie? Mr. McRae had seemed sincere when he retained Reece's services. But now Reece wondered if Mr. McRae had more on his mind than the welfare of his long-lost nieces. Why didn't he send his own lawyer? Perhaps he needed him for something else, but what? What would be more important than his own nieces?

Two Tails brushed her hands together after her fifth attempt to catch Marty's persnickety horse. "I can't git him if he don't want to be gitted."

Reece stood in front of Marty and spoke cordially, "Miss Rawlings, would you please retrieve your horse?" Enough time had been wasted.

"No." She looked him square in the face and with a challenge in her eyes.

Unbelievable. He figured he could conjure up all the politeness and manners in the world, and it wouldn't make a difference. Was she purposely trying to irritate him and be difficult or was it just her way? He took in a slow, even breath. "No? Why not?"

"That would be the same as helping you. I'll have no part in kidnapping my own nieces. You're a bigger fool than you look if you think for one moment I will cooperate with the likes of you."

Now what was he supposed to do? He couldn't leave her here; without her horse she would likely die, and with her horse she would come after them again. Looking over his shoulder was no way to live even if it was only for a few days.

She was smart enough to know he wouldn't hurt her, so a threat wouldn't work. The best thing was to take her with them and let her go once they reached Seattle. He felt like hauling her up and throwing her over his horse, but he already had one of the twins to carry on his horse. They just needed her horse or someone would have to walk.

"Would you rather walk to Seattle?" Maybe that thought would bring her to her senses.

"Yup."

He stared at her a long moment. She was serious. He threw up his hands. "Fine. Have it your way."

CHAPTER 8

Marty's wrists were tied together in front of her with Reece's bandanna. One end of a rope was tied around her waist, the other end secured to Wylie's saddle horn. Though Wylie wasn't happy about taking her along, he did seem to get some sort of pleasure out of dragging her behind him.

Reece looked back at Marty. Right now she was the safest place she could be — at the end of that rope. He wished it could be different, but Wylie would just as soon put a bullet in her at this point, and Reece wasn't about to let that happen. So for now, until he could think of something, she was stuck plodding along after them, though she didn't look as though she were merely "plodding" along. She held her head high like a queen, and her steps were sure and strong. But he knew she had to be tired, not only from the rigorous jaunt but from going on so little sleep if she had gotten any at all. She probably had been watching and waiting for her opportunity last night. Luckily, he was a light sleeper. He had felt watchful eyes on him all evening but figured it was just a coon or some other forest creature keeping an eye on what food it could scavenge. He had hoped it wasn't a hungry bear. But now, in hindsight, a ravenous grizzly would have been friendlier.

He had thought by allowing Marty to have her way and walk that she would see he *would* leave her horse behind. After they headed out she would ask, perhaps even beg, for her horse and behave herself. Well, her horse had followed them, and Marty walked with determination. He figured she would walk around the world before she would give in. He had to think of a way to get her horse and force her to ride.

Lord, I know I have been lax in praying lately, but if You could manage to get that stubborn woman on one of these horses, I would be mighty grateful.

Daniella and Daphne practically sat backward, turning around to look at their aunt with pitiful expressions. Reece, too, looked back often to check on Marty. He was concerned she would fall and hurt herself, but she had too much grit for that. However, over the two hours she had been walking, her head had begun to droop and her stride had weakened.

Twice Reece had tried to get Wylie to stop for a break for Marty's sake. Wylie either didn't hear him or was ignoring him. She had to be exhausted from lack of sleep. She couldn't have gotten any more than Reece, and he got precious little. How she was still going at all was a mystery to him.

He looked back at her again. She stumbled, but caught herself, barely, from falling all the way to the ground. His heart lurched. That was it! They were stopping. He brought the group to a halt, even though Wylie belly-ached.

"What are we stoppin' fer?" Wylie was obviously perturbed.

Reece knew if he said his real reason, to let Marty rest, Wylie would keep on going. "The girls need to go to the privy."

Wylie reluctantly stopped, grumbling and cursing under his breath.

Reece grabbed hold of Wylie's arm and spun him around. "Watch your mouth! I don't think Mr. McRae will appreciate hearing about the foul way you have been talking in front of his nieces."

Wylie jerked free and stalked off.

Reece handed his full canteen to One Tail. "Would you take this water back to your aunt?" Reece would have done it himself but thought she might be stubborn enough to refuse to take it from him.

She eagerly took the water and rushed back to her aunt.

In one fluid motion Marty sank weakly to the ground in a cross-legged fashion. She didn't want the two men to know how utterly tired she was. Her feet burned, and her body ached. She wanted to lie down where she was and not move for a week. She couldn't give up, wouldn't give up until her nieces were free. The only thing that had kept her on her feet was formulating her plan. She didn't quite have all the details worked out, but the plan was good.

Her thoughts were interrupted by Davey's sudden appearance. She sat down in front of her and held out a canteen. Marty gratefully accepted the water and guzzled it. She hadn't realized how thirsty she was with trying not to look tired and defeated.

"Davey, you and Dani have to get them to let the two of you ride Flash," Marty said between swallows.

"Why?"

"Just listen. When you get the chance, you and Dani ride back the way we came. Go as fast as you can and don't look back." Marty took another swig.

"But what about you?"

"Don't worry about me. They will let me go to chase after the two of you." Marty didn't really think they would let her go, but maybe they would be distracted enough for her to escape as well. "When you are out of sight of us, cut south. They will assume you are heading straight home."

Davey's eyes filled with tears. "But Aunt Marty, what about you?"

"Stop it, Davey. You got to listen." Marty kept one eye on their captors. "Find a town and wire Cinda where you are. She'll —" Marty stopped short because Wylie was eyeing them. Marty took another drink.

"Bring that canteen back over here, girl," Wylie snarled.

Davey got to her feet and scrambled back to where Dani stood. Marty hoped her nieces had the courage to go it alone. They had to. It was their only hope of escape.

Reece raised his voice. "She can't walk all the way to Seattle."

"Then leave the little witch here. I don't care."

Reece let out an exasperated sigh. "You know we can't do that."

"Sure we can." His dead serious glare belied his light tone. "We got rope, we got a tree, and there she'll stay."

Reece rolled his eyes and sighed again. "If we could only catch her horse, one of the girls could ride it."

While the two rats argued over whether Marty would come or stay, Davey whispered in Dani's ear. When Wylie stomped off in disgust, Davey swallowed hard and gathered her courage. "I could catch Flash."

Reece turned slowly to the girl and looked down at her.

Marty hoped he didn't suspect anything.

"You wouldn't help me catch your aunt's horse before. Why would you help me now?"

Davey dropped her head shyly and kicked at the ground. "That was before you were mean and made Aunt Marty walk all that way."

Yes! Davey could make you feel sorry for her for winning first prize because someone else had lost.

Reece took a deep breath and knelt in front of Davey. He looked her in the eye.

Don't waver, Davey. She hoped he would let her get the horse whether or not he suspected anything.

"If you can get that horse to cooperate, I promise your aunt won't have to walk anymore. Is it a deal?"

Davey nodded and headed for Flash. Reece looked amazed when the child walked right up to the grazing horse and climbed up into the saddle. The horse didn't even bat an eyelash or resist the girl's prodding. Davey stopped Flash near Reece and Dani.

"Throw me the reins," Reece said to Davey.

This was Marty's cue. "He won't be bridle led."

Reece turned to her and locked his gaze with hers.

She knew he was trying to intimidate her to see if she was telling the truth. Being a lawyer, he was probably well practiced at undoing a person with an incredulous stare. Well, Rawlingses weren't regular people; they were a tougher lot. He had met his match and then some.

"Flash won't be led by the bridle." She hoped her firm tone would convince him. She needed the reins in Davey's hands when they escaped.

Reece stared at her for a moment longer, then went to Wylie's horse and untied the rope. He marched over to her where she still sat on the ground and untied the rope from around her waist. "Then I'll lead him with a rope. You stay put."

Marty simply shrugged her shoulders. When Reece approached Flash, Marty made a clicking sound with her tongue, and Flash threw his head around, snorted, and stomped his feet. Reece stepped away from the agitated animal. Dani patted the horse's neck and whispered in his ear. He calmed down.

Reece brought the rope over to Marty and held it out to her. "You do it."

Marty glared up at him. "You really that stupid to think I'd help you?"

Reece squatted down in front of her with the rope held loosely in one hand between his knees. "I promised a little red-haired girl if she got control of the horse, her aunt wouldn't have to walk anymore. She did her part. I plan on keeping my promise. The only way I can, without your horse, is for one of your nieces to walk because you *will* be riding, one way or another."

She couldn't believe how gullible he was and snatched the rope from him, giving him a shove. He fell on his backside. She marched over to Flash and waited for Reece to catch up. She held out her bound wrists. "I can't do it with my hands tied."

"Don't try anything foolish." Reece untied her.

He was the fool, giving her yet another opportunity to escape. She would be foolish *not* to take it.

Wylie put a heavy hand on Dani's shoulder to keep her put. The little girl sucked in some air and closed her eyes tight.

Marty put the rope around Flash's neck and tied a knot that appeared secure to the untrained eye but was guaranteed not to hold. Reece took the other end.

"You put that kid on your horse," Reece said to Wylie.

"Oh, please no," Dani moaned.

"Can't you see she's afraid of him?" Marty glared at Reece. "You would have to be cruel to do that to a scared little girl."

"Then you can ride with Wylie because I

doubt you are afraid of anything," Reece shot back, grabbing hold of her arm.

"I ain't ridin' with her. She's trouble. Just tie her to a tree and leave her here," Wylie released his hold on Dani.

"I want to ride Flash," Dani demanded.

"I'm riding Flash. I caught him."

"That's not fair."

"Is, too."

"Is not."

While her nieces squabbled, Wylie muttered on about Marty being nothing but trouble. She would love to show him just how much trouble she could be. He wasn't going to have anything to do with her except to tie her to a tree for the wolves.

Marty smiled and almost chuckled aloud at Reece trying to concentrate amidst the confusion.

The hold he had on her arm tightened with his increased frustration. "Quiet!"

Her nieces didn't say another word and stared wide-eyed at him. Wylie slowly tapered off to silence as well but kept his back to the group. Reece released Marty and marched over to Dani. Dani's eyes got bigger as he approached. She squealed as he hoisted her up in the saddle behind her sister. "You can both ride the infuriating beast."

Marty smiled inwardly. *Fool.* She took a casual step toward Flash to see if Reece or Wylie were paying her any attention. Neither one noticed. She figured she could free Flash with one solid jerk, sending the girls on their way.

Then all she had to do was turn around, swing up, and take off on Reece's horse. She took a deep breath and made her move. She lunged forward and yanked on the rope hanging from Flash's neck.

"Gee-up!" She slapped the horse's rump, and Flash took off. Marty turned, making her move for the other horse. She would make it to his horse before him.

Reece grappled at Flash's reins. Though he touched them, he couldn't quite get a hold of them. Out of the corner of his eye, he saw Marty heading toward his horse. It would be trouble if she got away, too. All would be lost. He leaped forward and charged for his horse. He reached it at the same time Marty did and caught hold of her around the waist, lifting her off the ground, flailing.

"Let me go!" She beat the arm he had around her with her fists. He could tell by her slight startle that she hadn't expected him to catch her.

"They're gittin' away," Wylie hollered.

The girls were headed across a small meadow and closed the gap on the trees on the other side.

"They'll be back." At least Reece hoped so. He wasn't a gambling man, but right now he was betting on Marty.

Wylie pulled out his rifle. "I should have shot that horse when I first laid eyes on him."

He aimed at the racing pair.

"No!" Marty yelled, squirming in Reece's arm.

"Wylie, put it away." Reece moved between Wylie and the girls with Marty still in his grasp. "You could hit the girls."

"But they're gittin' away." Wylie lowered his rifle. The girls disappeared into the trees. "I'm goin' after 'em."

"Don't bother. Miss Rawlings will call back her horse," Reece said confidently.

"Over my dead body!" Marty folded her arms across her chest.

"I'd be more'n happy," Wylie snarled.

Reece took a deep breath. *Lord, it seems I can't do anything without You lately. I need this wild filly to cooperate.* "Call your horse," he said.

"What makes you think I can?"

"You and that horse are like one. I think he can read your mind and knows exactly what you want him to do. I heard you whistle to him last night when you tried to escape." Reece tightened his hold around her in case she didn't realize who was in charge here. "Now call him."

She struggled against him. "You can't make me."

He bet he could, and words would serve

him well for once with her. It was a matter of choosing the right ones. "The wilderness is a dangerous place for two little girls . . . all alone . . . unprotected." Reece leaned closer to her ear and lowered his voice. "They have no food. Do they know how to forage for food?" He paused to let it sink in. She stilled in his arm. "They have no weapon or way to protect themselves against predators. What do you suppose will find them first? Bear? Cougar?" His tone grew more sinister. "Maybe a renegade Indian or two? Those red-haired scalps would be quite a prize."

He felt the fight go out of her but doubted she would admit defeat.

She hadn't thought about the dangers her nieces were unprepared to face. She let out a loud whistle, waited a moment, and whistled again.

"Good girl." He was certain calling them back was not the end, not by a long shot.

"Let go of me." She wiggled to free herself.

"So you can try to escape again? I don't think so," Reece said.

"There they are." Wylie pointed at the woods across the meadow.

Flash came right up to Marty and greeted her. Marty rubbed his nose. "Good boy."

"He wouldn't keep going. We tried, but he turned around on his own," Two Tails explained in a whine.

"I know. It's not your fault. I was forced to

call him back." Marty squirmed in his hold.

If she thought he would let her go now that the twins were safely back, he had a surprise in store for her. She had gotten the better of him too many times already. He wasn't about to think of her as weak or helpless. She was as cunning and sly as a fox, a definite intellectual challenge. And that was rare.

"Wylie, tie the rope around the horse's neck," Reece said. He quickly covered Marty's mouth with his hand to prevent her from intentionally aggravating her horse. He knew who was in control of her horse. And it was high time he took control of this whole sorry situation. If that were even possible.

CHAPTER 9

Marty grappled at the hand covering her mouth. She couldn't budge it. The low-down, no-good, dirty weasel. Reece held her firmly. It was no use. She might be smart, but he was definitely stronger. She dropped her hands to her sides. She was too tired to fight him anymore.

His warm breath fanned her cheek, and his growing whiskers tickled her ear, sending a shiver through her. Again she jerked against his grip and the unusual feelings running wild through her from having this man hold her. She had never let a man get close enough to her to put an arm around her. It caused an odd feeling in the pit of her stomach and made her heart beat faster.

She watched as Wylie tied Flash to his horse. He gave her a gloating sneer. He had won for now, but she hadn't given up. Her next plan would be better, more thought-out. When her horse was secure, Reece took his hand from her mouth.

From behind his saddle Reece untied his bedroll with one hand, keeping a firm hold on Marty with his other. He threw the bedroll at Wylie. "Put this on the back of your horse." He hoisted Marty up into his saddle, keeping a good tight hold on the reins, she noticed.

She supposed he didn't want her riding off without him. The thought was appealing, but he didn't give her the opportunity.

He swung up behind her.

No chance of jumping off the back of his horse. Maybe she was better off trying to escape herself than trying to free the girls. Once she was free, she could set an ambush.

Marty sat up straight in the saddle and slightly forward, to keep space between her and Mr. Keegan. She held tight to the saddle horn to keep herself steady.

He nudged his horse up next to Flash. "This is in the way." He snatched off Marty's Stetson and handed it to Dani.

Marty reached for her hat but was unable to snag it before it was turned over to her niece.

Reece prodded his horse into a gallop. Wylie mounted up and was close behind.

After a few minutes, Reece slowed the pace to a walk and leaned forward. "I don't bite," he whispered in her ear.

She squared her shoulders and remained forward. He may not bite, but if he got any closer, she would.

Not having slept all night and walking most of the morning, coupled with the rhythmic plodding of the horse, made her drowsy. She was comfortable on a horse. Before long, Marty struggled to keep her heavy eyelids open but found it impossible. They finally shut, and her head dipped forward.

When her chin hit her chest, she jerked her head up, and her eyes flew open. She repositioned herself in the saddle and stretched her face by opening her mouth and eyes as wide as they would go. She blinked several times and raised her eyebrows up and down to try to revive herself. It worked for about thirty seconds before her eyelids shut again.

When her head dropped forward for the third time, Reece put an end to her misery. His one arm was partially around her, holding on to the reins, his hand resting on his knee. His other hand was planted on his upper thigh.

He wrapped his free arm around her waist and gently pulled her back into him until she rested against his chest. Her resistance was minimal. She was half asleep. Her head bobbed forward. It couldn't be very comfortable, not that sleeping on a horse ever could be. He took a chance she wasn't faking sleep and momentarily wrapped the reins around the horn. He slowly tipped her head back, trying not to wake her. She settled her head against his chest.

He rested his chin on her head. Holding her like this seemed so right. Like she belonged there. Why should he be so attracted to her? Why this woman who hated him?

She certainly didn't fit his idea of what a woman should be. And maybe his attraction to her was as simple as that. She was so different from any woman he had ever met, and it was going to get him in trouble. He kept expecting her to act meek and mild. She didn't do any of the silly things other women did to get what they wanted. She was strong and courageous. She boldly went after what she wanted and didn't cry if she got hurt or didn't get her way.

Now that he knew her better, he wouldn't underestimate her again. She wasn't about to give up until she had her nieces or died trying. Unfortunately, it was his job to see that she didn't succeed in the former, and he would do everything in his power to prevent the latter from happening as well.

When Marty woke, the sun was low in the sky. She couldn't believe she had slept the whole afternoon. Ahead of her she could see Dani and Davey being led by Wylie. Marty pulled away from Reece and sat up straight, not because she disliked being so close, but because her backside ached from sitting so long in the saddle. Reece kept his arm around her waist but didn't stop her from leaning forward.

He pulled the horse to a stop. "I think we both need to stretch our legs." He climbed down and offered a helping hand to her. She brushed it aside and jumped down on her own.

Reece clasped her hand. "To make sure you don't get lost."

Marty strained to free her hand but her efforts were in vain. She kept her hand stiff at first, then she slowly relaxed; she wasn't sure if she disliked his warm hand on hers or not.

Just after dusk they came over a rise. Nestled in the valley that spread out for miles to the north was a ranch house. Reece and Wylie had stayed there on their way out to pick up the girls and were invited back on their return trip. The ranch owner greeted them and invited them in for chow.

Daniella and Daphne were put up for the night in Sally's room, the rancher's step-daughter.

Marty bunked in a bedroom by herself. It looked like it had once been a lady's room with ruffled curtains, a lace doily on the wash table, and a pink ruffled quilt on the bed. Reece secured her wrists to the bedposts, loose enough so she could sleep comfortably, but not so much rope that she could free herself and hang him with it. Reece left with the promise to see her in the morning.

"Don't be surprised when you find us gone come sunup," she called after him.

Reece had planned to get a good night's sleep on a nice soft bed of hay except for two things gnawing at him: a ranch full of questionable men with a pretty, young woman just inside the house, and Marty's threat to be gone with her nieces by morning. So here he was sleeping on the hard floor in the hall outside of Marty's room and a few feet away from the little girl's room where Daniella and Daphne slept. He peeked in on them to make sure they were indeed there. He wouldn't put it past Marty if they weren't, but they were there all snug and fast asleep.

Reece spent most of the night listening to every little noise that drifted through the house. He checked on the girls five times before giving in to exhaustion.

Somehow, he managed to oversleep. The stirring downstairs woke him. The first thing he noticed was Sally's bedroom door ajar. He crept over and peeked inside. He flung the door open wide when he found no one there. He quickly glanced around the room. No one.

He stormed over to the room Marty was supposedly in and flung that door open as well. He was surprised to see her still bound. His temper flared.

"Where are they?" he bellowed. He hadn't thought it necessary to tie them up as well.

"Who?" she asked, struggling to wake up.

Or was it an act? He wouldn't put anything past her anymore.

"Don't act all innocent with me. The girls, that's who. Where are they meeting you? Where did you tell them to hide?" He got right down in her face. He wasn't just upset at them being missing and the inconvenience it would cause. He was also angry at her for sending them off by themselves again. Hadn't she learned anything from the first time?

"Dani and Davey are missing?" Marty tried to sit up.

"Like you didn't know."

"I had nothing to do with it. Untie me. I have to find them." She wildly twisted at the ropes.

"I would love to have you as a witness on the stand. You have a sweet, innocent look and those big blue eyes. A jury would be suckered in by anything you told them. A few tears and I would almost be convinced as well, but I know you better than that. Now what have you done with them?"

Marty balled her fists. "I don't cry," she said through gritted teeth. "I didn't have anything to do with them runnin' off. Now untie me so I can find them. So help me, if anything happens to them, I'll kill you."

"Bravo." He clapped his hands. "But I will find them myself. I pray you haven't sent them off to their doom." On that note he turned on his heels and left, closing the door firmly behind him.

"Wait! Take me with you. Come back and untie me, you no-good shyster," she screamed through the closed door.

Lord, Reece prayed, *help me find those girls and let them be safe.*

Marty twisted her wrists and yanked on the ropes. She would get free. She had to find her nieces. How could they be so foolish to try to escape by themselves? They wouldn't. Not without her. They were waiting, hiding. If she could get loose, they could all three escape. She worked with more diligence at the ropes. She needed to think instead of acting on raw emotion.

She was making progress when the door burst open. Davey and Dani skipped over to the bed. She sagged back against the headboard. They were safe. Her relief was short-lived when she realized they had not escaped.

Both girls spoke at once about baby kittens in the barn, six of them. They had snuck out early with Sally to see the newborn kittens.

Reece came in a few minutes later with a plate of food for her, his head down. He glanced up at her. He resembled a pup who had just been scolded.

"Aunt Marty, you're bleeding!" Davey squeaked.

There was a trickle of blood from Marty's wrist to her elbow. "I'm fine." She brushed the damage aside.

Reece looked up quickly at her and glared at her wrist. He handed off the plate to Dani and examined the injury.

"I said I'm fine." She tried to pull her wrist away.

Reece gave her a heartbroken look and whispered, "I'm sorry."

Marty saw pain and tenderness in his eyes. It was as if she could see right into his soul. She believed he was sorry, sorry for more than just her cut wrist, sorry for all he had done. The hostility she felt toward him dissolved in those two little earnest words, "I'm sorry."

"You girls untie your aunt. I'll be right back." He slipped out the door. Just as soon as they had untied Marty, Reece returned with some bandages and alcohol.

"You don't have to fuss over me." No one had fussed this much over her since her ma died fourteen years ago. "It's not that bad."

He reached for her wrist and turned it over. "It could get infected." He dabbed at it with a clean cloth and warm water, working gently, with more caution than necessary. He picked up a new cloth and poured whiskey on it. "This is going to sting like the dickens."

"Just do it. I've been hurt worse before." When he hesitated, she pushed his hand down. As the whiskey-soaked cloth touched her wound, she sucked in a quick breath between clenched teeth. He kept repeating he was sorry as he quickly cleaned the wound.

He let the wound get air while she ate her breakfast. Then he sent the girls downstairs to eat while he wrapped Marty's wrists. He wrapped and wrapped and wrapped.

"It doesn't need so much bandaging on it." She didn't think it needed any. It wasn't even bleeding anymore, just sore. So much fuss for a little rope burn.

When he wrapped her other wrist as well, she knew he was a real wimp. Though it was red, it hadn't bled. Fine, let him think she was a sissy. He would let his guard down. It would make escaping that much easier. When he reached for the rope to tie her back up, she realized how cautious he was. He was leaving nothing to chance.

"You don't need to tie me up. I won't try anything until we leave." It would be easier to escape without so many people around.

He continued in silence, and with it her stomach tightened. Something was wrong. The eerie silence was like spiders crawling up her back. "My word is good." Why wouldn't he look at her? Her gut was rarely wrong, and it was telling her something. She tried to jerk her arm free, but he held it firm and tied it to the bed.

When he had her secured, he looked up slowly into her eyes with pain and sadness in

his own. She could see it in his eyes.
He was leaving her behind!

CHAPTER 10

"No!" she shouted. "You can't leave me here." She fought wildly against the ropes like a rabid animal. "I have to go. Dani and Davey need me. Untie me. I have to go. I have to be with them. I have —" She seemed to realize her panic and stopped to take a long, ragged breath. "You can't do this. You can't leave me here."

"I can and regret that I will. I can't take you along. You're too much trouble." The girls disappearing this morning had been the last straw for him.

His job was to see the twins safely to Seattle to their uncle's care. Her job was to see he didn't accomplish his job. And Wylie was a mean cur who was still fuming about her punching him. If she caused any more trouble, Reece didn't know if he could stop Wylie from harming her, maybe even carrying out his threat to slit her throat. He couldn't let that happen.

"Please don't do this." She begged him. "I'll

be good, I promise." She struggled against the ropes.

He sincerely wanted to let her go. "Don't fight the ropes. You'll only reinjure yourself." He had wrapped her wrists with extra strips of cloth to protect them from the ropes and herself. He didn't know if it would do much good with her determination.

The twins were probably better off with Marty and her family. Would William McRae risk his own life for his nieces? No. Reece was sure of it. He had only met the man once. He had seemed sincere in his plea for his nieces' well-being. But had he gone to find them? No. He sent Reece and Wylie. How would an upstanding man like McRae know a scoundrel like Wylie?

But this young woman was completely committed to her nieces. She risked her life, more than once, to get them back. And she wouldn't give up now, Reece was certain. Marty would risk her life again. He had never seen anyone so fiercely loyal.

Remarkable, indeed!

He tapped her nose with his index finger. "I'll be back for you, little lady."
Lady. Ha! A lot he knew.

Marty refused to be sucked in by his earnest promise. She had believed his sorry and woebegone looks before and look where it got her. Even if he was telling the truth for a change, it would be a wasted trip. She planned to be far from this place. She drew comfort from knowing he would be with her nieces, and they wouldn't be at Wylie's mercy. He would protect them from harm, even if he was a lying shyster.

After two days of being tied up, Marty thought she was getting through to little Sally Davidson. Sally was eight years old and assigned the task of feeding Marty her three meals a day. Four times a day someone came to untie her and stand guard outside the door while she used the chamber pot.

Sally's blond hair had been cut unevenly above her shoulders as if someone had taken hold of the whole wad and whacked it off. Marty told the girl stories to pass the time, and she could tell the girl wanted to help her escape but seemed to need someone else to give her permission. Marty couldn't blame her, she was only a child, and Marty didn't want to get her in trouble.

"Could you just loosen the ropes before you leave? My wrists hurt." Marty held her breath, hoping Sally wasn't wise enough to suspect her motives.

Sally scrunched her face up this way and that as she thought about it. "I guess that would be okay." She leaned over to loosen the rope around one wrist.

"Sally Marie Davidson!" came a stern voice

from the doorway. "What are you doing?"

Sally jumped from the bed and was across the room in a single move. "Nuthin'." Her eyes were huge and said guilty as if she had screamed it. She twisted her foot on the floor.

In the doorway stood Nevin, Sally's twelve-year-old brother. He had the same blond hair but was round and pudgy. He squinted his beady little eyes and looked around the room, from his sister to Marty, then the food tray. He settled his gaze back on Sally. "You're only s'pose ta feed her. Now take the tray to the kitchen."

Sally picked up the tray and walked to the door. As she passed her brother, she paused long enough to stick her tongue out at him.

Before Nevin pulled the door all the way shut, he opened it a crack and poked his head back in. He started to say something then stopped.

"You want somethin'?" Marty was curious what was on the boy's mind.

"You sure your man's comin' back fer you?"

"He's not my man."

Nevin cocked his head. "But he said . . ."

"I don't care what he said. He's a lying, no-good rat who kidnaps helpless little girls."

The boy's eyes grew larger with every word. He eased back into the room. She had his attention and didn't want to lose it. "Them two cowards waited until the menfolks were gone, then they come along, tied us up, and run off with Davey and Dani."

At that moment Sally pushed back into the room, her timing perfect. "How would you feel if someone tied you up and stole your sister?" She paused to let him chew on that a moment and hoped he cared a little about his sister. "They are just little girls."

Sally stood up straighter, to show how big she was.

"They don't deserve to be ripped away from their home and family and be sold like cattle. You're lucky Sally's still here. I'm surprised they didn't take her when they left."

Sally's eyes spread wide as saucers.

Marty hadn't meant to frighten her, just convince the boy. She supposed she got a little carried away. "It's a good thing they were only needin' little girls with red hair."

Sally let out a puff of air.

"Nevin? Where are you, boy?" came a voice from downstairs.

"Pa," Sally whispered. Her wide eyes turned fearful. The two left quickly, like scared rats. He wasn't their real pa. He had married their ma and continued to look after them after she died in childbirth a year ago.

Marty had drifted off to sleep when Sally came in smiling like a beam of sunshine. It was hours later, and Sally had a lunch tray in her hands. She put the tray on the chair by the door and waltzed over to the wardrobe, flinging open the doors with flair. She pulled out a bright pink dress and held it up to herself.

"Isn't it pretty?" she said.

Marty rolled her eyes. If you liked that sort of thing, she guessed so.

"It belonged to Aunt Lilly. She's Pa's sister. She run off with one of the ranch hands." She skipped to the bed. "I picked this one for you to wear."

Marty crinkled up her nose. "Why would I want to put that thing on?"

"For your escape."

Marty's eyes widened. This conversation was suddenly interesting.

Sally explained how Marty needed to blend in with her pa's guests to sneak by them out to the barn. Sally untied her and left with Marty's clothes and went to the barn to wait for her.

The people gathered downstairs were dressed up, and Marty blended in, at least in appearance. She didn't know what the occasion was and wasn't about to hang around to find out. No one seemed to notice her, and she slipped out the back door to the barn as quickly as possible.

Once out in the barn, Nevin and Sally met her in one of the stalls. Sally returned her hat and gave her a bundle with her clothes in it.

"What are you three up to?" came a rugged voice from the stall opening.

The three spun around and stared wide-eyed at a young man with sandy-colored hair and brown eyes. He leaned lazily on the stall post chewing on a piece of straw. He couldn't have been more than twenty years old.

Marty seriously hoped he wouldn't be a nuisance and try to stop her. She hoped he thought she was simply a guest strolling through the barn. She sized him up and decided not to aggravate him. It would only make it more difficult to get away. "I intended to go riding." She moved forward to leave. "But I don't see a horse in this whole stable to my liking."

The young man put his foot on the adjacent post, blocking Marty's escape.

CHAPTER 11

Marty stared at the leg and boot blocking her path. He was going to make a nuisance of himself after all. She would try talking first to not draw unwanted attention, but if that didn't work, she would use other means of persuasion. "Please, move your foot. I would like to get by." She tried to sound pleasant, but the words came out forced and terse.

He lowered his foot slowly to let her pass. When she did, he leaned forward and said, "Flash's in the field."

Marty stopped one step past him. She turned slowly and looked up at him. What was he up to?

"I've had a terrible time with him." He strode over to the stable doors that opened to the field. "Can't get him to come into the stable. High-spirited . . . like his owner, I presume." He cocked his head toward her.

She glared at him, unsure of what to think of this stable boy.

"I saw you arrive with those two men and

the little redhead girls. Keegan asked me to look after your horse. He said if I didn't, you'd be pretty mad and to watch out. You don't look dangerous to me."

Just try and stop me.

"If you want your horse, you're going to have to get him yourself. He won't let me get near him since I unsaddled him the first night."

He didn't think she was capable of getting her own horse. She would show him. With her gaze still on him, she whistled for Flash. Flash's ears perked, and he turned her direction. The ranch hand looked in awe at the galloping horse. He didn't slow down at the fence but sailed over it and came to a stop at Marty's side.

Marty turned to her faithful companion and rubbed his nose. "Good boy." He rooted at her hand. "I'm sorry, boy. I don't have anything for you."

Flash snorted and bobbed his head.

"That's some animal you got there." He reached out and stroked his neck. "I wouldn't feel right about letting you ride by yourself."

"I can take care of myself."

"You gotta let her go," Sally whined. "You just gotta."

He looked down at Sally and knelt to be at her eye level. "And why is that?"

"Pa's gonna make her one of the entertaining girls if her man doesn't return," Nevin said in her defense. "It ain't right."

So some of those "ladies" were saloon gals in residence to keep his men happy and return some of his own money to his pocket. "I told you, he's not my man."

"She has to save Daphne and Daniella. Those bad men kidnapped them," Sally added.

The three explained the whole story to him before convincing him to let her go. "Nev, go to the kitchen and get her some grub for the trail. Sally, you climb up in the hayloft and give a holler if you see anyone coming."

Nevin and Sally scrambled away to their assigned tasks. The young man took Marty over to a pile of hay. He brushed the hay away and pulled back a tarp. There was Marty's saddle and all her gear, guns included. Her guns were clean and empty. She loaded her Colt and then the Winchester.

"You aren't going to shoot me now, are you?" He held up his hands in mock surrender.

But Marty's response was serious. "Only if you get between me and my nieces." She picked up her saddle and flung it on Flash's back. Nevin returned with the food.

Marty looked down at her dress. "I need to change."

"Here comes Butch," Sally yelled from the loft.

"No time now." The stable boy shoved her

up in the saddle. "Are you sure you want to do this?"

Marty nodded. "Thank you." She nudged Flash into a gallop away from the house, heading due west.

Marty rode hard and fast, weaving in and out of the trees until she was sure no one had followed her. She swung down off Flash and let him wander by a trickle of water, pooling by a large rock that she leaned against. Her heart thundered in her chest just as Flash's hooves had thundered on the ground. She had gotten away and was on her way to her nieces. *Hang on, Dani and Davey.* She looked west. *I'm coming.*

She changed into her jeans and riding clothes and stuffed the dress into her saddlebag. She walked for a while with Flash trailing behind her. It felt good to be moving after being rooted on that bed so long.

After about half an hour, Flash nudged her shoulder, and she climbed back on. They moved along at a good clip, but not the breakneck speed they had for their getaway. She went as far as she dared, even into the dark of night.

When she unloaded her gear, she noted that everything was there: her cook kit, ammunition, bedroll, even the coffee Cinda had packed for her. As if someone had expected her to need them. Did Reece know she would get away? Did he really intend to come back for her then? Why did it bother her that he might not? Maybe because she needed to believe he was a good man deep inside and wouldn't let any harm come to her nieces. It tore at her thinking some harm might have befallen them.

After she ate, she settled down in the cold mountain air and attempted to sleep but stared up at the stars instead. The night was clear and cold. She wondered if she should bother to pray. She doubted God would bother to listen to her. He probably didn't like her much because she wasn't much of a lady. And if He did, He would only get in her way and try to stop her.

She rolled to her side and stared into the fire. She was anxious to keep on the move but knew she needed rest to keep up her strength.

Cold and wet, Marty finally rode into the city called Seattle. The rain battered down on her. She had been riding in a steady downpour for the past two days. A hot bath and dry clothes would feel wonderful even if the only thing she had was a slightly damp dress.

Seattle was huge by Marty's standards. She had never been in a town this big before. Her small town of Buckskin was more or less an accident. The local ranchers grew tired of the distance they needed to travel for supplies, and it grew from there. Now there was a livery, saloon, telegraph and post office, general store, barbershop, blacksmith, and schoolhouse that doubled for the church when the circuit preacher was in town.

This Seattle was a bit overwhelming. Marty had never seen so many people in one place. She had read of big cities, but it was nothing like experiencing one. She looked around in wonder at the number of wooden buildings. How would she find her nieces in this big place? Should she knock on every door? And what if the McRaes lived outside of town? This wasn't going to be a simple retrieve and leave. She needed a foolproof plan. Simply kidnapping them wouldn't work here.

She rode by a saloon, a grocer, another saloon, a blacksmith, and another saloon. It seemed that half the places in town were saloons. Marty pulled into one of the livery stables across from a hotel. She boarded Flash and headed across the street for a room and a hot bath.

As soon as Marty entered the hotel lobby, she could feel several pairs of eyes on her. She eyed seven dirty, unshaven men gawking at her. They were not at all embarrassed at being caught. Even Marty had enough manners not to stare. She decided to ignore them and headed for the front desk.

"I would like a room."

The man behind the desk gave her an odd look. "You're a girl."

"I'm well aware of that shortcoming." The group of men gathered around the desk and Marty. "Now, may I have a room?"

"Yes, miss." He turned and retrieved a room key, number 17.

"I told ya she was a she," one of the older men said, throwing out his chest.

"Well, she don't dress like one. Anyone could've mistook 'er fer a boy," a tall blond said.

Marty rolled her eyes. The men continued to speak around her but not to her. She wished they would leave her alone. She signed the register. "Sir, where can I get a hot bath?"

"I'll have one sent up to your room immediately," the clerk said.

"My room?"

"Yes, miss. I can't let you go to the bathhouse down here."

"I'll take her bath up to her," said a particularly dirty man. She wondered if he even knew what a bath was.

"And I'll help her," said another man.

"I can manage on my own." She pulled out her Colt and spun the cylinder. "Any objections?"

The men shook their heads and stepped backward.

"You men git along," the desk clerk said. "The dining room will be open soon for supper. Now git." The men shuffled away in a huddle to the other side of the lobby and watched her.

"Miss, maybe you would prefer to stay at one of the nicer hotels," the clerk said apologetically. "We don't get many ladies here. You would probably be more comfortable in another part of town. I wouldn't feel right taking your money without letting you know."

Marty smiled stiffly and said, "I can take care of myself." Why did every man she met think she was some helpless ninny? And why were those men constantly staring at her? Hadn't they ever seen a girl before? It was probably that they had never seen one dressed in trail clothes. Well, she didn't care what they thought of her.

"What's with those men? Don't they approve of a girl wearing pants?"

"No, miss. That's not it a'tall. Out here men will take a woman jist about any way they can git one."

Marty raised an eyebrow.

"What I mean is, women are still pretty scarce around here, and the men aren't too particular." He realized how that sounded and immediately stammered, "Not to say that you're plain or somethin's wrong with you. You're right pretty. You'll probably have five or six men fighting over you. If you're looking for a husband, that is."

Marty narrowed her gaze. "Well, I'm not." She snatched her key and strode upstairs.

She could feel the men's eyes on her, and a chill ran down her back.

CHAPTER 12

The bathtub came quickly, and the hot water followed within a half hour. She slipped into the steamy water with a moan of delight. She ached all over from the long days of riding and the hard ground at night. She soaked her tired body until the water cooled and her skin wrinkled. She didn't normally sanction such luxury, but she hadn't expected to arrive until after dark. She had some extra time to plan and think.

After her bath, she donned the dress that was now dry and faced herself in the small wall mirror. As she stared at herself, she thought of her nieces and Mr. Keegan. Had he kept them safe? Were they even here? She combed through the mass of wet, dark curls with her fingers. She hated her hair when it was wet. The unruly curl in it sprang to life. It was just long enough to tuck behind her ears. Normally she wore her hat until it dried to calm it down.

She looked down at all the bright pink

ruffles circling 'round and 'round her. The ruffles were bad enough, but did it have to be so pink? She swished over to her trail clothes, hoping they were dry enough to wear down to supper. She grabbed hold of the sleeve of her shirt, her hand visibly wet. She let her gaze fall over the hideous dress. She was starved, and nothing was going to keep her from eating, not even a sissy, ruffle-ridden pink garment. She was tired and hungry, and if anyone so much as snickered at her, she would deck 'em.

The dress had no pockets, which forced her to take Ginny's reticule to put her room key and money in. She felt naked without her gun and strapped on her Colt, which made the ridiculous dress look even worse. If she had seen a woman dressed as herself with a gun strapped to her hip, she would have laughed out loud. She took off the gun belt and settled for the derringer. She locked her door and pretended she belonged in the ridiculous frock. She hiked it up, showing her worn work boots, but didn't care. How did women walk in these things all the time, when they couldn't even see where they were going?

As she descended the stairs, she took each step slowly to keep from tripping. When she reached the bottom and looked up from her feet, she was surrounded by five of the seven men from earlier. They had all washed up and combed their hair back, and a couple had even shaved.

"May we escort you to dinner?" one asked slowly and carefully.

These men were eager. She didn't see any way to avoid them, and they might prove helpful in her search, for they certainly knew the city and its people. She didn't take any of the offered arms, but walked with the men to the dining room. It was rather rustic like the rest of the hotel. Marty liked the no-frills atmosphere. Her clothes had enough for the whole building.

When she sat down at a table, the men crowded around.

A robust older woman came over to the table and pushed her way past the men. "If you're not eating, you're leaving."

"I'm having whatever she's having," one of the men said, pointing to Marty. All the others echoed him and grabbed chairs to sit down.

They might be acting silly, but at least they weren't laughing at her for wearing a dress. They seemed harmless enough. They didn't seem much different from her brothers, just hardworking men. She ordered roast beef, potatoes with gravy, and a biscuit.

Marty figured she could get all the information she needed from these men before her supper arrived. But none of them knew anything about a pair of redheaded girls nor had they heard of a Reece Keegan. A couple of them had heard of some bigwig by the name McRae but didn't know if it was a William McRae.

"I think his name was Aaron," another man said. "Yeah. Aaron McRae. He had something to do with the railroad."

Aaron McRae? Marty couldn't believe it. The twins' father here? But her sister said he died. Even Dani and Davey said he was dead. Had her unreliable sister lied to her own daughters?

So it wasn't really an uncle after all who was after them. Had her sister lied to them all? Was she protecting her girls from him? How would she fight her nieces' own father?

After she had eaten her meal, she said, "I will give a reward to the man who can find out where Mr. McRae lives or any information about my nieces." These men could probably use a little extra money, and the incentive just might be the thing to get her some results.

"What kind of a reeeward?" asked a man with a scraggly beard and mustache. "A kiss?" His eyes lit up, and the other men smiled and nodded eagerly, too.

Marty wasn't used to seeing men with facial hair. Her brothers were always clean shaven as her pa had been. She looked from one expectant face to the next, unsure what to say.

"I'll take that reward," came a voice with a familiar ring to it from the back of the crowd.

The men hung their heads and parted.

Reece Keegan stood dressed in an expensive East Coast suit looking dapper and handsome. She was startled by the fact she was glad to see him. She couldn't believe this was the same man, but he was, and she wanted a piece of him. "You!" She lunged for him with both fists balled, ready for a fight. "You can eat my fists."

He grabbed her wrists and struggled to control her to keep from being hit. "I should have known you wouldn't stay where I put you." A smile played at the corners of his mouth.

"Where are they?" She twisted her wrists.

He wrestled her arms behind her back. "I'm glad to see you haven't lost your spunk."

Marty growled. Spunk! She would show him spunk. She strained against his hold, but it made no difference so she gave up. Hard physical work had made her strong for a woman, but it still never compared to the natural strength of a man. It just wasn't fair.

The fact that she was actually glad to see him made her even angrier. After all he had done, how could she want to see this scoundrel? She rationalized he was a familiar face in a strange town.

Marty heard the cocking of several guns, all aimed at Reece's head. These men were useful after all.

"We seen her first."

Reece didn't seem rattled at all. Didn't this man know danger when faced with it?

"Call them off, Marty."

One side of her mouth turned up. "Why should I?"

"Because I'm the only one here who knows where Daphne and Daniella are."

Her smile slipped, and she tugged at her arms.

The guns moved closer to Reece's head. He tightened his hold on her. "Call them off."

She glared at him. "Back off, boys."

The men cursed but backed down and holstered their guns.

Reece turned to the group of men and said, "Miss Rawlings is through entertaining for the evening."

Most of the men grumbled, but one spoke up in her defense. "I don't think the lady wants you here."

Reece raised his eyebrows to the man then looked down at Marty. "Is that true, Miss Rawlings? Would you like me to leave?" The twinkle in his eyes said, "You'll never find them."

She gritted her teeth. "No, I don't want you to leave." She wanted him to leave, but at the same time she didn't. It was all so confusing.

"I'll be close by, miss, if you need me," said

the man who had spoken up for her. The others nodded that they would, too.

"Thank you, but I'll be fine. I can take care of myself."

The disheartened men left reluctantly with their heads hanging.

Marty stood in Reece's embrace waiting for him to let her go. For one fleeting moment she thought how nice it would be to be like other women, weak and helpless, falling into a man's arms and letting him take care of everything. It was hard always being strong. She quickly came to her senses. If she wanted something done, she'd have to do it herself.

Reece had had a knot in the pit of his stomach when he left her at that ranch. But it was necessary to keep Wylie from harming her. He needed to be in control of the situation, but part of him remained with her. There were just too many uncontrollable elements. A man who would take money from a stranger to hold a young lady without batting an eyelash or asking a single question was definitely a questionable man. He hoped she would be safe until he returned.

When the rancher's telegram came saying she had escaped, he wasn't sure whether to be relieved or worried. So he took hold of both emotions and waited for word of her arrival.

He was certain she could take care of

herself. He also knew there were many unknown dangers; even the strongest man could die out in the wilderness. He checked every hotel and livery stable in town and left word to get in touch with him if anyone saw a young lady matching Marty's description. Today it paid off. She was finally here and safe. Which was more than he could say for himself if she had anything to do with it. She was obviously still angry as a peeled rattler.

Reece released her slowly and was on guard for another attack. "What's your room number?"

"Seventeen. Why?"

"We need somewhere private to talk." He took her by the elbow to lead her away.

She jerked free. "I'm not going anywhere with you." She walked away.

"You will if you want to know where your nieces are."

Marty stopped in her tracks but did not turn around.

Reece came up beside her and motioned toward the dining room exit. "Shall we go?"

Marty sneered at his offered arm. She held her head high and walked with all the grace of a cowhand up the stairs. She kept her dress hiked in the front to keep from tripping on it. Reece followed close behind, shaking his head in amusement. One minute Marty could be wild and unorthodox, the next obedient and conventional with a tomboy slant, but always with a single determination — get her nieces back at all costs. She was single-minded, like a dog with a bone. She wouldn't let go.

Marty stopped at the door marked 17. Reece held out his hand. "The key."

"Why don't you jist tell me where they are? Then you can be on your way."

"Because there are a few things you need to know first." He wiggled the fingers of his outstretched hand, coaxing her to give him the key.

She jerked open her reticule and rammed her hand in, fishing for the key. She hated being backed into a corner. Who knew how long it would take her to locate the twins? She knew nothing about tracking someone in the city. Out in the wilderness she could track and make her way easily but not here in this unknown, sophisticated wilderness called Seattle.

Marty didn't know what to do until she felt the cold steel of the gun barrel. True it was just a single-shot derringer, but she could make that one shot count without causing death, at least not right away. With a sketchy plan in mind, she curled her fingers around the key and slapped it into his waiting hand.

CHAPTER 13

Reece unlocked the door and let Marty enter first. He swung the door shut, and as he turned he saw the miniature gun as she slipped it from her bag. Suddenly, life moved in slow motion. A myriad of thoughts dashed through his mind. If she still thought of him as a threat to her or her nieces, she would likely shoot him. He had to make her listen to reason, but not with a gun in her hand, even a small one. He had to get it away from her.

He lunged for her as she spun around, knocking her back. They fell together across the bed. She tried to maneuver the gun, but by the grace of God, Reece managed to pin her wrist to the bed. He pried the gun from her grip. "Not your usual weapon."

She growled at him and hit his arm and shoulder with her other hand.

He tucked the gun safely away, and he pinned her other wrist.

"You have one thought on your mind,

woman — putting a bullet in me," Reece said, exasperated and out of breath from struggling with her. He found it difficult to get control of her. She was strong.

"You're wrong. My only thought is of Dani and Davey. But anyone who stands in my way jist might have to dig out some lead."

He understood her better now and knew she would do whatever was necessary to get them back.

"Don't shoot me. I'm on your side." He wanted her to understand that he cared about her and her nieces.

"My side! You kidnapped 'em." She tried to twist free but fortunately he had the advantage.

"I was hired to bring them to Seattle to their uncle. It was wrong. *I* was wrong."

"Then you shouldn't have taken the job," Marty spat back.

"I know, but if I hadn't, Mr. William McRae would have found someone else, someone less favorable, who would." Reece let her think about it. She probably hadn't considered that.

He had to make her see this was not his doing. William McRae was the one responsible.

He could feel her relax a little, no longer fighting him. He felt something had changed in her opinion of him. It probably wasn't a big change, but at least it was a start. "I truly am sorry for what I have done."

"Now you're sorry. It's a little late for sorry."

"No, it's not too late. I want to help you get your nieces back. If you will only listen to me."

Marty twisted her wrists slightly in his grasp and glanced at his hold on her. "I don't seem to have much choice."

"This isn't my fault. You are the one who keeps trying to kill me. I'm only defending myself. And I'm getting real tired of you pointing guns at me." He glanced around the room and settled his gaze on an armchair. "If I let you up, will you promise to sit nicely in that chair over there and listen to what I have to say?"

Marty gave a quick nod of consent. He got up off the bed, pulling her by the wrists with him. He slowly released her, testing the waters. She stood defiantly.

"You promised to be good." Reece pointed his finger at her.

Marty rolled her eyes but said nothing and did not make a move to cooperate.

Reece figured she needed some prodding. "All right. Have it your way." He took hold of her wrists.

She yanked free and stormed over to the chair. She stared at it for a moment before plopping herself down and folding her arms across her chest. She gave him a you-may-have-won-this-battle-but-I'm-going-to-win-the-war look. He believed she would, too.

He paced back and forth with his hands clasped behind his back like he was giving a summation to a jury. "First of all, I would like to tell you how sorry I am for taking your nieces the way we did and tying you up."

"Sorry! It's too late for sorry." Marty rose from the chair.

Reece raised his eyebrows and pointed back at the chair as he saw the intent on her face to come after him. "Please sit down, Miss Rawlings. I don't want to have to tie you to that chair." He already hated the way he had treated her and her family and that he had frightened the girls. He wanted to do it differently, but Wylie had given him no choice. He really didn't want to manhandle her anymore, if he could help it. "Please, Miss Rawlings. I want to tell you where your nieces are, if you will just sit down and listen."

He was relieved when she moved back toward the chair, even though her look divulged her murderous intent toward him. If given the chance, would she really hurt him? He hoped the opportunity never arose for him to find out.

Marty wasn't sure she really wanted to listen to a man who could tear a family apart for the sake of money. What choice did she have? He possessed the information she needed to rescue her nieces from the clutches of William McRae.

She had met him a couple of times when she was five and her sister had gone to see his brother, Aaron. He gave her the creeps then, and the thought of possibly facing those cold gray eyes once more made her uneasy. If someone had to take her nieces, she supposed this Reece Keegan wasn't so bad. He had been kind and gentle with the two scared nine-year-olds. Actually, he seemed quite good with children.

She narrowed her eyes at him. He was sorry. She would make him sorry all right. She would sit here long enough to find out what she needed to know, then maybe she would tie him up. That way he couldn't stop her from retrieving them. See how he liked it.

On the off chance he was telling her the truth, she sat down. She seriously doubted he was capable of honesty; after all, he was only a lawyer. If anything had happened to either Dani or Davey, she would shoot both his kneecaps and watch him writhe in pain, then leave him begging for help.

"Your nieces are quite safe, I assure you," he began as if reading her mind.

"Your assurances mean nothing to me."

"Very well. But your nieces are still safe and will remain so as long as you don't cause any trouble."

"Are you threatening them?" Marty tightened her grip on the arms of the chair.

"No, I am not. But if William McRae thinks you are threatening what he wants, I don't know what he might do. He is not a man to be trifled with. Since my return, I have been learning as much as I can about the man."

Marty recalled what her supper companions had said about Aaron McRae being here. "What about the girls' father? He's the one behind this. He's here in Seattle."

"Their father never set foot in Seattle."

Marty huffed. He knew nothing. How was he going to be any help? "Aaron McRae was headed for Seattle. My sister came here with him. The men in the dining room said he was here. Maybe you can't find him, but I will."

Reece nodded with understanding. "Aaron McRae Senior did live here. Your sister married Aaron McRae Junior. He died six years ago in the eastern part of this territory. He and your sister never completed the journey to Seattle. Just why, I have yet to find out. Some sort of falling-out with the family is my guess."

"So Davey and Dani's father really is dead?"

It was more a statement of recognition than a question, but Reece confirmed it anyway. Marty felt a tinge of remorse and sympathy for her nieces. She knew the anguish of losing your parents at a young age.

"William McRae is a powerful man with a great deal of influence in this city. If he wanted to make trouble for you, believe me, he could make plenty. I would ask you to stay away from the hearing, so the McRaes won't be aware of your presence. Since that is unlikely, I'll give you a word of advice. Don't cause any trouble or let them know you might cause trouble."

Trouble was exactly what she had in mind, and from the arch of his eyebrows he could read it on her face. His eyes were warning against it.

She needed more information. "What's this hearing?"

"There is to be a hearing the day after tomorrow to determine permanent custody of Daphne and Daniella. A formality really as far as the McRaes are concerned. With no one to contest, they will be granted custody."

"Contest?"

"Object."

"But there is someone to *contest* — ME!"

"They don't know about you yet, unless Wylie has told them, but I doubt it. Their ignorance will work to our advantage."

Marty thought a few minutes on this new information. "If you think Mr. McRae will harm the girls, why did he want them in the first place?"

"When Aaron McRae Senior died, the family was shocked to find Aaron Junior named in the will. Aaron Senior believed his son would come around. He wanted his son to know he never gave up on him, and he loved him. Money is the only way the McRaes know how to show love."

The love of money is the root of all evil. Lucas had taught her that from the Bible. He also taught her that family was more important than money. And land was important because it kept the family together.

"The family made no effort to find him so he could receive his inheritance. Aaron Senior's lawyer spent his own money to locate his friend's eldest son, but by the time he located Aaron Junior, the young man had passed away, and your sister had moved. When the McRaes found this out, they jumped in, thinking that they could somehow get his money with him dead. If they could bring Lynnette into the fold, they could get Aaron's money from her. They thought the poor thing wouldn't know how to handle all that money."

Her selfish sister would have had no problem spending any amount of money . . . all on herself, of course.

"Three months ago they located a doctor whom your sister had seen in Spokane Falls. He said he had told her she should go home to her family. The McRaes figured if she had been seriously ill, she had returned to the Montana Territory with the girls, and if they were lucky, she had died. They persuaded a judge, a close personal friend, to grant them custody of the girls.

"This is where I came in. I was hired as an officer of the court to retrieve a pair of unfortunate girls who had been withheld from the family that *loved* them. I was even authorized to compensate your family for any inconvenience the girls may have caused while in your care."

"Compensate? Inconvenience?" Marty's anger boiled. "We would never take money for caring for our own flesh and blood." She hated this sittin'. She needed to be up, movin' around. If she got up, he might not tell her what she most wanted to know. But then, how hard could it be to find powerful William McRae?

"Basically, they figured you were some sort of poor dirt farmers who needed money. They can't comprehend that anyone would value people more than money."

She squeezed the arms of the chair and released, squeezed and released. "If they want the money, they can have it. We don't need it. We jist want Dani and Davey back."

"It's not that easy. Legally the money and the girls go together. A judge can't override Aaron McRae's will. Where the girls go, so goes the money. And the McRaes want that money."

CHAPTER 14

Reece took a deep breath. At least Marty was listening to him. "The only way to get the girls back is to do so legally. If the McRaes can't possess the girls legally, they can't touch the money. So we have to figure a way to keep them out of reach of the twins' money."

"We?"

"I would like to represent your family in the courtroom."

"Why would we want you?" Her tone accused him of all sorts of misdeeds.

"The hearing is the day after tomorrow. Even if you could secure a lawyer in the next twenty-four hours, he wouldn't have time enough to learn about the case and be prepared to face the McRaes' lawyer. Without adequate legal representation, you don't have a chance at receiving custody of your nieces. I'm your only hope. You're stuck with me whether you like it or not."

"Well, I don't like it. And I'm not so sure I'll be needing a lawyer at all."

Reece saw a glint of trouble brewing in her eyes. She was a loaded gun, cocked and ready to go off. "Promise me you won't do anything rash."

"I'll promise you nothing."

"Please, Miss Rawlings. If you snatch the girls and try to run with them, the authorities will come after you. They know where you would be headed. They would catch you. You would never be able to rest easy as long as you were looking over your shoulder for the McRaes' next move.

"I assure you I am a very fine lawyer." As soon as he got the words out he could see she was going to protest, and he knew why, so he said it before she could. "I know my assurance means nothing to you. But I did graduate top of my class and was very successful back east before coming to the Washington Territory. I have been quite successful here as well." But he had to admit he was so caught up in his own brilliance most of the time, he had forgotten to be human. That saddened him now.

"If you were so successful back east, why did you come out west?" Marty's pompous question rankled him.

"I wanted to prove to myself that my success wasn't because of who I was but because of my abilities."

"And who was it you *thought* you were?"

"Third son of one of the top lawyers in

Boston; destined to be the next partner in Keegan, Whitehurst, Keegan, and Keegan. I thought one more Keegan was one too many in the firm with my father, my brother-in-law, and my two older brothers. I wasn't sure if my success was really me or my family name. So I went where my name carried no weight to see if I could do it on my own. And I have."

"Modesty is not one of your attributes."

"I do what I do well. I won't hide the fact. My abilities will serve you well. You'll see when I get your nieces back."

"What if I don't want you for a lawyer?"

He knew he couldn't force it upon her. "If you come into the courtroom with another lawyer, one better qualified and equipped than myself, I will step aside." He bowed with a flourish. He knew full well she couldn't, but as long as she felt like she had a choice, she would be less resistant to his help.

Marty's thoughts jumped as she weighed her options. The only way to get the girls back free and clear was to go to court. The idea of court was like vinegar in her mouth. But she had to admit she would do better in court if she had someone who knew what to do. Someone like a lawyer. Unfortunately, the only lawyer she knew was the very man who had snatched her nieces in the first place. She squinted her eyes at him. Could she really trust him? She was out of her element here. She hated to admit it, even to herself, but she needed Reece.

If he was as successful as he boasted and the McRaes were as powerful as he said, would he really risk his standing in the community to help her? If he had any honor whatsoever, he would. Still she doubted it. She made no protest to his offer. How could she? Like he had said, she was stuck with him.

He looked at her, trying to read her thoughts.

"The hearing is the day after tomorrow at ten in the morning. I'll send a carriage around at nine-thirty to drive you to the courthouse."

"I can get there myself. You said it was only a few blocks away. I'm not helpless."

"I'm well aware of that fact. I just thought you would appreciate a ride. I guess not." He headed out the door, but looked back at her one more time.

Her heartbeat quickened, and she felt like she couldn't breathe for a moment. She didn't want him to leave just yet. Then she got angry. She was infuriated that a simple look from him could awaken strange feelings in her.

But she wanted to believe him. She wanted to trust him. That was another thing Lynnette had ruined, Marty's ability to trust others. If she couldn't trust and depend on her own family, whom could she trust? Herself. She made sure others could trust and depend on her. Next to herself, the only other person she trusted was her oldest brother, Lucas. Even with him there was a speck of doubt that maybe someday he, too, would let her down. The broken trust of a small child is hard to mend.

Marty walked into the lobby from a grueling day of shopping with a package under each arm. There were actually women who enjoyed that sort of thing. What an awful way to spend your day. It accomplished nothing productive, just wasted time. She would rather have been out slopping the pigs or cleaning stalls in the barn.

"The stores of Seattle will never be the same, I fear."

Marty spun around toward the familiar voice. She glared into the face of Reece Keegan. What did he want now? She turned to head up to her room.

Reece rushed over and blocked her path. "You're not even going to say hello?" He flashed her a brilliant smile.

There it was again, that little feeling and her heart thundered like a herd of stampeding cattle. The skunk. "I thought if I ignored you, you'd go away."

"Sorry. Like I told you yesterday, you're stuck with me." His smile turned mischievous. "Unless, of course, you have found a better lawyer."

She knew he knew she hadn't. "What do you want?"

"I thought we would talk about your family. Let's sit over here." He motioned toward some chairs on one side of the lobby. He ignored her protests and carried her packages for her, like a good gentleman. As she sat down, he said, "That color is very becoming on you. It brings out your blue eyes."

Marty didn't know what to say. She had never been complimented by anyone outside her family. It made her uncomfortable, so she looked down at her royal blue shirt. She liked the color and wore it often. She wasn't sure why; she just liked it.

"Now tell me about your family."

She furrowed her eyebrows and eyed him. "Why?"

"I need to know the kind of environment the girls were in and the people who surrounded them, so I can emphasize all the reasons the girls should live in Montana with the family they know and love." He scooted his chair so he was at an angle to Marty's chair and could look at her while they spoke. "Let's start with your brother, the sheriff." He seemed to be pleased with this angle.

"If you think I'm difficult, you haven't seen anything compared to Lucas." Lucas had raised Marty and her older twin brothers,

132

Trevor and Travis. They weren't as serious as Lucas, but if you tried harming the family, watch out.

She told Reece about her brothers, her sister-in-law, Aunt Ginny, and her nieces. She told of her parents' deaths when she was four. Lastly, she spoke of her sister's leaving, return, and her death.

After Reece had all the information he needed, Marty went up to her room. She unwrapped the dress she had bought and hung it up to keep the wrinkles from setting. The store clerk had told her to do so. She never cared before about wrinkles in her clothes, but her sister-in-law's aunt always said wrinkles were never in fashion for a lady. She didn't much care for being a lady, but she needed the judge to believe her capable of caring for her nieces.

The dress was the same color as the new blue shirt she wore. It had black stripes and was accented with black piping. Not one ounce of lace or a single ruffle was to be found anywhere on it. It was perfect, at least as perfect as a dress could be. She couldn't believe she had willingly bought a dress. A shiver ran through her. Only for someone she loved so dearly would she do such a distasteful thing.

The next day Marty stood before the small wall mirror assessing her total appearance. If she had to wear a dress, this one suited her fine.

She found a pair of lace gloves in the things Sally had packed for her. Her heart warmed as she thought of the girl and her brother. Marty wrestled the dainty gloves onto her hands. They were disgusting things and completely useless. They weren't sturdy enough to work in and sure as shootin' wouldn't keep her hands warm with all those tiny holes. They were good for disguising her callused hands.

When Marty stepped out of the hotel, the heavy mist hit her like a wet blanket. She wondered if the sun ever shone in this place. She had spent an hour trying to tame her curls and get her hair pulled back so she looked the part of a lady.

The drizzle wasn't too bad as long as she stayed next to the buildings, but when she had to cross a street, she ran into trouble. A curtain of water slapped her face. The streets themselves were nothing but mud, two inches deep. She had bought a pair of lady's boots yesterday as well, and now they were covered in mud and her stockings were wet. She held her dress up out of the way of the mud. At least that would stay clean. Now she wished she had accepted Reece's offer of a ride.

CHAPTER 15

By the time Marty reached the courthouse, her dark curls had popped out on all sides of her head. She took her handkerchief and blotted her face dry. She didn't dare touch her hair or it would worsen. She smoothed her wet dress and strode inside. There were a lot of people already there, but Judge Vance had yet to show.

Marty stopped to look for her nieces. All the staring eyes made her uncomfortable. She scanned the room for Dani and Davey. Where were they? Did she have the right place? Relief swept over her when she spied Reece. She was glad to see him even after all he had done. His unflappable, confident nature had a way of making Marty feel calmer, less on edge.

He motioned her to the front of the courtroom with him. Before she reached him, she spotted Davey and Dani. They tried to rise and go to her, but two women, one in her late thirties, the other around sixty, reprimanded them and kept them in their seats. In front of the women sat the red-haired William McRae with his attorney. Marty looked away quickly when he scrutinized her, trying to penetrate her soul. His stare resembled the weather — cold and gray.

Marty went over to Reece, hoping he could do as he boasted and get her nieces back. He was her lifeline. At least until she got her nieces back.

The McRaes huddled with their lawyer. They seemed to be discussing Marty. They were as distressed by her presence as she was by theirs. She longed to rush to her nieces. Their eyes beseeched her to take them away. She wanted nothing more than to do just that. She clutched the string of her bag.

Like the rest of the spectators, Reece stared at Marty. He couldn't help himself. She was stunning. She didn't realize the stir she caused among the men. She was trying to show the judge she was an ordinary lady. But there was nothing ordinary about Marty Rawlings. Reece noticed the new dress. She certainly hadn't brought it with her from Montana. That must have been what she bought yesterday.

Her hair was pulled up in a tidy bun on top of her cute head. Loose curls framed her face and lay at the nape of her neck. She was the picture of femininity. No one would guess otherwise, except for the masculine stride she tried to hide.

Reece knew what she was up to, at least in part. She wanted the judge and everyone else to think she was an ordinary, *helpless* lady. They would be unsuspecting when she sprung her trap. She was up to something, of that he was sure. He didn't know what exactly, other than that the end result would be her leaving town in a hurry with her nieces.

He noticed her working the handle of her reticule between her hands. Oh no. She hadn't brought her derringer, he hoped. He prayed she wasn't planning on holding them all at the end of her gun and taking the girls. It would never work. Everyone would know she would have only one shot. She wouldn't be that stupid, would she?

No, but she might be that desperate.

He reached over and grabbed her bag.

Marty looked up at him startled.

He pulled it from her grasp. "I'll hold on to this for you."

Marty started, but didn't protest. She knew now wasn't the time or place. She was almost thankful he had taken the temptation from her reach.

"I assume since you came alone, I am to be your attorney." Amusement twinkled in his warm brown eyes.

Marty rolled her eyes, but didn't dignify his

comment with a response. Reece smiled.

An elegant young woman behind Reece tapped him on the shoulder. "I have never known you to be so rude, Reece dear. Aren't you going to introduce me?"

Marty opened her eyes wider. *Reece dear?*

Reece forced a smile and turned stiffly to the woman. "Gina. This is Miss Martha Rawlings, Daniella and Daphne's aunt." He motioned toward Marty. He turned to Marty and continued, "Marty, this is Miss Gina Sadder," motioning toward the woman.

"It's nice to meet you. Marty, is it?" The woman smiled a counterfeit smile.

Marty got the distinct impression she meant the opposite. Judge Vance's arrival spared her from responding.

The judge was annoyed with the complication Marty's presence caused. In order not to show his favoritism and tip his hand, he had to hear both sides of what was supposed to be a quick hearing. The McRaes' lawyer played on the fact that these darling girls had been cruelly withheld from a family that loved them. To deny a grandmother from seeing her only grandchildren was heartless.

Reece stood up. "I will speak on behalf of the Rawlings family." He straightened the front of his coat. "There was no formal inquisition into the other family. Assumptions were made on little or no information. Very little was known about them. We cannot presume they are bad people simply because we don't know them." He continued extolling the virtues of both Marty's family and Montana Territory.

By the time he concluded, you would have thought the Rawlingses were royalty and Montana a glorious kingdom. Marty felt proud of herself and of Reece. She had experienced his competence firsthand. He could make anyone sound wonderful. She had heard the importance of speaking well. Reece was living proof. She could see for the first time the power of the right words.

The judge took a short break to figure out how to rule in favor of his bribe and not show blatant favoritism.

The courtroom was silent as Judge Vance returned, seated himself, and looked from the McRaes to Marty and back again. He cleared his throat. "I have come to a decision," he said loud enough for everyone to hear. "It's unfair for one family to have sole access to the girls without giving the other family time to get to know them. I grant William McRae temporary custody. There will be another hearing in six weeks. At that time I will consider the children's well-being and make a final judgment."

Shocked, Marty looked at Reece. How could he smile? He betrayed her with false hope. The weasel.

Reece rested his hand on her forearm.

"Don't look so worried. This is the best we could have hoped for under the circumstances," Reece whispered. "Now we have time to prepare properly. We will win in six weeks."

Marty's mind raced. Her nieces would be in the hands of William McRae for six weeks! She had to do something and abruptly stood.

Reece took hold of her arm. "Marty, sit down."

She pulled her arm free. "May I say something, sir?" she said to the judge.

Reece stood next to her and whispered sideways, "Address him as Your Honor. And don't be insolent."

Judge Vance reluctantly agreed.

"Your Honor," Marty said, unsure what to say next. "My nieces are frightened. How could you possibly think they would be better off with strangers?"

"Watch what you say," Reece said through gritted teeth.

She glanced up at him, then back at the judge. "What I mean is, they have traveled a long way and are in a strange place surrounded by people they don't know." Marty spoke slowly, choosing her words with care. "Any nine-year-old would be a little frightened. If they could be with me, they wouldn't be so scared." *And we could leave town the minute no one is looking.*

"What is it you want?" The judge sounded

irritated.

My nieces.

"What Miss Rawlings is proposing," Reece jumped in, "is to accompany her nieces to the McRaes' residence to help Daniella and Daphne adjust to their new surroundings. With Miss Rawlings there to help in the adjustment period, the girls would fare much better than without her." Reece saw the judge look over to the McRaes, so he quickly continued. "After all, we all want what is best for the girls. They must be first and foremost in our minds. What could be better than someone familiar to help them in this unusual transition?"

Reece had gracefully backed the judge into a corner, and the judge conceded. The McRaes were livid. Not only had they not received permanent custody and access to the money, but now they would have the enemy in their camp.

While Marty told Dani and Davey she would join them later at the McRaes', Reece sent for his buggy. Marty and Reece walked out of the courthouse together. Gina Sadder waited outside under an umbrella held by her carriage driver.

"I'll take you by your hotel first to pick up your things," Reece said, "before I drop you off at the McRaes'. I know you're anxious to be with your nieces."

"I can find my own way, but Miss Sadder

looks lost without you." Marty pointed at the woman standing beside an ornate carriage.

"Marty, be nice," Reece warned. "It won't help your cause to go ruffling Miss Sadder's feathers."

"What is that supposed to mean? She's a bird or something? Maybe a turkey? I know, a vulture," Marty said with a smart-alecky smile.

"She is first cousin to Dora McRae, William's wife." Marty looked up at him sharply. "The Sadder side of the family has more wealth and power than the McRaes." As they approached Gina Sadder, Reece lowered his voice. "And I *am* escorting you to the McRaes'."

Marty had an immediate dislike for this woman. She figured it would be easier to wrestle a grizzly than to say anything nice to her, so she chose to keep her trap shut, which she found almost as difficult.

The polite conversation between Reece and this woman droned. Marty wondered how people could talk so much and say absolutely nothing. When Marty's patience had been pushed beyond its limit and she was about to interrupt, Reece informed Miss Sadder they must go.

"It was a pleasure to meet you, Miss Rawlings." Gina forced a smile.

Marty forced her own quick smile, turned, and walked away.

"Good day, Miss Sadder." Reece caught up to Marty in a couple of strides. "That was rude, Marty."

Marty stopped and looked him square in the face. "I don't care." She walked on.

"You'll care if she decides to stir the fire."

CHAPTER 16

Marty didn't speak on the trip to her hotel or on the ride to the McRaes'. Her thoughts tumbled around in her head. She couldn't believe her feelings toward Gina Sadder. The woman had certainly done nothing to make Marty dislike her so. Then what was it? The frilly clothes and refined talk certainly weren't reasons to dislike a person, not really. After all, Marty's sister-in-law Cinda was as feminine as any woman, and Marty didn't dislike Cinda anymore. So what was it about this woman? It was . . . it was the way she — the way she what? What was it? The way she attached herself to Reece. Yes, that was it! Gina was possessive of Reece. That's what bothered Marty. Oh good heavens! Marty was jealous. She stole a look at Reece. He looked back at her and smiled.

Marty quickly looked back to her hands in her lap. It infuriated her that with a simple look and dashing smile he could evoke weak, mushy feminine feelings in her.

"You're awfully quiet." Reece turned slightly on the seat. "You look deep in thought. What are you thinking?"

How could she answer that? *You see, Mr. Keegan, I know you kidnapped my nieces and are a despicable lawyer, but I just can't seem to get you off my mind.*

"It's Daphne and Daniella, isn't it?" Reece said, interrupting her thoughts.

"What?"

"That's why you've been so quiet. You've been thinking about your nieces."

"I look forward to being with them," Marty said, not directly answering his question but covering her true thoughts. She looked around to try to clear her head.

"What is that building?" Marty pointed at a large building with pillars in the front. "Is it a church or something?" Marty had read of large cathedrals back east and in Europe.

"No, the churches in town are not nearly so grand."

"Some fancy hotel?"

"No, but it's beginning to look like one." Reece smiled.

Marty didn't catch his joke. "It must be something important."

"No, it's not important, but the people who live here would like to think so."

"It's a house? They must have a lot of children to need a house so huge."

"Not children, money." Reece pulled the buggy to a halt in front of the house Marty ogled.

Reece descended from the buggy. He turned and held a hand out to help Marty. She put her hand in his. "Who lives here?"

"You do."

Marty's gaze snapped to Reece as he took her by the waist and lifted her down. Fear rippled through her body. The McRaes lived here? What had she gotten herself into?

Reece retrieved Marty's one bag and her saddlebags from the back of the buggy. He came up beside her and offered her his arm. "Are you coming, Miss Rawlings?" he asked when she didn't take his offered arm. "You haven't changed your mind about wanting to be with Daphne and Daniella?"

"Of course not," she said, offended by the insinuation. She trudged up the stairs ahead of him, then she turned and looked back at him. "Are *you* coming, Mr. Keegan?"

Reece smiled and trotted up next to her. He looked down at her with warmth and tenderness.

She looked into his eyes. Who was this man that he could make her feel funny inside? She studied the feeling. If she could understand it, she could control it. It was as simple as that.

The door opened, startling her out of her trance. She turned to see a man in a black suit holding the door open, but it wasn't William McRae.

"Do come in," the man holding the door said in a slow, even tone.

Marty stepped inside and caught her breath.

"I'll announce you," the butler said and disappeared through double doors.

A winding staircase led to the upper floor, and a crystal chandelier hung high above the foyer. Marty's shoes tapped on the marble floor. She felt out of place surrounded by such elegance. These people could offer Dani and Davey the world. Maybe they would be better off here.

"Smile, Marty." Reece arched his hand through the air. "You're in the lap of luxury."

Marty looked up at him and forced a smile. She did not belong here. If it weren't for seeing Davey and Dani, she would turn tail and run like the coward she felt like.

"Aunt Marty!" Her nieces ran to her.

She knelt down and held them in her arms. They seemed happy. Maybe taking them home wasn't the right thing to do.

"Daniella! Daphne!" came a sharp voice. "You were told to stay at the table."

The girls stiffened and turned to the woman. "Yes, Aunty Dora," Dani said. Davey lowered her gaze and said nothing.

Dora McRae looked down her nose at the girls. "Return at once and finish your lunch."

The girls walked away slowly with their heads hung low.

Gina Sadder glided into the foyer. "Reece dear, you will stay for lunch."

"Yes, Mr. Keegan, do stay for lunch," Dora said without an ounce of sincerity. She turned to her cousin. "Gina, I find it interesting that it's been so long since you have graced us with your presence. Why did you choose today to drop by?"

"I wanted to congratulate you on your success in court and extend an invitation to a party Grandmother Sadder is holding in Miss Daphne and Miss Daniella's honor," Gina said.

Dora's eyebrows raised. "We'll be there. Now shall we go to lunch?" She led the way back to the dining room, passing a matronly woman. Marty hadn't noticed the woman standing there with her disapproving gaze.

Reece leaned close to Marty and whispered, "Silvia McRae, Aaron Senior's widow."

Gina slipped next to Reece and entwined her arm around his. "Shall we?" She looked toward the dining room.

Reece nodded and held out his other arm for Marty.

Marty latched on because he was the only one friendly toward her in this repugnant place and because Miss Sadder had firmly attached herself to his other arm.

As they passed Silvia McRae, she stopped

them. "Miss Rawlings, while you are in my house, I ask that you not cause any further disruptions."

Marty changed her mind. Her nieces definitely did not belong here any more than she did. The sooner she could get them out of here, the better.

Gina, undaunted by the tension in the room, kept the meal from being consumed in silence with her light chatter. She was like visiting royalty, the center of everyone's attention, even Reece's. Marty told herself she didn't care; she was with her nieces. Mentally she kicked herself because she did care and couldn't understand why.

Upon conclusion of the tense meal, Gina wormed an invitation out of Reece to drive her home, and they left. Marty hated to see him go, but he promised to visit the next day to see how things were going. Tessy, the twins' maid, showed Marty to her room across the hall from the girls' room. Before long Davey and Dani joined her.

"Aunt Marty, we missed you," Dani said, being the first one in the room.

Marty knelt down and hugged them tight. "I missed you, too."

"Are you going to take us home now?" Davey squeezed her around the neck.

"No, not yet. We have to stay here until the other hearing."

"Then can we go home?"

"Yes. I promise we'll go then." *Whether we win or not, the three of us will be leaving immediately following that hearing.*

Marty stared at the dishes before her. There were three forks, two spoons, two knives, a teacup, two stemmed glasses, and an ornately folded napkin resting in a gold leaf china soup bowl on top of a matching gold leaf plate. She didn't know what to do with all of it. Marty closed her eyes, trying to remember what Aunt Ginny had tried to cram into her head about "table etiquette," as she had called it.

Each piece of silverware had a specific purpose, and if you use the wrong one for the wrong thing, it's a social disgrace. Why hadn't she paid more attention to Aunt Ginny? Aunt Ginny always said, "You never know when you will be invited to a formal function and need to know these basic rules of etiquette."

Marty would just roll her eyes, wondering when she, of all people, would go to some fancy dinner out in rustic Montana. Even if she were invited by some mistake, she certainly wouldn't go. She would probably have to wear a dress. Now look at her. In a sissy dress at a fancy table.

Concentrate now, Marty. The larger spoon is for soup, and one of the forks is for de—

"Miss Rawlings, is something wrong?" Silvia McRae asked.

Marty quickly opened her eyes to find the McRaes, Dani, and Davey staring at her. "Nothing's wrong," she stammered. "Just saying grace."

"Why don't you say it aloud for all our benefit?" Silvia looked down her straight, pointy nose at Marty.

Marty cleared her throat and tried to swallow the lump there. *Me? Pray?* She bowed her head and blessed the food as she had heard Lucas do at every meal. After the amen, but before she raised her head, she quickly added a silent plea to help her make it through this meal with at least a little dignity. A calmness washed over her.

She was smart, and if she just watched what everyone else did and did the same, she wouldn't make too many mistakes. But she was not to get off that easily.

"Well, now we know where the twins learned their horrendous table manners," Dora said, crinkling up her nose while looking straight at Marty.

Marty wanted to truly show her manner and stick her tongue out at the pompous windbag but decided it would be wiser to restrain herself.

"Absolutely no breeding, like her sister. It's a good thing we rescued the twins when we did. Who knows what would have become of them?" Silvia's insult wasn't quite as direct. "I think manners are the first thing we should work on. We'll never be able to take them anywhere with their primitive behavior. I doubt there is anyone of breeding to be found in the whole Montana Territory."

We do, too, have breeding. There is horse breeding, cattle breeding, and one family even breeds rabbits. Marty smiled to herself. She had little respect for her sister, but next to this woman, Lynnette had looked pretty good.

William McRae didn't talk during the meal but kept a critical eye on Marty. He made her nervous. She wondered what was on his mind behind those cold gray eyes. Always watching. She could handle Dora's and Silvia's innuendoes, cutting remarks, and the way they talked about her like she wasn't there. But William's quiet, methodical staring could be her undoing. It was as if he could see into her very soul and was taking her apart . . . bit by bit.

CHAPTER 17

While Davey and Dani were asleep and the McRaes were huddled in the parlor, no doubt discussing their unwanted guest, Marty snuck into William's den. She wanted to see if she could find anything incriminating in his desk and blackmail them out of her nieces, if it came to that.

Wasting no time, she sat in the chair behind the massive oak desk and jerked the first drawer. It wouldn't open. She pulled harder. Still, it wouldn't budge. It was locked, as were the others when she checked them one by one. William McRae wasn't a very trusting man.

She found a letter opener and worked one of the drawers open. She shuffled through the papers in it. When the door opened, she looked up with a start and found a pair of cold, gray eyes staring back at her.

William had a smirk on his face, obviously pleased he had caught her. "Looking for something?"

"I . . . I was looking for some writing paper." Marty slipped the papers back into the drawer. "I wanted to write a letter to my sister-in-law and tell her we made it here safely."

William came around the desk and put a hand on the back of the chair, trapping Marty where she sat. "You won't find any writing paper in that *locked* drawer." With his other hand, he closed the drawer Marty had jimmied open. "I keep some writing paper on top of my desk next to the pen and ink." His hand came down firmly on a stack of blank paper. "What were you looking for?"

"I *was* looking for paper." Admit to this man who wanted to steal her nieces what she was really after? Not on her life! "I didn't see any there. I'll be sure to remember next time."

"I don't believe you. You were after something. You can use all the writing paper you want, but don't go snooping in my desk. Next time I catch you," he said in a cool tone, drilling her with his cold, stormy gaze, "I won't let you off so easily."

Next time, you won't catch me. Marty pushed the chair back hard and out of his grasp. "I'm tired. I think I'll write my letter tomorrow."

When she stood up, William stepped forward and backed her up against the bookshelves behind the desk. "Lynnette's little sister." He scanned her from head to toe.

154

"You were just a bit of a thing last time I saw you. Clinging to her skirt, as I recall. Do you remember me?"

She would have liked nothing better than to have forgotten him, but instead he gave her nightmares. Those cold, gray eyes staring, watching. "I'll be going now." She tried to move past him.

He put his hand up against the bookshelf, blocking her way. "You're a pretty girl." He reached up to touch her cheek.

Marty slapped his hand away. She glared at him and tried to leave in the other direction. He grabbed her by the upper arm and kept her from escaping.

"Git your hands off me," Marty growled through gritted teeth.

He just sneered at her with half a smile and moved his other hand from the bookcase to touch her hair.

"I said, git your hands off me."

He glared at her. "I heard what you said."

And you ignored me. She drew her fist back and socked him as hard as she could in the stomach, wiping the self-satisfied grin off his face.

He stepped back, doubling over.

"I said git your hands off me, and I meant it." Marty moved away from him and around the desk as Dora came into the room.

William held his stomach. "You little witch. You'll regret this."

Dora ran over to him. "William, what happened?"

"I caught her going through my desk, and she punched me."

Marty thought about protesting and telling Mrs. William McRae what her husband had really been up to, but figured Dora would believe her husband no matter how much Marty tried to argue. She may have even suspected or known her husband was a no-good, low-down snake, but she would always side with money. Those two deserved each other.

Marty moved to the door.

"Miss Rawlings," Dora called after her, "we know why you are here, so don't think you can just up and leave with the twins. We'll be watching you and the twins."

Marty left without a word and headed up to her room. Dora's threat of being watched didn't frighten her. She figured it wouldn't be too tough to take the girls, if she had a mind to. But she wanted to have them free and clear, so she wouldn't have to keep looking over her shoulder. No, Dora's threats didn't scare Marty — but Mr. McRae did. Marty would steer clear of him and his reach.

Out on the veranda in the back, Marty watched Davey and Dani gather leaves. Marty had been in the McRaes' house for nearly a week, the girls longer. It seemed like

156

an eternity. She had tried each day to search William's den again, but found the door locked each time. A man that distrusting was not to be trusted.

Dani and Davey came up on the veranda to show Marty the variety of beautiful leaves they collected.

"Listen," Marty said in a low voice to the girls so Rol couldn't overhear from his perch on the rail at the far end of the veranda. He was the watchful eye Dora had threatened Marty with. "We want them to question if they have done the right thing. You need to be rowdy and obnoxious and difficult, but don't overdo it so they suspect. Do you think you can do that?"

Dani and Davey looked at each other slyly, then turned back to Marty. "We can do it."

"And mix yourselves up," Marty added.

"They don't care about that," Dani said.

"They just call us the twins," Davey added.

"Like we are one person," they chimed in unison.

Couldn't they see that Dani and Davey were two unique people? No, Marty guessed they couldn't, not when they dressed the girls exactly alike and did their hair the same. Marty even had a hard time telling them apart in these getups, but their unique personalities still showed through. The three headed into the house but stopped in the hall when they saw Reece at the door talking with

Madam Silvia.

"I would like to take Miss Rawlings, Daphne, and Daniella for a buggy ride to show them our fair city." Reece smiled cordially.

Silvia McRae smiled back at him with contempt in her eyes. "You may take Miss Rawlings anywhere you like and keep her for all I care, but the twins do not leave the premises."

"A walk in your lovely garden then would be refreshing," he said. He seemed to be having difficulty keeping his forced smile intact.

"Rol will be keeping an eye on the twins to make sure they don't wander off and get lost."

"Of course," Reece said politely, though he looked like he wanted to tell her more. He tipped his head to her and stepped by her to where Marty was. He escorted Marty and the girls outside with Rol lurking close behind.

Marty enjoyed and even looked forward to Reece's daily visits. She depended on him. The strange feeling he caused was not quite as distasteful as she had once thought.

"Those are real nice dresses you have on, Miss Daphne, Miss Daniella." Reece held out each of their chairs and seated them at the table on the veranda. They giggled at him calling them miss.

"They're scratchy," Dani said, and both girls scratched under the high collar.

"They're awful," Marty said with disgust. "They can't do anything in them because they might get those *precious* ruffles dirty." She couldn't stand seeing her nieces cooped up in this dreary house trapped in useless clothes for active little girls. Marty felt confined as well and longed to ride off on Flash . . . anywhere, but she would not leave Dani and Davey alone for her own comfort.

"Don't get too discouraged, the time will go quickly, and you'll all be out of here," he said with a wink of encouragement to the girls.

A servant came and served them lemonade. They spoke of many things, and Marty almost forgot this distasteful place. The girls got antsy and ran off to collect more leaves.

Reece seemed relieved when the girls were gone and asked, "Are you accompanying the girls to the party tomorrow night?" He obviously wanted to ask her in private.

"Of course."

"I wasn't sure if the McRaes would allow you to attend." Reece spoke slowly, choosing his words carefully.

"They weren't, but I told them if I didn't go, Dani and Davey might not behave themselves. They asked if I had anything appropriate to wear to an elegant occasion. I assured them I brought my very best pair of Levi's." She smiled, remembering the looks on Dora's and Silvia's faces. "I thought they were going to faint at the thought of me showing up in pants. Dora moved faster than a jackrabbit with a coyote on his tail to find me one of her cast-off dresses. It was going to be given to charity anyway, and she figures I qualify as charity, and it's 'more than good enough for the likes of me.' "

"I'm sure you'll outshine Dora McRae no matter what you wear," Reece said. "Everyone who is anybody will be there. All of Seattle's society will want to know who is this mysterious girl with the beautiful, deep blue eyes." He took her hand and kissed it.

Marty couldn't help but smile at his compliment. Did he really like her eyes? Or was he just telling her what he thought she wanted to hear, like he did with everyone else? How could she know if he was sincere? He took great pride in his ability to manipulate words; after all, it was what he did. And as he said, he did it well. But how could he make her feel tingly inside with a look or his presence? He used no words. And he did come every day. Maybe he really meant it. She liked the thought of Reece possibly liking her, and she smiled self-consciously.

"Gina says her grandmother is sparing no expense for this party," Reece said.

Gina Sadder. Why did he have to go and mention her? She's beautiful, rich, and always acts like a lady. Marty couldn't compete. Miss Sadder had everything, including Reece. She

160

wondered if Miss Sadder knew he came to visit poor, backwoodsy Marty.

Reece had continued on about how wonderful the party was going to be, but Marty heard nothing after Gina's name. "I don't feel like being outside anymore." Her chair scraped the wooden floorboards as she jerked to her feet. "I'm sick of these trees."

Reece stood up with his hands out, palms up. "What?" All he could do was stare in confusion at the doorway Marty disappeared through. What had he done? He could not believe she didn't prefer the great out-of-doors, especially when the option was the McRaes' home.

"Where'd Aunt Marty go?" one of the girls asked, startling Reece out of his daze.

Reece studied the little girl. He could no longer tell the twins apart. At least before he could distinguish them from one another by their braids. Now, any uniqueness was being stripped away, molding them into a pair of perfectly matched dolls to decorate the furniture.

"In the house."

"Why'd she go inside?"

He shook his head. "I have no idea." He had been telling her about the Sadder party to assuage any fears she might have. An upscale party like this one could be overwhelming for someone who had never been to one. And Marty had certainly not had an opportunity before. Had he scared her? No . . . not Marty. But what then?

As his mind churned with thoughts of an untamed beauty, he feigned interest in Daphne and Daniella's leaves. The poor girls were prisoners here. If they were forced to remain in this house, would they have the grit and tenacity Marty did to keep their identities even with each other to rely on, or would the McRaes break them both?

Lord, forgive me for what I have done here.

CHAPTER 18

It amazed Marty how long it took these people to get ready for a stupid party. With all the baths, primping and preening, ironing clothes, curling hair, and dressing, it was an all-day affair. But not for Marty. She took a bath and towel-dried her hair. She didn't want to put her dress on one minute before she had to, and Tessy offered to do her hair. From bath water to the last pin in her hair was exactly one hour, which was too long. When she stepped in front of the mirror, she could hardly believe it was her reflection. She felt like a princess from one of those fairy tales Cinda would read to Dani and Davey. The light blue satin dress came off her shoulders slightly and was riddled with ruffles. She had had a choice between this one or a peach dress drenched in lace. She determined she had made the right choice when her nieces came running in.

"Ooooooooh," both girls crooned.

"Aunt Marty, you are soooo beautiful."

Marty eyed her. "Don't overdo it, Davey."

"Well, you do look beautiful, and I bet Mr. Keegan will think so, too," Dani said.

Marty doubted he'd even notice her with the elegant and refined Gina Sadder around. After all, it was Gina's domain, and she would surely monopolize Reece.

Marty and her nieces left her room and headed downstairs. The McRaes waited at the bottom like a big, happy family. Her thoughts drifted to her own family. Her brothers, Trevor and Travis, would certainly laugh at her for being all fancied up, and Tommy Jensen would tease her for weeks. She would wallop him. Then, a horrible thought crept in. What if someone at the party laughed at her? No one in Seattle had laughed at her so far for wearing a dress, but what if someone did? She couldn't very well wallop them at this fancy party. What would Reece think of her?

When they got to the Sadder estate, Marty noticed Reece right away, but he didn't see her. He was swirling around the dance floor with Miss Gina Sadder in his arms. Dressed in a pink gown with some transparent fabric over it that fluttered when Gina moved, she looked like a beautiful angel floating on a cloud.

The music stopped, and the dancers left the floor. An announcement was made about Silvia McRae's good fortune in finally being united with her long-lost granddaughters.

Marty saw Reece across the room with Gina firmly attached to his arm. Reece scanned the crowd until he laid eyes on her. He tipped his head to her and smiled. Marty looked away quickly as if she hadn't seen him, and soon the dancing resumed.

Marty moved to the back of the crowd. Several people's heads turned as she passed by. For the most part she ignored them. It put her on edge when some of them started whispering. She feared the whole room would burst into laughter, she being the target of their jokes. No one would miss her if she left. No! Wimps turned tail and ran; she was no coward. She held her head high and stared back at anyone bold enough to look at her for more than a moment.

A handsome, blond-haired man stared at her the longest, until he finally strode in her direction. He bowed and said, "Good evening, miss. My name is Tony Bittle."

Marty smiled politely, her nerves unraveling. "Good evening. I'm Marty — I mean, Martha Rawlings."

"Well, Miss Martha, may I have the pleasure of this dance?"

Dance? Marty looked from him to the dance floor, then back at him. "No, thanks. I don't —"

Reece came up next to her. "Miss Rawlings promised me this dance." Mr. Bittle backed out graciously, obviously irritated by being circumvented.

Reece took her hand. "Shall we?" he said, leading her to the dance floor.

"I don't like all these people staring. It's like being surrounded by a pack of hungry wolves just waiting to devour their prey. They know I don't belong. I can hear them whispering." Marty held back, trying to slow their way to the floor.

"You're right. They are whispering about you." Reece took her right hand in his left and put his right hand at her waist in the standard waltz position. "They are wondering who this beautiful, mysterious woman is. I even heard one woman say you must be a socialite from back east."

Marty looked up startled. *No.*

He nodded as if reading her mind.

She put her hand on his shoulder when he started moving her on the dance floor and immediately stepped on his feet.

He looked down at her, his mouth twitching up at the corners. He had unsettled her, and he knew it. "Shall we try again?"

Marty would need to concentrate hard to keep it from happening again. She took a deep breath and remembered what Aunt Ginny had tried to teach her and her brothers. Refinement, she called it. Marty hadn't cared for any refining. Reece and Marty made a couple of rounds on the dance floor.

"Marty?"

"What?" she barked, irritated at him for breaking her concentration. Did he want her stepping on his toes again?

"Have you heard a word I've said?"

"This is a dance floor; you're supposed to dance." She made no attempt to hide her irritation.

"There are no rules against talking while you dance."

Marty remained quiet, focused.

"Don't you want to talk?"

"I can't."

"You can't talk?" He stifled a laugh. "I've heard you talk before."

He was asking for it. "I don't do this dancing thing very well." She huffed. "I can't talk and concentrate on the steps at the same time." At that moment, she lost track of what her feet were supposed to do and they went their own way, stepping on Reece's feet. "See." Marty stopped in her tracks and threw up her hands.

Reece smiled down at her affectionately. "Since I really wanted to talk to you, let's take a stroll outside." He wrapped Marty's arm through his and guided her out the door.

"Look." He gestured toward the grounds. "These are completely different trees." They walked over to a bench that encircled one of the trees. The fall night was warm and dry for a change.

Marty relaxed at being off the dance floor and out of the crowded room with all its eyes condemning her.

Reece offered her a seat at the tree.

"I thought we were going to walk."

He got a glint in his eye and the corners of his mouth curved up slightly.

She narrowed her eyes. *Don't you dare say it.* "I can walk and talk at the same time."

"I just wasn't sure. My feet are a little tender."

Marty plopped down on the bench and folded her arms.

Reece sat next to her. "I'm sor—"

Marty stomped on his foot. She stood up and turned to him. "I guess you just aren't safe around me." She walked off.

With her little padded slippers she knew she hadn't hurt him, but he did look stunned for a moment.

He came after her. "Marty, wait." He grabbed her arm and pulled her to a stop.

She turned and looked at him. He studied her face. What was he looking for, tears? Hurt emotions splashed across her face? Tears and emotions would mean she cared, and he had the ability to hurt her. She just looked at him.

"I'm sorry. I shouldn't have teased you. I deserved it." He held out his other foot. "You can stomp on the other one if you like."

Although tempted by the offer, she declined. "You said you wanted to talk."

"I was wondering if you've found anything."
Marty gave him a quizzical look.

"I assume since you haven't tried to run off with your nieces, you are looking for something incriminating on one or all of the McRaes."

"Who says we haven't tried to leave?"

"If you had, *you* would no longer be living under their roof." He tapped her on the nose. "And with Rol keeping a lookout . . ."

"That watchdog doesn't scare me." Rol reminded her of the strongman she once saw in a traveling circus. She could not best him in a fight.

"He should." The lightness left his voice. "Rol could be dangerous if provoked. Don't aggravate him, Marty."

Marty shrugged her shoulders as if not to care. She had seen the potential danger in Rol's eyes. He was like a mountain lion ready to attack his prey. Waiting. Watching. Poised to spring into action if his prey dared move. Just waiting for a reason to strike. But he truly didn't scare her. She surmised he wouldn't pounce unless given reason to. Marty had nothing planned to give him reason to act. She intended to ride it out, at least until the hearing. If she didn't get custody of the girls, then Rol would have a chance to earn his keep.

"So have you found anything?" Reece asked, breaking her train of thought.

"No." She shook her head. "If there's anything to find, it would be in William's den. He keeps that locked now."

"Now?"

"He caught me going through his desk one day."

Reece's eyes widened. "What did he do? He didn't try to hurt you, did he?" Reece's concern seemed sincere and touched her in a place only he had managed to reach.

"When he declined to let me leave, I socked him in the gut. But don't worry. Dora was there to soothe his wounded pride."

"And how are things with Dora and Silvia?"

She turned her nose up and tried her best to imitate Dora's uppity voice. "They think my table manners are atrocious, my behavior unseemly, and my clothes are nothing but rags."

Reece smiled. "Don't let them get to you."

"I really don't care what they think of me. It's when they start picking at Dani and Davey I get riled, and they know it. They have quit for the most part. I think they're waiting until they're rid of me."

Marty loathed the thought of going back inside, so they walked around for a while.

"It's getting chilly." Reece removed his jacket and draped it around her shoulders, pulling it snugly around her. His voice softened, and he looked deep into her eyes.

"Is that better?"

Marty nodded. As they stood close, she returned his gaze and was warmed, not by his coat but his intense brown eyes. Marty had never before wanted a man to kiss her, but for an instant, she wanted this man to and wondered what he was thinking. Was he thinking of kissing her? When his gaze dropped to her mouth, she automatically licked her lips and bit on her bottom lip. His gaze slowly moved back up to her blue eyes and settled there.

"Reece dear," came a woman's voice from beyond them, breaking the spell. "There you are. I've been looking all over for you."

"Gina." Reece immediately stepped back from Marty when he heard her voice. "I was showing Miss Rawlings your lovely grounds."

"I see." Though her smile was as sweet as Aunt Ginny's sticky buns, she couldn't mask the suspicion in her eyes. "I would have thought Miss Rawlings would have left with her nieces."

"What? Dani and Davey are gone?"

"They left about a half hour ago. Silvia sent them home. It is late for *little girls* to be up." She raised her eyebrows at Marty.

Who cared if Gina thought Marty was too young for a man like Reece Keegan. At least she wasn't an old maid. She wanted to say so but decided it wasn't worth it. "I'm going, too." She hiked up her dress so she wouldn't trip on it and trudged off toward the house, leaving Reece and Gina together.

At the front door she asked the servant for her wrap and realized she was still wearing Reece's coat. When the servant returned with her cloak, courtesy of Dora, she held out the coat and asked him to please return it to Mr. Reece Keegan.

"I'll take it," Reece said from behind her. He put his coat back on and nodded for the doorman to fetch his overcoat. "I'll take you home. I've sent for my buggy to be brought around." Reece took the cloak from the man before he left and settled it on Marty's shoulders.

Gina appeared on the scene. "Reece, you aren't leaving, are you? It's still early."

Before it was late, and now it's early. Can't she make up her mind?

"I'm going to escort Miss Rawlings home."

"I would appreciate it if you would stay. I'll have one of our drivers take her home," Gina said, getting just the right amount of emotion in her voice to sound hurt.

Marty rolled her eyes. "I can take care of myself. I don't need anyone to drive me. I'll drive myself." Marty turned and went out the door. The two outside attendants came to attention when she exited the house. She hurried down the steps, but stopped and turned back to the house when she heard the door close a second time.

Reece came down the steps and stopped beside her. "My buggy should be around in a minute."

"I thought the queen bee wanted you to stay." Why hadn't he? Gina wanted him to stay as much as she wanted Marty gone.

Reece cupped her elbow in his hand. "Miss Sadder doesn't always get what she wants." A moment later his buggy arrived. They sat next to each other but without quite touching.

Once they were on their way, Reece shifted in the seat to look at her. "This changes things, Marty."

Marty turned toward him, confused. "Changes what?"

"I've insulted Miss Sadder by not staying at her request. If she wants to, she could make trouble."

"Trouble?"

"If she puts her power behind the McRaes, they could make things very difficult for you. She could use her leverage against me."

"Against you?" She wouldn't oppose Reece. It was obvious, even to a hick like her, that Gina Sadder was sweet on him.

He took a deep breath. "If I had to choose between your nieces' freedom and mine . . . I'd choose theirs."

His? How was his freedom in jeopardy?

"If I bow to her wishes, you could have the girls by morning. I don't think it will come to that. But I want you to know I will do anything to right my wrong . . . even marry a woman I don't love."

Marty's heart skipped a beat at the knowledge he wasn't interested in a sophisticated woman like Gina Sadder. "You could've stayed." But she was glad he hadn't. "I'm a big girl. I can take care of myself."

"I know." He glanced sideways at her. "You keep telling me that."

"So why didn't you stay?"

"I *wanted* to take you home."

Marty dipped her head to conceal her grin.

CHAPTER 19

Later that night, Marty trotted down the stairs on her way to the kitchen to get a glass of milk. She had tucked in Dani and Davey and waited for them to fall asleep. She passed Dora and Silvia in the foyer on their way to the den.

"I thought we had an elephant in the house with all that noise," Dora said to Silvia and with pinched lips gave a quick glance at Marty. Silvia raised her eyebrows and gave a graceful nod to Dora before continuing to William's den with Dora on her heels.

Even Dora's snide remarks and Silvia's insolent looks could not dampen her good mood. Reece had all but told her he preferred her over Miss Sadder and said he would see her in the morning. Marty continued on her way and had her glass of milk.

On the way back, she heard voices in the den. She couldn't help herself. She had to stop and listen. Silvia and Dora had slithered in moments before, but the voices she heard were both male, one William's, the other she was sure was Rol's.

"She's gonna be a problem," she heard Rol say. "She's just waitin' for her opportunity."

"Then we have to make sure she is never given the opportunity," William said.

"I just want her out of this house for good," Silvia said.

"I don't want to see her again before the hearing," William said.

"You won't have to worry about her ever bothering you again."

She recognized that third male voice. Wylie!

"My friend in California will see to it. When he buys something it doesn't wander off. He makes sure of it . . . one way or another."

"Good." William's tone was sinister. "I want you two to take care of it."

Marty's eyes grew big, certain they spoke of her. "You'll regret this." William's threat from when he caught her in his den echoed in her head. She hurried upstairs to her room. Whatever their scheme, with Wylie and Rol against her, it spelled big trouble.

She threw her trail clothes and boots on the bed. She spread her coat open and put in her Levi's, boots, chaps, and shirt. She folded the coat tight and tied the sleeves to secure it. She put the bundle under her arm and grabbed Aunt Ginny's reticule with the derringer in her other hand.

As she headed down the hall for the stairs,

she looked at the girls' door. She longed to take them with her, but there was no time right now. She would come back for them later. She continued to the stairs, then turned back to Davey and Dani's room. She couldn't leave without assuring them of her plan to return for them. They would feel abandoned.

She crept in and knelt between their beds. "Davey," she whispered, shaking her. "Wake up."

The girl rolled over and moaned sleepily, "What is it?"

"Shh!" Turning, she roused Dani.

When both girls were awake, Marty explained the necessity for her to go away immediately. She pledged to come back for them as soon as possible.

"We want to go with you now," Dani said.

Davey nodded her firm agreement.

"There isn't time. I just wanted to let you know before I left." Marty hugged them. "I love you both."

"We love you," both girls chimed together.

Marty got up with her bundle and went for the door. She opened it slowly and could hear voices clearly. They had left William's den and spoke at the bottom of the stairs. Someone was coming up.

Marty closed the door quickly. "They're coming." She scanned the room wildly and rushed over to the window. Good, a trellis. She opened the window and threw her clothes out to the ground. Hiking up her skirt, she heaved one leg out.

"Be good until I come back." She backed out the window. "Go back to bed and pretend you're asleep."

They stood teary-eyed, watching her descend.

Marty stepped on the hem of her dress, losing her footing, but didn't fall. She kicked it out of her way several times but it kept falling back in place. She couldn't hold it up because she needed both hands to maneuver. She would have to do her best. She wished she had had time to change clothes.

The ruffle at the hem got caught on the trellis. Marty tore it loose. She took another couple of steps, then her foot tangled in the torn ruffle. Her other foot lost its hold, and Marty found herself dangling by one hand for an instant before plunging ten feet. She hit the ground hard on her left side with her arm tucked under her, the wind knocked out of her. She got up on her hands and knees to catch her breath but felt dazed.

"Aunt Marty, are you okay?" a pair of frightened voices whispered.

Marty stood and looked up at them. "I'm fine." She motioned them away. Without seeing if they went, she picked up her bundle and scurried off for the stable.

Marty felt something wet on her forehead and wiped it away with her hand. Blood. She put her hand back to her forehead and felt for the cut. An inch-long gash along her hairline over her right eye oozed blood. It didn't hurt yet, but soon would. She must have hit it on the trellis during her accelerated descent.

Unable to run as fast as she wanted because of the pain in her side, she stopped to rest. She wiped away more blood on her dress and hurried to her destination.

She reached the stables, her breathing quick and labored. It hurt to breathe very deep. She wiped the blood again from her forehead to keep it from dripping into her eye, and then she ripped the torn part of the ruffle from the dress and with her injured left arm held it loosely against her forehead. With her right arm, she clutched her bundle tightly.

She moved quietly so as not to rouse the stable hand. His sleeping quarters were in the back. She went straight to where her saddle was stored, dropped her bundle, and uncovered the saddle. Her Colt and Winchester were still with it. Grabbing the saddle by the horn, she dragged it over to Flash's stall.

"Come on, boy. It's time to leave this place," Marty whispered to him and rubbed his nose. The horse's energetic nuzzle caused Marty to suck in a painful breath.

"Miss Rawlings, is that you?" asked the stable hand from behind her. "What are you doing out here this time of night?"

Marty spun around to face Oliver, dropping Flash's saddle. "I'm leaving." She turned back and struggled with the saddle.

"Let me get that for you," the old man said.

"Don't try and stop me," Marty warned.

"I won't." Oliver happily helped her.

She liked him. She used to come down to visit Flash and talk with him. In truth, she felt more comfortable around him than any of the McRaes.

He swung the blanket and saddle onto Flash's back and tightened the straps. He put her rifle in the holster and looped her gun belt over the saddle horn. He tied her blanket and tarp on the back and retrieved her bundle of clothes she had dropped. He turned to her and said, "Do you think you're fit to ride?"

"I can ride." She pushed away from the post that held her up. She sucked in a quick breath to stay the pain.

"I mean, banged up the way you are?" He pointed to her head. "I've got some bandages. They're the ones I use on the horses, but they're clean."

"No time for fussin'. I'll be fine." She moved to mount up.

He pulled out his kerchief and shook it loose. "At least let me tie this on it." He twirled the kerchief around so it was long and skinny.

She let him tie it around her head. It would

be easier not to have to hold her hand there. "Thanks."

He helped her up into the saddle, then led Flash to the door. Seeing that it was all clear, he opened the door wide. Before he released Flash's bridle, he said, "Be careful, miss."

Marty nodded and galloped away.

Running or even trotting hurt Marty's side, so once she was away from the house and grounds, she slowed Flash to a walk. Her first thought was to go to the nearest hotel, but what if William tracked her down? Did he just want her out of his house or did he want her out of town for good? She couldn't take the chance.

Maybe she could go to Reece. What if he was in on this? What if he had conspired with them all along? After all, the McRaes had hired him. Then he came to find her when she arrived probably at their insistence. Had he been stringing her along and distracting her from her goal so the McRaes could steal her nieces out from under her? No, she couldn't trust him, at least not right now. She looked heavenward, then dismissed God as an ally. She was alone.

Marty kept Flash moving. Eventually they strode out of town. She would sleep out under the stars where it was safe. She looked up, but there were no stars to be found. They were hidden by a blanket of clouds. It didn't matter. Clouds meant the night would be warmer than a clear sky.

She found a level spot to call home for the night. She eased off Flash but left him saddled in case she had to make a rapid departure. She didn't bother to take off her dress when she slipped on her pants, shirt, coat, and boots. She made a lean-to with her tarp, a couple of rocks, and a low tree branch, and bedded down for the night.

The euphoria she had felt a few hours before at the party had quickly worn off. The night had been like a fairy tale; but unlike Cinderella, Marty hadn't lost her slipper, and there would be no Prince Charming coming to look for her.

She had gotten caught up in the festivities, forgetting who she was and her reason for being here. She was a farmhand and belonged in the Montana country, not the city. She needed to rescue her nieces, not sit around waiting for someone else to do her job for her.

In the middle of the night she awakened; something dripped on her face. Rain. She should have known it would rain. She pulled her blanket over her head and went back to sleep.

"What do you mean she's not here?" Reece didn't care that he was raising his voice to matriarch Silvia McRae. "She was here yesterday!"

182

"Well, she's not here today," she said without batting an eyelash.

"No explanation, just she's not here." Reece was incensed. Marty always did the unexpected, kept him on his toes, but this was uncharacteristic. Leave her nieces? Never! Something was wrong. "I want to see Daphne and Daniella."

"I'm afraid that will be impossible. The twins cannot be disturbed. I would ask you to leave now." Silvia attempted to move Reece back to the door. "Good day, Mr. Keegan."

Daphne and Daniella ran through the foyer. They each grabbed hold of one of Reece's arms.

"She had to leave," one said.

Then the other continued, "They made her leave."

"She sneaked down the trellis."

They both had tears in their big blue eyes. Eyes like Marty's.

"And fell and got hurt."

"We saw her holding her head."

Marty had been hurt? Reece's stomach knotted. He could picture her hobbling away, hand to her head. She would go and take care of herself, determined to return for her nieces. Why hadn't she come to him for help?

"Tessy! Rol! Get the twins out of here. Take them up to their room."

Tessy and Rol did as they were ordered. As the girls were carted away, Gina Sadder sashayed over. "I'm sorry, Aunt Silvia. They got away from me." Gina feigned innocence. "You know how difficult nine-year-olds are to control." She sighed and batted her eyelashes.

Silvia gave her a suspicious look. She wasn't fooled.

"Walk me out to my carriage." Gina hooked her arm in Reece's.

Reece, still stunned by the news, let himself be led out and down the steps. Marty gone? Chased away. Injured!

"I have to find her," he said, snapping to. "Thanks for allowing me to see the girls, even if only for a moment."

After the words he had had with her the night before, he was surprised she was civil to him, let alone nice. He had tried to explain his departure from the party. When that was not met with understanding, he told her his feelings for Miss Rawlings went beyond professional. Although unsure of exactly what he felt, he did know his feelings were far more than any he had ever felt for a mere legal case. What was more, these were feelings he had never had for Gina.

"Don't get me wrong, Reece Keegan. I am deeply hurt and offended. I thought I meant as much to you as you do to me. A sort of game we played but would eventually end up together. Obviously I was mistaken. But Grandmother is right. I shouldn't stoop to

184

pettiness. So I am allowing my intense dislike for my cousin to override my own anguish. I will not join forces with Dora against you, but I will not help you, either."

"I understand." He couldn't ask her for more than that.

He helped her into the carriage. She held on to his hand. "A word of advice, Reece. Miss Rawlings is not for you. She's not like us."

No, she wasn't. Marty was like a breath of fresh air or a sweet morning rain. He was well aware of her differences and liked her more for them.

He pulled his hand free. "Thank you." He closed her carriage door.

"Don't thank me. I may change my mind tomorrow." Her eyes glistened with tears. The carriage rolled away.

Reece mounted his horse and headed for the stables.

"May I help you, Mr. Keegan?" Oliver asked.

Reece swung down off his horse. "I'm looking for Miss Rawlings's horse." Reece wanted to know if the man knew anything.

"Flash isn't here," he said. "Miss Rawlings went riding."

He did know something. "You helped Miss Rawlings with her saddle then?"

"It's my job."

"Kind of late for her to be riding, don't

you think?"

He sized up Reece and gave a quick glance around. "Real late, Mr. Keegan. In a big hurry. I didn't figure it'd do a lick of good tellin' her to wait 'til mornin'."

Getting Marty to do anything contrary to what she had her mind set to would be like getting water to run uphill. "Was she badly hurt?"

"Hard to say. Her forehead was bleeding." He touched his own forehead over his right eye. "You know how head wounds are. They don't have to be very big to do a heap of bleeding. She favored her left arm or maybe her side, I couldn't rightly tell," Oliver said.

Reece shook his head in concern.

"I asked her not to ride, but she insisted she was fine."

Of course. "Did she say where she was headed?"

"Nope. Just leaving in a hurry."

Reece swung back up onto his horse. He would find her. He had to.

"I hope you find her."

He hoped so, too, and nudged his horse into motion.

CHAPTER 20

When Marty woke the first time, it had been midmorning, and now the sun was dipping in the sky. In a couple of hours it would be dark again. All she had had to eat during the day were a few huckleberries she found clinging to some nearby bushes. She thought about hunting for game but without a fire, what was the point? Everything was too wet to start a fire.

The rain had let up in the early morning, but by noon it came down hard again. With the rain came a drop in temperature. Marty was cold, wet, hungry, and injured. At least her head had stopped bleeding, but it hurt along with her left arm and side. She just stayed in her lean-to wondering what to do next. Her eyes drifted closed. She had already accidentally taken two naps today.

Her eyes flew open with a start. She listened. She heard it again. Something was approaching. It was close. She scooted to a nearby tree and hid behind it. She pulled out her six-shooter and made sure it was loaded. Her rifle. She peeked around the tree. Sure enough, she had left it in the lean-to. That would give the invader a gun. She thought about retrieving it when she saw something move. She had no choice but to remain hidden.

She heard a horse blow and someone dismount. Had William sent someone after her? She stayed leaning against the tree and hoped whoever it was would leave.

"Hey, Flash," she heard Reece say from the direction of her horse.

Oh no, not Reece. She tipped her head back against the tree. She hadn't made up her mind about him yet.

"Where's your keeper?"

"Right here." Marty came out from behind the tree with her gun drawn. Joy and disappointment warred inside her at the sight of him. His familiar, friendly face was a comfort, but he could still be employed by William McRae.

"Marty." He stepped forward.

"Stay back." She held the gun a little higher so he couldn't help but see it.

He stopped. "You don't need that. I'm not going to hurt you." He held his hands out away from his sides.

"I don't know who I can trust." She found it difficult to concentrate on breathing normal to not show her pain, her weakness, as well as watch his slightest move. She couldn't let her guard down for an instant, or she could be doomed, if he was one of them. "You were on their payroll once, you could still be."

With his hands still held out away from his body, he backed up to his horse.

"What are you doing?" Marty asked.

"You look hungry. I have some biscuits and cheese in my saddlebag." He looked at her for permission to get the food.

Food sounded wonderful. Her mouth watered.

When she made no reply one way or the other, he turned slowly to his horse. "I'll just get it for you."

He brought the food over and sat down under her lean-to. "You're getting wet out there."

What difference did that make? The rain had soaked her to the bone hours ago. He was trying to help, but was he really on her side? Marty's head ached, making it hard to think, a searing pain shot through her side with every breath, and her arm had little mobility. She was a mess and needed help. She dropped her gun arm to her side. She had no fight left.

Reece patted the ground next to him. She really had no reason to trust him. Her first encounter with him had been a betrayal. What was to say everything since then hadn't been a lie, too? He longed to go to her and help her, but she was a woman who seldom needed help. Now was one of those rare times. He had to break through, regain her trust. She sat at the far edge of the lean-to. He handed her the food without making any move toward the gun or rifle. He would put his life in her hands if that's what it took for her to trust him. He needed to make her feel safe.

"Is it broken?" he asked when she had eaten all his food.

She looked down at her arm, then up at him and shook her head. "I don't know. It might be."

He got up and offered her a hand. "Come on. I'm taking you to a doctor." He was going to help her whether she liked it or not. He would carry her kicking and screaming if he had to.

She tucked the gun between her left hand and her stomach. He pulled her to her feet gently, not knowing the extent of her injuries. He folded her blanket and tarp, then tied them on her saddle. When he handed her rifle to her, she holstered her Colt and put the rifle on her saddle.

"I think you should ride with me."

"I can ride." She moved past his helping hand. "I can do it myself." She climbed up in her saddle with a grimace that tore at his heart.

Reece stood next to her and Flash. "Are you sure you're all right?"

"I'm fine." She turned Flash toward town.

Well, the food had helped her pride at least, and she didn't look so listless. Reece mounted and followed behind, keeping a close eye on Marty. If she so much as wavered in the saddle, he would be there to catch her, whether she liked it or not. When he first saw the bloody bandage on her head, his heart lurched at the sight. He expected it, but the sight was still startling. The fact she had made it through the night was a good sign.

Dr. Ford came out of his office and closed the door behind him.

Reece stood up. He had been waiting in the outer office while the doctor examined Marty. "How is she?"

"She'll be fine. My wife's helping her dress." He motioned Reece to sit back down on the couch. The doctor sat in a wing chair. "She has a cracked rib and two others that are bruised, but no signs of internal bleeding."

"Her arm, is it broken?" Reece asked.

"Surprisingly, no. It's banged up pretty good, has a lot of bruising. She's not going to be able to move it for a few days. I cleaned her head wound and stitched it up. The stitches will need to come out in a week or so."

Marty exited the exam room, dragging her feet. She had a fresh bandage around her head, her arm in a sling, and under her clothes her ribs had undoubtedly been tightly wrapped. The doctor's wife assisted her to make sure she didn't fall.

The doctor stood abruptly. "I told you to call me," he said to his wife.

"She was determined to do it herself." She shrugged her shoulders and held out Marty's dress to Reece. "She just wanted to wear her britches and shirt."

"Burn it," Marty said.

"What?" The doctor's wife seemed surprised, but Reece wasn't. "It can be mended and cleaned."

"I said burn it," Marty said with more determination.

Marty swayed and grabbed the back of the chair the doctor had been sitting in. Reece looked at Dr. Ford with concern. She looked worse off than when he had brought her in.

"I gave her laudanum for the pain."

"I don't feel any pain." Marty's words slurred.

"Exactly." The doctor gave Reece a sideways glance. "She should sleep through the night without any discomfort." He gave Reece a bottle of laudanum with instructions.

Reece nodded and went to help Marty outside. "I can walk," Marty insisted, but Reece had to catch her on her first step. She looked at him glassy-eyed. "I guess I need a little help."

Reece supported her under her good arm and helped her out to the horses.

"This isn't Flash," Marty slurred out, when Reece started to hoist her up onto his horse.

"I know."

"I can ride!" She swayed and put a hand to her head. "I *can* ride."

"I know you can, but I need something to hold on to."

Marty nodded and allowed him to put her up in his saddle.

Once he had her on his horse, he automatically took hold of Flash's reins and climbed on behind her. He put his horse's reins and Flash's in the same hand and wrapped his free arm gently around Marty's waist to keep her in the saddle. They plodded off down the road and on their way. Before Reece realized it, Flash was being bridle led without any trouble. He smiled and shook his head slightly. Quite a woman.

Marty leaned back, resting against Reece. He was warm and comfortable. She imagined him taking her in his arms, saying pretty things to her. She wore a beautiful, flowing dress with lots of lace and flowers in her hair. *What a dreadful thought.* She smiled. "I don't even like dresses."

"What?" Reece asked.

"I don't like dresseseses," she slurred.

"I know."

"So why would I think about wearing one of the foul things?"

"I think the medicine the doctor gave you is making you a bit confused." There was a hint of humor in his voice.

"Right. The medicine. Do you like dresses?"

"I don't think I would look particularly good in a dress."

She tried to picture him in a dress. "No, I don't think you would, either." The spinning in her head picked up speed. "Reece?"

"What?"

"I'm going to fall off the horse." She felt as though she was tumbling, slowly, endlessly.

"I've got you." Reece tightened his grip around her waist. "I won't let anything happen to you."

She grabbed his arm with her uninjured one to try to stop the reeling, to no avail.

"Good, because I've never fallen off a horse before."

"Milly!" Reece called when he reached his house. He swung down off the horse; Marty came with him. He caught hold of her above her waist and heard her moan in pain.

"I'm sorry," he whispered.

Marty attempted to stand on her own but leaned heavily on him. If not for his arm around her, she would be a heap on the muddy ground. He scooped her up in his arms and strode toward the door. Before he could call out again, the door opened.

In the doorway stood a robust middle-aged woman in a white apron with gray flecks in her brown hair. "Mercy, Mr. Keegan. Is she alive? I'll send for the doctor."

"We just came from there." He made his way into the house. "Doc said she'll be fine. He gave her some medicine. She'll sleep for a while."

"Put her in my room," the woman said. It was on the first floor next to the kitchen. "No sense in carrying her up all those stairs."

Reece lowered Marty to the bed. She sank deeper into the spiraling blackness. Afraid to be alone, she called out, "Lucas?"

"I'm right here," a voice answered, then a pair of hands grasped hers.

It comforted her to have him near, but confused her. Why did her brother sound like Reece? She held tight to his hand to keep from falling into the consuming darkness. Vaguely aware of the presence of another person, she faded into the unknown void.

Marty woke to the sound of whispers, though her eyes remained closed.

"Mr. Keegan, you really should get some sleep. It's not doing her one bit of good," a woman's voice whispered.

Who was she? His wife? A startling thought.

"I slept," Reece said.

"In a chair all night, beside the bed. That's no way to sleep," the woman scolded.

She sounded more like someone's mother. But she had called him Mr. Keegan. No mother would refer to her son as mister.

"I didn't want to disturb her. She's had a death grip on my hand all night."

Marty instinctively released him and jerked her hand away. She looked up into his hurt eyes and regretted her action. It had been done without thought. She wished he would take her hand again, but he didn't.

"She's awake now," the woman said with a pleasant smile. "You get off to bed and get some proper sleep."

"Are you feeling better?" Reece asked Marty, ignoring the good-intentioned woman.

"I feel a little dull, and it's hard to breathe." Marty was concerned for the first time about her physical well-being.

Reece grilled her on each of her injuries until he was convinced she was fine.

"This is Mrs. Atwater." He pointed to the woman beside him.

"Hello, Mrs. Atwater." Marty smiled.

"Please call me Milly."

"Milly is my housekeeper and substitute mother. You won't find a better cook in these parts." Reece leaned in closer. "I stole her from one of the logging camps."

"So you've had practice," Marty said.

He growled, then smiled.

"Stole. He plumb rescued me, that's what he did. Cooking for three hundred men and getting paid practically nothing."

"Best cook in the Pacific Northwest," Reece bragged. "If I were ten years older, I'd marry her."

"More like twenty, Mr. Keegan."

Marty could tell this was a go-round Reece and Milly had danced before.

CHAPTER 21

Reece sat behind his desk in his office at home, staring at the pages in front of him. One he had headed *Rawlingses* with a column for pros and another for cons. He had a similar page with *McRaes* written at the top. The Rawlingses' page was heavy on the pro side. Love topped the list; then, the girls knew the Rawlingses and loved them as well; they were dedicated and loyal; kindhearted. The list went on and on with positive qualities.

On the con side of the sheet, he had a hard time coming up with anything but finally wrote money. He didn't think it was a negative, but the judge and the McRaes would. In the short time he had been in Montana, he had seen that they were doing quite well. They didn't have as much money as the McRaes, but they were by no means the poor dirt farmers William had led him to believe. Lucas was obviously well thought of in the community to be acting sheriff.

Reece dipped his pen in the inkwell and

moved back to the pro column and wrote *sheriff.* That was a definite plus for their side.

Back on the con side he wrote *country.* Though Reece thought their living in the country was a good thing, he knew the other attorney would bring it up with emphasis on lack of education. The McRaes would no doubt send the girls to some faraway boarding school and then a stuffy finishing school. That would keep them out of the way until they grew up. He wrote education under country.

The McRaes' page looked very much the same except opposite. For every Rawlings pro there was a McRae con right on down the line. Reece dipped his pen in the inkwell and wrote *city/education* on the pro side. He knew how they thought and couldn't overlook this angle. He had to think of everything their attorney would to be prepared to counter it. Even then, he knew he couldn't win.

He pulled out another sheet of paper and dipped his pen back in the inkwell. *OUR CASE* he wrote in all capital letters across the top, a column for strengths and one for weaknesses. He stared long at the page, then let his head sag until his chin touched his chest and shook it. He didn't have a case. If this were an ordinary case with an honorable judge, they would have a chance.

The McRaes had the judge in their pocket. Unless Reece could prove that or something else to show they were unfit, Judge Vance would rule for the McRaes.

Reece lowered his head again. *Lord Jesus in heaven, forgive me for all these years of doing it on my own, for leaning on my own strength. I have defended people I believed were guilty because I never asked them outright and so could say I didn't know if they were to confess later. My conscience was clear. But in my soul, I knew better.*

Lord, touch Marty and heal her. Thank You for keeping her safe. You did something special when You created her.

I know in my mind, soul, and mostly my aching heart that Daniella and Daphne should live with Marty and her family. Show me how to do that. Give me the crucial bit of information I need to make William McRae back off and let the girls go. I can't do this without You.

Reece lifted his head and opened his eyes in time to see Marty heading for his front door. "Where are you off to?" From her startled, wide-eyed expression, he guessed she didn't know he was home. He couldn't drag himself too far from her. He didn't want to.

She came to his opened door. "I need to walk. I'll go crazy if I don't do something."

She had spent the first day resting in bed with enough laudanum in her to keep her from thinking about much of anything. The next day, she refused medication and got up to roam around.

He had wondered how long she could be kept down and was glad Milly had taken on the job of being the bad guy. Milly had her hands full and must have given up trying to keep Marty down. Either that or Marty had snuck past her only to be caught by him.

He got up from his desk chair and walked around to her. "Doc Ford said you should take it easy for a few days."

"I'm tired of resting. I'm not some sissy who needs to be coddled and pampered. I need to be useful."

She tossed her head slightly, not realizing how feminine the movement was. He wouldn't be the one to tell her. He liked her grit, loyalty, and honor. She was so true and honest. Then every once in a while he would catch glimpses of her denied femininity and his racing heart would stop for one brief moment. She was pretty near perfect in his eyes . . . with emphasis on the pretty.

Her sigh brought him back. "I did nothing at the McRaes', but I was with Dani and Davey. Now I can't even see them."

Silvia McRae had forbidden Marty and Reece to even set foot on their property. As soon as Marty had made her escape, Silvia had ordered the servants to burn anything she had left behind, including her Stetson. That loss was second only to her nieces.

"Come in here. You can help me." He offered her a seat on the couch.

She plopped down like a cowboy and sucked in a quick breath between gritted teeth.

He wanted to order her back to bed but knew it would not work. It wasn't necessary to ask if she was in pain. It was etched all over her face. And he wouldn't go over to her and fuss. If he did, he would pull her into his arms and carry her back to bed. She would be both offended and put off. But if he thought for one minute she was harming herself, he would drag her back to bed kicking and hollering and tie her down. He would give her the time she needed for the pain to settle.

She took an unsteady breath and leveled her gaze at him. "I don't know what good I'll be. I don't have a fancy education like you."

No fancy education would tell him what he needed to know. Reece sat in the chair adjacent to the couch. "Tell me about your sister."

"What?" She turned slowly to glare at him.

He was confused by her negative reaction. When she had told him about her family before, she had exhibited no emotion about her sister's death as she had for her parents'. He had dismissed it at the time but now wondered what was behind it. "Tell me about Lynnette, the girls' mother."

"Lynnette?" There was no mistaking the contempt in her answer. "Why do you want to know about her? She's dead."

What had happened to turn Marty against her own sister, a sister whose daughters Marty was totally devoted to? "I need to know everything about her. What she was like. What she said when she arrived with Daphne and Daniella. Her last wishes for them. Did she leave a will? Anything and everything. I need to know it all to get them back."

"I don't know what she wanted."

"She was your sister. Didn't she say anything to you about her girls before she died? Who she wanted them to live with?"

"I don't know. Maybe she said something to Lucas. I didn't see much of her. We weren't very close."

"Didn't you care she was dying?" He couldn't believe that this woman who cared so deeply for the girls could care so little for their mother.

"No, I guess I didn't." She lifted a shoulder and let it drop. "My sister was weak and self-ish. She thought only of herself. When things got tough, she left us. She was giving up once again and caved in to defeat without a fight."

"She was dying, for heaven's sake." Reece couldn't believe the cold words coming from this strong, passionate woman.

"She could have lived if she had had the

strength and the will. I know she could have."
Her tone suggested anger and hurt. "With
her husband dead she had no money, so she
left Dani and Davey for someone else to raise.
When they needed her most, she quit. She
didn't have to die. She could have lived on
the farm. Lucas would have taken care of her,
but instead she gave up, taking the easy way
out. That's her way."

Reece felt as though Marty's nieces being
left was a small part of a deeper pain. Still
waters run deep, and he suspected hers were
far reaching.

Marty got up and walked across to his desk
and fiddled with a paperweight. Reece came
over to her. She turned to him and continued
speaking, with her emotions in check. "It
wasn't the first time she abandoned her family. After Ma and Pa died, she ran off and got
married, leaving us alone on the farm."

She spoke in plurals, but the pain belonged
to her alone. Reece tried to think of when the
McRaes came to Seattle. Thirteen years ago.
He was back east then, in school. And Marty
was five years old. The same age as Daphne
and Daniella when their mother died, leaving
them. Her fierce loyalty stemmed from their
similar losses. He wanted to hold her, to
comfort her, but she shed not a tear. She was
too strong for tears or to be comforted. Lynnette's betrayal had made her that way. So he
stood there helpless, anguished by the pain

Marty denied.

The days dragged with no word about the twins. Marty's heart ached for them. She hoped Reece's plan would work. And to her surprise, she even prayed and felt . . . something. It was unlike any feeling she had experienced before, but she knew it was going to be okay.

She lay on her back on the couch in Reece's office with her feet propped up on the back of the sofa, the skirt of her dress tucked between her knees. Raindrops dripped from the outside sill and chased each other down the glass. This would be snow back home. She thought of playing in the snow with Dani and Davey and hoped they would have a chance to do it again this winter.

There were several benefits to Reece's plan. First and foremost, Marty would have a guarantee of getting Dani and Davey back, though her backup plan would guarantee that, too, if she could just get it worked out.

Second, Marty and her nieces could go back home and not be on the run for the rest of their lives. Either way she won. It was just that one way didn't make her a fugitive and an enemy of Reece.

Over and over she had tried to develop an alternative plan, should Reece be unsuccessful in court. She couldn't. Her heart wasn't in it. She wanted to trust that Reece would

205

and could do what he boasted. It felt like betrayal to distrust him.

She turned suddenly toward the door, sensing someone watching her. Reece stood in the doorway. He seemed a bit unnerved by her looking at him so abruptly and a gentle smile pulled at his mouth. How long had he been standing there? She swung her feet down to the floor. At the same time, her head popped up off the couch, forcing her upright. She sucked in a quick breath at the sharp pain in her side.

"You all right?"

"Fine."

Her hands ran over her skirt to smooth it, and she tried to act like a lady. She felt like a lady around him because he always treated her like a lady, regardless of how she behaved.

"I was watching the raindrops drip off the bare branches, wondering if it's snowing back home."

Reece crossed over to his desk. What was he thinking? What did that smile mean? He probably thought he had a primitive bumpkin with no manners at all in his house. She wanted him to like her or at least not be repulsed by her. At the same time she was irritated by how this man could turn her insides to mush. *Pull yourself together, Marty. He's only being nice because he feels guilty for what he did.* Flustered, she got up to leave.

"Don't go on my account," he said.

Marty turned to him. "I don't want to bother you." She pointed to the papers he held in his hands.

"You aren't bothering me. These aren't important." He put the papers down and came around his desk. "As a matter of fact, I need to talk to you." He motioned for her to have a seat. "I need to take a little trip." The caution in his voice made her nervous. "I leave first thing in the morning."

Marty's heart dropped like a rock down a well. He was leaving? Running out on her and her nieces? Marty stared at him in disbelief. How could he do this to her?

"I won't be gone long, maybe a week," he spoke quickly. "I'll be back in plenty of time for the hearing." Marty continued to stare and said nothing. "I need to talk to some people who knew your sister. I will be back. I promise."

"Lynnette. Everything is always about Lynnette." Marty stalked out of the room.

She went out to the animal shed to be with the one soul who was her constant companion. As she stroked Flash's neck, she sifted through her feelings. She had been at Reece's house for a week now and in Seattle for nearly three weeks. Although grateful for all Reece had done for her and her nieces, she couldn't wait for it all to be over. Marty wanted to get away from this place and her feelings. She trusted Reece and didn't exactly know why. She cared for him. Was she falling in love with him? What a silly thought. Marty Rawlings in love? She couldn't deny it. What else could it be? She had to stop these feelings right now. In three weeks she would have her nieces one way or another and be gone. There was no room for love. Besides, Reece would never love someone like her.

The next morning Reece left as promised. With him away, a hole opened up inside Marty. Though she tried to stop her feelings, they crashed over her like a raging river. It was good he was gone. It would give her time to get control of these strange new feelings.

"You don't like God?" Mrs. Atwater exclaimed.

Marty shook her head.

"We need to get you to church, child, and introduce you to the Lord God Almighty."

"I go to church and know who God is," Marty said.

"You say you know Him but don't like Him?" the woman asked, astonished. Marty nodded. After she had grilled Marty to the point where she was reasonably convinced Marty was a Christian, Mrs. Atwater asked, "Why is it you don't like God?"

"He don't like me." Marty could tell Mrs. Atwater was taken aback by the response.

"Child, He sent His only Son to die for you. I'd say He more than likes you. He loves you."

"He doesn't like the way I am," Marty tried to explain. "I don't dress and act the way a lady should. People, especially other Christians, look down on me 'cause I don't wear dresses, and I keep my hair short. People reflect who God is."

"Christians are an imperfect reflection tainted by sin. God takes each of us just as we are."

"I don't believe that. Like folks, He expects me to wear a dress and act like a 'proper' lady."

"You view God as you view people." Mrs. Atwater put a comforting hand over Marty's. "God is not a person. Can you think of no one who accepts you, child? Your family?"

Must Mrs. Atwater keep calling her child? After all, Marty was eighteen. "My brothers don't mind, but they seen me grow up this way."

"So they don't count?" she asked. Marty shook her head. "What about your nieces? From what Mr. Keegan tells me, those two little mites adore their aunty. They aren't taken in by the McRaes' wealth and finery."

"They are only children," Marty said as if that explained it.

"They don't count, either?"

Marty shook her head.

"Children can read people better than most adults. They can look inside and see who people really are. They aren't so easily fooled

209

by fancy words and pretty clothes. They see the heart. Your nieces love you for the person you are, not what you wear."

So. Marty just stared at her, raising her eyebrows.

Mrs. Atwater was silent for a couple minutes, then said, "What about me? I like you. It makes no difference to me if you're in a dress or pants. And before you go dismissing me, too," she said, quickly holding up her hand to keep Marty from protesting, "I'll have you know I was like the McRaes. I came from a wealthy family and looked down my nose at anyone who didn't wear the finest clothes." She paused, gathering her thoughts. "Harold, my late husband, and a crippled orphan girl named Molly showed me the way to the Lord and to accept people unconditionally. Harold was everything I wanted in a man: rich, powerful, and exceedingly handsome, but he was also a religious man. He wouldn't look twice at me until I did some charity work at an orphanage to get his attention. It was dirty, and the stench overwhelming. The children thought I was an angel and kept pawing at my expensive, yellow satin gown from Paris. I wanted to turn right around and leave, but Harold looked at me and smiled. I forced a smile and read story after story to the filthy little urchins.

"When it was time to leave, a brown-haired girl about seven or eight limped over to the door and held it open for me. She had hung back by herself because the other children teased her. When I thanked her, she looked up at me with her big brown eyes and smiled. She was so grateful just to be noticed. My cold heart cracked a tiny bit. I told her she needed gloves to be a proper door holder and gave her mine.

"As I got into my carriage she said, 'Thank you, Angel Lady.' It felt good to do something nice for someone else.

"Harold started calling on me. When Molly became ill, I wanted to go to her, but my family wouldn't allow it. Even with the best doctors and my angry prayers, Molly died. Harold said her last words were of me. 'I see her. She's right over there by the window. The yellow angel is taking me to Jesus.' She closed her eyes and was at peace." Milly's eyes moistened. She blinked back tears. "Shortly after that Harold led me to the Lord. And when I get to heaven, the first thing I'm going to do is give Molly a great big hug. If you look with the eyes of love like God does, everyone is beautiful, even a stuck-up socialite in the latest Paris fashions."

Marty shook her head. "I can't believe you were ever like Dora McRae."

"I was worse. I was an Eastern snob," she said with mocking airs. "We never would have associated with these West Coast types. Does the fact that I wear a dress make me a better person than you?"

"Most people think so."

"But what of God? God looks at the heart." She huffed out a frustrated breath. "Does money make William McRae a better person?"

"No!" Definitely not.

"Does it make Mr. Keegan a better person because he comes from back east? If your nieces didn't act the way others thought they should, would you love them any less?"

Marty didn't answer. She got the woman's point.

"It's what's on the inside that matters to God. You have a good heart. I think God is pleased with what He sees there."

Well, Mrs. Atwater was the only one who thought so, and that was only because she didn't know Marty too well.

"You're a lot like Moses, I'd say."

"Moses? Hardly." He was a man of God. God used him and spoke through him. Marty couldn't fathom even the remotest connection.

"Moses left Egypt because he felt the Hebrews were being unjustly treated. You left Montana because your nieces were unjustly taken. You both left the safety and comfort of your home for someone else's sake."

"A lot of people care about others." That did not put her on any level close to Moses.

"You both were unaware of the training you

would need one day. Moses fled to the wilderness where he would one day lead a great mass of people. He had to know how to live and survive there. Do you think he could have done that if he had stayed in Egypt?

"You were raised unconventionally so one day you would have the skills you would need to race after your nieces undaunted to rescue them. I know of no other woman and few men with your skills."

It wasn't so hard.

"Nothing is by accident. God has touched your life so you would be ready for this. Like Moses, with the Lord on your side, you will be successful."

Though Milly made a certain amount of sense, Marty couldn't quite stretch so far as to imagine God helping her. "But Moses was a man."

"God uses men and women alike. Our Lord spends patient years training us in hopes we will be willing to answer His call, and, honey, you answered with your whole heart.

"In the book of Judges, the Lord used two women to deliver the Israelites from the hands of the Canaanites: Deborah helped lead the army, and Jael killed the commander of the enemy's army. Not typical woman's work. So you being a woman has nothing to do with God's using you or not."

Marty thought long and hard about the things Mrs. Atwater said. Marty liked to think

God really did look kindly on her, even in Levi's, hauling grain or cleaning the barn. If God could like her as is, she could give Him a chance.

CHAPTER 22

It was a week into Reece's trip when Mrs. Atwater got a telegram saying it was going to take a little longer than he thought and to tell Marty he would be home soon.

After four more days without a word from Reece, Marty paced but was unable to soothe the knot in her stomach. Mrs. Atwater told her to relax, Mr. Keegan would be back in time. Marty wished she could be so sure.

She had lain awake night after night, making crude plans that were all doomed to failure. Her heart ached for her nieces. This was the longest she had ever been separated from them. She ached for the farm in Montana, for Lucas and the strength she had always drawn from him.

And she ached for something else she didn't understand. Montana was calling her, but she knew that it wasn't everything any-more . . . or more accurately, it lacked a certain person.

Mrs. Atwater had just served supper when

the front door opened. Marty rushed to the entryway with Mrs. Atwater in her wake.

Reece set down his stuff and looked up at the two women. "Good evening, ladies." He bowed with a broad smile and took a deep whiff. "Milly, I sure have missed your cooking." He wrapped an arm around her shoulders. He smiled at Marty. "You look happy to see me."

She was for many confusing reasons. She had to admit her elation. She had missed him, even though she tried hard not to think about him. "I'm glad you got back in time."

"I said I would be back before the hearing, and I have a week and a half to prepare."

"The hearing's in three days," Marty said.

"What?" His distress was obvious in his voice.

Mrs. Atwater nodded. "It seems William McRae talked Judge Vance into moving up the day. My guess is he heard about your little trip and wanted to have the hearing without you."

Reece's light mood turned serious. His eyes darted back and forth, his brows lowered, his face grew serious and thoughtful. He pulled out his pocket watch and glanced at the time.

"Now that you're back, it's good, isn't it? I'll have Dani and Davey sooner," Marty said, concerned by his mood change.

"Yeah. Everything will be fine," he said, but his thoughts seemed to have already run off without him. "Milly, don't wait supper." He turned and rushed out the door.

Marty stared at the door, too dazed to move. Why had the hearing date being moved up displeased him so much?

The next two days were torture for Marty. Reece wouldn't tell her what he had learned or how he was going to get her nieces back. He shut himself in his office and worked, worked, worked.

"Sit tight, child, and let Mr. Keegan wield his magic in the courtroom," Mrs. Atwater said as Marty paced about the house.

Marty couldn't sit around any longer, doing nothing. Too much of doing nothing for weeks. But what else could she do, legally, to help get the girls back? Nothing.

In her frustration, she jumped on Flash's back and rode away from the main part of town. Away from the courthouse. Away from the McRaes. Away from Reece and her growing feelings for him. A refined lawyer would never look at a dirty gal like her.

She rode hard and fast out of town, galloped through streams, and jumped fallen trees. Flash ran full steam until they came to a swift, deep stream. She realized the lathered horse had given his all. She jumped off to let him rest beside the stream. Still needing to run off steam, she took off on foot, dodging tree branches. Her lungs felt like they were on fire, and her ribs hurt. She could run no farther and collapsed on the ground, panting heavily, trying to squelch the pain.

She didn't know how long she lay there with her arm over her eyes. So consumed by her thoughts, she didn't hear him approach. She came to with his hot breath on her face. Big brown eyes set in a brown face loomed over her, long brown hair hanging between his eyes, and he brayed.

Marty reached up and petted Flash's nose. "I'm fine, boy." Suddenly aware of her surroundings and the dangers that could be lurking, she jumped to her feet. She had no gun for protection. She needed to stay alert. She headed back for town, aware of everything surrounding her.

She didn't know which was more foolish, having feelings for Reece, a well-educated man more than ten years her senior, or racing out on a storm of emotion into an unknown country with no protection.

"Which one should I wear tomorrow?"

Reece looked up. In his office doorway stood Marty with a dress draped over each arm. On her right arm was a stuffy gray dress, quite proper. It represented everything Marty was not: ordinary, stiff, formal. From her other arm hung a royal blue gingham with tucks down the front and a touch of eyelet around the neck and wrists. A matching blue sash at the waist tied in a bow in the back.

Reece sat behind his desk and studied Marty as she looked from one dress to the other. When he didn't answer, she looked up and caught him staring at her.

He raised his eyebrows. "What you're wearing is fine." He quickly looked down and pretended to read his notes.

"But I'm wearing pants. I don't think Judge Vance would appreciate it."

"I guess you're right." He liked her in breeches. It reminded him of her uniqueness. Not that he needed a reminder. "Then wear the one on the left," he said with a casual wave of his hand, like it didn't matter, knowing full well the left one was the blue one. That shade of blue brought her eyes to life and made them sparkle like stars in the sky.

"Your left or my left?"

"It doesn't matter." He put down his papers. "Your left." He got up and came around his desk and stood before her. With his finger under her chin, he lifted her face so she looked him in the eyes. "It doesn't matter what you wear. I'm going to get them back for you, one way or another."

He had quit denying his feelings for her when he had found her wounded in the woods. Reece had fallen in love with Marty. He wanted her to wear the dress for him, not the court. Anything to show she had interest in him other than a means to get her nieces back. Maybe when he settled this mess, he could tell her his feelings. But would someone as unique and spirited as Marty ever have feelings for someone so much older?

She squinted her eyes and studied him. "Why are you doing this?"

"Because I was wrong," he admitted boldly. "I never should have taken the girls. They belong with you and your family. I'm going to do everything in my power to correct the injustice I caused." Not only did he realize his error, he also believed fixing his mistake would redeem him in Marty's eyes. He needed her approval.

He raised a hand to her face and caressed her cheek with his thumb. "I'm sorry for everything I've done."

"What if we lose tomorrow? What then?"

He hated to see a trace of fear in her eyes. "Ye of little faith," he said with a smile. When Marty's stone-cold serious expression didn't waver, he pretended to be serious, too. "*If* we lose, then we go to my alternate plan."

Marty eyed him and raised an eyebrow. "Alternate plan?"

"We talk Silvia, William, and Dora into sending Daphne and Daniella to boarding school," he said.

"No! They would hate it at a boarding school." She shook her head. "I would go get them, you know that. Is your plan to make me a kidnapper, too?"

"The school I have in mind is well guarded.

No one will be kidnapping them. Besides, they will love it there. It's a quiet place in the Montana Territory, The Rawlings School for Girls." He smiled.

His heart beat faster at the smile that spread across her face. "Do you think they would go for that?"

"It would be the least troublesome for them. The girls would be out of their way, and they would have the money. You wouldn't have to worry about them coming after them again." He saw hope in her eyes. "If not, there is always plan C."

Marty raised her eyebrows. Reece could see she was impressed he had contingencies. "And what is plan C?"

"I help you kidnap your nieces," he said, as if it was ordinary business. "I have experience with that sort of thing."

She smiled *at him* this time, and his heart nearly jumped out of his chest.

"I have done this, and I will undo it. Whatever it takes." *Even marriage to Miss Sadder.*

In a way he wished she would cry. He longed for a reason to console her and to hold her in his arms. But her strength kept her from breaking down, and he loved her for it. Most men would be put off by her backbone, confidence, and determination. He treasured them.

■ ■ ■ ■

Later in the evening Marty heard violin music coming from behind Reece's closed office door.

Mrs. Atwater shook her head. "It's not good."

Marty thought it sounded fine. Very pleasing.

"He plays to calm his nerves before particularly difficult cases. It helps focus his thoughts." Mrs. Atwater headed for the kitchen, her head still shaking.

Was Reece worried? Would he really give it his all tomorrow? Marty stared at his office door as the instrument's mournful tone drifted through the air. He had nothing to lose; she had everything at stake. If only he could care for her, like a man cares for a woman. She was a fool. She couldn't let herself have feelings for this man, especially love. It would only get in the way when it came time to leave.

That was it. He was simply righting a wrong. She had hoped he was doing it for her, if only just a little or even for her nieces — but no. He was fixing a mistake in his life, and she was merely part of the problem. He wouldn't double-cross her now.

A little while later there was a knock at the door. A young man in his midtwenties, dirty from the trail and with several days' growth on his face, insisted upon seeing Mr. Keegan.

Mrs. Atwater invited the young man in out of the rain. "I'm sorry, Mr. Keegan is not to be disturbed."

The music stopped, and the office door opened abruptly. "It's all right, Milly. Come in, George." Reece welcomed the man into the office.

The door closed tight behind them. The man stayed for nearly half an hour before leaving. Reece donned his coat and hat and left a few minutes later. He didn't return for several hours.

Marty should have been asleep long before then, but she couldn't with Reece gone. She did not know why George had come. Did it have something to do with her or was it another case he was working on? Even after Reece returned, she tossed and turned. Finally, at dawn she threw back the covers and went riding to clear her head.

When she returned, Reece was seated at the table, eating breakfast. He seemed surprised by her riding attire. He probably didn't think she would take him literally about wearing anything she wanted. He pressed his napkin to his mouth. "I'll be back for you in one hour to take you to the courthouse." He left without a word about her clothing.

Marty's nerves filled her stomach and kept her from eating. She felt like throwing up.

Reece seemed so calm, but then he had been to court many times.

She sent up prayer after prayer, hoping God would listen to just one. She was becoming better acquainted with God. Marty had read the story of Deborah and liked it. She was no prophetess but felt God might be helping her.

Marty bathed and got ready, donning the blue dress. Mrs. Atwater helped her with her unruly hair. Reece seemed pleased. His broad smile stretched across his face. She tried to pump him for information.

His smile stretched wider. "It's a beautiful day."

Marty raised an eyebrow in question. It was raining, again.

Marty sat nervously in the courtroom and gave Dani and Davey an encouraging smile.

"Your Honor," William's lawyer began. "My clients waive all rights to the minors Daniella McRae and Daphne McRae and relinquish custody from this time forward."

A hushed whisper rippled through the courtroom.

"Do your clients wish to have any kind of visitation privileges?" Judge Vance asked, irritated.

"My clients feel suitable arrangements can be made out of court with the other party. We need not take up any more of Your Honor's valuable time."

The judge nodded, and William's lawyer sat down.

The judge turned to Reece. "Mr. Keegan, I assume your client hasn't changed her mind and still wishes custody of the minors in question?"

Reece stood. "Yes, Your Honor, Miss Rawlings does wish custody."

"Stand up, miss," the judge addressed Marty.

She wasn't sure her legs would hold her as she stood. She couldn't believe what she'd heard. Her nieces were free and would be coming home to Montana. Why had William changed his mind? She really didn't care as long as she got them back.

"Miss Rawlings, are you prepared to take on the responsibility of these two young girls?"

"Yes, sir . . . Your Honor." Marty's voice shook with excitement.

"Very well." He wrote something on the paper in front of him.

Marty's heart leaped for joy. She stole a joyous glance at Dani and Davey. They smiled back at her.

"How old are you?" Judge Vance looked her over critically.

"Eighteen," she said with her head held high.

The judge got a sour look on his face. "Mr. Keegan, I can't give custody to a child."

225

What? No. She couldn't lose them now. Not when she was so close.

"If it pleases Your Honor," Reece said, "I will take responsibility for the girls, and make suitable arrangements for them to return to their uncle and aunt in the Montana Territory."

"Very well, Mr. Keegan. Custody is yours until which time they can be returned to Montana. I hope you know what you are doing. Case dismissed."

With the slam of the judge's gavel, joy exploded in Marty's heart and raced throughout her entire being. Reece had done it!

She closed her eyes and turned her heart toward heaven. *Thank You, sweet Jesus.*

CHAPTER 23

Reece stepped aside to allow Marty and her nieces to enter his house ahead of him.

Milly greeted them with a warm smile. "These must be the two little misses I've heard so much about."

"Milly, these two beautiful young ladies are Daniella and Daphne McRae."

Marty never did like the sound of their last name and avoided even thinking about it, a reminder of Lynnette's betrayal. To her, they were Rawlingses, through and through.

Reece turned to the girls. "Daniella, Daphne, this is Mrs. Atwater."

Milly knelt down and gave each of them a big hug. "I've been waiting to meet you."

Dani pressed her face back into Milly's shoulder. "You smell like chocolate cake."

"And fried chicken," Davey added.

"And biscuits."

"Girls! That's enough."

Milly laughed. "It's all right." Milly turned from Marty back to the girls. "You two have a pair of very good noses. You have just named the lunch menu. You want to help me set the table so we can eat?"

The girls agreed and followed after her.

Marty turned to Reece as he was trying to help her off with her coat. She turned back around and let him help her. "How did you do it?" She still hadn't gotten over the fact that William, Dora, and Silvia had just rolled over and let her have her nieces back. She pulled one arm out of her coat. She couldn't figure out what Reece had threatened them with to cause the change. Had he made a deal with Gina Sadder? Marty pulled her other arm out of the second sleeve.

"We both know why the McRaes wanted Daphne and Daniella. Money. I simply reduced your nieces to mere paupers again." Reece hung her coat on the entry tree stand.

"You stole their money?" She didn't care what he did with the money as long as the girls got to come home.

"Let's just say I took it out of the McRaes' reach."

"How?"

"The money was willed to Aaron McRae Junior, not his children. Without a will, his estate is naturally passed on to his wife. With your sister gone, that left Daphne and Daniella to inherit the money. Their guardians would have complete control over it."

"That doesn't explain how you made them

paupers."

"I found some friends of Aaron and Lynnette's. He had a letter written from Aaron to Lynnette. I convinced a judge to declare the letter Aaron's will. The letter implied he wished Lynnette to have everything he could call his own. Of course, the letter was written before the girls were born."

"But with Lynnette gone, the money would still go to Davey and Dani."

Reece smiled. "Not if she had a will declaring someone else her heir."

Marty raised her eyebrows. Her sister had a will? Or had Reece fabricated one? Would he do that?

Reece went on. "Six months before Lynnette returned to Montana, she moved to Spokane Falls. There she worked as a housekeeper for an attorney and his family. They adored Lynnette and her daughters and were heartsick to find out about her illness. The man persuaded your sister to make out a will to protect her girls. She did, naming none other than big brother Lucas Rawlings as sole heir, knowing he would take care of her most valuable possessions, Daniella and Daphne. Little did she know he would inherit a fortune. The McRaes have no capacity to love a pair of destitute orphans."

"Lucas won't touch that money. It will all be there for Dani and Davey when they grow up."

"I don't doubt that."

After a few moments of contemplative silence, Reece caressed Marty's cheek with his fingers. "Stay," he whispered.

"What?"

"Stay. Here. With me."

"I can't jist stay."

His eyes searched hers. "You don't understand. I love you." He leaned forward and pressed his lips to hers.

Marty could hardly breathe. He loved her! She snaked her arms around his neck.

He pulled her close and kissed her cheek all the way over to her ear. "I want to marry you."

Her heart swelled with joy. He actually loved her. She hoped he cared but didn't think he could feel as she did. But it was no use.

She pulled away. "I can't," was all she could whisper. She turned away, unable to look at him. A strange moisture stung her eyes.

As he looked at her, he remembered when he first saw her. She came around the back of the wagon and marched up into the house, studying him. At the time he wondered what she was thinking. But now, he knew she was trying to gauge what kind of threat he was to her family. She was always thinking of her family. She would return to them.

He gently cupped her face and turned it

back to him. "Because of your sister?" She nodded. "You are not her. You're not deserting them. Just the opposite. You have done everything humanly possible." He paused, seeing tears pool in her loyal eyes. His argument wasn't swaying her. "They could stay here with us."

Marty shook her head. "Lucas would never give them up. He's like their pa."

And yours, too, he thought. He continued with his attempt to persuade her to stay. "We could put them on a stagecoach . . ." His words trailed off as he saw her shake her head. "They would be safe. I promise. Then you could stay."

"Stop it." She removed his hands from her face. "They are my responsibility. I promised I'd bring them back."

"Is there any use asking if you'll come back?"

The warring inside her shone on her face. She wanted to stay, but she couldn't. "I won't desert my family."

He took a deep breath and let it out. "It's not just the girls, is it? It's your brothers, and sister-in-law, the animals, the land."

"It's a part of me. It's who I am."

"I can't come back with you after what I did."

"I know." Marty hung her head. "Lucas is still sheriff."

He caressed her cheek with the back of his

fingers. She looked up at him. The very thing he loved most about her, her loyalty to family, would tear them apart. "Tell me you love me, too."

Reece had bought Daphne and Daniella each a horse, so no one would have to ride double. That was the least he could do after all the trouble he had caused them. He accompanied the three on their journey home. He finally knew that Two Tails was Daniella and One Tail was Daphne. He couldn't go all the way with them, but he would go as far as he could.

They were in Montana now, stopped at a river to rest and water the horses. Snow fell lightly, adding to the couple of inches already on the ground. He had gone farther than he knew was wise. He couldn't bring himself to part from her. He needed to know she was safe.

Daniella squealed. "It's Pa!" All heads turned to gaze across the river.

"Uncle Trevor and Uncle Travis, too," Daphne said.

Reece looked up at the ominous figures. His heart sank lower than he thought possible. It was over. The one he determined to be Lucas was flanked by two others nearly as big. There was no mistaking they were brothers. Marty's brothers. She wasn't kidding when she said her brother was big. Not only was he a substantial man, but he looked as angry as a peeled rattler. Why shouldn't he be? His nieces had been kidnapped, and his little sister was missing, and Reece had been responsible for tying up the man's pregnant wife. He was not a man with whom Reece wanted to tangle.

"The posse is here." His stomach twisted.

Marty looked from her brothers to Reece. His time with her had come to an end.

"Daphne. Daniella," Reece said to the girls but kept his gaze on Lucas, who was waiting, assessing. "Get on your horses and cross over to your uncles."

They eagerly complied. Once on the other side, Lucas greeted them but sent them on without even a hug. They disappeared into the trees beyond the river with the two younger brothers. Lucas waited for Marty. His rifle lay across his lap.

Reece turned to Marty and looked upon her face. He took off her hat, an old one of his, and combed his fingers through her hair. She would leave now. There was nothing he could say to talk her out of it. He wanted to kiss her good-bye. After glancing over at Lucas's grim face, Reece didn't think it was wise. He would have to settle for memorizing her face.

When Reece first looked into her eyes, she thought he was going to kiss her. That look was slipping away. He had changed his mind about kissing her, and the reason was looming behind her on the other side of the river.

As he stepped back away from her with good-bye on his lips, she stepped forward and took his face in her hands. She pulled his head down until his mouth met hers.

He closed his arms around her, holding her tight. She didn't want him to ever let her go. Marty wrapped her arms around his neck. He kissed her long and hard.

She pulled away as suddenly as she had kissed him. "Good-bye," she tried to say but no sound came out. Tears blurred her vision. She struggled to hold them back. She was losing the battle and wanted to leave before she did something silly like cry. She never cried. As she moved to leave, Reece clasped her hands and wouldn't let her go. She looked up into his face. His eyes were moist and glistening.

"Please," he pleaded.

Her throat constricted. A tear raced down each of her cheeks. She shook her head as she pulled her hands free and mounted Flash. He gave her hat back to her, and she looked down at him. More tears raced down her face. She had to go quickly if she ever was going to leave.

"I love you," she mouthed and goaded Flash into motion. She could feel Reece's gaze on her back, beckoning her to turn around. She kept her teary focus on Lucas's stern face and stopped at his side.

"Are you all right?" Concern was carved in his stonelike features.

Marty nodded.

She knew he was surprised by her tears. The last time he had seen her cry she was very little. "Did he hurt you or the girls?"

Marty shook her head.

"Go on," he ordered. "I'll be along in a minute."

Marty walked Flash several feet behind Lucas, then stopped and turned around. Reece's gaze was still fixed on her. She longed to race back across the river and into his arms, never to let go.

Lucas moved his horse to the water's edge and stopped. Reece got the message and got on his horse. He looked one long, last time at her. Turning, he rode away. She would likely never again see the man she loved.

Marty watched as he disappeared among the trees. "Good-bye," she mouthed with a quivering lip.

Marty and Lucas traveled side by side and remained a good distance behind the others.

Lucas looked sideways at his baby sister. She had grown into quite a woman. He broke the silence. "Do you love him?"

"It doesn't matter." Her hoarse voice quivered as she struggled to hold back tears.

He had wondered if he would ever see the

day when she fell in love and didn't realize it would be so painful . . . for them both. "I'm sure you would have no trouble catching up to him," Lucas said. "Lynnette was about your age, a little younger, when she married and left."

"I think I'm finally beginning to understand how she felt. But I'll never understand how she could leave."

"We all have to make our own decisions. She had to do what was right for her."

"At the expense of everyone else?"

He nodded. "Sometimes."

"Lynnette was selfish. I'll never leave you or the family. I'll always be there. You can count on me."

"I know." Though proud of her, it saddened him, too. She was a little too much like him. He had sacrificed what he thought was his future happiness for his brothers and sisters so they wouldn't have to do the same. He would give up everything he had to protect his family. Unfortunately, Marty had learned that lesson all too well. He could do nothing for her now except help her live with her decision.

"You won't tell Travis and Trevor I was sniveling like a ninny?" Marty dried her tears on her coat sleeve.

"I won't tell them a thing."

"Lucas, do you think God likes me?"

"Of course."

His reply came back so fast she felt it hit her, even though she knew that would be his answer. "I mean, do you think He approves . . . you know . . . of the way I dress and stuff?"

After a moment of contemplation, Lucas spoke again, "The Good Book says God does not look on the outward man — or woman — but the heart. Not many people, women or men, would go charging off across the country without a thought of themselves after two desperadoes."

Reece wasn't really a desperado.

"When God looks at your heart, I think He sees pure gold."

"I doubt that."

"It may be tarnished in a few places, but your motives are in the right place."

She had to wonder about that. Were her motives in the right place in the choice she had made?

CHAPTER 24

Back on the farm in Montana, Marty stood by the window in the royal blue gingham dress Reece had instructed Mrs. Atwater to buy for her. Spring was bursting out all over.

Travis eyeballed her, bewildered. He turned to his sister-in-law, who was rocking Lottie, the newest addition to the family. "It ain't Sunday, is it?"

"It *isn't* Sunday," Aunt Ginny corrected. Marty turned and watched as Ginny was fitting a shirt on Travis.

Looking sideways at Aunt Ginny, Travis took a deep breath and huffed it out. "Why is Marty wearing a dress?"

"Why don't you ask her yourself?" Cinda said in a whimsical tone.

He had a stunned look on his face like he hadn't thought to ask her himself. "Marty, why are you wearing a dress? It *isn't* even Sunday." He looked directly at Aunt Ginny when he said isn't.

"Because I want to." She planted her hands

on her hips and narrowed her eyes. "You want to make something of it?"

Travis held up his hands in surrender. "No. Just askin'."

"Hold still unless you favor getting poked," Aunt Ginny scolded.

Marty hadn't meant to snap at him. She turned back to the window.

"You look very nice, Marty. Royal blue is very becoming on you," Cinda said.

Marty already knew this particular shade of blue looked nice on her. She had been told it brought out the color of her eyes.

"She's just acting weird ever since she came back last fall. Weird," Travis said.

She felt weird. Tears swelled in her eyes. She had to escape before anyone noticed. She rammed on the old hat Reece had given her and made a swift exit.

"That hat don't go with her dress," she heard Travis say as she headed out the door.

She liked this hat. Reece's hat. In her opinion, it went with everything.

Her behavior was strange indeed. She didn't even flinch when Tommy Jensen teased her on Sunday for wearing a dress to church. She even let her hair grow. Now it touched her shoulders.

She strolled to the apple tree and pulled down a limb to drink in the smell of the blossoms. Nothing was the same anymore. For the first time in her life she wasn't completely happy on the farm surrounded by her family. Something was missing and always would be.

"It's a beautiful day," Lucas said from behind her.

It was a lovely spring day; she just couldn't enjoy it. Maybe if it were raining. "I suppose." She looked longingly to the west and sighed. "I thought it was the winter blues. You know, cabin fever, being closed in. Spring was supposed to cure me. It hasn't."

"Do you love him?"

She drew in a shuddering breath and shrugged her shoulders.

Lucas turned her to face him. "Martha Jane Rawlings, answer my question. Do you love him?"

Her brother had never used her full name. Marty tried to answer but couldn't quite form the words. She bit her bottom lip to keep it from quivering. Tears trailed down her cheeks as she nodded.

Lucas wrapped her in his arms.

After she regained control, he released her. "He always treated me like a lady, whether or not I acted like one." She paused and looked up at her big brother. She smiled with a tear-stained face. "Usually not."

"You could go to him. I won't stop you," Lucas said.

"I can't leave."

He understood. She could no more leave this place than he could, but it was good of him to give her a choice. "Come with me." He took her by the hand. "I have something sure to cheer you up. It's out front by the hitching rail."

She gave Lucas a nothing-is-going-to-help look. He pulled her along anyway.

It was probably some sort of animal if it was tied to the hitching rail. Certainly not a horse. Lucas knew she would never replace Flash.

When she was eight, she had seen a picture of an elephant at school and pestered Lucas for three months to get her one. When she was eleven, she wanted a hunting dog. Lucas said no, but when one of their horses foaled that spring Lucas said she could raise and care for the colt and saddle-train him. She named him Flash. She hadn't asked for another animal since. She didn't know what he could have possibly gotten her. Certainly not an elephant.

Anticipation churned in her as they rounded the corner of the house. The fact that her big brother was attempting to cheer her up with a surprise made her feel a little better. She determined to be enthusiastic no matter what it was and thank her loving brother.

Marty stopped in her tracks and stared. She couldn't believe it. Reece. He was here, leaning against the hitching rail as he had that first day. Her heart raced and she almost

241

forgot to breathe. "Reece!"

He turned to her and smiled. She hiked up her dress and ran to him. His arms enfolded her, and he kissed her. He held her for several more minutes without saying a word.

"What are you doing here?" Marty asked, breaking the silence.

He smiled. "I brought you a present."

"You didn't come all this way just to deliver a package."

"Why not?"

"Because you didn't. Now why are you here?"

"First the present." He walked her over to his horse and removed a big floral, lady's hatbox. Marty eyed it with suspicion. What would she do with a lady's hat? She would never be able to muster up enough excitement to convince him she liked it even a little.

"Open it." He tipped the box toward her.

She took a deep breath. *Here goes nothing.*

As she reached for the lid, Reece jiggled the box. "Careful, it might bite."

Marty looked up at his grinning face and furrowed her eyebrows to show him she did not find it funny. She supposed she was being a little silly. She grabbed the lid and jerked it off. She gasped and stared in the box. The lid slipped from her hands and landed at her feet. She reached into the box and retrieved a new gleaming white Stetson. This was one lady's hat she would have no problem wearing.

Reece set down the box. "Put it on." He plucked his old hat off her.

Marty raised the hat to her head. It fit perfectly. She smiled. "It's good enough to wear to church, I'd say."

Reece gave an approving nod and gazed at her as he had in Seattle.

"What are you doing here?"

"Delivering your new . . ." His voice trailed off and he shook his head in time with Marty's. "You don't believe me?" He clutched his chest. "The maiden doth wound me."

"You could have mailed it." Had Reece come on his own or had Lucas sent for him? No, Lucas wouldn't have sent for him, but he certainly wasn't opposed to his being here.

Reece's mischievous smile sent tingles through her.

"If you came just to bring this" — she tapped her wonderful new hat — "then I guess you can go now."

She turned to pretend to walk away, but Reece stopped her and drew her into his arms. "Not so fast. I'm not letting you get away again."

He kept his arms around her and looked deep into her eyes a moment before explaining. "I've been corresponding with Lucas. We had a long talk in town before riding out here."

She looked around, but Lucas was gone.

That's why he had taken the mysterious trip into town this morning and wouldn't let anyone go with him. Marty raised her eyebrows with hope and delight. "So you and Lucas are friends?"

"Not exactly." With love in his eyes, he caressed her cheek with his thumb. "Let's just say we have a mutual interest."

She put her hand on his and held it against her cheek.

"Marty." He held her face in both his hands. "I came here for one reason."

"To give me a hat."

He squeezed her face gently. "No. I came for you. I love you and want to marry you."

Her insides twisted. "You know I can't."

"Lucas has consented, with great reservation, but he has consented."

"Nothing has changed. I can't leave here." Her heart ached.

"I'm not asking you to. I'm staying here. It looks like you're stuck with me. Again." He smiled.

Marty's eyes brightened. "What about your lawyering and Mrs. Atwater?"

"I turned over the law practice to my partner. There are too many nasty bears in that forest. Milly and I converted my house into a nice little boardinghouse. She wouldn't let me give it to her outright, but I convinced her to run it. Everything's taken care of — my affairs back in Seattle, Milly, Lucas." He looked deep into her blue eyes. "I'm here to stay. The only thing left is for you to say yes."

She no longer fought the feelings he stirred in her. "Yes." It came out as a cross between a breath and a whisper.

He leaned down slowly and kissed her lips.

■ ■ ■ ■

A TIME TO KEEP

BY KELLY EILEEN HAKE

■ ■ ■ ■

To God, first and foremost, and to my critique partners and editors, without whom this book would not be what it is today.

PROLOGUE

Ireland 1874

Fifteen-year-old Ewan Gailbraith sidestepped yet another muddy puddle in an Irish thoroughfare. *"Be my braw lad and take good care of your mama for me, son."* His father's words echoed through his mind. *"I'll find good work and send ye the fare to come join me in America."* Ewan stubbornly trudged on in the face of the unseasonable downpour.

"Da left us nigh on a year ago." The lad aimed a fierce kick at a hapless rock as he neared his destination. "Surely this week we'll hae another letter." He drew up short at the old tavern banged together from a motley lot of old boards and prayed that old Ferguson would have an envelope for him.

He swung open the lopsided door. For once his arrival was unannounced by the creaky old hinges, now too waterlogged to protest. Ewan stomped his worn boots on the threshold to dislodge the worst of the mud and then bypassed the hearty welcome of the roaring fire in favor of approaching the tavern owner at the bar.

"Mr. Ferguson," he addressed, drawing up to his full height, "hae you any word from my da this day?" He clenched his teeth as the barkeep looked him over, as much to stop them from chattering as from biting back angry words at the miserable man who drew out his answers as long as the voyage to America.

"Aye." The man reached beneath his scraggly beard, into the pocket of his coat, and drew out a much-handled brown packet. He placed it on the weathered face of the bar and slid it toward the youth.

"Thankee." Ewan manfully resisted the urge to pounce upon the package, instead calmly nudging it off the bar and into the safety of his own threadbare pocket. His hand lingered over the small coin inside before drawing it out, placing it carefully on the bar, and turning away.

"You should warm yoursel' by the fire afore ye step outside again!" the barkeep's wife called to him.

Ewan hesitated, reluctant to waste even a moment before bringing his mam the news from his father, but saw the wisdom of the woman's words. He'd be no good to Mam if he caught a chill and couldn't work. He grudgingly moved toward the warmth of the flames, holding his hands toward the heat.

He kept ignoring the curious gazes of the old-timers who probably hoped he'd open the envelope before them all and give the town some new gossip to chew over.

He waited until he felt reasonably warmed, if not dry, and headed back into the gray rain. His long stride covered the soggy ground quickly in a bid to stave off the cold on his journey. With each step he took, the packet thumped against his side — a weight that would either ease his burden or add to it. Which would be the case, he knew not. 'Twas not his place to open the envelope before bringing it to his mother. His restless hands clenched at his sides as he neared their small, well-thatched cottage.

"Ewan!" Ma swung open the door and pulled him inside, clucking like a hen as she drew off his jacket and wrapped his hands around a warm mug of water. "I couldn't believe you'd taken off in this weather! What was so important it could not wait a day or two?"

Ewan jerked his chin toward the sopping wet jacket she started to hang on a peg by the door. "It has come, Ma." He watched her blue eyes widen in hope and surprise before her fingers deftly searched his pockets and withdrew the packet.

"Do ye ken what it holds, son?" She turned the envelope over in her hands as though loath to open it.

"Nay. I thought 'twas best we open it together." He put down the mug and walked over to his mother, placing his arm around her shoulders as he towered over her.

At his silent nod, she tore open one side of the envelope and drew two smaller ones from the packet. She opened the thinner of the envelopes first. They stood in silence as they each drank in the strong, sure strokes of his father's hand.

Ewan let loose the breath he hadn't known he'd held. Da was fine and well in America, and he sent his love and hopes that they'd all be together soon. Ewan gave his mother's shoulder a firm squeeze. She then slit open the other envelope to find a significant amount of money. "Oh, Ewan!" Tears of joy ran down his mother's tired face as she looked up at him. "He's well, and we're that much closer to joining him! Why, in another six months or so, we'll have enough to pay both our passages to America."

Ewan looked at his mother's smile and saw the lingering sadness in her eyes. Fine lines had sprung up around her eyes over the last few months and now gave away the disappointment she tried to hide. With each month her husband had been gone, Imogene Gailbraith had lost a bit more of her joy. In another six months, or even an entire year, Da would not recognize this slight woman as the beloved wife he'd left in his son's care.

Now's the time. 'Tis the right thing to do.

"Ma," Ewan began, taking her chilled hands in his own, "I've given the matter much thought, and I've come to a decision . . ."

CHAPTER 1

Montana Territory, Autumn 1886

"Look out!" Brent Freimont practically shoved Rosalind MacLean off the path as he rushed to plunge a bucket into the stream.

Rosalind gasped to see the normally fastidious young man's clothes all askew. "What's wrong?"

"No time." He hurried past her with the now-brimming bucket. Rosalind turned. Whorls of smoke were rising atop the maple trees.

"Fire!" Quickly she filled the unscrubbed pot, still dirty from the morning meal, with water and raced up the path after Brent. Water sloshed over her skirts and bare feet as she went, but she paid no heed. When she reached the line of trees, her suspicions — fueled by the acrid scent of smoke tinged with something even more unpleasant — were confirmed. Someone had set fire to the outhouse.

When she reached the site, several men

were already fighting the flames. Dustin Freimont and Isaac and Jakob Albright had obviously rushed over at the first sign of trouble.
She handed over the heavy pot with relief. It
hadn't been easy hauling it up the hill. She
drew in a deep breath and promptly began
sputtering. *Not the smartest idea I've ever had,*
she admitted to herself when she rushed once
again to the stream. Before long, they'd managed to douse the flames. All that was left
was a heap of sodden, smoldering wood —
and a lingering stench.

"What on earth happened?" Isaac turned
to Brent, outrage written plainly across his
handsome features.

"I . . . er . . ." Brent avoided his uncle's
gaze only to find Rosalind staring at him in
befuddlement. The young man blushed bright
red and mumbled something almost incoherent.

"What?" Isaac had plainly missed the
whispered confession.

"I was trying to smoke a cigar." Brent spoke
more loudly this time, though he seemed no
less embarrassed.

"You were *smoking*?!" Dustin Freimont
roared, having just come upon the scene in
time to hear his son's confession.

"In the *privy*?" Isaac's disbelief more closely
mirrored Rosalind's.

"Yes." Brent stared at the wreckage in

misery. "I knew better than to try it at home, Pa."

"You would've done well to take that caution a step or two further." Isaac grimaced. "Smoking near anything made of wood is foolish."

Rosalind stepped in. "I think he's learned his lesson." When she caught Brent's adoring gaze, she wished she'd remained silent.

Brent Freimont, a little less than two years her junior, had taken to giving her cow eyes whenever she so much as glanced in his direction. Since she was one of the few single girls in the area who wasn't his younger sister, Rosalind couldn't really blame him for his notice. Then again, she really couldn't encourage him either.

Dustin doled out the punishment. "He'll have learned his lesson once he cleans up this mess and builds a new outhouse."

"What happened?" Rosalind's dad stared at the charred mess. Mam, followed by Brent's mother, came hard on his heels.

Most days, Rosalind considered the proximity of their homes to be a blessing. When her mother and father had settled this land with the Freimonts and Albrights, they'd agreed to build their homes and barns on the strip of earth joining their properties. She'd grown up with Brent and, later, Marlene. Their parents, Delana and Dustin, lived within spitting distance of her family home. Two generations' worth of each family, all with homes on the same three acres of land.

Not too long ago, it had been three generations on each side. Rosalind looked toward the small cemetery where they'd buried Bernadine, Rawhide, and her Grandda Cade. The only one left was Rosalind's grandmother, Gilda Banning, who'd moved in with the MacLeans when Grandda passed on.

Any way Rose looked on it, she couldn't help but feel all of them were one big family. She knew that her family and Brent's hoped for a match to officially unite them. Try as she might, she couldn't fathom it. Brent seemed as much the scapegrace younger brother to her today as he had when he'd slipped wriggly tadpoles down the back of her dress on his sixth birthday.

Marlene ran up. "Oh, Brent. *Now* what did you do?"

By this point, it seemed as though everyone had gathered at the scene of the crime. Rosalind looked at the familiar faces with fondness, and a part of her wished she could make their dream of a marriage come true. However, that part was drowned out by the loud, insistent voice demanding that she be true to her own heart. Marriage was a lifetime commitment — a commitment she simply couldn't make to the young man who'd just burned down an outhouse.

"Clean it up and build a new one?" Brent's

voice jerked her back to the current problem. "Maybe I should take the opportunity to dig a new one altogether." Anyone who knew Brent could see that the idea of touching the filthy, smelly heap in front of him was enough to make him turn green.

"Good idea." Rosalind's da clapped him on the shoulder. "Clean up this mess and create an entirely new outhouse. Nice to see a man take responsibility for his mistakes and make amends."

Brent rubbed his shoulder sullenly, obviously unwilling to utter another word that might land him more work. One by one, all slipped away to tend to their own chores until Brent was left alone with Rosalind and his sister.

"I'm sorry, Brent." Marlene gave him a commiserating glance even as she looped an arm around Rosalind's shoulders and began to walk away. She bit back a snicker before she added, "This whole thing really stinks!"

She and Rosalind hurried away, failing to hold their giggles. They stopped when they were out of Brent's sight to talk about the contretemps.

"That wasn't very nice, making fun of your brother," Rosalind pointed out.

"There are worse things." Marlene gave a meaningful glance backward before wrinkling her nose. "I just don't understand what goes through his head sometimes."

"Nor do I. Though I wonder" — Rosalind plucked a late-blooming wildflower and twirled it between her fingers — "if others say the same about us."

"Who knows?" Marlene stretched and thought for a moment. "I'd probably say everybody reads us like we're open books."

"Surely not." Rosalind dropped the tiny flower and looked at the wide blue Montana sky that stretched ahead of them, broken only by the mountain peaks in the distance. "Human beings, like life, are never that simple."

"This life is simple," Ewan Gailbraith announced to the young man he'd be showing around that day and training for the remainder of the week. "You work hard, keep your mouth shut, an' help others when you can. Don't waste money or flash it around, stay away from Hank's chili, and don't start anything. Only other advice I can give you is to take care o' your tools and they'll take care o' you."

"Yes, sir." The wiry lad twisted his hat in his hands. "I don't mind honest work, so long as it's for honest pay."

"As a wheelwright, you'll be paid well for your skill." Ewan smiled. "In a couple of years, you'll hae enough saved to start a life anywhere you like. That's what most men do."

"Is that what you're planning to do, Mr. Gailbraith?"

Ewan gestured toward a freight car. "That's where we keep the raw materials." *When and where will I leave the railroad and begin my own life?* He kept talking business in an effort to distract himself from the question he refused to answer. "We build makeshift forges when and where we need them as the railroad builds from town to town. For the first week, you'll be transporting finished items and pre-sized strips down to where the track is being laid. It won't be too much longer before we hae to set up the forge farther down."

"I thought there was a small town a little ways farther down."

"There is. Saddleback is where we'll set up our next base. We'll be continuing the main line an' beginning an offshoot running through there, so you can count on staying there awhile. You'll end up trying your hand as farrier before long, I'd warrant."

"I apprenticed with a farrier for the last year." The young man sounded a bit more confident now.

"All to the good. I do both jobs myself." Ewan stopped for a moment and spoke more carefully. "Now, if you were apprenticing, why didn't you see it through?"

"My master drank too much one night and fell in the horse trough. I found him the next morning."

"Overfond o' t' bottle, eh?" Ewan gave the youth a measuring look. "There are some here who share that weakness. You seem a bright lad, but I'll offer you this warning: Don't indulge in drink, gaming, or some o' the loose women who follow the railroad. Any one of those vices will take your money and leave you feeling ill. I don't tolerate that sort of behavior from my men. Understood?"

"Yes, sir." The fellow stood a little taller. "I never held much stock by those ways myself."

"I'm glad to hear it." Ewan turned and continued walking. "Honest values and hard work will take you further than the railroad itself ever can."

CHAPTER 2

"The railroad will take this town and build it into a city." Rosalind could practically have danced upon the words she spoke to her father. He didn't respond while he ate the mid-morning snack she'd brought to his smithy. "Think of it — the workers who lay the rails are not so far off. I heard that they'll have reached us before the week is out."

"I'm thinkin' on it more an' more wi' each passing day, Rosey-mine." Da wore an expression she'd seen before only when he looked at his son. Pride tinged with regret for what could have been.

She and Luke were the joys of her father's life, but Da had hoped to pass on his trade to his son. With Luke's weak lungs, he would never stand at his father's forge, carrying on an age-old family tradition. Yes, she knew well the wistful gleam that crept into Da's eyes as he spoke of the progress of the "iron horse." But what could he possibly regret when they'd be linked at long last to the world beyond Saddleback? What opportunities lay at the other end of those rails?

"Da? What is it, exactly, you've been thinking on?"

"Sit down wi' me for a moment, lass." He gestured to a bench in the corner and sat down heavily. " 'Tis time and past for us to speak on a few matters."

"Da?" Worry sparked in her heart at the lines on her father's brow.

"Don't fret so, Rosey-mine. 'Tis nothing so dire as you may imagine." Her father drew a deep breath. "It seems to me as though 'twas only yesterday your ma came out here to join me. Her showing up wi' you in her arms was the sweetest moment of my life. I remember it so clearly. But I look on the memories that filled the passing years, and I know better. I see the stamp of time on your lovely face, Rosey, and can't deny that you've become a woman grown. If I were honest, I would say that I've known it for quite some time now."

Dread thudded in Rosalind's heart. Surely Da wouldn't tell her she must choose a husband and move on? Aye, most lasses wed long before their nineteenth year, but couldn't he see that it wasn't the right time for her?

"You are a beauty, just like your mother." Da's sudden smile brought a welcome rush of relief. "But with that beauty comes danger. A lovely lass without the protection of a husband can be a target for evil men."

"Da!" Rosalind burst out, desperate to stop his flow of words. "I know everyone expects me to make my choice soon, but I can't! Not when all I've ever known is this small piece of the world and the familiar faces on it! The railroad will give me the opportunity to see a bit more, meet new people, afore I settle down. Would you deny me that chance?"

"Nay, Rosey-mine, I wouldn't. Your ma and Delana cherish hopes that you'll choose to wed Brent. Nay, don't speak now." He held up one massive hand as though to ward off her alarm. " 'Tis your choice to make, daughter, but to my way of thinking, Brent 'tisn't the man for you. If he were, you would hae settled on him long ago."

Rosalind nodded, half-ashamed at the admission she'd be letting down her mother but half-relieved that her father understood and accepted her decision.

"I'll hae no part in shoving my lassie out of our home and into the arms of a man she doesn't love as deeply as I cherish your ma. And, were I to be completely honest, I don't know what we'd do wi'out you." Her father's grin made Rosalind's own smile falter.

Here, then, was the heart of the matter. Da knew she longed to explore the opportunities the railroad would bring, but he was reminding her of her responsibilities here at home. She helped Ma with the garden, cooking, housework, and sewing when she wasn't taking meals to Da or watching over Luke. If she followed her own dreams, she'd be leaving her family behind — and they needed her. Rosalind struggled against the sense of confinement pressing in upon her. She'd never abandon them, no matter what it cost her. She opened her mouth to assure her father that he could rely on her.

"What I mean to say is that we love you dearly, Rosey-mine, and I mean to warn you about the changes the railroad will bring." Her father's serious expression bore into her.

"Oh, I already know much of what to expect." Her enthusiasm rushed to the tip of her tongue. " 'Twill bring many people — farmers, traders, railroad officials, and more — to our small town. The number of families will swell, and our ability to send goods and receive modern niceties will increase dramatically. Should we want to visit Fort Benton or Virginia City, 'twill take naught but a fraction of the time we'd spend on horseback to arrive there and journey back. New friends, adventures just a ride away, and shorter waits for everything! The railroad is a marvel, Da. 'Twill change everything." *And I can hardly wait!*

" 'Tis glad I am to hear you've been thinking on the matter so seriously." Da nodded his approval. "Is that all you have to say on it, or will you be able to tell me of some o' the drawbacks the railroad brings along with all that shining opportunity?"

"Drawbacks?" Rosalind felt her brow crease as she considered this. "I suppose 'twill be awkward meeting new people and drawing them into our small community, but we'll all be the better for it, Da. And along wi' the opportunity will come more work for you — the more people, the more demand for your smithy, I know. I wouldna like to see you o'erworked." She gave him a stern glance.

"Nor would I," he agreed, a grin teasing the corners of his lips. "Though the work and pay will bring benefits as well — medicine for Luke, some of those newfangled laundry contraptions for your mam, delicious treats for us to sample at the general store . . ." He paused until he caught his daughter's eye. "And fine, fancy young men to turn a pretty lass's head."

"Oh, Da." Rosalind tried to ignore the heat rising to her cheeks.

"Now, you wouldna be trying to tell your old da the thought hadna crossed your mind?" His teasing made the blush deepen.

"I —" Rosalind's response was mercifully cut short by an interruption.

A tall, burly man stood in the entryway, powerful shoulders blocking out much of the day's light. Even though Rosalind couldn't see his shadowed features, she knew this wasn't one of her neighbors. It seemed as though the railroad — and the changes to come — had arrived.

Ewan blinked, trying to adjust his vision to the dimness inside the smithy. Slowly, he began to take note of the way things were set up. He liked what he saw.

The stone forge stood about forty inches high and forty inches square — large enough for big work and deep enough for the fire to most efficiently use the air from the great leather and wood bellows. He'd seen from the outside of the structure that the forge's chimney boasted a brick hood to carry out smoke and fine ash.

The anvil and slag tub stood close enough at hand to be immediately useful, but with a good, clear working space around them. The front and sides of the forge held racks and rings to hold hammers, tongs, chisels, files, and other tools. This in and of itself was not unusual; the fact that the tools had been put in their proper place immediately after use was. Most blacksmiths heaped their tools on the lip of the forge, having to quickly dig out the needed implement from beneath several of its fellows before continuing work.

Altogether, it was a well-built, well-stocked, and well-kept smithy far above and beyond what he'd expected to find in the depths of the Montana wilderness. Ewan tamped down an unexpected spurt of longing. It had been a long time since he'd worked in an honest smithy, instead lugging a cast-iron patent forge from work site to work site. The only advantage of a patent forge, in Ewan's opinion, was the mobility so highly prized by the railroad.

"Will you be needing anything now?" The resident blacksmith, a tall man who spoke with the lilt of home, stepped in front of Ewan.

Ewan shook himself free of the unbidden memories before speaking. "Perhaps." He looked around frankly, nodding in admiration, before continuing. "I'm Ewan Gailbraith, and I work wi' Montana Central as their head blacksmith. I step in to help wi' a bit o' the work of farrier and wheelwright." Ewan allowed his syllables to boast of his own Irish heritage. "We had some men decide to stay back at Benton, and I find myself a bit shorthanded as we make our way toward your town."

At the approval Ewan demonstrated for the smithy's workshop, the man seemed to thaw a bit.

"Now, then, that's a shame." The smith's eyes held a spark of interest. He gave an assessing look in return for Ewan's own appraisal.

"We're miles away from here, and the company will be moving t' make camp in this area any day now." Ewan noted the flicker of unease that crossed the older man's features

271

as he quickly glanced over his shoulder to the corner of the shop.

It didn't take much to see what concerned the man. A lovely lass stood in the corner, her demure pose belied by the avid interest on her face as she listened to their conversation. Within the darkness of the smithy, the colors of her braided hair and lively eyes were shadowed, but there was no hiding her lithesome shape and obvious intelligence. Ewan caught himself before his glance could become rude and resolutely returned his focus to the blacksmith.

" 'Tis good to know when we can expect the chaos ahead." The blacksmith thrust his hand toward Ewan. "Arthur MacLean, blacksmith of Saddleback."

"I'd a suspicion." Ewan grinned and returned the man's firm grip as he pumped his hand in welcome.

"This is my daughter, Rosalind." Arthur gestured toward the lass, and she stepped forward with lively grace.

" 'Tis grand to meet you, Mr. Gailbraith."

Ewan noted a pair of bright blue eyes framed by a riot of fiery curls. "And you, Miss MacLean." Intensely aware of her father's scrutiny, Ewan greeted her with all the formality a wary papa could require, even as he tried to hide his astonishment. Why had no one seen fit to warn him or the other supervisors that this small, out-of-the-way settlement held at least one pretty, unmarried female? This would greatly complicate things, as the workers saw precious few women along the work trail.

"Now that you've been introduced to Mr. Gailbraith, run home and tell your mam to be expecting a guest for dinner." Arthur MacLean folded his arms across his massive chest. "For now, he and I have some business to discuss."

Ewan refused to give in to the urge to watch Rosalind MacLean leave the smithy. He waited in silence until he could be sure the girl was out of earshot.

"Mr. MacLean," Ewan spoke before her father had the chance, "before we discuss smithy business, I would like to have a word about your daughter." He waited for the man's leery nod. Obviously, Arthur MacLean was a man who liked to have all the facts before he made a judgment. That boded well.

Ewan searched for words to put the matter delicately. Finding none, he plunged forward. "In large cities, men who so choose may find . . . companionship. However, it has been long days since we were at such a place. Lonely, less-than-civilized men will be descending upon your town by the dozens, and I will plainly tell you that I have fears concerning the well-being of your daughter."

"As do I." The man uncrossed his arms and rubbed the back of his neck. "We've another young lass or two in the area, as well. The only men they've ever known, they've grown up with. This is a small town filled wi' friends and extended family. None of the girls has any notion of how to handle strange men."

"I'm certain that you are able to protect your own, sir, but I hope that I may trust you t' warn the others of your community t' be diligent about watching o'er the misses." Ewan gave the man a meaningful glance. "I'll give the men a stern talking-to and set up what measures I can."

"I'll be taking your word on that, Mr. Gailbraith."

"Please, call me Ewan."

"Ewan. And you're to call me Arthur." MacLean gave a decisive nod. "Now that we've reached an agreement concerning what I deem the most important matter we could discuss, let's get down to business."

"Mam!" Rosalind rushed into the house. "Da sent me to tell you we'll be having a guest for dinner!"

"A guest?" Luke piped the question first.

"Aye. A Mr. Gailbraith, smith for the railroad. He came to Da's shop just now. He was still there when I left." Rosalind rushed about, tidying the flowers in a cracked mug, polishing a spot on the ornate metalwork of the stove grate, whisking dishes onto the table. "I'll pop in a batch of biscuits from the

274

dough I made this morning. They should be finished in time."

"Such a flurry," Mam marveled as she stirred the stew. "Is there aught you should be telling your mam before this important visitor walks through our door?"

"He's come to offer Da work, I think." Rosalind slid the biscuits into the bread oven. "And he brings news that the railroad men will be here any day!"

"I see."

Rosalind stilled as Grandmam caught her by the wrist and addressed her brother. "Luke, would you please go to the spring-house and fetch some butter and milk?" Once he was out of sight, she turned her sharp gaze upon her granddaughter.

Mam was the one who spoke up. "Rose, there's something we'd been meaning to speak wi' you about. 'Tis a delicate matter, but the time has come upon us sooner than expected." Mam had the same long look Da had worn scant minutes ago.

"Yes, Mam?" Rosalind wondered if it had to do with the same topic. *I hope it doesn't. Lord, I'm not ready to tell her my decision against Brent.*

"From all your talk, I know you are thinking that the railroad will bring many wondrous things — and so it shall. Yet the men who will build the rail line may not be so very wondrous, daughter." Mam paused meaningfully. "You've been sheltered here, surrounded only by friends and family. Now, strangers will begin to arrive in our midst — men who may not be as honorable or God-fearing as those you know. You must hae a care, Rose, not to become enamored wi' them or fall prey to any unscrupulous tricks. Be wary of these strangers, and guard your heart and mind, as well as your physical self. Do you understand me, Rose?"

"Aye, Mam." Rose nodded faintly. "Such dark thoughts about our fellow men, though! It puts a caution into my heart to hear you, who I've never heard say a harsh word over any soul, warn me so."

"See that you take heed. From now on, you are not to walk anywhere on your lonesome. You will hae your father, brother, myself, or someone known and trusted by us in your company at all times."

"Mam!" Rosalind couldn't stop the dismayed cry. *I already take Luke wi' me almost everywhere I go, and I'm always at the house or the smithy. The only moments I hae for my own thoughts and dreams seem to be while I'm traveling from one place to another. I didn't think they could clip my wings any further! Oh, heavenly Father, I don't see how I'm to bear it!*

"I know 'tis a sacrifice on your part, made necessary through no fault of your own, dear." Mam rubbed her hand down Rosalind's back. "Lovely young women usually learn to take such precautions at a far earlier age. You've had more freedom here than most."

Freedom? I've lived in the same small area my entire life! Until now my whole world consisted solely of Saddleback. Now, at my first opportunity to see anything different, I'm pulled ever closer to the bosom of my family. She paused, trying to see it from their view. *Da warned me. Mam and Grandmam did the same. . . .*

Lord, is this Your way? Parents protect their children, and though I feel I'm no longer a child, I know that they ask these things for what they deem my own good. Your Word tells me to honor my father and mother, and so I shall.

"I'll not go anywhere unescorted, Mam." The very words seemed to constrict her, but Rosalind knew that to struggle against her parents' wishes would only make them tie her still more tightly.

"I'm glad to see you being so sensible, Rose. 'Tis a sign of your maturity. Someday, not too far off, you'll hae a home of your own, and our little chats will be about how to rear your little ones." Mam, stirring the pot once again, had her back turned to Rosalind and so could not notice her daughter's expression of worry. She kept speaking. "If this man is a smith, he'll have a hearty appetite. Best see if you can slip in one more batch of biscuits, dear."

Rosalind smoothed back the irrepressible wisps of curls around her face before pulling the fragrant golden biscuits from the oven.

"Smells wonderful." Da's voice preceded him and Mr. Gailbraith, giving them last-minute warning.

"It does indeed," Mr. Gailbraith agreed, taking off his hat as he entered.

"Ewan Gailbraith, this is Kaitlin, my bonny bride." Da put a loving arm around his wife's waist. "And her mam, Gilda Banning. This is my son, Luke, and you've already met my daughter."

" 'Tis pleased I am to make your acquaintance, Mrs. MacLean, Mrs. Banning." He gave a slight bow to Mam and Grandmam. Then, turning in Rosalind's direction, he nodded his head and said, "Good to see you again, Miss MacLean." With a smile, he greeted Luke, pumping his hand heartily.

Rosalind busied herself, refusing to show any undue interest in the man now sitting at their table. The light of day revealed his hair to be deepest ebony, and his smiling eyes glinted a good Irish green. A strong jaw squared his face and framed a ready smile. All in all, he was even more handsome than she'd supposed. This, then, was the first stranger in their midst.

He doesn't seem dangerous at all. There is

something in him, aside from his broad shoulders and arms made thick from hard work, to remind me of Da. Perhaps this is the reason Mam warned me — I do not make a practice of seeing darkness in another. I know nothing of this man yet would be liable to trust him already. His very ease of manner and handsome appearance must make him every bit as dangerous as Mam fears these men may be. Now that I've been warned, I'll be sure to watch myself around him. For all I know, he's a threat.

CHAPTER 3

Miss Rosalind MacLean, Ewan decided, was a serious threat to his peace of mind. Standing near the window with the sunshine pouring a golden blessing upon her fiery locks and creamy skin, she delighted his eye and dismayed his heart. What red-blooded man among his workers would be able to resist such a siren? The light blue skirts of her dress swayed gently as she brought a basket of perfectly baked biscuits to the table.

No, no, no. Please, Lord, tell me she didn't bake those biscuits. Show me that she burns any morsel of food she tries to prepare. When she speaks, let her be missing a few teeth. At the very least, let her be clumsy enough to knock things over! When she gracefully set the hot biscuits down and gave him a soft smile full of perfect teeth, Ewan despaired. It took him a few moments to regroup with a few more cheery thoughts.

Perhaps she laughs like a donkey, eats with poor manners, or displays signs of becoming a nag. Maybe she isn't usually so clean as today or is content t' shirk her chores. She could have harsh words for others or be one o' those babbling women who causes men to shudder. There are still numerous off-putting faults she may possess to discourage suitors.

One half hour, one blessing, two bowls of stew, and three lighter-than-air biscuits later, Ewan leaned back. He watched as Rosalind MacLean graciously cleared the table, leaving a bewitching scent of roses and the silvery chime of her laughter as she passed. She'd been respectful to her parents, kind to her brother, welcoming yet reserved toward him, and maintained neither silence nor continuous chatter. Ewan stifled a groan, masking his discomfort by patting his almost-too-full stomach.

" 'Twas a delicious dinner, and I'm much obliged t' you all. I haven't eaten a meal so grand in ages."

"Will you be leaving, then, so soon?" Arthur sounded genuinely disappointed.

"I've work to attend to, and I'd not want to be holdin' anyone else from theirs." Ewan eyed what seemed a veritable mountain of dirty dishes.

"You can't make the time for some coffee and a bit o' shortbread, Mr. Gailbraith?" Rosalind's clear, cool voice washed over him.

"I *am* powerful fond of shortbread," he

admitted. "And I wanted to ask about something before I left."

"Yes?" Arthur's undivided attention seemed overly intent. "What can we tell you?"

"When and where is Sunday meeting held hereabouts?"

"It moves around," Luke MacLean said.

"Oh?" Ewan smiled at the lad. Had Arthur not already mentioned his son was twelve, Ewan would have estimated the slight lad to have reached only eight or nine years. Perhaps his small stature explained his absence from the smithy. He'd need to gain more height and breadth to do a blacksmith's work. "And where would a man be finding it come this Lord's day?"

"That'd be at the Freimonts' place, just north of us." Kaitlin passed him a mug of strong, hot coffee as Rosalind placed a plate of shortbread on the table.

"We meet at nine o'clock sharp," she advised. "Now, the Albrights hae the largest house hereabouts, but all the same we'll be on benches under God's own Montana sky. If you're late, you won't manage a seat."

" 'Tis glad I am to hear that you're a God-fearing man, Gailbraith." Arthur gave him a hearty clap on the shoulder. "If the railroad brings more like you, I'm thinking we'll hae no need t' regret its arrival."

"I can't speak for the others." Ewan felt the need to be honest. "They're rough men. They all work hard, eat as much as they can, as fast as they can, and seek diversion where they may. Some have been following the railroad for so long they can't be held to the same standard as city folk."

"All men should be held to the standard of God," Rosalind spoke up. "So long as they're honest and treat others as they'd like to be treated, we'll get along fine."

Ewan's heart sank. *How can she be so naïve? I just warned her that they're hard men who lack manners and don't care for niceties. There is no way to be plainer wi'out being too blunt for delicate female ears. Lord, please see to it that her parents discuss the matter wi' her!*

"Unfortunately," he began cautiously, "the law of the railroad camp seems t' be more along the lines o' every man for himself. The men hold certain loyalties to their work crews and such, but in the long run, they'll take what they want as long as they think they can get away wi' it."

"We'll all be sure to keep that in mind." Kaitlin sent her daughter a meaningful look, and Ewan rested more easily.

"How came you to be out in the Montana Territory?" He reached for a piece of buttery shortbread that melted almost as soon as he tasted it.

"Ah, now there's a story for those romance novels my daughter has a way of sneaking."

Arthur's words made Rosalind blush as pink as the flower for which she was named, but it seemed only Ewan had noticed. "I trekked out here nigh on two decades ago wi' naught but a pair of friends and a heavy load of determination."

"Aye. Naught else on account of him leaving his bride behind wi' her folks." Kaitlin's glance held more love than reproof, but the revelation that Rosalind's father had left his wife to travel across America struck a horribly familiar chord. The shortbread turned to sawdust as he tried to force it down his throat, and he slugged some coffee to wash it down. The bitter memories were harder to swallow. As long as he lived, Ewan would never understand how the promise of a new land could call a man away from his loved ones, leaving them alone and unprotected. *That's not fair,* he amended. *Arthur left his wife with her parents, so she wasna alone.*

"Imagine my surprise when I discovered I was wi' child." Kaitlin beamed and hugged her daughter close. "Our own wee lassie came into this world loud and strong. She would hae made you proud, Arthur."

"She already has, Katy-me-love. My only regret 'tis that I could not share the moment." Arthur's smile dimmed. " 'Tis a petty sorrow in the face of so many blessings, but one I will take to my grave regardless."

"Now, Da" — Rosalind left her mother's

side to kiss her father's cheek — "you may not hae been there for my first months of life, but your provision and love hae seen me through the years."

"Ah, I love you, Rosey-mine, just as I loved you when I caught my first glimpse of you being held in the arms of your mam, fresh from traveling thousands of miles to my side." He patted his daughter's delicate hand. "The Lord safely delivered two blessings that day."

"How wonderful for you," Ewan choked out, his own loss harsher in the face of their shared love. "So many never make it t' the promised land or to the waiting arms o' their loved ones."

"Too true." Rosalind's eyes held a compassion that seemed to sear his soul. "What of you, Mr. Gailbraith? Where is your family while you follow the railroad to provide for them?"

"I cannot say where my da is, the Lord took my mam o'er a decade ago, and I hae no wife." Ewan, aware of how gruff his voice sounded, summoned a semblance of a grin. " 'Tis good to see that you value what you're so blessed to have."

He shoved away from the table and strode to the door, plunking his hat on his head. "Thank you for your welcome and hospitality, Mrs. MacLean. I've much work to finish this day, so I must be going. I look forward to working wi' you, Arthur. Luke, Miss Mac-

Lean." With a tip of his hat, he walked out without a backward glance.

"Mr. Gailbraith seems nice enough," Rosalind ventured as she and her mother cleared the dinner table. Luke had volunteered to go to the Albrights' place and see about arranging an apple bee. The tree branches drooped, heavy with the weight of ripe fruit, but Rosalind felt the weight of unanswered questions.

"Aye." Mam's short agreement made Rosalind relax for but a moment. "*Seems* is just the right word to be using to describe him."

"His manners 'tweren't off-putting, he showed Da proper respect, and he asked after Sunday meeting." Rosalind stopped wiping down the board. "What concerns you?"

"What type of man does not know where his own kith and kin lay their heads?" Mam stoked the fire with more vigor than was strictly necessary. "A good son looks to his father in his twilight years, and that's a fact."

"We cannot know his reasons, Mam. There could be a perfectly good explanation." *Why am I defending the man? I've barely met him, and yet he's the first new man in town. Will Mam be so suspicious of everyone, or is it Mr. Gailbraith in particular?*

"Will you be telling me that a man with an honest explanation would all but bolt from the table?" Mam shook her head. "There's something amiss there."

"Mayhap." Rosalind went silent as she gathered the trenchers and pot to scrub by the brook.

"Be sure to fetch Luke afore you make your way to the stream."

"Yes, Mam." She stopped at the threshold when she thought of another question. "Is there aught else you find to dislike about him, or are we to be wary simply because he's not our neighbor?"

"I've already spoken wi' you, Rose. A young miss cannot be too careful around men, especially strange ones." Mam shooed her out the door, but Rosalind caught the statement made under her breath. "Particularly ones as handsome as Mr. Gailbraith."

Ah, so I'm not the only one to notice his fine looks, Rosalind mused. *And I suppose Mam saw the dark storm in the deep green of his gaze when he spoke on his family. No mother, no wife, no father in his life. 'Twouldn't surprise me a bit if 'twas pure loneliness as made him pull away, after hearing all about our happy family. It takes strength of a different sort than a blacksmith usually needs to live such a solitary life.*

"Rose!" Luke's voice made her look around sharply. Her little brother loped down the path toward her, cutting her search short.

"Hello, Luke. I've come to seek your escort

to the stream."

Her brother caught on to her joke and replied with an exaggerated bow. "Of course I will escort you, miss." He took the heavy pot from her hands and walked beside her, the top of his head barely reaching her elbow. At twelve years, he should have come close to his petite sister's shoulder.

Rosalind shoved the worry aside and listened to her brother's uneven breathing, noting a hint of a wheeze creeping into the sound as they passed the hayfields. "How are you?" She tried to keep her tone light.

"Now then, you wouldna be fussing o'er me, would you?" He teased a smile on to her face. "Surely not, on account of how you know of my hay fever. 'Twill ease when we near the brook."

And so it did. The harsh, raspy sound Rosalind so dreaded had faded away by the time they knelt by the cool, clear water. She watched as her brother scooped up some damp sand and scrubbed enthusiastically.

To those who didn't know of the difficulties Luke suffered from hay fever, running, smoke, and cold weather, it would be all too easy to see a healthy young boy. In truth, Luke's weak lungs made it so he could never take up blacksmithing, run with other children, help with the haying, or play overlong in the snow. At those times, his fight to breathe was nothing short of terrifying for those who loved him. And love him she did. Rose would do anything to see her brother happy and healthy.

"Hey!" Luke glowered at her in indignation, his scowl made comical by drops of the water she'd just splashed him with. At her grin, his anger disappeared, replaced by a crafty gleam. "Rose, if you mean to splash someone, you really should try to do a better job."

"Oh, now?" Rosalind shot to her feet, thinking to back away before her brother could retaliate. Too late. She blinked and sputtered after he doused her with an impressive splash. She planted her hands on her hips and glared at her brother. "And who's to say I meant to splash you, Lucas Mathias MacLean?"

"Ah." Luke didn't look at all repentant as he gave his thoughtful reply. "Then I suppose it serves you right for your carelessness."

Rosalind, unable to think of a suitable rejoinder, gave in to her brother's logic. "Why, you may have a point."

"Most usually I do."

"In that case, may I suggest you work on the virtue of humility" — Rosalind gathered the wooden trenchers — "so that others don't think poorly of you when you use your intelligence."

"Yes, Rose." His downcast eyes and soft voice made him the very picture of a humble young man — until he peeked up at his sister.

"How was that?"

She couldn't help but laugh. He joined in. Still laughing together, they started for home. Rosalind's merriment dried up when they passed the freshly cut hayfields and Luke's breathing grew raspy once more.

CHAPTER 4

"This is the patent forge supplied by the Montana Central Railroad Company." Ewan gestured toward the heavy equipment. "Thank you again for letting us set up near your forge. 'Tis a good location for the work we'll be doing in the area, and 'twill simplify things whilst we work together."

"Aye, 'tis no trouble." Arthur circled the "portable" forge, a monstrosity of cast iron. "Grand, the way you don't have to build a new forge every time you pick up and move. Comparatively, this sets up right quick."

"True enough," Ewan agreed. "But no one will convince me that a good stone or brick-built forge 'tisn't the very best to work wi'."

"I'll not even be tryin'." Arthur straightened up. "All the same, 'tis an incredible piece of modern machinery."

"Sure as shootin'." The young man named Johnny cast a fond eye on the forge. "She's a beaut, that's what I say."

"There's work enough to go around." Ewan

291

looked to the makeshift hitching posts where dozens of horses were tied, waiting to be inspected for shoeing.

"Let's get to it." Arthur walked confidently over to chestnut mare, running his hand over her withers and crooning for a moment before inspecting her hooves, one by one.

While Johnny worked to make the fire hot enough to temper iron, Ewan began with a tall bay. *Not a day too soon.* The gelding's hooves had overgrown the shoe by a long shot and would certainly begin to crack painfully if let go any longer.

He removed the too-smooth shoes one by one, cleaning each hoof before trimming it down. He fetched one of the shoes Johnny had heating over the fire and set it on the hard wall of the hoof, cautiously using hammer and tongs to shape the pliable metal to the best fit possible before nailing it in place.

Ewan worked efficiently, his job made simpler by Johnny's aid. All the same, he remained careful to soothe each horse and keep a wary eye on the back legs as he worked. Many a blacksmith, overconfident in his expertise, had become careless. Such men received a harsh kick to the ribs or skull and were often fortunate to survive at all. Ewan noted approvingly that Arthur showed the same awareness and appropriate caution. Things were going well.

"What say you to a bite of dinner?" Arthur

spoke up only after Ewan had finished shoeing a strawberry roan. "My wife and daughter packed enough for all of us."

"Aah!" Johnny straightened out. "I was beginning to fear you'd hear the rumble of my stomach between the blows of the hammer."

They settled in the shade of a large tree whose leaves, in bright shades of orange and deep red, covered the ground more than the branches. Arthur passed around cold bacon sandwiches and apples.

"How long have you worked wi' the railroad, then?" Arthur took a mammoth bite, almost halving his first sandwich.

"Just started a few days back." Johnny swallowed audibly before he reached for his canteen. "Ewan's been training me."

"Is that so?" Arthur eyed Ewan speculatively. "And how long has it been since you enjoyed the comforts of home?"

"Too long." Ewan shifted against the tree trunk, finding a less lumpy resting place for his shoulder. "Years, in fact."

"Years, eh?" Arthur savored a sip of cool water before popping the rest of his sandwich in his mouth and reaching for another. "Were you ever wi' the Northern Pacific Railroad Company?"

"Aye." Ewan frowned as he polished off his first sandwich. "I moved on after I realized the company didn't share my priorities."

"The Last Spike Snub?" Johnny stopped eating to stare at Ewan. "Is that whole mess what made you decide to leave?"

" 'Twas a symptom of the overall problem, aye." Ewan sampled his apple. The crisp fruit gave a tart but sweet flavor. *Tart and sweet, the same combination offered by old memories.*

"I heard tell of that about three years ago, but I don't know the details." Arthur poured some water into his cupped palm and combed it through his hair. "I'd like to hear your version of it."

" 'Twas a raging fiasco, to tell the truth." Ewan closed his eyes, remembering the up-swell of righteous anger against the company. "I know that the men had been pushed to finish the tracks before the worst of winter hit. When the two lines were ready to be joined, the owners of the company arranged a grand occasion to announce their success in bringing the railroad as far as the Montana Territory."

"That much I know," Johnny affirmed. "What I don't understand is how a happy event upset so many people."

" 'Twasn't the meeting of the railroads that caused problems," Ewan clarified. " 'Twas the way the company treated its own guests.

"Several important people, wealthy, power-ful, renown, were invited to meet at the Helena depot. These particular guests were transported to the site in the finest railroad cars o' the Northern Pacific. Sumptuous dining cars, Pullman sleeping compartments, and more were provided for these favored few.

"The bulk of the guests, however, weren't so fortunate. Dignitaries, people prominent in only the Montana Territory, and large landowners were also invited but left t' find their own transportation. They waited in the cold for the delayed train full of the other guests to arrive. At long last, the ceremony began."

"So they were upset that they weren't given the same treatment." Arthur mulled over his thoughts. "Since they were already in the Montana area, it stands to reason they would need to arrange their own transport."

"Sounds to me like some uppity folks got their noses out of joint over nuthin', if you ask me." Johnny rolled his eyes. "Can't imagine such a fuss over something so minor."

"That wasn't the end of it," Ewan warned before continuing. "Once the event actually began, only those who had traveled on the train cars were allowed inside the pavilion area t' hear the speakers. Everyone else was made to crowd in behind the platform, straining to hear. Even worse, the majority o' the seats inside were empty."

Ewan noted Arthur's darkening frown and nodded. "After the speeches were made and the spike driven in, 'twas time to dine. Everyone expected a grand feast after traveling miles to celebrate the occasion and waiting for hours in the cold. Many had day-long trips home t' look forward to."

"Stands to reason," Arthur proclaimed. "After being treated so poorly, they deserved some reward for their trouble, particularly as invited guests."

"And so they expected." Ewan paused to let that sink in. "The final blow was that only the train passengers, warmly ensconced in the new dining cars, were allowed t' take part in the feast. The multitude of guests — those who had traveled so far to bear witness to this historic occasion, waited patiently through delays, and suffered a grievous slight throughout the ceremonies — were told to go home. Precious few of those guests had even thought t' bring food, and a great many went hungry that day."

"Shameful." Johnny's jaw clenched. "I knew that a lot of people felt like it was a waste of time and that they'd been insulted, but I never knew the exact particulars. I don't read all that much, truth be told."

"Out here the news comes slowly. When we heard about it, there were far fewer details." Arthur turned his level gaze to Ewan. "You were right to sever ties wi' such people. It speaks to the strength of your character."

" 'Twasn't as though I were the only one

296

who left." Ewan shrugged. "And I'm of the opinion that Montana Central hired me more for the strength of my arm." With that, he got to his feet. "Let's get back to work."

"It'll never work." Rosalind flopped down in the barn's fresh, fragrant hayloft. Isaac had walked Marlene over. The two girls had finagled permission to snatch some leisure time, since they saw each other far less often now.

"Sure it will!" Marlene settled in next to her. "It feels as though we've hardly even seen each other in the past fortnight! Both our families have watched us with eagle eyes since the railroad men started lurking around."

"Wi' good reason. Some seem like good men, but others give me an uneasy feeling," Rosalind admitted. "Besides, it won't last forever. The railroad will hae to keep steaming along eventually."

"Do you really want it to take all the eligible young men away with it?" Marlene sat up straight. "Our very first opportunity to make new friends and meet men who aren't our neighbors, and it's all but snatched from us!"

"I'm not going to do it." Rosalind sifted a few smaller pieces of hay between her fingers. "I won't say I'm going to meet wi' you while you say you'll meet wi' me and we both hie off to find adventure. No matter how you try to justify it, 'tis dishonest and unsafe."

"You're right. Besides," Marlene huffed as she settled back into the hay, "we'd be found out before long, even if I could actually tell an untruth like it was nothing."

"If nothing worse happened," Rosalind reminded her best friend, glad to see her letting go of the rash idea. Usually they saw eye to eye despite their three-year age difference, but occasionally, Marlene's youthful exuberance got the better of her. "Although, I've had a few thoughts of my own. . . ."

"Do tell!"

"There is one way I can think of that will allow us to be useful, see each other regularly, and spend a bit of time with the railroad men in a protected setting." Rosalind paused until her friend nudged her arm.

"Out with it, Rose. You can't keep me waiting up here forever, and we need to work out the entire plan!"

"Our fathers wouldn't argue if we took in laundry and mending to earn some money. We're of the age where we'll be setting up our own homes soon." Rosalind shared a conspiratorial glance with Marlene. "Or if that idea doesn't tickle your fancy, I should think we could talk a few of our family men into making some rough picnic tables for us to run an outdoor café. We could use the summer oven and an open fire to make home-cooked meals for all those bachelors."

"That," Marlene sighed, "is surely the most

brilliant thing I've ever heard you say, Rosalind MacLean. No one could possibly object to such a worthwhile — and profitable — endeavor!"

"And I prefer almost any chore over laundry," Rosalind added.

"Me, too. I love the feel of clean clothes and sheets, but it's such monotonous, long, hot work, no matter what the season. Soap making is almost as bad." Marlene grimaced, then seemed to realize she'd gotten away from the important topic. "We'll have to convince our parents that we'll finish our own chores. How do we manage that?"

"We'll still milk the cows, gather the eggs, and help wi' breakfast in the morning. If we suggest that everyone eat the dinner we make, our mothers won't have to make any." Rosalind spoke the thoughts aloud as they came into her head. "We'll still help wi' supper and do our sewing in the evenings at the hearth. I suppose that leaves doing the weekly laundry on Saturday as the big problem. We could close down that day and the Lord's day — and only run the outdoor diner five days a week."

"Five days a week sounds good to me." Marlene gave a sly smile. "The men we're interested in will come to Sunday meeting anyway."

"Exactly." Rosalind let Marlene think she was simply bored and boy-crazy. *No one needs to know that I'll be saving the money I earn so I can travel on that railroad someday.*

"Let's go talk to Aunt Kaitlin now!" Marlene scrambled down the ladder in record time, looking up at Rosalind expectantly.

"You can't seem overly excited," Rosalind cautioned as she descended the ladder. "If you're too eager, they'll think it a whim and shut us down before we even open. We hae to present it in just the right way — thoughtfully and reasonably. Show them we're aware of the responsibility we'll be taking on and we're ready for it."

"When did you get so wise, Rose?" Marlene smiled and linked arms with her. "First, we convince your mother, then my mother. With them on our side, our fathers will surely consent!"

"That's the plan." Rosalind smoothed her hair back. "Men are the heads of the household, but women are the hearts, and every sensible person on earth knows which of the two is stronger."

CHAPTER 5

"Hae they gone daft?" Ewan rubbed his eyes but found no relief. "Do you see that? Tables and benches they've set up o'er near a summer kitchen?"

"I see it." Johnny didn't sound as though he disliked the sight at all.

"They're not planning on selling dinner. Surely they know better." Ewan thumped a moonstruck Johnny on the upper arm. Johnny's eyes still followed the little blond's every movement.

"I'm afraid not." Arthur's voice, heavy with misgiving, sounded behind them.

"I aim to be first in line," Johnny planned aloud, receiving glares for his enthusiastic support of the womenfolk.

"How did this come t' be?" Ewan struggled to maintain a calm demeanor. *Did I not speak wi' the man scarce three days past about keepin' the townswomen clear o' the workmen? This'll set the cats about the pigeons before I can so much as blink!*

" 'Tis the honest truth, I'm not all too certain." Arthur's brow furrowed in puzzlement. "I came home to find my favorite meal on the table, and Rosey talking about how she wanted to contribute to the growth of the community, and my sweet Kaitlin sayin' as how 'twas a good opportunity for the girls to learn the value of hard work in a business setting."

"And you said 'twas a foolish idea?" Ewan felt a sort of sinking in the region of his stomach at the older man's sheepish look.

"I said I'd hae to think on the matter, and the next thing I knew, Kaitlin left the table and came back with a fresh rhubarb pie and the sweetest smile you ever did see." He gave a rueful grin. "The next thing I know, I'm making benches."

"Good man," Johnny approved over Ewan's groan. "If I could say so, sir, I think you made a very wise choice. Excellent."

"We'll see." Ewan tried to think positively. *Lord, is there any possibility You could make the men so distracted by good, homemade food that they'll ignore any other . . . attractions?* He glanced over to where Rosalind and — what was her name? Arleen? — spoke animatedly, creamy cheeks flushed with excitement and effort.

Lord, I can see I'm coming to the right place

for help. 'Tis gonna take nothing short of a miracle.

Refusing to dwell on it, Ewan worked so single-mindedly that the morning all but flew by. He'd just set down a pair of tongs when Johnny yanked his arm and practically dragged him over to the table nearest the makeshift kitchen. Left without a choice, Ewan plunked down.

The rich, hickory smell of that pot of pork and beans doesn't tempt me in the slightest. Those steaming trays of sweet golden corn bread aren't enticing in the least. I'm here only because 'twould be rude to leave.

Ewan kept a litany of protective statements running through his mind, trying to convince himself that he wasn't pleased as punch to be the first man sitting at the table, with Rosalind smiling at him and ladling out a hearty serving of beans.

"Smells wonderful," he praised. "Such a clever idea to set up an outdoor diner where you'll have customers in droves." *Fool. And to think, I thought less of Arthur for giving his blessing. At least the man had a wife and daughter trying to convince him, and he made it all the way to dessert! I haven't even taken my first bite.*

Determined to stop himself before he said anything else, Ewan filled his mouth with pork and beans. *Mmm. Meaty, filling, slightly*

303

sweet, and perfectly cooked. He closed his eyes and took another bite before he realized Rosalind and the other girl were watching him and Johnny expectantly.

"Good," Johnny grunted, making short work of his bowl and slathering a piece of corn bread with butter. "Best thing I've tasted in months."

The girls' faces lit up at the verdict before they turned to hear Ewan's opinion.

"Best pork 'n beans I've ever had," he admitted. Rosalind practically beamed at his compliment, and Ewan accepted the truth. When Rosalind MacLean set her mind to something, whether it be her father's permission, a thriving business, or his own grudging approval, she found a way to get it. If he wasn't so busy savoring his piece of corn bread, Ewan just might have to think about how disturbing that was. He took a second piece, just for good measure.

"Well then, I think we're ready to open." With that, the blond girl rang the dinner bell loud and clear. Hungry workers came sniffing around in hopes of some good food. They were delighted to find it in plentiful supply. Word spread quickly, and soon the benches at the table creaked with the weight of satisfied customers.

Ewan's good mood evaporated as he took stock of the hungry eyes following the girls' progress around the tables. A few watched the saucy sway of Rosalind's skirt with more interest than they showed the food she placed before them. The only thing that helped Ewan's uneasiness was the knowledge that the girls' fathers were keeping close guard on the situation.

When the men finished clearing every morsel, they exited en masse, leaving soiled tables full of dirty dishes and corn bread crumbs in their wake. Even the girls' families left without offering to pitch in. Ewan frowned to see the amount of work the girls had before them. They looked anything but upset.

"We did it!" The girls chorused as they hugged.

"We might even need to make more tomorrow, just in case the men tell a few of their friends," Rosalind added.

"Word will spread," Johnny broke in. "Tomorrow will be a mad rush to get a spot at one of your tables. You'll be turning customers away in droves before you know it."

"It'd be a good idea to have your fathers and brothers — men you trust — overseeing a table each to make sure no fights break out." *If you can't beat 'em, join 'em.* "Things could get ugly if you're not careful."

"We hadn't thought of that." The blond — Marlene, Johnny had told him — showed signs of worry on her pretty young face. "Dustin, Da, Isaac . . . I don't think Brent is formidable enough to control a group of grown men, and Luke certainly can't. That's only three, and we have five tables." Rosalind bit her lower lip. She looked so delicate. Ewan knew he was sunk when she turned her brilliant blue eyes toward him with a speculative gleam. "Would you and Johnny consider helping us out in return for your dinner five times a week?"

"Absolutely!" Johnny grinned at Marlene. "Anything we can do to help, you just let us know. We'll take care of it."

"I'd be glad to pitch in." Ewan looked down at Rosalind. "And I'd still be more than willing to pay for your cooking. 'Tis worth far more than the asking price as is."

"You'll not pay for a meal at these tables, Mr. Gailbraith," Rosalind declared, unknowingly giving him a reminder that he had no right to be thinking of her as "Rosalind." She was Miss MacLean to him, and that was how things should be.

"I'll not argue the point, Miss MacLean." He gave her a polite smile. "At the moment, my stomach is far too full for me to gainsay you."

"Perfect." She clasped her hands together and turned to her friend. "Marlene, we did it. Everything worked out!"

As Ewan and Johnny walked back toward the forge, the afternoon's work stretching ahead of them, Ewan couldn't hold back one last doubt. *We'll see what happens tomorrow.*

"I never thought I'd see the day when I saw the use of your mother's o'erpacking, Marlene."

Rosalind set aside another clean plate. "Wi'out all these dishes, we'd be in a pickle."

"Be sure you tell her that last part." Marlene swished another one through the clean water. "It'll make her feel even better about helping convince Father to agree to this venture."

"I did fear Da might take back his agreement when he saw that bunch of hungry men swarming all around our new benches." Rosalind massaged the small of her back for a leisurely moment before returning to the task at hand. "Praise the Lord all went well today. Had the slightest thing gone wrong, that would hae been the end of it."

"Well, it's only the beginning" — Marlene scrubbed a particularly stubborn splotch of dried food — "which means we have plans to make and supplies to purchase before long."

"Aye. We should start by deciding what we'll be cooking for the rest of the week." Rosalind paused to consider what would be simplest to make in vast quantities. "Maybe shepherd's pie?"

"Agreed. Why don't we make it a policy to have some kind of soup or stew as the main dish every other day?" Marlene pushed back a few straggling locks of her golden hair. "With enough variety, the men won't complain. It's the simplest thing to make for so many . . . and hearty enough for working men."

"Let me think a moment." Rosalind ticked off types of stew and soup. "There's Irish, corn, and beef stew, and potato, parsnip, and split pea soup. . . . If we add a pork bone to Scotch broth, that will serve. Along wi' pork 'n beans, Welsh rarebit, and biscuits with gravy, we'll hae enough simple recipes to see us through."

"Exactly." Marlene rubbed her hands together in anticipation. "We'll need to stock up on all the vegetables we can buy and see about having the men slaughter another hog to keep us in provisions. We'll need cornmeal for johnnycake, flour for biscuits and bread. . . . How soon do you think we can persuade one of the menfolk to take us to the general store?"

"Soon, I hope, though we've already asked for their help at the tables every dinner. 'Tis glad I am to have enlisted the aid of Mr. Gailbraith and his friend. They'll help smooth things along."

"Johnny," Marlene murmured absently, dreamily swirling her finger in the sandy pebbles lining the brook.

"What?" Rosalind turned a gimlet eye on her friend. "When did you become familiar enough wi' the man to call him by his Christian name? Surely you hae not given him leave to address you so."

"I should say not." Marlene snapped back to attention. "He calls me Miss Freimont as is right and proper, but he invited me to call him Johnny. I haven't done so to his face," she added hastily at the warning glint in Rosalind's eyes.

"See that you don't. Mam says a young miss can't be too careful around strange men, no matter how affable they appear. Using each others' first name signifies a familiarity inappropriate between the two of you." Her warning delivered, Rosalind sank back on her heels and admitted, "Though I've had to remind myself of the same thing when I think on Mr. Gailbraith."

"Ooh!" Marlene squealed and abandoned the dishes altogether. "I knew it. I just *knew* it! You haven't so much as cast an interested glance at any other railroad worker."

"That's simply untrue." Rosalind grinned. "I gave that one man an interested glance when he claimed he owned the entire railroad."

"That's not the type of interest I'm meaning, and you know it, Rose." Marlene shook her head. "I meant the kind of interest that makes a woman's eyes widen and her knees go weak."

"Sounds to me as though such a hapless

woman wouldn't withstand a terrible fright."

"You know what I mean." Marlene shot her friend an exasperated glance. "The type of feeling that makes you want to call Mr. Gailbraith by his first name."

"Rubbish." Rosalind waved the notion aside. " 'Tis only that 'Ewan' seems to suit him far better than his surname."

"And you're in a position to know such things since when? Best come out with it, Rose. You've seen the handsome blacksmith quite often since he began working near your father. Don't pretend you haven't looked forward to seeing him around and perhaps exchanging a friendly greeting."

"I —" The intended denial stuck fast in Rose's throat. *If I were to be honest, I do look forward to Ewan's — Mr. Gailbrath's — warm smile and cheery wave.* Could his resemblance to Da while working over the forge be the only reason, or had a different sort of fondness crept into her heart over the past week?

"Aha!"

Rosalind realized her awkward pause had not escaped her friend's notice.

"I thought as much," Marlene crowed, sobering quickly when Luke popped into sight. "Luke's coming." She welcomed Luke brightly. "Come to lend a hand, have you? Well, we've plenty enough dishes to tote back and pack inside the crates." She leaned back toward Rosalind to give a whisper. "Don't think that this conversation is over, Rose!"

I was afraid of that.

oy and Rosalind to give a whisky. "Don't pull that this conversation is over." "Don't Luke, Edward rise.

CHAPTER 6

Ewan strove mightily to attend to his work, focusing on the iron he'd heated to a glowing red and now manipulated into the proper shape. Trouble was, he couldn't help but notice Rosalind MacLean, along with Luke and their blond friend whom Johnny seemed to have taken a shine to, riding past his forge in a buckboard and then heading into the small mercantile.

'Tis early in the morning. You've no call to be letting your mind wander from your work, Ewan Gailbraith. He sternly forced himself to concentrate on the task at hand and finished reshaping the implement before cooling it in the tempering bath.

A fine job, if I do say so myself. He gave a mighty stretch and glanced toward the general store. *'Tis no quick trip for a peppermint whim. The lasses hae been in there a goodly amount of time. Perhaps they're browsing as women are apt to do.*

He looked to his next task. 'Twould take

the better part of the morning to repair the broken wheel. Montana Central needed an official wheelwright to repair the wagons that carried loads of supplies away from the train cars and to the more remote areas where workers cleared the land and made ways through forest and rock. As it was, the work fell on his shoulders. He found it useful to know many skills, but he'd learned an unpleasant truth. The more kinds of work a railroad man was able to do, the more he'd be called upon to do. Whether he'd been hired on to do the task wasn't a big part of the equation.

Learning to do every scrap of work possible was how I helped support Mam after Da came to America. Any trade that involved working wi' iron, I turned a hand to.

"Ewan?" Johnny's hesitant tone caught Ewan's attention at once. Blacksmithing was good, honest work, but a simple mistake could cost a man dearly.

"Aye?" He quickly surveyed his new friend and found nothing visibly wrong. The tension in his shoulders eased.

"I'm finished with this bit." The younger man gestured toward the whorls of steam rising from the tempering bath as it cooled the heated metal within.

"Good." Ewan bit back a grin as Johnny cast a furtive glance toward the general store down the road. It appeared he wasn't the only one who'd noticed the ladies' destination this morning.

"And it occurred to me that I could use" — Johnny's brow furrowed — "an . . . er . . . well, this place could certainly use a few . . ."

"A few . . . what?" Ewan crossed his arms over his chest, delighting in his friend's awkward ploy to see the girls in the shop.

"Pounds of fresh-ground coffee!" His triumphant pronouncement made him nod sagely. "You know, to keep up our strength throughout the day. Nothin' like a pot of hot, strong coffee."

"Like this one?" Ewan hefted the pot keeping warm by the forge and made a show of peering around. "Seems as though we've a goodly enough supply to see us through the week." He put down the pot and nudged a sack with the toe of his leather boot.

"Oh." Johnny's face fell. "Right."

"Although" — Ewan decided to finally take pity on the poor fellow and give his consent — "it seems to me that you can never have too much coffee on hand. We might well invite Arthur over for a mug or two."

"Only neighborly!" Johnny untied his heavy, soot-stained leather apron and had it over his head in record time.

"I could do wi' a bit of a break, myself," Ewan admitted, pulling off his thick work gloves. *And seeing some of the pretty things on*

314

display at the store would be a welcome change.

Together, the pair made their way to the general store.

"Good placement they've set up," Johnny noted. "Smithy's in the middle of the village, and the store's nearby, but far enough away not to catch most of the ash."

"Wi' the railroad, this place will flourish into a thriving city before too long." Ewan shrugged off a vague discomfort at the notion. This place — with its endless skies, fresh air, mountains full of good pine, and tight-knit community — wouldn't maintain all its current charm in the face of progress. The thought saddened him, even as he told himself the railroad would ensure the survival of Saddleback.

"I hope it doesn't change too much," Johnny said, unwittingly echoing Ewan's own thoughts. "I'd hate to see the place turned into one of those crowded, gritty modern cities I've seen too many of."

Ewan gave a terse nod in reply as they stepped through the mercantile doors. A welcoming coolness settled around him as he made his way further into the well-insulated shop, wending his way past farming implements, seeds, buckets, sacks, rope, and various examples of leatherwork.

"Here we go." Johnny stopped in front of the large grinder but kept his head turned toward the back counter.

"Mr. Mathers!" The girl called Marlene greeted Johnny with a charming smile before giving Ewan a sedate nod. He didn't miss the way she nudged Rosalind with her elbow while doing so.

"Mr. Gailbraith." Rosalind's acknowledgment, while friendly, bore a hint more reserve than that of her friend's.

"Miss MacLean. Miss Freimont." He took stock of the mound of merchandise dominating the counter. "I'd be happy to lend a hand."

"Thank you." Her smile deepened, and a tiny dimple flittered in her right cheek. She got prettier every day.

"Welcome," Johnny jumped in. "We wouldn't let you little ladies haul a load this big."

"I'm glad to say we won't be carrying it farther than the wagon outside." Rosalind smiled. "Though 'twas such a lovely day for a walk, we gave a thought to leaving it behind."

"Although it is an awful lot of things, isn't it? Somehow it seems heavier when it's right in front of you than when you just write it down on a list." Miss Freimont pressed a hand to her heart. "Your help would be greatly appreciated. We remembered a few things not on our list once we got here."

"Must hae been quite a list." Ewan raised an eyebrow.

"Indeed." Rosalind pulled a piece of paper, filled with handwriting, out of her sleeve and squinted to read the tiny script. "Though I think we've all the supplies we could possibly need for the diner. Except for the vegetables." She turned to the shopkeeper. "We'll be needing to take a look at your carrots, parsnips, onions, and potatoes before we tally it all up." She headed for the large crates holding the produce.

Johnny's smile, if possible, grew wider as he dug his elbow into Ewan's ribs. "Looks like we can count on delicious dinners for the rest of the week, at the very least! I hope they make mashed potatoes — they're my favorite." He whispered this last.

"We'll be sure to consider that, Mr. Mathers." Rosalind's promise proved Johnny's whisper had carried a bit too far.

"Of course," Miss Freimont agreed with a twinkle in her eye. "After all, we want to keep our favorite customers happy."

Rosalind sucked in a shocked gasp at Marlene's blatant flirtation with the two railroad blacksmiths. Such forwardness! And yet, her disapproval was tinged with another, darker emotion she recognized as envy. *How can she be so at ease around these men?*

She relaxed when she saw a hint of rebuke in Ewan's — Mr. Gailbraith's — eyes. *So 'tis not just that I'm socially awkward. Such saucy*

317

*comments are too volatile for even Mr. Gail-
braith.*

"We want to make sure our cooking keeps
bringing patrons to the outdoor diner, of
course." Rosalind diffused the tension Marlene remained oblivious to. "And we especially appreciate your willingness to try the
dishes before we open every afternoon."

"Not as much as we appreciate your fine
cooking." Ewan's — Mr. Gailbraith's — smile
gave a sense of warm sincerity, and Rosalind
could tell he knew exactly what she'd been
trying to do when she spoke up.

To cover her sudden awkwardness, she
turned her attention back to her long list.
"Mr. Acton, if you'd let me know what we've
collected while I check it off my list, 'twould
greatly ease my mind."

"Of course," Mr. Acton agreed as he added
bushels of vegetables to the order. "Vegetables, eggs, flour, cornmeal, sugar, brown
sugar, baking soda, molasses, beans, a wheel
of cheese, vanilla extract, cinnamon, nutmeg,
salt, pepper, and coffee. Is there anything left
on your list, Miss MacLean?"

"Wait a moment. . . ." She looked at all the
crossed-off items one last time. "Salt pork."
Rosalind glanced up to find the railroad men
both looking as though the very mention of
that much food caused a corresponding
emptiness in their stomachs.

"If I may ask, Miss MacLean," the blacksmith ventured, "what are you planning on for today's dinner?"

"You'll hae to wait and see, Mr. Gailbraith." Rosalind shifted closer to the counter. "Though, if you had a request, what would it be?"

"After the pork 'n beans and shepherd's pie, I'd gladly tuck into any dish you set before me." His smile reached up to brighten his green eyes. "Though I must admit I bear a certain fondness for Irish stew."

"As do I, Mr. Gailbraith." She watched as the shopkeeper tallied their order.

"Seems we have a lot in common." His voice lowered so only she could hear, and the deep rumble sent a thrill down her spine. "Irish heritage, smithing families, and now favorite dishes."

"Here you are." Mr. Acton claimed her attention as she completed the transaction.

"Luke!" She called him away from the corner where he'd been admiring a few fancy toys. "We're ready to get going."

"Then let's head off." Ewan shouldered the heaviest load with manful ease. "For a man never knows what may lie ahead."

Is it my imagination, or was he looking at me as he said that? A giddy little bubble filled her heart at the idea, only to swiftly deflate as she remembered her mother's words — a woman could never be too careful with a strange man. *What lies ahead could be danger-ous.*

That sobering thought cast a cloud over the beautiful day.

Lord, You hae written that You love a cheerful giver, and Ewan lends a hand without thinking about it. How can I meet his selfless generosity wi' suspicion? Return distrust for help so freely given? And yet, Your Word tells that we are to seek wise counsel. How to behave around a man so strong and good-natured as Ewan, 'tis certainly beyond my own experience. If 'tis possible to join caution wi' caring, 'tis what I must do, though I cannot see how the two align. I've not the time to dwell upon the matter just now, but 'twill be in my thoughts. I ask for the wisdom to see and follow Your will.

"Oh!" Marlene's gasp caused Rosalind's gaze to follow hers. The modest buckboard, loaded down with their many purchases, was filled to bursting. Even the narrow bench up front for the driver held one of the crates of vegetables.

" 'Tis a small matter," Rosalind assured her. "Luke may drive it ahead, and we'll follow on foot."

"And what of dinner? We haven't the time to walk for a half hour before unloading the wagon and beginning." Marlene's voice came out low and rapid. "More time has passed while we were in the store than we planned for."

"Ewan and I are glad to come along," Mr. Mathers pronounced loudly, his eyes fastened on Marlene's upset expression. "We'll unload everything."

"Thank you!" Marlene seemed all but ready to hug the man, and Rosalind swiftly linked arms with her to avoid that catastrophe.

Luke drove the buckboard back to the outdoor oven that was the hub of the diner, and the other four followed more slowly on foot.

"Oof!" Marlene suddenly lurched forward, dragging Rosalind away from her thoughts and toward the hard-packed dirt.

Rosalind jerked her arm back, attempting to compensate for Marlene's lack of balance. The maneuver was successful, and neither of them landed facedown in the dirt, though Marlene seemed to feel the incident to have been very traumatic.

"I tripped over a root, just there!" Marlene pointed to a bare, even patch of earth, and Rosalind's eyes narrowed in suspicion. Marlene must have noticed, because she hastily swayed the tiniest bit to grasp hold of Mr. Mathers's arm. "Perhaps it was a rock that moved. Oh, I think I've turned my ankle." Her light lashes fluttered as though valiantly holding back tears, and Rosalind immediately regretted her uncharitable thoughts.

"Are you all right, Marlene?" She tried to loop Marlene's arm over her shoulders, but her friend pulled away and clung to Mr. Mathers instead.

"I'll be fine," she asserted a bit breathlessly as the young man slipped a supporting arm around her waist. "Yes, that's . . . better."

"I'd be glad to help you walk the rest of the way, miss." His offer couldn't have come any quicker, and he seemed loathe to let go of Marlene anytime soon — a fact Rosalind noted warily.

"How gallant of you," Marlene breathed, leaning gracefully against his stalwart support. "I'll be fine in no time at all. Usually I'm far more nimble." She cast her gaze to Rosalind, obviously expecting her friend to back her up on this.

"Yes," Rosalind agreed drily. "By far."

"Well, if Miss Freimont is up to it" — Ewan's voice had the vaguest hint of doubt — "we'd best continue. Miss MacLean?" He politely proffered his own arm to Rosalind, as was proper.

"I think 'twould be best." She tucked her hand in the crook of his arm, feeling the warmth of his strong muscles through the thin cambric of his everyday shirt. Suddenly feeling slightly out of breath herself, she gulped in the fresh mountain air in what came out as a sort of heavy sigh.

"Don't fret," Ewan patted her hand comfortingly. "Your wee little friend will be fine, of that I bear no doubt at all."

"Of course," she murmured, looking at the couple slowly making their way before them. Although Marlene leaned against the support Mr. Mathers so readily offered, her step showed no sign of an injured ankle.

Rosalind bit back a comment.

"To my way of thinking," Ewan said, his deep rumble soothing her ire, " 'tis simply an example of something I was taught long ago."

"Oh?" Rosalind quirked a brow, wondering what wisdom the handsome blacksmith would share with her. *A man like Ewan Gailbraith must know all sorts of things I wouldn't.*

"Sometimes," he bent his head closer to hers and spoke with a conspiratorial grin, "when it serves a purpose, people seem worse than they truly are."

CHAPTER 7

Ewan hefted a bag of flour into the old smokehouse the girls were using for storage. When he returned for another load, he was caught by the sight of Rosalind as she untied her sunbonnet and drew it off.

A soft breeze tickled the springy tendrils around her face while her hair caught the sun's light and burned with a brightness bold enough to warm a man's heart. He quelled a surge of disappointment when she dutifully donned the bonnet once more to conceal her crowning glory and protect her fair skin.

Lord, You truly hae made everything beautiful in Your time. 'Tis struck I am to see the loving stroke of Your hand around me, and the bearer of Your stamp so unaware o' it. Beauty is one thing; beauty wi'out the stain of pride gives even more pleasure.

"Are you certain?" Johnny, eagerly bringing Miss Freimont some cool water, sounded genuinely anxious. *Young pup.*

"Certainly." Marlene pointed the dainty toe

of her boot downward, then flexed it upward, causing the frills of her petticoat to froth over her ankle in a flagrantly feminine display. It worked, too. Johnny watched the motion, transfixed.

Ewan rolled his eyes. *If I didn't know any better, I'd say the minx had "tripped" on purpose to garner more attention. But surely no woman would use such an obvious ploy. . . .* He saw her laughing charmingly at something or other a besotted Johnny had said. The girl certainly had her eye on the lad. *Would she?*

He carried more sacks to the converted smokehouse, after taking a moment to clear his head. When he got back to the unloading, Ewan practically bumped into Rosalind as she came out of the tiny structure. Ewan quickly stepped back, getting a firmer grip on the goods he held lest they topple upon her pretty little head.

She gave him a ghost of a smile and side-stepped, obviously concerned with getting the work done in time to begin dinner. The tip of her braid bounced against the slim curve of her back as she walked the few steps to the wagon and reached up.

Now, there is a woman who wouldn't need to resort to petty wiles to catch a man's attention. She carries herself like a lady.

And she was carrying another sack back toward him. While she'd continued working, he'd stood and stared like an imbecile. Ewan swiftly deposited his load and strode past her to gather the last of the items. He cast an irritated glance to where Johnny still paid court to no-longer-maimed-but-not-helping Marlene.

"Oh no." He felt Rosalind's small hand press against his forearm where he'd rolled up his sleeves at the same time he heard her sweet, clear voice.

He almost dropped what he carried. "What's wrong?" He craned his neck to look down at her upturned face. Ewan watched in fascination as her cornflower blue eyes widened and her mouth opened in surprise at the unexpected intimacy of the moment before she yanked her hand back as though the brief contact had scalded her as it had him.

"I — I put those things aside so we could use them today." She looked toward the summer kitchen. "They need to go over there."

"Fine, then." He smiled, then looked at the bounty in his arms as his stride covered the short distance. Among other things, he held a modest crate filled with potatoes, onions, and carrots. A small sack held some precious spices, most likely salt and pepper. He cast a glance over his shoulder to see her exiting the old smokehouse with a piece of meat. He squinted to see it — lamb.

She's making Irish stew, just like I asked. The

realization flooded him with unexpected warmth. *Pretty Rosalind wi' the dancing braid and twinkling eyes wants to show her thanks for our help, and she found a circumspect way to do it. Aye, the lass is every inch a lady.*

Yes, he'd do well to keep a watch over Rosalind MacLean — and it wouldn't be a hardship to do so.

"Don't worry!" Rosalind turned Marlene away from where she stood staring at what seemed an impossible apple harvest.

Bushel upon bushel of the fruits filled the barn, emptied of its usual occupants to make room for this new purpose. Tart, yellow-green apples sat apart from their sweeter, deep red cousins, the bounty almost overwhelming.

All right, Lord. Truth be told, 'tis overwhelming. Every year the apple trees Delana brought here yield more and more fruit. Give us hearts grateful for Your provision, rather than thoughts of aching shoulders.

"This will take days!" Marlene frowned. "We'll have to shut down the diner."

With a pang, Rosalind realized she wouldn't see Ewan — *Mr. Gailbraith, Mr. Gailbraith, Mr. Gailbraith,* she reminded herself harshly — until Sunday meeting. Which was, if she recalled rightly, to be held in this very barn.

Can we finish the work wi' only Mam, Delana, Marlene, Grandmam, Mrs. Parkinson, and the

Twadley girls? She stared at the abundance of apples once more. *Surely not. And the men work at harvesting this time of year. 'Twas good of them to help pick the apples!* Rosalind sighed.

"I've an idea." Marlene whirled around giddily. "I'd warrant we could get the men to do it."

"Marlene! Your father, brother, and uncle hae more than enough to do in the fields. And Da works all the day long, too. We'll not shirk our fair share."

"So serious, Rose!" Marlene giggled. "I meant the men who come to our diner. What if we announced an apple bee? We'll have music and laughter and some supper to make the time go by."

" 'Twould be doable if we were to double whatever we make for dinner." Rosalind thought about it. "And to sweeten the deal, we could promise them apple cobbler wi' dinner later in the week."

"Now you're thinking!" Marlene scanned the open working space in the barn. "We'll bring in the benches for folks to sit on and our tables to hold the food. Mr. Twadley will bring his fiddle, and Luke's a whiz at playing the spoons. Brent would like the chance to show off with his harmonica."

"We'll hae an apple paring contest wi' the prize to be a fresh apple pie the next day." Rosalind thought of how best to make sure the work got done. "The men can take the pared apples to the cider press afterward. If enough men show up for the bee, we can get most of the work done in one evening!"

"Oh," Marlene spoke smugly, "they'll come. Just you wait and see. Tomorrow night, there won't be room enough for all the men who want to help."

The next afternoon, all the women of the town came from miles around to lend a hand. Soon, the wooden tables groaned under loaves of bread, pans of johnnycake, plates of biscuits, crocks of butter, platters of chicken, and two massive pots of Marlene and Rosalind's thick, creamy potato soup.

The diner benches lined the working area, with buckets and crates placed everywhere for the apple peels. Every hog in town would be well fed. Paring knives lay in rows; thick, brown string waited to hold apple slices for drying; and the cider press stood ready a short distance from the barn. Barrels next to heaps of straw were ready to cold-pack the fruit destined for the root cellars.

The men would come straight after the workday, and they'd work by lantern light until eyes drooped. With the barn doors thrown wide open, they'd carefully placed lanterns so as not to risk a fire.

The women took their places by the doors, closest to the waiting apples, as the men trickled in. Rosalind marveled at the difference in how they worked.

The women deftly turned their apples, sliding the paring blade smoothly beneath the skin to slick off the peel in one long rind of curlicues. The men attacked the apples as though whittling, moving the knives in short jerks to send shaved bits of peel flying into the buckets.

"I once heard," one of the Twadley girls confided to Rosalind and Marlene, "that if you peel the whole skin into one strip and toss it behind you, whatever shape the peel falls into on the floor represents the name of the man you'll marry!"

"What fun!" Marlene's hands moved with more cautious determination as she worked, though she kept her gaze fixed firmly on the men entering the barn. When Marlene straightened, her hands going still for the barest moment, Rosalind looked to the doorway.

There, his powerful frame gilded by the lantern light, stood Ewan. His broad shoulders all but blocked the smaller man who stood at his side.

Rosalind felt her breath hitch as Ewan stepped farther inside, his gaze passing over the barn's occupants and coming to rest on her. He dipped his head in acknowledgment before walking over to take a seat next to her father.

Mr. Mathers, much to Marlene's delight,

made a beeline toward her. She none too subtly scooted over to make room for him to plunk down, leaving Rosalind clinging to the edge of the bench.

Discomfited and not eager to examine why, Rosalind put down her knife and the apple she'd just finished paring. She dropped the long peel into the bucket behind her as she left for a drink of water.

Marlene's hastily smothered gasp made her turn around. There, obviously having missed the bucket, sat Rosalind's long apple peel, its curls resolutely shaped into an unmistakable letter *E*.

CHAPTER 8

"For pity's sake, Johnny." Ewan laid down his hammer as he caught his assistant giving him yet another odd look. "If you hae something to say, come out wi' it already."

"I — Oh, nothing." Johnny turned his back to Ewan.

"We're men. Quit shilly-shallying about and looking at me as though I've grown a second nose or sommat equally interesting. You're twitching more than a horse wi' pesky flies. 'Tis distracting."

"What do you think of Miss MacLean?" The younger man now wore a cautious, crafty expression Ewan found to be even more off-putting than the furtive glances.

"She's a fine lass." Ewan shrugged and said no more. *Pretty as a fiery sunset spreading o'er a blue sky, God-fearing, hardworking, deeply loyal, intelligent, kind . . . The list goes on. I won't be telling any o' that to Johnny, though.*

"I see." Johnny sounded more subdued,

disappointed even. "It's just that Marlene told me that she — Miss MacLean, that is — she got a sign last night at the apple bee. And —"

"Johnny!" Ewan bit out the name. "You're clucking like a gossipy hen, you know that?" *I don't want to hear about Rosalind getting a love-token from some other man. She deserves better than the fellows I've seen hereabouts, and that's that.*

"Fine." He sounded a bit huffy as he tossed a few last words over his shoulder. "If you don't want to know that she returns your high opinion of her but is too proper to say so . . ."

Ewan froze as Johnny's voice trailed off, tantalizing him with the thought that Rosalind might have noticed him the way he'd noticed her — the way he'd kept noticing her since the very first time they met.

"Oh?" He struggled to keep his tone neutral as he sought more information, but Johnny gave a shrug and said no more. "And this is leading to what?" he finally prompted more explicitly.

"Surely you don't expect *me* to say anything." Johnny inspected a piece of iron, obviously decided it wasn't ready, and thrust it back into the forge. "I don't want to sound like a . . . what was it?" His brow furrowed as he repeated, "A gossipy hen, right?"

"I may hae been a wee bit hasty," Ewan

admitted grudgingly.

"I'm glad to hear you realize that." Johnny, his lips firmly set, refrained from saying anything more. His silence was deafening.

"Johnny!" Ewan roared at long last. "Just tell me whatever 'tis that seemed so important naught but five minutes ago!"

"Marlene is of the opinion that Miss Mac-Lean thinks highly of you." Johnny stretched to get the cricks out of his muscles. "More highly of you than any of the men who've been sniffing around her lately. Marlene reckons her best friend has eyes for you, Ewan. I aimed to see if you returned her interest."

"Aye," Ewan admitted aloud for the first time. "She's a rare woman. But I'd hae no thought of courting her, you see."

"No, I don't see." Johnny gaped at him. "A pretty young lady who cooks like an angel and seems to like you above other men, and you have no thought of seeking her out? You're daft!"

"Now, Johnny —" Ewan stopped his protest before he uttered it. *Maybe he's right. How long hae I been thinking about settling down? And here the Lord brings me to the MacLean doorstep, where beautiful Rosalind is ripe for marriage.* "That may bear thinking on."

"Too right, it does." Johnny picked up his tongs once more. "I've already decided to speak with Marlene's father. Come spring, I'll have enough seed money to start my own spread. And in a year, I'll have a threshold to carry my bride over."

"You don't think you're being a bit hasty?" Ewan chose his words carefully, aware of the strength of Johnny's infatuation.

"I just said we'd wait a year before Marlene and I will wed."

"So you plan to settle down and want to see others do the same, eh?" Ewan couldn't resist teasing his friend just a mite.

"Something like that. You'd make a good neighbor, and Marlene wants to stay close to her friend." Johnny picked up his hammer. "Could work out to be a real good setup."

"Could be."

Ewan mulled over the information for hours, praying for guidance before feeling he had made the right decision. He strode over to Arthur's forge and waited until the older man finished what he was working on before he approached.

"Ewan!" Arthur drew off his gloves and apron, smiling in welcome. "What can I do for you?" He gestured for him to sit.

"You can give me permission to call on your daughter." Ewan figured Arthur was the sort of man who'd appreciate directness.

"I wondered when it would come to that." Arthur rested his heavy hands on his knees and closed his eyes. Even after a short acquaintance with him, Ewan knew him to be praying. He waited, respecting the man's need to seek God's will even as Ewan had before coming.

He's about to ask what my intentions are toward his daughter. Ewan straightened his shoulders and prepared to answer the question asked of would-be suitors by protective papas all the world over. He'd come with a ready answer to that.

"When you look at my Rosey," Arthur spoke slowly, drawing out the question to show its significance, "what do you see?"

Ewan paused to consider the unexpected question. He knew Arthur placed a great deal of importance on his reply, so he weighed his words carefully. There were as many ways to answer as there were things to appreciate about Rosalind herself.

"The first thing I saw was her beauty," he began honestly. " 'Twas why I spoke wi' you regarding her safety." At Arthur's nod of recollection, Ewan kept on. "Now, when I look upon her, I see a woman of warmth and integrity — a woman whose strength of character and generous heart I cannot help but admire. Her dedication to you and the rest of your family speaks well of her raising, and she carries herself as a God-fearing woman. She doesn't shirk from her duties, and I've yet to see her lose patience. In short," Ewan finished, admitting his hopes aloud for the first time, "when I look at your daughter, I see the woman I hope to share my life wi'."

He waited as Arthur thought over his response. *Did I say too little? Too much? Should I not hae mentioned her beauty? No, 'twould hae been dishonest and an obvious omission. Lord, when did feelings for Rosalind change my heart and priorities? Now everything seems to rest on this one conversation.*

"I'm well pleased wi' your answer, Ewan." Arthur gave an approving nod. "You see the beauty of her spirit and her worth beyond a pretty face and strong back. That's more than I can say for many a man hereabouts." He paused a moment. "You may court my Rosey, provided you agree to a few conditions."

Ewan waited to hear the conditions before he agreed.

"Should she reject your suit, you'll respect her decision. Should she accept it, you'll be treating her wi' the propriety an unmarried lady deserves at all times." Arthur's gaze bore into Ewan fiercely as he laid down his edicts, immovable as a wall of stone. "Her reputation will not be shadowed in any way."

"Done." Ewan reached out to shake his hand, but Arthur stopped him, holding up a cautionary palm before speaking.

"And before you speak wi' my daughter, we'll pray together. 'Tis no small thing, and we'll seek God's blessing afore all else." Arthur's expression turned wistful. "Should you win her heart and hand, it may well be I'll not see my daughter often."

This last thought hit Ewan with the force of a fist to the stomach. *He thinks I'll take her far away. Is that what marriage to her would mean, Lord? Dividing a loving family? I hae sworn never to separate kin — and I will not change my mind on the matter. Guide me, Father, that I not inflict such pain, as I hae suffered, on the family of the woman I hope to make my bride. And what if it comes down to marriage or her family, Lord? I'll not place her in that situation. Your eyes see ways I've no way of finding on my own. Help me trust You to see things through as You will, for the benefit of us both.*

"Look to your hair." Marlene's quick whisper caused Rosalind to glance over her shoulder.

"Why are Da and Ewan coming so soon?" She frowned in puzzlement. "Dinner is not near ready so early." Her breath caught in her throat as the icy hand of fear squeezed her heart in a suffocating grip. "Luke — he's unwell." Rosalind began to untie her apron strings as she hurried toward the approaching men, only to have Marlene snatch the strings and yank her backward.

"Calm yourself!" Marlene shook her head

in exasperation. "Why would Mr. Gailbraith be coming with your father to tell you such a thing? And why would your father not be running to seek your aid? They're not coming here to discuss your little brother." She gave Rosalind a knowing look. "They want to talk about you . . . and Mr. Gailbraith."

"Me and . . ." The iciness subsided, replaced by a pooling warmth. Marlene had always known more about these things than she did. "You think he's asked Da to come courting me?"

"Yes. Now duck as though to check the fire, and smooth your hair and pinch your cheeks so you look your best." Marlene rolled her eyes. "You should have guessed it long ago — the way he looks at you as though he'll tear any man apart who so much as casts you a friendly smile. Why do you think his table is always so calm at lunch? He scowls with a possessive gleam. I'm only surprised he didn't speak with you before he sought your father's official approval. Johnny's already talked to me, and we're agreed he'll speak to Father after next meeting."

Rosalind stopped fussing with her hair to stare at her friend. "Johnny spoke wi' you first? 'Tisn't it proper to go to the girl's father afore making any type of declaration at all?"

"No, silly." Marlene shrugged. "The man speaks with the girl, if he has any consideration at all, and then speaks to her father as though it's the first time he dared say anything. It appeases a father's pride and paves the way for family approval."

"But Ewan never said a word to me." Rosalind frowned. *'Tis his fault I'm caught so unaware! He's made this awkward by speaking wi' Da afore giving me so much as an inkling. Hmph. Marlene knows how 'tis done, and obviously Johnny does as well. Why am I to be blindsided in this ridiculous fashion?*

"Marlene, may I borrow Rosalind for a moment?" Da's question sounded ominously formal as he pasted a smile on his face.

"Of course, Mr. MacLean." Marlene turned to the oven.

"Let us go walk to the shade of that tree." Da pointed with one hand as he offered her the crook of his arm.

Rosalind accepted it, trying to avoid Ewan's intense gaze as the three of them walked a distance from where Marlene stood. When they came to a halt, Da squeezed her hand tenderly.

"Rosey-mine, there comes a time when a father looks for his wee lassie and finds instead a lovely young lady. Perhaps she's a lovely young lady who has caught the eye of a bachelor." He gestured for Ewan to come closer. "Ewan hae properly sought my blessing afore coming to call, and I've gladly granted him permission to court you. Provided, that is, you are willing to receive his interest." His grip tightened, as though letting her know he'd enforce her decision either way.

"I see." Gratitude for Da's unconditional support welled within her. *He approves of Ewan, and that's reason enough to accept, even if he didn't hae a ready smile and a kind heart.*

She looked up to see the cautious hope flickering in his sea-green eyes and knew her answer. "I'm willing, Da."

The grin breaking out across Ewan's face urged a smile in return as Da put her hand in Ewan's.

"I'll be leaving you two to speak for a short while then." He smiled and turned to walk back to where Marlene chopped potatoes. "Just a short while, mind!" he called over his shoulder, then left them in silence.

"Rosalind —" Ewan began. He didn't get far, as Rosalind checked to see if Da was watching, saw he wasn't, and lightly smacked Ewan's hand away. "What —"

"Listen to me, Ewan Gailbraith," she directed as she put her hands on her hips. "I'm willing to hae you pay me court and am flattered as well I should be, but 'tis a wee disgruntled I am, too, and that's a fact."

She shook a finger at his befuddled expression. "Don't look as though you don't ken

341

what I mean. 'Twouldn't have been overly difficult to give me some forewarning as to your intentions. I do not like to be caught unawares by anything, much less something of such importance." She finished speaking and waited for his reply. He had to understand straight from the start that he shouldn't be making such decisions without at least speaking to her first!

"I like hearing you say my name" was all he said.

"I — Did you not hear what else I said?" Rosalind demanded. " 'Tis vital you understand that I will not hae a husband who makes decisions first and speaks wi' me about them after the fact."

"Aye, Rosalind," he said, rumbling her name as though it were a blessing. "I should hae asked you first so as not to make things awkward for you." He took her hand in his once more, rubbing his thumb along her palm. "I value your thoughts and will seek them often. Does that put your mind at ease?"

No. If anything, my heart is beating fit to burst.

"Aye, that it does." She stepped slightly closer. "And 'tis honored I'll be to hae you come calling on me . . . Ewan."

CHAPTER 9

Ewan stared at where the heaping mound of corn ears took up even more space than the apples had not too long ago. And folks were pulling up wagonloads outside to replenish the pile as it diminished throughout the night.

"Good evening," he greeted Rosalind as he moved to sit beside her.

"Good evening," she replied. "At least, 'twill be a good night for me, I'm thinking." Her smile held a hint of mischief.

"Because we'll spend it together?" That's what made it a good evening to him, after all — sitting close enough to catch the light, fresh scent of roses her hair always carried.

"No. Well, that, too," she amended when she saw his chagrin. "I aim to beat you in the shucking competition. My two crates will be the first filled, I promise you." Her blue eyes sparkled in lighthearted challenge, needling him to answer it.

"Wi' these wee little hands?" He made a show of holding one of her dainty hands between his two large, rough ones. " 'Twill take you twice as long to do half the work, though 'tis certain I am you'll put forth a grand effort."

Ewan didn't release her hand until she pulled slightly away. Then she surprised him by pressing her soft palm against his calloused one, stretching her fingers as far as they'd go. They both looked at the contrast silently for a moment. His sun-darkened skin and broad digits dwarfed her creamy delicacy.

"Well" — Rosalind's soft voice sounded slightly breathless as she turned her gaze to meet his — "there you hae it. 'Tis plain as the very nose on your face that I'll be the swifter betwixt us." Her hand exerted a slight, warm pressure against his as though to push him into agreement with her misguided boasting.

"Nay." His fingers curled over hers as he shook his head. "There is no arguing wi' what your eyes surely tell you, lass."

"Of course, which is why I'll win." She drew her hand away and lifted her chin. "My hands are small and light, so I'll be able to move more quickly than your large fingers can manage."

"We'll see." Ewan waited for Dustin Freimont to welcome everyone to the corn husking and ask God's blessing on the night's work. He tensed, ready to spring into action as the man officially began the competition.

Ewan dove into the work with determined zeal, scarcely sparing a glance at Rosalind's progress. That brief glance was enough to still his hands for a moment as he watched her swift, confident motions add another shucked ear to her already too-full crate. *How did she do that?*

He redoubled his efforts, loathe to let her best him after he'd bragged so certainly of his victory. Husks flew through the air and littered the floor in front of them as he increased his frantic pace. Ewan froze in disbelief as Rosalind stood up, signaling that her crates were completely filled. She'd not only defeated him in their private challenge, she'd bested absolutely everyone hard at work inside the walls of the barn!

She walked up to Dustin and claimed her prize — a finely sewn quilt decorated with colored scraps fashioned into an intricate pattern of interlocking rings. She exclaimed over it, causing an old woman in the far corner to beam with delight.

"How did you manage that?" he whispered after she sat at his side once more. "Will you share the trick you use?"

"Ewan Gailbraith!" Rosalind scowled at him in mock disappointment. "How could you think I've any sort of trick? 'Tis plain hard work and" — she grinned in victory as she flexed her fingers in a silent display — "skill."

"I see I've underestimated you, Rosalind." He leaned close and whispered so only she could hear his next words. "You can be sure that I'll not be making the same mistake next time."

Her pink blush was all the victory he needed as they set back to work. Ewan's grin only faded when a shadow fell across him and he looked up to find a familiar young man standing before Rosalind, legs splayed, jaw set belligerently. He remembered the slight young fellow as Marlene's older brother but had an inkling he'd be remembering him differently soon.

"Rose," the youth addressed her with maddening informality, and Ewan had to remind himself that they'd probably grown up together, and thus it was an appropriate address. "Why don't you come over and sit with Marlene and myself?" He extended his hand to her, overconfident that she'd take him up on the offer.

"Brent, I'm quite comfortable here." Rosalind spoke kindly but firmly enough that the lad should have accepted her words.

"Rose" — Brent leaned closer and spoke in a low tone that carried plain as day — "you needn't feel obligated to sit near strangers out of a misplaced sense of politeness. Come sit with me and mine, where you belong." *Now.* This last wasn't said aloud, but came across as strongly as if it had been trumpeted.

Ewan got to his feet, unwilling to let the stripling order his Rosalind about or attempt to stake a claim to her affection. He needn't have made the effort. Rosalind fixed Brent with an outraged stare and crossed her arms as a further barrier.

"Brent Freimont, 'tis not your place to decide where I belong. And 'tis angered I am to hear you label me as one of *yours,* as though I were a prize sow displayed at the fair."

Realizing his error too late, Brent stammered an apology.

"I appreciated your kind invitation, Brent" — Rosalind gentled her scowl but kept her tone disapproving — "but when I politely expressed disinterest, you should have behaved like a gentleman and respected my decision rather than try to force your way."

"Yes, Rose." The boy made a swift bow and retreated back to where the rest of his family sat, obviously watching them all with an avid curiosity — and a hint of apprehension, as well.

Ewan returned his focus to where it belonged — Rosalind. She looked up at him, half-chagrined over the scene, half-defying him to question the way she'd handled the issue.

He sat beside her, moving as close as was decent, and gave voice to his opinion. "It seems as though I'm not the only one to underestimate you, Rosalind." He fingered the silken end of her braid to show support. "I'm only glad I'll have the chance to rectify that."

Men. Rosalind viciously ripped off another corn husk and threw it down before reaching for the next one. *Bad enough that Ewan discomfits me so, but to hae Brent saunter up and try to stake a claim as though I hae no say in the matter . . . Ugh. Incredible!*

"Which do you prefer, the apple bee or the corn shucking?" Ewan's question broke through her thoughts as though he knew what she was thinking. He waited patiently for her answer.

"Neither." Rose gave in to the contrary mood. "My favorite gathering is the sugaring-off. 'Tis the most fun and tasty."

"Sugaring-off? I'd the notion 'twas only done in Vermont or such."

"No, we've sugar maples here, as well." Rose took a shallow breath. "We don't harvest the sap until February. I suppose the railroad will hae moved on long before that." It was as close as she could come to asking what he planned for the future.

Will he continue to work for the rail lines, and take me wi' him to see all America? Excitement surged at the idea, even as her heart sank. *Could I leave Mam and Da and Luke*

348

behind if I knew 'twould be forever?

Intent upon harvesting some clue from Ewan's answer, she peeked at his face from the corner of her eye. They both continued divesting ears of corn of their husks.

"Aye." The single syllable came out forced, and Rosalind saw a shadow pass over his countenance. He said no more, and she did not press the matter.

Lord, I've always wanted to travel the length and breadth of the nation. All the same, I yearned for that adventure with certain knowledge of everyone here waiting to welcome my return. I always thought to settle nearby when I finally wed. It never occurred to me that the man I marry might hae different ideas. Now 'tis far too soon to press Ewan about the matter, but 'twill have to be addressed sometime. Give me the wisdom to handle my doubts and find peace in the path You place before me.

"Rosalind?" Ewan rose to his feet. "Would you fancy a drink o' water?" He gestured toward the large bucket.

"Aye." She smiled her thanks, relieved to see no sign of the shadow from earlier. He behaved as an attentive suitor should and now 'twas the time to take note of such fine qualities. No sense borrowing trouble, as Da would say.

She reached for another ear and peeled back some of the crisp green cover. A flash of deep red peeked out, and she covered it immediately.

Oh no! She could feel herself flushing a shade to rival the red corn. *I'll not kiss Ewan in front of the whole town! He'll be back in a moment.*

She looked about for Marlene. Rosalind had passed any red ears to her bolder best friend for years now. But Marlene sat next to Johnny — and Brent — across the way. *Oh bother.*

As Ewan shouldered his way back into view, Rosalind debated what to do. Would she dare slip the red ear into his pile? No. 'Twould still mean sharing their first kiss before everyone she ever knew. As Ewan stopped to say something to a man she didn't recognize, Rosalind dropped the ear and kicked it under the bench behind her skirts.

Ewan gave her an odd look as he handed her a tin of water, and she hastily gulped some to cover her unease. She smiled brightly and patted the bench beside her. Rosalind breathed a tiny sigh of relief as he settled onto the seat and began to share stories from his years working for the railroad.

"Now, I'll not be telling you all these are true, but men in the railroad camps hae been swapping stories for years. Some o' the tales sound reasonable enough to keep telling."

"Do you know any funny stories?" Rosalind

asked. "I've heard about the wrecks, and those make me sad."

"Nay." Ewan shook his head. "Those are warnings, not tales to be shared when a man sits beside a pretty lass."

His smile made her flush once again.

"I'll tell you a legend about one spendthrift builder and the clever foreman who outwitted him."

"That sounds good." She straightened. "Let's hear it."

"There was a builder named Mr. Hill, who kept a tight fist around the finances." Ewan's own fist tightened around the hapless ear of corn he'd just finished shucking. "He disapproved mightily of anything that could be seen as at all wasteful. Well, one day he was walking along the tracks, inspecting the work, and he spotted something in the dirt. Sure enough, he'd found a new rail spike lying deserted in the roadbed. Outraged, he stomped off to take the section foreman to task for such carelessness. They didn't have spikes to throw away."

"What a horrible man." Rosalind shuddered. "I'd hate to be that poor foreman, having to answer to that. What happened to him?"

"The quick-thinking foreman saw him coming, spotted the spike, and rushed to meet the builder. He hurries up to the man, stands tall, and says, 'Thank goodness you

351

found that spike, Mr. Hill. I've had three men looking for it for nearly a week!' "

Rosalind burst out laughing, only speaking when she finally caught her breath. "Oh, that's a good one. Should have taught that Mr. Hill a lesson. I'd like to think that really happened."

"Me, too." Ewan chuckled. "Can't you just picture the builder's expression? He probably gaped like a caught fish."

"Most likely," Rosalind agreed. "Tell another one, please! Out here we so rarely hear things like that. We just get news."

"Hmm." Ewan thought for a moment. "I could hae another story or so to coax a smile. 'Tis a grand reward for so little."

"Flatterer." Rosalind waggled a finger at him. "Fewer fulsome compliments and more humorous stories. I enjoy those more."

"All right." He took a moment, looking as though he enjoyed holding her interest. "Out in California, a railroad agent once got yelled at over doing things wi'out waiting for his orders to trickle down from faraway headquarters, as he should hae done. Then came a day, not long after, when the boss at headquarters received an urgent telegram from that selfsame agent: 'Grizzly bear on platform hugging conductor. Please wire instructions.' "

"No!" Rosalind's hands stilled as she looked up in shock. "Never tell me he waited afore helping that poor conductor!"

"I'm sure he took care of it before he ever sent the telegram," Ewan soothed. "The man was just trying to make a point. If he waited for official orders before doing everything, nothing would ever get done in time to do good."

"Well, in that case . . ." Rosalind relaxed. "If he kept his job, 'twas a rather clever way to argue his side of the matter."

"Aye, that's my thought, too." Ewan reached back for a mighty stretch and Rosalind, slightly more cautious since finding a red ear, peeled back a small section of husk as a safeguard.

Another gash of red blazed forth, and she hurriedly reached for another. As she grasped another ear, she let the red one roll off her lap. As before, she inconspicuously kicked it beneath the bench. Only this time, she kicked too hard. At the *thud* of the ear hitting the barn wall, Ewan looked back at her.

"What was that?" He looked around for the sound's source.

"Nothing." The word came out sounding as flustered as she felt. "You know, I'm starting to get a bit peckish." She hopped up. "Would you like me to fetch you an apple while I'm up?"

"Aye," he looked at her strangely. "A green one, please."

With a too-bright smile, she headed for the

tables, selected two shiny apples, and went back. Before sitting on the bench, she looked down. It wouldn't do to slip on one of those pesky red ears she'd let drop. Wouldn't do at all.

There were no ears on the floor. Startled, she glanced up at a beaming Ewan. In each of his upraised hands lay one of the red ears.

"Oooh!" A swell of raucous calls filled Ewan's senses as people took note of the two ears he held up for all to see.

"Who's your lucky lady, Gailbraith?" one of the men called out. "Let her know now so she can run away!"

"I know who he'll choose!" Johnny bellowed. Beside him, Marlene was beaming and casting Rosalind knowing looks.

Rosalind, for her part, had turned as petal pink as her namesake flower and sat down as though her knees had given out. She couldn't have looked any more enticing had she tried.

Though he thought it impossible, Ewan's grin widened. *I knew I saw her hiding something behind her skirts.* Sure enough, when she'd gone to fetch the apples, he'd found two partly unhusked ears of corn. Red ears. The thought of her squirreling away kisses charmed him. His Rosalind wouldn't hold up the red ear in triumph and boldly claim her forfeit. Instead, she clumsily hid the evidence. *Good thing I'm not shy.* Ewan clasped Rosalind's hand and purposefully drew her to her feet. Her eyes, impossibly wide, shone with a beguiling mix of anxiety and anticipation.

"There's only one woman I've eyes" — Ewan waved one of the cobs of corn — "or ears for." Resisting the urge to hold her close, Ewan kept her hand in his and leaned forward to press a chaste kiss on her soft lips. After the barest moment — a moment far too short, to his way of thinking — he drew back.

Amid the stares and cheers of the crowd, Rosalind held his gaze and raised her hand to gently touch her lips. The gesture nearly made Ewan reach for her again, but he saw the moment when she remembered the whole town watched her reaction.

Ewan addressed the crowd, diverting their attention from Rosalind as best he could. " 'Tis the truth, no man could ask for more than that." He held up the second red ear and pretended to consider it. "Now then, since I've experienced perfection, 'twould be churlish of me to deny another the same opportunity."

At his words, it seemed as though every man in the barn stood and shouted to be chosen. Ewan made a show of considering whom he'd pass the second red ear to before tossing it to Johnny. Envious groans shook the barn clear to the rafters.

As though I'd give it to some other man who'd choose my Rosalind. And honestly, any other man would be daft to choose another girl. Johnny, enamored of Marlene as he is, was the only safe choice.

And Johnny made the most of his good fortune, bussing Marlene with more enthusiasm than grace. With everyone's attention turned to the other couple, Ewan and Rosalind sank back onto their bench. Their moment of excitement had ended.

"Thief." Rosalind whispered the indictment under her breath and out of the corner of her mouth. All the same, her eyes held no matching reproach to make him regret taking action.

"Sneak," Ewan muttered back, grinning at her resulting gasp.

Long seconds stretched between them before she answered. "Aye," she admitted, biting back an impish smile.

"Aye." Ewan shouldered a bit closer, beginning to regret his gift to Johnny. "You know what that makes the two of us?"

"What?" The question in her eyes seemed less lighthearted.

"It makes us" — Ewan spoke seriously, to let her know he meant what he said — "a likely pair."

CHAPTER 10

"Is it true that the railroad will be moving on soon?" Marlene burst out with the question almost the instant Ewan and Johnny sat down for their pre-dinner-rush meal. "You've not even been here a month! Surely this type of haste isn't typical?"

Although Rosalind wouldn't have chosen to handle the issue in this manner, she shared Marlene's worries about whether the railroad would take their beaus away with it. She looked at Ewan, careful to school her features into a neutral expression. Whatever his decision — whether he stayed for winter or left now with plans of returning later — she planned on supporting it.

"Yes, sugar-pie." Johnny looked every bit as miserable as Marlene at the prospect of leaving. "We've lingered a bit long to enjoy the comforts of home-cooking and pretty smiles, so the foreman tells us we won't be able to delay any longer. Camp will be moved a good thirty miles away. We've no choice."

"Thirty miles!" Marlene sank down onto the nearest bench, tears dotting her pale eyelashes. "Can't they at least hold off until after Thanksgiving? That's only a few days away!"

"They say they won't risk losing our impressive pace." Ewan shook his head. "Though 'tis bound to slow. Tomorrow we head out."

"Why didn't they give us a warning?" Rosalind's firm resolve not to complain melted in the face of such an immediate separation. She bit her lip.

" 'Tis for the best." Ewan rolled his massive shoulders in a vain effort to relieve tension. "If they told the men ahead of time, they'd be prone to acting out. No man wants to go back to Hank's cooking in the midst of an empty wilderness — especially wi' winter coming. This late notice, 'tis a safeguard for all the town."

"But no safeguard against heartache." Marlene's whisper probably reached only Rosalind's ears, but she decided to take no chances Ewan would overhear such maudlin dramatics.

"Marlene, we've everything ready for the men. Why don't we leave off ringing the dinner bell just a wee little bit? The news has caught us all by surprise, and 'twould do us good to spend a few private moments together." She reached out to clasp Ewan's hand. "Why don't we walk a short distance afore dinner?"

"Aye," Ewan assented.

Marlene and Johnny didn't even follow, lost as they were in one another.

After walking only a short distance, Ewan began, "Rosalind, 'tis sorry I am this matter has come upon us so sudden. 'Tis said the men took such great cheer from your diner they laid track more quickly than was expected — too much of a good thing."

" 'Tisn't as though we thought the railroad would hole up here forever," Rosalind said, "but we did think 'twould be a bit longer before you packed up and moved away from us."

"As did I." Ewan put his hands on her shoulders. "I'd not intended to hae you make any sort of decision this quickly."

Surely he wouldn't propose now. Ewan wouldn't expect me to marry and leave my family wi' such haste! I can't!

"Ewan" — Rosalind stared down at the toes of her shoes, unable to look at him — "I'm sorry, but I can't go wi' you."

"I know." The surprise in his voice caused her to look upward. He seemed almost offended. "I wouldn't ask that of you, Rosalind. To separate from family . . . 'Tis a horrible thing."

"Then" — her brow furrowed in confusion — "what decision would you hae me make?"
What else is there for me to decide?

"Whether I go on wi' the railroad for now or make arrangements to stay the winter."

"Oh!" Rosalind threw her arms around him. "I'm so very glad!" She drew back after her initial burst of excitement and considered. "Won't the railroad need you? I'd not hae you leave them in the lurch when you've made a commitment. That you're a man of your word is one o' the things I admire so."

"Wi' winter coming on, the pace will slow. Johnny's capable of managing on his own by now. He's skilled enough." Ewan's gaze ran deep enough for her to drown in. " 'Tis my commitment to you I wouldn't want questioned."

"Oh." Rosalind suddenly found it difficult to speak past the lump in her throat. *If he asked me to go wi' him right this minute, I'd say yes. 'Tis good he will do no such thing!*

"But we've only been courting a wee while. I do not want to put you off by making such a decision wi'out speaking wi' you first." His eyes twinkled with suppressed mirth. "A wonderful lass once warned me against such terrible folly."

"And right she was. 'Tis grateful I am that such a wise woman took pains to show you the error of your ways." She gave him a sidelong smile. " 'Twill make you a much better neighbor this winter." She watched the grin break out across his face and knew she'd not regret her choice.

"I've a sneaking suspicion that same lass will find many ways to make a better man of me." They started back.

"Do you know," Rosalind teased, "I think you might be right."

At the sight of Johnny seated next to Marlene with his arm around her shoulders, Rosalind stopped walking. "Ewan, have you discussed this wi' Johnny to make sure he won't resent it?"

"Aye." He stepped back to stand beside her. Her sudden stop had left him ahead. "Johnny all but insisted I stay behind. Says he needs to have someone he trusts watch o'er Marlene while he's away for the winter. He plans to return come springtime."

" 'Tis good." Rosalind began walking once more but gave a loud sigh. " 'Twould be perfect if Johnny could stay wi' you. I know Marlene will miss him something awful in the months ahead." *And 'twill only be the harder when she sees that I still hae you.* She left the last thought unspoken. She wouldn't say anything that could reflect poorly on her friend. Marlene was entitled to some sadness at the loss of her first true love.

"We'll be sure to include Marlene in fun outings so she won't have time enough to dwell on his absence." Ewan folded her hand in his and gave a reassuring squeeze. "Spring will be upon us before she knows it, and for now, she has you. Such a blessing as that cannot be o'erlooked for very long."

Rosalind gave a gentle squeeze in return but said nothing as they came to stand next to Marlene and Johnny.

Marlene's sobs racked her petite frame, though Johnny spoke soothing words, promises he would return and they'd be strong for one another. "But I d–don't understand," Marlene gasped. "Why can't you stay if Ewan is going to? Why are you so set on leaving?"

"Now, sugar-pie," Johnny patted her back as one would an upset child's, bungling the earnest attempt to pacify her. "With Ewan gone, they'll need me all the more. We can't both abandon the crew all winter. They've no other blacksmith."

"Why doesn't Ewan go?" Marlene wailed, obviously only realizing the ugliness behind the words after she said them. "I don't mean that I don't want him to stay, too, but why are *you* going on with the railroad while *he* stays here in town?" There was no hiding the tinge of bitter accusation in the question.

Rosalind gaped at her in disbelief. Surely her best friend hadn't spoken such awful words? What would Ewan think?

"Marlene!" Johnny's stern disapproval startled her enough to stop the tears. "Ewan has every bit as much of a right to stay as I do. I counted on you easing his way while I went on ahead. Had someone told me to expect such an objection from my sweet sugar-pie, I wouldn't have believed it."

"I — I didn't mean it that way." Marlene sniffled apologetically. "Really, I do want Rose to be happy."

"That's my Marlene," Johnny encouraged. "Truth be told, Ewan is doing me a great favor by stepping down. I'll no longer be paid as only an apprentice. By sometime this spring, I'll be able to come back to you with enough to start a small home."

"Oh Johnny," she breathed, "do you mean it?"

"Of course I do!" He apparently couldn't refrain from adding, "It's only what I've been saying this whole time."

"Ewan, Rose, I'm so sorry for what I said." Marlene grasped their entwined hands in hers. "I wouldn't have you leave for my sake, Ewan. Really, truly I wouldn't."

Her earnest tone told Rosalind her best friend had earlier spoken out of frantic desperation. She forgave her on the spot. "I know that." Rosalind disengaged her hand to hug her friend. "This gives us that much more to look forward to come spring." She looked at Ewan and happiness bubbled inside her heart. *Though I hope there are things to look forward to now, as well.*

"Arthur?" Ewan made a beeline for the smithy as soon as he had a chance that afternoon. He waited for the older man's hammer to stop ringing before he went on. "I've a question to ask you."

"I assumed as much." Arthur's smile took the barb from the words. "Though I should warn you that Marlene spilled the news at lunch. I know you've spoken wi' Rosey and decided to stay the winter. I'll not be standing in your way, Ewan."

" 'Tis glad I am to hear it," Ewan said. "Now that I've made the decision, I'll have to find a way to make it work. I was wondering whether you could tell me who used to live in the smaller house so close to your own? As near as I can tell, 'tisn't in use."

"Ah. That used to be Gilda's home. She lived there wi' Cade — they were Kaitlin's parents you ken — up until Cade passed on two years ago." He shrugged. " 'Twasn't safe to let her live alone at her age, and she said the place held too many memories of Cade while she was grieving. So you've the right o' it. Gilda stays wi' us, and the house has stood empty for a bit." He cast Ewan a sidelong glance. "I know Brent Freimont hoped to purchase it as a home not too far in the future."

"Brent Freimont?" Ewan recalled the youth's treatment of Rosalind at the corn husking and his menacing glare after Ewan claimed his kiss. "He'll be having no need of it," he stated flatly. "Do I have your approval?"

"Aye," Arthur agreed. "Rosey has never looked on Brent wi' the affection he bears for her. 'Twouldn't hae been a good match."

"Do I speak wi' you or Gilda about renting the house through winter?" Ewan smiled at Arthur's assessment of Brent.

"I'm all for it, but you'll have to speak wi' Gilda. Though she lives wi' us, 'tis still the home of her heart."

"And I'll treat it as such." He thought of Rosalind's grandmam, the roadmap of wrinkles around her loving gaze and the way she'd looked him over when they first met. "She's a good woman, and I'll not be showing disrespect to her memories. Should she decide not to let me have the place, 'twill be simple enough to build a small soddy." He thought of living half underground, shut in by snow and walled in by solid earth for months at a time. He'd bear with dirt and burrowing bugs to win Rosalind, but all the same . . . "I do hope Gilda will let me rent the house."

"She'll be at home now, if you're half so anxious to ask as I'm thinking you are." Arthur gave him a wry smile. "Gilda seems to have taken a liking to you, if that helps."

"I'll take all the advantages I can get when it comes t' courting your daughter." Ewan nodded his appreciation and began to leave the smithy. "My thanks for your advice, Arthur."

He set off on the pleasant walk to the Mac-Lean homestead. *Lord, if 'tisn't Your will that I stay in the house, I'll accept that. You know I hope to make Rosalind my bride, but I've yet to see how to do so wi'out either taking her from her family or taking part of her da's livelihood. I can't do either, nor can I ignore the feelings I bear for Rosalind herself. Before winter ends, I pray that You will show me how to proceed. I will not ask her to be my wife until I'm sure 'tis Your will, though I know 'twill be a temptation. Help me remember to seek You first, Father, so I don't lead Rosalind the wrong way.*

By the time he reached the house, Ewan felt the mantle of peace that was God's way of showing him he did the right thing. He raised his fist to knock on the door only to have it swing open before his hand met the wood even once. Gilda Banning stood on the other side of the threshold, eyes canny.

"So you've come to ask about the house, hae you?" Her assessment left him speechless for a moment, and she let out a gleeful chuckle. "Come in, come in, then. Kaitlin and Luke went to gather some vegetables from the garden. We'll have a nice chat, you and I."

"Thank you." Ewan stepped inside, still thrown off balance by her greeting. "How did you know why I came before I asked?"

"I've seen a good many years, lad." She

sank into a carved rocker near the hearth. "I know you've come to talk about my home same as I know Brent Freimont had an eye on it, as well."

He took a ladder-back chair and dragged it beside her. "I do not seek it as a wedding gift," Ewan spoke carefully.

"I should hope not!" Gilda snorted. "After knowing our Rose for less than a month, you know how special she is, but you'd be a fool t' propose a marriage so very soon."

"Aye," Ewan agreed, relieved that he wouldn't have to defend himself on that score. "I come to ask whether I might rent your lovely house for the duration of the winter, and perhaps a bit into the spring. I'll pay well, Mrs. Banning."

"And 'twill be well worth the price, to my way of thinking." The old woman rocked slowly, as though contemplating the matter. "I've not much inside, you see, but I did leave a table an' chairs and an empty trunk or so. It has a fireplace rather than a stove, but I'd suppose you know that from the size o' the chimney." She nodded and suddenly turned a gimlet eye on him. "What are your intentions toward my granddaughter, Mr. Gailbraith, if you do not ask to buy the place after all?"

"I intend to court her honorably, Mrs. Banning."

"Psh. Call me Gilda." The old woman kept

her gaze pinned on him. "And I knew you were honorable, else Arthur wouldn't let you court Rose, and my granddaughter wouldn't see you, and I wouldn't hae allowed you to rent my house." She leaned forward intently. "I mean, what are your plans after you win her, lad? Will you settle here or take her away wi' you?"

"That I cannot say at the moment," Ewan confessed. "I've more than enough money saved t' settle into a home, but Saddleback already has a fine blacksmith in Arthur. Just the same, I don't believe in separating families." He noted the spark of understanding in her eyes. "What answer would you hae wanted?"

"That, I cannot say, lad." She leaned back once more. "We, of course, want her to stay, but that is our desire, not necessarily hers. Our Rose thirsts for a bit o' adventure. She feels she missed her big chance, being just a babe when my Kaitlin brought her to the wilds of the Montana Territory. She can't recall the journey, after all, and wants to see a bit o' the world."

"And I'm no closer to an answer." Ewan shifted in the chair. "I appreciate your insight, Gilda, and your generosity."

"As I appreciate yours. Now" — she smiled — "let's talk about the terms of that rental."

CHAPTER 11

"Marlene didn't take it very well when we packed up the supplies left at the diner." Rosalind frowned. "I wonder how long she'll be so blue. Surely this mood cannot last through the winter!"

"It won't." Mam stirred the hot tallow to keep it from lumping. "But the diner bore memories of her Johnny, and it brought her sadness to the surface. Give her a bit o' time."

"Aye." Grandmam dipped her too-thin candle in the wax again and drew it out, holding it aloft to harden. "She'll come 'round."

"I'm going to make the thickest candle ever." Luke eyed his already too-big contribution. "I'll make it thick enough that when I level the bottom, 'twill stand on its own."

"And if not," Grandmam noted, "we'll melt it down again. 'Twill not be a waste either way, and who knows? It may work."

Rosalind kept her doubts on the matter to herself, instead admiring the soft lavender-blue color of the candles. With each new layer of cooled wax, they took on a slightly darker shade.

" 'Twas so clever to soak the dried blueberries so they plumped and then juice them. It adds such a nice scent and lovely color." She dipped her candle once more and judged it to be thick enough. Rosalind hung it on the drying rack and began again. "The only drawback is they might make us hungry!"

"Mayhap next time we'll add a splash of oil of lilac instead of the blueberry juice." Mam surveyed the filling rack with satisfaction. "We'll be glad to have these come winter."

"Aye," Grandmam seconded. "If there's anything worse than being snowed in for months on end, 'tis being snowed in wi' only the hearth's light to see by. Makes it that much darker."

"Mam, may I give Marlene a candle or two for her nightstand?" Rosalind gave an appreciative sniff. "The treat might help to restore her good spirits. Coax a smile, even."

"I'm sure we can spare a few for such a good cause."

"You can give her mine, Rose." Luke generously held out the large, misshapen candle he'd been nursing the entire day.

"Oh, I'm not sure if 'twill fit in her candleholder, Luke." Rosalind gestured toward the monstrosity. "Best you keep it to read by. 'Twill be interesting to see how long 'twill last."

"Good idea, Rose." Luke headed back to dunk the thing yet again. "I don't think anyone's ever made one like this before."

"I believe you are the first, Luke." Mam ruffled his hair.

"Why don't you run o'er with these four?" Grandmam held them out to Rosalind. "You'll probably be glad to take a nice, quiet walk." Her eyes held a knowing glint as she looked at Rosalind.

"Aye." Rosalind took them thankfully. For the first time since the leaves had turned color, she'd have a moment to herself. With the railroad crew packed off, she could walk alone again.

She draped a light shawl about her shoulders to ward off the chill that warned of winter and set out down the well-worn path. The scents of fallen leaves and rich, dark earth freed by the harvest filled her senses as she moved along.

Father, I see the work of Your hands around me, and 'tis wondrous. Your imagination so far surpasses my own — all I seem to be able to think of is Ewan. How did he go from a man my parents warned me against to my possible future husband in such a short span of time? I remember praying not so long ago about trying to separate out my own impressions of the man wi' the caution Mam and Da exhorted me to use.

Now he has Da's approval, and while Mam had hoped for Brent as a son-in-law, she hasn't spoken against Ewan's courtship. Grandmam has even agreed to rent her house to him for the winter. Everything seems to point to an ideal match — can it be so easy? I know You guard o'er the seasons in our lives, but this time of beginnings seems almost too sweet. Why am I holding a fear that 'twon't last? Help me to trust in Your will, Father, as time ripens.

She knocked on the Freimonts' door, waiting until Mrs. Freimont opened it and ushered her inside with a welcoming smile.

"Rose! It is always good to see you." She took Rosalind's hands in hers and spoke more softly. "Perhaps you can cheer Marlene from her sullens. I will give her the rest of today to adjust to the idea of waiting for her young man, but that is enough."

"Aye." Rosalind nodded. " 'Twouldn't do to stay so for long. I'll hae a chat wi' her. She'll pull through this difficulty."

"Ja." Mrs. Freimont waved for her to go up into the loft where Marlene's bed reposed. Rosalind guessed that her friend had been up there since they'd come back from the diner.

"Marlene!" she called out in a hearty voice as she ascended the ladder. "I've come to see how you're doing this afternoon." She poked her head over the ladder to find Marlene sitting atop her bed, evidence of recent tears staining her white pillowcase.

Not a good sign, Rosalind inventoried, *though she's not crying now. That's more hopeful. Oh, unless she's cried so much she can't cry anymore. And I thought some blue candles would help?*

"Don't stand on the ladder all day," Marlene sniffed. "Come on up." She patted the mattress beside her and gave a ghost of a smile. "I promise I won't say anything awful."

"Hush." Rosalind stooped into the loft and sat beside Marlene. "I brought you a little something." She passed over the candles.

"They're purple! No, blue?" Marlene squinted in an attempt to determine. "Whatever did you put in the wax for color?"

"Mam added blueberry juice, and I thought they were a little more blue than purple, though I wouldn't argue wi' you on the matter." Rosalind took a deep breath. "Smell them."

"Mmm . . ." Marlene inhaled a few times before she put the candles down. "They make me want to eat some blueberries."

" 'Tis almost the same thing as what I said!" Rosalind laughed. "Still, I think 'twas a marvelous idea. Think of all the different things we could use! Raspberries for summer, apples for fall — and the berries at least would turn the whole batch pink."

"Custom candles," Marlene said. "Think of

373

it — candles to match the color of your quilt or curtains, whichever you like."

"What would you use for green or yellow?" Rosalind tried to think of anything that would work. "I can only think of green beans or such, and I wouldn't want that scent all the time."

"Nor I." Marlene thought a moment. "We could stir pumpkin juice with a stick of cinnamon and see how that turns out."

"Maybe. That would give us something like yellow. But I don't like the smell of raw pumpkin o'ermuch — just baked."

"That's what the cinnamon is for, Rose." Marlene leaned back on her elbows and stared up at the ceiling rafters. "I can't believe he's already gone. Here yesterday, and today —"

"Working to save up for your wedding," Rosalind broke in. "And we both know your da would say you're too young to wed for a while yet. Johnny's doing what's best for your future, Marlene. He'll come back."

"Do you really think so?" Marlene plucked at a loose string on her quilt. "He won't meet some other girl before then?"

"Not one who could cast you from his memory. God made you special, and none can compare." Rosalind's heart ached at her friend's forlorn look. "He'll be back afore you know it."

"I'll know it the second my Johnny walks

back into town," Marlene declared with her old confidence. "I know it will take a year or two before our home is ready — it takes so long to clear land, raise a house, and start a farm — but at least he'll be with me then. For now, I'll just have to think about something else." She looked at Rosalind with a speculative gaze. "So, how do you plan to get Ewan to propose?"

CHAPTER 12

"No, not like that." Grandmam shooed Rosalind away from the stuffed goose. "You keep it in the juices so it stays moist."

"I'd thought to add flour and such to make a bit o' gravy." Rosalind shrugged and slid a loaf of pumpkin spice bread from the old niche at the hearth. When Mam and Da first built the house, they'd not had a stove to call their own. Now, for Thanksgiving Day, every cooking contraption had been called into service.

"You make it right," Mam sided against Rosalind, "and there's no need for gravy."

"Da likes it for his potatoes and dressing," Rosalind pointed out. " 'Tis no insult to the bird."

"Aye." Grandmam's shoulders relaxed. "My Cade loved a dribble of thick gravy on his mashed potatoes, too. But you wait until the last possible moment — not until after the Thanksgiving Meeting."

"Right." Rosalind pinned an errant curl

behind her ear. "I should hae remembered that. When did I become such a muddled miss?"

"Oh" — Mam gave her a sideways look — "I'd say about the same time Ewan decided to stay through the lonely winter."

"Mam!" Rosalind shook her head but smiled at the truth in her mother's words. " 'Tis happy I am we've so much to be thankful for this Thanksgiving Day."

"And you want it to come off just right" — Grandmam shuffled back to her rocker — "and make sure you show Ewan he's made a sound decision, that's what 'tis."

"I hope I'm never so ungrateful as to o'erlook the others I'm blessed with." Rosalind walked over to give the old woman a hug. "Ewan's not the only one I thank God for."

"Aye." Mam came by to join the embrace. "Rose has the right o' it."

"All the same" — Grandmam settled back more comfortably after the moment passed — "I've the notion you ought to wear your best blue dress for the festivities today, Rose. It draws attention to your sparkling eyes."

"I'd already planned to," she admitted. "After all, Thanksgiving is a time when we thank the Lord by putting forth our best efforts!"

"Aye." Da stepped into the warmth of the house, trailed by Luke. " 'Tis glad I am to hear my women speak such humble thoughts."

Rosalind raised her eyebrows toward Mam and Grandmam — they had, after all, just been discussing a sort of vanity. Neither gave the slightest hint of amusement but carried on as though Da had the right of it.

It brought to mind Grandmam's old lesson: A still tongue gathers praise when a busy one catches naught but air.

"Luke!" Rosalind gently slapped his hand away from one of the carefully arranged platters of food. "You know that's for the community dinner!"

"But picnic eggs are my favorite!" His brown eyes pled for a wee taste.

"Just one." Rosalind handed him one of the boiled eggs, hollowed and refilled with a mashed mix of yolk, lard, pickle brine, and salt. They happened to be a favorite of hers, too. She popped one into her own mouth as she rearranged the platter to cover the empty spaces they'd made.

"We'll change into our Sunday best and make our way to the Freimonts' for the special Thanksgiving service." Da's declaration was the cue for everyone to fly into action, readying themselves to leave.

Rosalind helped prepare the dishes she, Mam, and Grandmam had worked on since the day before for carrying to Delana's kitchen. This Thanksgiving would bring a feast the likes of which Saddleback had never seen before!

With the work done, Rosalind slipped into her blue cotton dress, straightening the crisp white collar that framed her face with starched purity. She smoothed her hair one last time and pulled on her cloak and gloves.

"Is everyone ready?" Da turned to check, and Ma plunked the platter bearing the stuffed goose into his open arms.

Everyone else took up a dish or two before stepping outside, and Rosalind found Ewan about to knock on their door. She favored him with a smile as he took the basket of biscuits from her and offered her his arm.

"Thank you." She slipped her hand into the warm crook of his elbow and set off.

"My pleasure." He took care to shorten his stride, going slowly so she wouldn't have to rush to keep alongside him.

Such a thoughtful man. She peeked up at him. *And such a handsome one.* The Lord had outdone Himself the day He fashioned Ewan Gailbraith, and she meant to give thanks for it. After all, it wasn't every day a girl walked before the town in her best dress, on the arm of a kind, handsome suitor as they prepared to praise God for another wonderful year. No, days just didn't get any better than this.

The wide Montana sky stretched before them, clear as could be. The air crisped with the nip of winter's cold, but the sunshine chased thoughts of snow away. They reached the Freimonts' home in a few moments — far too soon, to Rosalind's way of thinking. She reluctantly slipped her hand from Ewan's arm, taking back the biscuits and following the women into Delana's kitchen.

The warm fragrance of baked apples wrapped itself around her like a welcome as she set the basket on one of two already-too-full tables. Pies, loaves of flavored breads, biscuits, muffins, corn cake, and maple sweeties vied for space between roasted chicken, turkey, and goose. Dishes of mashed potatoes, sweet potatoes, dressing, coleslaw, and Rosalind's deviled eggs crowded in alongside. She'd never seen such a feast — the women of the town had really outdone themselves this year. But though the kitchen seemed full of busy women, several of them were missing.

Rosalind took a swift tally. Jakob and Isaac Albright's mail-order brides bustled back and forth importantly as Delana and Marlene worked furiously over the red-hot stove. Mam, having made sure all the dishes were deposited in the warmth of the kitchen, was bundling Grandmam into a chair in the corner. A glance out the window showed the Twadley girls, along with the Hornton and Preston women, hovering close by, fingering each others' woolen capes and laughing in the spirit of the day. The men plunked benches into neat rows, preparing for the Thanksgiving service.

Rosalind gave a deep sigh of satisfaction. *All present and accounted for.* By God's grace, everyone in the entire community had gathered to give thanks.

Rosalind's gaze drifted past the chatting women to where Ewan held a serious conversation with the Freimont men. The earnestness of his gaze grabbed her heart, and his sudden smile brought a matching one to her own face.

This Thanksgiving, no one has more to be grateful for than I do. Thank You, Jesus, for bringing Ewan into my life. 'Tis more than I'd dared hope for.

Ewan looked up from his discussion with Dustin Freimont and spied Rosalind peeking at him through the window. At his quick wave, she grinned and ducked out of sight.

Ah, Lord, thank You for my precious Rosalind. Has it really only been a matter of mere weeks since You brought her into my life? He paused for a moment, considering the fact that he'd arrived in her hometown. *Or rather, You led me to her? Either way, the result is the same — we're together. For that, I'll be forever grateful, Father. Though the winter ahead may seem long and at times lonely when we're snowed in, apart from one another, the knowl-*

edge that she's nearby and safe will be a treasure I cherish. The only thing that could make this day — nay, this entire season — better would be if Johnny were here to share his joy wi' Marlene as I am able to share my happiness wi' my Rosalind. Father, keep an eye on the lad as he works through this winter. I've the notion You'll see him work harder than ever before. You've given him a new motivation in little Marlene. Thank You, Father.

At that final word, a cloud passed over Ewan's bright day, and he frowned in sudden sorrow. *And Lord, please watch o'er my own da, wherever he may be this day.*

Ewan looked up to see the townspeople taking their seats upon the rough benches that served as pews. He scanned the crowd to find Rosalind's family before wending his way toward them and settling himself beside her. As the light fragrance of rosewater reached his senses, he smiled once more.

Dustin Freimont stood before the congregation in lieu of the circuit riding preacher. The man cleared his throat, a last minute call for the attention of those still shifting about. When all were watching, he spoke. "We all know that today is the day of Thanksgiving, where we show our gratitude to the Lord above for the blessings He's given us, and we remind our loved ones how we appreciate them." He stopped to shoot a glance at the pretty, older blond woman Ewan recalled as Dustin's wife, Delana. "I'd like to start the day with a hymn. I believe we all know 'For the Beauty of the Earth.' "

Ewan sat back and let the song wash over him, joining in as the half-forgotten melody grew full with the voices of many.

"For the beauty of the earth,
for the glory of the skies,
for the love which from our birth
over and around us lies;
Lord of all, to Thee we raise
this our hymn of grateful praise."

How fitting, Lord. Wi' the beauty of the glorious skies above us and the rich earth beneath our feet, we are truly surrounded by Your love.

"For the joy of human love,
brother, sister, parent, child;
friends on earth and friends above;
for all gentle thoughts and mild:
Lord of all, to Thee we raise
this our hymn of grateful praise."

And this. When for the first time in years I am wi' people I love as I would family. And wi' Rosalind, who I bear husbandly affection for although we are not yet wed. This is fitting, for 'tis the people of Saddleback who are its greatest lure, and their souls Your greatest treasure.

The hymn came to an end all too quickly, but Ewan listened closely as Dustin began to speak once again, his Bible open to the passage he and Ewan had been discussing scant moments before. "Ewan Gailbraith, a newcomer to Saddleback, saw me rifling through the pages of my Bible in search of Psalm 65 this morning. And, while it is a wonderful passage advocating that we thank the Lord for His bounty, I seem to recall reading the same chapter and verse last year. But the Word of Christ" — he held up the Bible — "is full of wisdom, and Mr. Gailbraith directed my attention to the book of Deuteronomy. I'll be reading from chapter 8 this morning." With a nod to Ewan, he took a breath as though to begin. But no words came for a moment.

"Actually" — Mr. Freimont pinned him with an intense gaze before continuing — "I, for one, would be glad to have you do the honors."

Ewan blinked as the other man gestured for him to come up. Several others were nodding, and Rosalind went so far as to give him an encouraging nudge. He got to his feet and made his way before the congregation before accepting Mr. Freimont's Bible.

"This is irregular," Dustin Freimont admitted. "But it seems to me that the verse is fitting, and it's equally fitting to have the man who chose it be the one to speak on it." With this, he went to sit beside his wife, leaving Ewan alone before the population of Saddleback.

"Well," — Ewan cleared his throat — "I can't say I've ever filled in for a preacher before, so I apologize in advance for my inexperience. That being said, this is a verse I keep dear to my heart, and I hope you'll do the same.

"Deuteronomy, chapter 8, verses 7 through 10: 'For the Lord thy God bringeth thee into a good land, a land of brooks of water, of fountains and depths that spring out of valleys and hills; a land of wheat, and barley, and vines, and fig trees, and pomegranates; a land of oil olive, and honey; a land wherein thou shalt eat bread without scarceness, thou shalt not lack any thing in it; a land whose stones are iron, and out of whose hills thou mayest dig brass. When thou hast eaten and art full, then thou shalt bless the Lord thy God for the good land which he hath given thee.' "

Ewan paused to let the words sink in. "Now, I hadn't thought to speak on this passage, but a few things do come to my mind. First is that the Lord our God has brought us all into a good land, a land of brooks of water, valleys and hills, and wheat. . . . Those words weren't written about the Montana Territory, but they certainly do an excellent job of describing nature's bounty in this area." Several people were nodding, and he warmed to his speech.

"And when I see the good folk who've settled here, sensing that God has been welcomed into this community — and smell the food in the kitchen — it seems to me that we don't lack any good thing. And how appropriate 'tis that verse 10 speaks of eating and being physically full of the things God has given us in His care for our souls, that we may bless Him for all He's given us." He looked around, giving just one more comment. "So it seems to me, we should get to that eating so we can bless Him with full hearts and bellies!"

The men chortled their approval and everyone clapped, nodding their agreement with Ewan's assessment.

"Before we sit down to enjoy the fruits of our labors and the skills of our women's hands, I'd like to lead us in a simple praise — an old favorite." Ewan tilted back his head and sang the verse, singing it again as the townspeople joined in:

"Praise God from whom all blessings flow;
praise Him, all creatures here below;
Praise Him above, ye heavenly host;
praise Father, Son, and Holy Ghost.
    Amen."

As they all sat down to the best spread

Ewan had ever seen in his life, he looked over at Rosalind, and the words of praise echoed in his mind once again.

Your blessings hae flowed upon me, Jesus. I praise You above all others, and thank You for Your loving grace. Amen.

Chapter 13

After being uninhabited for so long, this place needs a bit o' upkeep, Ewan mused after a night spent trying to bundle up against chill drafts. *I'll see if I can get some pitch to fill in those gaps.*

He gulped his too-hot coffee in an attempt to warm up and ate his fried eggs straight from the pan. *No sense making extra dishes to wash when no one's around to quibble about niceties.*

Then he went to the firmly shut curtains and thrust them aside, eager to see the glow of the sun — and the warmth it promised. After working a forge for so many years, heat was more natural to him than cold would ever be.

He blinked at the view before him. *Snow!* A blanket of white covered the ground, coated tree branches, and dusted his windowpane. *No wonder 'twas so cold — a snowstorm blew in o'ernight.* Ewan pulled on an extra pair of socks, then struggled to jam his boots over them. He took his coat from the peg by the door and slid it over his shoulders before plunking on his seldom-used hat and mittens. Blacksmiths rarely had use for the things.

Girding himself for a cold wind, he opened the door and stepped outside. Before he so much as drew a breath of fresh air, something whizzed over to plunk on his jacket.

"I got him!" Luke pointed at him. "Did you see that throw? I just aimed and *thwunk,* he didn't know until 'twas too late!"

While the lad all but danced with pride, Ewan crouched down and scooped up some snow of his own. Packing it into a round ball, he waited for the right moment before he let it fly. *Whooosh-umph,* his snowball soared toward the boy, only to be intercepted by another expertly thrown one. He scowled as both burst into harmless pieces and fell softly to the ground. Then he looked to see who'd interfered with the lad's just desserts.

"Rosalind?" He looked in disbelief to where his lass, bundled in a woolen cloak, calmly packed her next volley. "You're firing at me?" Ewan put the shock of betrayal in his tone.

"Now, Ewan, I did no such thing." She neatly placed yet another snowball in the line before her. "I fired at your snowball. That's an entirely different matter, you know." The laughter in her voice made it hard not to smile in return.

"Two against one is clear as day," he growled. "This means war." He began packing snow as quickly as he could scoop it up, his jacket bearing the wet stains attesting to his opponents' ruthlessness. "Who fires on an unarmed man?" he roared, letting fly a few of his own shots. "Take that, and that, and — mmph!" A snowball hit him smack in the mouth before he'd truly begun.

"Nice one, Rose!" Luke shrieked with merriment, laughing so hard he began to cough.

"That's enough, now." Rosalind kicked apart her snowballs in a show of truce before walking over to her brother. "Let's go in for a sip o' cider, shall we?" She tugged his hat down.

"Will you cry craven the moment your opponent is ready to do battle?" Ewan protested the abrupt ending. "Stand and fight, or" — he lobbed a set of snowballs, each finding one of the siblings across the way — "surrender!"

"I said that's enough." The tightness in Rosalind's tone took him by surprise. "If you want some cider, come inside wi' us." She shooed young Luke into the warmth of the house and marched in behind him, leaving Ewan standing alone.

What? I've never thought o' Rosalind as fickle, but she abandoned the challenge quickly enough. Something hae set her back up, and 'tis best I find out what afore I make another misstep. Surely a reason lies behind her change of heart.

He resolutely made his way to the still-open door of the house. *There's a good sign, at least.* Ewan stomped the snow from his boots before venturing into the MacLean home.

Arthur raised a hand in greeting, Mrs. MacLean poured cider into mugs, and Luke, seated beside the roaring fire, coughed after sending some of his drink down the wrong way. Ewan noticed that Rosalind hadn't taken off her warm cloak.

"Ewan, would you walk me to the barn?" She laid a small, gloved hand on his arm. "I've yet to check on the livestock."

"O' course." Ewan led her out the door, walking with her in silence on the short trek to the barn. He waited.

"I wanted to apologize for being so curt." She stood before him, her hands worrying the fabric of her skirts. " 'Twas rude and uncalled for. 'Twill not happen again, Ewan, I promise."

"I thought that last snowball must have hit harder than I intended. Don't worry that I took offense at it, Rosalind."

"Aye. But in the future" — she looked up at him, big blue eyes earnest and pleading — "when I say 'tis time to go inside, I will ask that you not question it. The cold weather makes it all too easy to catch chill, and we've no doctor hereabouts."

" 'Tis wise of you to take care, Rosalind. I hadn't thought of the lack of doctors out here, and the last thing I would want is for you to catch ill." He could scarcely stand to speak of the possibility. "As soon as you say the word, I'll take you back inside. You've my word on it, and that's all you need."

"Thank you." She looked as though she wanted to say more but paused before adding, "Trust is a foundation to build on."

"Aye, Rosalind." He covered her shoulder with his hand. "And I'm aiming to build something to last a lifetime."

"Hae we enough snow to build a man?" Luke peered through the frost-covered window after the second snowstorm days later.

"There will be," Rosalind judged. "For now, we wait for the storm to end and the sun to come out and soften it for us." *And warm the frigid air enough so you can play awhile wi'out gasping for breath and coughing. Even then, 'twill be a small snowman. All too soon you'll be spending your days and nights near the warmth of the fire. Best to enjoy the outdoors for now.*

"This time I want to make a great big one." Luke stretched a hand above his head. "With Ewan to help, we can do it this year. Last time 'twas a sad and puny man we made, to be sure."

"Last year's snowman was my favorite,"

Grandmam spoke up as she rocked back and forth. "Reminded me of you when you were that small. 'Twould be better to build two of those than one great big man. Everyone tries t' build the same old thing."

"Oh." Luke frowned as he thought it over. "Maybe we'll try to make a small one and a big one, so they're friends."

"As long as the small one comes first, for Grandmam." Rosalind gave her a conspiratorial smile. They both knew Luke would only be able to make a small one, and should he start after his larger goal, would protest leaving it unfinished.

"Aye," Luke agreed generously, "for our grandmam." He hopped up and went over to press a kiss on her wrinkled cheek.

Rosalind smiled and continued knitting the scarf she planned for Ewan. *He doesn't hae one, and though he says nothing, I see that the cold bothers him just as it does Da. Fire is their element, and ice doesna agree wi' blacksmiths.*

In my worry o'er Luke, I was harsh wi' Ewan. He doesn't know of Luke's weakness, though he'll find out afore too long. For now, Luke lights up at the way Ewan treats him — like any regular lad. So long as it poses no risk, we'll let it be.

Her fingers stiff, Rosalind put away her knitting and went over to the trunk where the family Bible was kept. Kneeling, she drew it out, feeling cracks in the worn leather cover. She opened it to the first pages, full of family records.

Tears pricked her eyes at the names of Cade Banning and James MacLean. Her grandda and her baby brother were the most recent in a chain of loss stretching back over decades. She ran her fingers over the ink.

Gone but not forgotten. How long will it be until Grandmam's name joins that of her husband's? And how many harsh winters will Luke weather? Ten? Twenty? Will he marry and have wee ones of his own? I pray 'tis so.

Her gaze came to rest on the marriage register. It was Da's Bible, and so did not bear the date of Rosalind's grandparents' wedding. She traced the names of her parents — Arthur MacLean and Kaitlin Banning. *Will mine and Ewan be the next names written and kept here for our children to read someday?*

She turned the fine, brittle pages to the chapter she sought — Ecclesiastes 3 — and read to herself. *"To every thing there is a season, and a time to every purpose under the heaven: A time to be born, and a time to die; a time to plant, and a time to pluck up that which is planted."*

Life and death, side by side in the family records, and placed together in scripture, as well. Joy tempered with sorrow; a balance struck between the two.

Lord, all things are to come in Your time. As the seasons change, so, too, do we. This winter seems the most important season I've ever faced. Please help me grow into the woman You'd hae me be and, if 'tis Your plan, the woman Ewan will love. Come spring, a new beginning will bloom all around — I'll say honestly that I hope for a piece of that wellspring in my own life.

Rosalind carefully closed the Bible and placed it in the trunk once more. She looked up to see Da watching her, a question in his gaze. Ma unfolded extra quilts to place on the beds — the hearth wouldn't stave off cold when darkness fell.

I've not seen Ewan in two days. Only two days into a storm, and it seems as though he's been gone from me for weeks. He's snowed in, same as we are. Only Da goes outside, using the guideline to the barn.

Grandmam's house — and Ewan — sat much too far away to string a guideline. It was part of the reason she'd moved. With no way of knowing when the storm would end, Rosalind couldn't even look forward to a day she'd see him again. Marlene endured a distance much greater but with certain knowledge to help her bide her time.

It seems almost a worse torture to know Ewan is so close, but that I can't reach him. Rosalind took up her knitting once more. *Does he regret the decision we made? Is he wishing he had gone on wi' the railroad — wi' Johnny for companionship and work to hasten the long hours? My Ewan works hard day in and day out — how can he stand being cooped up in four walls, all alone, wi' so little to keep him occupied?*

Rosalind looked to the blocked window and couldn't help but wonder, *Is he thinking of me while I think of him?*

CHAPTER 14

Ewan shoved back the curtain without much hope of seeing anything but the wall of white that had stood between him and Rosalind for days on end. Was it wishful thinking or could he see the faint yellow glow of sunlight through the thinning snow?

Yes . . . yes. The blizzard has passed, and the sun is beginning its work. Soon I'll see my Rosalind again.

Ewan stoked the fire and put on some coffee before starting the porridge.

Lord, 'tis by Your grace I had the time to prepare for the winter ahead. Weeks ago, I'd worried 'twas too soon to ask Rosalind whether I should stay through the winter. Now I see 'twas Your timing, ensuring I could chop enough wood to last the cold of the winter.

I'd wondered whether 'twould drive me half mad, being trapped within four walls wi' no work to do and no one wi' whom to speak or pass the time. I was wrong to doubt the wisdom of Your will.

For too long I've worked, focusing on what needed to be done, falling onto my pallet at night wi' only the time to thank You for seeing me through the day and giving me a livelihood. I traveled across this new world, at first in search of my father, then in search of solace from my failure. Yet in all that searching, I lost my true focus.

Now I've taken time to seek You as I hae not in too many years. I don't deserve the grace of Your love nor the joy I find in Rosalind, but I treasure both. In the barren sleep of winter, a new beginning stirs to life. I aim to not lose sight of that, Lord.

Whistling, Ewan added a pinch of brown sugar to his porridge. He poured a mug full of the strong, steaming coffee, leaving it black. When he pushed away from the table, his glance fell on the just-finished project in the corner.

"More evidence of Your timing, Lord. Those snowshoes will come in handy soon," Ewan determined aloud. He opened the door of the house to a blockage of thick snow, scooped some into the pot he'd used to make the oatmeal, and cleaned it. He filled it with icy white once more before shutting the door and returning to the hearth.

While the water heated, Ewan dug out his razor and strop. With sharpened blade, small mirror, and warmed water, he set to. The raspy *scrape* of the razor, punctuated by an occasional *swish* in the water, filled the still house. Ewan ran a hand over his now-smooth jaw and nodded at his reflection. *Now I'm ready to see Rosalind.*

The strong, bitter scent of his coffee had him reaching for the mug again. He drained it in one long swallow. He looked around the cabin, checking off items. *Morning devotions done, bed made, breakfast eaten, pot cleaned, face shaven, snowshoes finished.*

He drummed his fingers on the tabletop. *I wonder . . .* He peered through the curtains again. *Maybe.* He grabbed the poker from the hearth and swung the door open again, giving the wall of ice an experimental prod. Since the door wasn't on the same side of the house as the window, the wall of snow here might be thicker. *Hmm.* No snow rumbled forward to fill the gap. He cautiously worked the poker farther and farther until his arm was thrust into the snow at the top of the door. Finally, there was no resistance. The snow, already thawing, piled only a few feet outside the door!

Ewan withdrew and shut the door, warming his half-frozen arm by the fire before donning his jacket, hat, and worn mittens. With the aid of the poker, he broke a sizeable opening through the snowbank and watched as the top portion collapsed down. Ewan kicked through it, smiling at the sight of the snowy hill nearby that must be Rosalind's home.

With the fire banked and his snowshoes tightly strapped to his boots, Ewan made his way. It was slow going, putting one foot before the other, cautiously testing the firm pack of snow before transferring his weight. Finally, he stood before the mound, seeing a corner of the roof poking out of the snowy whiteness.

Will it seem odd that I didn't wait a wee while longer for the snow to clear on its lonesome? Ewan's gloved hands clenched. *No matter. Everyone will be as eager as I am to taste some fresh air.* He dug into the snow, pushing it aside until he reached the wall. *It fell more deeply here — 'tis far thicker.* Ewan tapped on the unearthed windowpane, waited, and tapped again before the curtains drew back.

Luke pressed his nose to the windowpane and squinted through the frost. Ewan rubbed the pane clear of ice as Luke disappeared.

Rosalind's eyes widened when she saw him, and Ewan grinned. She pressed one small, bare hand against the glass, and he swiftly pressed his thickly gloved one over it on his side.

"I'll hae you out in a minute!" he yelled, knowing she understood him when she nodded and drew her hand back. He pushed the snow aside feverishly, packing it down in front of the door before giving a mighty knock.

"Ewan!" Rosalind swung the door open, the heated blast of air from within matching the warmth of her gaze. "You're soaking!" She pulled him inside.

Rosalind curled her fingers into the sopping fabric of his coat sleeve, pulling him close.

" 'Twould hae melted soon enough," she chided, tugging the coat from his broad shoulders. She laid it out by the fire and held out her hand for his dripping gloves. She twisted them as dry as she could before turning back. Rosalind found his green eyes watching her with a love that brought a warmth to her heart. He'd not said a word, just let her cluck over him like a fussy hen.

He raised a brow and held out one large hand in a silent invitation. She put her hand in his and stood close, reaching up to cup his clean-shaven cheek. *He shaved for me, just as he broke through the snow for me.*

"I couldn't wait another day." Ewan's deep rumble washed over her as he smoothed his free hand over her hair, his fingertips playing with the end of her braid.

"I'm glad you didn't." She returned his gaze until something new — chagrin? — flickered on his face. For the first time since she'd seen him at the window, Rosalind realized her entire family, from Grandmam all the way down to young Luke, was watching. She glanced at Da. She drew back the hand that cupped Ewan's strong jaw, missing the contact immediately.

"Don't just stand there." Grandmam shook her head, but all could see the smile on her face. "Sit down so Luke can help you with those snowshoes."

"I'll warm some mulled cider." Mam busied herself at the hearth as everyone sprang into motion.

"Good to see you, Ewan." Da spoke solemnly, but Rosalind heard the humor behind it. He put out his pipe.

"Ewan?" Luke flopped down at his feet, untying the snowshoes. "Will you help me make a snowman? A grand big one?" He held his hand high over his head.

Rosalind cleared her throat.

"Oh." Luke seemed properly chastened. "Two, then. A bitty one for Grandmam first, and then the grand big one?" His voice rose with anxious hope.

"Luke!" Rosalind intervened. "Ewan broke through the snow o'er his place and ours and only just sat before the fire!"

"Indeed," Mam added. "His things are wet with melted ice."

"I know." Luke seemed to shrink into himself, his thin voice tugging at Rosalind's heart. "I thought that so long as he was already snowy, 'twould be a good time, you

402

see." He stacked the snowshoes carefully by the hearth. " 'Twasn't my intent to be rude."

"Nor were you, lad." Ewan's smile robbed the room of any chill of discomfort. "Sound planning, to my way o' thinking. Now, if you can convince your bonny sister to lend a hand, I'd say this is as good a time as any." He shot Rosalind a quick wink.

"Rose?" Luke's shining eyes pled for her assent, and she couldn't withhold it.

"Aye, then. Let's both pile on our winter clothes." Rosalind frowned at Ewan's sodden coat and gloves.

"I've an old coat o' your da's in a trunk hereabouts." Mam moved some embroidered pillowcases off the top of the chest. "Should do a sight better than that mess. Ah, there." She shook out the old garment. "We don't want you catching a chill, Mr. Gailbraith."

"Thank you, Mrs. MacLean." Ewan accepted the coat and turned to Grandmam. "Now, Mrs. Banning, what's all this about a tiny snowman?"

"I'm of the opinion that snowmen should come in different sizes" — Grandmam eyed Ewan as he held Rosalind's winter cloak for her — "just as folks do. The small ones are most often more loveable."

"Aye." Ewan put his hands on Rosalind's shoulders, emphasizing the disparity between their heights. " 'Tis right you are."

"I disagree." Rosalind turned, tilting her

head back to look up at him. "Da is a big bear o' a man — same as you."

"And a more loveable fellow I've yet to meet." Mam walked over to Da and smiled up at him.

"Ready!" Luke's proclamation broke the tender moment as he led Rosalind and Ewan outdoors.

"Ooh." The chill wind made Rosalind shiver before she joined her brother. Together, they packed a base for the smaller snowman while Ewan began work on the larger.

Da and Mam came out to join them. "We thought we'd lend a hand."

"Ah." Mam took a deep breath of the clean, crisp air. "So nice to be outside again. And we have you to thank for that, Mr. Gail-braith."

"What use is the wide open when you've no one to share it wi'?" Ewan's smile sent a thrill through Rosalind.

"We're more than happy to share this beautiful day wi' you." Rosalind tried to imbue the words with the depth of her joy but feared she fell far short.

"I think this is done." Luke frowned in concentration as he gauged the base for the tiny snowman. "She wants it small."

"Here." Da plunked a large handful of hardened snow atop Luke's finished portion. "Let's start on the middle."

"I'll go see what branches and such I can

find." Mam headed for a copse of trees, leaving Rosalind standing alone.

Since Da helped Luke, she began packing snow to help Ewan. She tacked it onto the already massive chunk he worked to make round.

"How's that?" He stepped back to examine the misshapen lump.

"Well . . ." Rosalind gave the matter due consideration as she stepped around the beginnings of the sculpture. This one level reached her hip! "Seems to me . . ." She crouched down and made a show of inspecting it. "Yes . . . I know what will set it right."

"What?"

"If you look here" — Rosalind gestured him closer and bit back her grin as Ewan moved toward her — "it needs . . ."

"It needs what?" He looked down at the huge snow lump, then back up at her.

"Leveling off," she told him solemnly before shoving a goodly amount of the excess all over him.

"Hey!" Ewan straightened up, brushing snow from his face and shaking it from his coat.

Rosalind laughed as he gave a little dance to free his collar of the icy deluge. He stopped moving. Her breath caught. Bits of the ice clung to Ewan's coal-black hair, catching the winter sunshine as it melted. Standing tall and proud, he was magnificent.

"Rosalind." His voice lingered over her name as though relishing every syllable.

"Oh!" She spluttered as he took advantage of her gawking to exact revenge. He threw a spray of snow so it coated her. The icy specks melted on her tongue, stung her nose, and trickled into her hair where her cloak fell back. "You'll pay for that, Ewan Gailbraith!" She packed a snowball and advanced on him.

"I hope so." He snagged the snow from her hand and slipped a strong arm around her waist before she could react. His grin had a devilish charm. "I hope I get exactly what I deserve." The warmth in his gaze left no doubt what he meant.

Rosalind opened her mouth to tell him she felt the same . . . then shrieked as she felt her own snowball trickling down her back.

CHAPTER 15

"The pond is frozen over!" Luke barreled into the house a week later, his breath coming in hard gasps of excitement.

Ewan slapped his knee. "Well then. Sounds like we're going ice skating." He stood up. "I'll go get my skates and be right back."

"We'll be ready," Rosalind promised. "Though I'd like to go fetch Marlene, if you don't mind."

"You get your friend, I'll get my skates, and you" — Ewan mussed Luke's hair — "get ready." He set out, his long stride quickly covering the distance between the MacLean household and Gilda's house. He opened the trunk where he'd stowed most of his own possessions and withdrew the metal skates.

Holding them by the laces, Ewan walked back to Rosalind's home. Luke met him at the door, flushed and eager.

"Rose isn't back yet." The boy's voice lowered to a confiding whisper. "Marlene always takes a long time to do anything."

Ewan crouched down to look at the lad eye to eye. "Someday you'll see that pretty girls are worth the wait."

"But . . ." Luke frowned. "Rose doesn't make anybody wait if she can help it."

"I know." Ewan gave the lad a wink. "That makes her worth even more." He straightened up and saw the girls approaching . . . with a man escorting Rosalind — Brent Freimont.

"Luke" — he stooped once more and spoke with urgency — "who is that young man walking wi' your sister?"

"Oh. That's Brent Freimont, Marlene's brother."

"Yes, I know his name." Ewan tried again. "Has he been courting Rosalind for long?"

"Courting? He makes big eyes at her and sits next to her whenever he can." Luke scoffed. "Brent burnt down the outhouse a few months ago."

"He burnt —" Ewan stopped himself. There was more important information he needed right away. "And your sister?"

"No." Luke gave him a strange look. "He didn't burn Rose. 'Twas an accident wi' the privy."

"I meant," Ewan clarified, torn between exasperation and amusement, "did Rose encourage his attentions?" *The lad made a nuisance o' himself at the husking bee, but from the way Rose dismissed him, I thought he was*

408

no serious rival.

"Hardly." Luke snorted. "Everyone hereabouts thought she'd marry Brent, but she looks on him as a brother, same as me. Almost." He thought for a moment. "She likes me better."

"As do I." Ewan patted the boy on the shoulder and stood to his full height as the three companions joined them. His jaw tightened as he saw Brent's hand laid possessively over Rosalind's, which lay nestled in the crook of his arm.

"Thank you, Brent." Rosalind looked anything but pleased as she tried to disentangle.

Ewan's sudden good cheer vanished as Brent tightened his grasp, saying, "Of course, Rose. I'll escort you all the way to the pond. We wouldn't want you to stumble again."

"As I've already told you, Brent, 'twas naught but a bit of snow I was shaking from the top of my boot." Rosalind tugged free at last. "I did not stumble at all." She gave Ewan a beseeching glance.

As Brent reached for her hand once more, Ewan stepped between them. "I'd be pleased to carry your skates, Rosalind."

"Thank you." The heartfelt appreciation in her tone spurred Brent into action.

"I'll do that." He yanked the laces from her hand.

The lad fell for it! "Well, since your hands are full, I'll be happy to escort the lady."

409

Ewan smoothly offered Rosalind his arm. "Miss Freimont" — he gave a slight bow to Marlene — "good to see you."

"And you, Mr. Gailbraith." The amusement in her smile let him know she hadn't missed how he stressed the last word. "You've met my brother, Brent Freimont, haven't you?"

"Oh, we've met." Ewan looked at the lad in disgust before smiling at his sister. "Shall we go on to the pond?"

With that, he and Rosalind led the way, leaving Brent to trail behind. Ewan set a quick pace, deliberately putting more distance between Rosalind and him and the others.

"He needs time to come to terms wi' it, that's all." Rosalind spoke only when they were out of earshot. "Brent has nurtured certain . . . hopes, for a long while now."

"Hopes?" Ewan raised a brow. "Or expectations, Rosalind?"

"Expectations." Her whisper made him uneasy. "Expectations encouraged by his parents and my mother — but not by me." Her blue eyes transfixed him. "Though I never told him plainly. I should hae, long ago."

"He's not the sort to understand the subtle approach," Ewan agreed. "Though it should be clear as day by now."

" 'Tis clear to him now," Rosalind assured him. "He just hasn't accepted it yet."

"Accepted what?" He knew what she meant

but had an itch to hear her say the words aloud.

"That *you*" — her smile plainly told him she knew what he was up to and didn't mind humoring his whim — "are the only man I'm interested in courting."

"He's your brother," Rosalind grumbled to Marlene as Brent skated in circles around Ewan, edging closer in a blatant bid to make him uncomfortable. "Can't you do something?"

"They're competing over you," Marlene shot back. "And since when has my brother ever listened to a word I say — unless it's 'dinner'?" She watched as Ewan changed directions, leisurely skimming backward while Brent continued his annoying tactics. "Nice footwork, there. If you ask me, I'd say Ewan can handle Brent without any assistance from either of us."

"Of course he can." Rosalind beamed with pride. "Ewan's handled far more than whatever ice tricks Brent can throw at him. I just wish . . ." her voice trailed off.

"You wish what?" Marlene did a neat turn and stop, narrowly avoiding Luke as he zoomed around the perimeter of the pond.

"That Brent hadn't invited himself along." Rosalind sighed. "Not that he doesn't have every right to come to the pond, but . . . this was supposed to be a fun outing. And now . . .

well, you see." She gestured to where the two men had evidently decided to stage an impromptu race across the pond. "They're being . . ." She searched for a word other than *competitive* and came up short.

"Men?" Marlene zigzagged. "And you don't think it's even a tiny bit fun to have two men competing for your affection?"

"No!" Rosalind slid to a halt. "I'm not a prize at some country fair to be won by the man who can skate the fastest or eat the most pies in a single sitting. 'Tis pure foolishness, Marlene."

"Love makes fools out of us all, sooner or later." Marlene moved gently, leaving wavelike tracks in her wake as she circled Rosalind. "If a race or pie could bring Johnny back right now, I'd do it without thinking twice. But it's not so simple."

"No, it isn't." Rosalind reached out to clasp one of her friend's hands, and they skated side by side. "Here I am, going on about myself when my Ewan is scant paces away. Do you miss Johnny terribly, Marlene?" She gave a soft squeeze in sympathy.

"Part of me does," she admitted. "But I'm more worried about the part of me that's glad he went on with the railroad. I keep thinking that since he's gone now — when we'll be snowed in most of the time anyway — he'll be here in the spring. That's when we'll be able to see each other more. That's when he can start working the land he'll buy and building our house. If he stayed now, he'd be gone then. This way is best."

"Exactly!" Rosalind stared at her friend. "This is the way I knew you'd be once you'd thought it o'er."

"I did behave like the worst brat." Marlene flushed. "I'm blessed that you understood, Ewan forgave me, and Johnny wasn't scared away forever by my terrible temper!"

"You'll have to do far worse to frighten any of us away." Rosalind let go of Marlene's hand to do a quick spin. "We know what a wonderful woman lies beneath a passing mood. And in just a few short weeks, you've already unearthed her! Johnny will find an even better catch than he remembers when he comes back."

"I hope so — oof!" Marlene fell into Rosalind as Brent whizzed by too closely, throwing her off balance. Both girls crashed to the ice in an ungainly heap of arms and skirts and skates.

"Ooh," Rosalind moaned, rubbing the back of her head where it had met the ice so suddenly. "Are you all right, Marlene?" She disentangled her skates from her friend's and knelt beside her.

"Yes. I — I think so." She gingerly sat up, rubbing her elbow. "Just caught me off guard. Where is . . . Brent!" She glowered at her brother. "See what your showing off has done?"

As Ewan helped Rosalind, Brent yanked on Marlene's arms to pull her to her feet.

"I'll help!" Luke came speeding toward them, only to hit a slippery patch and come crashing down himself.

"Luke!" Rosalind pushed away from Ewan and raced to her brother's side. "Are you all right? Say something." Her brother's labored breathing chilled her in a way the hard ice and winter wind had not. "Let's get you back to the house."

"Knocked the wind out of you, did it?" Ewan lifted the small boy to his feet. "Well, I'd say we've done enough damage for one afternoon. Let's see if we can talk your mam into giving us some more of that wonderful mulled cider of hers." He led Luke to solid ground, and everyone unlaced their metal blades for the trek home.

Rosalind took care to walk slowly, leaving Ewan's side to hover around Luke. His flushed cheeks and continued coughing made her throat clench shut. *I was so busy worrying about myself and talking wi' Marlene, I didn't watch him closely enough. We should hae left before any o' this happened. 'Tis my fault he struggles so.*

Lord, please be wi' my brother. Put Your healing hand o'er him and help him to breathe. I'll sit him by the hearth and get him something warm to drink. Please don't let this episode worsen from my negligence, Father. His breath rasps and his chest heaves — please ease his breathing, Lord. Please.

Before they got to the house, her fervent prayers had been answered. While he still rasped, Luke's coughing had abated. She bundled him by the fire and gave him the first cup of hot cider, relaxing only when his faint wheeze was barely audible.

"Rosalind," Ewan spoke from behind her. "Why don't we walk Marlene and Brent home?"

"Of course." Rosalind shot him an apologetic smile. For a short time, she'd all but forgotten about everyone else!

The walk passed pleasantly enough, with Marlene and Brent soon ensconced in the Freimont house. Rosalind found herself suddenly alone with Ewan as they made their way back home.

Ewan waited until they were midway on the return to stop. "Rosalind, what's wrong?"

"Wrong?" Rosalind frowned. "Nothing. Marlene's seen the wisdom of Johnny's decision, neither of us suffered more than a bruise from the fall, and Luke's fine. What could be wrong?"

"Go back to the part about Luke being fine.

'Tisn't usual for a sister to fuss so o'er a twelve-year-old boy." Ewan peered at Rosalind. "He's nearing manhood, by then."

At about that same age, I was taking care of Mam wi' my father gone on to America. I worked hard and checked for Da's letters every day, trying to fill his shoes and hold everything together.

"He fell, too," Rosalind reminded him, but the answer didn't satisfy. Her gaze wouldn't meet his completely.

"I know." Ewan tilted her chin toward him. "I can see for myself that Luke's small for his age — small enough not t' spend all his time at the forge. But I've never seen him there. And today, when a small tumble knocked the wind out o' him, he gasped for breath all the way back home. So I'll ask you again, Rosalind . . ." He paused meaningfully. "What is wrong?"

"Will you start to treat him differently if something is?" she hedged, her eyes searching his face intently. "Or will you continue to see him as a normal boy and not coddle him?"

"You coddle him enough for both of us, t' my way of thinking." He said it gently, but firmly enough to reassure her.

"Luke's never been strong." She pulled her chin from his grasp to hold his hand in hers. "He was born wi' weak lungs. The doctors say 'tis nothing short o' a miracle he survived past infancy. He can't abide the smoke o' the forge — that's why he doesn't work wi' Da. We don't speak on it, as it pains them both."

"I see." Ewan nodded. "And the cold? 'Tis the reason he coughed and you stopped the snowball fight?"

"Aye," she admitted. "He had an episode then . . . and again today. I keep close watch o'er him so they don't worsen, but today I wasn't careful enough. It could hae been much worse."

" 'Twasn't your fault that he fell, Rosalind."

"No, but he'd probably begun rasping afore that even." She looked down at the toes of her boots. "I should hae checked on him sooner. He will not admit when he's done too much."

"What happens when it worsens?" He pulled her closer, putting his arm about her waist.

"He coughs so hard his body is racked wi' it. His chest heaves and he fights for breath until his face goes pale and his mouth turns blue. There's not a winter as goes by but he gets terribly ill. A simple cold sets him coughing, and it settles in his chest, and then" — the tears in her eyes when she looked up at him flooded his heart — "we all fight so he'll see the spring."

"Why didn't you tell me?" He cupped her cheek and used the pad of his thumb to wipe away her tears. "Let me help you."

"I didn't want you to treat him as though he were too fragile to do anything. He's a boy like any other and needs to laugh and play and feel useful. Luke brightens whenever you're around because you don't mollycoddle him." She bit her lip. "Da loves him and tries so hard to give him freedom tempered wi' safeguards, but Luke sees through it. I didn't want that for you or Luke."

"I understand." He took a deep breath. "And I'll treat him no differently. We'll leave it to you to shoo us back into the warmth of the house when you feel 'tis the right time."

"Thank you, Ewan." She rose on tiptoe to plant a soft kiss on his cheek.

He fought the urge to turn his head, knowing it wasn't the right time. Ewan settled for keeping his arm around her waist as they walked back to the house.

I may not be able to protect Rosalind from Luke's weakness, he reasoned, *but I can make it easier for her to look after him. A nice group we'll be . . . Rosalind watches o'er Luke, I'll watch o'er Rosalind, and God will watch o'er us all. May Christmas come to find us all hearty and full of joy.*

CHAPTER 16

" '. . . And the angel said unto them, Fear not: for, behold, I bring you good tidings of great joy, which shall be to all people.' " Da's voice rang with conviction as he read the Christmas story. " 'For unto you is born this day in the city of David a Saviour, which is Christ the Lord. And this shall be a sign unto you; Ye shall find the babe wrapped in swaddling clothes, lying in a manger. And suddenly there was with the angel a multitude of heavenly host praising God, and saying, Glory to God in the highest, and on earth peace, good will toward men.' Luke, chapter 2, verses 10 to 14." He reverently shut the family Bible.

Rosalind blinked, trying to clear the tears from her eyes. The wonder of that scene — the majesty of a newborn king come to save all men.

Jesus, You are so good to us. You sacrificed Your splendor to be born a man, and we did not appreciate it. The Prince of Heaven offered

419

a manger. Each time I hear the words, I marvel at Your greatness — the most powerful of all brought to us as a helpless babe. I struggle with pride, yet Your example shows the meaning of true humility. Thank You for Your loving grace, which brings us such undeserved joy.

Her tears stopped, and she found Ewan watching her, his own face shining with the light of love.

"We've so many blessings to be thankful for this Christmas," he said. "Christ's own love is mirrored at this hearth. 'Tis been many a year since I took part in such a celebration."

"We're glad to have you, Ewan." Rosalind stood and walked over to place a hand on his shoulder. His joy had been mixed with such wistfulness, she wanted to brush away the sorrow. "Shall we sing a few Christmas carols?"

" 'Tis been too long since I heard the Irish Christmas Carol." Ewan looked around hopefully. "Do you all know it?"

"Of course!" Luke hummed the tune. " 'Tis Grandmam's favorite."

"Aye, 'tis." Grandmam rocked back, smiling in remembrance and anticipation. "Why don't you start it for us, Mr. Gailbraith?"

"I'd be honored." Ewan cleared his throat and broke into the melody, his rich baritone flowing over the words as everyone joined in.

"Christmas day is come; let's all prepare
      for mirth,
Which fills the heav'ns and earth at this
      amazing birth.
Through both the joyous angels in strife
      and hurry fly,
with glory and hosannas, 'All Holy' do they
      cry . . ."

Rosalind closed her eyes and let the song wash over her. *My family is well, Ewan is wi' us, and we're celebrating the Lord's birth. What could be better?*

When the final note quavered in the air, she opened her eyes. "Any other favorites?"

And so they praised the night away, singing beloved hymns such as "O Come, All Ye Faithful," "Angels, from the Realms of Glory," and "Joy to the World."

When the candles guttered, eyelids drooped, and stomachs groaned with satisfaction, Ewan rose from the settle. "Will you walk wi' me a wee while?"

Rosalind looked to Da for permission. At his short nod, she swirled her thick cloak over her shoulders and stepped into the night with Ewan. Only a single candle and the light from the heavens illuminated their path. Rosalind could see her breaths coming in little white puffs of the frigid night air as he pulled her close.

"Ewan, why are we stopping?" Rosalind

stamped her feet to warm them as he set the candle on a sturdy log and took both her hands in his own. A curious warmth suddenly took away the chill.

"Rosalind," he began, "there is an old Irish marriage blessing. Do you know it?"

"Nay." Rosalind fixed her gaze upon him, understanding his purpose in bringing her outside. They were alone, under the stars, and he spoke of marriage!

She didn't dare breathe as he recited the blessing:

"May God be wi' you and bless you.
May you see your children's children.
May you be poor in misfortunes
and rich in blessings.
May you know nothing but happiness
from this day forward."

He paused, giving her time to savor the sweetness of the words. "Rosalind, God has blessed me simply by letting me know you." He sank to his knees, still clasping her hands. "I love you. Will you make me rich in His blessings and bring me even more happiness by saying you'll wed me?"

Tears streaked down her face as Rosalind let out the breath she'd been holding to kneel in front of him. "Yes, Ewan. Oh yes!" She threw her arms around him and sank into his warm embrace as his lips sought her own.

He pulled away a short while later and fumbled in his coat pocket. "Here." He held up a small, carved box, dwarfed by his palm.

Rosalind took it and opened the lid to find a simple gold band inside. She gasped as he drew it out and slid it onto her left ring finger.

" 'Twas my mother's." His hoarse whisper made her realize his eyes shone with unshed tears. " 'Tis all I hae left o' her, and I know she'd smile to see the beautiful bride I've given it to."

"And I'm proud to wear it," she whispered. "I love you, Ewan Gailbraith."

CHAPTER 17

"Still no word as to when the circuit rider will pass through?" Ewan worked to clear underbrush and rotten logs from around the bases of the sugar maples.

"None. 'Twas a harsh winter, so 'tisn't surprising." Arthur grinned. "Probably settled in somewhere to wait it out. Don't worry. Now that 'tis warm enough for the sap to run, he'll turn up."

"Good." Ewan carried a load of dead brush over to where they'd have the boiling place.

Lord, winter begins to change to spring, and still Rosalind is naught but my intended! Close to three months now, I've waited as patiently as I can. I'm anxious to make her my bride in truth, though I see the wisdom in Your timing. I've yet to determine where I'll set up household wi' my Rosalind. If I stay, I'll take Arthur's livelihood. Should I go, I separate her from the family I've come to love as well.

"Hold a moment, son." Arthur put a hand on Ewan's forearm, halting him. "I wanted a word wi' you. I know you want to be wed, and we've both been praying o'er where you'll settle. But I was wondering whether you're any closer to a decision?"

"I don't want to take Rosalind away from Saddleback," Ewan stated flatly before softening. "To tell the truth, I don't want to leave, myself. And yet, should I stay . . ." He let the thought hang, unable to speak of the harsh reality to the man who'd been so kind.

"You're worried you'll take away my customers." Arthur nodded. "I surmised as much when you asked my blessing. Hae you any solution to the problem?"

Ewan straightened his shoulders. "I've thought I might turn my hand to farming. I've a solid bit of money tucked away, more than I'd need for a good while. 'Twould do to seed a new spread, and I'm used to working wi' my hands."

"You're a blacksmith, son." Arthur clapped a hand on his shoulder, frowning. " 'Twouldn't do to try to change who you are."

For the first time, Ewan noted how the fine lines about the older man's mouth and eyes had deepened. Was it merely the strain of winter, or something else?

"I'm not a young man anymore." Arthur rubbed the back of his neck. "And I'm starting to feel my age. The cold brings a stiffness to my fingers and a tightness to my chest."

"I see." And Ewan could see what it cost the great man to admit it. "Wi' spring coming, that 'twill ease."

"Aye, for a while. But each year the stiffness hae lingered a bit longer, and the twinges hae turned to steady aches." Arthur looked ruefully at his strong hands. "I've seen forty-five years, Ewan. At this age, I'd thought to have a son beside me at the forge, taking on the lion's share o' the work."

Ewan glanced back to where Luke snapped dead branches a ways off. He looked back to Arthur. They both knew Luke wouldn't be the help to his father's business that Arthur had hoped for.

"Aye, you see what I'm saying. Kaitlin and I lost two babes between Rose and Luke — one too soon to tell whether the child was a lad or lassie, and one boy. Our James didna live to see his second year." Arthur's eyes burned with a fierce light. "And we both know Luke isna fit for smithing, and I won't hae him risking his life to try. I'll not lose my son to pride."

Not knowing what to say, Ewan simply nodded. He waited and listened, fighting not to compare Arthur with his own father. He'd begun to see where Arthur was heading with this conversation.

"Now the Lord hae seen fit to bring a fine man to my doorstep, who's won my Rosey's heart and hae proven himself a man of his word." Arthur paused. "And he's a blacksmith wi' no forge to call his own and loathe to take my daughter far from our family. 'Tis no stretch to see God's hand in this.

"I make a good living here, and wi' the railroad tracks laid, more business will be passing through than a lone old man can handle. Ewan, I'd be honored if you'd work by my side at the forge."

For a moment, Ewan couldn't speak, choked by an avalanche of thoughts. *I knew 'twas my lot to ever bear the burden of my poor decision. My da turned his back on me when I'd not yet reached the age o' sixteen. In all the years since he went to America, I've not laid eyes on the man, though I've tried to track him down.*

Now here's a man not bound to me by blood, calling me "son" and asking me to stand alongside him.

"I'm the one who's honored, Arthur." Ewan embraced his father-in-law-to-be with a hearty slap on the back. "Though you're no old man yet. You've a need for grandchildren before you claim that title."

"And that's another joy you'll be bringing me." Arthur stepped back. "I've high expectations," he warned.

Ewan grinned. "I plan to meet every one."

"Do you know what you'll do when the

circuit riding preacher finally does arrive?" Marlene drove a spike into one of the sugar maples. "Or has Ewan still said nothing about whether you'll stay in Saddleback or not? I pray you'll stay!"

"He's mentioned trying his hand at farming," Rosalind answered. "I think he fears taking away Da's business if he opens his smithy here, but neither of us wants to move very far."

"What happened to all your great dreams of travel?" Marlene stepped back as Rosalind pushed a trough into place beneath the hollow tube. "You've always said you want to see the world beyond our small corner of it. Not that I'm complaining if you're choosing to stay here with us, mind."

"I still do." Rosalind moved to the next tree with a cleared base. "Wi' the railroad tracks already laid, trains will start passing through. Ewan and I will hae the freedom to hop aboard whenever — and to wherever — we please and be back more quickly than I ever dreamed. Besides" — she gave a small smile — "I'm thinking marriage might be enough of an adventure to last a short while, at least. My own house will offer quite a change."

"Most likely," Marlene agreed. "I know I can't wait for mine! With spring upon us, my Johnny should be coming back any day." She peered about as though half expecting to see him pop out from behind the tree she just finished tapping.

"Or it could be a month," Rosalind gently reminded. Seeing the shadow creeping over her friend's face, she quickly changed the subject. "And what of Johnny? Will Da have to expect competition from your beau?" She said it lightly but couldn't hide the tinge of concern she felt. *Da, Ewan, and Johnny? 'Tis two too many blacksmiths for a single town, even wi' the railroad trade.*

"Oh no." Marlene brushed her concerns aside and tripped over to the next tree. "Johnny doesn't actually like smithing. Says it's hot, dirty, and loud. He'd prefer to be a wainwright, just working on wheels. I'm glad I won't be washing soot from his shirts every week! Does that put your mind at ease?"

"Yes." Rosalind didn't pretend not to know what Marlene meant. "Mayhap Da will be the blacksmith, Ewan the farrier, and Johnny the wainwright as Saddleback grows larger. The railroad will bring people. Our skilled menfolk will keep them nearby."

"That's a thought." Marlene handed the auger to Rosalind. "Of course, Johnny needs to come back and the preacher needs to show up before any of those plans will bear fruit!"

"Parson Burchill always had a fondness for maple sweeties." Rosalind moved on to the final tree in the immediate area. "Wi' the lure of those along wi' the welcome of warmer days, he'll turn up soon." She stepped back to survey her work. "I hope."

Talk turned to their hope chests as the girls made their way back to the sugaring-off shelter. They found everyone congregated there, waiting for the wooden troughs to fill.

The Twadleys, Horntons, and Prestons would be tapping trees nearer to home, so only a few households were represented out here. The MacLeans; Ewan; Marlene's parents; Brent, of course; and Marlene's uncles, Jakob and Isaac Albright, with their mail-order brides; made up the work crew. Grand-mam sat bundled by the boiling fire, oversee-ing everything to her heart's content. Fourteen neighbors welcoming spring and greeting each other after a long winter of snowy solitude — the sugar they'd make this day only sweetened the cheerful meeting.

They snacked on cold biscuits and cheese, chatting about anything and everything until it was time to get to work. The sap ran from the trunks in thick, gooey streams. As the hol-lowed troughs filled, everyone took care to replace them with empty ones and pour the bounty into buckets. The first troughs filled always made the very best sugar, so they boiled separately.

"Amazing how the ants always appear, isn't it?" Marlene brushed a few of the insects away, saving them from drowning in the sap. "And they never learn that the sap will kill them."

"Don't worry. You know the milk foam will bring all the bugs and bits o' bark to the top, and we'll skim it out," Rosalind teased. She knew that was Marlene's least favorite part of the sugaring.

"I remember," her friend spoke flatly. "Better out with the foam than floating in my syrup, though." She gave a shudder.

They hauled full buckets back to the boiling fire, handing them off to their mothers and Luke, who watched the sap boil with eagle eyes as it separated into syrup and sugar. A smaller pot hung with the other large ones, promising a special treat.

Everyone took turns emptying troughs, filling buckets, watching the boiling sap, and shooing away greedy squirrels and dogs that crept close enough to pose a threat. Humans weren't the only ones who had a taste for something sweet every now and again.

" 'Tis hard work," Ewan commented. "Though the rewards will be sweet enough to merit it. I'd not thought the animals would cause problems. Shouldn't the fire and noise scare them away?"

"You'd think." Rosalind walked with him to the farthest sugar maples to check the troughs. "But there're actually stories about livestock trying to steal a taste." She caught his disbelieving look. "Really! There's an old tale about a prize bull named Prince who popped his head into one of his owner's tins of hot sugar. The heat shocked him so that he ran off wi' the best of the batch stuck all around his muzzle, and the cows followed!"

"There's a yarn, to be sure." Ewan shook his head. "Though I don't doubt you believe 'tis the truth, Rosalind."

"What?" She stopped dead in her tracks. "You think that I'm easily taken in by false stories, do you now, Ewan Gailbraith?"

"No." He held up his hands in mute apology. "I just meant that you wouldn't knowingly pass on an untruth. You've too strong a character for something like that. 'Twas a compliment!"

"From the man who tells stories of conductors wi' bears and three-man-hunts for a solitary lost railroad spike." She shook her head. "They're naught but tales told to teach us."

"And what is the story of the bull and the maple sugar supposed to teach us?" Ewan folded his arms across his chest.

"To keep close watch o'er the things we value," Rosalind explained, "lest someone more daring come and take it away."

"In that case" — laughing, he swept her into his arms — "I suppose I should just keep a tight hold on you. Even though it seems Brent has accepted our engagement, I'd rather be careful."

"Ewan!" She reluctantly pushed away. "We've work to be doing. Now isn't the time to be stealing kisses — wi' half the town only paces away!" She moved to pick up the dropped bucket.

"Seems like the perfect time." He stepped close once more. He lowered his head and whispered in her ear, "After all, we're harvesting sweets today." With that, he pressed his lips to hers in a fleeting caress before swiping the bucket from her.

"You're incorrigible," she said, the sting of the reprimand stolen by her flushed cheeks and gentle smile.

"I'm in love," he corrected, sweeping her hand into his. "And in the mood to celebrate. Your da has asked me to work alongside him at the smithy. I'll not need to forsake my trade to turn my hands to a plow nor move us from Saddleback."

"Oh Ewan!" This time she threw her arms around him. "Why didn't you say so sooner? This is wonderful news — just perfect!"

"And so" — he planted a swift peck on her nose — "are you."

"I hate to disappoint," she warned, "but no one's perfect."

CHAPTER 18

"I hate to say it, Rosalind, but you were right." Ewan sat heavily on a log placed by the fire for that purpose. "You're not quite perfect, after all." He shook his head.

"I know," she responded, looking puzzled. "But what, in particular, has made you change your mind so very quickly?"

"How can you like this better than the corn husking?" He winked. "I happen to have some very fond memories of that day." His roundabout mention of their first kiss made her blush that delightful pink shade he'd come to be so fond of.

" 'Tis harder work than the corn husking," she admitted, not taking the bait. "And 'tis far colder, too, but my favorite part of the day is coming up now. You'll change your mind back soon."

"I look forward to it." He gave a mighty stretch.

"You'll need this." She handed him a small wooden spoon with a rather long handle.

"And you'll want to follow me." He watched as she took the last pot left on the fire — the smaller one that's sap had boiled down to a sludge-like syrup — and walked around the shanty and out of sight.

He hurried to his feet and followed, finding everyone eagerly crowding around Rosalind and her still-hot pot — each of them brandishing one of the curious wooden spoons like his. He watched as she set the pot on a sturdy old tree stump and backed away until she stood beside him.

Together, they watched as first Luke, then everyone else, dipped a spoonful of the thick syrup and hurried away, dropping the contents on a patch of hard snow a little ways off. Luke picked up his newly hardened piece almost right away and bit into it, his eyes closed with obvious enjoyment as he swallowed.

"This is the sugaring-off." Rosalind nudged him forward. "Go ahead — they'll all keep coming back for more until there's none left at all. Believe me, you'll want to try some for yourself."

Shrugging, Ewan stepped forward, waited for Luke to scurry away with his third helping, and loaded his own spoon with the hot, gloppy brown mixture. He went back to where Rosalind waited with her own portion and mimicked her as she flipped the syrup onto the hard-packed snow.

Almost immediately, the syrup froze into a hardened disk. Ewan picked it up and bit into the crunchy sweet that's cold flavor melted on his tongue. He started walking back to the pot before he finished the last bite of his first taste of the treat. He ignored Rosalind's laughter as he returned to her side with a heaping spoonful of the goop and eagerly flipped it onto the snow. He couldn't ignore her when she snatched his sweet from right under his nose.

"Thank you, sweetheart." She bit into it with relish. "So thoughtful of you to fetch more for me. Very gentlemanly!" she called as he tromped off once again to scrape the last spoonful from the very bottom of the pot as everyone watched.

Everyone but Arthur and his wife. Ewan noticed that Arthur began coughing as the day wore on and kept putting his hand to his head, as though in pain. He'd seen Mrs. Mac-Lean rubbing her husband's temples to comfort him, but he grew pale.

"Mam and Da are going home." Rosalind pinched the folds of her skirts. "Da has a headache he says is worsening. I heard him coughing. . . . I hope he isn't taking ill. Perhaps some extra rest will do the trick, and that's why Mam is taking him home for now. I'll need to keep a close eye on Luke. The days are warmer, but the nights bring a harsh chill as the sun sets."

"You're good to care so." He led her toward the fire. "And we're finishing up the boiling. 'Twill be done soon."

After the work ended, they all gathered around the fire in the waning light to share stories and laughter. Rosalind prevailed upon Ewan to tell more of his railroad legends, and he had to search his memory to find one worthy of the occasion.

"Ah. I'll tell about Mr. Villard's special train."

"Mr. Villard? The railroad owner who ran the Last Spike ceremony?" Jakob Albright frowned.

"The same one. And funny enough, this story — which has been sworn to me as true — takes place on the ride up to Independence Creek for that very ceremony." Ewan paused for effect, watching to see that he had everyone's attention before he began.

"Well, Mr. Villard brought his wife, their babe, and the babe's nurse along to be a part of his triumph. After a stop in St. Paul, Mrs. Villard made the appalling discovery that all the babe's linens were soiled — there were none clean in the hamper. Obviously, this just would not do. She notified her husband of the problem."

"Seems to me," Marlene's father, Dustin, commented, "that they should have packed enough of the linens to begin with."

"Or been responsible enough to do a wash,"

harrumphed Delana Freimont. "You'd think between the mother and the nurse, one of the two would have taken care of the matter long before."

"Aye," Ewan agreed. "But the fact of the matter was that they were stopped in St. Paul wi' naught but a hamper full o' soiled linen. Mr. Villard ordered the hamper be rushed to the Pullman laundry service, where it would be washed and returned before the train even pulled out of St. Paul."

" 'Tis good to own a railroad, I see," Gilda cackled. "To have your high and mighty wife send her laundry to the workers!"

"Now, I never met Mrs. Villard personally, mind," Ewan continued, "so I can't speak as to how hoity-toity a miss she may or may not hae been. But whichever the case, as the train made its way toward Helena, the distraught nurse came before her mistress and whispered that the hamper was nowhere on board. The whole thing had been left behind in St. Paul after all."

Ewan noted that Luke slipped away from the fire, and, after a short while, Rosalind followed after him. Unwilling to draw attention to their absence, he finished the railroad legend.

"So Mr. Villard ordered that an engine and car should be found immediately and made to follow their train at all speed to bring his wife the hamper of linens. And so the special

438

train, not weighted by a heavy load, sped o'er the tracks and managed to overtake the Villard family before they reached Helena.

"Flushed wi' the triumph of his idea, Villard watched the gleeful nurse open the hamper . . . and find naught but the same soiled linens."

Gasps and laughter sounded around the fire as everyone speculated on who Mr. Villard blamed for the entire affair and what they ever did about the baby. Who could imagine a special train sent to fetch a baby's laundry — and that laundry not done?

Ewan, for his part, searched the darkness beyond the perimeter of the fire, trying to find Rosalind and Luke. As they still did not appear, a frisson of tension shot down his spine. *After such a fine day, surely nothing is wrong?*

Something was very wrong. Rosalind could feel the unease as a palpable thing while she searched for her younger brother.

"Luke!" She whispered, at first, loathe to make a scene and embarrass him. Holding her lantern aloft to better see her way, she kept on. Darkness pressed in around the modest light, throwing shadows wherever she turned. "Luke!" she called more loudly after he still had not answered.

He knew better than to wander off into the woods alone — especially in the dark. He could fall or find himself in a much worse predicament. After a harsh winter, predators would be more aggressive. Luke should still be within earshot, but Rosalind heard no answering call to soothe her frayed nerves.

Lord, there are dangers out in the wild, but Luke faces even more. 'Tis growing colder by the moment. I've not checked in on him since before the sugaring-off. Please, do not let him be in trouble. For the first time in my memory, Luke's made it through the winter wi'out a severe illness. Now that spring is upon us, 'twould be cruel for his weakness to sicken him. Guide my footsteps and help me find my brother. Let him be safe.

"Luke!" Praying fervently between calls, she stopped and listened. There it was — the shallow rasp of Luke's breathing. She turned toward the sound, her lantern's light showing her brother sitting on the cold ground, his back against a tree.

"Rose." He gave a game smile. "I'm all right." But the words came out hard and fast — forced.

"No, you're not." She knelt beside him and threw her cloak around them both. *I've heard him speak like this afore — when he's holding his breath, trying to push back the coughing.* "Don't fight it, Luke. 'Twill go easier if you don't try to hold it back." She stood, pulling him to his feet.

Guided by the lantern light, she kept a slow pace, careful not to overexert him. He coughed and rasped and coughed in spite of her best efforts. Luke needed to be where the air was warm and where she could get a hot drink down him to ease his throat and breathing.

"When did the tightness begin?" She kept her voice steady, not accusing or angry or frightened. "How long?"

"The sugaring-off." His words ended in a horrible hacking that shook his entire frame.

Of course. Breathing in the cold air, then hurrying to eat frozen sweets would bring this on. And I was too wrapped up in Ewan to think of it. I didn't watch Luke as closely as I should.

"Why did you not say so?" Rosalind couldn't bite back the question. *Did it seem I would not care if he needed my help?*

"I didn't —" Coughs interrupted his answer, and they stopped mere yards away from the boiling fire. Finally, they subsided. "I didn't want to miss any of the fun. And" — he glanced sideways at her — "I didn't want you to miss any of it either."

"There will always be opportunities for fun!" She hugged him tight around the shoulders as they kept walking. "Don't you know that you're more important than any combination of sweets and stories? You're my brother and you always come first."

"Sorry." The piteous mumble wrung her heartstrings as they stepped into the flickering light of the big fire.

"Rosalind! Luke!" Ewan hurried over to greet them. "We were beginning to worry about you." He hunkered down to peer at Luke. One look obviously told him her brother wasn't well, because he scooped the boy into his arms before addressing everyone.

" 'Tis been a long day, and I'm as tuckered as Luke, here." He spoke loudly enough to hide the sound of the boy's ragged breathing. "So I'll be taking Rosalind home, now. We wish you all a pleasant night. I hope t' see you again soon."

With Rosalind's nod, he started out. She carried the lantern; he carried the more precious cargo. Even nestled against Ewan's warmth, Luke's coughing grew steadily worse before they reached the house.

"Mam!" Rosalind pushed open the door and rushed inside, dragging a chair as close to the roaring hearth fire as she dared. She hurried to put on a kettle of water while Ewan deposited Luke in the chair.

Mam took one look at her son's pale face, heard the labored breathing, and pulled out a warm quilt to wrap around him. She pulled off his gloves, chafing his hands as she knelt at his side. "How long has he been this way?" Her question sent another pang of guilt through Rosalind as she brewed the tea.

"He says his chest started feeling tight after the sugaring-off." Rosalind spoke for Luke, as he fought for breath. She scooped out some of the eucalyptus leaves and peppermint that had always helped to ease his coughing before and prayerfully would again.

"Why didn't he come wi' us when his da felt poorly?" Mam's face fell. "I should hae checked on him afore I took your father off." She smoothed back Luke's hair. "I'm sorry, son."

"No." Rosalind choked on the words as she finally handed over a mug of steaming tea. " 'Tis my fault. You left him in my care, but I didn't realize aught was amiss until he left the fire and did not immediately return to join us." She bowed her head. "I went after him and found him trying to stop the coughing."

"You weren't holding it in, were you?" Mam turned a harsh gaze on Luke as he breathed in the warm steam from his mug. At his sheepish nod, she sighed. "That always makes it worse."

"Aye." Rosalind sat wearily on the settle, beside Ewan. "As I brought him back to the fire, and then on to home, he worsened."

" 'Tis true." Ewan frowned. "I carried the lad and could feel it as he found it harder and harder to draw breath."

"You did what you could." Mam sat back

on her heels. "Thank you, Ewan, for helping Rose bring him home. Now we keep him warm and propped up, and hope that 'twill pass quickly."

Please, Father, Rosalind prayed as Ewan took his leave. *Please let this be a short episode. Do not let him worsen but instead feel better. Let Luke be well again come morning. Amen.*

CHAPTER 19

Four mornings later, Ewan knocked on the MacLean door, carrying a brace of freshly caught rabbits. *Wi' Arthur and Luke on the mend, nothing will go down half so good as hot rabbit stew — best thing to bring a man back to his feet.* When Rosalind, eyes heavy with dark circles, opened the door, his smile vanished.

"What's happened?" He shouldered past her, dropping the skinned game atop the wooden table. An unnatural stillness filled the house for a brief moment before both Arthur and Luke broke into coughing spasms, the sound shattering the silence.

"They were doing better." Rosalind's voice came in an exhausted whisper. "It seemed as though they were on their way to recovery just yesterday. But come nightfall . . ."

"Fever came upon them both." Gilda, rocking more erratically than Ewan had ever seen, spoke up. "Their breathing labored . . . the coughing racks their bodies. Nothing helps."

Ewan sat heavily on the settle, running a

445

hand over his face. For two days after he'd carried Luke home, Rosalind and Kaitlin had tended to Arthur and Luke night and day. Only yesterday it had seemed they'd turned the corner and the worst of it had passed. But now . . . He stared helplessly to where Rosalind stooped by Luke, propping him up on cushions to ease his breathing.

"When they're more upright, they take in more air," she explained as she noticed him watching. "That and the heat and the tea are all we can do for them. Mam's asleep now after staying up all night. They were improving —" She broke off in a stifled sob that wrung Ewan's heart.

He walked over to where she slumped by the hearth and fell to his knees. With his arms wrapped around her, her weary head nestled against his shoulders, she wept. Ewan prayed.

Lord, put Your hand on this home and Your children wi'in it. Bring healing to Arthur, ease to Luke's lungs, and rest to the women who've worn themselves weak with worry. This illness is more than we alone can handle, Father. We turn to Your wisdom and mercy, and seek Your blessings upon those we hold dear.

He stroked the soft strands of Rosalind's hair that had come free from her braid over the long night. He listened as her sobs quieted, until her breathing came long and deep in the even cadence of sleep. He shifted slowly, so as not to wake her. He swept her into his arms in one smooth motion and looked up at the loft ladder, where her bed must be.

I dare not climb it wi' her in my arms. Even were there no danger of bumping her head or worse, I'd not risk waking her.

"When she wakes, she'll take pains not to close her eyes for a scant moment, lest she sleep again," Gilda warned. "Lay her on the settle, so she can catch whatever rest she's able. Poor lass hae worn herself to a frazzle, helping her mam tend everyone these past days. The false hopes o' yesterday stole what strength she had left." The old woman kept rocking, her gaze flitting from one family member to the next in an unceasing vigil.

Ewan nodded, easing Rosalind down onto the furniture so gently she scarcely stirred. He pulled a crocheted afghan over her to keep her as comfortable as possible. That done, he stood, trying to think of ways he could help her — help them all.

Heavenly Father, when I was a wee lad, I caught ill in such a way. Mam did all the things Kaitlin and Rosalind have already seen to, but something tickles the edges of my memory — a warmth pressed to my chest, the strong smell making my eyes water. What kind of poultice did she use when all else failed to make me well? What made me feel better, though I disliked it? I remember thinking I'd never get rid of the smell . . . of what? What was that scent?

He looked at the shelves full of baking supplies, spices, teas, and herbal remedies. Nothing fit the memory. Ewan paced back and forth — from the hearth, to the table, and back again — keeping his distance from Rosalind for fear he'd wake her with his heavy tread. He passed the kettle, the pot, the skinned rabbits, and the door to the root cellar more times than he could count, vainly trying to recall Mam's treatment.

Hearth . . . rocker . . . table . . . root cellar door. Luke beside the hearth, stirring with fever. The rhythmic rocking of Gilda's concern. The scrubbed wooden surface of the table. The metal ring of the root cellar door — *the root cellar!*

He grasped the metal ring and heaved upward, descending into the cool darkness beneath without stopping to grab a candle. Without a light, he groped around, searching for the answer that had plagued him all morning.

There. Ewan's hands closed around the burlap sack and he followed the light back into the warmth of the house. He cautiously shut the cellar door, mindful not only of Rosalind's sleep but of Gilda's avidly curious gaze.

"Onions?" She peered in disbelief as he shook some onto the table. "You had a sudden hankering for onions, of all things?"

"I remembered an old remedy my mother used when I was young an' fought to breathe." He grabbed a knife and began chopping the pungent bulbs. "I could only recall the strength of the scent — how much I disliked it — but that it worked. She chopped onions, boiled them down, and wrapped the mash in flannel. Than she placed the hot poultice on my chest, changing it out for new whenever the old one cooled." Ewan kept his voice low even as he chopped. " 'Twas the only thing that finally worked. I thought it might do the same for Arthur and Luke. They'll reek of the stuff for what seems like ages, but 'tis more than worth it."

"Aye." Gilda's rocker gave a final, protesting *creak* as she got to her feet. "I'll put some water on to boil and then help you. If they must be replaced when they cool, we'll need a great many of those onions." She worked as she whispered, and Ewan slid the first batch of chopped pieces into the heating water.

The two of them worked quietly, the only sounds the soft bubbling of the onions, the *snick* of their knives, and under it all, the horrible rattling gasps as Luke tried to breathe.

Rosalind lifted her head from the settle, blinking to find herself there. *How did I . . . Oh no, I must have fallen asleep!* Yet another instance of her failing to take proper care of

449

Luke, and now her da. She swung her feet to the floor, tossing the afghan over the back of the settle.

"I didn't mean to fall asleep." She bustled over to where Luke lay, half propped up on a mound of pillows. "You should hae woken me." She looked pointedly at Ewan. "You know that."

"Aye." He plopped a steaming poultice on Luke's heat-pinkened chest. "I knew you'd want me to hae woken you. 'Tis why I didn't." With maddening calmness, he took another poultice to where Da lay on the great bed and changed it out.

"What are those?" Rosalind wrinkled her nose as she processed the pungent odor rising from the flannel packs. "Onions?"

"Aye." Grandmam stirred a pot. "Your Ewan remembered a remedy his mam used when he was but a lad."

"To a certain point." Ewan gave a wry grin. "I knew she made a smelly poultice, which eased the ache in my chest, but try as I might, I couldn't recall what she put in it."

"Lad near wore out the floorboards, pacing around while he tried to recollect what the mystery ingredient was. Finally, he looked at the root cellar door and remembered 'twas onions."

"I'd never hae thought to boil onions to ease a cough." Rosalind felt Luke's forehead with the back of her hand. "He's still o'er-warm." She cast a concerned glance over at Da, wondering whether the onions had wrought any effect on his symptoms.

"Arthur's taken well to it," Grandmam answered Rosalind's unspoken question. "He's stopped coughing, at least."

"Praise the Lord for that," Rosalind whispered, relieved that at least one of them was improving. Perhaps the onion treatment would eventually aid Luke as well. She looked to where he lay, half reclining, his breaths shallow and raspy. . . . No. She bent closer, listening intently.

No. Please, let me be wrong, she prayed, even as the ominous rattle came again. Luke fought not only tightness — there was fluid gathering in his lungs. With each breath, the rattling gurgle gave hideous warning. Rosalind dropped down, putting her arms about her brother and holding him close. *Come on, Luke. Fight it. Just keep breathing. Let the poultice do its work.*

Jesus, please, help him. This is as bad as he's ever been. His chest and ribs ache from the coughing. His head pounds wi' it. Only in this uneasy sleep does he find any respite. 'Tis grateful I am that Da begins to recover, but what of my brother? He's never been hardy — he can't take a prolonged illness. The tears she thought long shed came slipping to the surface once more as she battled for her brother the only way she knew how — on her knees. Prayer was the most powerful tool she could wield, if it served the Lord's purpose to grant her request. *If 'twasn't the Lord's will . . .* That didn't even bear thinking on.

Father, 'tis my negligence that is to blame. I should hae checked on him, watched him more closely. I should hae made him sip more broth and tea to ease his throat. I should never hae allowed myself to fall asleep when he needed me. Lord, don't let Luke suffer for my failings. Please, make him well. Let Ewan's treatment work for Luke as it has for Da. Please, Lord. Please . . .

The shrill of a steam whistle broke through her thoughts. Startled, she looked up to see Ewan bolt out the door, leaving his coat and hat behind as he raced off into the distance. He was heading for the train tracks.

Please, Lord. Don't let me be too late. Let the train stop. 'Tis the answer we've all been praying for — the train can bring Luke to the doctor at Fort Benton where a wagon through the cold could not. Let me be on time.

He ran faster than he'd ever imagined — not for his life, but for Luke's. Ewan pictured Rosalind's tired face, the bruised-looking circles around her eyes, and pushed himself even harder. He rounded the smithy and found the train — already stopped.

Thank You, Father.

Ewan rushed aboard to have a short conversation with the engineer, a man by the name of Brody whom he'd worked with before.

"Brody, I've a sick little boy not far off who needs the care o' a real doctor. Will you wait a very short while so I can fetch him? 'Tis a matter o' life and death." Ewan didn't take a breath until he'd gotten through all of his request.

"We'll wait." Brody shook Ewan's hand. "I'm glad to see the railroad put to such worthy use. We've only stopped now to let off Johnny Mathers. Go on, now. Get the boy."

God's timing. Ewan didn't even stay to look for Johnny, instead rushing back to the MacLean household. When he stormed through the door, Rosalind stared in cautious hope.

"They're holding the train for Luke." Ewan began grabbing the boy's coat off the peg by the door. "The railroad will get him to Fort Benton — and the doctor — when he wouldn't make it on the long wagon ride. Arthur, Kaitlin?" He strode over to the bed, waking them both. "The train is waiting to take Luke to Fort Benton. He needs a doctor's care. Will you trust me to look after your son?"

"Aye." Arthur nodded weakly. "Though one of us should go."

"Rose will go." Gilda stood up. "I'm too old to start a new journey, and Kaitlin should stay to help keep you on the mend."

"Aye, Rosalind should go," Kaitlin said, though Ewan could tell she was torn between staying with her husband and going with her son — any mother's greatest dilemma.

"I'm ready." Rosalind held a valise in one arm and her cloak in the other. "I've packed tea and blankets and socks . . . everything I can think of to keep him comfortable on the journey. If 'tis settled, we need to go before the engineer changes his mind and sticks to his schedule."

"That's my girl." Ewan scooped Luke into his arms and strode toward her. "We'll be back before you know it. I give you my word."

"Godspeed!" Kaitlin called with a break in her voice. "We'll be in constant prayer."

With that, Ewan and Rosalind hurried out the door and toward the waiting train — their last chance to help Luke. Ewan didn't relax until they were on the train, steaming toward Benton at full speed.

They spoke little during the journey. Rosalind kept anxious eyes on her brother, propping him up and giving him sips of water as he slipped in and out of consciousness.

Ewan repeated a litany of prayer. *Thank You, Jesus, for sending the train. Let it not be too late. Work through the doctor in Benton to heal our Luke. . . .*

If asked, Ewan wouldn't have been able to

say how long they spent on the train, only that it seemed much longer than it probably actually was. When they arrived, he tipped a porter to go fetch the doctor.

"He'll be all right now." Rosalind spoke words of hope, but her face was drawn with concern as she mopped Luke's brow. "He has to be."

"Hello?" A man clambered into the car with them, lugging a physician's bag. "I'm Dr. Carmichael. This must be the boy." Wasting no time, he knelt beside Luke.

Ewan and Rosalind watched with bated breath as he checked for fever and listened to Luke's breathing and heartbeat. The doctor's ruddy face grew long, his eyes dulling behind the round spectacles perched on his nose.

"I'm afraid it's not good news." Dr. Carmichael sat back, shoving his spectacles higher. "His fever is quite high and, I'd guess, has been for some time." He waited for Rosalind's despairing nod before continuing to share his assessment. "The cough has settled in his chest — pneumonia."

"What can we do?" Ewan strove to remain calm and find how best to serve Luke. "How do we help him now?"

"Make him as comfortable as possible. Keep him propped up, give him hot fluids, and make sure he's warm." Dr. Carmichael looked defeated as he spoke the words.

"We've done all that." Rosalind spoke in

desperation. "We've been doing it since he first fell ill. Is there nothing else?"

"The only other thing I'm sure you've already been doing." The doctor looked from one face to another. "Pray."

CHAPTER 20

"Is there no hope?" Rosalind turned to Ewan as the doctor left.

"Only if 'tis the Lord's will." His bleak stare offered little of the comfort she sought, though he reached out to take her hand in his. "Though I'll not pretend to understand it."

"No." A dry sob escaped her. "God won't take him away from us. We need him. God won't give us more sorrow than we can bear. Surely not. Luke!" She shook him, alarmed at how light he felt in her arms. "Luke!" Rosalind called louder, trying to rouse him where the doctor had failed. "Come on. Open your eyes."

His pale face seemed even more drawn, the dreaded tinge of blue creeping into his lips to steal him further away from her.

"Lucas Mathias MacLean," she ordered, ignoring the way her voice shook, "wake up this instant. Do you hear me, Luke? Open your eyes." She jostled him slightly.

"Rosalind," Ewan began, but her fierce glare silenced him.

"No. He'll listen. He'll wake up." She cupped Luke's face in her hands. "He's not so warm anymore. Maybe the fever is breaking." The blue tinge deepened, and his breathing grew shallow. "No. Wake up, Luke. You have to wake up." The whispered plea did no good.

"You have to!" This last came in a shriek as his chest rose and fell one last time and was still. His skin grew cold beneath her hands.

"No, Luke. Luke." She clutched him, leaning as close as possible. "Don't leave! Please, Luke. Don't go. It's my fault," she babbled, tears streaming down her face. "I know 'tis. I should hae taken better care o' you. I love you. I'll do better. I promise I'll do better, if you'll only just wake up. Smile at me one more time, little brother. Luke? Luke!"

But it was too late. She knew it by his unnatural stillness, the cold clamminess of his skin, the blue that was deeper than ever before in his lips and fingernails.

"Rosalind." She felt Ewan's warm hand on her shoulder, heard his deep, melancholy tones. " 'Tis over. He's gone."

"No!" The heartbroken whisper was all she managed before the swirling darkness claimed her thoughts.

At the parson's house, Ewan covered Rosalind with his own coat and sat by the fire to wait. She'd revived fairly quickly, though not before his own heart had skipped a beat in mortal dread. They'd made it through the short burial before she cried herself into unconsciousness once again. The train had moved on and wouldn't be taking them home to Saddleback. Arthur and Kaitlin wouldn't have even the cold comfort of burying their son.

"I brought you some tea to warm your bones." The parson's wife whisked in and set down the tray. "Though I'm afraid it won't help with the sorrow. Only God's grace and His time will lessen that burden." She glanced around before leaving them alone in the small parlor.

With Rosalind sleeping, Ewan had no company but his own grief, which came rushing forward in the silence. Tears welled in his eyes as he thought of lively little Luke, so welcoming, such a blessing to his family. He remembered how the boy had welcomed him to the table, threw snowballs with reckless abandon, skated as though he hoped to fly off the ice, and bolted down frozen maple syrup with more enthusiasm than sense.

Gone. Lost to us forever. Why, God? He buried his head in his hands, trying to swallow the tears and the pain. *Why now? Why Luke? I understand Your wanting him by Your side, but could You not hae spared him to us*

459

for a while longer, knowing he was Yours for all time? He struggled to understand, to accept, but failed. It seemed like years he sat in the chair, trying to fathom the reasons why Luke should be robbed of his life and his family stripped of their joy. No understanding came.

"Luke." Rosalind stirred, her eyes opening. For an all-too-brief moment, she seemed fine. Then remembrance clouded the bright blue, and she hugged her knees to her chest. "He's gone."

"Yes." Ewan walked over to sit beside her, drawing her close to offer what little solace he could. "He's gone to be with our heavenly Father now. We'll see him again someday."

"I know," she whispered. "But it doesn't make it easier today." She drew a shaky breath. "At least — at least he's where each breath he draws doesn't pain him. He's beyond the reach of that now. 'Tis all I can think of to be glad about."

" 'Tis no small thing," he soothed. "We always want what's best for the ones we love. Luke has that, and we should rejoice that he's found peace and joy with our Savior."

"Yes." She straightened her shoulders a little. "He's happy. I should be happy for him. And I am." She looked up at him, her eyes shining with tears once more. " 'Tis myself, and Mam and Da and Grandmam, that I grieve for. 'Tis our loss."

"Aye." Ewan rubbed his hand over her

460

back. " 'Tis certainly our loss. But, Rosalind" — he tipped her chin to keep her gaze fixed on him — " 'tisn't your fault."

"Ewan" — she tried to pull away from him — "you don't understand. . . ."

"I understand better than you think." He moved to cup her cheek with his palm. "You watched o'er him as best you could, and he cherished your love. There was nothing you could do about his weak lungs, or the illness, save stay by his side and offer what comfort and aid you could. You did all of that."

"No." She shook her head so vehemently that she freed herself from his grasp. "I could hae done more. I should hae watched him more closely. I shouldna hae fallen asleep. I should hae —" She gasped back a sob. "I should hae shown him every moment how much he meant to me — how I loved him."

"You did, Rosalind." He took her fidgeting hands in his. "It may not feel that way now, but you did. Wi' every smile, every snowball, every mug of hot cider . . . you loved him each day he was wi' us. I saw it, and I know he did, too."

"Do you think so?" She met his gaze, seeking reassurance.

"I'm certain." He shifted a tiny bit. "His life was never ours to keep, Rosalind." His eyes stung. "No one's is."

"Ewan?" Her gaze was searching. "What — what made you say that last part? Are you feeling poorly?" Her voice rose as she pressed the back of her hand to his forehead. "We'll call Dr. Carmichael again. . . ."

"No." He captured her hand and held it. "I wasn't referring to myself. I thought of my mother." He saw that she waited for him to share more. *Maybe my experience will help her through the grief,* he reasoned. *Besides, there's nothing I want hidden betwixt us.*

"When I was about Luke's age" — he winced at her hiss of indrawn breath but continued — "my da left Ireland to seek his fortune in America. He charged me to look after Mam and look after things while he was away. He planned to send money back to us so we could book passage to join him."

"Go on."

"It seems that Da was one of many, many men who had the same idea. Work was harder to find than he'd anticipated, and it took longer to gather the money. Months passed, then years. I worked at odd jobs — smithing, shoeing, whatever I could be paid to turn a hand to — and managed to keep food on the table and a roof o'er our heads. Every scrap o' money Da sent, we saved to buy our fare. But every day, the light in Mam's eyes dimmed just a wee bit more. She missed Da so."

"It must hae been hard for you both." She squeezed his hand.

"Aye, 'twas." He took a deep breath. "Finally, I could no longer bear watching her fade away before my eyes from missing him. As the man of the house, I made the decision to use our money for a single ticket. I sent her ahead, alone. The plan was for me to follow later. She gave me her wedding band, the only thing she owned of any value. If I needed to, she instructed me to sell it."

"How wonderful of you." She nestled close. "So selfless of you — to send your mam back to your da and ask to be left all alone. Such love. Your parents must hae been proud."

"No." The words thickened in his throat, but he managed to grind them out. "Mam never stepped foot on the American shore. Alone on a miserable ship, she caught an illness on board. Wi' no one to look after her, she died during the voyage."

"Oh Ewan." Her grip tightened. "That wasn't your fault." She spoke with fierce conviction. "You have to know that."

"I didn't know" — his voice became hoarse — "I didn't know about her death until Da wrote me. The letter reprimanded me for sending Mam alone when he'd left her in my care. 'Twas the last I ever heard from him." He ignored her shocked gasp and plowed ahead. "I saved money on my own, refusing to sell Mam's ring. When I made it to America, I spent years searching for him, but it didn't work." He paused and choked out the final words. "I don't even know whether or not he's still alive."

"Ewan." She held his head to her shoulder and rocked back and forth. "You can't blame yourself for your mother's death. You did the best you could by her. 'Twasn't fair o' your father to lash out at you. I'm sure 'twas done only in grief."

"Perhaps." He straightened up. "I've never told anyone about this." He traced the band of gold adorning her finger. "But you wear her ring, and you are to bear my name. We should hae no secrets betwixt us. And just as I had to come to terms wi' my mam's death, so, too, do you hae to stop blaming yourself for Luke's."

"Luke . . ." Her face fell at the mention of her brother.

"You did the best you could by him," Ewan softly echoed her own words. " 'Tisn't fair to blame yourself in your grief."

Silence stretched between them for a long while.

Finally, Rosalind spoke. "You're right." They sat for a while longer. "Ewan?"

"Yes, Rosalind?"

"Not too long ago, I was reading Da's Bible. I looked at the death records — and the marriage lines — and wondered what our future held."

"Oh?"

"And I turned to one o' my favorite chapters — Ecclesiastes 3."

" 'To every thing there is a season,' " he recited along with her, " 'and a time to every purpose under the heaven: A time to be born, and a time to die.' " They both stopped.

"And I thought how strange it was, that in the family records, birth and death are placed side by side and that it is the same in the scriptures." She bit her lip. "Ewan? When we have a son —"

"We'll name him Luke," he finished firmly. She nodded, a ghost of a smile breaking through her grief. "Rosalind, that chapter continues until it comes to another portion I think applies here."

" 'A time to laugh; a time to mourn'?" she asked. "For now is certainly the time to mourn."

"Aye, 'tis." He threaded his fingers through her hair. "Though I was thinking of the part that says, 'a time to lose; a time to keep.' "

"Oh." Rosalind thought for a moment. "We've lost Luke. What is there to keep? Our grief?" She seemed despondent at the very thought.

"No, though Luke will always be in our hearts." Ewan waited until her gaze met his. "You and I, Rosalind. Our love. The beginning of our life together. That is what we are to keep — hope for the future and trust that the Lord will see us through."

"Oh Ewan." She kissed his cheek. "How

right you are. And that is the way Luke would hae wanted it — that we allow for grief but look forward to the promise of tomorrow."

"And when we wed, my Rosalind," Ewan vowed, " 'twill be a time to keep."

EPILOGUE

Montana, 1889

"Can you believe it?" Marlene squealed, all but dancing for joy. "After two years of waiting, I'm finally married!"

"Wi' a home already built and a farm already in operation. Johnny's worked hard to make ready for his beautiful bride." Rosalind smiled. "I'm thinking 'twon't be long before you join your mam and me." She patted her rounded tummy with affection and looked at Delana, who was two months further along. "Isn't that right, Mrs. Freimont?"

"Ja." Delana laughed. "Though I hadn't thought to bear a babe near the time when my daughter would!"

"It's a wonderful surprise." Marlene leaned over her mother's swollen stomach. "She's going to be a sister, I think."

"Not mine." Rosalind cupped her hands over her own swollen midriff. "I bear a son. Ewan and I — we've decided to name him

Luke." Her eyes sparkled more with joy than sorrow, a sign of God's healing and the passage of time.

"What a wonderful idea!" Mam drew her into a tight clasp, her own eyes looking suspiciously moist. "Luke would hae liked that."

"Yes, he would." Marlene reached out to grasp both of their hands. "It's a lovely gesture, and I'm so happy for you!"

"We'll speak of it more when the babes are born." Delana smiled. "For now, we've much to celebrate. My daughter, a bride, and Montana declared an official state!"

"Yes. It's a grand day for a wedding — a day to be remembered." Johnny came up behind the women to steal a kiss from his blushing bride. "We're going to blow the anvils now."

They all hurried to the clearing, where Ewan and Johnny carefully overturned one anvil, pouring black gunpowder into the base's hollow before positioning the second anvil directly atop it. A thin trail of the gunpowder spilled over the side, waiting to be lit.

"And here we go! Everybody step far back, out of the way!" Johnny lit the trail of powder and rushed to Marlene's side. At that moment, the anvils began to dance, emitting a loud series of sparks until the pressure built up sufficiently to overturn the top anvil with

468

a spectacular *boom!*

When the gunpowder supply was exhausted — and everyone's ears rang with the sound of the merry tradition — Ewan stepped forward. Rosalind watched with pride as her husband waited for everyone's attention and began his speech.

"When I married my beautiful Rosalind o'er a year ago, 'twas a day of great joy. And also one tempered wi' sorrow wi' young Luke" — he paused for a moment as several people drew shaky breaths — "gone to heaven. But we know he would hae wanted us to celebrate."

He broke into a grin. "Now, after a long, patient wait, Johnny and Marlene hae wed on this joyous day. I'm both pleased and honored to speak an old Irish blessing upon their marriage and on all who are gathered here today. If my wife would join me . . ." He held out his hand, beckoning Rosalind to come to his side.

Surprised, she did so. Suddenly, she knew he'd planned the blessing to be a celebration of their own marriage, as much as Johnny and Marlene's. Looking into the deep green of his gaze, she spoke the ancient words with him:

"May love and laughter light your days, and warm your heart and home. May good and faithful friends be yours,

469

wherever you may roam.
May peace and plenty bless your world
with joy that long endures.
May all life's passing seasons bring
the best to you and yours."

■ ■ ■ ■

BEYOND TODAY

BY TRACIE PETERSON

■ ■ ■ ■

CHAPTER 1

On the way home from town, Amy Carmichael closed her eyes and rested her head
against the edge of the jostling wagon. She
was trying desperately to ignore the animated,
nonstop rambling of her twin sister, Angie.

Physically, Angela and Amy Carmichael
were identical. Considered too tall by most
of their peers, the girls measured at exactly
five feet, ten inches. Their stature was the
only thing their friends could find to criticize,
though, for the twins' perfect features and
tiny waists had been the envy of all. Now, at
nineteen, with dark hair the color of chestnuts
and brown eyes like velvet, the twins were
envied more than ever.

On the outside, the twins were a beautiful
matched pair, so much alike that they confused even their friends. But on the inside . . .

"You're not listening, Amy," Angie commented with a pout.

"No, I suppose I'm not. I'm really tired,
Angie." Amy tried to adjust her sunbonnet

for the tenth time. She pulled its shade over her eyes, squinting at the October sun that felt as hot as any summer day. She tucked a strand of hair beneath the bonnet, glad for the air's slight crispness that hinted that colder weather was coming.

"Just look at the dress Alice sent me," Angie whined.

Amy sat up and tried to show some interest. Angie was profoundly proud that their older sister Alice had broken away from the frontier prairie life, to live in a big city back east. Their sister understood Angie's passion for city life and often sent Angie hand-me-downs from her city finery.

Amy, on the other hand, had little or no interest in the clothes Alice sent. She'd rather be in calico or homespun any day. In consideration of Angie's feelings, however, Amy reached out and touched the shiny, pink satin. "It is lovely, Angie. You'll look quite the city girl in this."

"Oh, I know," Angie gushed, "and won't the boys be impressed."

Amy grimaced. "Where in the world will you wear it for them to see?"

"Why the barn raising, of course!" Angie continued to chatter away, while Amy waved to one of the neighbors in the wagon behind theirs.

As they made their way home, Amy looked often over her shoulder at the small parade of wagons behind them. She smiled. The harvest had been a good one this year. The corn, sold today for a record price, combined with August's summer wheat, guaranteed that the residents of Deer Ridge would head into winter fully supplied with not only their home grown foods, but also store bought goods and money in the bank; such security was a rarity indeed.

Things had gone so well in fact, that the twins' parents, Charles and Dora Carmichael, were planning a barn raising to erect a much needed livestock barn.

"What do you think he'll look like?" Angie questioned, continuing to rub the satin against her wind-burned cheek.

"Who?" Amy asked, wondering if she'd missed part of the conversation.

"The circuit rider of course. Think of all the wonderful places he's been. I get goose bumps just imagining all the things he's seen. It must be truly spectacular to travel to new places all the time." Angie sighed dreamily. "Don't you ever think of what it'd be like to live back in the city? Don't you ever want to make plans for the future, Amy?"

Amy smiled. "A future beyond today?"

"Oh bother with that," Angie said in frustration. "I remember Grandma always saying that and I hated it then, too. A person has to make plans."

"Why?"

"Just because they do." Angie's lips pressed together. "Besides, you're making plans for the future. You just don't know it. You're already rearranging the house in your head, just to accommodate the barn raising and the circuit rider's stay. Now don't tell me you're not, because I know you, Amy Carmichael."

Amy shrugged her shoulders. Arguing with her twin was pointless, so she said nothing at all.

Angie didn't care. She continued chattering as if the conversation had never taken a negative turn. That was the best thing about Angie, Amy thought as she half-listened to her twin; Angie'd argue her point of view, but she wouldn't run it into the ground by fighting.

"Amy," she said now, leaning forward as if to share a great secret. "I heard Mama say that the circuit rider used to live in Kansas City! Imagine that — Kansas City!"

Amy rolled her eyes. Between the satin dress and the circuit rider, Angie was completely daffy. Amy watched while Angie's fingers slid back and forth over the smooth material; she could tell that Angie's fascination with the gown was reaching the point where she would soon sink into an absorbed and silent contemplation. She would be imagining, Amy knew, what she would look like in the dress, what accessories would compliment it, how she should do her hair when she wore it. Amy smiled and sighed; she welcomed the silence.

While Angie dreamed of the party that would follow the barn raising, Amy, as her sister had predicted, calculated the work that would be involved during the day of labor.

Barn raisings were real celebrations, and the entire community would turn out to help. The plentiful harvest, coupled with the news of the circuit rider, made the best of reasons to celebrate.

Amy hadn't realized how much she missed regular church services, what her father referred to as the "calling of the faithful." Now they would have a regular circuit rider, and even if he only came every three or four weeks, it was better than nothing at all.

The small community of Deer Ridge had often contemplated building a church and hiring a full-time minister, but nothing had ever come of the plans, much to Amy's disappointment. She remembered the community meeting to decide which they would build and support first — a church or a school. With the many large families supplying donations of felled logs and other building materials, the school easily won.

Amy sighed as she remembered church services back in Pennsylvania. They'd left the civilized east, though, and moved to the wild prairie of western Kansas when she and Angie had been only seven.

Their older brother Randy had been elated at the prospect of an adventure. At seventeen, Randy saw this as an answer to the future. Pennsylvania farms were hard to come by and most of the land near his parents' home was already being farmed. Randy had known he could continue farming his father's land, but he wanted to make a stake for himself; homesteading in Kansas offered him the best chance.

Twelve-year-old Alice, though, had been miserable, just as Angie had been. They hadn't wanted to leave Pennsylvania. Alice had cried herself into the vapors and had to be put to bed, while Angie had whined so much that she received the promise of a spanking if she didn't settle down.

But despite the trepidations of two of the Carmichael daughters, the family farm was sold and the remaining possessions loaded into a canvas-covered wagon.

Unlike her sisters, Amy thought the whole thing great fun. She loved to run alongside the wagon on the way to their new promised land and hated being made to ride inside with the weepy Alice and whining Angie.

The memory made Amy feel cramped now as she sat squeezed between the supplies for the barn raising. "Pa?" she called up to the wagon seat in front of her where her father handled the team. "I'd like to stretch for a while. Would you stop so I can jump down?"

"Sure." Charles Carmichael smiled. Amy was so much like him — always moving, eager to be doing rather than watching.

Amy scrambled down, and because of the slowness of the heavily loaded wagons, she was easily able to keep pace on foot. Once again, she twitched her sunbonnet back in place. "Pa?"

"What is it, Amy?"

"I was just wondering if you knew anything about the circuit rider. Is he young or old?"

"Can't rightly say, but the district minister said he'd be on horseback. I can't imagine him being too awful old, if he's going to cover all this territory on horseback," Charles answered thoughtfully. "It'd be a might taxing on an older feller."

"And he'll be there for the barn raising and stay the night at the farm with us?" Amy already knew the answer, but she wanted to check the grapevine information she'd received from her sister.

"Yup. It's all settled and ain't we the lucky ones. New barn and a man of God all in the same day. Ain't we the lucky ones."

"More like blessed than lucky," Amy's mother, Dora Carmichael, put in from the other side of her husband. "Carmichaels don't hold no account in luck."

Charles laughed. "That's for sure, Ma. We'd never have gotten this far on Carmichael luck." The three of them laughed at this, though no one was really sure why. The Carmichaels had enjoyed a good life with many choice blessings, yet something in her father's words had amused them all.

No one who lived on the prairie ever chalked much of anything up to luck. Out here, surrounded by such a vast expanse of wilderness, human beings seemed to dwindle right down to the size of ants. They needed their belief in a pattern made by God, a design that He could see from up above, to give them strength; the thought of luck and chance spoiled the image. Maybe that's why they'd laughed. Whatever the reason, Amy was grateful for the laughter and the love.

Three weeks later found the farm in a frenzy of preparation for the barn raising. The entire community would turn out to help the Carmichaels put up their new barn, as well as celebrate the harvest and the arrival of the circuit rider.

Dora Carmichael spent hours sweeping the farmhouse floor. The Carmichaels were one of the few families in the community to have a puncheon floor, and Dora prided herself in keeping the long thin boards shining with a glow that rivaled even the finest city homes. Normally, once a month she would scrub the floor with a splint broom made from a piece of hickory — Dora always declared that this was the only way to "gussy up" the worn wood — but now with the circuit rider due to stay the night in the Carmichael house, Dora worked that broom until her arms ached.

The Carmichael farmhouse was by far the largest in the community. It was made now of logs and stood two stories high, but it hadn't always been so. The soddy house had come first. Amy remembered her disappointment the first time she'd seen their new home. It had been made of grass and mud, and the thought of living in a dirt house made Alice and Angie bawl. Amy didn't care for it any more than her sisters, but she looked past the sod and saw her father's pride.

Charles Carmichael had stood proudly with his hands on his hips, the hot, Kansas sun at his back, and sweat dripping down the side of his face. He was dirtier than Amy had ever seen him, but the promise of the future shown clear in his eyes, and his smile was as wide as the Smokey Hills River itself. He had built his family a house; now it was up to them to make it home.

Right then Amy decided to work extra hard to make each day pleasurable for her parents. And that was when she decided to adopt her grandmother's attitude of one day at a time, looking no further than that day for trouble, because tomorrow was sure to have even more time to plan for problems. And now, Amy thought with a smile, what with getting ready for the barn raising, she had plenty of work to keep her from worrying about anything that might come later on.

"Amy!" Her mother's call made Amy hasten to pull up yet another bucket of water from the well.

"Coming, Ma." Amy hurried back to the house, slopping water on herself as she ran. She was careful to leave her boots at the back door, as she entered her mother's freshly scrubbed kitchen.

"Just put the water on the stove and help me put these curtains up." Dora Carmichael motioned Amy toward the stove.

Amy poured the bucket of water into a large cast-iron pot and put the bucket outside the door. Wiping her wet hands on her apron, she reached up to help her mother place the red calico curtains at the kitchen window.

"Looks real good, Ma." Amy stepped back to get a better look. "That calico made up real nice for curtains."

"Well, it's not too bad if I do say so myself. Especially considering the fact that this was your sister's dress, just last week."

"Don't tell her and maybe she won't fuss." Amy laughed. Angie fought to have less homemade things in the house and more store bought luxuries.

"I just can't understand that sister of yours. Never could understand Alice either." Dora sighed. "Don't they ever stop to think that somebody had to make those things the store buys and resells?"

Amy laughed and put her arm around her mother's shoulders. "Angie only thinks about which one of her beaus she's going to marry and what big city she'll go live in. I don't imagine she thinks about much more than that."

The late October temperatures were unseasonably warm and the window stood open to let in the steady southerly breeze. The calico caught the wind and fluttered like a flag unfurling. "They sure do look nice, Ma," Amy repeated.

The 20th of October found the Carmichaels' homestead overrun with friends and family. Amy and Angie's brother Randy was the first to arrive. His growing family was seated in the bed of the wagon behind him.

Amy helped her nephews, Charlie and Petey, from the wagon bed, before taking her two-year-old niece, Dolly. Her very expectant sister-in-law Betsey smiled at her gratefully.

"How have you been feeling, Betsey?" Amy questioned as the pregnant woman scooted herself to the back of the wagon.

"I've definitely been better. I think it would have been easier to ride bareback, than to sit another mile in this wagon."

Amy laughed at the rosy-cheeked blond and

offered her a hand down, but Randy came and easily lifted Betsey up and out, placing a loving kiss on her forehead before he set her feet on the ground. At the site of her father offering kisses, Dolly reached out her arms, and said, "Me, too!"

Everyone laughed, but Randy leaned over and gave Dolly a peck on the cheek. "Now, Lilleth Carmichael, I expect you to mind your manners today."

The little girl cocked her head to one side, as if confused by the use of her Christian name, instead of the nickname her brother had given her. Then four years old, Petey had been unable to pronounce Lilleth, and so he announced that he would call her "Dolly," because she looked just like a baby doll he'd seen in Smith's General Store. From that point on it had been official, and Lilleth became Dolly.

"Come on, Betsey. Ma's already got a comfortable spot picked out for you under the cottonwood tree," Amy said. Taking hold of Betsey's arm she led her to the waiting chair.

The farmyard was soon a riot of people and livestock. Randy and Charles had picket stakes already set up for the horses, and the wagons were used as tables or places to sit when taking a break from building.

Amy was to be in charge of the children, thus freeing the women to quilt, cook, and visit. Some of the more ambitious ladies were even known to get into the act of helping with the construction. Why, Cora Peterson sometimes shinnied right up to the roof supports to put in a few well-placed nails. She said it kept her young, and at seventy years of youth, nobody was going to argue with her.

As the sun rose above the horizon in a golden, orange glow, the final preparations were taken care of. Tents were quickly erected for the purpose of neighbors spending the night, thus saving them the long trip back to town, only to turn around the next day and return to hear the circuit rider preach at the Carmichael farm.

Tables bowed from the weight of food, and the array of tantalizing, mouth-watering delights was never to be equaled. Amy had to laugh, knowing that the overflowing plenty was not even the main meal but for the purposes of snacking only. Huge cinnamon rolls and fresh baked breads lined the tables, along with jars of preserves and jams of every flavor, as well as a variety of butters, apple, peach, and even plum. Someone had thought to bring several long rolls of smoked sausage, which were quickly cut into slices and eaten between bread, before the first log was in place. All in all, everyone deemed it a great day to build a barn.

CHAPTER 2

"The preacher's a'comin! The preacher's a'comin!" The children ran toward the two approaching horses.

The excitement was uncontainable among the Deer Ridge residents, and even Angie stopped flirting with Jack Anderson. Another of her boyfriends, who just happened to be Jack's brother Ed, rode into the farmyard with the biggest man anyone in Deer Ridge had ever laid eyes on.

Amy was out of earshot, and so she missed seeing the circuit rider as his six foot, six inch frame bounded down from his huge Morgan horse. Angie, on the other hand, was ready and waiting.

"This is Pastor Tyler Andrews," Ed Anderson told them. Ed was the town's bank teller and the one person Angie figured had a pretty good chance of getting her out of Deer Ridge.

"Howdy do, Parson," Charles Carmichael said, taking the man's mammoth hand in his own.

The giant man smiled. "Please call me Tyler." His voice was rich and warm. "Pastor and Parson sound much too stuffy for friends." Taking off his hat, he revealed sweat-soaked golden curls. Angie thought they were divine.

She batted her thick black lashes while her dark eyes slid appraisingly over Tyler. He dwarfed everyone around him, but his brown eyes were welcoming and friendly.

Without warning, Angie reached out boldly and took Tyler's arm. "You simply must meet my mother, Dora Carmichael. Oh, and over here is Mrs. Stewart. Her husband owns the bank. And this is Mrs. Taggert — her husband is Doc. He's that man over there in the dark coat." Tyler had to laugh as the tall, willowy girl fairly pulled him through the mass of people, completely ignoring Ed Anderson.

If anyone in Deer Ridge was surprised by Angie's outburst, no one said a thing. Angie was always livening up things, and today wasn't going to be any different. She had a way about her that endeared her to people about as quickly as she annoyed them. Angie, though, never had any hard feelings; she was simply being Angie, and most people understood that.

Only a handful of people missed getting introduced to the massive preacher by Angie. Most of them were under the age of ten, though, and the only adult not yet privileged to make Tyler's acquaintance was Amy.

Amy had taken the children to play hide-and-seek and Red Rover in the orchard. She loved the children best. They were demanding, but their wants were simple. They continually asked for drinks and help to the outhouse, but Amy found them easier to be with than the adults. She could simply play with them all morning, and they accepted her just as she was. At the noon meal, the weary and worn children would join their folks and be ready to nap in the afternoon.

"Watch me, Amy! I'm gonna jump out of this tree," eight-year-old Charlie called to his aunt.

"If you break your leg, don't come crying about it afterward," Amy called over her shoulder as she hoisted Dolly to her other hip. She was glad she'd chosen to wear her older blue gingham for playing with the children, since Dolly was taking turns chewing first on the collar of the dress and then the sleeve.

"Poor baby," Amy said as she smoothed Dolly's downy brown hair back into place. "Are you getting new teeth? I bet Grammy has some hard biscuits for you to chew on. We'll just see if she doesn't."

Amy put two of the older girls in charge of watching over the others and went in search of a teething biscuit for Dolly. As she rounded the corner of the Carmichaels' two-story log home, Amy could see that the barn was already sporting a frame on three sides. She glanced around, wondering if the new minister had arrived. Spying her mother, Amy made her way to inquire about the preacher and the biscuit.

"Dolly needs a teething biscuit, Ma," Amy said, trying to pull her collar out of her niece's mouth. "Those back molars of hers are causing her fits."

"There's a whole batch of hard biscuits on the table in the house," Dora answered and reached up for her granddaughter. Dolly would have none of it, however, and turned to bury her face in Amy's hair.

"You ought to tie your hair back, Amy," Dora suggested. "She has your hair a mess."

"I tried putting it back three times," Amy answered. "It keeps coming free, mostly because of a little boy named Petey, who thinks it's fun to snatch my ribbon." Amy laughed. Betsey and Dora laughed, too.

Amy turned to go to the house when she remembered the circuit rider and turned back. "Is he here yet, Ma?"

"Who?" Dora asked, wondering if her daughter was finally taking an interest in one of the community's eligible men.

"The circuit rider, of course. Who else did you think I was talking about?"

"Oh, no one in particular." Her mother smiled. "I was just hoping, that's all."

"Now, Ma. Don't get started on me and husband hunting. I'll know when the right man comes along. He just hasn't come along yet. So is the preacher here or not?"

"Sure is. See that spot of gold on top of the east edge of the barn frame?"

Amy craned her neck to see the man her mother was pointing out. She could barely see him, but he was there and she felt satisfied just knowing it.

"I'm sure glad he made it. It's going to be fun having a preacher and regular church services again."

"We haven't done so bad with the home services," Dora said, supporting her husband's perseverance in holding some type of Sabbath service for his children and grandchildren.

"Of course not, Ma. I just think it will be nice to get together with the others. Is he nice? What's he look like? I can't really see him too well from here." Amy strained to get a better look without being too obvious.

"Well," her mother answered, "I must say your sister was certainly taken with him. Angie latched on to him first thing, so you'd best ask her if you want to know what he's like. I just barely said hello, before Angie was dragging him off again." Dora laughed and added, "About the one thing I could tell about him is that he's a big man. Taller than your pa and shoulders broad as a bull."

"That's for sure." Betsey struggled to get into a more comfortable position.

Amy decided not to seek out the new preacher. After all, if Angie had already set her cap on him, what chance would the poor man have of freeing himself up to meet the likes of Amy?

I don't need to meet him now, Amy decided, going back to tend the children. *I'll get to hear him preach tomorrow and maybe even tonight. Let Angie make a fool out of herself. It seems to give her such pleasure.*

Amy was enjoying the children so much, she was surprised when someone rang the dinner bell.

"You children run on now and find your folks," she said. "It's time to eat — and I heard tell somebody brought cherry cobbler for dessert." She steered the children in the direction of the lunch tables.

She managed to deposit Dolly into Dora's arms with only a few complaining whimpers from Dolly, and then she went to make sure the other children made it back to their mothers. She glanced around again for a glimpse of the preacher, but he was seated among a huge group of people and she couldn't get a good look at him. She would just have to wait to satisfy her curiosity.

"So that would make you thirty-one years

old," Angie said, after mentally calculating the figures she'd just heard Tyler recite.

"That's right, Angie." Tyler grinned. He liked this young woman, so lively and vibrant. She seemed to pull everyone around her into an atmosphere of celebration. "I've been riding the circuit for seven years, with most of my time spent in Missouri. My folks live outside of Kansas City."

"Kansas City!" Angie squealed. "Oh, do tell me what Kansas City is like. I want so much to go there. Have you been to any other big cities? I want to hear about them, too!" Angie rambled on, giving Tyler no time to answer.

But before the meal was finished, Angie had managed to learn a great deal about life in Kansas City. She also knew that Tyler Andrews had become a minister after losing his bride of several months to an influenza epidemic.

Stuffed from the heaps of food ladled onto his plate, Tyler excused himself to clean up. Meanwhile, Ed and Jack Anderson had taken as much ignoring as they could tolerate from Angie, and as soon as Tyler got to his feet, they came to reclaim her.

Tyler listened to Angie fuss over the two men and laughed to himself. He shook his head in wonderment, nearly running over Charles Carmichael.

"Pastor Tyler," Charles said, unable to bring

himself to use only the man's first name. "I hope you're finding everything you need. The conveniences are behind the house, although I'm sure you could've figured that one out. Feel free to walk around." Charles patted his full belly. "I think I'll take a little nap while the others rest."

"Thank you, Mister Carmichael," Tyler said.

"No, no," Charles protested, "just call me Charles. Everybody else does."

"Only if you'll call me Tyler."

Charles laughed and stuck out his right hand. "It's a deal, Tyler. Although never in my life have I called a man of God by his first name."

"Then it's about time." Tyler shook the man's hand vigorously. "Formalities hold little account with me. We're all one family, after all."

"That we are. That we are," Charles agreed and went off in search of a place to rest. He was going to like this new preacher, he could tell already.

Amy placed the two full buckets of water on either end of the yoke. Careful to avoid spilling any of the precious liquid, she hoisted the yoke to her shoulders. She carried the water to a huge cauldron, normally used for laundry and soap making, and dumped it in. After several trips to the well, she lit the kindling and logs beneath the pot so that the water would heat for washing the dishes.

Satisfied that the fire was well lit, she went back to hauling water. She hummed to herself, enjoying the temporary quiet in the aftermath of lunch. The final two buckets hoisted at last to her shoulders, she was startled to find the weight suddenly lifted. She whirled around.

Her mouth fell open as she stared up at Tyler Andrews's giant form. After several seconds, she stammered, "I, I, ah —" She couldn't think of anything to say.

Tyler grinned. "You amaze me, Angie. I wouldn't have thought a little lady like you could've raised this thing, much less carry it very far. How in the world did you manage to give your beaus the slip?" He chuckled, amused by the stunned expression on the face of the woman he thought was Angie.

Amy felt her legs start to shake. What in the world was wrong with her? She hoped she wasn't coming down with a spell of ague, or malaria, as some of the city doctors referred to it. It ran rampant at times, and while Amy and Angie had been lucky to avoid it, Amy knew her mother suffered severe bouts of it.

She struggled to find something to say and finally blurted out the only thing that came to mind. "You must be the circuit rider. I'm glad you decided to come to Deer Ridge."

Tyler looked at her strangely for a moment. What kind of game was Angie playing now? She'd nearly broken his arm dragging him from person to person this morning, and then at lunch she flirted with him unmercifully. Now, she acted as though she'd never met him.

Amy felt her heart pounding louder and faster, until she was certain Tyler could hear it from where he stood. She put her hand to her breast as if to still the racing beat. Tyler Andrews was as handsome as any man she had ever met.

When Tyler just watched her, his brows knit, Amy suddenly realized that he was confused. Apparently, though not surprisingly, Angie hadn't told him she had a twin sister. Amy took a deep breath. "I'm sorry, you must think my manners are atrocious. I'm Amy Carmichael, Angie's twin sister."

A broad smile crossed Tyler's worried face. "That's a relief. I thought for moment you were touched in the head. You know, too much sun."

Amy smiled. "No, just not as forward as my sister. Sorry if we confused you. We're really not up to mischief." She heard her own words, and she thought her voice sounded normal enough, despite the alien feelings inside her body and the clutter of confusion in her mind. "Well," she added with a grin, "at least *I'm* not up to mischief. Once you get to know us, you'll be able to tell us apart. We may look alike, but that's about it."

Tyler laughed out loud. "So there are two of you — and I'll eat my hat if you aren't identical."

"We are that, Pastor," Amy agreed and added, "in a physical sense. We do have our differences, though, believe me."

"I can see that, too."

Tyler had forgotten about the weight he still held, but Amy noticed the water and motioned for Tyler to follow her. "You'll burn your muscles out good, standing there like that, Pastor," she said. She wondered whether she should take one of the buckets and ease his burden.

"Just lead the way," he answered, "and please don't call me pastor. I've just worked through that with your pa and finally he's calling me Tyler. I'd like it if you'd call me that, too." He followed Amy to the cauldron.

She took the pails off the yoke hooks and emptied them into the cauldron before answering. "All right, Tyler." She smiled a little, tasting the name for the first time. "And you call me Amy."

Tyler placed the yoke on the ground and extended his hand. "It's a deal."

Amy held out her hand, and Tyler took hold of her small tanned arm with his left hand, as his right hand grasped her fingers. The touch of his warm hands made her shiver. "There's a chill to the air, don't you think?" she said, despite the warm sun that beat down on their heads. She thought she saw a glint of amusement in Tyler's eyes.

What in the world was wrong with her?

CHAPTER 3

Despite the jittery feeling that ran along her nerves, Amy found herself comfortable in the company of Tyler Andrews. She showed him around the farm, pointing out things she loved the most.

"There's a path down past the old barn that leads to our orchards," she told him, guiding him back to the construction site of the new barn. "But I can show you later." She noticed that a few of the men were already back at work, and while she was enjoying her time with Tyler, he was probably anxious to get back to the company of men.

In reality, nothing could have been further from Tyler's mind. He was delighted at his good fortune and Amy's company. He'd ridden the circuit for over seven years, always embracing each new community, always enjoying his service to God. But in the back of his mind he had always had the desire to settle down. That desire had made Tyler carefully consider each and every community that he pastored — as a possible home.

Now, as he watched Amy Carmichael speak in her soft, quiet way about the life she loved here on the plains, Tyler began to think he might see the possibility of a lifetime partner — and maybe even a home.

Amy brushed back a loose strand of brown hair and took her red hair ribbon out of her apron pocket. "I tried three times to retie my hair — and each time one of the ornery boys I was caring for this morning pulled it from me and left my hair disheveled. I do apologize for being so unkept." Amy tied the ribbon in place. "Now that the children are napping, I should be safe."

Tyler chuckled, and Amy was surprised to see a strange look of amusement spread across his face. His laughing brown eyes caught the sunshine and reflected flecks of amber in their warmth. There were tiny creases at the corners, betraying his love of laughter.

What manner of man was this preacher? So full of life and laughter. So comfortable and happy to share the small details of life on the farm. Amy smoothed down the edges of her dress collar, now hopelessly wrinkled from Dolly's chewing; she didn't even feel the hand that reached up and pulled loose her hair ribbon.

As the chestnut bulk fell around her face, Amy gave a gasp of surprise. She looked up to see a mocking grin and arched eyebrows, as Tyler dangled her ribbon high above her head.

"Boys will be boys no matter the age, Miss Amy," Tyler said and then put the ribbon in his shirt pocket. Amy started to protest, but Tyler had already moved away to retrieve a hammer. She stared after him, long after he'd climbed the ladder to help her father.

"Better shut your mouth, Amy, or you'll catch flies in it," Angie teased. "Isn't he wonderful!" It was an exclamation, not a question, and Angie fairly beamed as she continued. "He spent lunch with me and told me all about his life. Do you know, his parents still live near Kansas City and they go to the opera and the symphony. Can you imagine it, Amy?"

"No, I truly can't," Amy admitted. The things that attracted her twin held little interest for Amy, and while she hated to hurt her sister's feelings, she couldn't lie.

"If I were to marry that man," Angie continued, "I could probably live with his parents in Kansas City, while he rode the circuit. Wouldn't that be a dream? Everything in the world at your fingertips!"

"For pity's sake, Angie. The man just arrived in Deer Ridge, and already you're acting as though he's proposed." Amy didn't want to admit the twinge of disappointment she was feeling. Her sister was used to getting her own way when it came to men. Most of them simply fell at her feet whenever she batted her eyes, and now Angie was contemplating the new minister as if he were a prized hog at the local fair. Amy shrugged her shoulders.

"Things move pretty fast among frontier folk," Angie mused with a coy smile. "But I think I would like to get to know this Tyler Andrews better. I'm going to see to it that he dances at least half the dances with me tonight. I'll bet I can have him proposing before the night is over."

"Angie!" Amy gasped. "You don't even know this man. You surely don't love him, so how can you even think of trying to snag him into marriage?"

"I can love anybody, dear sister. In fact, love is the easy part. I haven't met a man yet that didn't make me feel happy and loved."

"What about the man?" Amy asked and noticed the smile leave Angie's face. "Don't they deserve to be loved by their wives?"

"Well, don't get vulgar about it." Angie feigned a shocked expression. She hated it when Amy revealed a flaw in her ideals, and now she tried to distract her twin by deliberately misunderstanding. "Of course, whatever is expected of a wife would come along with the marriage. I'm sure it can't be too unpleasant."

"You know very well I'm not talking about

that," Amy said with a blush. "I'm talking about caring and supporting. That's the kind of loving I'm talking about."

Angie tossed her precisely placed curls. Unlike her twin, she had little trouble keeping her hair pinned, despite the number of suitors that followed her around the farm. "You are such a bother, Amy. I don't want to argue with you, so let's just drop it for the time. I like Tyler, and he likes me. If something more comes about tonight, then it must be meant to be."

With that, Angie bounced off in the direction of the newly arrived Nathan Gallagher. Nathan was Deer Ridge's only lawyer and the third of Angie's more serious boyfriends. Amy shook her head and sighed. Sometimes her sister could be infuriating.

By nightfall the barn was completed, with the exception of some indoor work, and it was as fine a structure as any farmer could ever hope for. Its completion signaled time for supper and everyone knew what would follow that — the dance!

Amy was busy with kitchen work, but she found her thoughts still caught by Tyler. She couldn't help but remember the way his eyes seemed to laugh even before his face cracked a smile. She had already memorized each feature of his handsome face, she realized, and she nearly found herself tracing its lines in the potatoes she was mashing before the clatter of pans behind her brought her back to reality.

She looked around her to see if anyone had seen how silly she was acting, but the bustling group of older women seemed to scarcely notice her presence. Most of the other women Amy's age were outside, enjoying the company of the young men. Through the open window, Amy could hear Angie's exuberant laughter. No doubt she had cornered Tyler again and was working him into her snare.

Amy threw down the potato masher. Why did Angie have to be like that? Trying to ignore the sound of her sister's joy, Amy took the large bowl of potatoes to the table and fled to the safety of her room.

After an hour or more had passed, Amy rejoined the festive crowd. She had changed her grass-stained dress and now wore a soft muslin gown that had been dyed a shade of yellow. The dye was made from goldenrod plants, and the color was called nankeen. The gown was simple, with gathers at the waist and a scoop-necked bodice that had been trimmed with handmade tatting. The bodice was a bit snug, as the dress had been made nearly three years earlier, and it accentuated Amy's well-rounded figure and tiny waist.

She had pulled back her hair at the sides and pinned it into a loose bun at the back of her head. Tiny wisps fell stubbornly loose, framing her heart-shaped face, but Amy felt satisfied with her appearance. She shouldn't let Angie's zeal for life annoy her — and she certainly shouldn't let her irritation make her miss the fun of the evening.

Amy stepped into the yard just as the fiddles began tuning up for the dance. Her father had hung several lanterns from poles and trees, and their light cast a hazy glow over the party. The light was so soft, so muted, that Amy felt as though she were in a dream.

She couldn't help but hear Angie's vivacious voice, though. Her twin stood with several girls her own age, telling them about the pink satin gown she wore. Amy sighed and turned toward the dessert table to help the older women cut pies and cakes.

"Amy!" a voice called out from the sea of people.

Amy was surprised to see Jacob Anderson, younger brother of Ed and Jack, pushing his way toward her through the crowd.

"Hello, Jacob." Amy smiled. "I didn't know you'd be here tonight. I thought you were still in Hays."

"I wouldn't have missed a chance to dance with you. My, don't you look pretty tonight. How come you won't marry me? We could run off to find our fortune in gold. You know they're pulling nuggets as big as sows out of the Rockies. We could have it all, Amy." Jacob took hold of Amy's elbow. "Come over here where it's quieter and talk with me a spell."

"Oh Jacob," Amy sighed. "I have a great deal of work to do. Ma counts on me to help out, seeing's how Angie's always so preoccupied." She allowed Jacob to lead her to the back of his family's wagon and accepted his hands on her waist as he lifted her to sit on the edge of the wagon bed. "I can't stay long."

Jacob stood in front of her, his boyish face illuminated by the glow of a lantern that had been mounted on the wagon. "You know how I feel about you, Amy." He took hold of her hands. "I can't stand not being around you and when you're not around, you're all I can think about."

Amy shook her head. Poor Jacob. He wasn't at all interesting to her. He was only a year older than her and so immature with his wild dreams of gold in the Rockies. "How you do go on, Jacob Anderson. How come you aren't taking after Angie, like your brothers?" Amy smiled, hoping to lessen the seriousness of Jacob's face.

He smiled sheepishly, not wanting to admit that he *had* been interested in Angie, but his brothers had threatened to skin him alive if he so much as dared to speak with her. "Don't you think your sister has enough beaus?" he said instead. Amy was every bit as pretty as her sister and she was always kindhearted, listening to his gold rush stories. That made up for a lot, Jacob reasoned.

Amy pulled her hands gently from his. "Jacob," she began, "you know I'm not interested in being courted by you. Why do you keep after me like this?"

Jacob pushed a hand through his blond hair and shrugged his shoulders. "I keep thinking it can't hurt to try. Sooner or later you're bound to come to your senses. Why you're already older than most of the unmarried girls in the county." He grimaced as he realized what he'd said. "I'm sorry, I didn't mean it like it sounded."

Amy laughed and pushed herself off the wagon to stand eye to eye with her suitor. "I know you didn't, Jacob. Don't worry, I'm not Angie and I couldn't care a fig how old I am. I won't marry anyone until I'm in love and know that it's the man God wants me to marry."

Amy left Jacob to contemplate her words and joined her mother at the food table. An array of pies, cakes, cookies, and fruit breads lined the long wooden planked table. Amy noticed that here and there someone had placed a cobbler or custard dish, and someone had even gone to the trouble of making a tray of fruit tarts.

"Did I see you with the youngest Anderson boy?" Dora was ever hopeful that Amy would find someone who interested her.

"Yes, Jacob proposed again, in a round-about way." Amy laughed. "And, I told him no, in a most definite way."

"One of these days, girl, you're going to have to settle down with someone." Dora reached out to caress her daughter's cheek. "But until you do I'm mighty glad to have you here with me. You're a blessing child, both to me and to your pa."

"I could never doubt that for a minute!" The masculine voice belonged to Tyler Andrews, and Amy felt her face grow hot with embarrassment.

"I've been looking all over for you," Tyler said with a grin, amused that Amy was so self-conscious, while Angie had boldly flirted with him through a half a dozen reels already. "Come share a dance with me and let me see if twins dance differently from one another."

Amy laughed. "I don't dance nearly as well as Angie. In fact, I quite often avoid the activity if at all possible." Her heart pounded in an unfamiliar way, and she noticed her mouth felt suddenly dry.

Tyler wouldn't be put off. He surprised both Dora and Amy by coming around the table to take Amy's hand. "I won't take no for an answer. Now, if you'll excuse us, Mrs. Carmichael, I intend to waltz with your daughter."

Dora Carmichael nodded and smiled as Tyler fairly dragged Amy toward the other dancers. Amy flashed a look over her shoulder at her mother. Dora shrugged in amusement at the stunned expression on her daughter's face.

"Maybe," thought Dora aloud, "just maybe he's the one." The thought gave her a great deal to contemplate as she watched the new circuit rider take her daughter into his arms.

Amy stiffened at the touch of Tyler's hands on her waist. She felt her hands go clammy and wished she'd remembered to bring her handkerchief with her. She was glad for Tyler's towering height, because usually she had no choice but to look directly into the eyes of her dance partner. With Tyler, however, she was granted the privacy of his chest.

"Relax, you'll do just fine," Tyler whispered into her ear.

But instead of relaxing, Amy felt a shiver run up her spine. Her stomach did a flip, and she felt weak in the knees. "I don't think I can do this," she murmured beneath her breath.

"Of course you can," Tyler said with knowing authority. "Look at me, Amy."

Amy's head snapped up at the command. Tyler's face was only inches from hers, and the look he gave her seemed to pierce her heart. She'd seen looks like this before, but usually they were intended for her sister.

She swallowed hard and unknowingly tightened her grip on Tyler's hand, as she stepped on his toe. She frowned. "I told you I wasn't any good at this."

Tyler laughed and whirled her into the flow of the other waltzers. "You dance perfectly well, Miss Carmichael. I fear it's my inept skills that caused your misplaced step."

"How gallant of you, sir," Amy said, playing the game.

"My pleasure, ma'am," Tyler teased, and Amy found herself relaxing almost against her will.

When the dance ended, Tyler suggested a walk. "You did promise to show me the orchards."

"I did?" Amy tried to remember. "Oh well, come along then."

Tyler took hold of her arm and allowed her to lead. As they passed from the warm glow of the lighted farmyard into the stark brilliance of the moon's light, Amy felt her breath quicken. She chided herself for being so childish. *Next thing you know,* she thought, *I'll be swooning!*

Tyler's large, warm hand securely held her arm to keep her from stumbling. He had no way of knowing, of course, that Amy knew this land as well as her own bedroom. He was being chivalrous, as she'd noticed him to be with everyone. Tyler Andrews, she told herself, was simply a gentleman; the caring way he treated her meant nothing special.

Familiar laughter rang out, and Amy and

Tyler saw a very busy Angie talking nonstop to a group of four or five men. She was flitting about inside a ring of suitors, as she made promises for upcoming dances.

"That sister of yours is something else," Tyler commented. Amy's response stuck in her throat. She'd always wished she could be more like Angie, and now even Tyler seemed to be as captivated with her twin as most men were. But before she could reply, Tyler continued. "You two are so different. Such a contrast of nature. I thought twins were supposed to be alike."

Amy giggled. The sound touched Tyler's heart with the memory of another tender-hearted woman. A young bride who'd only lived as his wife for a few months before losing her life to influenza.

Seeing Tyler's frown, Amy's laughter died. Her worried look made Tyler say, "I'm sorry. For a moment you reminded me of my wife."

"Your wife!" Amy nearly shouted the words. "I didn't know you were married." She was gripped with guilt for the thoughts she'd been having. Thoughts about how nice it would be to be married to Tyler Andrews. Now she'd coveted another woman's husband.

"I *was* married." Tyler put Amy's racing thoughts to an abrupt halt. "She died over ten years ago. We'd only been married four months when she caught influenza and died."

"I'm sorry." Amy truly meant the words.

510

She'd seen a great deal of death here on the stark, lonely plains of Kansas.

Tyler smiled the sad sort of smile Amy knew people to get when remembering something bittersweet. "Don't be. She was a frail thing and she was ready to meet God. I've learned not to mourn, but to rejoice because I know she's happy and safe. It was her fondest desire that I not wallow in self-pity and mourning. She even made me promise to remarry."

"I see."

"Losing her made me realize the void in my life. It was then that I decided to become a minister. Circuit riding just seemed to come as a natural way for me, what with the fact that I wasn't tied to one spot. It's been a good life, but I can see the time coming when I'll be ready to settle down to one church and one town." Tyler didn't add the part of his heart that said "and one woman."

"It would be wonderful if you could settle in Deer Ridge," Amy said, not thinking of how her words might seem to Tyler.

"I was just thinking that myself." Tyler smiled at Amy's blunt honesty. "What about you, Amy? Do you have any plans for the future?"

Amy laughed, the sound like music in the night. "You mean beyond today?"

Tyler felt his heart skip a beat as Amy leaned back against the trunk of an apple tree. Her face was lit by the white glow of the moon, and Tyler decided he'd never known a more beautiful woman in all his life.

"That was the general idea," Tyler whispered in a husky tone that was barely audible.

Amy smiled up at Tyler, knowing he didn't understand the Carmichaels' family joke. "I've learned to take it a day at a time. There's too much that's unpredictable in life. My grandmother used to tell me 'Never make plans beyond today!' " Her voice was soft, almost hypnotic, and when she fell silent, Tyler stood completely still, captivated by the moment and the feelings he had inside.

The night was unseasonably warm and the sweet scent of apples still clung to the ground and air around them. Amy couldn't understand why her chest felt tight every time she tried to breathe deep. Or why, when she looked at Tyler looking at her the way he was just now, she felt moved to throw herself into his arms. What kind of thought was that for a good, Christian girl?

Used to speaking her mind, Amy suddenly found herself blurting out a confession. "I don't understand what's happening to me. I feel so different. Ever since you appeared at the well, I just feel so funny inside."

Tyler refrained from smiling at this sudden outburst. He was amused to find a woman so innocent and unaware. Surely she must feel the same way he did. After ten years of loneliness, Tyler felt a spark of hope.

Amy frowned as she contemplated her emotions, and Tyler couldn't help but reach out and run a finger along the tight line of her jaw. At his touch, she relaxed. His fingers were warm, and she stood very still, hoping he would not take his hand away.

"Tyler, I . . ." Her voice fell silent, and she lost herself in his eyes. The moment was too much for either one of them, and Tyler pulled her against his huge frame, bending her ever so slightly backward to accommodate his height.

When his lips touched hers, Amy found herself melting against his broad, muscled chest. Molded there against him, Amy thought she would die from the flood of passion that filled her. Was this love? she wondered as his mouth moved against hers.

Tyler pulled away only enough to look deep into Amy's eyes. Amy suddenly realized that she'd wrapped her arms around Tyler's neck; the impropriety of romancing the district's circuit rider made her pull away.

"I'm so sorry." She backed out of his arms and found herself up against the trunk of the tree. "I didn't know, I, uh . . . I didn't mean to do that."

Tyler laughed and pulled Amy back into his arms. "Well, I did," he said and lowered his lips to hers one more time.

CHAPTER 4

Sunday morning dawned bright and clear, and the temperature remained warm. Friends from far and wide crawled out from tents, where they had slept on pallets on the ground, and lifted their faces to the sunlight. As the sun rose higher over the brown and gold corn shocks, the shadowy fingers of night disappeared.

Amy watched from her bedroom window. She'd had to spend the night with her sister, because Angie's room had been taken by several of the elderly women in the community, and Amy had had to endure Angie's account of Tyler's life until the wee hours of the morning. She couldn't explain to her twin that Tyler had kissed her, nor could she explain the feelings he had stirred inside her heart.

The fact was, Amy didn't know what to say or think. After all, Tyler Andrews was the new minister, and Amy was nothing more than one of his flock. Or was she?

When Amy finally came downstairs, she could tell by the way people were gathering up their breakfast dishes that the hour was late. Angie had long since departed, anxious to find Tyler and see how he'd fared the night before. Amy was glad she'd chosen to linger upstairs. She felt apprehensive, almost fearful of facing Tyler. What must he think of her after she had wantonly allowed him to kiss her, and not once but twice?

Amy didn't think she could sit in the congregation with family and friends, listening to Tyler Andrews preach, while all the while she was thinking of his kiss. Somehow, she must have led him on; after all, he was a man of God, and surely he had better self-control than she did. Tyler would have no way of knowing how grieved she was by her actions the night before, and Amy longed to apologize.

Amy purposefully avoided the busy kitchen and chose instead the quietness of the back sitting room. *Dear God,* she prayed silently, *I don't understand what happened last night and I don't understand the way I feel. I'm truly humiliated at the way I acted and I ask You to forgive me. I asked You long ago to send a strong Christian man into my life, a husband I could love for a lifetime. And* — she felt tears form in her eyes — *if Tyler Andrews is the man You have in mind — please show me. I don't*

*mean to be a naive and foolish child, Lord —
but like Pa sometimes says, "I need a good
strong sign — one I can't miss." Please God,
please don't let me feel this way towards Tyler
if he's not the one. Amen.*

Someone began ringing the dinner bell,
signaling the time to gather for the services.
Amy made her way out the back door of the
house and around to where the residents of
Deer Ridge were congregating.

She spied Tyler in the crowd, shaking hands
and sharing conversation with just about
everyone. She also noticed Angie standing to
one side of him, her eyes eating up the sight
of him in his Sunday best. Amy could almost
hear Angie's thoughts as she eyed the cut of
his stylish black suit. The string tie he wore
at the neck was secured with a tiny silver
cross, and beneath the creased edge of his
pant legs, his black boots were polished to a
bright shine. All in all, the massive man was a
fine sight.

Amy tried to slip past Tyler and Angie
without having to speak, but Angie didn't let
her. "I saved you a seat, sleepy head," Angie
said, taking hold of Amy's arm.

Tyler turned to Amy. Her long brown hair
was neatly pinned up, and the wispy strands
that fell in ringlets worked with the high-
necked collar of her blouse to form a frame
for her face. He looked at her for several mo-

ments before she allowed herself to meet his eyes.

"I thought you'd sleep right through breakfast!" Angie said. "And you tossed and turned so much last night, I thought I was going to have to kick you out of bed to get any sleep."

Amy turned crimson as she caught sight of Tyler's grin. She wanted to run to the safety of the house, but Angie's grip on her arm was firm, and her twin was already rambling on. "I never knew you to get so worked up over a get-together. I swear you mumbled all night long and fairly thrashed me to death."

Amy could no longer stand it. She turned to Angie and with very little charity, flashed her a look that produced instantaneous silence from her twin. Tyler wanted to laugh out loud, but didn't want to add to Amy's embarrassment. He loved the innocence in her eyes, and the knowledge that she'd spent as restless a night as he had gave him even more confidence that she was the woman to end his searching. Confident that God would show him in time, Tyler knew he could wait. After all, he'd waited this long.

"Ladies, if you'll take your seats, I'll start the service," he said with a tender glance at Amy.

Amy immediately relaxed. His look was almost apologetic. She couldn't figure out if the apology was for her sister's comments or for his actions the night before, but either way, he was kind to care. Amy had never known a man to be so considerate of her feelings.

The congregation fell silent when Tyler stepped forward. He'd refused to stand in the back of a wagon, as one person had suggested, for he knew he needed no extra height while he preached. Instead, he'd asked only for a small table upon which he could place his Bible.

Amy couldn't help but notice the way he cradled the beloved book. She could tell by the way he caressed the cover with his large calloused hands that this Bible meant the world to him. It was clearly his life's blood, and confirmation came in the powerful words that followed.

"People without God are nothing," he began. "They have no purpose, no destiny — no life. They are useless in matters of importance and worthless tasks are all they know." The words rang out loud and clear, and no one, not even the children, said a word.

"People without God don't know which way to walk, or where they're bound. They don't have even the slightest solid path to follow and they are lost from the one road that matters." Tyler's intense stare moved from person to person. As he made eye contact with the community people, he could see whose life was saved and whose wasn't, by the looks on their faces. Some met his stare with a confident nod; those were souls who'd clearly accepted the truth of the Word. Other's seemed to squirm uncomfortably at the contact he made; these knew the truth of the words but weren't following them. One or two stared in disinterest and seemed pre-occupied with other things; these souls were not yet open to the urging of God's Spirit or they'd chosen to ignore Him altogether.

When Tyler's eyes fell upon Angie, she straightened up in her seat and gave him a sweet smile. And then his eyes moved on to Amy. She was fairly on the edge of her seat, so hungry to hear the Word preached that she was oblivious to the fact that this was the same man who'd held her so intimately the night before. When Tyler's gaze met her eyes, he saw the need there. A need for God's Word — a need to hear the truth reconfirmed, over and over. A woman after the heart of God.

Tyler pulled his eyes from her face before continuing. "Jesus said, in John 14:6, 'I am the way, the truth, and the life: no man cometh unto the Father, but by me,' " Tyler paused to let the words sink in.

"Think about it, folks. Jesus made it real plain to the people of His time. But not only that; He made it simple and clear for the people of our time and for those whose time has not yet come. He's the only way. He's the only truth. He's the only life!"

The richness of his booming voice seemed

to penetrate Amy, and she began to tremble from the very power of the hand of God upon this man. Tyler Andrews was clearly God's chosen servant. Several people around Amy murmured an "Amen," or "Hallelujah," but Amy remained fixed and silent. At that moment, she longed only to be nourished upon the Word.

"You all have a purpose in life," Tyler was saying, "and if you aren't living that purpose, you're missing a very special pleasure that God has reserved just for you. Some of you know that purpose, others don't. Some of you share a common purpose, and others of you are fixed upon a solitary path. But that purpose, that way God has established for you, leads everyone in the same direction. It leads to His arms and to His very heart. It leads you home."

The silence that fell was nearly deafening. Amy felt a warmth spread through her body as she thought of walking home to God. Yes, that's exactly how it was to be a Christian. You had a definite direction and a path that was sure. Then at the end of your way, you got to go home to the Father — your very own Father.

"Do you know the way home?" Tyler asked the congregation. "Is your path clearly marked? It's a simple step to the right path and your heavenly Father is waiting at the other end of the road. He's waiting for you to come home."

Tyler offered salvation through Jesus to the residents of Deer Ridge, and Amy was deeply moved by the sight of grown men weeping in their acceptance. Women who'd struggled under the heavy burden of the loneliness and tension of prairie life gave up their loads and placed them at the feet of God.

After Tyler closed, the congregation lingered to sing and praise God. People gave their testimonies, stories Amy had never heard, stories that blessed her heart and gave her hope and reason to also praise God. This was why the calling of the faithful was so important. This was the fellowship of God's people that she had so sorely missed. These were her brothers and sisters, and how dear they were to her, how rich the love she felt for each one.

The gathering turned into a celebration again. After the services, leftovers from the night before were joined with a few new foods, and lunch was served. While they ate, the residents of Deer Ridge urged Tyler to return to their community as soon as possible.

"We've missed having a man of God in our town," the town's schoolmaster, Marvin Williams, said, shaking Tyler's hand. "When you come back, we'll use the schoolhouse for the services." There was a hearty confirmation from the crowd that had gathered around Tyler.

Tyler took out a small black book and pencil. "I can be here in three weeks on a Saturday. That's when I'll be back in this part of the district again."

"Then it's settled," someone called out from the group. The murmured affirmation was enough to confirm the entire matter.

As families began to pick up their belongings and wagons were repacked, Amy couldn't help but feel a sadness to see them go. Sometimes the isolation of the prairie wore heavy on her soul.

Rebuking herself for her attitude, Amy realized that she'd have little time to feel sorry for herself with all the work left to do to get ready for winter. Mentally, she began a list.

November was always butchering month. The men would be getting together to butcher the hogs. This was planned for the first true cold spell, and Amy knew that wouldn't be far off. Then there was the matter of the apple preserves, jellies, and butters that she still needed to put up before the apples went bad. Then they'd can some of the meat, smoke the rest, and make soap with the fat.

Amy moved around, picking up messes whereever they caught her eye, and continued to think of the things she needed to take care of in the weeks to come. She was so lost in thought that she hadn't been aware of Tyler's watchful eye.

When she looked up, though, her eyes immediately met his. He stood casually against a cottonwood tree, arms folded across his chest, a gleam in his eye. Amy glanced around, wondering where Angie was and why she wasn't captivating Tyler's attention.

A smile spread across Tyler's face, as if he could read her thoughts. She blushed and quickly lowered her eyes to the work at hand. Tyler, however, wouldn't allow her to get away that easy.

"I'd like to have a minute or two alone with you," he said, taking the dirty plates from her hand. He placed them back on the table and turned to her. "That is, if you don't object."

Amy felt her pulse quicken. "Of course I don't object," she answered. Her hands were trembling as she wiped them on her apron and allowed Tyler to direct her away from the crowded farmyard.

"I suppose you'll be leaving soon." She hated to say good-bye, but she knew it was inevitable.

"Yes," Tyler answered.

They walked past the new barn, and Amy realized that Tyler was leading her back to the orchard. As soon as they were well away from the noisy neighbors, he slipped his hand from Amy's arm and into her hand. They continued to walk in silence for several moments until they came to the spot where they'd kissed the night before.

"Amy." Tyler paused to look down into her face. "I have to say something to you before I go."

Amy felt her stomach tighten and her legs began to tremble. "All right."

He abruptly dropped his hand and turned away from her, as if he had something to say that was painful and distasteful. Amy twisted her hands together, burdened by the thought that perhaps he wanted to reprimand her for the night before. She waited, head bowed and hands clenched, while Tyler seemed to contemplate something of extreme importance. When he finally turned back to her, Amy couldn't bring herself to face him. She kept her head lowered.

He reached out and gently lifted her face. When he did, he saw her cheeks were damp with tears. "What's this all about?" he whispered softly.

Amy choked back a sob, certain that God was going to tell her Tyler Andrews was not the man for her. "I, uh . . . , I'm sorry," was all she could manage to say.

"Sorry? For what?"

Amy began to wring her hands, but Tyler took one of her small hands in each of his larger ones. "Have I offended you?" he questioned gently.

"Never!" Amy dared to look up into his compassionate eyes. The worried expression she saw there touched her heart, and silently she wished there was an easy way to apologize.

"Then what's the trouble?" Tyler asked.

"I was just afraid that *I'd* offended *you,*" Amy finally managed to say.

Tyler chuckled softly. "And how, my dear Amy, do you imagine you might have accomplished this offense?"

Amy swallowed hard, unable to concentrate on anything but the touch of his hands on hers. "I thought maybe you brought me out here to talk about last night."

"I did."

"Then I was right. I'm really sorry about acting so loose with you." Amy licked her lips nervously. "I'm really not generally so forward. In fact, Mother worried that I'd never take an interest in anyone. Honestly, that was my first kiss." Amy's honesty was telling Tyler a great deal more than she'd expected.

She continued to try to make amends. "Just please forgive me. I know you're a minister and all, but I guess I was just, well . . ." Her words drifted into silence. She really had no excuse for what she'd done.

"You think I brought you out here for a comeuppance? Is that it?" Tyler asked in a serious tone.

"Yes." Amy hung her head.

Tyler gently brushed his finger against her closed lips. "I'm responsible for what happened last night," he whispered. "Yes, it was a bit forward and I, not you, am the one who should apologize." He broke into a broad smile. "But I am glad that I was the first one to kiss you and," he added with a certainty that caused Amy to tremble anew, "I intend to be the only one who has that privilege."

Amy stared openmouthed for a moment, but then the real meaning of Tyler's words sank in. She smiled, realizing Tyler wasn't upset with her at all.

"You look so charming when you smile," he whispered, tracing the line of her jaw with his finger. "Then again, you look wonderful even when you aren't smiling."

Amy cocked her head slightly to one side and put her hands on her hips. "Just what are you up to, Tyler Andrews?"

"I just wanted a chance to tell you a proper good-bye." He grinned.

"Good-bye, then," Amy said with a hint of laughter in her voice. She started to walk away, but Tyler reached out and pulled her back. Amy couldn't suppress a giggle. Her heart was suddenly light; Tyler was obviously as interested in her as she was in him.

"Oh no, you don't," he said. "You must be a more mischievous person than I thought. I thought Angie was the manipulative one, always teasing with people's feelings and such."

Amy stiffened and felt her muscles go rigid. Her smile was replaced with a look of serious intent. "I wasn't teasing with your feelings, Tyler."

"I know," he replied soberly and added, "and neither am I."

"Three weeks is a long time," Amy murmured.

Tyler took her face in his weathered hands and looked deeply into her eyes for what seemed an eternity. "Three weeks is just a heartbeat, Amy. Just a heartbeat."

CHAPTER 5

By the end of the first week, Amy had put up seven quarts of applesauce, fifteen quarts of apple preserves, and twenty-four pints of apple butter. She also helped her father and mother with the butchered hogs. She stuffed sausage casings until she thought she'd drop, and she helped her mother hang so much meat in the smokehouse that not a spot was left to put even one more ham. When all that was done, she and her mother canned enough meat and vegetables to bulge the pantry shelves.

The second week she missed Tyler more than she had the first, but Amy plunged into anything that kept her mind occupied and her hands busy. She ripped rags into strips and braided them into rugs, then worked in a fury through her mother's great pile of mending, much to the amazement of everyone. She counted the days down and then dissected the days into hours and counted those, too.

Taking advantage of a clear but cold day,

Amy was boiling a kettle of lye for soap, when Angie came sashaying through the yard.

"Ma wants me to see if you need any help." Angie pushed out her lips in a pout.

Amy knew better than to solicit Angie's help. Angie was hopelessly clumsy at most every household task. Ma had said on more than one occasion that they'd all be lucky if Angie did move back east to a big city with servants.

"No, Angie. I was about to add the grease and you know how careful I have to be with the amount. I'd rather just work alone."

"Good," Angie said with a sudden smile. "Do you realize that Tyler will be returning in little more than a week? I've asked Ma to help me make a new skirt. I needed one anyway, but I think it will be glorious to wear it for Tyler the first time."

Amy bit back a angry retort and poured grease into the cauldron. She couldn't stand the way her sister was acting these days. Most all their lives the twins had been comfortably close — not like people thought twins ought to be, but close enough. They really had very little in common, but still a bond had tied them together. Now, though, that bond seemed to be fraying.

"And Betsey said she heard him telling Randy that he was quite taken with me," Angie said, dancing around the cauldron to keep warm.

Amy's head snapped up. "What did you say?"

"I said, Tyler told Randy that he was quite taken with me," Angie repeated.

"He said that?" Amy nearly forgot to stir the soap.

"Well, he didn't use my name, but Betsey said that Randy was certain he meant me." Angie ignored the look of displeasure on Amy's face.

Amy wiped the perspiration from her brow and continued to work over the fire. She was certain Tyler hadn't meant Angie. How could he after the things he'd said? She wished she could ask Angie for more details without arousing suspicion, but Angie would pick up her interest in a flash. Besides, Amy reminded herself, Tyler had voiced his own interests and they certainly did not include Angie.

Angie was growing bored with Amy's lack of attention. "I'm going back into the house. Ma will be here to help shortly," she finally said and turned to walk away. Then she stopped abruptly and came back to where Amy was working with the wooden tubs for cutting the soap. "I almost forgot, Ma said that we'll need about ten dozen bars of hard soap. She wants to give some to the Riggses since Anna Beth is due to have her baby any day. All the women in town have agreed to take care of something and we get to provide soap."

Amy nodded and tried to mentally calculate how much rosin she'd need to add to make the soap set up and how much soft soap she'd have left over for their other house cleaning needs. "Tell Ma by my best calculation that'll leave us with five barrels of house soap."

Angie nodded and went on her way, while Amy still worried about Angie's attraction to Tyler. She'd never really cared before about her sister's flirtatious ways, but now with Tyler in the picture her sister grated on her nerves like fingernails on a slate. What if Angie ruined everything for her? What if Tyler ended up liking Angie's fun-loving nature more than Amy's quieter one? Maybe she should tell Angie that she cared for Tyler. Maybe then Angie would leave well enough alone.

Amy remembered then a verse from the Bible: "The Lord shall fight for you, and ye shall hold thy peace." The words of Exodus 14:14 seemed to haunt Amy throughout the day and by nightfall she was thoroughly convinced that she should hold her tongue and say nothing to her sister about her feelings for Tyler.

When only two days remained until Tyler's return, Angie made an announcement that stunned Amy into an even deeper silence. "I've decided that I'm going to marry Tyler."

Amy slapped the bread dough she'd been

about to place into pans onto the floury board and began to knead it some more. She thrust her fingers deep into the soft mass again and again; Angie had stirred an anger inside her that Amy didn't want to acknowledge.

"I see," she managed to say at last.

Angie pulled up a chair, certain her sister would want to hear all the details. "His parents still live in Kansas City and that's perfect for me. I could go and live with them and maybe I could even convince Tyler to get a big church in the city and quit the circuit. I just know I'd love Kansas City."

"What about Tyler?" Amy found herself asking against her better judgement.

Angie laughed. For her, the situation was as fun as a good game of croquet. "Why, I'd love Tyler, too. What did you think, silly goose, that I'd marry a man I didn't love? I think Tyler is one of the greatest men I've ever known and I just know we'd be right for each other."

Just then Dora Carmichael entered the kitchen to find Amy nearly destroying the bread dough. "Amy, what in the world are you doing?"

Amy looked down at the sorry mess. "Sorry, Ma, I was a bit preoccupied."

Angie flashed Amy a look that demanded silence regarding their discussion, and Amy said nothing more.

"Mercy," Dora said as she pulled out a chair and sat down. "I'm feeling a bit peaked."

Amy placed a hand on her mother's forehead. "Ma, you've got a fever. You go on up to bed and I'll bring you some sassafras tea." Amy pulled her mother to her feet.

"I hate to leave all this work to you girls." Dora knew full well the load would fall to Amy.

"Nonsense, Ma. You're sick and you have to get to bed before the shakes set in. Do you think it's the ague?" Amy remembered her mother's bouts with the sickness.

"Can't rightly say that it feels that way, but time will tell. Better get the quinine anyway." Dora headed toward the stairs. "Angie, you make yourself helpful," she called over her shoulder.

Angie grimaced. "Ma must think I don't do a thing around here," she pouted, but Amy had no time to care. She had to tend to her mother, for she knew that prevention was crucial here on the frontier. If they were to have any chance at all of heading off a bad bout of ague or a serious fever of some other nature, Amy knew they'd need to work fast.

When Saturday morning arrived, Dora was still sick. She'd suffered with the shakes and fever for over two days, but Amy felt certain her mother was getting better now. The only problem, however, was that this was the day Tyler would preach in Deer Ridge, and Amy could not leave her mother alone.

When Charles came in to check on his wife, Amy assured her father that she'd see to everything. "Just go on to the services, Pa, and tell everyone hello for me." Amy tried not to sound too disappointed.

Angie had already put a deep dent in Amy's sense of well-being by prancing through the house wearing her new blue plaid wool skirt. Every other word was Tyler this, and Tyler that, and Amy thought she'd scream before the buckboard finally pulled down the drive for town, with Angie securely blanketed at their father's side.

When her mother was dozing comfortably, Amy went to stoke the fire in the stove. She couldn't stop the tears that flowed down her cheeks when she thought of missing Tyler's service. How cruel life was and how unfair.

She tried to pray, but her heart wasn't in it. Instead, she found herself whispering over and over, "Help me, Father, to understand. Help me to understand."

By midday, Dora was feeling well enough to sit in a chair for a while and take some beef broth. Amy knew this was a good sign and tried to feel more cheerful. She tried to chat lightheartedly with her mother, but Dora could sense that something was amiss. Amy assured her mother that nothing was wrong.

When the hall clock chimed four, she helped Dora back to bed and went downstairs to tend to the other household needs. Soon, she heard first the wagon, then Angie's animated laughter. Amy was anxious to ask her father what Tyler had preached on and hurried out to the barn, meeting Angie halfway.

"How's Mama doing?" Angie's voice was filled with real concern. No one could accuse Angie of not loving her family, despite her absorption with her own self.

"Much better," Amy answered. "She's napping now, but she was up earlier and even ate a little."

Relief passed across Angie's face. "I think I'll peek in on her and then I'm going to bake some muffins," she said and walked past her sister toward the house.

"Why in the world would you want to bake muffins, Angie? You know you hate to cook."

Angie whirled on her heel and put her finger to her lips, indicating that Amy should be quiet. Amy cocked her head slightly and then realized that her father was talking to someone in the barn. Angie hurried into the house, while Amy made her way to the barn in time to find her father and Tyler sharing a hearty laugh.

Amy's mouth dropped open. She had no idea he would accompany her father back to the farm and she looked down at her dress, realizing that it was stained and smudged from the ashes in the fireplace. She knew she must look a fright, but Tyler smiled warmly at her as though he'd genuinely missed her.

"How's your ma doing?" Charles asked Amy when he'd finished hanging up the tack.

"Much better, Pa. She's resting, but wanted to see you when you got home." Amy tried to keep her voice even. In truth, her nerves were rattled, all because of the smiling giant who stood behind her father.

"You've done a good job by your ma, Amy. I'm deeply grateful for your love of her," Charles said, reaching out to give his daughter a warm embrace. "I'm going to go see your ma now. Tyler, if you need anything, I'm sure this little lady will be happy to accommodate you."

Amy blushed a deep scarlet, and when her father was out of earshot, Tyler let out a hearty laugh. "Well now," he said with a teasing tone, "how about accommodating me with the same kind of greeting your Pa got?"

He crossed the distance between them and lifted Amy into the air to whirl her in a circle. "My, but I've missed you. How in the world can you stand there so calm and quiet? I wanted to give out a yell when I saw you there."

Amy had to laugh. "Put me down, Tyler." She said his name with pleasure. How she loved this man! Now that she saw him again, she admitted the fact to herself. She chided herself that she might be feeling a mere childish crush, but her heart told her otherwise.

Tyler allowed her feet to touch the ground, and his hands left her waist. How he'd missed her! But had she missed him, too? Tyler couldn't help but wonder. She seemed interested enough; she always responded positively to his touch, and she was honest to a fault. He knew he'd have only to ask her how she felt, and she'd no doubt spill her feelings. *But could she love me, could she really love me,* Tyler wondered to himself, *the way I love her?*

"So." Amy pulled away from Tyler's hold. Somehow she felt safer with some distance between them. "Why did you come to the farm today? I suppose Angie wouldn't have it any other way."

"Your sister does make it hard to say no," Tyler laughed.

Amy frowned, and Tyler couldn't help but notice the furrows that suddenly lined her forehead. She had been all laughing and smiles one minute and now she looked sad, almost miserable. Tyler had no way of knowing that Amy was contemplating Angie's plans to marry him.

A scream came suddenly from the house. Tyler and Amy whirled and ran across the yard. Smoke was pouring out of the kitchen door, and Angie stood screaming for help.

"Something's burning!" she exclaimed,

nearly hysterical. "Oh Amy, do something!"

Tyler and Amy shared a brief look, and then Amy moved past her sister into the smoke-filled kitchen. "Didn't you think to check the oven before you fired up the stove? I had your supper warming there and now it's burned." Amy threw a look back at Angie. "Don't just stand there crying, Angie, open the windows." She looked past her sister to the towering man who stood behind her and added, "Tyler, would you go upstairs and tell Pa what happened? I'll take care of this." She took a potholder in one hand and covered her mouth with the other in order to ward off the smoke.

In a few minutes, Amy returned outside to deposit the hopelessly burned food. Angie soon joined her after opening the windows to let out the smoke. After the smoke had cleared, Amy went to work fixing them something else to eat, while Angie took the opportunity to court Tyler.

Amy tried not to feel angry about things, but it was difficult. She kept worrying that Angie was using Tyler and that somehow he would come to care more about her twin than about Amy. She attacked a ham, slicing off thick pieces to fry on the stove, all the while considering how frustrated she felt playing second fiddle to her more rambunctious sister.

When she had mixed up a batch of muffins, she started to relax a bit. *If God wants you to have Tyler for a mate,* she reminded herself, *no amount of interference from Angie will matter.*

Outside, Amy could hear the wind pick up and felt a chilly blast, cold enough to merit closing the windows. Placing the muffins securely into the oven and checking to make certain the temperature wasn't too hot, Amy went around the house closing the windows.

She had just walked into the front parlor when she heard Angie's voice. Apparently she had taken Tyler to the front porch swing in order to share her heart with him. "It must be wonderful to see so many different places, but don't you ever get lonely, Tyler?" Before Tyler could answer, Angie asked him a second question. "I mean, don't you ever think of getting married again?"

Amy felt her ire rising at her sister's brazen behavior. Angie was being totally improper, even if Amy *had* wondered the same things.

Tyler's laughter caught Amy's attention, however, and she found herself eavesdropping to hear the answer to Angie's questions. Did Tyler get lonely? Did he want another wife? Angie wasn't as patient as Amy, and she prodded Tyler to speak. "Well?"

"I do get lonely, Angie. These open prairie plains are enough to do that to any man. And, yes, I do plan to marry again."

"I see." Angie thought a moment and then said, "Why don't we go into the parlor, Tyler? I'm getting a chill out here, what with the sun going down."

Amy heard the creak of the porch swing as its occupants got up. She had no recourse but to leave the parlor windows open and go out the back way. She wasn't about to have Tyler or Angie catch her listening to their conversation.

She hurried to the kitchen and pulled the golden brown muffins from the oven. They were plump, just barely crisp on the tops, and Amy knew they were some of the finest she'd ever made. She hurriedly placed them on the table and added bowls of plum jelly and freshly churned butter. Then she turned her attention to the ham steaks and put some potatoes on to boil.

Soon the table began to take on the look of a proper supper, and Amy felt satisfied that she'd worked through her anger. She loved her sister and hated to think anything could come between them.

Amy was just about to call her family to supper when her father appeared in the kitchen doorway. Behind him were Tyler and Angie.

"It's getting mighty late, Tyler. Why don't you plan on staying the night with us?" Charles Carmichael invited.

"Oh, do say yes, Tyler," Angie gushed. "I

do so want to hear more about Kansas City."

Amy glanced up, her soft brown eyes betraying her own desire for Tyler to stay. With a chuckle, Tyler sniffed the air. "How can I pass up the opportunity for such great cooking and company? My schedule's pretty tight, but I'd be happy to stay. Thank you."

"Well, it's settled then." Charles smiled. "I'll ready a room for you."

CHAPTER 6

Amy had more than her fill of Angie's fussing over Tyler. Angie hadn't really done anything improper, but Amy felt jealous of the control and confidence her twin boasted.

After clearing the supper dishes and putting the kitchen in order, Amy decided to retire to her room and leave Tyler to Angie's wiles. Going quietly to check on her mother first, Amy found that Dora was feeling much better. She gave her mother a dose of quinine and a drink of cold water and then sought out the sanctuary of her room. She was contemplating her feelings for Tyler and the promise she felt God had given her about waiting, when a knock sounded at her door.

"Yes?" Amy called.

"Amy, Carl Riggs is downstairs," said her father's voice from the other side of the door. Amy opened the door to reveal his worried face. "It's the baby, Amy. Carl thinks that Anna Beth is dying in childbirth. He needs you to come midwife 'cause Doc is out of town."

Amy smiled, trying to ease her father's worry. "Of course I'll go, Pa. But every man I've ever known thought his wife was dying in childbirth. It's probably nothing at all."

Charles placed his hand on his daughter's arm. "Carl says there's a great deal of blood, Amy."

Amy's expression changed immediately. "I'll get the birthing bag. Will you saddle the horse for me?"

"I can take you in the wagon if you like."

"No, there won't be time. I'll have to ride like all get-out as it is." Amy pulled on a heavy coat she used for outdoor chores. "I'll be downstairs in just a minute."

Charles nodded and hurried to saddle the horse for his daughter.

Amy grabbed what her mother had dubbed "the birthing bag." It held the supplies the Carmichael women had found useful over the years during childbirth chores. Amy knew it had a collection of herbs for easing pain and bleeding, as well as the routine tools necessary for bringing new life into the world.

She fairly flew down the stairs and ran headlong into Tyler. She was startled to find his hands reaching out to steady her.

"I think I'd better come, too," he said solemnly. "If the woman is truly dying, she may need me, too."

Amy nodded, her eyes worried. "It doesn't sound good any time there's a lot of bleeding." She glanced around the hallway for Mr. Riggs. "Where's Carl?"

"He went with your father to the barn. Come on and I'll carry this for you." Tyler took the birthing bag.

Angie stood by the door, looking helpless and without purpose. Amy turned to her, realizing her discomfort. "Angie, you'll need to care for Ma. I gave her the quinine just a few minutes ago, but you might want to look in on her shortly." With those few words, Amy redeemed her sister's obvious lack of nursing skill. With that behind her, Amy lifted her skirts and ran for the barn.

The Riggses lived in a two-room soddy about two miles from the Carmichael farm. Amy was off her horse and flying through the soddy door before the men had even managed to dismount. "Anna Beth," she called as she entered the bedroom.

Amy was shocked by the blood-drenched sheets and bedding. Anna Beth had to be bleeding a great deal to have soaked through the quilted blankets that had been placed on top of her.

"Amy Carmichael," a weak voice called out, "is that you?"

"It is, Anna Beth. Ma's sick in bed, so I'm here to help you with the birthing. We need to get these wet things off you." Amy started removing the quilts as Tyler and Carl entered the room.

"Dear God," Carl moaned at the sight of the blood.

"Carl, I need you to get water boiling on the stove. Then I want you to cut me some strips from any extra sheets you have. It's really important. I know you'd rather be here with Anna Beth, but I need you out there." Amy motioned toward the kitchen. "Can you do it?"

Carl nodded, almost relieved to leave the sight of his dying wife. Tyler stood fast in the doorway. "What can I do to help?"

"Oh Tyler, we need to get her out of all this blood. Can you lift her while I cut the nightgown away?" Amy pulled the last of the bloody quilts away.

"Just show me what to do."

Anna Beth's weak voice barely whimpered a protest, as the contractions ripped through her abdomen. Amy could tell by the flow of blood that the birth of Anna Beth's child would also be the death of her.

"Anna Beth," Amy called to the barely conscious woman. Amy shook her head, for in truth Anna Beth was barely a woman. Anna Beth Riggs was only sixteen, but on the frontier, adulthood came early and birthing was the ultimate arrival of womanhood.

Amy wiped the woman's head with a cool

cloth. She knew she could do very little for her. Amy's only real hope was to save the baby and pray that God would help the mother. But in order to accomplish even the delivery, Amy was going to have to pull the child from the birthing canal.

"Anna Beth, your baby is having a hard time being born. I need to help him," Amy said softly. She glanced up to meet Tyler's intense stare. He seemed concerned for Amy's well-being, as well as for the dying woman. Amy shook her head at him, for her own feelings could not possibly matter at a time like this.

"Amy, save my baby, please! Do whatever you must," Anna Beth whispered and then turned to Tyler. "Pastor, will you pray for us?"

"Of course, Anna Beth." Tyler took hold of the woman's hand. "Father, we lift up Your daughter, Anna Beth. She's fought a hard fight, Lord, and we ask that You ease her burden and give her rest. We ask for the safe delivery of her child and Your healing touch upon both. Steady Amy's hands to do what she must, that we might all bring You glory. In Jesus's name, amen."

Amy felt warmed by the prayer. She placed a hand on the struggling woman and patted her reassuringly. "Anna Beth, you just rest a minute. I need to talk to Tyler and tell him what I need him to do. I'll just be right at the end of the bed, so you won't be alone." The woman nodded, and Amy motioned Tyler to the foot of the bed.

"This won't be easy, Tyler. I'll need you to hold her down and still. I'll have to reach up inside and pull the baby down. It's not a pretty sight and it won't be pleasant work. Can you help me? I know Carl won't be able to stand it."

Tyler took hold of Amy's upper arms and held her firmly for a moment. "I'll stay by your side no matter the cost. You can count on me to be there for you." Tyler's words somehow seemed a promise of something more.

Amy nodded. "We must work fast or we'll lose the baby, too. It may already be too late."

Tyler and Amy took their places at the bedside, and Amy explained to Anna Beth that she had to hold as still as possible. "Tyler is going to help you, Anna Beth. It won't be very easy for you and it's going to hurt." Anna Beth nodded and accepted Tyler's hands upon her shoulders.

Amy rolled up a washing cloth and gave it to Anna Beth. "Bite down on this." Obediently, the woman heeded her instructions.

At Tyler's nod, Amy went to work. For the first time since their arrival, Anna Beth screamed, and then she lost consciousness. Amy worked unsuccessfully to rotate the breech-positioned baby and finally managed to pull the child out, bottom first.

547

The baby boy was stillborn.

Amy glanced down at Anna Beth, who was just starting to stir. The blood was flowing even harder now, and Amy knew no amount of packing would ever keep Anna Beth alive.

Anna Beth's eyes fluttered open. She looked first to Tyler, then at Amy. Amy pulled out a soft flannel blanket that Anna Beth had made for her baby and wrapped the child lovingly in its folds. She talked gently to the baby, as if it were alive.

Tyler stood by in utter amazement, not certain what Amy was doing. He watched in silence as Amy washed the tiny, red face of the infant and smoothed back the downy black hair on his head.

"Anna Beth," Amy said as she brought the infant to his mother. "Your son is a might worried."

Anna Beth perked up at the words that she had a son. "What is it, Amy? Can I hold him?"

"Of course you can." Amy placed the small bundle in Anna Beth's arms. "Does he have a name?"

"Carl Jr.," Anna Beth whispered, trying feebly to stroke the baby softness of her son's cheek.

"Anna Beth," Amy whispered as she stroked the woman's hair, "Carl Jr. is afraid to be without you. He wants to know if it would be all right to go on to heaven and wait for you there."

Tears fell down Anna Beth's cheeks, but Amy's remained dry. Her eyes revealed her pain, however, and Tyler longed to take her away from the death scene in the Riggses' bedroom.

"That would be fine, little boy," Anna Beth murmured to the baby. She cupped his cheek with her hand. "Mama will be right there. You go on ahead. Mama's coming soon." She glanced up and smiled at Amy. Her eyes were filled with a sad knowledge, but also with peace. "Thank you, Amy." She pulled her son close and closed her eyes. She sighed, glad that the pain was over. And then Anna Beth joined her son in heaven.

For several moments, no one said a word. Amy continued to smooth Anna Beth's hair, unmindful of her action. Tyler reached out and took Amy's hand from across the bed.

"Yea, though I walk through the valley of the shadow of death, I will fear no evil: for thou art with me," he recited.

Amy looked up into Tyler's eyes, grateful for his comforting presence. This was only her second time to deal with death in childbirth, and it wasn't any easier than the last time.

"Thank you, Tyler," she said. Letting go of his hand, she squared her shoulders. "I'll get the bodies ready for burial. Will you tell Carl?"

"Of course."

■ ■ ■

Nearly two hours later, Amy and Tyler left the stunned Carl and rode back to the Carmichael farm. They'd both tried to convince Carl to come back with them, but he wanted to be near his family. He'd requested that Tyler perform the funeral the next day and Tyler readily agreed.

At nearly two o'clock in the morning, they made their way across the open prairie. Amy was quieter than ever, and Tyler knew her mind was on Anna Beth and the baby.

"Childbirth is a risky thing," he said. "I sometimes wonder how a woman can bear a normal delivery, much less as much pain as that woman had to endure tonight."

"It's the joy of the child to come," Amy said absently. She smiled sadly. "I know I'm not a mother, but I've heard enough to tell their story. I think maybe it's the things that cost the most pain that are the things most worth having, the things that bring us the most joy."

"You believe that to be true about children?" Tyler's question seemed louder than he'd intended, somehow amplified by the vast expanse of the open plains.

"I suppose I do," Amy murmured.

"You only suppose? Don't you plan to have children, Amy?" After what they had witnessed tonight, he wouldn't blame her if she said no.

"Beyond today," Amy said, "I don't have any plans." She tried to laugh, making light of her life-long doctrine.

"Maybe that's because you've never had the right person to plan with."

"Maybe," Amy admitted. "But I feel God wants me to just take a day at a time. I think it keeps me better focused than looking at the big picture."

"What do you mean?"

Amy pulled her coat collar around her throat. The night had turned cold and a shadowy ring had formed around the moon. The air tasted like snow.

She could tell that Tyler's eyes were still on her. He was waiting for an answer to his question, and throwing caution to the wind, Amy decided to be honest with him. "Angie always has plans a plenty. She revels in them like some people glory in a large account of money. Angie knows what she wants in life, or at least she thinks she does. She wants to live in the city and have the world eat out of her hand. And believe me, Tyler" — Amy paused to look at Tyler's silhouetted profile — "she's used to getting what she wants."

"But what about you?" Tyler asked, frustrated by this talk of Angie when Amy's feelings were what concerned him. "What do you want?"

Amy smiled. "I want whatever God wants for me. I'm not always very patient, but I know His promises are rich. I don't want to miss out on a single one of His gifts."

Tyler's mouth curved. "That's a bit evasive, don't you think?"

"Perhaps."

The lights from the front room of the Carmichael farm were now in view. Just a few more minutes and they would be home. Amy felt the weariness deep in her bones. She felt as if she could sleep forever.

Silently, she braved a glance at the man who rode by her side. She was surprised to find him watching her with an unreadable expression on his face. Amy offered a weak smile.

"I'm glad you were with me tonight," she whispered and turned toward the barn.

Tyler sat back thoughtfully in the saddle. She was quite a woman, this Amy Carmichael, he thought to himself. In his heart, he knew she was much more to him than just another member of his flock.

CHAPTER 7

Charles Carmichael took one look at their faces and then shook his head sadly. He took his daughter's hand in his. "You gave it your best and God was with you, child. You mustn't blame yourself."

Amy leaned against her father and sighed. "I know, Pa. We tried to talk Carl into coming home with us, but he didn't want to leave them."

Charles nodded. "I don't think I would've left your ma either. He'll have to work through this in his own way. No one can grieve for you, Amy. No matter how many others shed their tears, the pain is still your own. We'll keep him in our prayers, and I'll ride over tomorrow and see how I can help."

"Thanks, Pa." Amy was too close to tears to say anything more.

With the horses cared for, Charles led them back to the house. "I'll show you where we put your things, Tyler." Tyler nodded and gave Amy a quick glance before following her father up the stairs.

"Don't forget to turn down the lamp, Amy," Charles called over his shoulder.

"I won't. Good night, Pa." Almost as an afterthought, she added, "Good night, Tyler."

In the empty downstairs, the silence fell around her like a cloak. Amy felt drained and cold in the aftermath of what had taken place. She went to the front room and stoked up the fire before easing her weight onto the sofa. Staring into the flames, she felt her composure crumble.

Tears fell down her cheeks, until she was sobbing quietly into her hands. Why did bad things happen to people who loved God? It seemed so harsh. So unfair. Why, if a person put their trust in the Lord, didn't He relieve their suffering and keep them from the horrors of the world?

Without warning, Amy felt herself being swept to her feet. Tyler's warm fingers took her hands from her face. Staring up at him with red eyes, Amy's tears began anew.

"Hush, it will be all right." He pulled her into his arms. Amy laid her face against his broad chest and sobbed.

Her tears raged for several minutes, while Tyler waited patiently for her to regain control. He stroked her hair and whispered over and over in her ear that it would be all right. The words, though plain and simple, were a comfort, not only for what they said, but because of who said them.

"I'm sorry," Amy murmured, finally feeling able to speak. Tyler's arms were still around her, and she wasn't ready yet to pull away from the safety she felt there.

"Don't be." Tyler pulled her with him to sit on the sofa. "You can't bear the pain for all the world."

"I try so hard to be strong. I want so much to be of some use to God," Amy whispered. "I guess sometimes I'm just not cut out for His work."

"Nonsense." Tyler's firmness surprised Amy. "God knows what each man and woman can bear. He knows how your heart breaks for those who suffer — but He knows, too, how He can use that pain in you to do the work of His kingdom. If your heart wasn't so tender, the Lord wouldn't be able to use you so much."

"It just seems so unfair." Amy allowed Tyler to pull her head against his shoulder. "There's a part of me that wants to cry out and ask why this thing has happened. There's even a part of me, I'm ashamed to say, that questions how God can allow folks to suffer so."

Tyler smiled, though Amy never saw it. Hadn't he himself had those questions, those doubts? "That's pretty normal, Amy. Everybody wonders at something, sometime."

"I don't know, Tyler." Amy pushed away to look him in the eye. "I feel so helpless. Life out here is so hard. Sometimes I wonder if Angie doesn't have the better idea — escape to the city and live a more protected life." Before Tyler could say a word, she continued, "But then, I see a sunrise across the open prairie or hear the coyotes when the moon is high, and I know I could never leave it. For all its unmerciful hardships, I'm at home here and here I'll stay."

The words brought a flood of emotion to Tyler's heart. For a moment he'd feared she'd tell him she planned to move away with the first man who offered her an easier life in the big city. Hadn't he just listened to that very plan from her sister's lips earlier in the day? Now, he felt relieved by Amy's declaration. He was more certain than ever that Amy Carmichael was the woman God intended him to marry.

Amy started to wipe her face on her apron but then noticed the blood stains. "Christ spilled His blood for us," she whispered. "Although He was a man, I think He must have understood the pain a woman feels in childbirth. He knew what it was like to bleed, to feel pain, to die while giving life to another. So why do I feel so discouraged and sad? That should be enough."

"It is enough," Tyler agreed. "Enough for our salvation and reconciliation with God.

But although our eternal life is safe and assured, that's no guarantee we won't run into pain and hardship in our everyday, physical life. Like everyone, we must endure hardships and trials, just as Jesus said we would. Remember?"

Amy frowned for a moment, trying to remember what scripture Tyler might be quoting. She shook her head when nothing came to mind and waited for Tyler to enlighten her.

"Jesus was preparing for His death when He told His disciples in John 16:33, 'In the world ye shall have tribulation: but be of good cheer; I have overcome the world.' He made it real clear that we will have trouble in this life of ours. But the good news is that He's already overcome anything the world can throw at us."

"That's all fine and well." Amy's lips pressed tight together. She sighed and then burst out, "Of course He overcame the world. He was God. He had the power and the ability to overcome anything He chose. I know it sounds selfish, but how does that help me? I still have to go through the trials and heartaches. How do I comfort myself or find ease from the pain when its Jesus that has overcome, not me?"

Tyler read the agony in her eyes. He touched her face gently. "Because He overcame, we have the power to do the same.

When we accepted Him as Savior, He came into our hearts. He became one with us, and now we share in His life. We share His suffering — but we also share His triumph. That's why He told us to be of good cheer. We're a part of Him now, and that means we've already overcome. We just don't realize it sometimes."

Amy stared thoughtfully into the fire for a moment before nodding her head. "Of course," she whispered. "That makes so much sense. How could I have thought He was being a braggart, when He was simply trying to bolster the disciples' courage?"

Tyler nodded. "That's right, Amy. He knew we wouldn't be able to bear the load alone. When He died on the cross, He bore the pain of the entire world. He knew all about Anna Beth and her little boy. And He knew how you would hurt tonight. He's already taken that load onto Himself. All you have to do now is let Him have it. You have to let go of the pain you're feeling." Tyler smiled. "It's a funny thing, but sometimes it's almost harder to trust God with the hard things in our life than it is to trust Him with the happier things. Believe me, I know."

Amy smiled and sat back against the sofa. "You make it so easy to understand. I think that's why I've missed having church and a regular minister so much. I read the Word every day, but so often its meaning eludes me. Thank you for being patient with me, Tyler."

"I think, Amy, that when it comes to you" — Tyler reached for her hand — "that I have an infinite amount of patience." He looked into her face. "Maybe we could pray about this together."

"Yes, please." Sudden joy leapt up from the depths of Amy's pain. How often she had dreamed of a man with whom she could pray about the sorrows and troubles of the day. A man who truly sought God's heart for the hidden answers and meanings to life's questions.

They prayed together silently, and then each shared their petitions aloud. Amy felt as though a revival of sorts was taking place just for them. For hours, in spite of the fact that dawn was fast approaching, they sat and prayed, talking about the mercies of God and their hope for the future.

Finally, Amy couldn't stifle a yawn, and Tyler pulled her to her feet. "Come on, sleepy head. You've had a busy night and you'd best get some sleep. From the sounds of the wind outside, I wouldn't be surprised to find a foot of snow on the ground by morning."

Amy had to laugh as she cast a suspicious glance at the mantel clock. "It's going to have to snow mighty hard and fast in order to meet that demand. After all, it's nearly morning now."

Tyler chuckled and pulled her along with him toward the stairs. "It could snow three feet by daylight, I wouldn't care one bit. I think I might rather enjoy being snowed in with you, Amy Carmichael."

Tyler's words very nearly came true. First light greeted the Carmichael farm with a raging blizzard that dumped snow on top of snow, burying everything in a blanket of white.

Dora was up and feeling better when Charles returned from the barn and morning chores. "My," she exclaimed, brushing snow off his shoulders, "but you look frozen clear through!"

"It's a bad one out there." Charles shook the worst of the snow from his coat before hanging it up on the peg by the back door.

Angie burst into the kitchen all smiles and sunshine. "Good morning." She nearly sang the words. Glancing around for Tyler and Amy, she suddenly frowned. "Where is everybody?"

"Well, part of us are right here," Dora chided her daughter. "As for your sister and the pastor, I don't know."

"Well, I do." Charles stepped out of his wet boots. "They didn't get back until late last night. Anna Beth and the baby died."

"Oh no, Charles." Dora's stricken expression matched her husband's heavy heart.

"Poor Carl. And poor Amy, having to deal with that alone. I should have been with her."

"She was pretty upset," Charles agreed, "but you know Amy. She held her ground. I wouldn't bother to wake up either one of them." He turned his eyes meaningfully toward Angie. "They need their rest."

Angie's lower lip threatened to quiver into a pout, but noting her father's stern expression, she managed to shrug her shoulders and leave well enough alone. Dora quickly put her daughter to work making bread, lest Angie change her mind and go about some type of noisy task. Angie was unhappy about the arrangement, but in light of her father's presence, she did as she was told.

Much to her surprise and pleasure, Angie found her patience rewarded when Tyler popped his head into the kitchen doorway nearly an hour later.

"Smells mighty good in here," he said with a grin toward Dora.

Dora was pushing bacon around the frying pan and looked up with a smile. "I thought you might be hungry. We've already eaten so you just make yourself comfortable at the table and tell me what you'd like to eat."

Tyler did as he was told and soon found Angie at his side. "Would you like some coffee?" she asked sweetly, eager to please.

"Sure would," he replied.

Dora barely managed to find out what Tyler wanted to eat, because Angie immediately monopolized him. Dora thought privately that their conversation seemed more like an interrogation than a conversation, with Angie in the role of interrogator.

At last Angie fell silent and sat looking dreamily at the man while he shoveled in forkfuls of Dora's scrambled eggs and potatoes. He squirmed a little under her steady stare, wishing she would turn her eyes somewhere else, but he didn't want to hurt her feelings. When she began her interrogation again, he tried to answer her questions when he could; if he didn't know the answer, she seemed just as content to move on to yet another subject.

At last, with hearty praise for Dora's fine cooking, Tyler moved from the kitchen. He allowed Angie to lead him to the front room where he'd spent most of the night talking to Amy. He couldn't help but think of her when Angie spread out her red calico skirt on the sofa and beckoned Tyler to join her there.

Leaning against the mantel, Tyler laughed. "I swear, Miss Angie, you have more energy than a woman ought to have."

Angie giggled and took his words as a compliment. "I do believe," she said, "that it's the company of one particular circuit rider that brings out the best in me."

This was the comment that a bleary-eyed Amy overheard from the doorway. She had thought to greet them both, but instead she backed away. Going to the kitchen, Amy found her mother taking fresh baked loaves of golden bread from their tins.

"Morning, Ma."

"Amy!" Dora set the pans aside. She hurried to her daughter's side and embraced her. "I'm so sorry about Anna Beth. I wish I could've been there to keep you from bearing that alone."

"I wasn't alone," Amy replied softly. "But I wish you'd been there, too. I keep thinking that maybe it was my lack of experience that kept me from saving them."

Dora pulled back with a shake of her head. "No. You have no power over life and death, daughter. Only God has that. Besides, you've helped in more births than I can even name. Sometimes, no matter how skilled we might be, there's just nothing we can do. Anna Beth was a mere girl. Obviously the whole thing was too much for her. We have to trust she and her baby are both in God's hands."

Amy nodded. "Tyler stayed with me and helped. I was sure glad he was there. He helped me afterward, too."

"Oh?" Dora felt hope flicker once again. She noticed the underlying softness to Amy's voice.

Amy nodded. "We stayed up and talked quite a while last night. Pa had shown Tyler to his room, while I decided to sit a spell and think on things. Pretty soon, though, I was blubbering like a baby — and Tyler was there to comfort me."

Dora hid her smile. "I see."

"Oh Ma." Amy had a look in her eyes that left her mother no doubt as to her daughter's heart. "The best part was that he knew just what to say and then he prayed with me. Not just a short little prayer, but he really prayed. We must have talked to God for over an hour before we got it all said."

Dora squeezed Amy's shoulder and offered her a chair. Saying nothing, the two women sat down to the table, and Dora reached out her hand to take Amy's. Through the hallway drifted Angie's laughter, causing a frown to form on Amy's lips. Glancing up at her mother, Amy suddenly felt a kindred spirit with the woman who'd given her life. Dora smiled sympathetically, yet it was something more than just that.

"You know, don't you?" Amy questioned. "You know what I'm feeling inside."

Dora nodded. "I've waited long enough to see you feel it. I knew when love came to you it would come like a rushing wind that knocked you off your feet and took away your breath."

"That's just how it is, too," Amy agreed. She found comfort in the fact that her mother knew her so well. Angie's boisterous laugh sounded again and Dora patted Amy's hand.

"Don't give it a second thought," she re-assured. "If God is for you, who can be against you?"

Amy nodded, finding comfort in her mother's words.

Hours later, the storm still showed no signs of abating. Tyler donned heavy boots and clothes to help Charles with the chores that wouldn't keep, while the womenfolk worked to keep the house warm and made sure that hot food and coffee were waiting.

Amy tried not to feel angry when Angie managed to control Tyler's time. She even bit back an angry remark when Angie set the table for dinner and placed Tyler between herself and Charles.

But by the time dinner was over, Amy had more than enough of Angie's brazen behavior and blatant designs. After washing the dishes, Amy managed to slip unnoticed to the back parlor. She sat down and considered her feelings in silence.

"I don't mean to be jealous, Lord. It's just that I can't hold a candle to my sister. I wish I could have more confidence like Angie, but it's just not me," she whispered aloud.

No, it isn't you, a voice seemed to whisper to her heart. Amy sat back and closed her eyes. Was God trying to speak to her? She relaxed for a moment, listening to the gentle silence, before feeling the need to say more.

"Forgive me, Father. I'm sorry for being so mean-tempered. Forgive me." She felt a peace spread throughout her body. She wasn't Angie and she'd never be as lively and vivacious as her sister, but that didn't mean God hadn't given her qualities of merit that were all her own. Qualities that she already knew attracted Tyler.

"All right, Father." She folded her hands in her lap. "What do I do now?"

CHAPTER 8

"Are you avoiding me?"

Amy's head snapped up, surprised that Tyler had managed to get away from Angie long enough to seek her out. She tried to choose her words carefully before replying.

"No," she answered finally. "I just figured your attention was pretty well taken." She bit her lip, immediately wishing that she'd said something else.

"Your sister does have a way about her, doesn't she?" He laughed and came closer to where Amy sat.

"She always has," Amy replied rather flippantly. The anger was starting to surface again, making her feel she was a miserable failure after all her efforts to put her bad feelings aside.

Tyler suddenly became aware of Amy's feelings. She was obviously put out with the way Angie had monopolized his time. Why hadn't he seen it before? Reaching out, he pulled Amy to her feet and encircled her in his arms.

"Don't you know yet?" he whispered.

"Know what?" Amy's voice was a bit breathless. His actions had taken her by surprise.

"It's you I care about, not Angie. It's you who's captured my heart." Tyler's eyes pierced Amy's facade of strength. Her mouth formed an O, but no sound escaped her lips. The sheepish curl of Tyler's lips widened into a full-fledged grin. "That's what I like best about you, Amy. You're unassuming and so innocent. You have no idea what you do to me. Why, just one look at those big brown eyes and my heart does flip-flops inside. I love you, Amy."

Amy was grateful for the arms that held her. Her knees felt like jelly and she was certain that she swayed noticeably at Tyler's declaration. "I think I'd better sit down," she said weakly.

Tyler stared at her with concern. "Did I say something wrong?" His worried expression steadied Amy's legs.

"No," she managed to say, her voice so hoarse that it sounded nothing like normal. "You said something very right."

"I had hoped you felt the same way. I know we're moving things pretty fast, but I feel like we've lived a lifetime of experiences in the few short times we've spent together. After last night" — Tyler sighed — "after last night,

I knew. I knew without a doubt that I loved you."

He'd said it again. Amy felt a wash of excitement and wonder flood over her. "I still think I'd like to sit down," she whispered, and with a smile that lit up his eyes, Tyler assisted her back into the chair.

Amy was elated by Tyler's words, but in the back of her mind a nagging doubt crept in to spoil the perfect picture. Angie! Tyler immediately noticed the change in Amy and pulled up a chair to sit directly in front of her. "You might as well tell me what's on your mind, 'cause I'm not going away until you do."

Amy grimaced and nodded. "All right," she said with a sigh. "It's Angie. She fancies that you're the one man who can get her away from small town life. She's set her cap for you, I'm afraid, and a more determined force you will never have to reckon with."

Tyler rubbed his chin thoughtfully and shrugged his shoulders. "I'm honored that she thinks so highly of me, but it doesn't matter. She's a nice girl and I realize you look a great deal alike, some might even say identical, although I've noticed some differences. Anyway, Angie's not for me. I've no desire to live in the city. I've done that and it chokes the life out of me."

"But don't you see," Amy pleaded, "this thing will be between us. I love my sister and

I don't want to hurt her. She'll think I worked against her, knowing what she had in mind for you, and that I stole you away from her. I can't have that kind of rivalry between us. I've fought too long and hard to avoid it."

"Is that why you don't have any other suitors?" Tyler asked softly.

"Yes, I suppose it is. The one man in this town who's paid me the slightest attention has only done so because his brothers forbid him to chase after Angie. You see, they both want her for themselves and refuse to have another rival for her attention." Amy couldn't believe she was sharing all of this with Tyler.

"I just don't want her hurt, Tyler," she stressed. "Angie's just being Angie and she really isn't trying to hurt me. She's just so used to me backing away from her conquests and leaving her to her designs."

"And what about this time?" Tyler asked with a raised brow. His face held a look of amusement that eased Amy's tension.

"This time, I'm not backing away," she replied in a whisper.

"Good," Tyler countered, "because I wouldn't let you if you tried." He reached out to hold her hand. "I can deal with Angie."

"How, without hurting her and making this an issue between sisters?"

"Leave it to me," he answered lightly. "I've had to deal with hundreds of mommas and their daughters. All who have set their strategies toward seeing me married. I've fought them off this long, I reckon I can handle one very lively Angela Carmichael."

Amy shook her head with a sadness in her eyes. "I don't think it will be that simple, Tyler. She's got a tender heart, in spite of her outward appearance of invincibility."

"Trust me, Amy. I will work this thing out so that it's Angie, herself, who loses interest. She'll cast me aside quick enough when she learns that I've no intention of living in the city or even moving close to one. When I make it clear that the open Kansas prairies are my home, she'll no doubt find a way to ease herself away from me."

Amy's face lit up. For the first time since this problem developed, she saw a way around having to battle with Angie for Tyler. "It just might work," she smiled.

"Trust me," Tyler said with a wink, "it'll work."

Amy made herself scarce for the rest of the day so that Tyler would have time to speak with Angie. Because of the storm's relentless tirade, the entire family was trapped inside the house through the whole long day; Tyler would surely have plenty of opportunities to get his message across to Angie.

When suppertime came, Amy joined her mother in the kitchen to help prepare the meal. Angie wandered in, seeming rather dejected, and Amy felt certain that Tyler had made his plans known to her.

"Angie, you can set the table while Amy cuts this bread," Dora said, noticing that Angie was just moving about aimlessly.

Angie did as she was told, setting the plates absentmindedly on the red checkered tablecloth they used for every day. Soon, Dora was calling the men to supper, and Amy found herself privileged to sit beside Tyler, while Angie quietly ate her dinner beside their mother. Apparently, Tyler's plan had worked.

After supper, everyone gathered in the front parlor to talk and share stories of days gone by. Charles and Tyler shared a game of checkers, while Amy and Dora worked on quilt blocks. Angie excused herself to her room, much to everyone's surprise. Everyone except Amy, who knew that her sister had seen her dreams defeated in one swift blow. Her heart ached for her, and silently Amy prayed that God would send a man for Angie. One who would understand her needs and love her.

The wind died down around eight-thirty, and Amy found herself so tired that she, too, decided to excuse herself. Dora put aside her sewing and, with a nod to her husband, expressed her desire to also retire.

Charles stood and put a loving arm around

his wife. "It's been a real joy having you here, Tyler. I'd like nothing better than if we could find a way to keep you on full-time as our parson. I intend to speak to the townsfolk and see if they aren't of the same mind. Do you suppose you might be interested in settling down in a tiny town like Deer Ridge?"

Tyler cast a quick glance at Amy and then smiled broadly at Charles and Dora. "I might be persuaded."

Charles laughed. "Somehow I thought you might be willing to consider it." With that, he and Dora went upstairs, leaving Amy and Tyler to follow.

Amy took one of the oil lamps and handed it to Tyler. "In case you want to read," she said and moved to extinguish the other lamps.

With nothing more than the soft glow from the fireplace and the lamp that Tyler held, Amy turned to study him for a moment. "Thank you," she finally said. "Thank you for caring and helping Angie through this."

Tyler moved forward and put an arm around Amy's shoulders. "I simply told her the truth," he answered. "I told her my heart could never be in the city."

Amy smiled knowingly and climbed the stairs with Tyler at her side. At the top, they stood for a moment before Tyler placed a brief kiss on Amy's mouth.

Amy felt a happiness like she'd never known, and her expression clearly revealed her heart. Without words, she went to her room, while Tyler moved in the opposite direction to the guest room.

"Thank You, God," she whispered against her closed bedroom door. She hugged her arms to her breasts and smiled, knowing that tonight's dreams would be the sweetest of all.

By morning the weather had cleared, leaving pale blue skies and sunshine against the snow-white prairie fields. Huge drifts of snow had piled up against the house, barn, and fences. Anything that stood out as an obstacle to the blowing snow found itself insulated in white.

Tyler shared morning devotions with the Carmichaels before announcing his departure. Amy was happy to see that Angie was acting more like herself and smiled when her sister spoke of the Anderson brothers for the first time in weeks. Tyler was happy to see the recovery of Angie's lively spirit, as well. He'd felt confident that he could disinterest Angie in him as husband material, but like Amy, he was worried that she might somehow place the problem between her and her sister.

"When will you be back our way?" Charles asked, while Dora began clearing the breakfast dishes from the table.

"I plan to spend Christmas here," Tyler replied. "That is, if you think folks around here will approve."

Charles laughed. "I think they'll more than approve. It'll be our first Christmas with a real parson in charge. I'll see to it that plans get made for a real celebration. We'll have the kids put on a play or something and the ladies can all make those goodies we enjoy so much."

"I'll look forward to it then," Tyler said enthusiastically.

"Where are you headed after you leave here?" Dora asked. "I'd be happy to pack you some food for the road."

"I'd appreciate that, Dora. I promised to stop by the Riggses' place for the funeral. With this snow, I doubt many folks will be able to get away, and it will be difficult at best to make a proper grave. I want to offer Carl as much help as I can."

"Of course," Dora replied. "I don't imagine we'll be able to make the funeral." She glanced up to see her husband shake his head.

"I don't see how," Charles agreed. "I'm still not sure what kind of damage the storm has done. If we can, we'll go over later on and see what kind of help we can offer."

Amy remained silent throughout the exchange. She hated the idea of Tyler leaving, and yet what else could he do? That was his job and if she were to marry him, it would be a big part of her life as well.

The thought of marriage to Tyler made Amy smile, and without her realizing, the attention of everyone in the room turned toward her.

"Looks like Amy's already a world away," Charles laughed.

Dora nudged her husband good-naturedly. "Now, leave her be, Pa. She's just day-dreamin'."

Amy blushed and lowered her head. No doubt they all knew full well what she was thinking about. Angie was the only one who seemed not to notice.

"Well, I for one will be glad when winter is over," Angie declared, moving to wash the dishes.

"Winter's just set in, Angie," her father mused. "You'd best just set your mind for a few more months of cold."

Tyler laughed and got to his feet. "I'd best get a move on."

Dora set about to make sandwiches for him to take along, while Amy packed some ginger-snaps and sugar cookies. She was glad for some task to occupy her hands; otherwise, she feared she'd just sit and twist them until everyone knew she was upset and asked her why. Surprised by the flood of emotions that threatened to run out of control, she silently prayed that she'd not cry when Tyler departed.

When the moment did arrive, everyone bid Tyler farewell and managed to inconspicuously disappear, leaving Amy and Tyler alone.

"I'll miss you," Tyler said, pulling on his heavy coat. Amy nodded, afraid to speak. She lifted her eyes to his and saw the love shining clear. Mindless of proper manners, Amy threw herself into Tyler's arms and clung tightly to his broad frame.

"It won't be that long," Tyler whispered against her buried face. "And when I come back, I intend to ask you something quite important, so you'd best be ready to give me an answer."

Amy lifted her face to his and nodded. "I'll be ready," she replied. "I promise."

CHAPTER 9

Amy felt a giddy anticipation in the days that followed Tyler's departure. She missed him terribly, yet she felt as though she shared a private secret with him. Over and over, she remembered his words to her when they said good-bye, and she was certain that when he returned, he would ask her to marry him.

The snow kept them homebound for five days, but then a warm southerly breeze blew in and melted most of the drifts. Soon soggy brown puddles were all that remained. During the thaw, the twins' older brother Randy arrived to announce the birth of his new son.

"He's a big one, for sure," Randy boasted. "I measured him myself and he's pert near twenty-three inches long."

"My," Dora remarked in amazement. "He is good-sized."

"Congratulations, son." Charles gave Randy a hearty slap on his back. "How's Betsey doing?"

"She's fine. Tired, but fine. Doc was there

this morning and said she needs to get plenty of rest. Other than that, he thinks both of them are good and strong."

"I'd be happy to come keep house and tend the children," Amy offered her brother.

"I was kind of hoping you might say that," Randy said with a smile. "I know it'd be a real peace of mind to Betsey. She doesn't trust me in her kitchen."

At this the family laughed. Even Angie teased him good-naturedly, "You must take after me."

"Naw," Randy teased right back, "nobody is as bad as you are in the kitchen. At least I can make coffee."

Amy smiled, remembering the day Angie had filled the house with smoke when she had tried to impress Tyler with her culinary skills.

"He's got you on that one, Angie," Charles laughed. Then turning to Amy, he said, "You'd best get your things together."

Amy nodded and hurried upstairs. She was grateful for the job that awaited her, knowing that it would keep her mind occupied until Tyler returned.

She calculated the days left until his return, and then she smiled again. Maybe she'd even be married before the year was out! The idea warmed her like a toasty quilt. She hugged her arms around herself, imagining what Tyler would say when he saw her again, and then she laughed out loud at herself when she realized what she was doing.

"I'm always telling folks to take one day at a time — but ever since Tyler's come into my life, it's all I can do to keep from dreaming away my days," she said aloud. "Maybe Tyler was right. Maybe I found it easy to keep from planning beyond today, because I had no one to plan for or with."

She threw the things she would need at Randy's house into a worn carpet bag. Then she headed downstairs to join her brother. She determined in her mind to take life one day at a time, just as she always had before she met Tyler, but her heart was already rebelling at the idea.

In the weeks that followed, Amy found that caring for Betsey and the baby was the easy part of her responsibilities. The hard part was keeping Charlie, Petey, and Dolly amused. Blustery winter weather confined them to the house, and out of boredom, they insisted on constant attention.

Amy tried to fuss over each one of them. She took great joy in getting to know the newest Carmichael, baby Joseph whom everyone already called Joey, but she tried to remember that the needs of the other children were just as important as the baby's. Dolly, used to being the youngest, had her nose slightly out of joint when it came to sharing attention with her baby brother. She didn't want to give up without a fight the important job of being the family baby.

Amy soothed her niece by telling her it would be far more fun to help with Joey, than to cry over the attention he got. Dolly was a bit young to understand logical reasoning, but Amy found a sugar cookie usually helped matters greatly.

Petey and Charlie were intrigued with the ruddy-faced bundle, but the attraction wore off quickly. Soon they were begging to bundle up and go outside, and then they tracked in mud and snow from their outdoor adventures.

Before long, Betsey was up and around, and the need for Amy to stay lessened with each passing day. Finally, when Christmas was only a week away, Amy bid them good-bye and headed home.

"Only a week," she told the horse on their journey to the Carmichael farm. "Only one more week and Tyler will be back."

The horse flicked his ears and plodded faithfully along the soggy prairie. Amy gazed out across the fields and sighed. The land was so open here, so vast and empty, yet life was only asleep; Amy knew when spring arrived the prairie would come to life once again.

Even the gray skies overhead could not dampen her spirits, and Amy found herself humming a tune. She loved thinking about a life with Tyler. She wondered where they would live and whether she would travel with her husband on his circuit. Most circuit riders rode alone, she thought, and frowned at the lengthy separations their wives must know.

Maybe Pa will talk the town folks into giving Tyler a job right here, she thought. *Especially if we're married.* The idea pacified her concerns, and Amy's thoughts turned to what she'd do once she arrived home.

She rode into the yard just before noon and found an animated Angie awaiting her. They walked together to the barn, but when Amy prepared to unsaddle her horse, Angie reached out to stop her.

"I was hoping you'd ride into town with me," Angie said. "I haven't done much Christmas shopping, and now there's only a few days left."

Amy froze, realizing that she'd not prepared anything for Tyler in the way of a Christmas gift. What should she do for him? Should she make something or purchase some trinket at Smith's General Store? Her mind raced with ideas, totally blocking out Angie's ramblings.

"You aren't listening to me!" Angie exclaimed at last.

Amy stroked the horse's mane and sighed. "Sorry, Angie. I was just thinking about what you'd said. I managed to make something for Ma before I left, but I don't have a thing for Pa or you." She carefully didn't bring Tyler into the conversation.

"Then you'll go with me?" Angie asked hopefully.

"Sure." Amy smiled. "Let me get my money and a bite to eat, and I'll be ready."

Angie flew into the house to tell their mother what the girls had planned. Angie even made a sandwich for Amy in order to hurry things along.

The girls rode side by side, saying little until they neared the small town of Deer Ridge. To call it a town seemed a bit of a boast, but it was all they had and Amy loved it. The handful of buildings made up what folks affectionately called "Main Street." On one side stood the general store and bank, along with several smaller establishments, including the barber shop and Doc Taggert's place. On the opposite side of the street was Nathan Gallagher's law office, the livery stables and blacksmith's shop, and farther down from this was the new school building. Opposite the school building at the other end of town was the hotel/boardinghouse.

Smith's General Store was the main attraction for the small community, however. Folks gathered here to discuss the weather and crops, new babies and deaths, and whatever else came to mind. Socializing wasn't an everyday occurrence, it was a luxury, and if one had to make the trip into town, he or she had the responsibility of bringing back all the news that bore repeating.

Tying their horses to the hitching post, Amy and Angie pulled their coats closer as a blast of frigid prairie wind pushed them along. "Pa says it's going to snow tonight for sure," Angie said with a shiver.

"He's usually right about those things," Amy replied and added, "so we'd best get to it and get back home."

Angie paused for a moment outside the clapboard storefront. "Uh, Amy," she said hesitantly.

Amy turned and eyed her sister suspiciously. "What are you up to, Angie?"

"Nothing," Angie hedged, "it's just that I saw Nathan go into his office across the way and I thought, I mean . . ."

"Go on and see him." Amy shook her head. "You and I neither one will enjoy this trip if you don't attend to all of your beaus. I'm sure Ed Anderson will be slighted if you don't make the rounds to the bank as well."

Angie laughed and gave her head a toss. "I don't care if he is. He hasn't been to see me in over a week."

"And Nathan has?" Amy teased.

"Well, no," Angie admitted. "But Nathan's practice keeps him busy."

Amy had to laugh at the idea of an abundance of law work in Deer Ridge. "The idea of a railroad spur coming this way is the only thing that keeps Nathan Gallagher busy. Tell them all hello for me," Amy replied. She left Angie contemplating her words.

Inside the store, the potbelly stove was nearly glowing red from the hearty fire that Jeremy Smith had built to keep his customers warm. Several of the community's prominent members stood discussing important matters when Amy entered. The gentlemen tipped their hats, and the only other woman, Mrs. Smith, came quickly to Amy's side.

"Land sakes, child, whatever are you doing out on a day like this? Come get warmed up." The gray-headed woman pushed her way through the men, dragging Amy with her to the stove.

"Angie and I needed to do a bit of last minute shopping. You know," Amy whispered in the woman's ear, "for Christmas."

Betty Smith nodded and shared the excitement of the moment with Amy. "Who are you still shopping for?"

"Pa and Angie," she said right away, and then with a quick glance around her to make certain no one could overhear, she added, "and the new pastor."

Betty smiled, revealing two missing teeth. "I heard tell he'd spent a deal of time out your way. Is there something I should know about you and him?"

Amy blushed and lowered her head. "No, but when there is, I'll let you know."

"Why, Amy Carmichael!" the woman exclaimed a bit louder than she'd intended. Ears around them perked up, so Betty pulled Amy away from the crowd and toward the back of the store. "I'll bet your ma's plumb tickled pink. She's always a frettin' that you'd never find anyone to settle down with."

Amy felt her face grow even more flushed. Did everybody have to know her business? Seeing her discomfort, Betty began showing Amy some of the trinkets they'd stocked with Christmas in mind.

"That silver mirror is pretty," Amy said and immediately thought of Angie's love of primping. "I'd imagine my sister would like that very much."

"Where is Angie?" Betty asked, setting the mirror aside.

"Oh, you know Angie. She had to make the rounds."

Betty laughed, because she did know Angie and her love of flirting with half the town.

Amy continued to shop for the next half hour or so before finally settling on the mirror for Angie and a brass-handled jackknife for her father. Buying a gift for Tyler proved to be an easy task when Amy spied the newest collection of books. Tyler had mentioned his love of reading, and with this in mind, Amy quickly sorted through the stack and picked out Dickens's *A Tale of Two Cities.*

Thumbing through the book, Amy remembered her father telling about a series of public readings that Charles Dickens had performed in America. The man had taken the country by storm, and his works were quite popular.

Tucking the book under her arm, Amy glanced around to see if Angie had returned. Most of the other customers had filtered out, and now, with the exception of the self-appointed Mayor Osborne, who was in a heated argument with Jeremy Smith, the store was empty.

"Betty?" Amy called into the back room where she'd seen Betty take her other purchases.

The woman emerged with two brightly wrapped packages. "I thought this might dress them up a bit," she said proudly. "And don't be fretting that I'll charge you, 'cause I won't. I just happened to have it left over from my own things."

"Oh Betty, it's wonderful. Thank you!" Amy held out Tyler's book. "I'm going to take this as well. I'd be happy to pay for it to be wrapped."

"This for the pastor?" Betty asked with a grin. Amy nodded and waited while the woman disappeared into the back to wrap the book.

When she'd paid for her things and Angie still had not appeared, Amy could do nothing but try and find her sister. She tucked her gifts into one of the saddle bags, then made her way across the street to Nathan Gallagher's office.

Opening the door to the law office, Amy peeked in. No one was in the outer room, and she saw no sign that Angie had ever been there. Amy started to step out when she heard voices coming from the other room. Thinking that Nathan and Angie were talking in his office, Amy quietly moved to the door and started to knock.

Her hand was nearly against the wood when she heard Nathan's voice bellow, "I don't care what you think! We'll take the bank money on Christmas morning when that fool of a pastor is teaching the town about charity and love."

Amy's heart pounded harder, and she froze in place. Her hand was still lifted to knock, but for some reason she couldn't bring herself to move.

"Gallagher, you're a hard man," a voice commented. "I guess I'll take my share and be on my way. You can do this job on your own."

"Have it your way, but go out the back door. I don't want anyone seeing you." Nathan's voice was clearly agitated. "Oh, and here." Amy heard a clinking thud as something hit the floor. "Don't forget your money."

The other man grumbled, and then she heard the sound of a door being opened and closed. Amy hadn't been able to bring herself to move, but she suddenly realized what a precarious position she'd placed herself in. She backed away slowly from the closed door.

She'd made it halfway to the front door, when she stumbled into a spittoon and sent it crashing over with a resounding clang. Nathan was through the door in a heartbeat, staring dumbfounded at Amy. He tried to decide for a moment whether she was coming or going, but Amy didn't give him any time to figure it out before she turned to run for the door.

He was on her before she'd taken two steps, gripping her wrist with his steely hand and dragging her back to his office for privacy.

"What are you doing here, Angie?" he asked, mistaking her for her sister.

"I, I . . ." Amy tried to speak but the words wouldn't come.

"What did you hear?" Nathan shoved her into a chair.

Amy shook her head. "Nothing. I came here to find my sister."

"What would Amy be doing here?" Nathan frowned and then his eyes narrowed. "You're not Angie." His words seemed to hang forever on the air.

"Yes," Amy finally admitted. "Angie and I were shopping and she said she was coming to visit you. I was just trying to find her so that we could go home." Amy timidly came up from the chair, only to have Nathan whirl around and slam her back down.

"Stay there!"

Amy trembled, but she did as she was told, while Nathan moved quickly to lock his office door. She cast a quick glance toward the back door, knowing if she could somehow make it there, she'd be safe.

Nathan came back to where she sat, putting himself between her and freedom. He rubbed his jaw for a moment and stared at her, his hard eyes boring into her face. "You know, don't you?"

Amy tried to look innocent and shook her head. "Know what?"

"Don't play games with me, Amy. You aren't going to ruin my plans. I can't have you out there bringing the town down on me. You overheard my plans or you wouldn't be so afraid of me."

"I'm wasn't afraid until you grabbed me and dragged me in here," Amy said angrily. "I don't know why you're treating me like this, but when my pa and brother find out, you won't have time to worry about any plans you've made." She prayed he'd be convinced that she hadn't overheard his conversation

590

with the now absent stranger.

Nathan moved away from her, thinking. As a lawyer, part of his job was to study men and what they had to say, determining whether or not they were telling the truth. He had to admit, Amy Carmichael was either a very good actress or she truly hadn't overhead his plans. Still, if she hadn't heard him talking, why was she running from him?

When Nathan turned his back to retrieve a drink he'd poured earlier, Amy bolted for the back door. She had managed to get it open before Nathan slammed her against it.

"I won't say anything!" Amy exclaimed without thinking. Nathan was twisting her arm behind her so violently that she thought she'd pass out from the pain.

"I thought you didn't know anything," Nathan sneered. "How can you say anything about something you didn't hear?"

Amy knew he'd caught her and she hung her head in dejection. "What are you going to do with me?"

"That, my dear, does present a problem," Nathan said, pulling her back to the chair. "I have no desire to kill anyone over a matter of a mere several thousand dollars. Still" — he paused to push her into the seat — "I won't have you mess this up for me."

Amy said nothing, waiting and watching while Nathan contemplated her fate. "I suppose," he continued, "if I can keep you out of the way until after the job is done, I won't have to kill you."

Amy blanched at his statement, making Nathan laugh. "Don't worry, little Amy. You just cooperate with me and I'll figure this out. Otherwise — well, let's just say, it won't be a merry Christmas at the Carmichaels'."

CHAPTER 10

Amy struggled against the ropes that bound her hands and feet. She tried to yell, but the gag Nathan had placed firmly over her mouth muted any sound that came from her throat.

Quieting for a moment, Amy listened to hear if Nathan was still in the building. He had dumped her in the storage closet with orders to keep quiet or else. When he told her he had to get her horse out of sight, Amy knew he meant business; she could hardly believe this was the same man who had courted Angie. "Please," she had tried to say through the gag, but Nathan locked the closet door and left her alone in the darkness.

He had tied her hands tightly behind her back so she would have no chance of freeing herself. Nevertheless, Amy worked at the ropes until her wrists were chafed and sore. She felt her eyes fill with tears, but she refused to give in to her misery. Somehow, she had to get out of this.

■ ■ ■ ■

Angie finally made her entrance into Smith's General Store, only to find Amy already gone. Betty assured her that Amy had gone in search of Angie when her shopping was completed, so Angie took the time necessary to finish her own Christmas shopping, certain that Amy would return any minute. When she didn't, Angie started to get worried. After paying for her things, Angie went outside and looked up and down the street.

The sun was already well to the west, and Angie knew they'd stayed a great deal longer than they should have. Noticing Ed Anderson as he came out to lock up the bank, Angie ran toward him.

"Ed, have you seen Amy?" she asked breathlessly.

"Angie!" Ed grinned. "Why didn't you tell me you were coming to town?"

"Didn't know myself until just today," Angie replied. "I'm looking for Amy. She rode in with me to do some shopping, but now I can't find her."

Ed laughed. "Deer Ridge isn't that big. She must be around here somewhere. Did you check over at the post office — or maybe Miller's Hotel? You know how Mrs. Miller likes to visit."

"You mean gossip — and no, I hadn't

checked there." Angie smoothed her hair and smiled up at Ed, but her lips were still tight with worry. "I was visiting with Mrs. Miller earlier, myself. Maybe Amy and I just crossed paths."

"That's probably it," Ed agreed. "Would you like me to walk with you over to the hotel?"

The worry eased from Angie's face. Ever the flirt, she batted her eyes and extended her arm. "I would simply love it!"

Passing by the store again on their way down Main Street, Ed noticed the solitary horse that stood outside. "You girls didn't ride double, did you?"

"What are you talking about, Ed?"

Ed pointed toward Angie's horse. "You said you rode in together. Did Amy ride her own horse?"

"Yes, yes, she did," Angie replied. She shrugged her shoulders. "Maybe she was mad at me for taking so long and she got tired of waiting for me. I'll bet she rode on home without me. That would figure."

"Sure would." Ed laughed. "I guess the joke's on you for taking too much time visiting around the town."

Confident that this was true, Angie allowed Ed to help her up onto her horse. "She's probably already home sitting safe and warm in front of the fireplace."

"If you give me a minute," Ed said, "I'll go

saddle up my horse and ride part of the way home with you. I promised Ma I'd bring out some supplies tonight for her baking, so I've got to go that way anyway."

Angie's face lit up, and her frustration with Amy disappeared. "I'll wait right here for you."

Dark had nearly fallen by the time Angie finally rode into the farmyard. She'd had the most wonderful time with Ed, and she was still wearing her dreamy expression when her father met her in the barn.

"I was beginning to get worried," Charles said, helping her from the saddle.

"I'm sorry, Pa. I took time to try and find Amy, and before I knew it, the sun was sinking lower and lower. Ed Anderson rode out as far as the creek with me, so I didn't have far to come alone."

"Alone?" Charles frowned. "Where's your sister?"

Angie's mouth dropped open. "You mean she's not here?"

"No." Charles's voice was flat. "What made you think she was?"

"We separated in town because I went to see Mrs. Miller at the hotel. She'd promised to make me some lace as a Christmas present for Amy. I stayed too long I guess, 'cause when I headed back to the store, Amy was already gone. I went to look for her after I finished my shopping, but I couldn't find her anywhere." Angie twisted a curl around her finger nervously. "I saw Ed Anderson locking up the bank, so I went and asked him if he'd seen Amy. He hadn't, but he offered to look for her with me. That was when we noticed her horse was gone."

"Amy's horse was gone?" A frown lined Charles's normally cheerful face.

Angie nodded. "We figured she'd gotten mad at me for taking so long and had headed home on her own. That's why I came on home myself. I thought she'd be here."

Charles was already pulling the saddle off Angie's horse. "You give this horse some feed and water. I'm going back in town to look for your sister. Tell your ma what happened, but try not to tell it so as she worries too much. Amy's probably still looking for you, so there ain't no reason to get her frettin'."

Angie nodded. She was starting to feel anxious for her twin. Amy was not the type to act irresponsibly, Angie realized, and she should have known Amy would never have gotten mad and left her. Angie quickly cared for the horse and hurried inside to tell her mother what had happened.

Amy knew it was only a matter of time before Nathan returned. She pondered what he might do with her in order to keep her from spilling his plans. She still couldn't fully

597

comprehend that the handsome young lawyer planned to rob the town of its harvest money.

Without even realizing what she was doing, Amy began to pray. *Lord,* she thought, *I need help out of this one, for sure. Please send someone to rescue me. And keep me from the harm Nathan Gallagher plans for me. Please,* she added, *help me not to be afraid.* It was only a brief prayer, but it strengthened her spirits, and Amy began to have hope that she would somehow escape.

Waiting there in the dark, her mind turned to thoughts of Tyler. He would be arriving any day now, and Amy wondered if he would be the one to find her. She fell into a daydream where Tyler rode up to Nathan's office and pulled her out of the closet, into his strong arms. *How terribly romantic,* she thought, and had to laugh at her nonsense.

She'd no doubt be home long before Tyler returned. But thinking about that was just a romantic, for then he'd ask her to marry him, and she would of course say yes. She fell deep into another daydream.

The sound of someone entering the law office caught her attention. She began to pound her feet against the floor and threw her shoulder against the wall of the closet. The door to the closet swung open, and light from a lantern blinded Amy's eyes for a moment.

"Quiet down — or else," Nathan whispered harshly.

Amy sat still while her eyes adjusted to the light. Nathan placed the lamp on the floor and began searching his pockets for something.

"I've decided to take you out of here," he said while pulling a handkerchief from his pocket. "I have a problem, though. I can't very well parade you down Main Street, now can I?"

He laughed at Amy's expression and continued. "I paid a visit to Doc Taggert. Well, actually to his office. You might say I allowed myself entrance through the back window in order to retrieve this." He held up a corked bottle of liquid.

Amy shied away, trying to scoot back against the closet wall. She was only too certain of what Nathan had in mind. He uncorked the bottle and poured a liberal amount of the contents onto his handkerchief before continuing. "This way, it will be a lot easier on me and you both."

Amy shook her head furiously. She kicked at Nathan when he moved closer to her. Her strangled protests couldn't make it past the gag, but Nathan understood their meaning well enough.

"Don't fight me, Amy. I can't let you spoil this for me. I've worked too hard and too long on this. You're a good girl and I don't want to hurt you. Now just cooperate with me and it'll all be over in a short time."

Amy felt a scream rise up inside her, only to die as Nathan pulled her forward. He held the cloth firmly against her face, and in spite of her thrashing from side to side, the chloroform did its job. Amy had a burning sensation in her nostrils and throat, and then the darkness overtook her.

She came awake slowly, almost like she'd been a part of some strange dream. She lifted her aching head and tried to focus on the images around her, but nothing made sense. Dropping her head back, she waited for a few moments, hoping her head would clear before she tried to lift it again.

Her lips felt sore and dry, and she ran her tongue across them. She remembered the gag then — it was gone! With that memory, everything else came back to her. She was lying on a bed somewhere, and she swung her legs over the side, realizing that the ropes had been cut from her hands and feet. She sat up, her head swimming.

Her head pounded with the echo of each beat of her heart, and her throat was scratchy and sore from the chloroform. When she could finally focus a bit better, she noticed a small table across the room from the bed. On it, a lantern offered the room's only light.

Amy got to her feet slowly, testing her

weight against her wobbly legs. When she felt confident she could stand, she walked to the table and inspected the items on top of it. Nathan had left her a jar of water, a loaf of bread, and the light.

Looking around the room, Amy surmised that it must be a dugout or root cellar. She climbed the two dirt steps that led to a wooden door and pulled at the handle to open it. It wouldn't budge — but then she really hadn't expected it to. Heaving a sigh, she stepped away and took a more careful inventory of the room's contents.

There was the makeshift bed she'd been lying on, the table, and nothing else. Overhead was the dirt and grass ceiling that was typical of dugouts, but with no stove and no hole in the roof for a flue, Amy decided this must be someone's deserted storage cellar.

She returned her gaze to the table, then again to the door, and at last sat back down on the bed. She was trapped without hope, and the silence of her prison broke her like nothing else could have. She lay back on the bed and began to sob.

CHAPTER 11

Charles Carmichael pounded on the door to the general store. After several moments, Jeremy Smith's scowling face appeared in the window.

"You know we're closed," he called from behind the glass.

Charles was undaunted. "Jeremy, have you seen Amy?" he bellowed.

His expression erased Jeremy's scowl. He opened the door and shook his head. "Not since earlier when she was shopping."

The lines in Charles's face grew deeper. "She's missing," he said heavily. "I've looked all over for her. I covered the miles between here and home as best I could, but I didn't see any sign of her anywhere. I was hoping she'd be somewhere still in town."

"I'll get my coat and a light," Jeremy said. He knew no one would be able to rest until the young woman was found.

"I'm going to ride out to the Anderson place," Charles said. "If they haven't seen anything of her, then I'll bring George and his boys back with me to help with the search. Would you get the men together here and wait for us?"

"Sure thing, Charles. We'll be waitin' for you right here."

Confident that Jeremy would help, Charles mounted his horse and rode as fast as he dared to the Anderson farm. Snow was beginning to fall as he dismounted, but Charles barely noticed. He charged toward the house, ignoring the barking dogs, but the commotion brought George Anderson to the door before Charles could knock.

"Charles!" George exclaimed. "What are you doing out here on a night like this? A guy would have to be pert near crazy to brave the winds tonight."

"You haven't seen Amy, have you, George." Charles's words were a statement rather than a question. He wiped the snowflakes from his face, and took a deep breath. "She went into town with Angie and never came home."

By this time Ed and Jack had joined their father at the door. "I thought she'd ridden out ahead of Angie," Ed said. "I helped Angie look for her until we noticed her horse was gone. We figured she'd gone home."

"If she headed toward home," Charles said, fear making his voice gruff, "she never made it. I've got Jeremy Smith getting the men together in town. I wanted to ask —"

"No need to ask, Charles," George interrupted. "Boys, get your brother and tell your ma what's happened."

Ed and Jack quickly returned with Jacob, closely followed by Emma Anderson. "Is there anything I can do, Charles?" Emma asked.

"Pray," Charles suggested. "Just pray for her safe return. I know your prayers will be joined by an awful lot of others petitionin' God for the same thing. I just have to believe that Amy will be safe in our Father's hands."

"I know she is," Emma said firmly. "And I'll be praying for both her and for you men as you search." She reached out to squeeze Charles's hand, then watched as her family prepared to leave with Charles.

"Bar the door, Emma," her husband told her as they left. "We don't know what's amiss and there's no sense taking chances." He kissed her lightly on the cheek, picked up his rifle, and followed his sons outside.

Alone in the cold, damp room, Amy shivered and hugged her arms around herself. She was grateful she still wore her heavy coat, but she was still cold. She pulled the thin bed blanket around her to add to her coat's warmth and tried to breathe slowly and calmly. She could do nothing now but wait. Surely Nathan wouldn't just leave her here to die; after all, he had provided food and water for her.

She got off the bed and paced back and forth across the room, trying to warm herself by moving around. Her thoughts turned to home, and she bit her lip while her eyes burned with tears. Her parents would be frantic, and Angie would blame herself. Amy breathed a silent prayer that God would ease their worry, and she asked again for a speedy rescue.

She tried to focus on pleasant thoughts and not give in to the fear and hopelessness of her situation. She was uncertain how long she had been unconscious, and she wondered what day it was. Days might have already passed, she told herself, and rescue could be very near. Clinging to that hope, she ate a small piece of the bread, allowing herself no more than a brief swallow of the water. She knew rationing could be essential, because she had no guarantee that Nathan would return to supply her with more.

As the hours dragged by, she spent most of her time praying and remembering. The air grew colder, and she feared she might freeze to death before anyone could find her. She felt more and more sleepy, but she knew sleeping could be dangerous in the cold, and so she forced herself to stay awake by reciting Bible verses and signing hymns.

"Father," she said aloud. Even the sound of her own voice was welcome in the silence. "I need a miracle. I don't know what's happening out there or even where I am, but You know, and I know You're watching over me. Please let them find me in time, Lord — and if not, then teach me how I can help myself get out of this." She didn't add a closing "amen," for she knew her prayer would continue again when the stillness became too much for her once more.

Tyler approached the Carmichael farm with the giddy excitement of a schoolboy. He'd arranged to have three weeks away from his circuit, while another rider took his place during his absence. During those three weeks, he intended to make plans with Amy for their wedding.

Snow covered the ground now, and Tyler was reminded of the storm that had kept him at the Carmichaels' long enough to share his true feelings with Amy. He smiled to himself, thinking of how worried she'd been about her sister's feelings. That was one of the things he loved most about Amy. She was always looking out for the folks around her before ever considering her own needs.

Without stopping at the house first, Tyler went directly to the barn. He cared for his horse and then ran across the yard to the house. Slightly breathless, he knocked on the door. A red-eyed Dora opened it.

"Tyler!" she gasped in surprise. Her face twisted with emotions that Tyler could not identify, and then she turned to her husband. "Look, Charles, it's Tyler."

The skin on the back of Tyler's neck prickled when he saw how haggard both of Amy's parents were. They ushered him into the kitchen without a word and motioned him toward a seat. When Dora and Charles had sat down with him, he leaned toward them, waiting for them to speak.

"What is it?" he asked finally. He knew in his heart he wasn't going to like the answer. "Has something happened to Amy?"

Dora began to cry anew, and Charles put his face in his hands. "She's gone," he said. The sorrow in his muffled words made Tyler believe she was dead.

"Dear God," he breathed, feeling his own heart break. "What happened? How did she . . . ?" He fell silent, unable to utter the word.

Dora instantly realized what he was thinking. "She's not dead, Tyler! At least we pray to God she's not."

Relief washed over him, but the sick feeling that filled his stomach refused to leave. "Then what are you saying?"

Charles leaned back in his chair and shook his head. "She's been missing ever since she went into town with Angie. They went Christmas shopping four, no, five days ago, and Amy hasn't been seen since."

Tyler's heart pounded in his ears, nearly drowning the words Charles spoke. "We got a search party together," Charles continued, "but there wasn't a clue anywhere. It was like she simply disappeared off the face of the earth."

"Is anybody else missing?" Tyler asked.

"No," Charles replied. "Everyone else is accounted for. None of her friends have seen her. Even her horse has disappeared."

"Her horse?"

Charles nodded. "She and Angie both rode horseback into town. When Angie saw that Amy's horse was missing, she presumed she'd ridden home without her. Angie's beside herself. She blames herself for not sticking around and waiting."

Dora sighed. "I've tried to talk to her, but she won't even open her door."

Angie tossed fitfully in her bed. She'd tried to sleep, but whenever she closed her eyes a cold foreboding settled upon her and she felt a misery that she'd never known. People often said twins were bonded to one another, and although she had never experienced it before, Angie couldn't help but wonder if what she was feeling now was actually the echo of Amy's suffering.

The knock at her bedroom door brought her upright in the bed. "Leave me be, Ma," Angie called in a ragged voice.

"Angie, it's Tyler. Please open the door and talk to me."

Angie swallowed hard and felt a trembling start at her head and go clear to her toes. Her mother had already told her how much Amy cared for Tyler. She'd also told Angie that she was quite confident Tyler cared deeply for Amy. Angie couldn't help but believe Tyler would blame her for Amy's disappearance. "And why shouldn't he?" Angie muttered to herself.

"Angie," Tyler persisted. "Please open the door. It's not your fault that Amy is gone — but you may be the only one who can really help us find her."

At these words Angie jumped to her feet and threw open her door. "How?" She stared into Tyler's face. "How can I possibly help her?"

Tyler studied the young woman before him. She was the image of his Amy, but in some ways she was different as well. The differences were especially clear now after the days of worry and grief Angie had spent alone. She had dark circles under her eyes, and her face was gaunt and pale.

Tyler put his arm around Angie's shoulders. "Come downstairs and let's talk."

Angie nodded and allowed him to lead the way. When she saw her parents waiting in the kitchen, she nearly turned to run back to her room, but Tyler's grip was firm.

They looked so old, Angie thought, taking the chair Tyler pulled out for her. Did they hate her for doing this to them? Would they ever forgive her for leaving Amy? Angie buried her face in her hands and sobbed.

"I should have never left her. This is all my fault and you all hate me now."

Dora looked at her in stunned silence, while Charles nearly dropped the cup of coffee he'd been nursing.

"Nobody blames you, Angie," Tyler said. "Nobody except yourself."

Angie looked up at him with tear-filled eyes. "I feel like Cain in the Bible," she cried. "I was my sister's keeper and now . . ." She couldn't say any more and put her head on the table to cry.

Tyler put his arm around her. "Father," he prayed, "please comfort Angie in her pain. She feels responsible for her sister, but we know that isn't the case. Help her, Lord, to see that her parents love her a great deal and that no one holds her accountable for Amy's disappearance. Father, guide us to Amy and show us the way to bring her home. In Jesus' name, amen."

Angie's tears slowed, and finally she leaned back in her chair and sighed. Her father reached out and covered her hand with his own. Taking in another deep, ragged breath, she steadied her nerves. "What do you want to know?" She lifted her face to Tyler's imploring eyes.

"Just start from the beginning and tell me

everything," he said with a smile of hope. "Don't leave out anything, no matter how insignificant it might seem."

Some time later, Tyler rode into Deer Ridge. He wouldn't rest until he'd questioned people himself, and so he made his way to where several of the townspeople stood talking in a cluster in front of the store.

"Howdy, folks." He climbed down from his horse. "I heard about Amy and was hoping to help locate her." He wasted no time with formalities.

"I think Injuns took her," the hotel owner, Mrs. Miller, stated firmly.

Cora Peterson scoffed at this. "Tweren't no Injuns, Bertha. Don't you ever think Injuns got better things to do than snatch up white folks? Might as well blame the Swedes."

"Well, it could of happened," Bertha Miller sniffed. "It hasn't been that long since Little Big Horn. They might be feeling riled at white folk, and Amy might just have been in the wrong place at the wrong time."

At this Cora's husband, Bud, stepped in and waved the woman away. "Don't get her started on Little Big Horn or we'll never get to hear what the preacher has to say."

The crowd smiled, in spite of their worry, and even Bertha seemed to relax a bit. Tyler was grateful for the break in the tension he'd known since first learning of Amy's disappearance.

He talked with the folks for a few more minutes before heading into the general store. At the sound of the front door being opened, Jeremy Smith came from the back room. For once the store was strangely void of activity. *Maybe,* thought Tyler, *people are too tense to relax inside the store the way they would normally.*

"Good to see you, Parson," Jeremy Smith said, extending a hand over the counter.

"It's good to be back, although I had hoped for more pleasant circumstances," Tyler replied.

Betty Smith joined her husband, fear clearly etched in the weathered lines of her face. "Pastor Andrews." She greeted him with a nod.

"I'm glad we're alone," Tyler said, glancing around him. "I hoped you could give me the details about the day Amy disappeared. I promised her folks I'd help look for her."

Betty's eyes misted with tears. "You know, she bought you a Christmas present." The words were out before she realized it. "I'm sorry, I shouldn't have spoiled the surprise, but . . ."

"It's all right, Mrs. Smith." Tyler smiled. "I know Amy would understand and I promise to be surprised." Tyler was deeply touched to think that Amy's thoughts had been on him.

He stayed long enough to listen to the

Smiths tell every detail they could remember. When the couple fell silent, Tyler mulled the information over for a moment and then asked one final question.

"You say she was going to look for Angie when she left here. Where might she have thought to find her?"

"My guess," Mrs. Smith answered, "would be that Amy figured she was visiting her beaus. Ed Anderson would have been over at the bank and Nathan Gallagher's office is across the street."

Her husband nodded in agreement, and Tyler took a deep breath. At least he had a place to start.

CHAPTER 12

Talking to Ed Anderson revealed nothing more than Tyler already knew. Ed went over every detail patiently, even though he'd already told his story a dozen or more times to the Carmichael men. He understood Tyler's anxiety because Charles had told him in confidence that Amy and Tyler had feelings for one another. Ed tried to offer Tyler comfort, and he promised he'd continue to search for Amy as his time allowed.

Tyler picked up his hat and coat and headed for the door.

"You know, Tyler," Ed said, returning to his desk, "Nathan Gallagher has been pretty quiet about this whole thing. You might want to see if he knows any more than I do. If he'll talk to you."

"I was headed over there now," Tyler said. "I'll stress the need for his cooperation."

Ed smiled at the towering pastor's back. No doubt he would get his point across to Mr. Gallagher.

Tyler let himself in the law office and tossed his hat and coat on the nearest chair. "Hello!" he called.

Nathan Gallagher came from his office with a look of surprise. "You're the circuit rider, aren't you?" He looked Tyler up and down.

"That's right," Tyler responded. "I'm also a good friend of the Carmichaels. I'm trying to help them locate their daughter."

Nathan stiffened slightly. "I see. And just what has that to do with me? I've already told Mr. Carmichael I know nothing about Amy's whereabouts."

Tyler was taken aback by the man's cool manner. Everyone else had greeted him with somber cooperation and earnest concern, but Nathan Gallagher seemed not only indifferent to Amy's plight but almost angry at the interruption.

"Folks tell me that Amy was last seen looking for her sister," Tyler said. "Everybody knows that Angie has a number of gentlemen callers, one of which is you. I figured it might be possible that Angie came to see you the day Amy disappeared — and that Amy might have come by here looking for her." Tyler leaned against the wall in a casual manner, making it clear to Nathan Gallagher that he intended to stay until he got some answers.

"It's true that I've called on Angie before," Nathan acknowledged. "But Angie didn't come to see me that day. Amy wouldn't have any reason to come here without Angie."

"She would if she were looking for her sister," Tyler said. "That would be a logical thing to do, now, wouldn't it?" His eyes were intense, watching Gallagher's reaction.

If the lawyer thought he was good at reading people's expressions, then Tyler Andrews was a genius at it. He noticed the way Nathan's eyes darted from side to side to avoid his own, and he saw the way Nathan's hands fidgeted in his pockets.

Nathan shrugged, feigning nonchalance. "I guess that's reasonable, but Amy didn't come here. I told her father that and now I'm telling you."

"I'm just trying to find her," Tyler said calmly. Inside, however, he was boiling at Nathan's lack of concern.

"Well, I believe you've done all you can here," the lawyer said firmly. "Now if you'll excuse me, I have work to do."

Tyler allowed him to return to his office without another word. Something told him that Gallagher knew more than he was saying, but Tyler could not force him to reveal what he knew. Frustrated, Tyler pulled on his coat and hat and retrieved his horse from the front of the general store. Then he turned toward the Carmichael farm, eager to see if Randy or Charles had learned anything more.

When at last Tyler arrived back at the farm, he felt more discouraged than he'd ever felt in his life. Amy was out there somewhere, maybe hurt, definitely scared, and he couldn't help her. He wanted so much to let her know that he cared, that he would always care, but he had no leads, no answers to the questions that could help him find her.

When he approached the house, his heart jumped. Amy's horse was tied out front alongside another that he didn't recognize. Had she been found? God surely must have heard his prayers. He nearly flew off his horse and into the house.

"That's Amy's horse!" He pushed into the kitchen without so much as a knock.

Randy Carmichael stood against the stove warming his hands. "I found it in Hays," he said without looking up. "The livery owner said a man came in several days ago and sold it to him, tack and all, for twenty dollars."

"Did he get a description of the man?" Tyler asked.

"He did," Charles said, coming in from the other room. He nodded down the hall. "Dora and Angie are pretty upset by this. I told them to leave the discussion to us."

Tyler nodded. "It's probably best." He turned to Randy and asked again about the man.

"Livery said the man was about six foot tall," Randy answered. "Heavyset, scraggly red beard, and hair down to his shoulders. He wasn't dressed well, and the livery owner was surprised when he only wanted twenty dollars for the horse. The man told him that he just needed to unload the animal and that twenty was plenty. That's when the livery man got suspicious."

"Was anything missing?" Tyler asked. "Was there any sign of what might have happened?"

Randy shook his head and took the cup of coffee his father handed him. "No, even the Christmas gifts Amy bought were safely stashed in the saddlebags. There was no sign of blood or anything else that might give us a clue."

"Well, then, she wasn't taken for the money," Tyler thought aloud.

"You think she was taken then?" Charles asked, pouring a cup of the steaming liquid for Tyler.

Tyler nodded. "More so now than ever. If she'd gone out ahead of Angie and gotten hurt or lost her way somehow, the horse would have come on home. Nobody is missing in town, but that still leaves the area surrounding it. Were any of the local men interested in Amy? I mean, would they have taken her by force?"

"Naw." Charles shook his head and made a face, as though the thought was ridiculous. "We've been here a long time, Tyler. Ain't no one round here who would try to get a woman that way. Besides, I don't know

618

anyone who was even interested in Amy. You know how it is between Angie and Amy. Angie's always courting and Amy never was. The only one marginally interested in her was Jacob Anderson and he's been most devoted to helping us look for her."

"If someone did take her," Randy began, "and I'm inclined to believe someone did, what reason could they possibly have had? What purpose would it serve to take Amy?"

"That's what I'm trying to figure out," Tyler replied softly. He took a long drink from the mug and set it on the table. "By my calculations there is only about an hour on the day Amy disappeared that her whereabouts were unaccounted for before Angie noticed her horse was gone. The time from which Amy left the store until Angie began looking for her was only forty-five minutes, maybe an hour at best. Somewhere in that hour is when Amy was taken. Since no one remembers seeing any strangers in town, Amy had to have been taken by someone familiar to her. Maybe she was even talked into helping someone she knew well and went willingly with them."

Charles rubbed his jaw, then looked at his son. Randy nodded; Tyler's words made sense.

"So what do we do from here?" Charles asked.

Tyler rubbed his own stubbly chin for a

moment, noticing absently that he needed a shave. "We make a list," he finally said. "We make a list of everyone in the area. Then we plot the names on a map. You take part of it, Charles, Randy a part, and I'll take another part. I'll stick to the town, since I'm not all that familiar with the outlying farms. You and Randy can divide your lists with someone you trust, like the Andersons. Then we'll go door to door, farm to farm. We'll question everybody and leave no stone unturned."

Charles frowned. "That might make our neighbors feel we don't trust them to come forward with what they know."

"They'll understand." Tyler drained the coffee from his cup, then added, "They won't be offended if you remind them that should this have happened to one of their own family members, you'd expect them to do the same."

"I'll get some paper," Charles agreed and left the room.

"I'll get the horses in the stable," Randy offered, "and then I'll help you map this thing out."

Tyler tried to ignore the anguish in his soul. He had forced his voice to remain calm and even while he talked with Randy and Charles, but inside he was gnawed by a fear that said if Amy's horse had turned up as far away as Hays, then Amy, too, could be long gone from Deer Ridge.

Running a hand through the waves of his hair, Tyler decided not to say anything to the family. No sense taking away what little hope they had. Tyler would keep the fear to himself that with each passing day, Amy was getting further and further from his reach. He whispered a prayer and sat down at the table, prepared to work.

Making the list and map took them most of the evening. When it was completed, Tyler divided it in thirds, with the larger of the shares going to Charles and Randy.

"I'm heading home." Randy stuffed the paper in his pocket. "I'll be back early and we can get started then."

"We'll be ready," Charles replied and bid his son good-bye.

The silence that fell between Charles and Tyler was numbing. Each man wanted to comfort the other, but neither had any words for what they were feeling. Each bore a burden so heavy that the weight drained them of energy. Finally, Charles reached out and placed his hand over Tyler's. Tyler lifted his eyes and saw the tear-stained cheeks of a worried father.

"If God be for us," the pastor whispered, "who can be against us?"

Tyler spent a restless night in the Carmichaels' spare bedroom. He could hear Dora crying off and on from down the hall, and from time to time Angie joined in from the privacy of her own room. A verse from the Bible came to Tyler, the verse that describes Rachel weeping for her children and refusing to be comforted. The verse so haunted Tyler that at last he got up and opened his Bible to Jeremiah 31:15.

"Thus saith the LORD; A voice was heard in Ramah, lamentation, and bitter weeping; Rachel weeping for her children refused to be comforted, because they were not."

Tyler shuddered, but then he found the Lord leading his eyes on to verses sixteen and seventeen, and the words he read now brought him hope.

"Thus saith the Lord; Refrain thy voice from weeping, and thine eyes from tears: for thy work shall be rewarded, saith the Lord; and they shall come again from the land of the enemy. And there is hope in thine end, saith the Lord, that thy children shall come again to their own border." He read the words silently, then again aloud.

A weight lifted from his shoulders, and he fell to his knees in prayer. First he offered thanksgiving for the scriptures God had led him to, and then he began to petition his Father for Amy's safety.

When Randy arrived the next morning, the entire family gathered for Tyler to lead them in devotions and prayers. He shared the precious verses he'd read the night before. "We must put our hope in God," he reminded them. "He is our only hope right now, but He won't let us down. He is the only One who can reach out and help Amy. We must put her in His hands." Tyler waited for them to absorb his words, and then he added, "We can trust Him with Amy's life, for He loves her even more than we ever will."

At these words, Dora seemed to sit straighter and even Angie lost her mask of fear. A light had been given them in their darkness, and they stood at a crossroads that would lead them to a wonderous peace of mind.

"You're right, Tyler," Charles said finally. "We've been fighting this thing too hard on our own. If we're to ever get anywhere, we must let God work it out." Angie, Dora, and Randy nodded in unison.

After breakfast the men readied their horses and prepared to leave. Dora and Angie stood by helplessly watching, until Angie could no longer stand it.

"Can't I go along and help?" she asked her father.

"No, you'd best stay here. We still don't know what we're going to find out there. I'd rather you be here to care for your mother." Charles gave Angie's cheek a gentle stroke.

"But it's awful just waiting here," she protested.

Dora nodded. "Feels like we're not doing our part."

"Somebody should be here," Tyler said before Charles could reply. "In case Amy makes it home on her own. If you're both here, then Angie can ride out and let the rest of us know."

"I suppose that makes sense." Dora put her arm around Angie. "And," she added softly, "we can continue to pray."

Angie saw the wisdom in their words, and though she longed to be at some other task, she agreed that they needed to stay at the house.

"We'll be back by dark," Charles said, mounting his horse. The cold leather creaked and groaned as he settled his body in the saddle. "Looks like it might snow again, so you'd best stay inside."

"What about the chores, Pa?" Angie questioned.

"We took care of everything before you ladies got up. You just stick indoors and stay warm," Charles instructed. He hated to leave them alone, but he knew he had to trust God to watch over them if he was to go look for his other daughter. He gave Dora a loving look and then turned his horse to follow Randy and Tyler across the yard.

"Kind of like leaving the ninety-nine," he

murmured aloud.

"What was that?" Tyler questioned.

Charles smiled and pulled up even with Tyler. "I was just thinking that leaving them here is like the shepherd who leaves the ninety-nine to go look for the one."

Tyler returned the smile with a nod. "That it is. I guess now we know just how precious that one can be."

CHAPTER 13

Tyler stood in the center of Deer Ridge's Main Street and stared down at the list. He decided to start with Miller's Hotel, since six of the people on his list resided there. He spoke first to Mr. and Mrs. Miller and then was happily received by Marvin Williams, who was enjoying his holiday break from teaching.

Marvin, however, knew next to nothing about the entire affair, and so Tyler moved on to Nathan Gallagher's room. He knocked, but receiving no answer from the other side of the door, he again moved on. He could pin Gallagher down at his office later, he decided.

The town barber and dentist, Newt Bramblage, was also absent from the hotel, but Mrs. Miller reminded Tyler that he'd probably be happy to answer any questions while giving Tyler a shave.

The only other resident was an elderly woman who rarely left her room. The woman had a delicate constitution, and so as not to upset her unduly, Mrs. Miller questioned her for Tyler. The woman, not surprisingly, had no knowledge of Amy Carmichael's whereabouts; she went still further, however, and insisted that since she was not given to gossip, she would have nothing to share in the future, even in the unlikely event that she should fall privy to such knowledge.

Tyler thanked the Millers and moved on down the street to where Doc Taggert was shoveling snow in front of his building. "Doc," Tyler called and climbed down from his horse. He tied the reins and offered to take over the shoveling if Doc would speak to him about Amy. He finished the remaining work quickly, and Doc invited him inside for coffee and biscuits.

"My wife, Gretta, always worries that I'll starve before I come home for lunch." Doc smiled. "Then she wonders why I don't have much of an appetite at supper."

Tyler laughed and helped himself to the offered refreshment. "I'll happily share your misery." He bit into a fluffy biscuit.

"I don't know what I can do to help you." Doc took a seat behind his desk. "I don't believe I saw Amy at all the day she disappeared."

"Did you work in your office that day?"

"Sure did," Doc replied. "I was here pert near all day. I'd just gotten in a shipment of medicine and had to inventory it before I could close up and go home. I was just leaving when — say, wait a minute."

Tyler leaned forward. "What is it, Doc?"

"I didn't see Amy that day," Doc said thoughtfully, "but I did see Angie."

"Oh." Tyler sat back hard against the wooden chair. The disappointment was clear on his face.

"Yes," Doc remembered. "She was just crossing the street and heading into Nathan Gallagher's office when I was locking my front door."

Tyler leaned forward again. "You saw Angie going into Nathan's office?"

"That's right."

"How did you know it was Angie? I'd think from a distance it would be pretty hard to tell the twins apart. I'm not sure even I could do it. What made you so sure it was Angie and not Amy?"

Doc shrugged and scratched his jaw. "I guess I just assumed it was Angie. After all, Amy wouldn't have any reason to visit Gallagher. He's not at all her type. Besides, everybody knows Angie considers him one of her more serious gentlemen callers."

"But —" Tyler opened his mouth, then closed it again. His eyes narrowed, and he took a deep breath. "You're sure it was the same day that Amy disappeared?"

"Positive."

Tyler grabbed his hat. "Thanks, Doc. I think you've helped me a great deal."

Without another word, Tyler hurried from Doc's office. He left his horse behind and walked to Nathan's office. Nathan had insisted that he'd not seen Angie or Amy on the day Amy disappeared — and now Tyler had proof that he'd lied.

"Gallagher!" Tyler slammed the office door behind him.

Nathan came from the inner office with the same look of surprise that he'd worn the visit before. "What in the world is going on, Preacher?"

"Doc Taggert says he saw Angie come here to visit you the day Amy disappeared." Tyler's voice was flat.

Nathan's mouth hardened. "He's mistaken, Andrews. I told you that I didn't see Angie that day."

Tyler stepped forward, barely able to control his temper. "Doc was sure about what he'd seen."

"Doc is an old man." Nathan laughed. "He simply has his days mixed up. Angie never came to see me that day." Nathan's voice was confident. The more time that passed, the closer he was to accomplishing his goal of robbing the town on Christmas. Without a clue to Amy's whereabouts, Andrews was simply grasping at straws.

"I'm going to get to the bottom of this."

Tyler's tone left Nathan little doubt that he would do just that.

"Well, you aren't going to get to the bottom of it here," Nathan replied.

Tyler backed away, fearful that if he remained within punching distance of Nathan, he'd lose control and flatten the man. "I'll be back." He looked at Nathan for another moment, his eyes dark with anger.

"You do that, Preach." Nathan crossed his arms across his chest and smiled. "I'll be here — and I won't have any more information for you then than I do now."

Tyler stalked out of the office and climbed into his saddle with a growl that made his horse's eyes roll. Tyler knew that Gallagher was keeping something from him, but he had no proof. His only recourse was to head back to the farm and question Angie. Perhaps she'd lied about seeing Gallagher for fear her folks wouldn't like her forward actions. Maybe she *had* seen him and covering that up made her feel even guiltier about Amy. Tyler shook his head and urged his mount forward. He would have to question Angie in private and promise to keep her secret.

Amy forced herself to wake up, but the effort cost her every ounce of determination she had. She was weak from lack of food and numb from the growing cold. She had no idea how much time had passed, and so she tried to concentrate on the present moment only. She could not anticipate the future, and remembering the past now only made the present seem worse. She was no longer living even one day at a time; instead, she knew if she was to survive she must live moment by moment.

She wasn't worrying anymore about whether Nathan would steal the harvest money. Now she thought only of whether or not he would free her before she succumbed to cold and thirst.

Each minute seemed as long as an hour. She still had a little water left, but she was afraid her thirst would drive her to swallow the remaining drops in one gulp. Again and again she reached out to take the jar in her hand, but each time she forced herself to put it back on the table. She had to make the water last. Without water, she would surely die.

With each passing moment, the room seemed smaller, as though the walls were closing in on her. She tried the door over and over, and shouted until her voice was hoarse. The longer she considered her plight, the more certain she felt that Nathan intended to leave her to die. Finally, her desperation drove her to action.

"My only hope of getting out of here is through the roof," she said aloud. She took the lamp and water from the table and put them on the floor. Next, she looked around the room, trying to figure out where the roof might be the weakest and easiest to penetrate. She moved the table to one side and gingerly tested it to see if it would hold her.

The table wobbled, but it held as Amy put her full weight on it. Weakly, she climbed to her feet on the tabletop and then had to duck down to keep from hitting the ceiling overhead. She pulled at the cold, packed dirt with her hands until she cried out from the pain. The dirt was frozen by the winter's cold, and Amy's numb fingers were no match for it.

Glancing around the room, Amy looked for some tool to make her job easier. She found nothing that looked promising, though, and so she continued to labor with her hands. God would give her strength, she reminded herself. "God is my strength," she whispered again and again while she scrabbled with her numb hands at the frozen ceiling. "God is my strength."

Tyler pushed his overworked gelding to gallop across the prairie until they reached the Carmichael farm. Tyler dismounted quickly and left his mount in the barn. He knew he should care for the horse, but the snow was coming down heavier than before and time was of the essence. He patted the patient animal apologetically and turned toward the house.

Before he could reach the door, Angie burst through it. "What is it? Did you find her?" she cried. "Mother is sleeping, but I can wake her."

"No, Angie." Tyler pulled her into the house with him. "I have to talk to you alone. It's very important."

Angie's brow wrinkled. "Me? Why me?"

"Sit here with me." Tyler pulled one of the kitchen chairs out for Angie.

Angie did as he asked, but her apprehension mounted with each silent moment that passed. Finally, Tyler found the right words to begin.

"Angie, I know this might be a delicate matter to broach, but if it weren't so important, I assure you I would never question what you told me before." Tyler took a deep breath. "Doc Taggert and I talked this morning. It seems he remembers you going to Nathan's office the afternoon Amy disappeared."

Angie shook her head. "I already told you that I didn't see Nathan that day. I spent my time with Mrs. Miller. I let Amy think I was going to go calling on some of my beaus — but that was just so she wouldn't suspect the Christmas present for her I was planning with Mrs. Miller. Mrs. Miller can tell you I was with her the whole afternoon."

"Yes, she did say that." Tyler sighed. "Look, Angie, I'm not calling you a liar — I'm just desperate to know the truth. If you went to Nathan's and felt ashamed — or if you were concerned about your folks — or one of your other beaus — catching wind of it, I promise to keep it to myself. It's just that when I questioned Gallagher about it, he swore to me that he'd not seen you either. And yet he acts suspicious about the whole thing. I need proof that he's lying to me."

"You think he's hiding something?" Angie asked in surprise.

"Could be. Is he hiding your visit?" Tyler's tone was gentle. "Is he protecting you, Angie?"

Angie shook her head vigorously. "No! I did not go to see Nathan Gallagher that day. I would have if I'd had time after I finished with Mrs. Miller, but I lost track of the time. By the time I returned to the store, Amy was already gone. I figured she'd be back soon, and so I finished my shopping. When she still hadn't come back, I decided to find her. I stepped outside the store and saw that her horse was still there, so I knew she was nearby. That's when I went to talk to Ed —"

"Wait a minute, Angie," Tyler interrupted. "You just said that when you came out of the store, Amy's horse was still there."

Angie looked at him in astonishment. "Yes! Yes, it was there! That's why I went to ask Ed if he'd seen her. He was outside locking up and — oh Tyler, what does it mean?"

Tyler got to his feet. "I don't know yet. What I do know is that Doc is confident that he saw you entering Nathan's office."

"But I didn't," Amy insisted.

"If you didn't," — Tyler took a deep breath — "then it had to have been Amy that Doc saw!"

"Of course." Angie's eyes narrowed thoughtfully. "And if Amy went to Nathan's to find me, and Nathan swears he didn't see either of us, then he's lying. And that means he probably has done something with Amy."

"That's just about the way I figure it," Tyler muttered. "Tell me, Angie, has Nathan said anything to you about leaving town?"

Angie started to shake her head and then stopped abruptly. "He did say he wouldn't be here at Christmas. I remember, because I asked him to accompany me to your service and the festivities afterward and he told me he couldn't."

"Did he say where he was headed?" Tyler moved closer to Angie and put his hands on her shoulders. "Think hard, Angie. Did he give you any idea at all?"

Angie thought for moment and then shook her head. "No. He just told me he couldn't escort me and left it at that. I wish I could be more help." She sniffed back tears. "That lying, no-good skunk. He better not have hurt my sister. I just wish there was something I could do to help her."

Tyler put his arm around her and patted her shoulder. "It's all right, Angie. You've given me more to go on than anyone else. You've at least pointed the way. Now listen to me carefully. I want you to wake your mother and tell her what we know. Then I want you to ride out and find your father. It's snowing again, so dress warm and ride quickly."

"What do you want me to tell him?"

"Tell him to find Randy and meet me in town. Since Nathan's still in town and Christmas is tomorrow, he must be planning to make his break tonight. We'll have to be there to follow him and hope that he'll lead us to Amy."

Angie dried her tears and agreed to Tyler's plan. "I'll send them, don't worry about a thing. Just please, please find Amy."

"I'll do my best," Tyler promised, heading for the door. "You just do what I've told you and keep praying."

CHAPTER 14

Tyler went straight to Nathan's office, but he found it dark and the door locked. He glanced down the darkening street to the boarding-house, wondering if Nathan had taken refuge in his room, or if he had fled town altogether. Tyler could only pray that he'd not find the latter to be the case.

"Pastor Andrews," a voice called from behind him, and Tyler turned to find Jeremy Smith.

"Evening." Tyler's manner was preoccupied.

"Gallagher's gone home for the night," Jeremy said, gesturing toward the locked of-fice. "I saw him leave not ten minutes ago for the boardinghouse."

Tyler let out all his breath at once. "I guess I'll talk to him later," he said and started for his horse.

"Pastor," Jeremy called out, "you will be giving us a service tomorrow, won't you?"

Tyler turned and saw that several other people had joined Jeremy. "Yeah, Pastor," another man added, "the family's sure been looking forward to Christmas morning service."

Tyler had nearly forgotten his promise to preach. His worry for Amy was shutting out all other thought. "I'll be there," he replied, knowing that his voice lacked its normal enthusiasm.

"Good, good," Jeremy said, satisfied that the matter was settled. "The kids are going to put on a play for us, and I've got sacks of candy to give them after you preach. It's going to be a lot of fun for them. I know you're mighty worried about Amy, but I wouldn't want to spoil things for the young 'uns."

Tyler agreed that they should not spoil the festivities, but his heart wasn't in his words. He knew only God could mend the hurt that bound him inside.

Excusing himself, he pushed past the men and got on his horse. "I'll see you all tomorrow morning." He rode out past the hotel, casting a suspicious glance upward at the second story windows.

He manuevered his horse into the shadows of nearby trees and dismounted. From where he stood, he could watch the boardinghouse, and he realized that he might learn more by waiting for Nathan to move than by questioning him further.

Grateful that the snow had let up, Tyler decided to board his horse at the livery and stake out the boardinghouse from the livery loft. From there, he would have a view of everything around, and he'd be able to spot Randy and Charles when they made their way to join him.

If the livery owner thought the new pastor was strange for wanting to sleep in the loft, he made no mention of it as he accepted Tyler's money.

Tyler saw to his horse's care and feed, then threw his saddle bags over his shoulder and made his way up the rough ladder to the loft. Tossing the bags aside, Tyler eased the heavy wooden shutter open just enough to peer down the road. All seemed quiet. Only the soft glow from the windows of the surrounding homes broke the fall of darkness.

Tyler studied the boardinghouse a moment longer, noting the side stairs that led to the second floor. Gallagher would have to come out one of three ways, Tyler surmised. Either by the front or back door or these side stairs. Whichever he chose, Tyler was ready.

Tyler was prepared for a lengthy stay, but within a half an hour, he was rewarded by the appearance of Nathan Gallagher on the side stairs. He watched as Nathan moved away from the hotel and came toward the livery. Tyler wondered if Nathan had chosen to depart Deer Ridge now. Easing away from the window, Tyler heard the livery door open below. He held his breath.

After a moment, crawling at a snail's pace on his hands and knees, he eased his six foot six frame to the edge of the loft. Looking over, Tyler flattened himself in the straw and watched the dark-hatted head below. Nathan seemed to be waiting for someone to appear. He checked his watch several times and paced the floor below, making the horses stir.

Tyler could hardly force himself to remain still. He kept thinking of Amy and wondered if Nathan had hurt her. Every time her brown eyes and smiling mouth came to mind, Tyler had to bite back a growl. He wanted to throttle the man, but he knew Gallagher's type wouldn't respond to force. *Lord, I need patience and steadfastness,* Tyler prayed. Feeling the cold bite into his skin, he could only hope that Nathan would lead him to Amy soon.

The back door to the livery swung open then, and a man appeared in the shadowy light. Tyler saw that he matched the description of the man who had sold Amy's horse.

"Gallagher?" the man called, and Nathan stepped into the light.

"Here," he replied. "Did you do the job?"

"You paid me to do it, didn't you?" the man growled. "Still can't figure selling a fine piece of horseflesh like that for only twenty dollars. Why, the saddle alone —"

"I don't want to hear what you think,"

Nathan interrupted. "That's precisely why your brother isn't working with us anymore. Because he thought too much."

"Well, what do you want me to do now?" the man asked.

"Come back to my room with me. We'll take the side stairs and no one will see you." Nathan motioned the man to leave the way he'd come.

Tyler wished he could follow them, but he knew he wouldn't have enough cover to get close enough where he could be out of sight and still hear the conversation. All he could do was watch the two men walk away, knowing full well that one or both of them knew where his beloved Amy was hidden.

The men had no sooner disappeared into the hotel than Tyler spotted two riders approaching. He figured they would be Randy and Charles, and he bounded down the ladder to meet them in the street before they could go in search of him.

The Carmichael men were anxious for whatever news Tyler could share. He told them what little he knew, including the whereabouts of the man who'd sold Amy's horse. He and Charles had to grab Randy's shoulders to keep him from storming over and calling the man into the street.

"It won't get Amy back," Tyler insisted, while Charles kept a firm grip on his son's arm.

"Tyler's right," Charles said. "You can't just barge in over there and spill your guts. If Tyler is right, and Nathan plans to make some move between now and the morning, we'll be here to see what it is."

"Each of us needs to stake out a different spot," Tyler suggested. "I'll bet Doc would let one of you use his place."

"We'll work that out, Tyler," Charles agreed. "You stay here and we'll do what we have to."

"If anyone sees or hears anything that bears notifying the others about, don't waste any time. We may only have minutes to act." Tyler's voice was grave.

Randy nodded and swallowed his anger. "I hope your plan works."

Tyler looked first at Randy and then Charles. "I pray it does, too."

Loneliness settled over Tyler after Charles and Randy had gone. Whenever he was near Amy's family, he felt at least a small link with her, but now nothing distracted him from the image of Amy cold and afraid somewhere, perhaps hurt, needing him . . . Nothing could comfort him.

No, that wasn't true, he realized as he settled himself in the loft again. God was with him and God was with Amy. That was comfort enough.

An hour passed before the scraggly-looking

man reappeared on the side stairs of the boardinghouse. Tyler watched the darkness, straining to see where the man would go next. He was surprised to see him return to the livery.

Without thought for his safety, Tyler perched himself on the edge of the loft landing and waited for the man to appear. The door groaned as it was pushed open and then closed with a thud. The man had taken only two or three steps when Tyler jumped from the loft and threw his full weight against him. Delivering a well-placed blow to the burly man's face, Tyler knocked him nearly senseless.

Tyler quickly bound the stranger's hands and feet, hoping he could finish before the man's head cleared. His task accomplished, Tyler manuevered the heavy man to one side of the livery and went for a bucket of water to revive him.

The frigid water made the man jump, and his eyes flew open. "What the —" The man noticed Tyler for the first time. "Who are you, mister?"

"I'm Tyler Andrews, the circuit rider for these parts. I'm also the man who hopes to marry Amy Carmichael as soon as she's found," Tyler replied.

The man shook his head. "Don't know no Amy Carmichael." He reached his tied hands up to his bruised jaw. "Why'd you do this?

Sure don't seem like a very parson-like thing for you to be doing."

Tyler studied the man carefully. He seemed to be genuinely surprised that Tyler would have any interest in him. "I know you're working with Nathan Gallagher. And I know you sold Amy's horse in Hays."

"I did sell a horse for Gallagher," the man admitted, "but I didn't know who it belonged to. He just told me to get rid of it quick-like and I did."

"It doesn't matter." Tyler drew closer. "What does matter is that you'd best tell me where Gallagher has Amy and you'd best tell me right now."

The man shook his head. "I'm telling you, mister, I don't know any Amy. There ain't been any woman involved in my dealings with Gallagher."

Tyler grabbed the man by the collar and yanked him forward. "Then you'd best tell me what you and Gallagher are up to and let me judge for myself."

The man's eyes narrowed, as if he were considering Tyler's words. "I don't reckon Mister Gallagher would like that," he finally replied.

Tyler's face twisted. He tightened his grip on the man and slammed him back against the wall. "I don't reckon Gallagher's going to take the beating that you are when I go across the street and retrieve Amy's pa and brother.

Of course, that's going to be after I get done with you myself. After that, I figure you'll be right glad to go to the gallows."

The man blanched. He wasn't getting paid enough by Gallagher to take the gallows for him. Especially if Gallagher had done in some woman in the process of setting up his scheme. Looking into the preacher's face, the man met his deadly stare. What he saw there was more than enough to unnerve him.

"I'll talk," the redheaded man declared. "I ain't going to hang for something I ain't done."

"You'd best get to it then." Tyler's voice was ominously calm.

"Gallagher plans to rob the bank tomorrow morning," the man replied. "He has the combination to the safe and while the town is celebrating Christmas at the school, he's going to let himself in and clean out the harvest money."

Tyler nodded. The man's explanation made everything fall into place. Somehow, Amy must have overheard Gallagher's plans. That was why he had taken her hostage. At last her disappearance was starting to make some sense.

"How do you and your brother figure in this?" Tyler asked, surprising the man with his reference to his brother.

Rather than question the preacher, though, since the huge man seemed to be feeling a might testy, the red-haired man hurried to answer his question. "We arranged to get Gallagher's stuff out of town. Then we were to act as lookouts while Gallagher took the money. We aren't involved in any killings, though, and I never did see any woman. That's the God's honest truth, preacher."

"Gallagher never said anything about a woman overhearing his plans? He never told you that the horse belonged to Amy Carmichael?"

"No, sir, he never told me nothing. He got mad at my brother and told him to git. Told me I could have his cut if I wanted to keep on with the plan. It sounded like easy money, so I told him I would. When he told me to take the horse to Hays, he just told me to get rid of it without a scene and to take whatever I could get without haggling the price. I did that and came back here to let him know and get ready for tomorrow."

Tyler realized the man was most likely telling the truth. He studied him for a moment before speaking. "So you aren't supposed to see Gallagher again until tomorrow?"

"I ain't supposed to meet up with him until after the job's done," the man admitted. "I'm supposed to wait between the bank and the school and make sure no one interrupts Gallagher. After that, I'm supposed to ride out and meet him at the river."

Tyler nodded. "Good enough. I'm going to

have to lock you up, but maybe once this is done with — and if Miss Carmichael is found, unharmed — just maybe the judge will go easy on you for cooperating with me."

The man grumbled at Tyler's plan, but he knew he had nothing to bargain. He nodded weakly and resigned himself to captivity.

Tyler locked the man in the tack room and hurried to find Charles and Randy. He located Charles first and together they went to retrieve Randy. He quickly explained to them what he knew.

"Look," Tyler said, the excitement clear in his voice. "Gallagher plans to rob the bank tomorrow while we're having Christmas service. We've got to play this thing out carefully and give him no reason to believe that anything is amiss. Most likely he'll be ready to use Amy as insurance for his plans."

"What'll we do?" Charles asked cautiously.

"We'll act as though nothing has changed," Tyler said. "Randy, you go on home to your family and, Charles, you do the same. Get everybody up and around for the services and bring them on in, just like you planned."

"We can't just pretend nothing's happened," Randy protested.

"Of course we can." Tyler's firmness hushed Randy's objection. "It's the only way we can smoke Gallagher out of his hole."

"The Andersons will need to know," Charles said. "They've been so good to help look for Amy. I know they'd want to be in on this."

"Good. In fact," — Tyler had a sudden thought — "we'll need Ed to be inside the bank before Gallagher gets there."

"What do you have in mind?" Charles asked. He looked at the preacher and shook his head, and his lips curled a little. "Never would have thought no parson could be as mean as you are."

"Even Christ got angry enough to physically throw the money changers out of the Temple," Tyler answered. "When He saw true evil, He was just as 'mean' as I feel today."

"What do you have in mind?" Charles repeated.

Tyler smiled, feeling assurance for the first time. He'd finally nailed Gallagher down. "Well, I see it like this . . ."

Chapter 15

The sleepy people of Deer Ridge emerged from the warmth of their homes and made their way to the schoolhouse for Christmas morning services. Tyler stood outside the school welcoming the families as though nothing was amiss. He saw pain and fear in the eyes of some of the people and wished he could ease their minds even a portion.

Wagons came rattling in from the farthest reaches, and those who dared to make the snowy trip were anxious to seek the warmth of the school building. Dora and Angie Carmichael arrived well bundled in the buckboard, with Charles riding alongside. Close behind them was Randy and his family in their wagon, with Randy's horse tied on the back. Tyler nodded to the two Carmichael men and felt a calm assurance that everything was falling into place.

He cast a quick glance down the street to where the bank stood. Ed Anderson had taken up his place there some hours earlier, and Tyler knew that the other Anderson men were waiting out of sight in order to lend a hand in the capture of Nathan Gallagher. All was progressing as planned.

"Let's hurry inside, folks," Tyler called to the gathering crowd. "We've got a good fire going in the stove and Brother Smith has kindly furnished hot cider for everyone."

The children clapped their hands at this, and the adults offered brief smiles of gratitude. Tyler knew their discouragement and worry. Wasn't his own heart nearly broken? Didn't his own mind strike against him with torturous thoughts that Amy might already be dead?

Please, Father, he prayed silently, *help me be strong for these people. Help me to help them through this. And be with Amy wherever she is. Let her know that help is on its way — that we haven't forgotten her.*

Amy struggled to climb again onto the table. She had little strength left to even walk, much less to put forth the energy required to knock a hole in the roof. She had no way of knowing how much time had passed, but in spite of the care she had taken, she was out of water now, and the lamp was nearly out of oil.

Always before, Amy had forced herself to ignore her dilemma and to concentrate instead on the task at hand. Minute by minute, she reminded herself that she could lie down and die, or fight to escape. Up until this moment, she had always chosen quickly to fight. Now, however, she was tired, cold, hungry, and completely defeated in spirit.

"God," she whispered in a hoarse voice, "I know You're here." She felt like crying, but tears had long since stopped coming. "I've got nothing else to give, Lord. I'm spent and we both know it."

Just then a huge clod of dirt worked loose from the roof and fell, striking Amy across the face. The pain it caused was brief, but the sunlight it let in was stunning.

Amy stared up in disbelief at the small hole. Bits of snow came in with the dirt, and Amy instantly reached out to pull a handful of the moist whiteness into her mouth. Her lips and tongue seemed to suck up the snow instantly, and eager for more, Amy reached out again and again.

The stream of sunlight offered only shadowy light to the room, but it was enough to encourage Amy. She felt as though God had spoken to her directly, and she worked at the hole with fresh strength, scraping and clawing, until all of her fingers were cut and bleeding.

But she was too weak to work for very long. When her legs would hold her no longer, Amy let herself sink down on the tabletop to rest. After a moment, she rolled from its surface and took herself to the bed, hoping to regain even a little more strength so that she could continue her work.

She closed her eyes and felt the air grow colder. She hadn't thought about the fact that by making a hole in the roof, she would lose what little warmth she'd maintained in the dugout. Opening her eyes, Amy glanced up at her handiwork, then sat up abruptly. Her newfound hope ebbed into despair. The hole was hardly more than eight inches across, too small to do her any practical good. All of her hard work had rendered nothing more than this!

She began to sob, though her eyes refused to produce tears, and she slumped down again on the bed. Hopeless despair filled her heart and all reasonable thought left her mind.

"I'm going to die," she cried. "Oh God, I can't bear this!"

Her body was spent, and she had no energy left to urge her on. For a moment longer she struggled to call forth the will to fight, but then at last she gave up and offered God her life, praying that death would be quick and painless.

The exhaustion of the past week had overtaken her, and she had no strength left to fight death any longer. Without even bothering to pull the filthy cover around her, Amy let her mind drift into dreams of her family and Tyler.

It must be close to Christmas, she thought. *Will they still have the Christmas service? Will they sing the old songs?* she wondered.

Strains of music rose through her memories. The haunting melody of "Silent Night" brought her tired mind peace. "All is calm, all is bright." She mouthed the words. "Sleep in heavenly peace." *Yes,* she thought. *I will sleep in heavenly peace.*

Tyler stood at the front of the school room for only a moment. He looked out at the community gathered there, and then he made a brief statement. When he had finished, stunned silence echoed through the room.

"You must help us," Tyler beseeched the crowd. "Amy Carmichael's life depends on it. I don't mind telling you good folks, her life has come to mean a great deal to me."

Several couples exchanged brief knowing smiles before they turned back to the preacher, awaiting further instruction. Moments later the congregation joined in song. The music rang out loudly as Mrs. Smith played a donated piano, and the gathering did their part to assure anyone listening from outside that the service was well underway.

Meanwhile, Tyler hurried out the back door and came quietly around the school to where his horse was hitched. In one fluid movement, he pulled the reins loose and mounted the animal's back. Then, without making a sound, he pushed the horse into a gallop across the snow-covered plain.

Nathan heard the singing and knew his time had come. He smiled and congratulated himself on the simplicity of his plan. He was Morgan Stewart's lawyer, and Morgan Stewart was the bank's owner. He was also the only one besides Ed Anderson who had the combination to the safe. That was he *was* the only one before he had hired Nathan as his lawyer. Then he had allowed Nathan to keep the carefully guarded secret in a confidential file with Stewart's other important papers.

The whole thing had been too simple, Nathan laughed. He'd only had to place himself in the community for a couple of years and earn their regard and trust. Then when the opportunity of a good harvest presented itself, Nathan knew his time had come.

He threw the last of his belongings into already bulging saddlebags and made his way down the side stairs of the hotel. He would miss Mrs. Miller's apple dumplings, he thought, but with thousands of dollars in his keep, he could no doubt buy tasty apple dumplings elsewhere.

He went to the livery and saddled his horse,

loading his bags before leading the animal down the empty street. The bank sat there like an unguarded jewel, and Nathan felt his pulse quicken.

Down the street, the townspeople broke into yet another Christmas carol, oblivious to the evil that lurked just steps away. At least that's what Nathan presumed.

Quickly, he hitched the horse behind the bank. He looked up and down the empty alleyway, and then with great caution, he picked the lock on the bank door and let himself in.

With the door closed behind him, the singing voices were muted. He steadied his nerves with a deep breath and moved toward the safe. One step, then two, and everything was quiet, just as it should be. But as he lifted his foot a third time, a voice stopped him cold.

"Hello, Gallagher." Ed Anderson sat ever so casually to one side of the room, contemplating the revolver he held in his hand.

Nathan's eyes narrowed and he whirled on his heel, his own gun quickly drawn from his coat pocket. "Anderson!" He leveled the pistol.

Ed seemed unmoved. His sober gaze never wavered. "Where's Amy?"

Nathan had forgotten the girl, and now he nearly laughed. "Somewhere you'll never find her."

"Now, that doesn't seem to be a very

reasonable way to act," Ed said.

Nathan sneered. "Drop your gun, Anderson. I have a quicker hand than you, and I won't hesitate to shoot."

"Oh?" Ed raised a brow. "Then you won't mind when the whole town is alerted by the noise?"

Nathan realized Ed was right. He paused a moment to rethink his plan. "Where's the money?" he asked, noticing that the safe was open.

"Where's Amy?"

But Gallagher refused to give in, and Ed realized he'd have to draw him out. "Look," Ed began, "we know you're using Amy as your protection. I realize that once you leave here, you'll go get her and force her to ride with you so that none of us will follow."

Nathan smiled smugly. Anderson had just given him his new plan of action. "That's right. If you try to stop me, Amy will die."

"I kind of figured that." Ed's voice was cool. "I just figured maybe you'd strike a deal. Like I give you the money and you give me Amy. Maybe we could have a trade-off down by the river."

"No," Nathan refused firmly. "I'm not a fool to fall into a predictable plan like that. You'll give me the money now and you won't follow me — or you'll never see Amy Carmichael again!"

Ed got to his feet and took a step toward

Gallagher. The look on his face was threatening, and Nathan waved him back with the gun. "If I have to, I'll shoot you — whether the town hears me or not. When they come running, I'll just tell them that I stopped you from robbing the bank. Of course, you'll be dead and dead men tell no tales. Then where will your precious Amy be?"

"All right, Gallagher," Ed said between his clenched teeth, "you win."

"Of course I do. Now, give me the money and leave me to ride out of here. Remember, I'll have the girl and there won't be anything to stop me from killing her."

Ed nodded and motioned to the safe. "The money's still inside."

"Get it," Nathan commanded and stepped back. "But first, lose that gun."

Ed looked angrily at Gallagher for a moment and then put the gun down on the desktop. He crossed the room to the safe and pulled out two full money bags.

"Put them on the table by the door," Nathan motioned, and Ed did as he was told. "Now, get down on your belly and don't even think of following me. Not if you want me to release the Carmichael girl unharmed."

Ed began to get down on the floor. "What assurance do I have that she hasn't already been harmed?" he asked.

"None." Nathan leered. "But what other choice do you have?"

Ed shrugged his shoulders and lay down on the floor. He waited until Nathan had grabbed up the money and exited the bank before raising his head. Then glancing around cautiously to make certain Gallagher wasn't waiting for him, Ed got to his feet, pulled on his coat, and ran out of the bank.

He mounted his horse and circled the building. Gallagher was long gone, much to Ed's relief, but the tracks in the snow pointed the direction he'd fled, and Ed knew that his brothers and Amy's family would already be tracking the man. Hopefully, he'd lead them straight to Amy.

CHAPTER 16

Amy's mind registered sounds, but she told herself she was dreaming. She thought she heard a horse's whinny and the sound of movement on the ground above her, but try as she might, she couldn't push herself to investigate.

She forced her eyes open, only to be blinded by a flood of brilliant light as the door creaked open. She waited, uncertain whether she was dead or alive. Either way, she could only wait, helpless, for whatever happened next.

She felt herself being lifted, and for a moment she wondered if God had come to take her to heaven. The thought comforted her, and she waited limp in the arms that bore her, hopeful that she'd find her celestial home on the other side of the door.

Instead, cold air hit her face, and Amy roused ever so slightly. Trying to focus on the face overhead, she felt a deep foreboding. This was definitely not her heavenly Father who carried her.

"You didn't expect me to come back, did you?"

Amy shook her head, not in reply to the question, but because she was unsure of the words. Her mind was so muddled, clear thinking so beyond her strength, that she could only bide her time.

"The whole town has been looking for you," the voice said. "Especially that fool Andrews."

Amy's foggy mind grasped at the thought of Tyler Andrews. His name was like a lightning bolt, jolting her with energy. She remained silent, however, feigning the near unconscious state that she'd been in before. She still didn't have enough energy to fight this man, but no longer was she apathetic, ready to give up.

"Now," the voice spoke again, "everyone in town is going to have a little more to say about Nathan Gallagher."

Nathan! Of course, now Amy remembered. Nathan had brought her to the dugout. She forced her mind to remember the events, and through the clouds she pulled together bits and pieces. *Yes, yes,* she thought, *I remember; Nathan planned to rob the bank.*

All of a sudden Amy found herself slammed stomach side down against the back of a horse. Just as quickly, Nathan mounted behind her and half pulled her body across his lap.

"They won't be so inclined to do me in," he said with a laugh, "when they see what's at stake."

"I wouldn't count on that, Gallagher," a voice called.

Nathan whirled his mount around to meet the angry faces of Tyler Andrews and Randy and Charles Carmichael.

Tyler could barely maintain his seat at the sight of Amy, half-dead, sprawled across Nathan's lap. He gripped the reins so tight that both hands were balled into gloved fists. More than anything, he would have liked to strike those fists against Gallagher's head.

Randy Carmichael was feeling none too patient either. He moved his horse forward a step. "Let her go, Gallagher."

Nathan laughed and revealed his pistol. "I can easily shoot her," he replied, cocking the hammer. "And I will if you try to stop me from riding away from here."

"But then" — Tyler's voice was steady — "you'd have no hostage. And instead of bank robbery, you'd be facing murder."

Nathan shrugged. "I don't intend to rot in any prison, either way."

The sound of Tyler's voice had cleared Amy's head a bit more. She moved it ever so slightly to get an idea of her circumstances. The tiny movement caught Tyler's eyes, but

Nathan seemed not to notice.

I've got to keep him talking, thought Tyler. "Look, Nathan," he began, surprising Charles and Randy with the smooth, open way he spoke, "this doesn't have to end badly. You know what you've done is wrong, but a lot of people have gone astray besides you. You know that God offers forgiveness and new life to all those who ask, no matter what they've done. Why not start over?"

"I don't need a sermon, Preach," Gallagher said.

Tyler moved his horse closer, his eyes never leaving Nathan's. "It's more than a sermon, Nathan, and you know it. If you died right now, you'd have to face God. Are you ready to do that? Are you ready to risk eternal damnation and separation from God?"

"I don't intend to die right now," Nathan said evenly.

"But you will if you don't hand Amy over," Randy promised, his voice tight.

Nathan shrugged. "But then you'd be responsible for her death."

Amy stiffened at the words being bandied over her head. Tyler's horse came forward another pace, making Nathan's horse prance nervously.

"Stay where you are, Andrews," Nathan demanded. "I know what you're trying — and it's not going to work."

"I'm not above begging." Tyler's voice was

off-hand. "I don't want you to hurt her. I care a great deal about her. In fact, I love her and want her to be my wife."

Nathan laughed. "How touching. But I could care less."

"I guess I've pretty well figured that out." Tyler tried to control his temper. "Point is, I can't help trying. A man such as yourself must surely be in a position to understand that. After all, you're also facing a most precarious situation."

"I've had enough of this," Randy interrupted. He narrowed his eyes. "Gallagher, you let my sister go now or you'll have to deal with all of us."

"I thought I already was dealing with you," Nathan said, unmoved by Randy's declaration. "I seem to be managing satisfactorily." He grinned.

"Not quite." Ed Anderson came out of the trees. His brothers, Jacob and Jack, followed. Now six horsemen surrounded Nathan. Slowly he began to realize that he was losing the battle.

"God can still save your soul, Gallagher," Tyler edged the huge Morgan he rode another step forward. "But right now, you're the only one who can save your hide."

Nathan's horse shied at the Morgan's nearness and whinnied nervously. Tyler refused to back off and pressed his luck. Nathan quickly brought the gun up from Amy to level it at

Tyler, just as the Morgan nudged his head against Gallagher's mount.

Amy took that opportunity to dig what was left of her ragged fingernails into the horse's side. Nathan's mount reared. While Nathan fought to hold on to the reins, Amy slid backward off the horse. She used every ounce of her remaining energy to roll to the side. After that, she could do nothing more than lie there and await her fate.

Without warning, Tyler leapt across his horse, knocking Nathan to the ground. The pistol fired harmlessly into the air as it flew from Nathan's hand. Within moments, four other men were helping to restrain Gallagher, while Charles Carmichael jumped to the ground and lifted Amy into his arms.

"Pa?" she whispered. Her throat was raw, and her voice was barely audible.

"I'm here, Amy," he answered with tears in his eyes. "You're safe now."

Tyler was at her side immediately. He pulled off his coat and wrapped it around her shivering body. In Amy's confused state of mind, she found his worried expression almost amusing, but the overgrown stubble of his beard amused her even more.

"You need a shave." She croaked the words against his ear.

Tyler lifted his head and laughed loud and hard, though tears shone in his eyes. Even Charles had to join in the laughter. "That's my girl," Tyler said, lifting her in his arms.

Randy left Nathan to the capable hands of the Andersons. They'd already agreed to be responsible for getting Gallagher to Hays. Ed was the one witness who would be able to confirm the bank robbery, and the others would no doubt be called upon if needed at a later date.

"Merry Christmas, Sis," Randy said, laying a hand on Amy's dirty cheek. Tears gleamed in Randy's eyes, too.

"Quite a present," she replied weakly.

"Let's get her to Doc," Tyler said, heading for his horse with his precious cargo.

"I can take her," Randy offered. He reached out his arms, but his father's hand pulled him back.

"I think you'd have a fight on your hands if you tried to separate them now," Charles said softly.

Randy nodded. "I suppose you're right. If it were Betsey . . ."

"Or Dora," Charles interjected. "There comes a time when fathers and brothers have to step aside. Now, come on, let's get back to town."

Tyler held Amy close, whispering endearments and encouragement all the way back to Deer Ridge. She snuggled against the warmth of his coat, thanking God silently for sending help in time to rescue her from

Nathan's plans.

She opened her eyes briefly and gazed up into the haggard face of the man she'd come to love more dearly than life. With a smile, she whispered, "I love you, Tyler Andrews."

Tyler shook his head with a grin. "You're something else, Amy Carmichael. You endure all of this and now you want to finally get around to telling me that you love me?"

"Just thought you'd like to hear it." She smiled, closing her eyes.

Tyler leaned down and placed a kiss against her forehead. "You bet I want to hear it. I want to hear it every day of my life for the rest of my life!"

The entire town was waiting and watching for the riders to return. When they caught sight of Tyler's huge horse, they strained their eyes to identify the bundle he held. Cheers went up when Randy and Charles moved ahead to announce that Amy was alive, but extremely weak. Charles handed his reins to Randy and went quickly to Dora and Angie to assure them that Amy was safe. There were tears of joy on their faces as they followed arm in arm to Doc Taggert's office. In hushed conversation, the townspeople gathered behind them and followed in the street to gather outside the doctor's office.

Tyler waited outside with Charles, while Dora and Angie went inside to be with Amy while Doc Taggert examined her.

"Where's Gallagher?" Jeremy Smith asked the question everyone wanted to know.

"The Andersons are taking him to Hays," Tyler replied. His mind was not on the question, though. He had been reluctant to leave Amy's side, and now he ached to know if she would be alright.

"Then he's alive?" someone else called out.

Randy moved through the crowd with Betsey at his side. Their children were being tended back at the school by one of the town's women, while baby Joey was safely tucked in the crook of his mother's arm.

"He's alive," Randy said, coming to stand beside his father. "He could just as well be dead and so could Amy, if it weren't for Tyler's patience." A smile crossed Randy's face. "Good thing for Gallagher, 'cause patience ain't exactly one of my own virtues."

The crowd laughed, and then Charles hushed them all. "I want to thank all of you for your help in finding Amy. We're stuck out here so far from everybody else in the world that we've truly become one big family. Without working together, we'd probably all perish."

Murmurs of agreement went through the crowd before Charles could speak again. "Truth is, and you folks need to understand this, Tyler Andrews saved this town from disaster. See, Gallagher didn't just take Amy, he planned to clean out the bank as well. Amy overheard his plans and that's why he kidnapped her."

The exchange of looks between the people varied from anger to plain shock. Their hopes and dreams were pinned on their savings and earnings.

"Look, I know you folks feel the same way I do about having a full-time parson around these parts. I think we pretty much owe that to Tyler and I'd like to propose we hire him on as Deer Ridge's first pastor." Charles sent a beaming smile toward the man he knew would one day be his son-in-law.

Cheers from the crowd confirmed that Deer Ridge's residents felt the same way the Carmichaels did.

"It's the least we can do," Jeremy Smith said to the crowd. "We wouldn't even have the money to last through the winter if it weren't for Andrews getting wind of Gallagher's plan."

"That's right," Mrs. Smith agreed enthusiastically. "I think Pastor Andrews is just what this town needs."

Tyler held out his hands to quiet the enthusiastic response of the people before him. "I appreciate the offer," he said.

"Well, what do you say?" Amos Osborne, Deer Ridge's self-appointed mayor, questioned Tyler. "Will you pastor our community? I'm sure I speak for all the folks here in saying we'd be most honored to have you stay on. We might even be able to build a church in another year or so — that is, if we get another good year behind us." Everyone nodded in unison and waited for the towering man to speak.

Tyler's heart was touched, but his mind was on Amy. "I'll pray about it," he replied.

Just then Angie appeared at the door with a smile on her face. "Doc says Amy is half-starved and dehydrated. But she didn't suffer much from the cold, and he says she ought to be just fine in a few days."

Tyler reached out and gave Angie a hearty hug at the news.

"Whoa, preacher," someone called. "You got the wrong sister!" Everyone laughed, and Tyler's face reddened.

"Don't worry," Angie laughed. "I'll pass that hug on to the right one." With a wink, she turned and went back into the building.

Bit by bit, the crowd dispersed and regathered at the schoolhouse where the festivities for Christmas started anew. Once Tyler was certain Amy was out of any real danger, he agreed to return and preach the service he'd promised. The atmosphere was one of genuine love and happiness, with each and every person knowing just how far God's protection and love had extended to them that Christmas.

The kids made clear that they considered the holiday theirs, and after their simple play about the shepherds seeking the Christ Child, they lined up to receive candy from the Smiths. Soon the entire affair burst into a full-fledged party, with sweets and goodies spread out on a lace tablecloth. Someone brought out a punch bowl and cups, and soon everyone was toasting the day and the man whom they hoped would stay to become one of Deer Ridge's own.

Finally, Tyler led them in a closing prayer. "Father, we thank You for the gift of Your Son. We can't begin to understand the sacrifice You made on our behalf, but we praise You for Your love."

Several people murmured in agreement before Tyler could continue, "You've watched over this town in a most wondrous way this day — and in a very unique and special way You brought us all together. For a while, we forgot our differences and divisions. For a very precious time, we were able to stand here before You, knowing with surety that Your gift was given equally to us all. In that gift we are given hope, forgiveness, and eternal life. Thank You, Father. Amen."

There were few dry eyes in the room when Tyler finished. Beyond a murmured thank-you or pat on the back, no one said a word to the young pastor as he left the school. They all knew where his heart was hurrying him.

CHAPTER 17

Amy restlessly pushed back her covers and started to sit up. She'd been in bed four days now; because of her mother's continual care, she was very nearly herself again. In spite of this, however, no one seemed inclined to let her out of bed.

"Oh no, you don't, young lady." Her mother came into the room with a tray of food.

"I can't just lie here eating all the time," Amy protested. "I'll get fat and lazy!"

"You could do with a little more meat on your bones." Dora laughed. "As for lazy, that will be the day pigs fly."

Amy giggled and sat back reluctantly against the pillows. "I truly feel fine, Ma."

"I know." Dora put the tray across her daughter's lap. "You just let me pamper you a bit more. Soon enough, if I have that young preacher of yours figured out, you'll be gone from this house and my care — so let me enjoy it while I can."

Amy frowned slightly. Since the day after

her rescue, she had not seen Tyler at all. She'd asked her father about him yesterday, but Charles had shrugged his shoulders. Perhaps Tyler needed to tend to business, he told her.

"You can just wipe that frown off your face," Dora commanded good-naturedly. "Tyler will be back."

"I hope so." Amy's voice lacked confidence. She glanced down at the tray on her lap; it held a bowl of beef stew, two biscuits, and a glass of milk. "Didn't I just eat an hour ago?" she asked with a laugh.

"Just be quiet and eat." Dora tucked the covers around her daughter. "I used Cora Peterson's recipe for the stew. I seem to recall that was your favorite."

Amy took a mouthful of the thick stew and nodded. "Mmm, it's perfect."

Dora smiled at this announcement and turned to leave. "Now, if you need anything at all, just ring." She nodded at the bell by Amy's bedside.

"I promise." Amy tried to give the stew her attention. When her mother had left the room, though, Amy sighed and pushed the tray back.

"Where are you, Tyler?" she whispered into the silent air. She didn't want to eat or rest anymore. She wanted to talk to Tyler. She needed to hear his voice and know that everything was truly all right.

Boredom was her enemy, and Amy wanted nothing more than to be up and about. At least if she were back to her regular duties, Tyler's absence wouldn't be so noticeable.

After ten or fifteen minutes, her mother reappeared. She gave the tray a glance and frowned. "You haven't eaten much of it." She looked at Amy for a long moment, and then she surprised her daughter by going to the closet and pulling out a long flannel robe. "Here." She handed Amy the robe and took the tray. "Put this on and I'll let you sit at the window."

Amy's smile stretched nearly from ear to ear. This was the first time her mother had agreed to let her get up for any reason other than the absolute necessities. Hurriedly, in case her mother changed her mind, she thrust her arms through the robe's sleeves.

Dora put the tray on the table by the window. "Now, seeing as how I'm being so nice to you, oblige me by eating a little more of this." She went back to help Amy to her feet. "You promise to just sit here, now?" Dora settled Amy in the chair. "No big ideas about trying to get up on your feet?"

"Of course not." Amy smiled.

Dora sniffed and looked at her daughter suspiciously. "You just mind what your mother says, girl." Her voice was stern, but the corners of her mouth curved up.

A knock at the bedroom door made them

both turn. Charles peeked his head inside with a grin. "I found someone wandering around the yard below, hoping to get a chance to talk with our Amy," he teased. Pushing the door open wide, he revealed a grinning Tyler Andrews.

"Tyler!" Amy jumped to her feet.

"Sit back down!" Dora commanded. "You promised."

Amy obediently did as she was told, but a slight pout on her lips told them all that she wasn't happy about it.

"Now, if you promise," her mother stressed the words, "to stay put, we'll let Tyler visit you for a spell."

Amy nodded and made the sign of an *X* over her heart. "Cross my heart," she said solemnly.

Her parents and Tyler laughed. "I guess that's the best we can hope for," Charles said. "I'll get you a chair, Tyler," he added. "Be right back."

Dora smiled and exited the room quietly. Meanwhile, Amy tried to keep herself from leaping across the room into Tyler's arms.

"You shaved," she said with a grin.

"I was told it was quite overdue." Tyler returned her grin.

Charles entered the room with a kitchen chair, then just as quickly left. Tyler brought the chair to the table where Amy's food still sat untouched.

"You'd best eat that." He pointed to the stew.

"I'm not hungry," Amy said softly.

Tyler frowned. "You're still not feeling well?"

Amy made a face. "I feel fine. But Ma's been feeding me every five minutes — or so it seems. All I've really wanted to do was get up and . . ." She stopped abruptly and looked deep into Tyler's warm gaze.

"And?" Tyler prompted.

"And talk to you," she admitted. "Where have you been? I was beginning to get worried that I'd have to saddle up and come looking for you."

Tyler reached out and took hold of Amy's hand. He looked down at her fingers and then gave them a squeeze. "I'll never be far from you. I promise."

Amy felt warmth spread from her hand, up her arm, until it finally engulfed her whole body, leaving her trembling. "I've missed you," she whispered. "I never even had a chance to thank you for all that you did. Pa told me you were the one who figured things out. He told me that without your devotion to the search, I'd most likely have died."

Tyler said nothing. He knew the words were true, but they seemed unimportant just now. "I had to find you," he whispered.

"Yes," Amy said. A hint of amusement played at the corners of her mouth, but she made her voice carefully serious. "Mrs. Smith told me that she accidently told you about your Christmas gift. I suppose it was necessary to find me in order to be sure you got it."

Tyler looked surprised at her words, almost taken back for a moment, and Amy laughed. "Don't be so serious, Tyler. I was teasing."

Tyler shook his head and smiled sheepishly. "I guess it's going to take me a while to get used to the idea that you're really here with me safe and sound — and even a little obnoxious. I was so afraid I'd lost you."

Amy smiled, but her eyes misted at the expression she saw on his face. "But I'm all right now, thanks to you and Pa and everyone else. God watched over me. Even when I gave up hope, He stood fast and provided for my rescue. I won't spend the rest of my life having you look at me that way." Her voice was firm.

Tyler pulled his hand away. "Look at you what way?"

"Like I'm about to disappear into thin air. Or" — she lowered her voice to a whisper — "die."

Tyler considered her words for a moment. "I know you're right. I have to learn to trust your safety to God. But you did disappear into thin air — and you came awfully close to dying. Gallagher would have left you there in that soddy if we hadn't interfered. I don't

676

think you could have survived much longer." He shook his head, his eyes dark.

"I know." Amy reached to take back Tyler's hand. "After what happened to your wife, I can understand how you must feel. But we are all in God's hands. And you must let go of your worry. I want to get on with my life. I want to make plans."

Tyler's face relaxed, and after a moment his mouth curved into a smile. "What? Beyond today?" he teased.

"Yes." She looked up at him. "You were right. It's easy to take one day at time when you have no one to plan for a future with. Now that I have you, I find my head just bursting with plans. But I don't think it can be all bad to make plans. Even Proverbs says that we can make our plans, counting on God to direct our path. I'll still try to live one day at a time. I don't want to miss even one of the wonderful blessings God has given me in the here and now. But while I'm doing that, I'm also going to look forward to the days to come. Just so long as our plans for the future are grounded in God's Word."

"Then maybe you'll need this." Tyler pulled his well-worn Bible from his coat pocket. He handed the book to Amy and watched as she gently ran her fingers across the cover. "Merry Christmas."

"I don't know what to say." Amy looked up at him with tears in her eyes. "I can't take your Bible." She blinked the tears away and saw now the amusement in Tyler's eyes.

"Well, you're right," he said. "I won't be able to get along without that Bible very well. That's why I have a confession to make."

"Oh? And what might that be?" Amy's voice was suspicious.

"The Bible is just a part of your Christmas gift."

"And what might the rest of my gift be?" Amy leaned forward.

Tyler shrugged, then held out his arms. "Me. It's a package deal. To get the Bible, you have to take me, too. We kind of go together."

"I see." Amy hugged the Bible to her.

"Will you marry me, Amy Carmichael?" Tyler's voice was serious now.

"Of course I will." Amy breathed out a heavy sigh. "I was beginning to wonder how I was going to propose to you, what with you taking so long to ask that particular question. All this talk about Bibles."

Tyler laughed and got to his feet. He started to pull Amy up into his arms, and then suddenly he stopped and pushed her back down. "I forgot. You promised your ma you'd sit."

Amy frowned, but Tyler quickly remedied the situation by pulling his chair close to hers. Leaning over, he pulled her against him with one hand and lifted her face with the other. "I love you, Amy." He lowered his mouth to hers, his lips both gentle and firm.

Amy melted against him. She felt her heart nearly burst with love. When he pulled his lips away at last, she opened her eyes slowly and met his amused stare.

"When?" she whispered.

"I beg your pardon?"

She narrowed her eyes at him, but his golden hair beckoned her fingers, and she reached up to push back a strand before she answered. "You know very well what I mean, Tyler Andrews." She pursed her lips primly. "When can we get married, Parson?"

Tyler grinned. "I'll have to check my schedule and see when I can fit you in. Pastoring is a mighty big responsibility, you know. It might be a spell before I can get back to these parts and . . ."

Amy jerked away from his arms. "Don't tease me, Tyler Andrews. If I have to, I'll hitch up the team and drive us to Hays myself." She sighed and then added firmly, "I've never been pushy about anything in my life — until now. But I'm beginning to think Angie may have been right all along. She sees a thing she wants and goes right after it. Well, now I intend to do the same."

Tyler's raucous laughter filled the air, bringing Charles and Dora to the doorway.

"What's going on?" Charles gave Tyler and Amy an amused look.

"Your daughter," Tyler said, still laughing,

"is threatening to to hitch up the team and drive us to Hays so we can get married. I was just picturing the sight in my mind. Barely off her death bed, clad in her nightgown, hair all wild and crazy behind her" — he paused, and Amy turned crimson at his description — "and she's going to drive us to Hays."

"It's always the quiet ones who'll surprise you," Charles advised Tyler. With an arm around his wife, Charles added, "And I speak from experience."

Tyler laughed all the more at that, and even Dora couldn't help but join in. Soon, Amy gave up trying to be serious and chuckled in spite of herself. With Tyler Andrews for a husband, she had no doubt she would always have laughter in her house.

From that moment on, Tyler and Amy spent many hours together planning and preparing for their wedding. Tyler shared with her his prayerful consideration of the town's offer to become the full-time pastor, and Amy rejoiced when he decided to accept the job. She'd happily follow him anywhere, she knew in her heart, but she loved Deer Ridge and her family, and she was glad to stay close to all that she cared about.

She soon learned that Tyler's absence during her recovery had included a trip to Hays, where he had managed to find another preacher who would not only take over Tyler's circuit, but also returned to Deer Ridge with him. With the other preacher officiating, the wedding was to take place on New Year's Day. Amy couldn't imagine a better way to start the new year.

When the day came at last, she stood proudly beside the huge man. The drawn, nervous look on his face almost made her giggle, but her own nerves weren't much more settled than Tyler's appeared to be. She listened carefully to the words spoken by the circuit rider, and then she repeated her vows. Without a doubt in her heart, she promised to love, honor, and obey this man she loved so much.

Tyler's voice was firm and grave as he repeated the same vows. When he took her hand and placed a small gold band on her finger, tears of joy and wonder slid down Amy's cheeks.

Then the ceremony was over. Tyler pulled her into his arms, kissing her in front of the entire community. With a loud voice, he declared to one and all that they were joined in God's sight and in love.

The community cheered heartily as the ceremony concluded. They congratulated the young couple until Amy thought her hand would be permanently numb from shaking the hands of so many people.

Charles and Dora came to greet their children, and Amy smiled radiantly when they called her Mrs. Andrews. Angie in her wedding finery, a new gown of blue taffeta that had come from Hays, danced rings around everyone. The entire community was convinced that she'd be the next to marry. The only question was which one of her many suitors Angie would finally settle on.

"We're mighty glad to see you up and around, Miss Amy," Jeremy Smith said when his turn came to congratulate the newlyweds. He turned then to Tyler and broke into a broad grin. "And we're mighty happy, Preacher, to know we'll get to hear your preaching every week and not just once a month."

Tyler pulled Amy close. She lifted her face to see the look of pride and joy in her husband's eyes. "Deer Ridge will be a good place to call home," he replied, looking down into Amy's face. "A right fine place to plan a future."

Amy smiled. "You mean a future beyond today?" she whispered.

The joke was lost on Jeremy, but Tyler smiled as he looked down at Amy and nodded. "You can count on it, Mrs. Andrews." He gave her a wink. "I'm planning on spending a good long time with you beyond today. A whole lifetime, in fact."

■ ■ ■ ■

Myles from Anywhere

by Jill Strengl

■ ■ ■ ■

With love to Tom, Annie, Jimmy, and
Peter Stengl.
I thank God for each of you every day.
Every mother should be so blessed!
Thank you again to Paula Pruden Macha
and Pamela Griffin —
two living proofs that long-distance
friendship is possible. Love you both!

PROLOGUE

CHILD PRODIGY MISSING. STATEWIDE
SEARCH UNDERWAY FOR MYLES VAN HUY-
SEN, MUSICAL STAR, read the headlines of
the August 21 edition of the city paper. A
passerby stepped on the newspaper where it
lay crumpled beside the tent door, and a
breeze lifted the top page, sending it drifting
across the midway.

A boy glared at the paper from beneath the
brim of his cap, hoping his prospective
employer had not read it closely. Why did
Gram have to make such a big deal about
everything?

"You say you're willing to work hard, kid?
How old are you, anyway?"

"Eighteen. Ain't got no family." He
struggled to sound illiterate yet mature
enough to merit the two extra years he
claimed.

"Kinda puny, ain't ya?" The owner of the
traveling circus chomped on his unlit cigar.
"You're in luck, Red. One of our fellas went

687

down sick a week back, and we've been struggling since. It ain't easy work, and the pay is peanuts, but you'll get room and board, such as it is. Go see Parker in the animal tent and tell him I sent you."

"Yes, Mr. Bonacelli. Thank you, Mr. Bonacelli."

"You may not be thankin' me when you find out what you'll be doin'. What's yer name, Red?"

"Myles Trent." It was his name minus its third element. If he so much as mentioned "Van Huysen" the game would end for certain.

"Hmph. I'll call ya Red."

Visions of becoming an acrobat or animal trainer soon vanished from Myles's head. During the next few months, he worked harder than he had ever worked in his life, cleaning animal pens. It was nasty and hazardous work at times, yet he enjoyed becoming friends with other circus employees. Whenever the circus picked up to move to the next town, everyone worked together, from the clowns to the trapeze artists to the bearded lady. It wasn't long before Myles began to move up in the circus world.

Bonacelli's Circus made its way south from New York, then west toward Ohio, playing in towns along the highways and railroads. During the coldest months, the caravans headed south along the Mississippi; spring found them headed north. Months passed into a year.

Lengthening his face to minimize creases, Myles wiped grease paint from his eyelids. Behind him, the tent flap was pulled aside. Someone came in. "Antonio?" he guessed.

"Hello, Myles."

His eyes popped open. A handsome face smiled at him from his mirror.

Myles froze. His shoulders drooped. He turned on the stool. "Monte."

The brothers stared at each other. Monte pulled up a chair and straddled it backward. "I caught today's show. Never thought I'd see my musician brother doing flips onto a horse's back. You've built muscle and calluses. Look healthier than I can remember." There was grudging admiration in his voice.

"The acrobats and clowns taught me tricks."

"I've been hanging around, asking questions. People like and respect you. Say you're honest and hardworking."

Myles's eyes narrowed. "I love the circus, Monte. I like making people happy."

"You're a performer. It's in your blood."

Myles turned to his mirror and rubbed blindly at the paint. "Why so pleasant all of a sudden?"

Monte ignored the question. "Gram wants you back. She's already spent too much on detectives. I'll write and tell her I found you before she fritters away our fortune."

"I'm not going back."

"I didn't ask you to. The old lady sent me to keep an eye on you. She never said I had to go back . . . at least not right away." One of Monte's brows lifted, and he gave Myles his most charming smile. "The Van Huysen Soap Company and fortune will wait for me. No reason to waste my youth in a stuffy office, learning business from a fat family friend. I think I'd rather be a circus star like my runny-nosed kid brother."

"You've seen me. Now get lost." Hope faded from Myles's eyes. "You'll spoil everything."

"Believe it or not, I do understand. That was no life for a kid. I've often wondered how you endured it as long as you did. Getting out of that Long Island goldfish bowl is a relief. Always someone watching, moralizing, planning your life — whew! You had the right idea. I could hardly believe my luck when Gram sent me after you."

"She trusted you," Myles observed dryly. "What are you planning to do?"

"Does this circus need more workers? I'm serious. This looks like the life for me."

Myles huffed. "Nobody needs a worker like you, Monte. Why don't you go find yourself a gaming hall and forget you ever had a brother?"

"Gram would never forgive me if I returned

without you."

"You could tell her I'm dead."

Monte pondered the idea in mock gravity, dark eyes twinkling. "Tempting, but impossible. Family honor and all that. You'd show up someday, then I'd look the dolt at best, the knave at worst. Part of the family fortune is yours, you know. I wouldn't try to filch it from you. I'm not as rotten as you think, little brother. I do feel some responsibility for my nitwit prodigy sibling."

The next morning when Monte left his borrowed bunk, Myles was gone. No one had seen him leave. Running a big hand down his face, Monte swore. "Gotta find that crazy kid!"

"Are you here with good news or bad, George Poole?" the old lady grumbled from her seat in a faded armchair. A few coals glowed upon the hearth near her feet. "I trust you have disturbed my afternoon rest for good reason."

"Yes, Mrs. Van Huysen. You may see for yourself." He thrust a newspaper into her hands and pointed at a paragraph near the bottom of the page. "An associate of mine in Milwaukee — that's a town in Wisconsin — heard of my quest, spotted this article, and mailed the paper to me."

"Kind of him," Mrs. Van Huysen said, fumbling to put on her glasses. Holding the folded-back paper near her face, she blinked.

"For what am I looking?"

"This, madam. The article concerns a small-town farmer who, years ago, served a prison sentence for robbery and murder. Last summer, new evidence was discovered and the man's name was cleared of the crimes. Judging by the article's tone, this Obadiah Watson appears to be a fine Christian man. It is a pleasure when justice is served, is it not?"

"Yes, yes, but what has this to do with my grandsons?" Virginia Van Huysen struggled to keep her patience.

"Let me find the line . . . ah, right here. You see? The article mentions a certain Myles Trent, hired laborer on Watson's farm." Poole's eyes scanned his client's face.

"I fail to see the significance, Mr. Poole. You raised my hopes for this?"

"Don't you see, madam? Your grandson's name is Myles Trent Van Huysen. Oftentimes a man in hiding will use a pseudonym, and what could be easier to recall than one's own given name?"

"Have you any proof that this man is my Myles? And what of Monte? There is no word of him in this article. The last I heard from the boys, they were together in Texas. Isn't Wisconsin way up north somewhere? Why ever would Myles be there?" Pulling a lacy handkerchief from her cuff, Virginia dabbed at her eyes. "In Monte's last letter he told me that he had surrendered his life to the Lord. Why, then, did he stop writing to me? I don't understand it."

Poole tugged his muttonchop whiskers. "I cannot say, dear madam. The particular region of Texas described in your grandson's most recent letters is a veritable wasteland. Our efforts there were vain; my people discovered no information about your grandsons. It was as if they had dropped from the face of the earth."

"Except for the note your partner sent me about the game hunter in Wyoming." Virginia's tone was inquisitive.

"An unfortunate mistake on Mr. Wynter's part. He should have waited until he had obtained more solid information before consulting you. Be that as it may, madam, unless this Myles Trent proves to be your relation, I fear I must persuade you to give up this quest. I dislike taking your money for naught."

"Naught?" Virginia lifted her pince-nez to give him a quelling look.

Poole nodded. "We at Poole, Poole, and Wynter are ever reluctant to admit defeat, yet I fear we may be brought to that unfortunate pass. It has been nine years since Myles disappeared and nearly six since Monte's last letter reached you. If your grandsons are yet living, they are twenty-five and twenty-eight now."

"I can do simple addition, Mr. Poole," Virginia said. "Have you given up entirely on that hunter?"

"The fellow disappeared. He was probably an outlaw who became nervous when Wynter started asking questions. You must keep in mind that your grandsons are no longer children to be brought home and disciplined. They are men and entitled to live the lives they choose. I fear Myles's concert career will never resume."

Virginia clenched her jaw and lifted a defiant chin. "I would spend my last cent to find my boys. Look into this, Mr. Poole, and may the Lord be with you."

CHAPTER 1

Shall not God search this out? for he
knoweth the secrets of the heart.

PSALM 44:21

Summer 1881

"Move over, Marigold."

The Jersey cow munched on her breakfast, eyes half-closed. When Myles pushed on her side, she shifted in the stall, giving him room for his milking stool and bucket. Settling on the stool, he rested his forehead on Marigold's flank, grasped her teats, and gently kneaded her udder while squeezing. His hands were already warm since she was the sixth cow he had milked that morning. Marigold let down her milk, and the warm liquid streamed into the bucket. Myles had learned that it paid to be patient with the cows; they rewarded his kindness with their cooperation.

"Meow!" A furry body twined around his ankle, rumbling a purr that reminded Myles of a passing freight train. Other cats peered at Myles from all sides — from the hayloft, around the stall walls, from the top of Marigold's stanchion. Their eyes seldom blinked.

The plump gray and white cat had perfected her technique. She bumped her face against Myles's knee, reached a velvet paw to touch his elbow, and blinked sweetly.

"Nice try, you pushy cat, but you've got to wait your turn. I'll give a saucer to all of you when I'm finished."

"Why do you reward them for begging? It only makes them worse." A deep voice spoke from the next stall where Al Moore was milking another cow.

"Guess I like cats."

"I . . . um, Myles, I've got to tell you that I'll be heading over to Cousin Buck's farm after dinner. I've got to talk with Beulah today . . . you know, about my letter."

"I'll be there, too. I'm working in Buck's barn this afternoon — mending harnesses and such."

"Things have changed since Cousin Buck married Violet Fairfield last year and took over her farm, Fairfield's Folly," Al commented sadly. "I mean, in the old days he kept up with every detail about our farm, but he's too busy being a husband and papa these days."

"He doesn't miss much. Must be hard work, running the two farms." Myles defended his friend.

"I run this place myself," Al protested. After a moment's silence he added, "You're right; I shouldn't complain. I just miss the old days; that's all. Anyway, to give Cousin Buck credit, being Beulah's stepfather must be a job in itself, and now with Buck and Violet's new baby . . ." His voice trailed away. "Buck has made major improvements at the Folly farm this past year. Guess that's no surprise to you."

"I do have firsthand knowledge of those improvements," Myles acknowledged. "Working at both farms keeps me hopping, but I don't mind. I'm glad Buck is happily married. I've never worked for better people than you and your cousin."

"Since I'm taking the afternoon off, I'll handle the milking this evening. How's that?" Al asked. "Don't want you to think I'm shirking."

Myles smiled to himself. "Don't feel obligated, Boss. You always do your share of the work. Be good for you to take a few hours to play."

"But you never do. Wish you'd relax some; then I wouldn't feel guilty."

"Maybe you and I could toss a baseball around with Samuel this afternoon." The prospect lifted Myles's spirits. He liked nothing better than to spend time with Obadiah "Buck" Watson's three stepchildren. The retired cowboy preferred to be called "Obie," but Myles had known him for years as "Buck" and found it impossible to address or even think of his boss by any other name.

"That would be great!" Al sounded like an overgrown schoolboy.

Myles stripped the last drops from Marigold's teats. Rising, he patted the cow's bony rump. "You're a good girl, Goldie." He nearly tripped over the pushy gray cat as he left the stall. With a trill of expectation, it trotted ahead of him toward the milk cans, where several other felines had already congregated.

Myles found the chipped saucer beneath a bench. Sliding it to the open floor with one foot, he tipped the bucket and poured a stream of milk — on top of a gray and white head. Myles smiled as the cat retreated under the bench, shaking her head and licking as much of her white ruff as she could reach. Another cat began to assist her, removing the milk from the back of her head. "Pushy cat, Pushy cat, where have you been?" Myles crooned.

He filled the saucer until it overflowed; yet it was polished clean within seconds. A few cats had to content themselves with licking drops from the floor or from their companions. Myles tried to count the swarming animals but lost track at twelve.

"Too many cats," Al remarked, emptying his bucket into a can.

"They keep down the rodent population," Myles said.

"I know, but the barn's getting over-crowded. There were a lot of kittens born in the spring, but most of them are gone. I don't know if they just died or if something killed them."

Myles squatted and Pushy cat hopped into his lap, kneading his thigh with her paws and blinking her yellow eyes. She seemed to enjoy rubbing her face against his beard. He stroked her smooth back and enjoyed that rumbling purr. Myles knew Al was right, but neither man had an answer for the problem.

"Say, Myles, what if . . . I mean, are you . . . do you have any plans to move on? Might you be willing to stay on here over the winter and . . . I'm not sure how to say this." Al ran long fingers through his hair, staring at the barn floor.

Myles rubbed the cat and waited for Al to find the words. He had a fair idea what was coming.

"I'm hoping to marry Beulah and take her to California with me — to meet my parents, you know. We would probably be gone for close to a year, and I can't leave Cousin Buck to run both this place and Fairfield's Folly alone. I would take it kindly if you would . . . well, run my farm as if it were yours, just while I'm away, you understand. I would make it worth your while. You don't need to answer me now; take your time to think it over."

Myles nodded. In spite of his determination to keep his own counsel, one question escaped. "Have you asked her yet?"

"Asked Beulah? Not yet." Al's boots shifted on the floorboards. "That's the other thing that worries me. She's . . . uh . . . I don't know that she'll take to the idea of a quick wedding. We've never discussed marriage . . . but she must know I plan to marry her. Everyone knows."

Myles glanced at his young boss's face. "Will you go if she refuses?"

Al looked uncertain. "I could marry her when I get back, but I hate to leave things hanging. Another man could come along and steal her away from me. Maybe I could ask her to wait." He collapsed on the bench, propped his elbows on his spread knees, and rested his chin on one fist. "She's really not a flirt, but I can't seem to pin her down. Every time I try to be serious, she changes the subject. What should I do, Myles?"

Myles rose to his feet and began to rub his flat stomach with one hand. "You're asking an old bachelor for courtship advice?" He hoped the irony in his voice escaped Al's notice. "I've got no experience with women."

"No experience at all?" Al's face colored. "I mean . . . uh . . . . Sorry."

Myles shrugged. "No offense taken. I left

home at sixteen and bummed around the country for years."

"What did you do to keep alive?"

"Any work I could find. No time or opportunity to meet a decent woman and had enough sense to avoid the other kind. When I drifted farther west it was the same. You don't see a lot of women wandering the wilderness."

"So where are you from?"

"Anywhere and everywhere." His lips twitched into a smile that didn't reach his eyes. "When your cousin hired me and brought me here to Longtree, that was the first time I'd been around women since I was a kid. Guess I don't know how to behave around females."

"I didn't know you were afraid of women. Is that why you almost never go to church or socials?"

Myles lifted a brow. "I didn't say I was afraid of them. More like they're afraid of me."

"If you'd smile and use sentences of more than one syllable, they might discover you're a decent fellow."

This prompted a genuine smile. "I'll try it. Any other advice?"

Al cocked his head and grinned. "That depends on which female has caught your eye. Want to confide in old Al?"

"I'd better cast about first and see if any

female will have me," Myles evaded.

Al chuckled. "Too late. I know about you and Marva Obermeier."

"About me and . . . whom?"

"Don't look so surprised. Since the barn raising at the Obermeiers' when you and she talked for an hour, everyone in town knows. She's a nice lady. If you want a little extra to hold and like a woman who'll do all the talking, Marva is for you."

"But that was —" Myles began to protest.

"Things aren't progressing the way you want, eh? You ought to spend evenings getting to know her family, getting comfortable in the home. Try teasing her and see what happens. Nice teasing, I mean. Women enjoy that kind of attention from a man."

"They do?"

A collie burst through the open barn door. Panicked cats scattered. Both men chuckled. "Good work, Treat."

Treat grinned and wagged half her body along with her tail, eager to herd the cows to pasture. "Cats are beneath your notice, eh, girl?" Al said, ruffling her ears.

Al carried the milk cans to the dairy. Myles untied the cows and directed Treat to gather them and start them ambling along the path.

Udders swaying, bells clanging, gray noses glistening, the cows did their best to ignore the furry pest at their heels. While Myles held the pasture gate open, Treat encouraged the little herd to pass through. Myles gave one bony bovine a swat before latching the gate behind her. "As usual, last in line. No wandering off today, my ornery old girl."

The sun was still low in the sky and already the temperature was rising. Myles swung his arms in circles to relieve the kinks. He glanced around. No one watching. He performed a few cartwheels, a round off, then a front flip to back flip in one quick motion. He straightened in triumph, flushed and pleased, arms lifted to greet the morning. The cows and Treat were unimpressed.

"Good thing you're used to my antics. Hey, Treat, maybe I'll see Beulah today." Myles slapped his thighs until the dog placed her front paws on them. He ruffled her fur with both hands. "What do you think, girl? Think Beulah will smile at me?"

Then his grin faded and his heavy boots scuffed in the dirt. Little chance of that while Al was around. Of all the stupid things Myles had ever done, falling in love with his boss's girl was undoubtedly the worst.

Deep in thought, Beulah Fairfield dumped used dishwater behind her mother's gladiolus. Something jabbed into her ribs, and the last of the water flew skyward. "Oh!" She spun around, slapping away reaching hands. "Al, stop it!"

Al took the two back steps in a single bound

and held the kitchen door for her. "Testy woman. Better make myself useful and return to her good graces."

She was tempted to suggest that he choose another time to visit, but her mother had chided her several times recently for rudeness. "Thanks." Beulah forced a smile as she entered the kitchen before him. His return smile seemed equally fake. "Is something wrong, Al?"

He let the door slam behind him. "Nothing much."

Beulah hung the dishpan on its hook and arranged the dishtowels on the back of the stove to dry. "Would you like a cup of coffee?"

"Uh, sure. Yes, please."

"Please take a seat at the table, and I will join you presently."

In another minute, she set down his coffee and seated herself across the table from him. His forehead was pale where his hat usually hid it from the sun; his dark hair looked freshly combed. Beulah knew her apron was spotted, but she was too self-conscious to change to a fresh one in front of Al. Her hair must be a sight — straggling about her face. "I've been canning tomatoes all morning." She indicated the glowing red jars lining the sideboard.

Before Al could comment, Beulah's sister Eunice burst into the room. The hall door hit the wall and china rattled on the oak dresser. "It *was* your voice I heard in here! Why did you sneak around to the back door, Al? I was watching for you out front."

A black and white dog slipped in behind Eunice and thrust her nose into Al's hand, brushy tail beating against the table legs. "Watchful, shame on you! Get out of the kitchen." Beulah attempted to shoo the dog away.

"She's all right." Petting the dog, Al gave Eunice a halfhearted smile. "I didn't sneak. My horse is in the barn, big as life. I rode over with Myles. He's mending the whiffletree the horse kicked apart while we were pulling stumps."

"Myles is in our barn?" Beulah asked.

"Still want to go for a ride today, do you?" Al asked Eunice as if Beulah had not spoken.

The girl flopped down in the chair beside him. "Of course we want to ride with you. My brother has to finish cleaning the chicken pen, but he's almost done. I finished my chores. Won't you teach me to jump today? Please?" She laid her head on Al's shoulder and gave him her best pleading gaze, batting long lashes.

He chuckled and roughed up her brown curls. "Subtle, aren't you, youngster? We'll see. I'd better talk to your parents before we try jumping. To be honest, Blue Eyes, I want to talk with your sister in private for a minute, so could —"

The door popped open again, this time admitting Violet Fairfield Watson, the girls' mother, with a wide-eyed baby propped upon her shoulder. "Would one of you please take Daniel while I change his bedclothes?" She transferred the baby to Beulah's reaching arms. "Thank you, dear. Hello, Albert. Will you stay for supper tonight?"

"I . . . um, thank you, but no, not tonight, ma'am. I . . . I've got to do the milking. I promised the kids we'd go for a ride this afternoon, but then I've got to get home and . . . and get some work done."

Violet gave him a searching look. "Hmm. Is something wrong, Al?"

Blood colored his face right up to his hairline. "Actually, yes. I got a letter from my mother yesterday. She wants me to come home to California. I'm the oldest son, you know. It's been five years since I was last home, and my folks want to see me again."

"I see." Violet Watson sent Beulah a quick glance before asking Al: "Do you plan to leave soon?"

"I'm not sure, ma'am. That depends . . . on a lot of things. I'll have to work out a plan with Cousin Buck — Obie — for care of the farm. I can't expect Myles to handle everything alone for so long. I mean, he's just a hired hand."

"How long is 'so long'?" Eunice asked, her

expression frozen.

"I don't know. Could be up to a year. The train fare between here and California is no laughing matter. I have to make the visit worth the price."

"Yes, you do need to speak with Obie about this, Al." Violet looked concerned. "That is a long time to leave your farm."

Al held out his hands, fingers spread. "I know, but what else can I do? They're my parents."

"But, Al, a whole year? What will we do without you?" Eunice wailed.

Wrapping one long arm around the girl, Al pressed her head to his shoulder. "Miss me, I hope. I'll be back, Blue Eyes. Never fear."

Rocking her baby brother in her arms, Beulah watched Al embrace her sister. *No more pokes in the ribs, no more mawkish stares. I wonder how soon he will leave?*

Baby Daniel began to fuss. Beulah took the excuse to leave the kitchen and wandered through the house, bouncing him on her hip. He waved his arms and kicked her in the thighs, chortling. She heard the others still talking, their voices muffled by intervening doors.

My friends all think I'm the luckiest girl in the world because Al likes me. He is handsome, nice, loves God, has his own farm — he'll make a great husband for someone. But that some-

one isn't me!

She strolled back into the hall, studying the closed kitchen door. No one would notice if she slipped outside. Snatching a basket from a hook on the hall tree, she headed for the barn. Her heart thumped far more rapidly than this mild exertion required. Shifting Daniel higher on her hip, she reached for her hair and winced. No bonnet, and hair like an osprey's nest. Oh well; too late now. If she didn't hurry, Myles might finish his work and leave before she had a chance to see him.

A tingle skittered down her spine. Without turning her head, she knew that Myles stood in the barn doorway. The man's gaze was like a fist squeezing her lungs until she gasped for air. Daniel squawked and thumped his hand against Beulah's chest. He managed to grasp one of her buttons and tried to pull it to his mouth, diving toward it. Beulah had just enough presence of mind to catch him before he plunged out of her arms.

One ankle turned as she approached the barn, and she staggered. Daniel transferred his attention to the basket hanging from her arm beneath him. He reached for it and once more nearly escaped Beulah's grasp. "Daniel, stop that," she snapped in exasperation, feeling bedraggled and clumsy.

"Need a hand?"

Swallowing hard, Beulah lifted her gaze. A little smile curled Myles's lips. One hand rubbed the bib of his overalls. The shadow of his hat hid his eyes, yet she felt them burning into her.

"I came for eggs," she said, brushing hair from her face, then hoisting Daniel higher on her hip. "For custard."

"Your brother Sam headed for the house with a basket of eggs not two minutes back."

"He did?" Beulah felt heat rush into her face. "I didn't see him."

Daniel grabbed at a button again, then mouthed Beulah's cheek and chin. She felt his wet lips and heard the fond little "Ahh" he always made when he gave her kisses. Unable to ignore the baby's overtures, she kissed his soft cheek. "I love you, too, Daniel. Now hold still."

When she looked up, white teeth gleamed through Myles's sun-bleached beard. "Thought Al was with you."

"He's in the kitchen with my mother and Eunice. Daniel and I came out for the eggs. Are you — will you be here long?"

"Might play baseball with Samuel and Al. Glad you came out for a visit."

Myles appeared to choose his words with care, and his voice . . . that rich voice curled her toes. Did he know she had come outside in hope of seeing him? Why must her mind palpitate along with her body whenever Myles was near? She was incapable either of analyzing his comments or of giving a lucid reply.

"You haven't been to our house for a while, and I haven't seen you at church all summer."

His smile faded. He took a step closer, then stopped. Did Myles feel the pull, almost like a noose tightening around the two of them and drawing them ever closer together? She had never been this close to him before. Only five or six feet of dusty earth separated them.

Tired of being ignored, Daniel let out a screech and smacked Beulah's mouth with a slimy hand. Pain and anger flashed; she struggled to hide both. "Daniel, don't hit."

The baby's face crumpled, and he began to wail. Sucking in her lip, Beulah tasted blood. "I think it's time for his nap." She spoke above Daniel's howls. "I'll try to come back later."

Myles nodded, waved one hand, and vanished into the barn's shadows. Beulah trotted toward the house, patting Daniel's back. "Hush, sweetie. Beulah isn't angry with you. I know you're tired and hungry. We'll find Mama, and everything will be fine."

Al held the door open for her. "What are you doing out here? What's wrong with the little guy?"

"Where's my mother?"

"Upstairs. You going riding with us?" he called.

"No, you go on. I've got work to do." She barely paused on the bottom step.

"Play ball with us later?"

"Maybe." Beulah hid her grin in Daniel's soft hair.

Once Daniel was content in his mother's arms, Beulah returned to the kitchen to work and ponder. Sure enough, a basket of brown eggs waited on the floor beside the butter churn. Samuel must have entered the kitchen right after she left it.

Beulah found her mother's custard recipe on a stained card and began to collect the ingredients. *I'm just imagining that Myles admires me. Probably he watches everyone that way. I scarcely know the man. No one knows much about him. He could be from anywhere — a bank robber or desperado for all we know. It is ridiculous to moon about him when I can have a man like Al with a snap of my fingers. Myles is beneath me socially — probably never went to school. Could never support a family — we would live in a shack . . .*

Al's words repeated in her mind: *Just a hired hand. Just a hired hand. Just a hired hand . . .*

CHAPTER 2

And when ye stand praying, forgive,
if ye have ought against any:
that your Father also which is in heaven
may forgive you your trespasses.

MARK 11:25

Custard cooled on the windowsill. Untying her apron, Beulah peeked through the kitchen window. Outside, a baseball smacked into a leather glove. She heard her brother Samuel's shrill voice and good-natured joking between Al and Myles. *He's still here!* She hung her apron on a hook, smoothed her skirts, and straightened her shoulders. Once again, her heart began to pound.

Eunice slammed open the kitchen door. Damp curls plastered her forehead; scarlet cheeks intensified the blue of her eyes. "We had a great ride, Beulah! You should have come."

Beulah wrinkled her nose.

Eunice splashed her face at the pump. "It hurts Al's feelings that you never want to ride

712

with us."

"I'm sure I don't know why."

Lifting her face from the towel, Eunice protested, "But you're supposed to want to spend time with him. People in love want to be together all the time, don't they?"

"How would I know?" Beulah said. "And I can't see how being in love would make me want to ride a horse. Hmph. You need a bath. I can smell horse from here."

"You're mean, Beulah." Eunice rushed from the room.

Beulah rolled her eyes. Pinching her cheeks, she checked her reflection in the tiny mirror over the washbasin. "Guess I didn't need to pinch my cheeks. They're already hot as fire."

Beyond Beulah's kitchen garden, the two men and Samuel formed a triangle around the yard. The ball smacked into Al's glove. He tossed it to Samuel, easing his throw for the boy's sake. Samuel hurled it at Myles, who fielded it at his ankles, then fired another bullet toward Al. Around and around they went, never tiring of the game.

"Hi, Beulah!" Al greeted her with a wave. "Want to play? We've got an extra mitt."

"No, thank you." *He must be crazy.* "Don't want to spoil your fun."

"We would throw easy to you," Samuel assured her.

"I'll watch." Beulah moved to the swing her stepfather, Obie, had hung from a tall elm.

After tucking up her skirt lest it drag in the dust, she began to swing. The men seemed unaware of her scrutiny. They bantered with Samuel and harassed each other. Her gaze shifted from Myles to Al and back again.

Al's long, lean frame had not yet filled out with muscle. A thatch of black hair, smooth brown skin, beautiful dark eyes, and a flashing smile made him an object of female fascination. How many times had Beulah been told of her incredible good luck in snaring his affection? She had lost count.

Leaning back in the swing, she pumped harder, hearing her skirts flap in the wind. Overhead, blue sky framed oak, maple, and elm leaves. A woodpecker tapped out his message on a dead birch.

Sitting straight, she wrapped her arms around the ropes and fixed her gaze upon Myles. He was grinning. Beulah felt her heart skip a beat. Myles had the cutest, funniest laugh — a rare treat to hear. What would he look like without that bushy beard? He had a trim build — not as short and slim as her stepfather, Obie, but nowhere near as tall as Al.

The ongoing conversation penetrated her thoughts. "So are you planning to go, Al? Will you take me with you? I've always wanted to see a circus. I bet my folks would let me go with you," Samuel cajoled.

Al glanced toward Beulah. "I was thinking

I might go. It's playing in Bolger all weekend. The parade arrives tomorrow."

Samuel let out a whoop. "Let's all go together! Eunice wants to go, and you do, don't you, Beulah? Will you come, too, Myles? Maybe they'll ask you to be a clown. Myles can do lots of tricks, you know. Show 'em how you walk on your hands. Please?"

Beulah's eyes widened.

Myles wiped a hand down his face, appearing to consider the request. "Why?"

"I want you to teach me. C'mon, Myles! Beulah's never seen you do it."

She saw his gaze flick toward her, then toward Al. He fired the baseball at Al, who snagged it with a flick of his wrist. "You can walk on your hands? Where'd you learn that trick?"

"I worked for a circus once. The acrobats taught me a thing or two."

Beulah fought to keep her jaw from dropping.

"No kidding? I'd like to see some tricks. Wouldn't you, Beulah?" Al enlisted her support.

Beulah nodded, trying not to appear overly interested.

Myles studied the green sweep of grass. "All right." He removed his hat. "Can't do splits or I'll rip my overalls," he said with a sheepish grin.

"If I tried splits, I'd rip more than that," Al

admitted.

Myles upended and walked across the yard on his hands, booted feet dangling above his head. He paused to balance on first one hand, then the other. With a quick jerk, he landed back on his feet, then whirled into a series of front handsprings, ending with a deep bow. His audience cheered and clapped.

"Amazing!" Al said. "I never knew you could do that."

"Your face is red like a tomato," Samuel said.

Beulah met Myles's gaze. Did she imagine it, or did his eyes reveal a desire to please? Heart pounding again, she managed an admiring smile. "Who needs to see a circus when we have Myles?"

He seemed to grow taller; his shoulders squared. "You would enjoy a real circus."

"So let's go!" Samuel persisted. "Beulah, you've gotta help me ask Mama. With Myles and Al taking us, I'm sure she'll say we can go."

"Do you want to take us?" Beulah asked, carefully looking at neither man.

"It might be fun," Al wavered.

"I do." Myles's direct answer took everyone by surprise. "I'm going for the parade and the show."

Beulah and Eunice hurried into the kitchen. Beulah tied her bonnet beneath her chin, set-

716

ting the bow at the perfect angle. "Does this bonnet match this dress, Mama?"

Violet cast her a quick glance. "It's sweet, dear."

"Now you stay close; no wandering off by yourself," she warned Samuel while combing back his persistent cowlick. "Being ten does not mean you're grown up." The boy squirmed and contorted his face.

Obie watched them from his seat at the kitchen table, his chest supporting a sleeping baby Daniel. Amusement twitched his thick mustache.

"I'll behave, Mama," Samuel said. "Do you think there will be elephants in the parade, Pa? Maybe bears and lions! Myles used to be in the circus. He says it was lots of work. I think I'd rather be a preacher when I grow up."

His stepfather lifted a brow. "Preachers don't have to work, you figure?"

"Reverend Schoengard doesn't work much. He just drives around visiting people and writes sermons."

Obie chuckled. "Our pastor more than earns his keep. You don't get muscles like his by sitting around all the time."

Eunice was still braiding one long pigtail. "I'm so glad it stopped raining! Now it's all sunny and pretty — the perfect day for a circus. Are they here yet?" She hurried to the window and peered toward the barn.

Obie tipped back his chair and balanced on his toes. "They're hitching the horses to the surrey. Should be ready soon."

"Can I go help, Pa?" Samuel begged.

"Ask your mother."

"You may. Try not to get too dirty." Violet released her restless son. "I'm trusting you to keep your brother in line, girls. Don't get so involved with your friends that you forget to watch Samuel."

"We won't, Mama," Beulah assured her mother. A crease appeared between her brows. "Our friends? I thought just the five of us were going."

Obie grinned. "I imagine half our town will head over to Bolger this afternoon. Circuses don't come around every day."

"Here come Al and Myles!" Eunice announced, bouncing on her toes.

Beulah bent to kiss Daniel's soft cheek. "Bye, Papa and Mama. Take care and enjoy your free day."

Al was less than pleased when Samuel squeezed between him and Beulah on the surrey's front seat. "Can't you sit in the back? It's crowded up here, and I need elbow room."

The boy's face fell. "Can't I drive a little? Papa lets me drive sometimes. The horses know me."

"I'll climb in back," Beulah offered quickly, rising. When she hopped down, one foot tangled in her skirt and she sat down hard in the dirt, legs splayed. Her skirt ballooned, displaying a fluffy white petticoat and pantaloon. Horrified, she clapped her arms down over the billowing fabric and glanced toward Myles. He was loading the picnic basket behind the surrey's rear seat. Had he seen?

"But, Beulah," Al protested. "I wanted to — Are you all right?"

Beulah scrambled to her feet and brushed off her dress, cheeks afire. "I'm fine."

"I'll drive, if you like," Myles said. "I don't mind sitting with Samuel."

Al looked abashed. "I don't either. It doesn't matter, really." He settled beside the boy and released the brake. "Climb in."

In the surrey's backseat, Eunice had one hand clamped over her mouth. Her shoulders were shaking. She looked up, met Beulah's eyes, and started giggling again. Beulah felt a smile tug at her mouth. Frowning to conceal it, she climbed up beside her sister and smoothed her skirts. "Stop it!" she hissed.

"You looked so funny!" Eunice nearly choked.

Myles hauled himself up to sit on the other side of Eunice. He must have visited the barber that morning. His beard and hair were neatly trimmed. He watched Eunice mop her eyes with a crumpled handkerchief, but made no comment.

Beulah leaned forward. "Are you excited to

see a circus again, Myles?"

He looked at her with raised brows. "Guess I am. It's been a long time."

Conversation flagged. While Samuel chattered with Al, the three in the backseat studied passing scenery with unaccustomed interest. Beulah longed to talk with Myles, but about what? Her mind was blank.

After a while, Myles cleared his throat. "Lots of traffic today."

"Must be for the circus," Al said. "I think I see the Schoengards up ahead."

Samuel's ears pricked. "Scott is here?"

"You're sitting with us, Sam." Beulah leaned forward to remind him.

"I know. I know," he grouched, pushing her hand from his shoulder.

The streets of Bolger were already crowded. People lined the road into town, standing in and around buggies and wagons. Al parked the surrey beside a farm wagon, easing the team into place. "We can see better from up here," he explained, "and we've got shade." He indicated the surrey's canvas top. "Did you bring water, Beulah?"

Samuel stood and waved his arms, shouting, "Here it comes! I see it!"

A roar went up from the crowds, and Beulah clutched her seat. The horses objected to the commotion. Al had his hands full quieting the rearing animals.

"May want to drop back," Myles advised.

"Especially if this circus has elephants."

"You all climb out," Al growled. "Don't want Sam to miss the parade."

Beulah climbed down, but Eunice chose to remain in the surrey. "Al needs company," she said. "You three can find us after the parade."

Grabbing Samuel's hand, Beulah tried to find a place with a clear view. "This way," Myles said, waving to her. He found a front row spot for Samuel, and Beulah clutched her brother's shoulders from behind.

Two elephants wearing spangled harnesses led the parade. Pretty women rode on the beasts' thick necks, waving to the audience. A marching band followed, blaring music that nearly drowned out the crowd's cheers. Beulah watched clowns, caged beasts, a strong man, fat lady, a midget, and several bouncing acrobats. Costumed men shouted invitations. "Come and see the circus! Come to the show!"

Beulah clapped and waved, smiling until her cheeks ached. The crowd pressed about her and waves of heat rose from the dusty road, but she was too enthralled to care. Samuel hopped up and down, waving both arms. "It's a real lion, Beulah! Do you see it? And that huge bear! Was it real?"

When the music died away and the last cage disappeared into the dust, Beulah stepped back — right on someone's foot. Hands cupped her elbows; her shoulder bumped into a solid chest. "Oh! I'm so sorry," she gasped.

"We'd better find Al and Eunice," Myles said. His eyes were a dusty olive hue that matched his plaid shirt.

Beulah shivered in the heat. "Yes. Yes, of course." He turned her around and started walking, guiding her with one hand at her elbow. Beulah walked stiffly; she was afraid to wiggle her arm lest he remove his hand.

Samuel capered beside them, turning cart-wheels in the trampled grass. "Have you ever seen a bear that big, Myles? And they've got two elephants, not just one. This is the greatest circus! Did you see those men wearing long underwear do back flips? Why don't they wear clothes, Myles?"

Myles chuckled. "Not underwear, Sam. They wear those snug, stretchy clothes to make it easy to move. It's a costume, you could say. There's the surrey." He waved an arm at Al.

Samuel took off running toward the surrey. "Did you see it? Weren't the elephants great, Eunice?" His sister agreed.

Al's smile looked forced. "We could see pretty well from here. Too well for the horses' peace of mind. They don't care for elephants and lions. I'm hungry. Ready to dig into that supper basket?"

722

■ ■ ■ ■

Myles followed the Fairfields and Al into the big tent and took a seat at one end of a bench. Ever since the parade, Al had hovered over Beulah like a dog over a bone. Now he made certain she sat at the far end of the bench. Beulah looked up at Al just before he sat beside her. Myles lifted a brow. That pout of hers was something to see.

Although Myles knew he was a far from impartial observer, he was certain something had changed between Al and Beulah. True, they had never been a particularly affectionate pair, but they appeared to enjoy an easy camaraderie.

No more. Beulah seemed almost eager to escape Al's company. Her attention wandered when he spoke, and her gaze never followed his tall form. Al's dark eyes brooded, and his laughter sounded strained.

Perhaps they had quarreled. It was too much to hope that their romance had died away completely. Everyone in town knew that Al and Beulah would marry someday. Everyone.

Myles studied the sawdust center ring, arms folded across his chest. There was a tightness in his belly. He tried to rub it away. Not even the familiar sounds and smells of the circus could alleviate his distress.

"Are you hungry again, Myles?" Eunice asked over Samuel's head. "We could buy some popcorn."

He tried to stuff the offending hand in his pocket, then crossed his arms again. "I'm not hungry, but I'll buy you a snack." Rising, he approached a vendor and returned with a sack of buttered popcorn. "Don't know how you can eat again so soon, but here you go." Eunice and Samuel piled into the treat, knocking much of it to the floor in their haste.

"Hey, look. Isn't that Marva Obermeier?" Al pointed across the tent. "If you hurry, you could find a seat with her, Myles. We'll join up with you later."

The well-meaning suggestion was more than Myles could endure. Without a glance at Al or Beulah he turned and left the tent. Stalking around the perimeter of the big top, ducking under guy wires, he made his way toward the living quarters.

Evening shadows stretched long on the trampled grass between tents and wheeled cages. From the shadows of one caravan, a large animal gave a disgruntled rumble.

"You there! Mister, the public is not going back here," an accented voice called from behind him.

Myles froze. It couldn't be! He turned slowly, studying the approaching clown. No mistaking that green wig and the wide orange smile. "Antonio? Antonio Spinelli!"

The clown halted. Myles saw dark eyes searching his face. "Who are you?"

"Myles Trent. I'm the boy you taught how to tumble years ago. You used to call me Red, remember?"

Antonio stepped closer, his giant shoes flopping. "Red? The bambino who feared the heights and the bears?" He held out a hand at waist level then lifted it as high as he could reach, and gave a hearty chuckle. "My, how you grow!"

Myles gripped the clown's hand and clapped his shoulder. "I never expected to see you again, Antonio. You're a sight for sore eyes! How's your wife?"

"Ah, my Gina, she had a baby or two or three, and now she stay in the wagon while the show it goes on. We do well, we five — two boys and a dolly." The proud father beamed. "I teach them all to clown as I did you, Red." He scanned Myles once more. "You looka different with that beard on you face. And your hair not so red anymore. You marry? Have a family?"

Myles shook his head. "No. I've got a girl in mind, but she doesn't know it yet."

Antonio laughed again. "You wait until my act, she is over; then you come and see Gina. Tell us all about your ladylove. Yes?"

Myles nodded. "For a quick visit. I'm here with friends."

"This girl in your mind?" Antonio guessed.

725

"Yes. Problem is, another fellow has her in mind, too."

Antonio pulled a sober face, ludicrous behind his huge painted grin. "That a problem, yes. Now you must put yourself into the lady's mind, that's what! I must run. You stay." He pointed at Myles's feet.

"I'll wait." Myles nodded.

The little clown hurried toward his entrance. Soon Myles heard laughter and applause from the big top, then screams of delighted horror. The aerialists must be performing. He imagined Beulah watching the spectacle, and his smile faded. *If only I could sit beside her, enjoying the show through her eyes.*

The Spinelli family lived in a tiny red coach parked behind the row of animal cages. Myles had to duck to keep from bashing his head on the ceiling, and his feet felt several sizes too large. The redolence of a recent spicy meal made his eyes water.

Antonio's wife, Gina, was thrilled to see him, kissing him on both cheeks. She shoved a pile of clothing from a chair and told him to sit, then plied him with biscotti, garlic rolls, and a cup of rather viscous coffee. Myles took one sip and knew he wouldn't sleep all night. It was a pleasure to hear the Spinellis' circus stories, yet he could not completely relax and enjoy their company.

A tiny girl with serious dark eyes claimed

his lap and played with his string tie while he talked. "This is our Sophia," Gina explained. "The boys, they are helping with the horses. Such a crowd tonight! Never did I expect it in the middle of nohow."

"Nowhere," Myles mumbled.

"We had a problem with the bear today. Did you hear?"

"Gina." Antonio shook his head. "We are not to speak of this."

She touched her lips with red tinted nails. "Oh, and I was forgotting. You will not think of it." She shook her dark head and changed the subject. "So you work at a farm? You are happy at this farm, Red?" Gina had put on weight over the years, yet she was still an attractive woman.

Myles shifted little Sophia to his other knee. "I am. I hope to acquire land of my own before long and raise a family along with cattle and crops."

Gina nodded. Her mind was elsewhere. "And you were such the performer in those days! Our Mario is much like him, don't you think, Antonio? Such a fine boy you were, and how we missed you when you disappeared. It was that brother who chased you off, no? Never did I care for him, though he was your flesh and blood. What become of that one?"

A tide of bitterness rose in his soul. "Monte is dead." Antonio's intense scrutiny produced an explanation. "He was shot by bandits in Texas. Gambling debts and cattle rustling."

The little clown nodded. He had not yet removed his wig and greasepaint. "And you cannot forgive this brother."

Myles sniffed. "Why should I forgive him? He's dead."

"For your own peace of mind. You have the look of a man carrying a heavy load, Red. It will break you, make you bitter and old while you are young."

Myles made a dismissive movement with one hand and watched his own leg jiggle up and down. "I'm starting over here in Wisconsin. The past is gone, forgotten."

"You have not forgotten; oh no. Grudges are heavy to carry. The past will haunt you until this burden you give to God. Remember how the good Lord tells us that we are forgiven as we forgive others? Why should God forgive you when you will not forgive your fellowman?"

Myles placed the dark-haired "dolly" on her feet and rose. "I'd better return to my companions. It was a pleasure to see you again, Gina." Gloom settled over his soul.

After Myles made his farewells, Antonio accompanied him back to the midway. Darkness had fallen, making support wires and ground stakes difficult to see. Myles felt the need to make casual conversation. It would not be right to leave his old friend in this dismal way.

"This seems like a successful circus," Myles said, ducking beneath a sagging cable. "Are you satisfied with it?"

Antonio shook his head. "Ever since Mr. Bonacelli, he sell out, things not go so well. Lots of us come from Bonacelli's Circus — some of the animals, even. The new owner, he cut the pay and the feed to make a profit. The animals not so happy anymore."

"Is the bear the one that came at me while I was cleaning his cage?" Myles grimaced at the memory of falling through the cage doorway with hot breath and foam on his heels.

"The very same." Antonio frowned. "He's a bad one, sure. You were right to fear the beast. He only get meaner as he get old. He ripped up our animal trainer we had who liked his corn liquor too well."

"I can believe it. Was it the same bear that made trouble today?"

Antonio glanced around. "Not to speak of this!" he whispered.

"Those cages don't look sturdy. I wouldn't want my little ones playing near them if I were you."

Antonio nodded and pushed Myles toward the main entrance. "Gina keeps the bambinos to home. You not to worry, my friend. Ah, it looks like the show, she is over. You had best find your friends quick. Is this lady with the yellow hair the one who lives in your head?"

Myles glanced up to see Marva Obermeier approaching. "No. She's just a friend." But a moment later Marva was attached to his arm. Myles introduced her to Antonio, attempting to be polite. The clown's eyes twinkled.

"I didn't know you knew any clowns, Myles," Marva chattered in her amiable, mindless way. "Wasn't that a tremendous show? It was so exciting when . . ." Myles tuned her out, scanning the passing crowds.

He spotted Al's broad gray hat. "Al!" Waving his free arm, he gave a sharp whistle and saw his friend's head turn. "Over here!"

Marva was excusing herself. "My papa is beckoning — I must go. It was nice to meet you . . ."

Myles tuned her out again, focusing on Al until he spotted Beulah behind him. "Here she comes — the tall girl in the blue dress. Beulah Fairfield."

Antonio regarded Myles with evident amusement. "Your other lady friend is gone. Did you notice?"

Myles glanced around. Marva had disappeared. "Did I tell her good-bye?"

"You did." Still grinning, Antonio turned to study Beulah.

Myles made his introductions all around. Samuel was thrilled to meet a real clown and plied the man with questions. Antonio answered the boy patiently.

"How long ago did you two know each other?" Beulah asked.

"This fine fellow was but a lad with hair like fire," Antonio said, eyes twinkling.

"It has been about eight years," Myles said. "Antonio and his wife were newly married. Now they have three children."

"Myles tells me he has thoughts of family for himself." Antonio wagged one finger beside his ear. "Time, she is passing him by."

Myles felt his face grow hot.

Al gruffly reminded them that home was still a good drive away. Antonio bade the Fairfields and Al farewell. Beulah held the clown's hand for a moment. "It was so nice to meet an old friend of Myles. His past has been a mystery to us, but now we know you, Mr. Spinelli."

Beulah's smile had its usual effect: Antonio beamed, shaking her hand in both of his. "But mine is the pleasure, Miss Fairfield, to meet such a lovely lady. Red is a mystery to Gina and me always — so secretive and shy! But in him beats a man's heart, I am knowing. He is needing a great love to banish these burdens he carries and fill his life with laughter and music."

Myles knew a sudden urge to hurry the little clown away before his heart's secret was broadcast to the world. Al relieved his distress by hustling Beulah away. "Give them time alone, Beulah. They haven't seen each other in years. We'll meet you at the surrey, Myles."

As soon as they were out of earshot, Antonio shook his head mournfully. "And this Al, your fine friend, is the other whose heart beats for Beulah. For him it is a sad thing, Red. She must be yours."

Myles lowered one brow. "What makes you say that?"

Antonio waved at the starry sky. "I read it in the stars? But maybe the stars, they are in a young lady's eyes." He laughed and patted Myles's arm. "You will have joy, Red. Gina and I, we will remember you and your Beulah in our prayers each night. Remember what I say about forgiveness — I know this from living it, you see. Don't imagine you are alone. Everyone has choices in life. Think of Beulah — you cannot offer her an unforgiving heart. The poison in you would harm her."

The man was like a flea for persistence. Nodding, Myles pretended to ignore the stinging words. "You will write to me? I live in Longtree, the next town over."

"I not write so good, but Gina will do it. Maybe when the season ends, we come to see you and your little wife."

Myles smiled and hugged the smaller man's shoulders. "Thank you, Antonio. You have given me much-needed encouragement."

Buck met the tired travelers in front of the

barn and helped unhitch the horses. "Why are you up so late, Papa? Is Mama still awake?" Eunice asked sleepily.

"Mama and Daniel are asleep. Get ready for bed quietly, children. Go on with you now." Buck shooed his flock toward the house. "We've got church in the morning."

"Thank you, Al. Thank you, Myles. It was a wonderful circus," Beulah paused to say. Her eyes reflected the surrey's sidelamps.

"You're welcome," they each replied.

"See you at church," Al called after her. "May I come pick you up?"

Myles jumped. That would be a sign of serious courtship. Hidden in the shadows behind the surrey, he gritted his teeth and braced himself for her reply.

"Thank you for the offer, but no, I'll see you there," Beulah's voice floated back. "Good night."

Al smacked a harness strap over its peg and tugged his hat down over his eyes. Without a word, he led his horse from its stall and saddled up. Myles felt a pang of sympathy for his friend.

Buck finished caring for the team while Myles saddled his mare. "Got a job for you Monday," Buck said.

"What's that?" Myles asked.

"We got two pasture fence posts snapped off; musta been rotted below ground level. I found Mo among our cows. He may be only a yearling, but he's all bull. I propped up the fence well enough to hold him temporarily; but we've got to replace those posts soon."

"I'll run the materials out there," Al promised.

"And I'll fix the fence," Myles said.

CHAPTER 3

Let all bitterness, and wrath, and anger,
and clamour,
and evil speaking, be put away from you,
with all malice.

EPHESIANS 4:31

Clutching a novel under one arm, Beulah peeked into her mother's room. "I'll be at the pond if you need me, Mama."

Bent over the cradle, Violet finished tucking Daniel's blanket around his feet. Straightening, she turned to smile at her daughter. "Enjoy yourself, honey. Would you bring in green beans for supper tonight? Samuel caught a dozen bluegill this morning, and beans would be just the thing to go with fried fish."

"He's getting to be quite a fisherman," Beulah observed. "Whatever will we do when school starts up and we lose our provider? You're right, beans sound delicious — or they would if I were hungry. Is Papa around, or did he go into town today?"

Violet led the way downstairs. "He went to help Myles repair the fence the bull broke. Which reminds me . . . I know it's asking a lot of you, dear, but would you be willing to carry water to the men? They're way out at that northwest pasture beyond the stream."

Beulah followed her mother into the parlor. "Of course I will, Mama. I'm going out anyway."

"You're a dear! You might take along some of those cookies you baked."

Beulah felt slightly guilty about her mother's gratitude, since her motive was not entirely altruistic. "That's a good idea. If I hurry, I'll still have time to read a chapter or two."

Violet settled into a chair and picked up her mending. "Darling, I want you to know that I've noticed your efforts to be cheerful and kind, and so has Papa Obie. You're my precious girl — I want other people to see and appreciate your beautiful spirit along with your pretty face."

"Do you really think I'm pretty, Mama?" Beulah tried to see her reflection in the window. "Everyone says I look like my real father, and he was homely. At least, I remember him as kind of ungainly and bony with big teeth."

"You have your father's coloring and his gorgeous brown eyes. Your teeth may be a bit crooked, yet they are white and healthy. You

736

have matured this past year, and I think you must have noticed that boys find you attractive. Al certainly does."

Beulah looked down at her figure. "I guess so. I wonder why men are attracted by a woman's shape. When you think about it, we're kind of funny looking."

Violet laughed. "Trust you to say something like that! As for me, I'm thankful that men find women attractive and vice versa. It makes life interesting."

"So it isn't wrong for a girl to enjoy looking at a man?"

"Wrong? Of course not," Violet answered absently. "I enjoy looking at my husband."

"When a girl is interested in a man, what is the best way for her to let him know it?" Beulah perched on the edge of the sofa. "A subtle way, I mean. Without actually saying so."

Violet looked at the ceiling, touching her needle to her lips. "Hmm. Subtle. How about meeting his gaze and smiling? A touch on his arm, perhaps. Touching can be hazardous, however. A lady doesn't want to touch a man too much or he will lose respect for her."

Beulah's lower lip protruded and her brows lowered as a certain memory of a clinging blond recurred. Her mother's advice seemed faulty. A shy man like Myles might be different. He might prefer a woman who took the initiative. "How does a lady know if a man returns her interest?"

737

Violet's lips twitched. "She will know. Most men are straightforward."

"But how will she know for certain? If a man stares at a girl, does that mean he is interested?"

"That depends on the stare." Violet frowned. "Who has been staring at you?"

"It's a respectful gaze. Don't worry." She hopped to her feet. "Thank you, Mama. I'd better hurry before the day is gone."

Although she took a shortcut through a stretch of forest, the trek to the back pasture was more arduous than Beulah had anticipated. She crossed Samuel's log bridge over the brook, then hiked up the steep bank, nearly dropping the water jug once.

"Why did I think this was such a good idea?" she grouched, hoisting the jug on her hip. "I'll be a sweaty mess again before he sees me." Mosquitoes and deerflies hummed around her head, dodging when she slapped at them. Her arms ached until they felt limp, and her feet burned inside her boots.

Through the trees she caught sight of Papa Obie's mustang Jughead and open pasture-land beyond him. The horse's patches of white reflected sunshine as he grazed. Wherever Jughead was, Beulah was certain to find Obie nearby.

Sure enough, there were Obie and Myles, ramming a new post into a hole. Both men had removed their shirts; their damp undervests gaped open to reveal sweaty chests. Suspenders held up faded denim trousers, and battered hats shaded their eyes.

"Hello," she greeted, picking her way between stumps. "I brought water and cookies."

"Beulah!" Obie straightened. "You're an angel of mercy. We've needed a drink yet hated to stop before we finished this post." He exchanged a glance with Myles. "Let's take a break." Myles nodded, and the two men sat on nearby stumps.

Wiping his face with a red kerchief, Obie drained the dipper in one long draught. "Thanks."

Beulah's hands trembled as she handed Myles the dipper. Hazel eyes glinted in his dusty face. He, too, poured the water down his throat and wiped his mustache with the back of one hand. "Thank you."

"More?"

Each man accepted two more drinks, and the jug felt much lighter. Then they gobbled up her molasses cookies. "These are delicious, Beulah . . . but then your cookies always are," Obie said.

She peeked at Myles to see if he agreed. "My favorite." He lifted a half-eaten cookie.

Satisfied, she settled upon a low stump near Obie's feet and arranged her skirts. "How much longer must you work in this heat? Is this the last post?"

"Yes. Once we brace this post and attach the crossbeams, we'll be done. Nasty work." Obie shook his head, betraying a former cowboy's natural aversion to fences. "Myles did most of it before I got here. Planned that well, didn't I?" He grinned at the hired man, and Myles acknowledged the teasing with a smile.

"Ready?"

Myles nodded, and the two returned to their work.

Beulah stayed. Myles never spoke to her, but several times she caught his eye and smiled. He did not smile back. Her heart sank. *He is in love with Miss Obermeier! Whatever shall I do?*

"Beulah, would you bring me the hammer?"

She hurried to comply.

"If you would hand me that spike . . ." Obie requested next.

This time she hovered. "May I help?"

"Not now," Obie puffed. "Better stay back."

Myles lifted the rails into place and Obie hammered in the spikes. The hair on the hired man's forearms and chest was sun-bleached. Sweaty hair curling from beneath his hat held auburn glints. His trousers bagged around slim hips.

From this close range Beulah could locate his ribs and shoulder blades. Sinews protruded in his neck and chest as his muscles strained. When Mama was pregnant with Daniel, Beulah once sneaked a peek at a human anatomy book in the doctor's office. Myles might have posed for the model of muscles and bones, so many of them were visible beneath his skin.

He glanced up; Beulah looked away, too late. Her body already dripped sweat; now she burned on the inside. *What must he think of me, staring at him like a hussy?* She strolled away, fanning her apron up and down. Grasshoppers fled buzzing before her.

When the last rail was in place, Beulah helped the men gather their tools. Obie loaded his saddlebags. "Thanks again, Myles." He swung into Jughead's saddle. A wisp of grass dangled from the gelding's mouth. "Will you see Beulah home, then check on Cyrus Thwaite for me? He hasn't been eating well since his wife died, and I want to make sure he's all right."

"Yes, sir, I will."

Obie's silvery eyes smiled, and one brow arched. "You two take your time. Behave yourselves."

Now what did he mean by that? Beulah wondered.

Jughead sprang into motion, hurdling brush and stumps in his way. Within moments he had disappeared from view.

Beulah looked at Myles. "Why didn't you bring a horse? I thought cowboys preferred

741

to ride. Or are you really a clown?" she tried to tease.

Wiping one sleeve across his forehead, he clapped on his hat. Every inch of exposed skin glistened red-brown, and his undervest was sopping. Though he was pleasing to behold, Beulah tried to remain upwind.

"First a clown, then a cowboy, now a farmer." One grimy hand began to rub his belly. "No point in making a horse stand around while I work. The boss was in town this morning; he needed a horse."

"Don't forget your shirt." She scooped it up and held it out.

"Thanks." He slung it over his shoulder and picked up her water jug.

He wouldn't even meet her eyes. Beulah's temper rose. "You don't need to escort me home. You must be tired." She picked up her book.

"Let's cut through Mo's pasture."

Not twenty yards down the sloping pasture, placidly chewing his cud, lay Mo. Shading her eyes, Beulah cast a wary glance at the dormant bull. "Is it safe?"

"He knows me." Myles bent to step through the fence rails. "Come on."

She slipped through the fence easily enough, but her skirt caught on a splinter and Myles had to release it. Beulah kept glancing toward Mo. The bull watched them walk across his field. Slowly he began to rise, back end first.

"Myles, he's getting up!" Beulah caught hold of Myles's arm.

He looked down at her hand on his arm, then back at the yearling Jersey.

Clutching his arm, she let Myles direct her steps and kept both eyes on the bull. Mo began to follow them, trotting over the rough ground.

"Any cookies left?" Myles asked.

"Some broken ones. Why?"

"Mo likes sweets. Don't be frightened, child. He's too small to harm you."

Child!

When the bull approached to within a few yards, it bawled, and Beulah let out a yelp. "Here, give him the cookies!" She shoved the sack into Myles's hands, then cowered behind him. The man's cotton undervest was damp beneath her hands, but the solid feel of him was reassuring. Beulah could hear her own heartbeat.

Myles extended a piece of cookie. "Come and get it, Li'l Mo. You've had your fun, scaring Beulah. Now show her what a good fellow you are."

Shaking his head, the young bull pawed the ground and gave a feinting charge. Myles held his ground. Mo stretched toward the cookie, nostrils twitching. When the bull accepted the treat, Myles took hold of the brass ring in its nose. "Good lad." He stroked Mo's neck and scratched around the animal's ears. "This is one fine little bull."

Beulah began to relax, peeking around Myles's shoulder. "I can't believe he was once a tiny calf. Samuel named him 'Moo-moo.' Remember that day when my mother drove us to your farm — Al's farm — by mistake? Or were you there that day?"

"I was there. I helped deliver this fellow that very morning." With a farewell pat for Mo, Myles turned to Beulah. "I remember how cross you looked that day. You've got a pretty smile, but your pout is like nothing I've ever seen." His grin showed white through his beard.

Beulah gaped, hands dangling. She took a step back and tucked her hands under her elbows. "I — I was not cross; I was worried."

"With your lip sticking out and your eyes stormy, just like now." His hat shaded his face, yet Beulah caught the glint in his eyes.

She covered her mouth with one hand, conscious of her overbite. Eyes burning, she turned and picked up the water jug. If Myles knew how she felt about him, he would laugh, and the whole town would know about Beulah's infatuation within days. Marva would regard her with pity and mild amusement.

"Are you all right, Beulah?" Myles took two steps in her direction. "I didn't mean to hurt your feelings."

"I'm not angry; I'm hot." Water sloshed in

the jug. Beulah eyed the sweaty man. "You look hotter." Without pausing for reflection, she dashed the water into his face.

Water dripped from his nose and beard and trickled down his chest. "Did I deserve that?"

He didn't seem angry. A nervous giggle escaped before Beulah could stop it. "You needed a bath."

His eyes flared, and Beulah knew she had better get moving. Picking up her skirts, she dashed for the fence, intending to vanish into the forest. But an arm caught her around the waist. "Not so fast." Without further ceremony he tossed her over his shoulder and picked up the empty jar. Her book flew into the tall grass.

"What are you doing?" she gasped. "Put me down!" He surmounted the fence without apparent difficulty and headed into the woods.

Beulah found it hard to breathe while hanging head down over his shoulder, and her stomach muscles were too weak to lift her upper body for long. In order to draw a good breath she had to put both hands on his back and push herself up. "Myles, a gentleman doesn't treat a lady this way! Please put me down. This is . . . improper," she protested. The grasp of his arm around her legs was disturbing, the solid strength of his shoulder beneath her stomach even more so. There was a roaring in her ears.

"Very well." He hefted her and flung her from him. Beulah fell with splayed arms and horrified expression only to land with a great splash. She had enough presence of mind to shut her mouth before water closed over her head.

Flailing her arms, she managed to right herself, but her face barely cleared the surface when she stood on the rocky bottom. The source of the roaring sound was now clear: the stream poured into this little pool over a lip of rock suspended twelve feet above the surface. The churning water tugged at Beulah's billowing skirts, and bubbles tickled her arms.

"How dare you!" she gasped, sudden fury choking her. "I could have drowned!"

An exaggeration, but the sharpest accusation she could think of at the moment. She had to shout for him to hear her.

Myles stood above her, his boots planted wide, arms folded on his chest. Dapples of sunlight played across his hat and shoulders. "It's not deep," he protested. "I swim here often." His smile was infuriating.

"I can't swim with my boots and clothes on," she blurted, then choked on a mouthful of water. "You . . . you monster! You are no gentleman!"

"I had not observed you behaving like a lady."

"Ooooh!"

Desperate for revenge, she thrashed over to the steep bank and reached for his boots. One frenzied hop and she caught hold around his ankles. No matter how hard she tugged, he remained unmoved. She paused, gasping for air. "Where are we? I've never seen this place."

"Just over half a mile above the beaver pond. The waterfall made this hole, perfect for swimming. It's one of my favorite places on earth."

Beulah tried to look over her shoulder at the lacy waterfall, but her bedraggled sunbonnet blocked her view. Hoping to catch Myles unaware, she gave his feet another sharp jerk, lost her grip, and slid back into the pool. Sputtering with fury, she surfaced again, arms thrashing. Her teeth chattered, although the water was not terribly cold. "Help me out of here!"

He frowned, considering, then removed his hat and boots. After stacking his garments well out of Beulah's reach, he dove into the pool and disappeared.

Beulah let out another little screech, then scanned the pool for him with narrowed eyes. He should pay for this outrage.

He did not come up. Beulah began to feel concerned. Had he hit his head on a rock? "Myles?" she inquired.

"Myles, where are you?" She stepped forward, took a mouthful of water, and coughed.

"Myles!" Her hands groped, searching for his body. This pool was too shallow for safe diving. Panic filled her voice. "Myles!"

" 'Ruby lips above the water blowing bubbles soft and fine, but, alas! I was no swimmer, so I lost my Clementine.' " The voice in her ear was a rich baritone.

"Oh!" Beulah's anger revived. "You are dreadful! I thought you had drowned — that's what you wanted me to think!" Even more infuriating was her helpless condition. It was difficult to appear righteously angry when her face barely cleared the surface. Exertion and excitement made her huff for every breath. "How can you be so mean? First you say I'm ugly, then you drop me in the water fully clothed, and then you pretend to drown? And I thought you were a nice person! You're horrible! Cruel!"

"Who said you're ugly?" He caught her by the waist and lifted until her head and shoulders rose out of the water. His hair lay slicked back from his high forehead. She could count the freckles on his peeling nose.

"Let go of me!" The grip of his hands sent her heart into spasms. Her corset's ribs bit into her flesh. She pulled at his fingers, kicking wildly.

He shook her. "If you don't hold still, I'll drop you back in the pool and you can find your own way out."

Her struggles ceased. She gripped his

forearms, feeling iron beneath the flesh. *I can't cry! I must keep control.*

"Now who said you were ugly?"

"You did. That was unkind! I can't help having crooked teeth any more than you can help having red hair and freckles!"

He blinked. She saw his eyes focus upon her mouth. She clamped her lips together.

"I never noticed that your teeth are crooked."

"But you said . . ."

"I said I'd never seen a pout like yours. It's like a tornado brewing. Wise people stay out of your way." He grinned. "I would never call you ugly. Your temper, however, deserves that designation, from all I hear."

Beulah gaped into his face.

"Go ahead and flay me alive. I can take it." He smiled.

Her mouth snapped shut. The backs of her eyes burned.

"I've got to put you down for a minute. My arms are giving out." He turned her to face away from him. She placed her hands on top of his at her waist, thankful for her trim figure and sturdy corset.

Hefting her back up, he slowly walked toward the far side of the little pool. As they passed the waterfall, Beulah looked up and felt spray on her face. "Wait!"

Myles stopped, lowering her slightly. Beulah reached out and touched the sheet of falling water, surprised by its power. "Ohhh, this is wonderful!" Rainbows glimmered in the misty water. She lifted her other hand, straining her upper body toward the falls.

"I can't hold you like this anymore," Myles protested, then let his arms drop.

Startled, Beulah caught hold of his wrists and began to protest; but Myles pulled her back, wrapped his arms around her, and supported her against his body so that her waist was at his chest level. "Go ahead and enjoy the waterfall," he ordered from between her shoulder blades.

Beulah's pounding heart warned her that she had exceeded the bounds of ladylike deportment. "Have you ever walked beneath it?"

"I have." She was sliding down within his grasp.

"Can you walk through it while holding me?" She looked over her shoulder at him and recognized the intimacy of the situation. His arms pressed around her waist and rib cage. He lifted his knee to boost her higher in his grasp.

"Are you — are you sure — are you sure you want me to?"

CHAPTER 4

Seek ye the LORD while he may be found,
call ye upon him while he is near.

ISAIAH 55:6

"Please do!" she begged.

His arms shook both with strain and with excitement. Knowing he should flee temptation, Myles found himself unable to deny Beulah's request. Hopefully she would attribute his strangled voice to physical effort.

Again hefting her higher in his grasp, he walked toward the waterfall, feeling stones turn beneath his feet. Keeping one arm wrapped over his, Beulah lifted her other arm over her head to greet the cascade as it tumbled over their heads. Water filled their ears, noses, and eyes, dragged on their clothing, and toiled to pull them under. When they emerged on the far side, Beulah coughed. Water dribbled from her every feature. She had slipped down within his grasp, her bonnet was gone, and her arm now clung around his neck. Long eyelashes clumped together when she blinked those glorious brown eyes. Her smile lighted up the grotto. "I will never forget this, Myles."

She was a slender girl, yet she felt substantial in his arms, better than anything he had ever imagined. Oh, but she was lovely with her questioning eyes and her lips that seemed to invite his kisses! Her free hand crept up to rest upon his chest; she must feel the tumult within. His breath came in labored gusts.

Shaking, he gripped her forearms and shoved her away. He shook his head to clear it, reflecting that another dunk under the waterfall might benefit him.

"Myles —" she began, then fell silent. Although she was obliged to cling to his arms to keep from sinking, he felt her withdrawal. Her chin quivered with cold.

God, help me! I love her so, the wild little kitten.

Without another word Myles hoisted her into his arms, this time in the more conventional carrying position, and slogged across to the far shore. When Beulah turned to crawl up the bank, he caught a glimpse of her face. "Beulah?"

Her booted foot slipped and thumped him in the chest. With a soft grunt, he caught hold of her ankles and gave her an extra boost until she could sit on the mossy bank.

Water streamed from every fold of her clothing. Her hair dripped. Her face was crumpled and red. Her woeful eyes turned Myles to mush.

"Are . . . are you all right?" Assorted endearments struggled on his lips; he dared not speak them aloud. He touched her soggy boot, but she jerked it away, staggered to her feet, and rushed off along the bank of the creek.

When Myles emerged from the forest near Fairfield's Folly, Watchful rose from her cool nest beneath the back porch and came to greet him, tail waving. Thankfully she was not a noisy dog. Myles left the jug on the porch and turned to leave, but the kitchen door opened.

"Hello, Myles."

Myles removed his hat as he turned. "Hello, Mrs. Watson."

Violet Watson cradled Daniel against one shoulder, jiggling him up and down. "My, but it's hot today! I happened to see you out the kitchen window." Her blue eyes scanned him. "I see you've been for a swim."

"Yes, ma'am."

"I must admit, a dip does sound tempting. So Beulah reached you men with the water and cookies?"

"Yes, ma'am. Please extend my thanks for all of her thoughtfulness."

Violet smiled. "I'll do that. She must still be reading at the pond. That girl does love to read, and she seldom finds time for it these days. I'm afraid I depend greatly on her help around the house. Maybe I need to give her more afternoons off like this."

Myles nodded, feeling dishonest. He knew Beulah had returned home already, for he had followed her wet trail through the forest. She must have sneaked inside. "I enjoy reading, too."

"Really? Do you also enjoy music? Beulah and I are both fond of music, but we have so little opportunity to hear good music around here."

His ears grew warm. "I enjoy music." Realizing that he was rubbing his stomach, he whipped the offending hand behind his back. Violet didn't seem to notice.

She leaned against the door frame. "I play the piano a little. Obie bought me a lovely instrument for Christmas, you know, but I do not do it justice. Beulah plays better than I do. Do you sing or play an instrument?"

"Yes, ma'am."

"I'm thinking of planning a music party after harvest, just for our family and a few friends. Might you be willing to join us?"

"I'd be honored, ma'am." Myles shifted his weight. "I must be going. Have an errand to run."

"Are you going to see Cyrus Thwaite? That poor man has been so lonely since his wife died. I'm certain he doesn't eat well. Let me pack you a sack of cookies for him."

Myles handed over the empty cookie sack. Little Daniel reached for it, trying to bring the strings to his open mouth.

When Violet returned the full sack, she gave Myles a sweet smile. "Good-bye, and thank you."

Myles's mare whinnied as she trotted up the Thwaite drive. "Hello the house!" Myles called. Swinging down in one easy motion, he left his mare's reins hanging. A knock at the door brought no response. Myles entered, feeling mildly concerned. Cyrus seldom left his farm since his wife, Hattie, died last spring.

Myles scanned the kitchen, taking a quick peek into the pantry. The sacks of flour and sugar he had delivered the week before had not been touched. Only the coffee supply had been depleted. Dirty cups were stacked in the dry sink, but few plates had been used. He set Violet's sack of cookies on the table.

"Cyrus?" he called, quickly inspecting the rest of the untidy house. Stepping outside, Myles felt the relief of fresh air. A breeze had risen, swaying the birches beyond the drive. "Cyrus?" he bellowed, heading for the barn.

There — he heard a reply. From the barn? Myles broke into a jog. Chickens scattered as he approached the barn door. The cow lowed, turning her head to gaze at him. "Why aren't you out at pasture?" Myles left by the barn's back door. "Cyrus, where are you?"

"Here, boy." Cyrus waved from across the pasture. He appeared to be leaning on the handle of a spade. At his feet lay a gray mound. Two vultures circled overhead, and crows lined the nearby pasture fence. The swaybacked old mule must have keeled over at last. But by the time Myles crossed the field, he realized that the animal had met a violent death. Its body was mauled.

"What happened?"

Cyrus lifted a long face. "You know how he could unlatch doors; he musta let hisself out last night, poor ol' cuss. Myles, I may be crazy, but this looks like a bear's work to me." He lifted a silencing hand. "I know there ain't been a bear in these parts since Hector here was a long-eared foal, but what else could break a full-growed mule's neck like this?"

Myles studied the claw marks on the animal's carcass. "Why would a bear want to kill an old mule? Surely it might have found better eating nearby." A suspicion popped into his mind.

"Mebbe it's sick or wounded or plain cussed mean. Would ya help me bury what's left of Hector?" Cyrus looked halfway ashamed to ask. "Cain't jest see m'self leavin' him for the vultures and coyotes. Thought I'd bury him on this here knoll."

Myles nodded and returned to the barn for

another spade.

To give Cyrus credit, he worked harder at eighty than many men worked at thirty; but his body lacked the strength to lift heavy loads of dirt. All too soon he was obliged to sit down. "Was a time I could work like you, boy, but that time is long past." He wiped his forehead with a grimy handkerchief. "I been putting lots of thought into what's to become of this here farm. Hattie wanted to leave it to Obie, but I don't see much point in that. He's already got more land than he can work."

Myles paused for a breather, leaning on his spade. One callused hand absently rubbed his belly. "You might sell it and live in town. Bet you'd enjoy living at Miss Amelia's boardinghouse, eating her good cooking morning and night. Lots of company for you there."

Cyrus looked pensive. "You paint a tempting picture, Myles boy. I reckon I'd like that mighty well, but I can't see myself selling this farm. Hattie and me built it up when we was young, expecting we'd have a passel of younguns. Never did, though. I figure this land is worth more to me than it would be to a stranger. It's played out. We planted it so many years, took all the good right out'n it."

Myles began to dig again. "I hear there're ways a man can put soil right again by planting other things like beans and peas in it. Some scientists claim it'll work."

Cyrus shook his white head. "I'll never see the backside of a plow again. But if you had a mind to buy, I might reconsider selling. I'd rest easy knowing it was in your hands, Myles." His eyes drifted across the weedy pasture to stump-ridden fields beyond.

"If I —" Myles stopped working to stare at his spade. "You'd sell to me?"

"That sounds about like what I said, don't it? This place needs someone who'll put work and love into it. You've done a sight of work hereabouts already, but I know you've been itching to do more, to make the place what it oughta be. You're a good man, Myles Trent, and I think you're a man God will use — no matter if folks claim you don't believe in Him. I know better."

Myles met the old man's gaze. "How do you know?"

"You're plumb full of questions that demand answers, and you ain't the kind who'll quit before he finds them answers. God promises that a man who seeks Him will find Him, if he searches with all his heart."

Myles shifted his grip on the handle. "I can't buy your place, Cyrus. No money. I've laid a little by each year, but not enough."

Cyrus pondered, deepening the lines on his brow. "Don't know why, but I got this feeling about you and my farm, Myles. I think God has something in mind, though I cain't begin to tell you what it is."

A deep sigh expanded Myles's chest. When he exhaled, his shoulders drooped. "Unless He plans to drop a fortune into my lap, I'll be a hired hand till the day I die."

"You might could marry rich," Cyrus suggested with a wicked grin. "Naw, I don't mean it. You find yourself a good wife and make this place into a proper home again."

Myles quickly began to dig. Cyrus chuckled. "Why is finding a wife such a chore for you young fellers? I just up and asked Hattie to wed me and got us hitched. No fuss and feathers about it, yet we stayed happy together sixty years. Bet there's more'n one lady in town who'd be eager to accept a fine feller like you. Why not chance it? Might want to wash up first; try hair oil and scented soap. Females like such things."

"A man doesn't want to marry just any woman," Myles objected. His thoughts whirled.

Scented soap. Van Huysen's Soap.
Money. His money.
Farm. His farm?

"Why not? One woman is same as another." Cyrus's grin displayed almost toothless gums. "Comely or homely, fleshy or scrawny, they kin all keep a man warm on long winter nights. Hattie was never what you might call comely, but then I weren't no prize winner myself!" He cackled. "One woman — that's all you need."

When the hole was deep enough, Myles dragged the carcass over and shoved it in. "That should be deep enough to keep varmints from digging ol' Hector up," he said. Cyrus helped him fill in the hole and tamp it.

"Hope that bear took off for foreign parts," Cyrus remarked. "We don't need a killer loose in these woods."

"I'll warn our neighbors about the possibility of a renegade bear. Want to come to supper at Miss Amelia's boardinghouse with me tonight?"

Cyrus's faded eyes brightened. "That'd be fine. You got a buggy?"

"We can hitch my mare to your buggy," Myles said. "I'll talk with Buck about getting you another mule or horse. You can't stay out here alone with no transportation."

On the way to town, Myles's mare tossed her head and tucked her tail whenever he clucked to her. "Cholla takes being hitched to a buggy as an insult," Myles explained when Cyrus commented on the mare's bad mood.

"Is she yours or Obie's?"

"Mine. Caught and tamed her myself out in Wyoming. Not so pretty to look at, prickly like the cactus she's named for, but she's got legs like iron and a big heart." Myles fondly surveyed his mare's spotted gray hide, wispy tail, and unruly mane.

"And a kind eye. You can tell a lot about a

horse by its eyes," Cyrus added.

Miss Amelia Sidwell greeted them at her boardinghouse's dining room door. "Pull out a chair and tuck in. Evenin', Myles. You been taking too much sun."

"You're looking pert today, Amelia," Cyrus commented. "Fine feathers make a fine bird."

Miss Amelia appeared to appreciate the compliment, favoring the old man with a smile. Her blue-checked apron did bring out the blue in her eyes. "What brings you to town, Cyrus? Ain't seen you in a spell." Her voice was as deep as a man's.

"Your cooking draws men like hummingbirds to honeysuckle," Myles assured her, straddling his chair. He returned greetings from other diners, most of whom he knew.

A stranger stared at him from across the table. Myles nodded, and the gentleman nodded back, then looked away.

Amelia scoffed. "Hummingbirds, indeed. More like flies to molasses, I'd say." She ladled soup into Cyrus's bowl. "Got more of you blowflies than I kin handle these days. I'm thinkin' of hiring help."

"You, Amelia?" Boswell Martin, the town sheriff, inquired in his wheezy voice. "I can't imagine you finding help that would suit. What female creature ever found favor in your eyes?"

Never pausing in her labors, Amelia snapped back, "Miss Sidwell to you, Boz

Martin — and I'll thank you to keep your remarks to yourself. If that's a chaw in your cheek, you'd best get yourself outside and rid of it. I never heard tell of a man eating with tobacco tucked in his cheek, looking like a hulking chipmunk. If you don't beat all!"

The sheriff meekly shoved back his chair and stepped outside while the other diners struggled to hide their mirth. Myles again met the gaze of the dapper gentleman with bushy side-whiskers. The two men shared an amused smile.

"I ain't never seen you before, mister." Cyrus directed his comment toward the stranger. "You new in town or jest travelin' through?"

"I arrived in town Tuesday," the gentleman replied. "I am George Poole, lately from New York. I have business in this area."

"Welcome to Longtree, Mr. Poole." Cyrus and Myles reached across the table to shake the newcomer's hand. Poole's handshake was firm, his gaze steady.

The sheriff returned to the table and began to shovel food into his mouth.

"Boz?" Cyrus said. "I lost my mule today — looked like a bear's work."

Sheriff Martin gave the old man a skeptical look, still chewing.

Cyrus forestalled the inevitable protest. "I know there ain't been a bear in these parts for twenty years, but I know what I seen. The

762

varmint broke ol' Hector's neck and left huge claw marks. I'm thinking you ought to organize a hunt before the critter tears up more stock."

Martin nodded and spoke around a mouthful of stew. "I'll get right on it."

"Don't talk with your mouth full," Amelia ordered, reaching over the sheriff's shoulder to place a freshly sliced loaf of bread on the table. Within moments the platter was empty. "You lot behave like hogs at a trough," the gratified cook growled.

"Talk of bears puts me in mind . . . that circus left Bolger this morning," one diner said. "I heard rumors they lost an animal in this area. Did you hear anything about it, Sheriff? Last thing we need in these parts is a roaming lion."

This time Boz swallowed before he spoke. "Nope. Ain't heard a thing."

Again Myles recalled his circus friend Gina Spinelli's slip of the tongue about a rogue bear, but he said nothing. Surely a missing circus bear would have been reported to the authorities. Or would it?

Mr. Poole turned his steel blue eyes upon Miss Amelia. "That was a wonderful meal, madam. The best meal I've eaten in many a year."

Amelia fluttered. "Why, thank you, Mr. Poole. I'm right glad you liked it. I've got apple dumplings and cream in the kitchen."

"May I take my dessert later this evening? I'm afraid I cannot swallow another bite at the moment." He laid his folded napkin beside his empty plate and pushed back his chair. When he stood, the top of his head was on a level with Amelia's eyes.

Work-worn hands smoothed her starched apron. Myles noticed that her gray hair looked softer than usual; she had styled it a new way instead of slicking it back into a knot. "Certainly, Mr. Poole. You let me know when you're ready for your dessert."

Poole excused himself from the table and left the room, apparently oblivious to the stunned silence that followed Amelia's reply. "But, Amelia —" the sheriff protested.

"Not another word from you." She withered him with a glance. "Not a one of you what cain't fit in your dessert when it's offered. A fine gentleman like Mr. Poole isn't used to stuffing his face, so's a body must make allowances." With a sweep of her skirts, Miss Amelia returned to her kitchen.

Sheriff Martin scowled. "That woman's gone plain loco. A few bows and compliments, and even the best of women plumb lose their heads."

"Jealous, Boz? Maybe you'll get further with the lady if you try bowing and complimenting." Old Cyrus chuckled. "Wouldn't hurt to bathe if you're right serious about courting."

Boz's already florid face turned scarlet.

"Reckon she'd take notice?"

"A woman likes it when a man takes pains on her account. Amelia likes things clean and neat."

"Clean" and "neat" were two terms Myles would never have applied to the sheriff. He was startled by the concept that Sheriff Martin wished to court Miss Amelia. Not that the man was too old for marriage — Boz hadn't yet turned fifty. But hard-boiled Martin had never struck him as the marrying kind.

Then again, what made any person wish to marry? A craving for love and companionship, he supposed. The longing to be needed, admired, and desired. The urge to produce children to carry on one's name. Myles could appreciate the sheriff's inclination.

"I'm thinkin' on asking her to the church social Friday," Boz growled, shoving food around on his plate. "How you think I oughta go about it, Cy?"

Enjoying his new role, Cyrus sized Boz up, rubbing his grizzled chin. "You need to head for the barber for a shave and trim, then buy yourself new duds. And no tobaccy. Amelia hates the stuff. Might better drop it now than later."

Boz rubbed his plump jowls with one dirty hand, making a raspy noise. He nodded. "I'll do it." Amid raucous ribbing from the other men at the table, the sheriff rose, hitched up his sagging belt, and headed for the door.

"No dessert, Boz?" Amelia stood in the kitchen doorway, a loaded plate in each hand.

"Not tonight. Got business to attend. Thank you for a wondrous fine meal, *Miss Sidwell.*" Boz bowed awkwardly and made his exit.

Shocked by his unaccustomed formality, Amelia stared after him, shrugged, and plopped dumplings in front of two diners. When she served Myles and Cyrus, she fixed Myles with a shrewd eye. "You takin' Marva Obermeier to the church social, Myles? She's counting on it."

The fork stopped halfway to his mouth, then slowly returned to the plate. "Miss Obermeier?" His stomach sank. "Why would she expect that?"

"You'd be knowing better than I," Amelia snapped and headed back to her kitchen.

Myles gave Cyrus a blank look. The old man lifted a brow. "It's all over town, Myles. Didn't you know?"

The dessert lost its appeal. "I think I've only talked to her twice."

"You mean to say you ain't sweet on her?"

"No. I mean — yes, that's what I mean to say; no, I'm not sweet on her. I hardly know the woman."

"I reckon you'll be getting to know her real soon." Cyrus chuckled.

CHAPTER 5

Wrath is cruel, and anger is outrageous;
but who is able to stand before envy?
PROVERBS 27:4

Cyrus was no prophet, but he came uncomfortably close. And "uncomfortably close" was an apt description of Marva herself. The blond lady was not unattractive; in fact, in her rosy, plump, blond fashion, she was pretty.

"I'm so happy to see you here tonight, Myles. You've been neglecting church lately." She wagged a finger in his face and moved a step closer. "My papa says I should claim you for my partner at charades."

Myles took a step back. "Why is that?"

"He says you're a natural performer. Have you ever been on the stage?" Marva spoke above the noisy crowd, leaning closer.

"In a way," Myles hedged, shifting backward. "Have you?"

Marva chuckled in her throaty way. "I? Not unless you count school recitations. I play piano in church, but that's different. No one looks at me. Are you warm, Myles? Would you like to step outside for a while?" She stepped closer to make herself heard.

"No, no, I'm fine." Myles moved back and bumped into the wall. He cast a desperate glance around, only to spy Beulah across the room. She sipped lemonade from a cup, then laughed at a comment from her companion. Myles felt a pinch in his chest at the sight of Al's broad shoulders and smooth dark hair. So Beulah had come to the social with Al. The romance must have revived.

"Myles?" He heard someone repeating his name and struggled to focus on Marva's blue eyes.

"Myles, are you all right? You look pale all of a sudden."

"Maybe I do need fresh air." He walked to the door, wishing he could bolt. Across the porch and down the steps, between small clusters of talking, laughing people — fresh air at last. He drew a deep breath and lifted his gaze to the evening sky. A few pink stripes still outlined the horizon; stars multiplied above them.

"It's a lovely night, Myles. I'm glad you brought me to see the sunset." Marva spoke at his elbow, linking her arm through his. "Do you want to take a walk?"

Considering his options, he accepted. "Why not?" He started across the yard surrounding the building that served Longtree as both church and schoolhouse.

Marva trotted to keep up. "Slow down, Myles! We're not racing. Wouldn't you like to stroll away from other people where we can talk?"

"The games will start soon. Wouldn't want to miss them." Myles shortened his stride, but maintained a rapid gait.

Marva began to puff. "I had no idea you enjoyed games so much, Myles. Aren't we rather old for such things?"

"You never outgrow having fun. They're having a spelling competition tonight along with charades." Fun was the furthest thing from his mind at the moment. Surviving the evening without a broken heart would be challenge enough.

When they returned to the steps, Myles escorted Marva through the door. A large woman greeted her. "Marva, darling, you look lovely tonight. I'm sure Myles thinks so!" Without waiting for a response, she rambled on. "I was just saying to Ruby that your recipe for corn fritters is the best I've ever tasted. You add bits of ham to the mix, right?"

While the women discussed cooking, Myles melted into the crowd. "Pardon me. Pardon," he repeated, trying not to be pushy. Arriving at the refreshment table, he reached for a glass of lemonade.

"Hello, Myles." His outstretched hand froze in place as he recognized the pink taffeta dress across the serving table. Slowly his gaze moved up a slender form to meet eyes like chips of black ice. Beulah held a ladle in one hand, a cup in the other. "Are you having a pleasant evening? Miss Obermeier looks particularly lovely tonight, flushed from the cool night air."

Myles wanted to return a snappy remark about Beulah's equally blooming complexion, but his mouth would not cooperate. Was it her beauty that immobilized him, or was it her chilly stare?

"Would you like two cups of lemonade?"

"One will do. Uh, do you need help? I mean, with serving?" He worked his way around the table until he stood at her side. Was this a good time to apologize for throwing her into the pond?

She studied his face with puzzled eyes. "No, but you could offer to fetch more lemonade. Mrs. Schoengard and my mother are mixing more at the parsonage. We spent half the day squeezing lemons. I never want to do that again. Caroline Schoengard, you know, the pastor's wife?" she added in answer to his blank look.

"Oh. Yes. Are you having a nice time?"

"It's all right. Far more people showed up than were expected. Poor Mrs. Schoengard was distraught until Mama offered to help.

Will you get the lemonade for me? This bowl is nearly empty."

"Right away." He thought he heard Marva call his name as he stepped out the back door, but he pretended not to hear. What a joy this evening would be if he could spend it at Beulah's side! How he longed to partner her at games, to share casual conversation and develop a friendship, to have talk circulate town that Myles Trent was sparking Beulah Fairfield.

Violet met him at the parsonage door. "Why, Myles, how nice to see you!"

He doffed his hat. "Beulah sent me to help. Is the lemonade ready? Her bowl is empty."

"Wonderful! Caroline," Violet called back over her shoulder, "people are drinking the lemonade even without ice."

"I haven't heard any complaints," Myles said. "Lemonade is a treat. Just right to wash down the sandwiches and fried chicken."

"Hello, Myles." The pastor's wife appeared in the kitchen doorway, wiping her hands on a towel. "A Chicago friend of my husband shipped the lemons to us. Wasn't that kind? Far more than our family could use." A lock of blond hair clung to Caroline's forehead.

"You must get off your feet for a while, Caroline," Violet fussed over her pregnant friend.

"I'm fine." Caroline ignored her and led Myles to the kitchen. "Thank you for the help, Myles. We were about to send for someone to carry this kettle."

Myles wrapped his arms beneath the kettle's handles and lifted. Lemonade sloshed against his chest. Violet gasped. "I knew we should have put it into smaller containers. I'm sorry, Myles. That thing is so heavy —"

"It's all right. If you'll open the door . . ." Myles walked through the house, across the dark churchyard, and up the church steps. Violet and Caroline called further thanks after him, but he was concentrating too hard to reply.

Beulah backed away from the serving table while Myles emptied his kettle into the cut glass punch bowl. Only a few drops trickled down the kettle's side to dampen the tablecloth. Several gray seeds swirled at the bottom of the bowl. "There." Myles set the kettle on the floor and brushed at his shirt. Already he felt sticky.

"You've spilled lemonade all down the front of you; but then, you've probably noticed," Beulah remarked.

"I couldn't help it. Did pretty well coming all that way with a full kettle."

Beulah picked up a napkin and rubbed at his spotted sleeve. "Yes, you did. Thank you, Myles." Her gaze moved past him. "Marva is looking for you."

He cast a hunted glance over one shoulder. "Guess I'd better run. If she asks, tell her I got covered in lemonade and decided to go home."

"You mean, for good?" Beulah's eyes were no longer icy. Her hand touched his forearm. What was it about her mouth that made him think of kissing every time she spoke to him? "Won't you come back?"

Myles placed his other hand over hers and squeezed. "By the time I came back, the party would be about over. It's all right. I'm no socialite anyway. Never have been."

Someone asked for a cup of lemonade. Beulah poured it with shaking hands while Myles admired the downy curve of her neck. The pastor stood up to announce the start of the spelling match, and the milling crowd began to shuffle.

"If you leave, how will Marva get home?" Beulah asked beneath the buzz of conversation. He bent to listen, and her breath tickled his ear. His hand cupped her elbow. Did he imagine it, or did she lean toward him?

"The same way she came, I guess. Why?"

Beulah bit her lip, studying his face. Myles swallowed hard. Suddenly she bent over the table to wipe up a spill. Her voice quivered. "People never will learn to clean up after themselves. Thank you for your help tonight."

"My pleasure. And Beulah . . ." His courage expired.

"Yes?" She looked up for an instant, then dropped her gaze and licked her lips.

"Miss Beulah, may I have some lemonade?" Across the table, a little girl smiled up at Beulah, revealing a wide gap between her teeth.

"Certainly! Looks like you've lost another tooth, Fern. Are you competing in the spelling bee tonight?"

"Of course, Miss Beulah. You sure do look pretty. Wish I could put my hair up."

"It won't be too many years until you can. And thank you."

Beulah filled another cup. "You were saying, Myles?" She took hold of his wrist and pulled his hand away from his stomach. He hadn't even realized he was rubbing it again.

Heat rushed into his face. "Nothing important. I'll see you around." He didn't want to sound like an echo of little Fern. Beulah wasn't just pretty, she was beautiful tonight with her gleaming knot of dark hair, satin skin, full red lips, and those eyes that took his breath away . . . but he had no idea how to tell her so without sounding foolish.

She faced him. "Oh. Well, good night." Her lips puckered, suspiciously resembling a pout. A fire kindled in Myles's belly, and his hands closed into fists. The intent to drag her outside and bare his soul, come what may, began to form in his mind.

"Ready for the spelling bee, Beulah?" Al asked, sliding behind the table to join them. "Hey, good to see you here, Myles! I saw Marva a minute ago. Better start making your move; you know, like we talked about." He gave Myles a wink and an elbow to the ribs.

"Oh. Yeah." Myles said.

"Myles is just leaving," Beulah said in a voice like ice cracking. She linked arms with Al. "I've been looking forward to this all day," she cooed, gazing up with limpid eyes.

Al blinked in surprise, then grinned. "Me, too!"

Myles stared, his fists tightening.

"Don't stand there like a stone statue, Myles; go find Marva," Al advised. "You and I have the prettiest gals in town."

Myles skulked out the back door, his heart dragging in the dust. He vaulted to his mare's back and wheeled her toward the street.

"Leaving already, Myles?"

"Sheriff Boz? What are you doing out here?" He reined Cholla to a halt. She champed her bit and pawed at the gravel road.

"Patrolling the town. It's my job."

"Miss Amelia turned you down," he guessed. "I saw her with that New York man tonight."

Boz hooked his thumbs in his sagging gun belt. "Marva turn you down?"

"I've never asked her anything," he grumbled. "Better luck next time, Boz."

"Nothing to do with luck. I been praying for a good wife, and Amelia's the one God showed me." He rubbed his chin. "It'll just

775

take time to convince her."

"But, Beulah, you promised to be my partner!"

"I told you, I've got a headache. Ask Eunice; she's good at charades." Beulah slumped into a chair behind the serving table and rubbed her temples. "You already won the spelling competition. Isn't that enough?"

Al propped big fists on his hips. "How can a headache come on that fast?"

She shot him a sour look. "You expect me to explain a headache? It's all this noise, and I can hardly breathe."

He folded his arms across his chest and stared down at her. "I'd be happy to take you outside. Beulah, the games won't be any fun if you don't play. I'll sit with you until you feel better."

"No! Please leave me alone. I think I'll go over to the parsonage and ask Mrs. Schoengard if I can lie down."

Al helped her to her feet. "I'll walk you there."

He was so considerate that Beulah could not be as uncivil as she felt. As they passed the line of tethered horses and buggies, she looked for Myles's spotted mare. Cholla was gone. "Does Myles really plan to court Marva?" The question could not be restrained.

"I guess so. I . . ." Al gave her a sideward

glance. "Why?"

"I wondered why he left so abruptly right after you advised him to 'make his move.' "

One side of Al's mouth twitched. "No matter what the man says, I think he's afraid of women. He's all right with girls like you and Eunice, but a real woman scares him speechless. Maybe I'll give him more advice and see if I can help."

Beulah reared back. "Albert Moore, I'm eighteen now, and I'll have you know that I'm just as much a woman as Marva Obermeier is!"

"Don't you think I know you're a woman? Beulah, that's what I've been trying to talk with you about these past few weeks, but you'll never give me a chance." On the parsonage steps, Al pulled her to a halt and gripped her shoulders.

Beulah flung his hands off. "That was a cruel thing to say, Al," she raged. "Myles doesn't see me as a little girl, even if you do! Leave me alone. I don't want to talk to you tonight."

The door swung open. Violet appeared, pulling on her gloves. "Is the party over? I was just heading that way — Beulah?" She stepped back as Beulah rushed into the house, gripping her head between her hands.

CHAPTER 6

Casting all your care upon him; for he
careth for you.

1 PETER 5:7

Beulah was in her kitchen garden picking yet
another batch of green beans for supper when
Al caught up with her late the following
afternoon. "I did it." He slapped a pair of
leather gloves against his thigh.

"Did what?" Beulah asked coldly, adding
two more beans to her basket.

"I finally told Cousin Buck about my
mother's letter and my plan to go to California. He's disappointed in me for 'running out
on my responsibilities,' as he phrases it. But,
Beulah, when *will* be a good time to go back?
My parents will die of old age before it's ever
a convenient time."

"It is a difficult situation for you," Beulah
agreed, trying to forget her grudge and be
courteous. "I imagine Papa will calm down
and begin to see your side of the situation.
Presently he is thinking only of the work

involved for him in keeping two farms running. Do you think you might sell off stock?"

"Our Jerseys? Never! We've worked years to build up our herd. Now that we have a silo for storing feed, we can keep our cows producing milk over the winter. This is not the time to cut back."

"But if there is no one to milk the herd, I can't see —"

"Myles will be here to milk them. Now that the creamery has opened, our farms should start pulling a profit instead of barely keeping us out of debt."

"Then this is poor timing for you to leave your farm, Al. It sounds to me as if you need to make serious choices about which is more important to you, your farm or seeing your parents."

"Nonsense," Al said. "After we bring in the crops, one man can keep the farm going over the winter. There's no reason Myles can't keep things rolling until my return. He should be pleased to have a steady job. During the past few winters he's had to cut ice blocks on the lakes or work up north in the logging towns to support himself."

Beulah turned back to her beans. "Papa Obie says Myles has worked hard for three summers and has little to show for it. Papa thinks you and he ought to grant Myles some land to start up his own farm, or at least give him a partnership. I heard him talking about it with Mama." There was a buoyant feeling in her chest when she spoke Myles's name.

A line appeared between Al's thick brows. "I don't like that partnership idea. Myles is a good fellow, hardworking and honest, but the Bible says we should not be unequally yoked together with unbelievers."

"Myles is not a believer?" Her voice was dull, giving no evidence that an ice pick stabbed at her heart.

Al lifted a significant brow. "Buck hopes that in time God will reach Myles's heart, but I haven't seen any change." He reached over to pick himself a ripe tomato. "If Myles wants land of his own, he should homestead somewhere. There is plenty of land for the taking in this country if a man has the ambition to find it for himself. Why should I give him any of mine?"

"I thought you wanted him to stay here and milk your cows. He can hardly homestead for himself while he's doing your work." *Myles cannot leave, not ever!*

"True," Al admitted. "But he has plenty of time; he's not old." He tossed and caught the tomato with one hand.

"You're younger than Myles," Beulah observed.

"Why are you so interested in Myles Trent?" The tomato slipped from his hand and smashed into the dirt. "First last night, and now today."

"What are you talking about?" Her cheeks flamed, but perhaps Al would not see. "I simply think your attitude is selfish. Kindly stop destroying my produce."

For a moment she heard only puffing noises as Al struggled to restrain hasty words. When he spoke again, his voice was humble. "I'm sorry I said that about Myles; he's a good fellow. Beulah, please . . . I didn't come here to argue. I need to talk with you. It's important."

"Al, I've got to go make supper; I've taken far too long picking these beans. Mama must be wondering if I ever plan to come back inside." She moved along the row of vegetables toward the house.

His mouth dropped open. "But, Beulah —" He started trotting along the outside edge of the garden to intercept her. "Honey, I tried to talk with you last night and you put me off. We can't go on like this! I've got something important to ask. Don't you want to hear?"

"Some other time, Al. I'll see you later." With an insincere smile, she darted up the steps.

Staring after her openmouthed, Al suddenly flung his hat to the ground and let out a roar. "That cuts it! I'm not even sure I want to marry you anymore, you . . . you . . . *woman!*"

"So when are you getting married?" Eunice asked, plopping down on Beulah's bed.

781

"What?" Beulah stopped brushing her hair and stared at her sister.

"Didn't Al ask you to marry him?"

"Whatever gave you that idea? Do you want me to marry Al?"

"If you marry him, he can't go away." Eunice wrapped her arms around her knees and flung her head forward. Her brown hair, several shades lighter than Beulah's, draped over her knees and arms, hiding her face.

Beulah began to braid her hair. "I don't want to marry Al, Eunice." Red-rimmed eyes gazed from the mirror. Lack of sleep was catching up with her.

The girl's head popped up. She stared at Beulah between wavy locks. "That's silly. Everyone knows you're in love with Al. He's been courting you almost since we arrived in Wisconsin."

"I'm not in love with Al, and I don't want him to court me."

Eunice tossed her hair back. Anger sparked in her ice-blue eyes. "You're afraid to go to California, aren't you? I wouldn't be afraid. I'd go anywhere with Al."

"Then you marry him." Beulah smacked her brush down on the dressing table and rose. Her nightdress fluttered around her legs as she paced across the room. "I don't want to marry Al whether he goes or stays, Eunice. He is not the man I love." She rubbed her hands up and down her bare arms. What had happened to her gentle little sister? What had happened to the entire world? Everything seemed strange and mixed-up.

"Then who is? I can't imagine anyone nicer or handsomer than Al. You haven't got a heart, Beulah. I don't think you'll ever get married."

Beulah swallowed the lump in her throat. "I would rather be an old maid than marry a man I don't love. What has gotten into you, Eunice? This isn't like you."

Biting her lips, Eunice sprang from the bed and rushed out of the room. Beulah heard the girl's feet thumping along the hallway.

Beulah lay in bed, staring toward the ceiling. *It's not as if I've never bickered with Eunice before, but this fight was different. What is wrong with me? Why do I hurt so much inside?*

There was a quiet knock at the door. "Come in."

Light streamed from the candlestick in Violet's hand as she peeked into the room. "I've just come from Eunice's room, and she told me of your quarrel. Beulah, do you need to talk?"

Beulah nodded, and a shuddering sob escaped. Rolling over, she buried her face in her pillow and cried out her misery. Warm hands rubbed her shoulders and stroked her hair.

At last Beulah turned back, mopping her

face with a handkerchief. "Oh Mama, I'm so unhappy."

"I know. Papa and I have been concerned about you."

"I don't know what to do."

"Tell me."

Beulah blew her nose and propped up on one elbow. She thought for a moment. "I don't know where to begin."

"Why not begin with what hurts?"

Beulah bit her lip. "I'm in love, Mama . . . and oh, it hurts so much! He sees me as just a girl — at least, Al says he does. And I think he doesn't respect me anymore because I touched him too much. And Al says he isn't a believer — but I can't believe he could be so nice and good if he isn't."

Violet frowned. "That cannot be true. Al has always proclaimed his faith in Christ, and we have no reason to doubt him."

"Yes, but he says Myles isn't. Mama, do you think he really wants to marry Miss Obermeier?"

Her mother blinked. "Beulah, do you mean to say you're in love with . . . Myles Trent?"

Beulah nodded.

"Oh my!" Violet's shoulders drooped. "I had no idea. Papa told me . . ."

"Told you what? Don't you like Myles, Mama?"

"Of course I like him. He's a good man. Obie thinks highly of him. It's just that . . ."

She couldn't seem to put her thoughts into words.

"He's only about twenty-five, and I'm eighteen now. Oh Mama, just looking at him sets my soul on fire! I know he isn't handsome like Al, but he's so . . . so . . ."

Violet sighed. "I understand. He has the same masculine appeal as your papa. It's something about these cowboys, I guess. What did you mean by 'touched him too much,' Beulah?" Her voice sharpened.

Beulah studied her wadded handkerchief and confessed the waterfall story. "He didn't kiss me or anything, Mama, but I wanted him to." Her eyes closed. "Mama, he's so strong and gentle! It was the most wondrous moment of my life . . . and the worst. I can't help thinking about him all the time and wishing he would hold me again."

Violet brushed a hand across her eyes. "Oh dear. I had no idea . . . What kind of mother am I to let this go on under my nose?" Her hand dropped to her lap and her shoulders squared. "Darling, you know that Myles has told your papa little about his past. It's not that we don't like him, but I fear he may be hiding from the law — you know, under a false name."

Beulah bolted upright. "Mama, how can you say such a thing? Myles has always been honest. Papa and Al trust him. And he is so polite. I know he has an air about him — sort of mysterious and dangerous, I guess — but that doesn't mean he is a criminal!"

The line between Violet's brows deepened. "I don't mean to accuse him, dearest, but we cannot be too careful with our daughters. You are a beautiful young woman, and it sounds to me as if you tempted Myles almost beyond his strength to resist. If he does intend to marry Marva — which would perhaps be best for all concerned — you need to leave him alone."

"Mama, how can you say it would be best for him to marry Marva? I told you that I love him!" Beulah caught her breath on a sob.

Violet stood up and began to pace across the room. "But Beulah, what about Al? Eunice tells me that you don't want to marry him, but, darling, he is steady and dependable — he's your friend, and he loves you. I can't help thinking . . . Well, to be perfectly candid, my dear, you have a tendency to be contrary. Are you certain you're not deciding against Al simply because everyone expects you to marry him?"

Beulah wrapped her arms around her knees and glowered. "Mama, Al is my friend, but he is more like an irritating brother than a lover. When we first met he treated me like fine china; then he got used to me and started acting like himself, and, honestly, Mama, he is so immature and annoying! I can think of few prospects worse than facing Al across the breakfast table every morning for the rest of my life."

Violet stared, shaking her head. "Oh dear," she repeated. "I must talk with Obie. We may have to let Myles go . . . and that would be difficult, what with Al leaving for California soon. How could we find a replacement?"

Beulah scrambled to her knees, clasped her hands, and begged. "Mama, please don't send him away! He has done nothing wrong — it was entirely my fault!" She thumped a fist into her quilt. "And why shouldn't I marry him if I love him? Even if he sinned in the past, he is an honest man now, and he would be a good husband to me."

Violet seemed to wilt. "Beulah, how can you even consider marrying a man who does not love and serve God? I knew you had strayed from the Lord these past few years, but I thought you understood how vital shared faith is to a marriage."

Beulah sat back on her heels and hung her head. "You won't even give Myles a chance, will you, Mama? How can you be so sure he isn't a believer? He doesn't drink or swear or gamble, and there is goodness in his eyes." Resting her head upon her knees, she began to cry again.

Violet sat down and stroked the girl's long braid. "Beulah, I do want to give Myles a chance — he is a fine young man, and I can see why you admire him. I will ask your papa to talk with him about his faith and about his intentions toward you. But in the meantime, I think it would be best if you spent more time with your girlfriends and stayed away from Myles Trent. Not that we will ban him from the house, but . . ."

"Do you mean I have to hide if I see him coming?"

"I simply don't want you to seek him out, dearest. If he approaches you, be gracious, of course, as I have taught you. Darling, I will be praying for wisdom and guidance — for your papa and me as well as for you."

She bent to kiss Beulah's damp cheek.

CHAPTER 7

Let nothing be done through strife or
vainglory;
but in lowliness of mind let each esteem
other better than themselves.
PHILIPPIANS 2:3

"Thank you for coming, Mrs. Watson. And thank you for bringing Beulah. Maybe soon we'll be working on her wedding quilt." Sybil Oakley waved good-bye from her front porch as Violet clucked her gray mare into a quick trot.

Beulah waved to her friend until trees hid the girl from sight. "It's hard to believe Sybil is getting married." Beulah sighed.

"She has grown up quickly this past year. You know, many women would have flown into a temper if you'd pointed out flaws in their quilts. Sybil accepted your criticism graciously."

Beulah fanned herself. "I wasn't trying to be unkind."

"Neither were you trying to be kind. Darling, you must learn to think before you speak, or you'll chase away all your friends. You're gifted in many ways: beauty, talent, and intelligence. You don't need to point out other people's faults to make yourself look better."

Beulah was silent. The mare's hoofs clopped along the road, sloshing in occasional puddles. Maple and birch trees were beginning to show patches of yellow and red.

"I'm sorry, Mama. I'll apologize to Sybil next time I see her." Her voice was quiet.

"I've noticed that Al doesn't talk to you when he comes over. Did you quarrel with him, too?"

Beulah braced herself for a pothole in the road. "Not exactly. I think he's mad because I won't let him talk mushy to me. He tries to get romantic, and it makes me uncomfortable. He is my friend, and that's it."

"Have you told him how you feel?"

She wrinkled her nose. "No, but if he doesn't catch on by now, he's dumber than I think."

"Don't be unkind," Violet said. "You haven't told him about your infatuation with Myles, have you?"

"Mama, of course not! It's none of his business — and besides, I don't want to make him mad at Myles. I haven't seen Myles since the church social." Beulah felt glum.

"I did hear that he had dinner with the

Obermeiers the other night. I hope he settles down with Marva. She needs a good man to love and spoil."

Beulah closed her eyes against a stab of jealousy.

Singing to herself, Beulah wiped off the table. There was a quiet knock at the open kitchen door behind her. "Samuel is outside. He can play until dark," she called.

"Beulah?"

She spun around, putting a sudsy hand to her heart. "Myles?" It came out in a squeak. "I–I thought you were one of Sam's friends come to play. Papa Obie and Mama are at Cyrus Thwaite's house this evening, and Eunice is at a friend's house. It's just the boys and me at home," she babbled. "And the baby is asleep. I haven't seen you in weeks! Did you need to see my papa?"

Behind him, the sky was pink and filmy gray. A bat darted above the fruit trees, and a fox yapped in the forest. "No. I came to see you. I brought this." He held out a book. "Found it in Mo's pasture this morning. You dropped it that day, didn't you?"

That day — only the most important day of Beulah's life. Feeling conscious of her bare feet and loose braid, Beulah wiped her hands on her apron and reached for the book. "Thank you." It smelled warm, like sunshine and wildflowers. The cover was warped and the pages looked wavy.

"It got wet."

"I can still read it." She looked up.

What would Mama do? Shoulders back. Head high. Cool, even tones. Gracious and hospitable. "Will you come in for coffee and cookies?"

His boots shifted on the floorboards. "First I need to . . . to apologize for throwing you in the creek. That's been weighing on my mind. You were right to be angry — my behavior was inexcusable."

Beulah watched his right hand rub circles on his flat stomach. Why did he always do that? It made her want to touch him. *I can't love a man who doesn't serve God. I can't! Gracious and hospitable, that's all.*

"I forgive you. It was my fault, too. I threw water at you first."

"No hard feelings?"

She glanced up. The entreating look in his eyes reminded her of Samuel. "Would I ask a man to carry lemonade for me if I held a grudge against him?"

Myles smiled. "Guess not. Or maybe you knew I'd spill it all over myself and wanted to get back some of your own."

Beulah opened her mouth to protest, but Myles laughed. "I'm teasing. You're easy to provoke."

Warmth filled Beulah's heart and her cheeks. "So they say. I'm trying to improve. I

792

wish you would smile and laugh more often. Your laugh makes me want to laugh. Now will you come in for coffee and cookies?"

His eyes twinkled. "Thank you. I will."

She lowered her chin and one brow. "What's so funny?"

"You. I'm glad you're back to normal. Those elegant manners make me nervous."

Beulah laughed outright. Forgetting her resolve to be aloof, she grabbed him by a shirt button and dragged him into the kitchen. Planting a hand on his chest, she shoved him into a chair. "Sit. Stay."

He seized her wrist in a lightning motion. "Bossy woman. If you request, I am your humble servant. If you order . . ." He shook his head. "Another dunk in the creek might be imminent."

"You use awfully big words for a hired hand." Beulah tugged at her arm. "Is that a threat?"

"A warning."

"I guess your apology wasn't genuine." She pouted, thinking how nice it would be to slip into his lap. He smelled of soap and hair oil. "Don't you want to be friends?"

Pressure on her arm brought her closer. "Is that what you want from me?" The low question set her heart hammering. His face was mere inches from hers. Beulah licked her lips.

Scrabbling claws skidded across the floorboards; then Watchful shoved her face and upper body between Beulah and Myles. Panting and wagging, the dog pawed at Myles's chest.

He released Beulah to protect his skin from Watchful's claws. "Down, girl. I'm glad to see you, too." He forced the dog to the floor, then thumped her sides affectionately. Glancing toward the door, he said, "Hello, Sam."

Samuel stamped his boots on the porch, tossed his hat on a hook, and flopped into a chair. "Howdy, Myles. You come for cookies?"

"Just trying to sweet-talk your sister into giving me some. See if you can influence her."

Beulah propped her fists on her hips. "Not necessary. Samuel, you wash your hands first and bring in the milk, please." She moved to the stove and poured two cups of coffee.

The boy made a face at her back but obeyed.

"Bossy, isn't she?" Myles observed.

"You said it!" Samuel pumped water over his soapy hands, then ran outside to the springhouse.

Beulah's spine stiffened. She set a steaming cup in front of Myles. "Sugar? Milk?"

"Black is fine."

She felt his gaze while she took cookies from the crock and arranged them on a plate. "I'm not bossy," she hissed.

"Do you prefer 'imperious'?" His eyes crinkled at the corners. "You're rewarding to

794

tease, and you somehow manage to be pretty when you're cross. Unfair to the male of the species, since you seem to be cross much of the time. I have observed, however, that your smile is to your frown what a clear sunrise is to a misty morning. Each wields its charm, yet one is far more appealing than the other."

Confounded by this speech, Beulah settled across from him. She was pondering an answer when Samuel clattered up the steps, carrying the milk. "Save some for me," he protested, seeing Myles pop an entire cookie into his mouth.

Still chewing, Myles wrapped his forearms around the plate of cookies and gave Samuel a provoking smile. "Mine."

Samuel pitched into him. Myles caught the boy's arms and held him off easily, but Samuel was a determined opponent. Beulah watched helplessly as they wrestled at the table. She rescued Myles's coffee just in time. "Boys, behave yourselves!"

The chair tipped over, and Myles landed on the floor, laughing. "Truce," he gasped. "I'll share."

Samuel was equally breathless and merry. "I beat you," he claimed. He thumped Myles in the stomach, and the man's knees came up with a jerk.

"Samuel! Don't be mean!" Beulah jumped to her feet. "Are you all right, Myles?"

Samuel gave her a scornful glare. "Don't be

silly. I couldn't hurt him."

Myles sat up, resting an arm on his upended chair. "Aw, let her protect me if she wants to. I like it." Rubbing his belly, he smiled up at Beulah, and she felt her face grow warm.

Myles and Samuel talked baseball and fishing while they finished off the cookies. Sipping her coffee, Beulah listened, watching their animated faces and smiling at their quips and gibes.

"So where's Al?" Samuel looked at Beulah, then at Myles.

Beulah collected the empty dishes and carried them to the sink. Leaning back in the chair with an ankle resting on his knee, Myles stroked his beard. "Reckon he's at home."

"Why didn't he come with you?"

"He didn't know I was coming."

"He was here last night," Samuel said. "Eunice and I played marbles with him. Do you want to come play catch with me tomorrow?"

"Just might do that. Better enjoy free time while we have it. Harvest starts in a few days, and from then on, we work like slaves." Myles rose and stretched his arms. "Guess I'd better get on back."

"Bye, Myles." Samuel left the room without ceremony.

Taking his hat from the table, Myles twisted it between his hands. "Thank you for the cookies and the good company, Beulah. Can't remember when I've had a nicer evening."

"I can't either." Beulah clasped her hands behind her. "I'm glad you came over." She backed away, giving him room to pass.

His eyes searched her face. "So am I." He clapped on his hat and disappeared into the night.

CHAPTER 8

He healeth the broken in heart,
and bindeth up their wounds.
PSALM 147:3

Rapid footfalls approached the main barn from outside. "Myles? Al? Is anyone here?" Beulah called.

"I'm here," Myles answered. He set aside the broken stall door and rose, brushing wood shavings from his hands. "Al is out. Do you need him?"

Beulah stopped in the barn doorway, eyes wide, chest heaving. "I . . . well . . ." She hopped from one foot to the other, her gaze shifting about the barn. "Oh, what can it hurt? I need your help! Please come quickly, Myles."

"Are you ill? Hurt? Come, sit down here." He indicated the bench.

"No, no, I need help," she panted. "I found a cat caught by a fishhook down near the beaver dam. Do you have something I can use to cut it loose?"

A cat? Myles put his hammer into his neat toolbox and selected a pair of pliers. After plucking his hat from a hook on the barn wall, he pulled it low over his forehead. "Lead on."

"I hope I can find the cat again." Beulah was beginning to catch her breath. Her bound braid hung cockeyed on the side of her head; her sunbonnet lay upon her shoulders.

"We'll find it." He followed her outside into blinding sunlight.

She pulled her sunbonnet back into place and retied the strings. "Do you like cats? I've never been fond of them, but this one purred when I touched it. Even if it hissed at me, I still couldn't leave it to die. Could you?"

"Of course not." Myles frowned, seized by a premonition.

When they entered the forest Beulah took the lead. Myles followed her slim form through the trees, keeping close behind her. He heard the cat wailing before they crossed the dam.

"Lucky you heard her instead of some hungry animal." Myles pulled aside branches. Sure enough, there was a familiar round face with the white blotch on the nose. Sorrow and horror formed a lump in his throat. "Hello, girl. How long have you been here?" He snipped away a tangle of line until only a short piece dangled from the cat's mouth.

Slipping one hand beneath her, he lifted Pushy free of the brush and cradled her in his arms. That rumbling purr sounded again, and the cat closed her golden eyes. Myles rubbed behind her ear with one finger, and she pushed her head into his chest. Dried blood caked the white bib beneath the cat's swollen chin. She made a little chirruping noise, her usual greeting.

He felt movement within her body, and the lump in his throat grew, making it difficult to speak. "I think she's expecting kittens."

"Really?" Beulah breathed out the word. "Can you help her, Myles?" She stroked the cat's side, then let her hand rest on Myles's arm.

"I'll try. Let's take her home."

Back in the barn's tack room, he dug with one hand through a box of medical supplies until he found a bottle of ointment. "Please find a blanket to wrap her in."

Beulah returned empty-handed. "The only blankets I can find are stiff with horse sweat and covered in hair. Will my apron do?" she asked, untying it.

He wrapped the cat in Beulah's calico apron, securing its legs against its body so that it could neither scratch nor squirm. Pushy let out a protesting howl, but relaxed and began to purr when he rubbed her head.

Beulah looked amazed. "This is the friendliest cat I have ever seen!"

Myles gave her a quick smile. "She's a special one. She won't stay wrapped up long, so we've got to work quickly. You hold her head up and her body down while I cut off the end of the hook."

Beulah did as she was told and watched him work. The cat struggled when Myles had to dig for the hook's barb, which protruded beneath her chin. Then *snip* and the barb fell upon Beulah's apron.

"Now we must hold her mouth open so I can slip out the rest of the hook." Myles demonstrated how he wanted Beulah to hold the cat under her arm. Once she had the cat in the right position, he pried its mouth open and struggled to grip the hook with the pliers. Pushy squirmed, gagged, and growled. Myles heard claws shredding Beulah's apron. His hat landed upside down on the floor.

"Got it." Myles held aloft the bit of wire and string. "Better get cotton over that wound before . . ."

Too late. Blood and pus oozed from the wound and dripped upon Beulah's lap. Myles snatched a cotton pad from the worktable and pressed it against the cat's chin. "Sorry about that."

Beulah said nothing. Her eyes were closed.

"Beulah? You . . . uh, might want to clean your dress there." He dropped cotton wool on the spot.

"I — I'm not very good around blood," she

whispered.

Myles snatched the cat from her lap and pushed Beulah's head down toward her knees. "Lower your head until the faintness passes."

The apron dropped to the floor. Pushy struggled, trying to right herself. Her claws raked across his chest. "Yeow!" Myles tucked her under his arm, and she relaxed. "Stupid cat."

"Do you think she will live?" Beulah's voice was muffled.

"I hope so. Although I'm sorry about your dress, it's a good thing all that mess came out of her jaw. I'll put ointment on her face and hope her body can heal what we can't help."

"I've been praying for her." Beulah lifted her head. Her face had regained color. She took the jar of ointment and removed the lid.

"Have you? Good."

"Do you believe in God, Myles?" Beulah held out the jar.

"I believe there is a God."

She smiled. "I thought you must. Al said you weren't a believer."

He found it hard to meet her gaze. "Al can't be blamed for that. I guess I've been fighting God. Painful things happened in my past, and I blamed Him." Myles dipped a finger into the ointment. "I've had a lot of talks with Buck — Obie — about God."

802

"I know who you mean. All of Papa's old friends call him Buck — it's his middle name. So you don't blame God now?"

Myles evaded the question. "It isn't logical to blame God for the evil in the world."

"Feelings are seldom logical," Beulah said.

His hands paused. "True. Which is why it's dangerous to live by one's feelings." Myles held Pushy's head still as he smoothed ointment over her chin. She resumed her cheery purr.

"Pushy here must wonder why I am hurting her, yet she trusts me. This simple cat has greater faith than I do." There was a catch in his voice.

"She is your cat, Myles?"

"She lives in our barn. I named her Pushy because she finds ways to get me to pet her and feed her. I realize now that I hadn't seen her around for days, yet I didn't think to search for her." He fixed his eyes upon Pushy, trying to hide his face from Beulah. She would think he was foolish to become emotional over a cat. Pushy closed her eyes and savored his gentle rubbing.

So lightly that he scarcely felt it, Beulah skimmed his hair with her fingers. "You can't be everywhere and think of everything the way God does, Myles. I'm sure Pushy forgives you. You didn't intend to let her down. It was a human mistake."

"We humans make a lot of mistakes." Bitterness laced his voice.

"My mother says that's why we need to be patient with each other." She sighed. "People can be so annoying, and my first reaction is to say something nasty. My mother says it's because I'm proud and think myself better than other people."

Myles lifted his head until he could feel Beulah's touch. "Do you?"

"Think myself better? Sometimes I do," she said so softly he could hardly hear. Her fingers threaded through his hair. "Deep inside I know I'm not better, though. I don't like being mean."

Her touch made it difficult to concentrate. Myles closed his eyes. "You're being nice to me right now. My grandmother used to rub my head like this."

"You look as if you might start purring." Beulah laughed.

Hearing laughter in her voice, he smiled. "P-d-d-r-r-r. I can't do it like Pushy does."

Pushy climbed from his arms into Beulah's lap, tucked in her paws, and settled down to purr. The two humans paid her no attention. Myles shifted his weight and sat close to Beulah's feet. She put both hands to work, rubbing his temples and the nape of his neck. "I've got chills down my spine, this feels so good," he said, letting his head loll against her hands.

"Your hair ranges in shade from auburn to

sandy blond."

"Yeah, but it's still red hair."

"Did you used to get teased about it?"

"My nickname was 'Red.' "

"The clown called you that, I remember."

"Antonio and everyone else at the circus. Wish I had dark hair and skin that didn't freckle."

"Like mine?"

"Yours or Al's."

"I used to get teased about my big teeth and about being skinny." She spoke quietly. "I've never told that to anyone but my mother before."

"It hurts, being teased." He reached back and patted her hand.

After massaging his shoulders for a few minutes, she touched the left side of his chest. "Is this your blood or Pushy's?"

Myles looked down, surprised to see a spot of red on his tan shirt. "Mine, I think. She scratched me."

"You had better put ointment on it," Beulah advised. She held out the jar.

Myles unbuttoned three shirt buttons, then his undervest and glanced inside. "It's nothing." He covered it up.

"Let me see."

"Yes, Mother." Feeling sheepish, he exposed the triple scratch, which was reddened and puffy. "I thought you couldn't bear the sight of blood."

"Turn this way." Beulah leaned over the sleeping cat and wiped a fingerful of ointment into the wound until his chest hair lay smeared and flattened across the scratches. "I've never done this before." She pursed her lips in concentration. Myles tried to swallow, but his mouth was too dry.

She looked up and smiled. "There, that should feel better soon." The smile faded. "Did I hurt you? I tried to be gentle. Those scratches are deep."

"Uh . . . Pushy needs a drink." His voice sounded like gravel in a bucket. "I'll fetch milk from the springhouse." Myles scrambled to his feet and rushed from the barn, shaking his head to clear it. The temptation to haul Beulah into his lap and kiss her had nearly overcome his self-control.

He lifted the bottle of milk from its cold storage in the little man-made pool. Conflicting thoughts raced through his mind.

She doesn't know. She thinks I'm a Christian man like Buck and Al. If she knew me, really knew me, would she trust me, touch me with her dear hands? Myles shook his head, teeth bared in a grimace. *Antonio said I'm poison — full of bitterness and hatred. I would destroy her, the one I love. God, help me! I don't know what to do!*

He rubbed his face with a trembling hand. *Yes, I do know what I should do. If I were an honorable man, I would tell her to leave me alone, tell her to marry Al and be happy.*

When he returned to the barn, Beulah still sat on the bench with Pushy in her lap. The girl's eyes were enormous in her dirty face, and she was chewing on her lower lip. She opened her mouth, but Myles spoke first. "Sorry I took so long. Let's see if Pushy can drink this."

"She's asleep."

"I imagine she'll wake when she smells the milk. Set her on the floor here." He filled the chipped saucer.

Myles was right. Pushy was desperate for the drink, yet she could not lap with her swollen tongue. She sucked up the milk, making pained little cries all the while.

"I thought you were angry with me when you rushed outside," Beulah said.

"Why would I be angry?" Myles kept his eyes upon the cat.

"I shouldn't have touched you like that; you won't respect me anymore."

He let out an incredulous little huff, smiling without real humor. "Won't respect you? That's unlikely." He stared at a pitchfork, unwilling to grant her access to his chaotic thoughts. *Do you know what your touch does to me? Do you dream about me the way I dream about you? Could you be content, married to a wretched, redheaded hired man? What would you think if you knew my past?*

"Does your stomach hurt?"

Myles snatched his hand from his belly.

"Eunice says you must be hungry a lot because you rub your belly so much."

He felt warm. "Nervous habit."

After several saucers of milk, Pushy made an effort to groom. As soon as she lifted her paw to her mouth she remembered the impossibility of using her tongue, but she wiped the paw over her ear anyway.

"Do you think her kittens will live?"

"I felt one moving while I held her. Unless she eats, she will not have milk enough for them." Squatting, Myles rubbed the back of the cat's neck with one finger, and the purr began to rumble. "I'll chop some meat for her tonight. It will have to be soft and wet. I'll keep her in my room until she is well. Poor Pushy. I think she has wanted to be my pet all this time, but I was too busy to notice how special she is."

"You *are* too busy. I hardly ever see you. I wish you would come by for coffee again some evening. My parents wouldn't mind." Beulah rose and shook out her rumpled apron. "I think even I would enjoy having a cat like this one. She's special."

Rising, Myles watched her fold the stained garment. She looked smaller without that voluminous apron. Her simple calico gown complemented her pretty figure. The sunbonnet hung down her back.

The ache in his soul was more than he could endure. *I'm not an honorable man. Al can't have her! I want Beulah for my wife. Whatever it takes, God. Whatever it takes.*

"Would you like to own Pushy?"

"I'm sure she will be happiest here with you." Beulah smiled. "I don't think my mother would want a cat. We already have one animal in the house, and that is enough. I had better be going home now. No one knows where I am. Take care of Pushy, Myles . . . and thank you for coming to her rescue. You may think I'm bossy, but I think you're wonderful!" Rising on tiptoe, she kissed his face above his beard.

He slipped his arms around that slim waist and pulled her close. Her face rested within the open vee of his shirt; her breath heated his skin.

"Why did you do that?" Myles asked gruffly, his cheek pressed against her head.

"I saw my mother kiss Papa Obie that way not long after we met him." She sounded defensive. "She told me she did it to demonstrate gratitude for his kindness."

"No wonder Buck is besotted with your mother." Eyes closed tight, he spoke into her hair.

"I was trying to show affection." Beulah's arms wriggled free and slid around his waist. "Now I understand why Mama likes it when

Papa holds her. It's nice."

When her hands pressed against his back, he released her and stepped away. "Come. I will walk with you as far as the dam."

Beulah looked shaken. Myles could think of nothing to say, so they walked in silence.

"Did I shock you?" she asked meekly.

"No."

Beulah had been walking ahead of him on the narrow path, but now she stopped to face him. "I wish I knew what you were thinking. Sometimes I feel as if you are laughing at me on the inside. I must seem young and naive to you."

"Believe me, I'm not laughing," he said. "Do I seem old and dried up to you?"

"Of course not, but you never seem happy. Even when you smile and laugh, there is sadness in your eyes." She tipped her head to one side and searched his face. "Do you ever wish you could talk with someone about . . . about things? I don't think I really know you, Myles. You're like a carrot — most of you is underground."

His lips twitched at her choice of analogy. Fear of overwhelming her prevented him from revealing even a fraction of his desire to be known and loved. "I'll let you know when the carrot is ready for harvest."

"Now I know you're laughing at me!" Dark eyes accusing yet twinkling, she gave him a little shove and hurried away along the trail.

"Good-bye, Myles."

"Beulah?"

She glanced back.

"You can demonstrate gratitude to me anytime you like."

Aghast, she turned and ran into the woods. He chuckled.

CHAPTER 9

Thou openest thine hand,
and satisfiest the desire of every
living thing.

PSALM 145:16

Myles found the Bible in the bottom of an old saddlebag, smelling of mildewed leather. A spider had nested on the binding — years ago from the looks of it. The title page bore his name in his brother's hieroglyphic script: "Myles Van Huysen, from his brother Monte, 1875."

His squared fingertip caressed the page. "Monte." Memories assailed him: A childhood filled with Monte's derogatory name-calling and cruel tricks whenever Gram's back was turned. Years of adolescent jealousy and competition. Then Monte showing up at the circus — mocking, yet for once honest about his feelings and plans.

Myles stared vacantly at the saddlebag. In Monte's final days something had happened to change him, to turn him from his reckless ways. Was it the shock of finding himself a hunted man? Was it the realization that someone wanted to kill him? Myles shook his head. Danger had never fazed Montague Van Huysen.

He recalled faces around the campfire, cowboys of assorted sizes and colors squatting to drink scalding coffee before heading out to keep watch over the herd. Monte had smiled, a genuine smile containing no scorn, when he handed over the brown paper parcel. "Happy birthday. The boys gave you a lariat, so I got you something you didn't want. It took me years to stop running from God; hope you're quicker to find Him."

Now, clutching the Book to his bare chest, Myles closed his eyes. "You were right, Monte. I didn't want it. Nearly tossed it away when I saw what it was. Wish I had. Stupid to carry an old book around with me all these years."

He opened it at random. "Isaiah. Never could make heads or tails of those long-winded prophets." Frowning, he looked at the heavy log beams overhead. "All right, God," he growled, "*if* You exist, explain Yourself to me. Beulah says I'm unhappy. Antonio says I'm carrying a burden of unforgiveness. I don't see how I can be held responsible for the wickedness of other people!"

Rising, Myles began to pace back and forth

across the small room, his Bible tucked under one arm, a finger holding his place. "I'm not the one who sinned. First my mother gave up on living and left me to Gram. Then Gram favored Monte and made me work like a slave. Monte never gave me a moment's peace; then he followed me around the country all those years as if he really cared what became of me. It's his fault he got killed —" A surge of emotion choked Myles's voice. Grimacing, he struggled to hold back tears. Vehemently he swore.

Sorrow and loss were incompatible with his anger at Monte. Myles clenched his fists and screwed up his face. "I hated him, God! Do You hear me? I hated him! I'm not sorry he died." A sob wrenched his body. "I hate him for being such a fool as to get himself killed. I hate him for being an outlaw. I hate him for being so kind to me right before he died, just so I would mourn him!" Tears streamed down his face and moistened his beard.

He climbed onto his bed, bringing the Bible with him. Flat on his back with the Book lying open on his chest, he continued, "You tell me to forgive people if I want to be forgiven. Ha! What they did was wrong, God! I can't pretend it wasn't and absolve them from guilt." Self-righteousness colored his voice, yet speaking the words gave him no relief. "They didn't ask to be forgiven. They weren't even sorry. I hope they all burn in hell. What do You think of that?"

He pressed upon his aching stomach and groaned aloud. Antonio's words rang in his head: *"You cannot offer Beulah an unforgiving heart."* Poison. Hatred. The bitterness was eating him alive from within.

"Can You offer me anything better?" he demanded.

If I want God to explain Himself, I'd better read what He has to say. He's not going to talk to me out loud. As if this Book could answer any real questions.

His finger was still holding a place in Isaiah. Myles opened the Book, rolled over, and focused on a page. " 'Ho, every one that thirsteth, come ye to the waters, and he that hath no money; come ye, buy, and eat; yea, come, buy wine and milk without money and without price,' " he read aloud.

How can he that has no money buy something to eat? His soul was thirsty, but this couldn't be speaking about that kind of thirst. Myles read on: " 'Wherefore do ye spend money for that which is not bread? and your labour for that which satisfieth not? hearken diligently unto me, and eat ye that which is good, and let your soul delight itself in fatness.' "

So maybe it really is talking about feeding the soul. I suppose spending "money for that which is not bread" means trying to fill the emptiness inside with meaningless things. Maybe only

God can fill that aching void, the hunger and thirst in my soul.

His gaze drifted down the page. " 'Seek ye the LORD while he may be found, call ye upon him while he is near: Let the wicked forsake his way, and the unrighteous man his thoughts: and let him return unto the LORD, and he will have mercy upon him; and to our God, for he will abundantly pardon.' "

Myles stared into space and brooded. Much though he hated to admit it, his hatred and anger were wicked. He was that unrighteous man who harbored evil thoughts. He was in need of pardon.

He read on: " 'For my thoughts are not your thoughts, neither are your ways my ways, saith the LORD. For as the heavens are higher than the earth, so are my ways higher than your ways, and my thoughts than your thoughts.' "

Myles snapped the book shut, eyes wide. A chill ran down his spine. There was his answer: God does not need to explain Himself. Period.

Myles suddenly felt presumptuous. Insignificant. Like dust. He tucked the Book under his bed, blew out the lamp, and lay awake until the early hours of morning.

If Buck Watson was surprised when Myles started asking him questions about Scripture, he didn't say so. The two men spoke at irregular intervals, sometimes drawing a simple conversation out over hours.

"There are parts of the Bible I can't understand," Myles said as he raked hay on a newly cut field. He felt small beneath the dome of cloudless blue sky. Trees surrounding the pastures flaunted fall colors, reminding him of the passage of time.

"Such as?" Buck prompted.

The two worked as a team, tossing hay into a wagon. The mule team placidly nibbled on hay stubble. Myles looked at other crews around them, their burned and tanned backs exposed to the autumn sun. "I was always told to obey God's commands and He would take care of me. But the Bible tells many stories about good people who were killed or tortured. I've had bad things happen in my life. Wicked people seem to reign supreme; tornadoes, floods, and droughts come; and God sits back and does nothing. The Bible says God is the Author of good, not of evil. I know He knows everything and doesn't have to explain Himself to us lowly people, but my head still wants to argue the point."

"Man has free will to choose good or evil, and those choices can affect the innocent. The whole earth suffers under the curse of sin, and we all feel its effects. Sometimes God intervenes; sometimes He doesn't."

"But why? If He's all powerful, loving, and holy, why doesn't He prevent evil or crush wicked people?" Myles stabbed too hard, driving his pitchfork into the earth.

Buck considered his answer, brows knitted. "There are things we won't know until we reach eternity. You see, Myles, our faith is based not upon what God does but upon who He is. God tells us that He is just, loving, merciful. We must take Him at His word and know that He will do what is best. He doesn't explain Himself. He doesn't guarantee prosperity and good health. But He does promise to be with us always, guiding and directing our lives for His purpose. Once you place your faith in Him, you will discover, as I have, that He never fails, never disappoints. He will give you perfect peace if you will accept it." Buck forked hay atop the mound in the wagon bed.

"Peace." Myles studied Buck's face and beheld that perfect peace in action. God's reality in Buck Watson's life could not be denied. There was no other explanation for the man.

Myles lifted his shirttail to wipe his sweating face. Over the course of the day, he had peeled down to an unbuttoned shirt. Buck worked shirtless; his shoulders were tanned like leather beneath his suspender straps. "I do want the kind of peace you have," Myles admitted. "I know I'm a sinner, but I'm not as bad as some people."

"When you stand before God, do you think

He will accept the excuse that you weren't as bad as some other guy? What is God's requirement for entrance into heaven?"

"I don't know," Myles grumbled.

"Then I'll tell you: Perfection. No sin. None."

Myles jerked around to face his boss. "But that's impossible. Everybody sins. If that is so, then nobody could go to heaven."

A slow smile curled Buck's mustache. "Exactly. The wages of sin is death, and we are all guilty. Doomed."

Myles shook his head in confusion. "How can you smile about this? You must be wrong."

"No, it's the truth. Look it up for yourself in Romans." Buck's gaze held compassion. "But here is the reason I can smile: God loves us, Myles. He is not willing that any should perish. You see the quandary: God is holy — man is sinful. Sin deserves death — we all deserve death. No one is righteous except God Himself. Do you know John 3:16?"

Myles thought for a moment. "Is that the one about 'God so loved the world'?"

Buck nodded. " 'For God so loved the world, that he gave his only begotten Son, that whosoever believeth in him should not perish, but have everlasting life. For God sent not his Son into the world to condemn the world; but that the world through him might be saved.' "

Myles stared into space. "I think I'm beginning to see . . ."

"I would suggest that you start reading the book of Matthew. Read about Jesus, His life and purpose. He is God in the flesh, come to save us. Ask God to make it clear to you."

Myles climbed atop the pile in the wagon, arranging and packing the hay. His brow wrinkled in thought.

"Jesus died in your place, Myles, so you could go to heaven," Buck shouted up to him. "He loves you."

To Myles's irritation, tears burned his eyes. He turned his back on Buck and worked in silence. His work complete, Myles jumped down and leaned against the wagon wheel. A muscle twitched in his cheek, and his body remained taut. "I still have questions."

Gray eyes regarded him with deep understanding. "Nothing wrong with that. God wants you to come to Him with your questions."

Myles glanced at his friend and drew a deep breath. "Buck, I haven't forgotten your past. I don't know how you continued to trust God all those years, especially while you were in prison through no fault of your own."

"I had my ups and downs," Buck said. "Times of despair, times of joy. But I clung to God's promise to bring good out of my life. Sometimes that promise was the only thing I had left."

"But didn't you hate the men who did it to you? I mean, they're all dead now. You've had your revenge. Although I never understood why you went and tried to lead that rat Houghton to God before he died. I should think you would *want* him to rot in hell!"

Buck stopped working and studied Myles. "Hmm. I see." He rested both hands atop the rake's handle. "I tried hating, Myles. For months, I hated and brooded in that prison, vowing revenge on the lying scum who put me there. Then a friend read me a parable Jesus told about forgiveness; you can find it in the book of Matthew, chapter eighteen. That story changed my life."

Myles grunted. Forgiveness again. He didn't want to hear it.

Buck took a deep breath. "Myles, it comes down to one question: Are you willing to make Jesus your Lord or not?"

Myles stared at a distant haystack and brushed away a persistent fly. There was one thing he could do to make his past right. "I must return to New York."

Buck lifted one brow. "Oh?"

"I'll never have peace until I let my grandmother know where I am and apologize for running away. I can't bring my brother back for her, but I can give her myself. This is something I know God wants me to do." Myles slipped a hand inside his open shirt and scratched his shoulder. "Maybe I should write a letter. If I go back, I might lose everything that's important to me here."

Buck looked into his soul. "Beulah?"

"You know?"

"I'm not blind. Her mother asked me to question your intentions."

Myles swallowed hard. "What about Al?"

"Wrong question. What about Myles? Listen to me, my friend. You can't make your heart right with God. Only Jesus can do that for you."

Myles's head drooped. "I know I'm not good enough for Beulah. A friend told me once that I would poison her with the bitterness in my heart. I've got to work this thing out with God."

Buck crossed his arms, shaking his head sadly. "Until you do, better leave Beulah alone."

Myles lifted his hat and ran one hand back over his sweaty hair. Then he nodded. Climbing into the wagon seat, he loosed the brake, called to the team, and headed for the barn. Buck moved to a new spot and began to rake.

Al and his crew waited near the barn to unload hay into the loft. After turning his load over to them, Myles watered his team at the huge trough. One mule ducked half its face beneath the water; the other sucked daintily. Myles pushed a layer of surface scum away with one hand, then splashed his face and upper body with the cold water. Much better. He slicked water off his chest with both hands, then plastered back his unruly hair.

Just as he finished hitching the team to an empty wagon, Beulah's voice caught his attention. There she was at the barn, serving cold drinks to the hands. Slim and lovely, dipping water for each man and bestowing her precious smiles. Myles suddenly noticed his raging thirst. Eyes fixed upon Beulah's face, he started across the yard.

Better leave Beulah alone.

Myles halted. Shaking his head, he closed his eyes and rubbed them with his fingers. The woman was like a magnet to him. Buck was right to warn him away from her. *Guess I'll have to do without the drink.* He jogged back to the wagon, leaped to its seat, and slapped the reins on the mules' rumps. "Yah! Get on with you."

"Myles!"

Shading his eyes with one hand, he looked back. Beulah ran behind the jolting wagon, her bonnet upon her shoulders. Water sloshed from the bucket in her hands. "You didn't get your drink. You can't work in this heat without it."

Myles hauled in the mules and wrapped the reins around the brake handle. She hoisted the bucket up to him. Myles took it, holding her gaze. "Thank you." Lifting the dipper several times, he drank his fill.

"Why didn't you come talk to me?" she asked. "I've hardly seen you for days and days. How is Pushy? Any kittens yet?"

"Not yet. She's healing well. She . . . she sleeps between my feet." Myles lost himself in the beauty of Beulah's eyes.

"Myles, are you feeling all right? Maybe you've had too much sun." Accusation transformed into concern. "Why don't you come inside for a while. Your face is all red."

Temptation swamped him. What would it hurt to relax for a short time? When Beulah's gaze lowered, he realized that he was rubbing his belly again. She smiled when he began to button his shirt. "Don't bother on my account. You must be roasting." She touched his arm. "Your skin is like fire. Maybe you need another dunk under the waterfall."

Startled, Myles met her teasing gaze. "I washed in the trough. I'll be all right. Buck is waiting for me." His skin did feel scorched where her hand rested on his arm, but it wasn't from sunburn.

The smile faded as her eyes searched his face. "If you're sure . . . Myles, what's wrong?"

"I can't talk with you, Beulah. Not until — You don't even know me, who I really am."

"I know all I need to know. Did my mother tell you not to talk to me?" She sounded angry.

He studied her delicate hand, wondering at

its power to thrill or wound him. "No."

"You're still coming to our music party Friday, aren't you?"

"I'll be there." He handed her the bucket. "Better get back to work." Holding her gaze, he tried to smile. "You, too. Lots of thirsty men around here."

She nodded and watched him drive away.

Streams of milk rang inside a metal pail. Al spoke from the next stall. "I've got to leave soon in case we get an early snow. Thanks for all your help preparing this place for winter."

Myles grunted.

"I've given up on marrying Beulah. I don't know why I ever thought she'd make me a good wife. She's pretty, but looks aren't everything. A man wants a woman to be his friend and companion. Beulah flirts one minute and treats me like anathema the next. She about snapped my head off this afternoon. Something was tweaking her tail, that's certain."

Myles chewed his lip. "She hasn't been herself lately. She's got lots of good qualities."

Al snorted. "At the moment I'd be hardpressed to name one."

"She's your friend. Don't say anything you'll be sorry about later, Al. Just because she isn't meant to be your wife doesn't mean she's not a good woman."

Al grumbled. "I know you're right. But still, I'm thanking the Lord that He prevented me from proposing marriage. What a fix I would be in if she had accepted!"

Myles leaned his head against a tawny flank, fixed his gaze upon the foamy milk in his bucket, and drew a long breath. "I'm thanking Him for the same thing."

"What did you say?"

"I said I'm thanking God that you didn't propose to Beulah."

"Thanks. Say, when did this come about, you talking to God?" Al's grinning face appeared above the stall divider.

"Recently. Been talking to Buck a lot. I've got a past that isn't pretty, but I know I need to make things right. I wrote a letter to my grandmother. Plan to mail it tomorrow when I go to town."

"Will you be able to keep my farm going this winter?"

"Not sure I should make promises at this point, Al."

He sighed. "I guess I understand. Wish I had peace about going to California. I don't feel right about it, and God isn't answering my questions."

As soon as he was alone, Myles allowed a grin to spread across his face. He punched the air in delight, kicked his feet up and stood on his hands, then dropped to his knees. "Thanks, God! I can hardly believe it, but thanks! Soon as I gave in to You and wrote that letter — whizbang! Al is out of the running! Now if I can sell my part of the soap business and buy Cyrus's farm, then . . ."

"Myles, good to see you."

Pausing on the boardwalk in front of the general store, Myles stared at the speaker. The voice was familiar, but the face? "Sheriff Boz?"

Gone was the tobacco-stained walrus mustache. Looking pounds thinner, Boz Martin sported a crisp white shirt and string tie. The star pinned to his vest sparkled. His gun belt no longer completely disappeared beneath an overhanging paunch. He grinned, showing yellow teeth. Myles had never before seen the man's mouth.

"Don't know me, eh?"

"I haven't seen you at Miss Amelia's in a while."

"Been staying away. I'm hopin' she'll be surprised, too."

"I'm sure she will be. You look . . . fine."

Boz stood taller, puffing out his chest. "Town's jam-packed with drifters, harvest workers. Lot of riffraff, if you ask me. We had to break up a fight at the Shady Lady last night. You hear about it?"

Myles shook his head.

Boz deflated slightly. "I'll be just as glad when that lot moves on. That New York character, Mr. Poole, left town last week, so I've got hopes Amelia will notice me again. Poole was mighty interested in you, Myles. Can't know why."

"How do you mean, 'interested'?"

"Asked a lot of questions around town. You going to Buck and Violet's party tonight? I can't make it, and neither can Amelia."

"That's too bad. Seems like half the town was invited. The Watsons have a lot of friends."

Peering intently across the street, Boz rose on tiptoe, fingering his gun belt. "That Swedish family south of your place lost a pig a few nights back. Looks like Cyrus's bear ain't left the county after all."

Myles turned to see what was distracting Boz, but saw nothing unusual. "Be glad to help on a hunt. We've been keeping our stock close to the barns, just in case."

"Ain't Al headin' west soon? Hear he's taking Beulah with him."

Myles fingered the letter in his pocket. "Al's catching the train south tomorrow. He's traveling alone."

Boz shifted to one side, frowning past Myles. "That so? Those two make a purty pair."

Blinking in surprise, Myles studied his friend's vacant expression. Another curious glance over his shoulder cleared up the mystery. On the walkway near the livery stable stood Miss Amelia, conversing amiably with the town barber. Myles shook his head and grinned. "Actually, Boz, I'm planning to elope with Beulah tonight after the party. We're moving to Outer Mongolia to open a millinery shop for disgruntled Hottentots."

"Yup. I saw that match coming almost as soon as she stepped off the train."

Myles chuckled. "Never mind. I'll see you later."

Still distracted, Boz waved two fingers. "Later, Myles."

When Myles left the general store, Boz had joined the conversation across the street. Smiling, Myles shifted his bundle under one arm. *Good old Boz. Hope he gets his Amelia.*

The letter was in the mail. Soon Gram would know both where Myles was and what had happened to Monte. *Is that enough, God?*

Cholla dozed at the hitching rail with her eyes half-shut. "Howdy, girl. Bought myself new duds for tonight. Hope you'll recognize me all duded up." The horse rubbed her ears against his hand and lipped his suspender strap. Myles's voice trembled with anticipation. "Think I'll stop at the barber next and get me a shave. Don't know if Beulah likes my beard or not, but I'm through hiding my identity. Maybe tonight I'll tell her about my past. Maybe she'll like the sound of 'Beulah Van Huysen.' "

"Myles!"

He turned on his boot heels. A buxom figure in a calico dress hurried along the boardwalk. Myles stiffened. He wanted to run, but his boots had grown roots.

"Goodness, but it's warm today," Marva panted, waving a hand before her flushed face. Her eyes were vividly blue. "They say it's going to storm tomorrow, maybe even snow, but I can't believe it! The trees still have most of their leaves. Mr. Watson got his corn in, didn't he? I saw the reaping machine pass our farm yesterday on its way out of town. Papa got our crops in days ago, but then he doesn't farm that much acreage."

She pressed white finger marks into his forearm and shook her head. "You're so brown, Myles, like an Indian! It's not good for fair-skinned people like us to take so much sun. I hope you wear your hat and shirt all the time."

Behind Marva, the Watson buggy stopped at the railing. Samuel and Eunice remained in the buggy while their mother stepped down and tethered her horse.

"Hello, Marva, dear. So good to see you. Hello, Myles," Violet said in her gracious way.

"I'm looking forward to the party tonight, Mrs. Watson," Marva said as Myles tipped his hat. He tried to smile, but his face felt like dried clay. Marva chattered on, "This will be the social event of the season, I'm certain. I'm inviting Myles to join our family for supper before the party."

Violet gave Myles a look. "How nice! I look forward to seeing your parents, Marva. Is your mother better?"

"Much better, thank you. She and I have practiced a duet, and my papa brought out his fiddle for the occasion. I also look forward to hearing Myles sing. He has a marvelous voice." Marva took Myles by the elbow and pressed close.

Myles attempted to disengage his arm, but she clung tenaciously. Heat rose in his face.

He saw one delicate eyebrow lift as Violet met his gaze. "I, too, anticipate hearing you sing, Myles. Good day to you both."

Without moving away, Marva rattled on as if she had never been interrupted. "I'm sure you must be longing for good home cooking. It's been weeks since you visited us, and my papa keeps asking where you've taken yourself. I told him you've been harvesting for nearly everyone in the county, but he won't be happy 'til you join us for a meal. We can have supper first, then drive to Fairfield's Folly together." The dimple in her right cheek deepened. "What's your favorite pie?"

"Blackbottom. My grandmother used to bake it." Pushing at her hands, he detached himself from her grip. "Miss Obermeier, I really don't —"

"I'll do my best to equal your grandmother's pie. Where are you from, Myles?

You seldom speak about yourself." Her gloved hand rested on his chest.

"There's little to speak of." Myles tried to slide the conversation closer to his horse. "Miss Obermeier, I don't think you —"

Marva followed. "Good friends don't use titles, Myles. Please call me Marva. I like to hear you speak my name."

"I must go now. Work doesn't wait for a man." Perhaps it was rude to mount Cholla then and there, but Myles was desperate to escape. Tonight was the night to let Marva know that his heart had already been bestowed elsewhere. His problem was how to communicate any message at all to a woman who never stopped talking.

"Be there at five." Marva rested her hand on his knee in a proprietary way. "Don't forget."

"I'll come after the cows are milked." He spun Cholla around.

Eunice and Samuel waved as Myles passed their buggy. "When's the wedding, Myles?" Eunice teased, and Samuel clasped his hands beside his face and batted his eyes in a fair imitation of Miss Obermeier. Had Myles not been so irritated, he might have been amused.

Glancing over his shoulder, he saw Marva laughing and waving at him. What had gotten into the woman?

Cholla sensed his anger and wrung her tail in distress. As soon as she passed the outskirts of town, Myles let out a "Yah!" Cholla leaped into a full gallop.

CHAPTER 10

Beloved, let us love one another: for love is
of God;
and every one that loveth is born of God,
and knoweth God.

1 JOHN 4:7

Miss Obermeier finished playing a hymn. A patter of applause trickled through the room as she returned to her seat between Myles and her mother. She leaned over to whisper to Myles. He inclined his head to listen. Marva's pale hair gleamed, and her fair skin contrasted with Myles's ruddy tan.

"Wonder why Myles didn't wear his new duds," Al muttered as Cyrus Thwaite began a mouth organ solo of "Camp-town Races."

Beulah met Al's gaze. "He bought new clothes?"

He nodded. "Today. A fancy suit, like for a wedding. Told me he had an announcement to make. I'm guessing there will be a wedding soon."

Beulah jerked as if she had been slapped.

"Maybe it didn't fit," Al mused. "Too bad. Marva looks like a queen, and Myles looks like . . . like a farmhand. I've got to help the man loosen up."

Eunice leaned around Al, frowning and holding a warning finger to her lips. "Don't be rude!" she whispered.

Beulah took shallow breaths. *I won't look. I cannot bear to see Myles sitting with that woman.* Her heart had started aching the moment she saw Myles hand Miss Obermeier down from a buggy, and the pain grew steadily worse. Marva's parents already seemed to regard Myles as a son-in-law.

He never made me any promises, yet I thought there was something special between us. Maybe he does think of me as a child to be amused.

Biting her lower lip, Beulah smoothed the skirt of her sprigged dimity frock. She had been so proud of this dress with its opulent skirts and tiny waist. Violet had fashioned a ruffled neckline that framed the girl's face, revealing the delicate hollow at the base of her throat and a mere hint of collarbone. Now the white ruffles seemed childish.

Marva's royal blue satin gown showed off her white shoulders. Beulah wondered that Marva could keep her countenance in front of Reverend and Mrs. Schoengard. "I think her dress is improper for an unmarried lady."

Al gave her a wry look. "Trust you to say so."

"Shhhh!" Eunice leaned forward again.

Beulah flounced back in her seat. *I was excited to have Myles come tonight. Now I wish he had stayed home. I wish I had never met the horrible man.*

David and Caroline Schoengard rose to stand beside the piano. Violet settled on the stool and opened her music. "We will sing 'Abide with Me,' " Caroline announced in a trembling voice.

Beulah watched the pastor shape his mouth in funny ways as he sang the low notes. Mrs. Schoengard was now heavily pregnant. Their voices were pleasant, but once in a while Caroline strained for a high note and fell short.

Al shifted in his seat and tugged at his stiff collar while the Schoengards returned to their seats. "Is it almost over?" he whispered.

The only people present who had not yet performed were Al, Myles, and Obie. Beulah knew her stepfather could not carry a tune. He attended Violet's party to be an appreciative audience, he said. And Al would "rather be dead than warble in front of folks."

"Myles, will you play for us?" Violet requested. "Don't be shy; none of us are music critics."

Myles rose, approached the piano, and

turned to face his small audience. Candlelight flickered in his eyes and hair. "I'll play, but I have something to tell all of you afterward." His gaze came to rest upon Beulah. "Something important."

She sucked in a quick breath, lifting one hand to her throat.

Myles placed the piano stool and seated himself. He drew a deep breath and flexed his fingers, seeking Beulah's gaze. The message she read in his eyes at that moment banished her jealousy and insecurity.

He began to play a lively composition. His hands flew across the keyboard with complete mastery. Broad shoulders squared, heavy boot working the pedal, he looked incongruous, yet perfectly at home. His very posture denoted the virtuoso.

Myles completed the piece with a flourish. "Schubert," he said into the ensuing silence. A murmur stirred the room's stuffy air as people audibly exhaled.

"Wow," Al said.

"That was unbelievable, Myles," Violet said. "Never before in my life have I heard —"

"I had no idea you knew how to play piano," Marva protested. "You always let me play and never said a word!"

"You never asked me," Myles said. "This is what I planned to tell you all tonight. My true name is Myles Trent Van Huysen, and during my childhood I was a concert pianist and singer. At age sixteen I ran away, and many years I have wandered the country seeking purpose for my life. Thanks to Buck Watson, I found that purpose here in Longtree. I apologize for keeping my identity a secret all this time. I was wrong to deceive you. With God's help, I am doing my best to make reparation to those I have wronged."

Obie and Al approached Myles with outstretched hands. Beulah watched the men clap Myles on the shoulders and embrace him, expressing forgiveness and acceptance. Soon everyone had gathered around the piano, eager to greet this new Myles.

Beulah joined the crowd, trying to appear happy. What did this mean? Was Myles planning to leave town and return to his concert career? He suddenly seemed far away and beyond her.

"Sing for us, Myles," Violet pleaded.

"Yes, please do," other voices chimed in.

"A love song," Marva requested.

"A love song." Myles appeared at ease in his new role of entertainer . . . but then, the role was not new to him. Acrobat, pianist, singer — what other surprises did the man hold in store? Was there anything he could not do?

Beulah recognized the tune he began to play, but never before had she heard such elegance in the old, familiar words. Myles affected a Scot's accent that would fool any but a native. His voice was smooth, richer than butter.

"O, my love's like a red, red rose,
That's newly sprung in June."

Beulah felt herself blush rose red when Myles caught and held her gaze.

"As fair art thou, my bonnie lass,
So deep in love am I,
And I will love thee still, my dear,
Till a' the seas gang dry."

He was singing the love song to her! Beulah gripped the piano case with both hands, feeling the music reverberate in her soul.

"And fare thee weel, my only love,
And fare thee weel a while!
And I will come again, my love,
Tho' it were ten thousand mile!"

The song ended. Myles lowered his gaze to the keys, releasing Beulah from his spell. "Hope you like Robbie Burns," he spoke into a profound silence. "It was the only love song I could think of at the moment. I know some opera, but didn't think you'd care to hear me sing in Italian."

Beulah drew a deep breath; it caught in her throat.

"Never cared much for fancy singing, but that beats all," Al admitted. "I think I'd be pleased to listen for as long as you cared to sing — and in any language you choose."

"How long had it been since you played the piano?" Violet asked.

Myles figured for a moment. "More than nine years. It's a gift, I guess — being able to play any song I hear. I didn't play those pieces flawlessly, of course, but usually I can play and sing almost anything after hearing it once or twice."

"Amazing! I heard no mistakes. Myles, you have thrilled our souls. Thank you for sharing your gift," Violet said. "I hope you know that you are part of our family, whatever your name."

The entire group murmured agreement.

"If anyone is thirsty or hungry," Violet continued, "we have cider and cookies in the kitchen. You are all welcome to stay as long as you like."

Everyone seemed to relax, and conversations began to buzz. Cyrus and Pastor Schoengard asked Myles to play requests, which he obliged. Strains of "My Old Kentucky Home" and "It Is Well with My Soul" accompanied the chatter. Samuel chased another boy into the parlor, laughing and shouting. Their mothers shooed the boys outside.

Beulah drifted toward the kitchen and claimed a cup of homemade cider. The drink felt cold and unyielding in her stomach, so she left her cup on the counter. She wanted to wander outside amid the fruit trees, but the night was cool and her dress was thin. She could retire to her room for the night, but that would negate any chance of talking with Myles. Wrapping a shawl around her shoulders, she took refuge on the porch swing.

The front door opened and closed. "May I speak with you?"

Startled, Beulah looked up. Moonlight shimmered on a full skirt and fisted hands. Marva's face was hidden in shadow.

"Yes."

The other woman joined her on the swing, making it creak. A moonbeam touched Marva's beautiful hair and traced silver tear streaks on her face. Muscles tensed in her round forearms as she repeatedly clasped her hands.

"Myles loves you." Marva gulped.

Beulah had no idea what to say. *Dear God, please help me to be kind and good.* She pulled her shawl closer and saw Marva do the same. They would both freeze out here on the swing.

"Are you going to marry Al?" Marva asked.

"No."

"Why not?"

"I don't love him that way."

Marva sighed. "You're so young. Do you have any idea what you want in a husband?"

"I know that I don't want to marry a man who is like a brother to me."

"So you would steal a man from another woman?"

Beulah stiffened. "Of course not! What a

—" She nearly choked on her own hasty words. Maybe Marva's insinuation was unkind, but it was the desperate charge of a broken heart. What might Beulah be tempted to say under similar circumstances? She felt sudden sympathy for Marva.

"You already had Al. Why did you try to steal Myles from me?" Tears roughened Marva's voice.

"I didn't know you loved him, Miss Obermeier. I wasn't trying to be cruel to you, honestly!"

Marva covered her face with her hands. "It's not fair! It's just not fair."

Beulah patted Marva's shoulder. "My mother tells me that God is always fair. If He doesn't allow you to marry Myles, then He must have someone better in store. You've got to trust Him, Marva. He doesn't make mistakes."

Marva lowered her hands and sucked in a quivering breath. "You're nothing like I thought you were, Beulah Fairfield. Everyone talks about your sharp tongue and quick temper. They must be jealous. You're really a sweet girl." Her tone was doleful. "No wonder Myles loves you. You're both pretty and nice."

"So are you," Beulah said. "Just now I asked God to help me be kind; it doesn't come naturally to me."

Marva gave a moist chuckle. "Me, neither. I came out here wanting to scratch your eyes out! It's easy for you to talk about God bringing someone better along; but when you get to be twenty-six with not so much as a whisker of a husband in sight, you'll know how I feel. Of course, you're likely to be married and a mother several times over by the time you're my age."

She stood up, leaving Beulah in the swing. "When my parents come outside, will you tell them I'm in the buggy?"

"I'll tell them. Are you sure you're all right, Marva?" She followed the older girl down the steps.

Marva shivered. "I'll recover. Humiliation isn't fatal."

"I don't know. I've come close to dying of it more than once."

Marva reached out and hugged Beulah. "Maybe my heart isn't as broken as I thought it was. I feel better already. Myles is a wonderful man, but he never did seem to care for my cooking, and sometimes when I talked to him I saw his eyes kind of glaze over. Guess I'd better be patient and wait for God's choice instead of hunting down a man for myself."

Beulah found it hard to restrain a giggle, but Marva waved off her efforts. "Go ahead and laugh. I know I'm silly." She grinned. "You know, I once even considered Sheriff Martin as a marriage prospect. I didn't consider him long, but the thought crossed my mind."

"Marva, he's old enough to be your father!"

Marva chuckled. "I know. Oops, here come my parents. You'd better get inside before you freeze. I'll see you at church, Beulah."

"I would take it as a favor if you would sing in church," Reverend David Schoengard said in a hushed voice. "God could mightily use a talent like yours."

"I hope He will," Myles replied. "When the time is right, I will let you know."

"Don't wait too long," David advised.

"I am still learning what it means to honor Jesus as Lord. You know that story about the lost sheep? That's me."

"The church door is open to lost sheep."

A small boy tugged at the pastor's leg. "Dad, Ernie hit me."

"Excuse me a moment, please." David squatted to listen to his son.

Myles scanned the room.

"Looking for Beulah?" Al asked. Leaning one elbow on the piano, he sipped a cup of cider. "She's talking with Marva, I think. I spotted the two of them on the porch swing not long ago. If you need help splitting up a cat fight, call on me."

"How did you —"

"Please, don't ask! Anyone with half an eye could have read the look on your face while you sang to Beulah tonight, old friend. I'm thinking you'd better soon have a serious talk with Buck, or he'll be after you with the shotgun." Al's grin was pure mischief. "I'm also thinking I'll have to miss that train tomorrow. Don't you want me to stand up at your wedding?"

"You're not angry?"

"Naw. When two people are right for each other, it's obvious. And vice versa. Beulah and I blended like horseradish and ice cream. You'll be good for her; she needs someone to keep her in line. You should have seen her writhing in jealousy when you showed up with Marva tonight." Al chuckled. "She must have been dying when I talked about what a handsome couple you and Marva made."

Myles felt his face grow warm. "I intended to tell Marva tonight —"

"I don't think you need to say a word. She knows. Her parents just left. They looked pretty sad."

His shoulders slumped. "They're good people, Al. And Marva's a nice lady. I feel bad about hurting her."

Al shrugged. "Some of us are slow to catch on. I wasn't the quickest hog to the trough, myself. Don't know why I couldn't see the attraction between you and Beulah before now. It sticks out like quills on a porcupine. But there will be another girl for me — one who appreciates my humor and thinks I'm great." He grinned.

Myles had to smile. "You're chock-full of brilliant analogies tonight. Porcupine quills?"

"So are you going to talk with Beulah or not?"

He found Beulah on the porch swing. Watchful lay at her feet. The dog flopped a fluffy tail. "Isn't it too cold for swinging?" Myles asked.

Huddled beneath her shawl, Beulah stared up at him. "I guess it is. I needed a place to think, but I've discovered that the front porch isn't private."

Myles leaned a hip against the railing, gazing out past the barn. His left leg jiggled up and down. "Al told me Marva talked to you."

"She was crying at first, but when she left she was laughing. I like her, Myles. She is funny and nice. I think she could be a friend."

He shifted against the rail. "I was planning to explain to her tonight. About you and me, I mean."

Her voice was too bright. "I enjoyed your singing. I don't understand why you hid your talents for so long."

The comment interrupted his train of thought. "It's a long story."

From somewhere beyond the barn came a commotion. Watchful lifted her head, ears pricked. Myles followed the dog's gaze, but saw nothing. Hackles raised, growling softly, the dog trotted down the steps and headed for the barn. The white tip on her tail was visible after the rest of her disappeared.

"Myles?" Beulah stopped swinging and leaned forward. "What is it?"

Watchful began to bark. Myles had never heard such a noise — the dog sounded frantic, terrified. His ears caught the bawling of cattle, trampling hooves.

"I don't know, but I'm gonna find out."

Running feet approached, and two small figures appeared in the moonlight. Myles heard the boys panting before he could identify Samuel and his buddy, Scott Schoengard. "Myles!" Samuel said, stumbling up the steps. "There is something big in the yearling pen — something that roars!"

CHAPTER 11

We roar all like bears. . . .

ISAIAH 59:11

"I called Watchful, but she won't come. Go save her, Myles! That monster will kill her!" Samuel was sobbing.

Myles threw open the front door. "Buck! Al! Trouble at the barn."

Buck snatched up a lantern and a rifle, tossing another gun to Myles. Al caught up with them halfway across the yard. The yearling pen was ominously quiet except for Watchful's shrill yelps. Leaning against the split rail fence, Buck lifted the lantern. On the far side of the pen, many wide eyes reflected the lamplight. A young cow bawled.

"Watchful, come." The stern command brought the collie to heel, ears flattened, tail between her legs. Every hair on the dog's body stood on end. She still yammered at intervals. "Hush, Watchful." Instant silence. She pressed against Buck's leg and shivered.

Buck unlatched the gate, and the three men

stepped into the pen. Myles felt the hair on his nape tingle. A cursory examination of the corral revealed that the invader was gone.

Buck studied the muddy ground with a practiced eye. He pointed out bunches of woolly hair on a fence post along with glutinous streaks of blood. "It was a bear."

Myles counted the cattle. "One yearling missing. The Hereford-cross with the white patch on his left hip."

Al measured a print in the mud with his hand. "That was one big bear. It lifted that steer over the fence."

"We'll track it come morning. I don't follow giant bears into dark forests," Buck said with grim humor.

Al crossed his arms. "That monster could have come after one of the children."

"Sam and Scott were playing near the barn," Myles said. He swallowed a wave of nausea at the sudden mental picture of what might have been. "God must have been protecting them. I'll be ready for the hunt first thing tomorrow, Buck."

"Me, too."

Buck lifted a brow at his cousin. "Don't you have to get ready for your trip, Al? Your train leaves at four o'clock tomorrow afternoon."

Al glowered at the ground. "Might know I'd have to miss the fun. All right. I'll feed and milk in the morning, one last time, so you two can hunt."

Something cracked in the darkness near the gate. Watchful's ears pricked. The men spun around, guns lifted. A ghostly figure drifted closer. "It's me — Beulah."

"What are you doing?" Al snapped. "Don't you know there's a bear out here somewhere?"

Beulah clutched her shawl. "I didn't know until now." Her voice sounded small.

"Back inside, Beulah," Buck ordered. "Your mother will worry."

"I'll escort her." Myles stepped out of the corral.

"No lingering."

"Yes, sir." Myles had never before heard that protective note in Buck's voice. He followed Beulah toward the kitchen door. She drifted beneath the apple trees, crunching leaves beneath her feet.

"I love all our trees and the beautiful fall color, but now comes the hard part — raking," she said in a quivering falsetto. "Did you like the cider? My mother and I made it from our apples."

Myles touched her arm. "Beulah."

She turned. Her eyes were dark pools in her pale face. "Oh Myles, you aren't really going to hunt that bear, are you? I'm frightened!"

She cared! "I've hunted bears before. Buck and I will hunt this one down in no time. A few shots and it'll be over."

Her hand fluttered up to rest upon his chest. Myles wrapped his fingers around her upper arm. "Buck told me not to linger, but I must tell you tonight. I love you, Beulah. I want to marry you. I want it more than anything." His voice cracked.

He heard her suck in a quick breath. "Do you know God yet, Myles? Mama and Papa both told me to wait until you gave your life to Him. You said something tonight about making your peace with God's help. Did you mean it?"

"I did. I do. I wrote to my grandmother and apologized for running away. I imagine she will contact me soon, and I expect to make a quick trip to New York to wrap up business affairs." His voice trembled with eagerness. "I'm planning to buy the Thwaite farm, Beulah. For us. You and me. How does that sound?"

He wanted to hold her in his arms, but the rifle in his right hand made that impractical.

Beulah touched his beard with two fingers. "It sounds wonderful . . . but are you sure you want to be a farmer? You can do so many things. I've never known anyone like you."

"I'm sure." He leaned the rifle against the back steps and took Beulah into his arms. "Are you sure you want to marry a farmer?"

She captured his face between her hands and gently kissed his lips. "Please don't go away, Myles. Not ever."

"What?" he mumbled, conscious only of his need for another kiss. Her lips warmed beneath his, and her hands gripped his shoulders. Myles kissed her again and again until the cold, dark world faded away. Nothing existed except Beulah, sweet and pliant in his arms.

The kitchen door opened, catching them in a beam of light. "Beulah, it's time for you to come inside," Violet said.

The couple sprang apart, wide-eyed and breathing hard. Beulah grabbed for her falling shawl and rushed past her mother into the house.

"Myles, I believe you need to talk with Obadiah before you meet with Beulah again."

Myles heard the iron behind Violet's mild tone. Gathering his scattered self-control, he nodded and picked up the rifle. "This is Buck's."

Violet took it from him. "Al is waiting for you out front." She started to close the door then paused. "I know you love my daughter, Myles, and I'm not opposed to the match. But as her mother, I must be careful of her purity."

Guilt swamped him. "I understand. I am sorry, ma'am. It won't happen again."

"See that it doesn't. Good night, Myles Van Huysen."

Myles stepped into predawn darkness, feeling the chill through his wool coat and gloves. A recent dusting of snow on the ground might make tracking more difficult. Cholla was displeased to see him so early, but she accepted her bit after Myles warmed it in his palm. "We're on a hunt, girl. Like old times."

Cats waited around Cholla's stall, making noisy petition for milk. "Sorry, friends. No milk this morning." Myles thought of Pushy, still sleeping on his bed, and grinned. These cats would rebel for certain if they knew she got her own saucer of cream each morning and evening.

He tied a scabbard to his saddle and shoved his loaded rifle into it, then packed extra cartridges into his saddlebags. "Hope we're back in time to escort Al to the station." He would miss his young boss and friend.

Cholla broke into a canter, tossing her head and blowing steam. Myles hauled her back to a jog. "Too dark for that pace, my lady. We'll get there soon enough."

Buck waited in the yearling paddock. By the first light of dawn, he studied the bear's spoor. Buck nodded greeting as Myles joined him. "Big bear, like Al said. Amazing claw definition for a blackie. I'd say it was a grizzly if I didn't know better."

"Powerful, whatever it is, to carry off a yearling steer. It obviously has little fear of man."

"Makes my heart sit in my throat to think how the children have walked and ridden about the property at all hours these past weeks. And all the while this monster was afoot."

Myles had been having similar thoughts. "Have you heard the rumors that a bear escaped from the circus? If this is the bear I think it might be, our lives have been in constant danger. That grizzly hated people."

Buck swung into his saddle. His jaw clenched in a grim line. "Whether it is or whether it isn't, our job is to end the creature's life."

The bear's trail was easy to follow; it had dragged the carcass through grass and brush. Less than a mile up the creek, they found the remains of the young Hereford crossbreed. "There lies our next year's winter beef supply," Buck grumbled, still on horseback. "This bear has an eye for a tender steak."

Jughead and Cholla snorted and shied at the strong scent of bear. "Steady, boy. That bear should be miles from here by now." Buck patted his gelding's neck, but the horse would not be quieted. "I don't like this." Buck exchanged glances with Myles, then studied the surrounding brush and trees. Plenty of hiding places for a bear.

Cholla reared slightly, eyes rolling. "What if it stayed around to eat from the kill again?" Myles asked and hauled his gun from its sheath.

Buck swung his mount around, rifle at the ready. "It could happen. This bear doesn't seem to follow standard bruin behavior. Let's see if he's still around." He gave a whoop.

"That should frighten every critter in the county." Myles chuckled. The laughter froze in his throat. Not twenty yards away, a huge cinnamon-brown form rose out of a patch of mist. The bear's roar was more than Cholla could endure. With a rasping squeal, she reared high, pawing the air. Myles forced her back down, but it was impossible to fire while fighting his horse. The bear made a short charge, then paused to rise up and roar again. Foam dripped from its open jaws.

A rifle cracked, and the bear flinched. Infuriated, it charged at Jughead. The mustang bolted with Buck sawing at his reins and shouting.

Myles brought his rifle around, but Cholla chose that moment to shy sideways into the trees. The shot went wild, and Myles lost a stirrup. Furious and frustrated, he decided to let the screaming horse loose and try his chances on foot. He leaped to the ground, and while the bear made a short dash toward Cholla, Myles fired. In his haste, he hit the hump on its back.

Instantly the bear spun around, spotted Myles, and charged with incredible speed. Myles caught a glimpse of flaming eyes, yellow tusks, and a red tongue. Without a thought he cart-wheeled to one side, made a front roll, and propelled himself upward to catch hold of a tree branch. He swung his legs up as the bear charged beneath him, still roaring.

All well and good, but now his rifle lay on the ground. "Buck, I'm up a tree!" Could he be heard above the animal's fury?

The bear quickly figured out where Myles was and returned to the tree. Its roars were deafening, and it pushed against the tall pine, making it wave wildly. Then, to Myles's horror, the bear began to shinny its great bulk up the trunk. Even as Myles scrambled to move higher, one great paw slapped into his leg and pulled. He let out a shout, clinging to the trunk with all his strength. "God, help me!"

Shots rang out in rapid succession. Buck stood ten feet away in plain view, pumping bullets into the beast's back. The bear gave another roar, then a grunt, and dropped to the ground in a heap.

Myles hugged the tree trunk, laughing in hysteria. Relief made his arms go limp. Had he eaten breakfast, he would surely have lost it. Pain knifed through his leg. "Thank You, God. I'm alive."

"Amen." Buck's voice sounded equally shaky. "You all right, Myles? I'm so sorry — I never dreamed my yell would bring the bear down on you like that. I thought he had you for a moment there."

"I think he got my leg. That beast went up a tree like a squirrel — I've never seen the like."

"It is a grizzly. I guessed it from the tracks, but I didn't believe my own eyes."

Myles tried to climb down the tree, feeling weaker than a kitten. His leg was wet. His head felt swimmy. "Check its neck, Buck. I have an idea he's wearing a collar, or used to be."

Buck bent over the carcass. "Biggest bear I've seen in years." He reached a hand into the coarse fur. "You guessed it, Myles. A leather collar with a short length of chain. Those rumors about the circus bear were true. I can't believe no one reported this!"

"No doubt the owner feared negative publicity. They probably expected to find the bear before they left, but he was too smart for them."

"Maybe he was smart, but a circus animal wouldn't know how to survive in the wild. Stealing stock was his only option. Look how skinny — no fat surplus for hibernation. He would never have lasted the winter. I can't help feeling a little sorry for the old bruin." Buck shoved the inert body with his boot.

"Not me. This isn't the first time that old buzzard came after me." Myles released his hold on a branch and dropped to the ground. His leg buckled. He fell to his knees and grabbed it. The hand came away red. "Buck, I need help."

Rushing to his side, Buck pulled out a knife and cut away the trousers. The smile lines around his eyes disappeared. "Looks nasty. Got to stop that bleeding."

CHAPTER 12

Peace I leave with you, my peace I give
unto you:
not as the world giveth, give I unto you.
Let not your heart be troubled, neither let it
be afraid.

JOHN 14:27

While Beulah mixed pancake batter, gazing dreamily through a frosty windowpane, she saw Jughead trot into the barnyard, riderless and wide-eyed. "Mama!" Dropping her work, she raced upstairs. "Mama, Jughead came home without Papa. Something bad has happened, I just know it!"

Violet nursed Daniel in the rocking chair. Her body became rigid; her blue eyes widened. "Let's not panic. Papa might have released Jughead for some reason." She bit her lip while Beulah wrung her hands. "Send Eunice over to tell Al. He'll know what to do."

Dead leaves whisked across the barnyard, dancing in a bitter wind. Frost lined the wilted flower border, and ice rimed the water troughs. His reins trailing, Jughead hunted for windfalls beneath the naked apple trees. Beulah's gentle greeting made the horse flinch and tremble. He allowed her to take his reins, however, and seemed grateful for her attentions. She patted his white shoulder, feeling cold sweat beneath his winter coat.

In the barn, Eunice was saddling Dolly. Excited and frightened, the younger girl chattered. "Can you believe how cold it is today? And yesterday I didn't even carry my coat to school. Good thing there's no school on Saturday or I wouldn't be home right now. Good thing Al hasn't left yet. Maybe he'll decide not to go to California after all. Maybe . . ."

Beulah tuned out her sister's prattle. If anything had happened to Papa or Myles . . . Beulah hauled Jughead's saddle from his back and hung it on the rack. Would Papa want her to blanket the horse now, or was Jughead warm enough with only his winter fur? Taking the gelding to his stall, she slipped off his bridle. The slimy snaffle bit rattled against his teeth, but Jughead was too good-natured to hold that against Beulah. He bumped her with his Roman nose and heaved a sigh, seeking reassurance.

Beulah patted his neck and rubbed his fuzzy brown ears, resting her cheek against his forelock. "Papa will be all right, Jughead.

Don't worry."

"I'm leaving now, Beulah." Dolly's hooves clattered on the barn floor as Eunice mounted.

"Be careful. And hurry, Eunice."

After Dolly galloped up the driveway with Eunice clinging to her back, Beulah closed the barn door and returned to the house. Her face felt windburned when she removed her wraps.

Wandering from room to room, she looked for chores that needed doing. No one was hungry for pancakes, so she covered the batter. At last she decided to bake bread and cookies. The men might come home hungry. Her thoughts kept returning to Myles and Papa.

Dear God, please keep them safe! I love them both so much.

While the bread rose and the first batch of cookies baked, she sat at the table and tried to soak up the stove's radiated heat. Wind howled around the eaves and rattled the windows. Beulah shivered.

Violet entered the kitchen and sniffed. "It smells good in here, Beulah. You've been working hard." She spread a quilt on the floor and set Daniel on it, handing him a spoon and two bowls for playthings. Sitting at an awkward angle, he crowed and waved both hands in the air. He grinned at his mother, and Violet smiled back.

Beulah stared. "How can you be so calm, Mama? Papa could be in terrible danger out there, and it looks like snow again!" She waved a hand at the window.

"God is with him, Beulah. I've been praying since you told me about Jughead, and God assures me that He is in control. Remember Philippians 4:6–7: 'Be careful for nothing; but in every thing by prayer and supplication with thanksgiving let your requests be made known unto God. And the peace of God, which passeth all understanding, shall keep your hearts and minds through Christ Jesus.' If I chose to worry about Obie every time he went into a dangerous situation, I would be in a home for the insane by this time." Violet smiled.

Daniel leaned too far forward and fell on his face. Unfazed, he grabbed the spoon and batted it against a bowl.

Beulah studied her mother's expression. "But how, Mama? How can you trust God this way? You can't see Him, and you know that bad things happen sometimes."

Violet poured herself a cup of coffee. "When you truly know the Lord, you know that evil and pain are the furthest things from Him. He is all the joy and meaning in life, dearest. Without Him, life is nothing. It's the Holy Spirit who gives us peace, Beulah, along with love, kindness, and every other spiritual fruit. He doesn't force Himself into our lives

— we have to allow Him to fill and use us for God's glory."

Beulah removed the cookies from the oven and put in another batch. "Last night I asked God to help me be kind to Marva, and He did. I have given my life to Jesus, and I know He is working in me, but I don't have the peace I see in your life and Papa's. Most of the time I don't even want to be kind and good. Hateful things come out of my mouth before I think them through!"

Violet rose and wrapped an arm around her daughter's drooping shoulders. "Darling, don't you understand that all people are that way? None of us in our own strength can be always kind or loving or unselfish. Those traits belong to God alone. And yet God can use anyone who is willing to be used by Him. You say He helped you last night? Then you know He can change your heart when you allow Him."

"I'm willing right now, but I might not be tomorrow," Beulah admitted. "You know how ornery I am."

Violet squeezed the girl's shoulders. "Yes, the tough part is surrendering your will to His will. I understand entirely. Where do you think you got your ornery nature? It wasn't from your father."

"Then how do you do it, Mama? How can you be so full of faith and patience and everything?"

"Remember when Jesus talked about taking up our cross daily? He meant that every day we must die to ourselves and let Him live through us. That is the only way to have lasting peace and joy in your life — and it's the only way to have faith through any crisis. When you know God well, you will understand how completely He can be trusted with your life."

Beulah nodded, thinking over her mother's words. She sampled a cookie, chewing slowly. "Mama, I need to talk with you about Myles. Last night, right before you told me to —"

Watchful began to bark from her post at the back window.

"Someone is coming," Violet said. Both women rushed to look outside. Behind them, Daniel began to cry. Violet hurried back to pick him up.

"They're back!" Beulah exclaimed. "Al and Eunice are with them."

"Thank the Lord!" Violet rejoined her at the window.

"I'm going out there to greet them," Beulah declared. She hurried to the entry hall for a coat and hat, then rushed down the steps and across the yard. "Papa! Myles, are you all right?" Both men looked pale and drawn.

Obie caught her before she could spook the horses. "We killed the bear, but not until after he took a swipe at Myles. Got to get the doctor out here right away. Help us take Myles into the house, and I'll ride to town."

"I'll go with you," Al offered. "I'm not leaving today. I'll catch a train next week. I can't run off to California when Myles is hurt."

Nobody argued. Beulah rushed back to the house to inform her mother, and together they decided Myles should have Samuel's bed. The men carried Myles up the stairs just as Beulah tucked in the top bedsheet. The sight of his bloody boot and trouser leg stopped her breath for a long moment. "Oh Myles!" she exclaimed. Her head began to feel light and foggy.

"It's not so bad. You should see the other guy." He gave her a crooked smile. "I'm pretty thirsty."

"I'll get you a drink. Do you want water or coffee or milk?"

"Water."

As she left the room, she heard her mother order quietly, "Al, help me cut the boot from his foot. Beulah, we need a basin of hot water."

"Yes, Mama." All the way downstairs and while she worked, Beulah prayed: *Lord, please fill me with Your Spirit today and help me to show love, peace, joy, and every other fruit. Please help my dear Myles! Help the doctor to heal his leg like new. And please keep me from fainting when I see all that blood.*

She held the basin with towels to prevent

sloshing water from burning her hands while she mounted the stairs. A bucket of cold water for Myles weighted her right arm.

"Put it there on the bureau," Violet said. "Thank you, Beulah. Al and Papa have gone for the doctor."

Beulah offered a dipper of well water to Myles. He propped himself on one elbow and drank. "Much better." When he returned the dipper, their hands touched. Beulah felt her lips tremble. She could not meet his gaze.

Beulah dropped the dipper into the bucket. On the floor at her feet lay the shredded shirt Obie had used to stanch Myles's blood. It was leaving a stain on the floorboards. Beulah closed her eyes and breathed deeply. *Don't think about it,* she told herself. She gingerly picked up the shirt and wrapped a clean sheet around it. Blood soaked through.

"You may toss out that old shirt." Violet was tearing a sheet into strips. "Then again, I suppose we can boil it and use it for rags."

Beulah trotted downstairs and put the bloody cloth in a pot to boil, then ran outside and was sick behind the withered perennial bed. Her head still felt light afterward, but at least her stomach had settled. The cold, fresh air helped.

"The bleeding has slowed," Violet was saying when Beulah returned to the room, "but you'll have to be stitched."

"I thought as much." Myles looked pale.

"Beulah, will you please check on Daniel?" Violet asked. "I think I hear him stirring."

Beulah gave Myles a longing look, then hurried to obey her mother.

Daniel had pushed up with both hands to peer over the side of his cradle. His little face was crumpled into the pout that always appeared just before he started crying. He grinned when he saw Beulah and flopped back down on his face, crowing and kicking at his blankets. Beulah melted. "Oh sweetie, I do love you! I wish you would sleep right now, though."

"I'll take him for you, Beulah." Eunice stood in the doorway. Curls had escaped her braid to frame her round face, and the hem of her dress was soaked. Her blue eyes looked lost and lonely. "Is Myles going to die? You should have seen that bear. It was huge. Papa says it charged at Myles and he swung into a tree like a monkey." She wiped a fist across her eyes and sniffed. "Please let me take Daniel. I don't know what else to do." Tears clogged her voice.

A wave of love for her sister warmed Beulah's heart. "Myles lost a lot of blood, but I don't think he'll die. Of course you may take Daniel. You'd better change into dry clothes first. If you don't, you'll be coming down sick next thing, and we don't need that." Her voice softened. "Thank you for riding for help this morning. You're pretty wonderful."

Eunice's dimples appeared before her smile. She nodded and hurried to her room. Beulah settled into the rocking chair and cuddled Daniel close. He was too busy and awake to snuggle, so she let him sit up and amuse himself by playing with her buttons while she sang "Auld Lang Syne."

Eunice spread Daniel's blanket on the floor and set up his blocks before she took the baby from Beulah. "We'll be fine. I think the doctor is here; someone arrived just now."

"Thank God! And Eunice, Al decided he's not leaving today." Beulah smiled at the overjoyed expression on her little sister's face. "He'll catch the train next week."

Eunice caught hold of Beulah's skirt as she whisked past. "Beulah, I'm sorry I said you were heartless. You love Myles, don't you?"

Biting her lip, Beulah nodded. "But don't you tell anyone!"

The dimples appeared again. "I won't. He's not Al, but I like him a lot."

Peace filled Beulah's heart as she returned to Samuel's bedroom. Next thing she knew, she was being shooed from the room. How she wished Myles would request her presence! Not that Mama would have allowed such a thing. Not that Beulah could have endured the sights or sounds of a sickroom without passing out on the floor.

Beulah hurried to the kitchen to prepare more coffee and cookies for everyone. Someone — Eunice? — had removed the batch of cookies from the oven and punched down the bread dough. It was ready to bake.

Dear God, it's hard to be helpful when all I want is to be with Myles. I guess this is the best way for me to serve today. Please help me to have a cheerful attitude and to give thanks.

Obie and Al were grateful for the hot food. Beulah joined their sober conversation midway through and gathered that someone besides Myles was hurt. "*Who* got shot last night, Papa? What happened?"

Obie wiped his nose with a handkerchief. "The sheriff. One of those drifters who's been causing trouble in town all month had a drop too much at the tavern last night and took offense when Boz offered him a night's rest in jail. Before anyone could react, the man pulled a gun and shot Boz from point-blank range."

Blood drained from Beulah's face . . . again. "Will he live, Papa?" she croaked.

Obie shook his head. "They carried him home, and Doc dug out the bullet, but he's afraid it nicked a lung. Boz has powder burns on his chest, and he has trouble breathing."

Beulah bit her lips and screwed up her face. The tears overflowed anyway.

Obie patted her hand. "Miss Amelia is taking care of him while Doc is here with Myles. Boz couldn't ask for better care. We just need to pray. He has peace about eternity, thank the Lord." Obie drew a shaky breath and blinked hard. "He's my oldest friend. The deputy is keeping order in town for the present. The man who shot Boz is behind bars. I'm hoping to visit him after church tomorrow."

"I'll go with you," Al offered.

"You could take him some of my cookies." Beulah wiped her face with her apron and tried to smile.

Light snow fell Sunday, but Monday dawned clear and warmer. Eunice and Samuel threw snowballs back and forth as they left for school, but the snow blanket had dwindled to a few patches by noon.

While Mama nursed Daniel, Beulah peeked in to check on Myles. His foot lay propped on pillows. In repose, his pale face had a boyish look. His eyes opened, but Beulah slipped away before he spotted her. Violet had made it clear that Beulah was never to be alone with Myles in his sickroom.

Outside, Watchful began to bark. Beulah went to her own room and peered down at the driveway. "Mama, someone is coming. I don't recognize the horses."

Violet sounded harassed. "Would you greet our guest and make excuses for me, dear? I'll be down when Daniel is finished."

Beulah untied her apron and hung it on a hook, patted her hair, and opened the door.

An elderly woman stood on the top step. Behind her, the buggy turned around and disappeared up the driveway. "Hello, dear. Is this Obadiah Watson's home?"

"Yes, it is."

Watchful suddenly rushed past the woman into the house, whisked Beulah's skirts, and bounded up the stairs. "I'm so sorry," Beulah gasped. "That was my brother's dog."

The lady straightened her bonnet. "Does a man named Myles Trent work here?"

"Yes, but he does not live here."

The lady's face fell. "But they told me . . . Oh dear, and I let that hired rig go . . . I was so sure Myles would be here."

Beulah hurried to explain, "No, don't worry — you see, he is here right now. Upstairs in bed. He was injured the other day. Are you — Could you be his grandmother?"

The woman lifted a trembling hand to her lips. "Yes, I am Virginia Van Huysen. Is my grandson expected to live?"

Her tragic eyes startled Beulah. "Oh yes!" she quickly assured. "He is recovering nicely. It was a bear that attacked him."

"I see." The woman looked bewildered. "My Myles was attacked by a bear?"

Beulah recalled her manners. "Please come inside. My mother will be down in a few minutes; she is caring for my baby brother. I'm sure Myles will wish to see you."

Mrs. Van Huysen gave her a weak smile and

stepped inside. "I hope so. I'm sorry, child — it has been a long and tedious journey. My train arrived in town only this morning. Mr. Poole was supposed to meet me in Chicago, but he did not appear."

"I see." Beulah said nothing. She could neither ask questions nor remain silent. The lady seated herself on the horsehair davenport at Beulah's invitation. They sat and stared at one another.

"Would you like me to tell Myles that you have arrived?"

"He did not know I was coming." There was sadness in the woman's reply. "How old are you, child?"

"Eighteen. I am Beulah Fairfield. Obadiah Watson is my stepfather. Myles has worked for him these past three years, mostly during the summers."

"I am pleased to make your acquaintance, Miss Fairfield. You are a pretty child. Do you play the piano?" She indicated Violet's instrument.

"A little. Nothing to compare with Myles. He played for us the other night for the first time. It was amazing."

Mrs. Van Huysen lifted her brows. "So, he still can play. Hmm. Did he sing for you?"

Beulah could not help but smile. "Yes! It was wonderful. He told us that he was a concert pianist in New York, and he told us his real name for the first time. Did you receive his letter?"

"Letter? Myles has not written to me in years."

"But he did! Just last week. He wanted to apologize to you for running away to join the circus when he was a boy. Did Myles live with you always?"

"The boys lived with me after their parents died."

"I didn't know his parents were dead. My father died years ago, but my mother is happy with Mr. Watson. He is a good father to us." Beulah paused. "Did you say 'the boys'? Does Myles have a brother?"

Mrs. Van Huysen suddenly rose. "Please take me to Myles now. I can wait no longer."

Beulah led her to the staircase. "This way, please."

Mrs. Van Huysen worked her way up the stairs. Beulah wanted to offer her arm for support but feared rejection. "This way," she repeated, pushing open the door to Samuel's bedroom.

Myles appeared to be asleep. Blankets covered him to the chin, and his eyes were closed. "Myles?" Beulah whispered, moving to the far side of the bed. He did not stir. The room still smelled of blood, ether, and pain.

Mrs. Van Huysen stood at his other side. "Myles, my dear boy!" Her lips moved, but no other sound emerged. Tears trickled over her withered cheeks.

Beulah touched Myles's shoulder. "Myles, wake up. There is someone here to see you." Her own eyes burned. "Myles!" She gripped his shoulder and shook gently. Her fingers touched warm bare skin. Startled, she jerked her hand away.

His eyes popped open and focused on her face. "Beulah. I was dreaming about you." His hazy smile curled her toes. His hand lifted toward her face.

"Look who is here to see you, Myles," she whispered, unable to speak loudly. She glanced at his grandmother, and a tear slipped down her cheek.

Myles turned his head. Beulah saw his eyes go wide, and his mouth fell open. A moment later he was sitting up, clutching Mrs. Van Huysen and nearly pulling the lady from her feet. "Gram!" His voice was a ragged sob.

Beulah crept from the room.

Chapter 13

Thou wilt keep him in perfect peace,
whose mind is stayed on thee:
because he trusteth in thee.

ISAIAH 26:3

"You're so tiny, Gram. Did you shrink, or have I grown?" Myles asked.

Virginia patted his hand and smoothed his forehead, just as she had during his childhood illnesses. She smiled, but her expression was far away. "You must tell me about Monte sometime, Myles. Right now is convenient for me."

He pulled his hand out of her grasp and ran it over his rumpled hair. "I know. I've been hiding things too long, from myself . . . from everyone." He drew a deep breath and released it in a sigh, praying silently for strength. "This won't be easy."

Virginia watched him with sad yet peaceful eyes.

"Monte was wild, Gram. I know you thought he was a good boy, but it was all a sham. He loved to gamble, drink, and smoke . . . although I can say with confidence that he was never a womanizer. You raised us to respect women, and Monte kept that shred of decency as far as I know. With his charm, he might have been worse than he was."

Tears pooled in his grandmother's eyes, but she nodded. "I knew, Myles. It nearly broke my heart to see the way you two boys fought and despised each other. I prayed for wisdom and did everything I could to encourage love and respect between you. It never happened. For some reason, Monte considered you a rival from the day you were born."

Myles sat stunned. "You knew? I thought you doted on him."

"Certainly. I doted on the both of you. What grandmother doesn't dote on her grandsons, flawed though they may be?"

"Then why did you keep me isolated from everyone except private tutors and force me to practice for hours every day? It was a terrible life for a boy! I thought you hated me and loved Monte."

Virginia looked stunned. "I wanted the best for you, Myles. God gave you a wondrous gift, and I felt it my duty to give you every opportunity to develop and enjoy that gift of music. I thought your complaints stemmed from laziness, and I refused to listen. Oh my dear, how wrong I was! My poor boys!" Wiping her eyes, she insisted, "Tell me about

Monte. I must know."

"When you sent him after me, he took advantage of the opportunity to sample every pleasure the world had to offer. He was delighted to escape his responsibilities. He did plan to return someday, but then circumstances prevented it."

Virginia shook her head. "I knew I had lost him. Releasing him to find you was a last effort to show him that I trusted and respected him as a man. He proved himself unworthy, as I feared. He did write to me occasionally over the years, however, as you did. I never understood why that precious correspondence ended."

Myles absently unbuttoned his undervest. "The last place we were together was Texas; you knew that much. We had a steady job brush-popping longhorns for a big rancher. Monte started running with a group of gamblers. They were the ruin of him. It wasn't long before he started rustling a beef here and there to support his habit, and the boss became suspicious."

Tears trickled down Virginia's cheeks again, but she nodded for him to continue.

Myles twined a loose string around his finger and tugged. "Then all of a sudden Monte changed. I don't know exactly what happened — well, maybe I do — but anyway, one day he was wild, angry, and miserable; the next day he was peaceful, calm, and had this radiant joy about him. He told me that he had made his life right with God. I thought he had lost his mind. Both of us hated church and anything to do with religion, yet here was Monte saying he had found Jesus Christ. He tried to talk with me about God — even gave me a Bible for my birthday."

"Thank You, Jesus!" Virginia moaned into her handkerchief.

"One day we were riding herd, almost ready to start a drive north. Monte was across from me, hunting strays in the arroyos. A group of riders approached him. I took my horse up on a small bluff and watched. I had a bad feeling — something about the situation made me nervous. The best I can figure, the riders were men to whom Monte owed money, probably demanding payment. I saw Monte's horse rear up; Monte fell off backward and vanished. The sound of a shot reached me an instant later. Panic spread through the herd. Within seconds I was riding for my life, hemmed in on every side by fear-crazed longhorns."

The string broke free and his button dropped beneath the blankets.

"And Monte?"

"I never found him, Gram. By the time we got that herd straightened out — a good bit smaller than it was when the stampede started — we were miles from the location of the fight, and it was pouring rain. I hunted for days, but found no trace of Monte or his mustang. The horse never returned to the remuda; it must have died in the stampede, too."

Virginia sobbed quietly.

"I don't know if the men who killed Monte were aware that I witnessed his murder, but I didn't take chances. I was nineteen, scared, stricken with regret and sorrow. I hightailed it out of Texas and never went back. Once or twice I thought about writing to you, but shame prevented it. Not until God straightened me out this summer did I have the courage to confess my role in Monte's death."

"You weren't to blame, Myles." The idea roused Virginia from her grief.

He sniffed ruefully. "Had I not run away from home, Monte would never have been in Texas."

"Then he most likely would have died in a back alley in Manhattan. It is not given us to know what might have been, my boy. We can only surrender what actually is to the Lord and trust Him to work His perfect will in our lives." Virginia's voice gained strength as she spoke. "Monte is safe with the Lord, for which fact I am eternally grateful. Myles, dear, can you ever forgive me for my failings as a grandmother?"

Myles nodded. A muscle in his cheek twitched. "I forgive you, Gram. You meant well." He blinked, feeling as if a small chunk had broken from the burden he carried. To his surprise, forgiving his grandmother was an agreeable experience. Love welled up in his heart, and he opened his arms to her.

Weeping and smiling, Virginia fell into his embrace without apparent regard for her dignity.

Beulah carried a tray upstairs and knocked at the closed door. The voices inside stopped, and Mrs. Van Huysen opened the door. "That looks lovely, dear. Thank you." She stepped aside, and Beulah carried the tray to the bureau.

"Are you two having a good visit? Were you comfortable last night, Mrs. Van Huysen?"

"Yes, dear. Thank you for the use of your bedroom. I'm sorry to put everyone to such inconvenience."

"It is no trouble. We are all pleased to meet Myles's grandmother."

More than a day had passed since Virginia's arrival. Beulah's family had begun to wonder if the two Van Huysens would ever rejoin the world.

Myles eyed the steaming bowls and the stack of fresh bread slices. "What kind of stew?"

Beulah felt her face grow warm. She gave his grandmother an uncertain glance. "Bear."

Virginia's face showed mild alarm.

Myles laughed aloud. "Poetic justice. I hope

he was a tender bear. Don't worry, Gram; Beulah is the best cook in the state, with the possible exception of her mother."

"I don't doubt it."

"I hope it's good stew," Beulah said weakly. "Papa says the bear was skinny and tough. He showed me how to prepare it so it would taste better, but I don't know if you'll like it."

Myles shoved himself upright. "Beulah, will you ask Al to feed Pushy? She must be wondering what happened to me."

Beulah avoided looking at him. "Al says Pushy is lonely but well. She reminded him to feed her. No kittens yet."

"You need to take a look at the stitches in my leg, Beulah. There are fifty-seven. Doc did a great job of patchwork. Maybe you could learn a few new designs for your next quilt. Beulah sews beautiful quilts, Gram. She can make almost anything."

"Indeed?"

"Did you see the bear when they brought it in, Beulah? Wasn't he immense? You should have seen that monster climb a tree. He would have had me for sure if Buck hadn't packed him with lead. Say, that water looks good. Would you pour me a drink?"

Beulah felt his gaze as she poured two glasses of water from the pitcher. She glanced at his grandmother and caught an amused smile on the lady's face.

Virginia suddenly rose from her chair and

smacked Myles's hand. "Stop that belly rubbing. Never could break you of that." She addressed Beulah obliquely. "Myles suffered chronic stomachaches as a child. He used to wake me every night, crying for his mother. At least he no longer totes around a blanket."

Myles slumped back against the pillows. "No secret is sacred."

Beulah smiled. He would be embarrassed for certain if she gave her opinion of his habit — she found it endearing.

"Myles was a sickly, scrawny child — all eyes and nose. It's amazing what time can do for a man. I never would have known you in a crowd, Myles — although one look into your eyes would have told me. Doesn't he have beautiful eyes, Beulah? They are like his mother's eyes, changing hue to suit his emotions. I would call them hazel."

"Sometimes they look gold like a cat's," Beulah observed.

"Has he told you that he was being groomed for opera? His beautiful voice, his ability to play almost any piece the audience might request, and his subtle humor packed in the crowds. He was truly a marvel — so young, yet confident and composed. Even as a little child, he was mature beyond his years. I thought I was doing the best thing for him, helping him reach the peak of his ability. How wrong a grandmother can be!" She shook her head sadly.

"We've already discussed this, Gram. It's in the past and forgiven, remember?" Myles sounded embarrassed.

"Myles told me about the letter he wrote last week." Virginia shook her head. "I never received it. My private detective, Mr. Poole, recently discovered Myles's whereabouts after long years of searching. I find it odd that Myles wrote to me even as I was coming to see him. But the Lord does work in mysterious ways."

"God told me to write to you, Gram," Myles said gruffly, "even though He knew you were coming."

"At any rate, I plan to telegraph Myles's old agent tomorrow and set up a return performance. The musical world will be agog; his disappearance made the papers for months. His reappearance will take the world by storm, I am certain."

"Gram," Myles began, sounding somewhat irritated.

Beulah backed toward the door. "That's wonderful. You had better eat before the stew gets cold. I'll be back for the dishes."

She heard Myles call her name as she ran down the steps, but she could not return and let them see her distress. *Myles is leaving!*

"Beulah is a pretty thing and well-spoken," Virginia commented. "Exquisite figure, although I'm sure you have noticed that fact."

"I have."

"Your fancy for the child is evident, and even I can see why she attracts you." Her gaze shifted to Myles, and she pursed her lips. "The bluest blood in New York runs in Van Huysen veins."

"Blended with the good red blood of soap merchants, sea captains, and a black sheep or two. From all I hear, some of Beulah's ancestors might have looked down their aristocratic noses at one or two of my wild and woolly ancestors." His mustache curled into a smirk.

Virginia merely poked at her stew.

"So you like Beulah, Gram?" Myles dipped a chunk of bread into his stew and took a large bite.

"I suspect there is more to that inquiry than idle curiosity. Do you intend to wed the child?"

"I do." One cheek bulged as he spoke.

His grandmother considered this information. "Would she blend into our society, Myles? Her manners are charming, but they are country manners, nonetheless."

"If she won't blend in, then I wouldn't either. It's been a long time since I lived in your world." Myles ate with relish.

Virginia frowned. "Yours is a veneer of wilderness, I'm certain. Cultured habits will return, given the proper surroundings. I do hope you plan to shave soon. Facial hair does not become you."

"It was a disguise. Not a good one, but it fooled me." Myles smiled wryly. "All of this is immaterial, since, as you know, I do not intend to remain in New York. One farewell concert, sell the business, and back here I come to purchase a farm." His voice quivered with excitement.

Virginia lifted a trembling hand to her lips. "Um, Myles . . ."

"Buck Watson told me again and again that God blesses when we surrender our lives, and I'm living proof of that fact. It struck me one day that my resistance to facing my past was preventing me from having the future I longed for. You can stay in Long Island if you like, Gram, or we could sell that old house and move you out here. There's room in the Thwaite farmhouse, and I plan to build on anyway. The farm needs money and work, that's certain, but neither should be a problem."

Virginia finally succeeded in breaking into his soliloquy. "About the business . . . there is something you need to know, Myles."

Beulah scooped the mess of raw egg and shattered shells from the hardwood floor and dumped it into a pail. Goo had settled in the cracks between boards.

"I didn't mean to, Beulah. The floor was slippery, and I fell flat." Samuel hovered around her, shaking his hands in distress.

"Mama needed those eggs. I feel awful."

Beulah sat back on her heels and sighed. "The chickens will lay more eggs tomorrow, I'm sure. We still have two from yesterday. Don't worry about it. I'm thankful you're not hurt."

Samuel crouched beside her. "Are you feeling all right, Beulah? Is Myles dying? Is Sheriff Boz dying? Why are you being so nice?"

Beulah frowned, then chuckled. "As far as I know, no one is dying. Papa says the sheriff is holding his own. I simply don't see any point in being angry about smashed eggs. You didn't intend to break them, and someone has to clean it up. I'm not busy right now like Mama is, so I'm right for the job."

Her brother laid a hand on her shoulder. "Thanks, Beulah. You're a peach." With a fond pat, he hurried from the room.

When the floor was no longer sticky, Beulah sat back with a satisfied sigh. "That wasn't so bad."

"Beulah," Samuel called from another room. "Mama wants you to collect the dishes from Myles's room. And can you set beans to soak?"

"I will." When the beans were covered and soaking, Beulah washed her hands and checked her reflection in the blurry mirror. Her hair was reasonably neat, and the chapping around her mouth had cleared. She touched her lower lip, recalling Myles's ardent kisses. "Will he ever kiss me again?" she whispered.

Glancing at the ceiling, she sighed again. *Lord, please give me peace about the future. I know You are in control, but I always want to know about things right now! Please help me to control my emotions around Myles and to seek Your will.*

Minutes later, Beulah knocked at the bedroom door. "Myles?"

Silence.

She pushed open the door. He lay with arms folded across his chest, staring out the window. "Myles, do you mind if I collect your dishes?"

He did not so much as bat an eye. Biting her lower lip, Beulah began to load the dinner dishes onto her tray. Mrs. Van Huysen had picked at her food. Myles must have enjoyed his stew.

"Please stay," Myles begged as Beulah prepared to lift the tray. He reached out a hand. She was startled to see that his eyelids were red and swollen.

"Myles, what's wrong? Where is your grandmother?" She wrapped his cold hand within both of hers. "Are you hurting?"

His other hand fiddled with a buttonhole on his undervest; the corresponding button was missing. "Yes." He pressed her hand to his cheek and heaved a shaky sigh.

"I'm so sorry!" Beulah settled into the chair beside his bed. "Would you like me to read to you?"

"No. Don't go so far away."

Beulah blinked. "Far? I'm right next to you. Where is Mrs. Van Huysen?"

"Lying down, I think. I don't care. Nothing matters anymore."

She reached out to feel his forehead. "You're cool and damp. Would you like another blanket?"

When she would have returned to the chair, he grabbed her around the waist and pulled until her feet left the floor. Sprawled across him, Beulah felt his face press into her neck. "Myles, let me go! What if my mother walked in right now? She would murder me!"

"I need you, Beulah. Just hold me, please! I won't do anything indecent, I promise."

Hearing tears in his voice, she stilled. "Myles, what is wrong?" Her hand came to rest on his upper arm. It was hard as stone. His entire body was as tense as a bowstring.

"Do you love me, Beulah?"

Her teeth began to chatter from pure nerves. Something was not right. She felt a terrible heaviness in her spirit. "Yes, I love you. I do. Myles, whatever is wrong? I'm frightened." Pushing up with one arm, she regarded his face. "You were bright and cheerful when I brought lunch. Is the pain that bad? I'll get Mama."

"No!" He gripped her wrist. His eyes were glassy and intense. "Will you marry me right away? We can start over somewhere else, maybe homestead a place."

She shook her head in confusion. "I thought you planned to buy the Thwaite farm and settle here. Why should we marry right away? You're acting so strange, Myles."

He emitted a bark of laughter. "Plans? I have no more plans. Not ever. Plans involve depending on someone else. I will never again trust anyone but myself. And you, of course. You'll be my wife. We can live by ourselves out West."

The dread in Beulah's chest increased. "Please tell me what has happened." She twisted her arm, trying to escape his vise-like grip.

He suddenly released her and flung both forearms over his face. "Same old story. I trust someone, they let me down. Everyone I have ever depended on has failed me. Everyone. Most of all God. As soon as I start trusting Him even the slightest bit, the world caves in. If you desert me, too, Beulah, I think I'll crawl away and die."

She reached a hand toward his arched chest, then drew it back. "But God will never fail you. Why do you think He let you down?"

Myles sat up in a rush of flying blankets. Eyes that reminded Beulah of a cornered cougar's blazed into her soul, and an oath blasted from Myles's lips. His white teeth were bared. "Enough of this insanity! The entire concept of a loving, all-powerful God is absurd. A fairy tale we've been force-feeding children for generations. A superstition from the Dark Ages. I don't ever want to hear you talk about God to me again, do you hear?"

Beulah's mouth dropped open.

His fury faded. "Don't look at me like I'm some kind of monster! I need you, Beulah!" Flinging the blankets aside, Myles swung his legs over the far side of the bed and tried to stand on his good leg.

Seeing him sway, she sprang around the foot of the bed. "What are you doing? Myles, get back in bed or I'll call Papa." She stopped cold, realizing that he wore nothing but winter underwear. Hot blood flooded her face, and she rushed back to stand by the door.

He whipped a blanket from the bed and wrapped it around his waist. Jaw set, he hopped to the window and looked down on bare trees and blowing snow. "That's how I feel inside: cold, gray, and lifeless."

"That's because you've turned your back on God." Beulah was surprised to hear herself speak. "What happened to you, Myles? Why are you acting this way?"

He huffed. "I'll tell you what happened.

For years Buck has been telling me about God, about salvation. Finally I decided to try this thing out, trusting God. I wrote to Gram. I started giving God credit for the good things happening in my life. I even started believing that He was with me. When I read the Bible it was as if He talked to me."

Beulah studied his broad shoulders and felt her dreams crumbling.

"I began to believe that He had wonderful plans for my life — marriage with you, the farm I've always wanted, and friends who like me for myself, not because I'm a Van Huysen. I've never wanted the money; I've been proud to support myself and lean on no one . . . except maybe Buck. But since God told me to reconcile with Gram, I figured He must intend me to make use of my inheritance. I didn't want much; just enough to buy a farm and set us up with a good living. Then I found out that you loved me — life was looking incredibly good. Gram came, asked me to forgive her, and I did. Great stuff. Everything coming together."

He fell silent.

Beulah settled into a chair, hands clenched in her lap.

"Then the cannonball drops: There is no money. The family friend who ran the Van Huysen Soap Company mismanaged it into bankruptcy, sold out to another manufacturer, and is now president of that company.

He swindled it all away and left Gram holding massive debts. She sold off most of our stock and commercial properties to pay the debts, then mortgaged the family house to pay for the detectives who found me. There is no money. None."

Beulah tried to sound sympathetic. "Don't the police know how that man cheated your grandmother? Isn't there something you could do to help her?"

"There is no money to pay for lawyers, and apparently Mr. Roarke covered his legal tracks. It looks as shady as the bottom of a well, but no one can prove anything."

"Poor Mrs. Van Huysen. I can understand why you are upset. Had you been there to keep an eye on the business, this might not have happened to her."

Myles turned to fix her with a glare. "Don't you understand, Beulah? Gram is fine; she still has the old house and a small stipend to live on. The money lost was *my* money! This is the end of *my* dream. I have no money to buy a farm, and I can't support a family on my pay as a hired hand. We cannot stay here. Either I must return to New York and try to break back into the music world — which would not be an easy task no matter what Gram says — or I must head out West and find land to homestead."

Beulah's chest heaved, and her heart thudded against her ribs. That heavy, ugly feeling weighed on her spirit. "So when it looks like God is answering your prayers the way you want, you believe in Him. As soon as things don't go your way, you decide He doesn't exist? That isn't faith, Myles. That is opportunism. And I thought *I* was a selfish person! I don't care what you decide to do. Whatever it is, you'll do it without me."

Picking up the tray, she stalked from the room.

CHAPTER 14

And Jesus answered and said unto him,
What wilt thou that I should do unto thee?

MARK 10:51

Al entered the sickroom without knocking.
"Myles, you won't believe what happened!"
Spotting Mrs. Van Huysen, he pulled off his
hat. "Hello, ma'am."

"Good morning, Albert," Virginia responded cordially.

"I sure enjoyed visiting with you last night.
Myles, do you know this grandmother of
yours whupped me at checkers? It was an
outright slaughter."

"Myles never cared for the game," Virginia
said when Myles remained silent. "He is good
at chess, however." A moment later, she rose
and gathered her embroidery. "I'll let you
boys chat awhile." The door clicked shut
behind her.

Al settled into the empty chair, long legs
splayed. "It stinks in here. Like medicine."

Myles tried to scratch his leg beneath the

bandage. The skin showing around the white cloth was mottled green and purple. "What's the news from town? Doc tells me it looks like Boz will pull through."

"If good nursing has anything to do with it, Boz will be back on his feet within the week. From all I hear, Miss Amelia treats him like a king." Al's eyes twinkled. "She had him moved to her boardinghouse, and her front parlor is now a hospital room. Nothing more interesting to a woman than a wounded man, but I guess you know all about that."

Myles grunted. "So what's your big news?"

Al slipped a letter from his chest pocket. "Today I got this letter from my folks asking me not to come west until spring. Can you believe it? Today! Think about it: If you hadn't let that bear rip your leg off, I would have been on my way by now and missed their letter. No wonder I didn't have peace about leaving! They don't even want me yet. I have no idea what I'll do with my farm next year, but it doesn't matter — God will provide, and I've got all winter to think and prepare. So if you need to go to New York, don't hesitate on my account."

Myles tried to smile. "That's good news, Al. I felt guilty about delaying your trip."

"Now that you're rich and all, you won't be needing a farm job, I reckon," Al said, looking regretful. "I feel funny about things I must have said to you in the last year or two, me thinking you had less education and fewer advantages than I had!" His grin was crooked. "That will teach me to judge people by appearance."

"You always treated me well, Al. You have nothing for which to apologize."

"Why are you so gloomy? Is your leg hurting?"

The innocent question sparked Myles's wrath. He bit back a sharp reply and folded his arms on his chest, staring out the window.

"Hmm. Beulah is moody, too. My powers of deduction tell me that all is not well in paradise."

"Shove off, Al. I'm not in the mood for your jokes." Myles scowled.

Al pursed his lips in thought. "Want to talk with Buck?"

"I want to get out of this house, pack up, and head for Montana."

"What happened, Myles? I thought your life was going great. Beulah loves you, you've cleared things up with your grandmother, you've got a music career and money to burn."

"I'm not rich, Al. The money's gone."

"Oh. All the money?"

"Every cent."

Al looked confused. "But Beulah wouldn't care whether you're rich or not. She loved you as a hired hand."

"Whatever I do, wherever I go, she says

she's not going with me. Guess she only loved me if I stayed here in town." Bitterness left a foul taste in his mouth.

"That doesn't sound like Beulah. She could make a home anywhere if she set her mind to it, and she's crazy about you, Myles."

Myles gave a mirthless sniff.

"Sure you don't want to talk to Buck?"

"I know what he'll say. He will tell me I need to forgive those who have wronged me and give control of my life over to God. I've heard it all before."

Al lifted a brow. "Sooo, tell me what's wrong with that answer? Sounds to me as if the truth pricks your pride, pal."

Myles rolled his eyes.

"C'mon, Myles. Think this through. Are you content and filled with joy right now?"

Myles slashed a glare at Al, but his friend never blinked. "Fine. Don't answer that. Think about this: How could your life be worse if God were in control of it?"

Myles opened his mouth, then closed it. His head fell back against the headboard. "I've never had control anyway."

"Exactly. You're at the mercy of circumstances with no one to turn to. The only things you can truly control in your life are your behavior and your reactions."

"Sometimes I can't even control myself."

"Without God, we're all losers. Look at Buck. The stuff that happened to him was like your worst nightmare. He could be the most bitter, angry person you ever met, but he chose to trust God with his life, and look at him now!"

Myles nodded. "And you, too. You didn't get angry about Beulah."

Al shrugged. "It wouldn't have done any good to get mad. Anyone can see she isn't in love with me, and to be honest, my heart isn't broken. The point is, once you decide to trust God with things, He turns your messed-up life into something great. I'm not saying you'd have it easy from then on, or that all your dreams would come true; but no matter what happens, your life would be a success. The Bible says in First Peter, 'Humble yourselves therefore under the mighty hand of God, that he may exalt you in due time.' You can never lift yourself up no matter how hard you try."

After a moment's thought, Myles lowered his chin and shook his head. "I don't see it, Al. I understand that God is far above me, holy and just, almighty and righteous, but loving? I don't know God that way. Sure, He saved me from the bear, but look what has happened to me since."

"When was the last time you read about Jesus?"

"The last time I read the Bible? I was reading in Genesis the other night."

"I think you need to read the Gospels now.

The Old Testament is important, too, but you need to understand about Jesus first. Where is your Bible?"

"At our house next to my bed. Don't bring it here, Al. I want to go home. Can you talk Buck into taking me home? It's driving me crazy, being here in the same house with Beulah. She hasn't spoken to me since we fought yesterday. Gram is good to me, but I'm getting cabin fever."

Al looked into his eyes and gave a short nod. "I'll talk to Buck."

Beulah watched the wagon disappear up the drive. Her eyes were dry. Her heart felt as leaden as the sky. Returning to her seat, she picked up her piecework and took a disinterested stitch.

Violet observed her from across the parlor. "The house already seems quiet, doesn't it? I will miss having Virginia around to chat with. She is the most interesting lady. She refused my offer to stay here. I hope she will be comfortable at the men's house. They don't have an indoor pump, you know, and the furnishings are rather crude."

"Is Daniel sleeping?" Beulah asked in her most casual tone.

"Yes. Samuel is at Scott's house, and Eunice is reading. Did you hear Al's news?" Violet snipped a thread with her teeth.

"Several times over. I told Eunice first; then

she told *me* about three times so far. I'm glad he's not leaving for a while. We would all miss him. I think Eunice has romantic feelings for Al."

Violet chuckled. "I've noticed. She has good taste. Maybe I'll have Albert for a son-in-law someday after all. I hope so. He's a dear boy."

Beulah concentrated on tying a knot. "She's only thirteen, Mama. Maybe I should have married him."

Violet's hands dropped to her lap. "Pardon?"

Beulah winced, wishing she had kept the stray thought to herself. "Al wouldn't marry me now if I proposed to him myself, and I'm not in love with him anyway, but I can't help wondering if I couldn't have been happily married to him. After all, lots of people make marriages of convenience and end up happy together. Al is annoying, but he's steady and safe."

Violet lowered her chin and stared at her daughter. "What about Myles?"

Beulah pressed her lips together and jerked at a tangle in her thread. "Myles is not the man I thought he was. He is selfish and bitter." She swallowed hard.

Setting aside her mending, Violet joined her daughter on the couch. "Tell me."

Beulah leaned against Violet. Her shoulders began to shake. Wiping her eyes, she grumbled, "I hate crying, Mama, but it seems as if every time I try to talk about something important, I start bawling."

"It's a woman's lot in life, darling." Violet pushed a lock of loose hair behind her daughter's ear and smiled. "I understand, believe me."

Between sobs and sniffles, Beulah poured out her heartache and disappointment. ". . . so I told him he could go without me. I thought he was kind and wise, Mama, but yesterday he acted like a brute. And all because of some money he doesn't have. I'm so thankful I found out what he is really like before I married him!"

Violet stared at the fireplace, pondering her reply. "So now Myles is a brute. All the good things you loved about him mean nothing."

Beulah wiped her eyes and nose with a handkerchief. "I could never be happily married to a man with such a terrible temper, Mama. He swore in my presence and never apologized!"

"If Myles has truly turned his back on the Lord, then I agree that you should not marry him. But if, as your papa believes, he is on the verge of surrender, it would be a shame for you to give up on him. He adores you, Beulah, and I think he would make you an excellent husband."

Beulah's head popped up. "Mama! How can you say that after what I just told you?

He told me never to mention God's name in his presence again!"

"He was distraught. I'm sure he didn't mean it. I understand he had a long talk with Al about God this afternoon, and he plans to start reading the New Testament when he gets home today. Darling, every man has faults. I hope you realize that. Even Al would lose his temper, given the right provocation."

"Papa never shouts at you."

A dimple appeared near Violet's mouth. "No, but that's because he talks softly when he gets angry. The angrier he is, the softer his voice."

"You don't mean it, Mama," Beulah said, eyes wide.

Violet rubbed a little circle on the girl's back. "I mean every word. Darling, you had better learn quickly that only God can offer you complete security and contentment. No man can fulfill your every need, and most of them wouldn't want to try. The average man enters marriage thinking that a wife's purpose is to fulfill *his* needs. Unless you recognize the fact that all people are basically selfish, you will be in for a rude awakening when you marry. Myles has plenty of faults, but so have you, my dear."

"If people are so terribly selfish, how can a marriage ever be happy?"

"That's where the Lord makes a difference. In His strength, you and I can learn to love our men with all their human flaws and failings. That is one of the greatest joys of marriage: to give and give of yourself to please your beloved. Usually a good man will respond in kind, but you must understand that there is never a guarantee of this. Your part is to love at all times, without reservation."

Beulah wilted. "How can I do that, Mama? You know how selfish I am!"

"In the Lord's strength, dear. If you truly love Myles, you will accept him just as he is and be grateful for the opportunity to shower him with the love and attention he craves from you. There are few things in life more fulfilling than pleasing your husband, Beulah." Violet spoke with the authority of experience.

Beulah sat straighter. "I want to be exactly like you, Mama. You make Papa so happy that he glows when you're near. I want to make Myles that happy."

Violet squeezed her shoulders. "That's my girl! Now you keep on praying for Myles, and when he is ready to receive your love, I think you will know it."

Beulah hugged her mother. "You're wonderful. I feel so much better! Now, I have this idea for my wedding dress that I've been wanting to discuss with you. Do you have a moment?"

Eyes twinkling, Violet nodded.

Pushy kneaded a dent for herself in the middle of Myles's back. He groaned when she settled down. "You must weigh a ton, cat. When are you going to fire off those kittens?"

Pushy purred, vibrating against him. "You really missed me, didn't you?" Her affectionate greeting had warmed his heart.

He returned to his reading. The book was fascinating. For the first time in his life, Myles could visualize Jesus among the people, teaching, healing, loving.

The parable of the unforgiving servant in Matthew, chapter eighteen, struck a nerve. He recognized himself in the cruel, vindictive man who punished a debtor after he himself had been forgiven a much larger debt. The simple story was an eloquent reprimand and admonition.

"I understand, Jesus," Myles said, bowing his head. "This story is about me. Please forgive me for my anger at Monte. I want to forgive him as You forgave me. If he's there with You now, please tell him for me. Tell him I love him. I forgive Mama for dying and leaving me behind. She must have been terribly lonely after Father was killed in the war. And I forgive Mr. Roarke for swindling us, too. I don't imagine he's deriving much true pleasure from his ill-gotten gains. I feel almost sorry for him. You know that the real reason I refused to forgive people all those years was pride. I thought I was better than others. I was wrong."

Humility was an easy burden in comparison to the bitter load he had carried for so many years. Myles felt free and relaxed, yet still rather empty.

"Where is the joy, God? Are You really here with me? What's wrong with me? Maybe I'm spiritually blind."

Pushy purred on.

Sighing, Myles returned to the Book. The story enthralled him, and when he reached the end of Matthew, he continued on into Mark, absorbed in the story of Jesus from a slightly different perspective. His eyes were growing heavy when he reached chapter ten, the story of blind Bartimaeus begging at the roadside.

Then, for some reason, he was wide awake. His mind pictured the pitiful man in rags who cried out, "Jesus, thou son of David, have mercy on me."

Jesus stopped and asked the fellow what he wanted. Jesus didn't overlook the poor and helpless among His people. He cared about the blind man.

Myles read the next part aloud. " 'The blind man said unto him, Lord, that I might receive my sight.

" 'And Jesus said unto him, Go thy way; thy faith hath made thee whole. And immediately he received his sight, and followed Jesus in the way.' "

Myles stopped and read it again. Slowly his eyes closed and his hands formed into fists. The cry echoed from his own heart. "Lord, I want to see! Please, help me to see You as You truly are."

He contemplated Jesus. "The kindest man who has ever lived. He came to reveal You to mankind. He was Emmanuel — 'God with us.' God in the flesh. So You *are* a God of mercy, patience, and infinite understanding. Lord, I believe!"

Myles wept for joy.

CHAPTER 15

For I determined not to know any thing
among you,
save Jesus Christ, and him crucified.
1 CORINTHIANS 2:2

His bandaged foot wouldn't fit into a stirrup,
so Myles decided to ride Cholla bareback. A
wool blanket protected his clothes from her
sweat and hair, and he laid his walking stick,
a gift from Cyrus Thwaite, across her withers. "Take it easy, girl," he warned, gripping a
hank of her mane in one hand as he sprang
to her back and swung his leg over. "I'm running on one foot, so to speak." The swelling
had receded and the vivid bruising had faded
to pale green and purple, but Myles could
put little weight on the foot as yet.

"Myles, you be careful," Virginia called
from the front porch as he passed. "Visit your
friend and the barber and come straight
home. Do you hear?"

"I hear." Reining in the fidgeting mare,
Myles grinned at his grandmother. He could

endure her motherly domination for the sake of her good cooking and excellent housekeeping skills — abilities he had never before known she possessed. "You're quite a woman, Gram."

"Away with your flattery," she retorted, not before he glimpsed her pleasure.

Cholla trotted almost sideways up the drive, head tucked and tail standing straight up. Its wispy hair streamed behind her like a shredded banner. "You're a loaded weapon today, aren't you?" Myles patted the mare's taut neck. "Sorry; no running. The roads are too icy."

A few miles of trotting took the edge off Cholla's energy. She still occasionally challenged her master's authority, but her heart was no longer in it. Myles felt her muscles unwind beneath him.

Although it was good to be out in the open again instead of cloistered in his stuffy room, fighting the horse drained much of Myles's strength. When he dismounted in front of Miss Amelia's boardinghouse, he lost hold of his walking stick. It clattered to the frozen mud. Cholla shied to one side, and Myles landed hard. His bad foot hit the ground. Clutching Cholla by the chest and withers, he gritted his teeth and grimaced until the worst pain had passed.

"Steady, girl," he gasped. Balancing on one foot, he scooped up his stick. It wasn't easy to tether Cholla with one hand, but he managed. Hopping on one foot, using the stick for balance, he made his way to Amelia's porch.

"What on earth are you doing, Myles?" Amelia said, flinging open her front door and ushering him inside.

"I came to see Boz," Myles gasped. "Isn't he here?"

"You come on into the parlor and sit yourself down." Amelia supported his arm with a steely grip. "That's where Boz keeps himself." She lifted her voice. "You got a visitor, Sheriff. Another ailing cowboy on my hands. Just what I needed. You two sit here and have a talk. I've got work to do." Leaving Myles in an armchair, she brushed her hands on her apron, gave each man an affectionate look, and departed.

Boz drew a playing card from his deck, laid it on a stack, and gave Myles a crooked smile. "How's the foot?" His right shoulder was heavily wrapped, binding that arm to his side.

"Mending. You don't sound so good." Myles shifted in his chair.

Boz did not immediately reply. "I ain't so good, Myles," he finally wheezed. "Bullet nicked a lung and severed a nerve in my shoulder. It kinda bounced around in there. Doc did his best, but he doesn't expect I'll regain the use of my arm."

Myles blinked and stared at the floor.

"I know what you're thinkin'," Boz said. "Not much good in a one-armed sheriff. I reckon God has other plans for my future."

Myles met the other man's steady gaze. Slowly he nodded, amazed by Boz's cheerful acceptance of his fate.

"Amelia says I can work for her. She's been needing to hire household help, and she cain't think of anyone she'd rather have about the place."

"You?" Myles stared blankly until he caught the twinkle in his friend's eyes. "Boz, are you joshing me?"

The former sheriff's face creased into a broad grin. "She reckons it wouldn't be proper for me to stay here permanent-like, so she proposed marriage."

Myles began to chuckle. Boz put a finger to his lips. "Hush! Let the woman think it was all her idea, at least until after we're hitched."

Myles sputtered with suppressed merriment, and Boz joined in. Soon the two men were wiping tears from their faces. Boz groaned, holding his shoulder and wheezing. "Stop before you do me in."

The door opened, and Amelia backed into the room carrying a tray. "I brung you coffee and cakes." Her sharp eyes inspected their faces. "Doc says the sheriff needs quiet. Hope I didn't make a mistake by letting you in, Myles."

"He's all right, Amelia. Laughter is good

for what ails a man. What you got there? Raisin cookies?" Boz perked up.

"Yes, and snickerdoodles. Mind you don't eat more'n is good for ya, Boswell Martin."

Nearly an hour later, Myles grinned as he heaved himself up on Cholla's back. "Next stop, the store, then on to the barbershop." The horse flicked her ears to listen.

Thank You for leaving Boz with us here on earth, Lord, Myles prayed as he rode. *And thank You for giving him his heart's desire. He's waited a long time for love, but from the look in Amelia's eyes while she fussed over him today, he's found it.*

Myles picked up his mail at the general store. There was a letter addressed in strange handwriting. Curious, he paused just inside the doorway, balanced on his good foot, and ripped open the letter.

Dear Myles,

Antonio tells me what to write, and I do my best.

Antonio pray for you every day. He say have you dropped your burden yet? I hope you do, Myles. We want your best for you.

You can write us here in Florida. We stay until summer season open. We want to visit you, but have not the money.

Antonio want to know if the bear was found. He feel bad about keeping it secret. Our circus, it was bought by another man when the owner was put in jail. He cheat one man too many, Antonio say. Things better for us now, but we want a home that does not move.

Antonio speak much of settling down to open a bakery. Is there need for a bakery in your town?

God bless you.
Antonio and Gina Spinelli

Myles determined to write back at his first opportunity. Antonio would be pleased to hear news of his mended relationship with God, and if any town ever needed a bakery, Myles was certain Longtree, Wisconsin, did.

As Myles rode past the parsonage, someone hailed him. He reined in Cholla and waited for the pastor to approach. "Hello, Reverend."

David Schoengard's ruddy face beamed as he stood at Cholla's shoulder and reached up to shake Myles's hand. "Good to see you about town. We've been praying for you. From all I hear, yours was a serious injury."

"Thanks for the prayers. God has been healing me . . . inside and out."

David's eyes gleamed. "Ah, so the lamb has found its way home?"

"More like the Shepherd roped and hog-tied an ornery ram, flung it over His shoulder, and hauled it home. I'm afraid I was a tough case, but He never stopped trying to show me the truth."

The pastor chuckled. "I understand. Are you ready to profess your faith before the church?"

Myles tucked his chin. "Is that necessary?"

"Not for your salvation but it would be a wonderful encouragement to other believers to hear how God worked in your life. I'm also hoping you'll honor us with a song someday soon."

Staring between Cholla's ears, Myles pondered. "I do need to ask forgiveness of people in this town. Guess this is my chance. I'll do it, if you think I should, Reverend."

"I appreciate that — and please call me Dave, or at least Pastor Dave. I'm no more 'reverend' than you are." He patted Cholla's furry neck.

Myles nodded. "All right, Pastor Dave. Do I need your approval on a song?"

"I'll trust you to choose an appropriate selection. And thank you. Caroline will be excited when I tell her you agreed to sing."

"How is she doing?"

"She has a tough time of it during the last weeks before a baby arrives, but she handles it well. My mother is at the house to help out. She and Caroline are great friends."

David cleared his throat. "If you don't mind me asking, how are things between you and Marva? Or is it you and Beulah? Caroline and I were never sure."

Myles scratched his beard and took a deep breath. "Marva and I are friends. There never was more between us. And Beulah isn't speaking to me at present. I . . . uh . . . let's just say she got a glimpse of Myles Van Huysen at his worst, and she didn't care much for what she saw."

"I see. Have you apologized?"

"Not yet. I haven't spoken with her since God . . . since He changed me. I don't know how to approach her. I mean, she pretty much told me to leave her out of my future plans."

"The change in you could make a difference, Myles. Faint heart never won fair maiden."

"Yes, I need to figure out a plan. I'd better be on my way. I've got orders not to dawdle."

"Your grandmother?" David stepped away from the horse. "I enjoyed meeting her last Sunday. Quite a lady."

Myles nodded. "Beulah is a lot like her. Feisty." He smiled. "If you think of it, I could use a few prayers in that area, too. You know, for wisdom and tact when I talk to Beulah."

"Every man needs prayer in the area of communication with women," David said with a straight face. "See you Sunday." With a wink, he turned away.

Myles squirmed in the front pew, elbows resting on his knees, and rubbed one finger

914

across his mustache. His chin felt naked, bereft of its concealing beard. His heart pounded erratically. Lines of a prepared speech raced through his head.

Marva Obermeier played the piano while the congregation sang. She never once looked in his direction. Myles could not sing. He knew he would be ill if he tried. Why had he volunteered to sing so soon? He wasn't ready. It was one thing to entertain a crowd for profit and another thing altogether to sing in worship to God while other believers listened.

"Relax, Myles. The Lord will help you." Virginia leaned over to pat his arm.

He nodded without looking up.

Was Beulah here, somewhere in the room behind him? Would she change her mind when she saw how God was transforming his life, or had he forever frightened her away? With an effort, Myles turned his thoughts and heart back to God and prayed for courage and peace. *This is all new to me, Lord. I feel like a baby, helpless and dependent. Can You really use me?*

His foot throbbed. He needed to prop it up again. Pastor David was making an announcement. Myles tried to focus his mind.

"A new brother in Christ has something to share with us this morning. Please join me in welcoming Myles Trent Van Huysen into our fellowship of believers."

Myles rose and turned to face the crowd,

leaning on his crutch. Expectant, friendly faces met his gaze. He swallowed hard. "Many of you know that I have been living a lie among you these past few years. Today I wish to apologize for my deceit and ask your forgiveness."

There was Beulah, seated between her mother and Eunice. Her dark eyes held encouragement and concern. She pressed three fingers against her trembling lips.

"My grandmother, Virginia Van Huysen, has prayed for me these many long years. She never gave up hope that God would chase me down. I stand before you to confess that I am now a child of God, saved by the shed blood of Jesus Christ. My life, such as it is, belongs to Him forevermore. I do not yet know how or where He will lead, but I know that I will humbly follow." His voice cracked.

Marva sat beside her father in the fourth row. Although her eyes glittered with unshed tears, she gave Myles an encouraging smile.

"I'm having difficulty even talking — don't know how I'll manage to sing. But I want to share my testimony with a song."

He limped to the piano. After leaning his crutch against the wall, he settled on the bench. This piano needed tuning, and several of its keys were missing their ivories. One key sagged below the rest, dead. Myles played a prolonged introduction while begging God to carry him through this ordeal.

Lifting his face, he closed his eyes and began to sing Elizabeth Clephane's beautiful hymn:

"Beneath the cross of Jesus I fain would take my stand . . ."

Myles knew that the Lord's hand was upon him. His voice rang true and clear. The third verse was his testimony:

"I take, O cross, thy shadow for my abiding place —
I ask no other sunshine than the sunshine of His face;
Content to let the world go by, to know no gain nor loss,
My sinful self my only shame, my glory all the cross."

The last notes faded away. Myles opened his eyes. His grandmother was beaming, wiping her face with a handkerchief. He collected his crutch and stood. Someone near the back of the room clapped, another person joined in, and soon applause filled the church. "Amen!" Myles recognized Al's voice.

Pastor Schoengard wrapped an arm around Myles's shoulder and asked, "Would anyone like to hear more from our brother?"

The clapping and shouts increased in volume. " 'Amazing Grace.' " It was Cyrus

Thwaite's creaky voice.

" 'Holy, Holy, Holy,' " someone else requested.

Pastor David lifted his hand, chuckling. "This is still a worship service, friends. Please maintain order and do not overwhelm our new brother." He turned to Myles. "Will you sing again, or do you need rest?" he asked in an undertone. "Don't feel obliged, Myles. There will be other days."

Myles stared at the floor, dazed by this openhearted reception. He smiled at the pastor. "It is an honor." He returned to the bench and began to play, making the ancient spinet sound like a concert grand.

CHAPTER 16

But as it is written, Eye hath not seen, nor
ear heard,
neither have entered into the heart of man,
the things which God hath prepared for
them that love him.
1 CORINTHIANS 2:9

"Whoa, girl." Myles hauled the horse to a stop and set the buggy's brake. On the other side of a pasture fence, Al and Buck kept watch over a smoldering fire, feeding it with branches and dead leaves. Smoke shifted across the sodden field, hampered by drifting snowflakes.

Myles hoisted a large basket up to the seat beside him, unlatched the lid, and peeked inside. Indignant yellow eyes met his gaze. "Meow," Pushy complained.

"I'll be right back, I promise. I need to talk to Buck for a minute. You should be warm enough in there." Leaving the basket on the floor, he climbed down and vaulted the fence, hopping on his good foot before regaining his balance.

Cold seeped through his layers of clothing. "Not a great day to be outside," he commented to the other men as he approached. "That fire feels good." He held out gloved hands to the blaze.

"Need to get rid of this brush before winter sets in for good," Buck answered, forking another bundle of dead leaves into the fire. Flames crackled, and ashes drifted upward. "This is the best weather for it. Little danger of fire spreading."

"Um, I need to talk with you, Buck. Do you have a minute?"

Al looked from Myles to Buck and back. "Need privacy? I can head for the house and visit the family."

Myles shifted his weight, winced at the pain in his leg, and tried to smile. "Thanks. Would you take the buggy, Al? I've got Pushy and the kittens with me — planned to let Beulah see them. I'm afraid they'll get cold."

Al smirked and shook his head. "You and those cats! All right, I'll deliver the litter to Beulah, but that's all. Should I tell her you're coming?"

Myles nodded. "Soon."

He stood beside Buck and watched Al drive away. The rooftop of Fairfield's Folly was visible through the leafless trees surrounding it. Smoke drifted from its chimneys. Myles could easily imagine Beulah working at the stove or washing dishes.

"How's the leg?"

"Better every day."

"Good. Violet is in town visiting Caroline and the Schoengard baby," Buck said. "Had you heard? Little girl, arrived last night, big and healthy. They named her Jemima after Pastor David's mother."

"That's wonderful! A healthy girl, eh?" Myles fidgeted. "Great news."

"Beulah is watching Daniel. Samuel stayed home from school; said he was sick. I have my doubts." A smile curled Buck's thick mustache and crinkled the corners of his eyes.

"Beulah is home?"

"That's what I said. Washing laundry, last I saw."

"I, uh, need to talk with you. About the future. I mean, about Beulah and me. I need advice."

Buck threw a branch on the fire. "I'm listening."

Myles shifted his gaze from the fire to the house to the trees and back to Buck. He crossed and uncrossed his arms. "I'm not sure where to begin."

Buck smiled. Sparks flew when he tossed a large pine knot into the blaze.

"I want to ask your permission to marry Beulah, but I don't know how soon I'll be able to support a wife. I must return to New York and give a concert tour. Along with a few remaining stocks and bonds and whatever is left from the sale of the family house after I pay off debts, the money I earn should be enough to purchase the Thwaite farm. Cyrus agreed to hold it for me . . . at least for a few months." Myles spoke rapidly. Realizing that he was rubbing the front of his coat, he stuffed the errant hand into his pocket.

"Do you plan to propose before you leave or after you return?"

"I don't know." Myles rubbed the back of his neck, pushing his hat over his forehead. "Do you think she will accept my proposal at all? I mean, I haven't spoken with her — not a real conversation — since the time she blew up at me. I can't leave without knowing, but at the same time it would be tough to leave her behind once we're engaged. What do you think I ought to do, Buck?"

"Have you prayed about this?"

"God must be sick of my voice by now. I've been begging for wisdom and guidance. I feel so puny and stupid. After years of regarding God with — I'm embarrassed to admit this, but it's the truth — with a superior attitude, I'm feeling like small potatoes these days."

"God likes small potatoes. They are useful to Him."

Myles shoved his hat back into place. His smile felt unsteady, as did his knees. "If Beulah won't have me, I'll set up housekeeping with my grandmother. Gram has decided she likes Longtree better than New York, believe it or not. Most of her old friends have died, and she prefers to live out her earthly days with me here. She's a great lady."

"That she is. And what are her plans if you marry?"

"She would be willing either to settle in town at Miss Amelia's boardinghouse or to stay with us at the farm, whichever Beulah would prefer. Gram has money of her own, enough to keep her in modest comfort for life." Myles tossed a handful of twigs into the fire, one at a time. "Do you . . . do you think Beulah will see me today? I mean, is she still angry? I was terrible to her that day — I swore at her, threatened her, and manhandled her."

Buck shook his head. A little chuckle escaped.

"What are you thinking?" Myles asked in frustration.

"Beulah and her mother have been sewing a wedding gown these past few weeks while you've been stewing in remorse and uncertainty. She forgave you even before you professed your faith at church. Beulah's temper is quick, but she seldom holds a grudge. I hope you know what a moody little firebrand you're getting. That girl will require plenty of loving attention."

Myles gaped as a glow spread throughout his soul. "She's been making a wedding dress? For me?"

"Actually, I believe she intends to wear it herself," Buck said dryly.

Myles was too intent to be amused. "And I have your permission to propose?"

"You do. Violet and I are well acquainted with your industry and fidelity, my friend. You will be an excellent husband to our girl."

Myles stared at the ground, blinking hard. "And I had the gall to believe God had deserted me," he mumbled. Biting his lip, he turned away. "I don't deserve this."

Buck wrapped a strong arm around the younger man's shoulders. "I felt the same way when Violet accepted me."

"You did?"

Buck laughed aloud. "Go talk to the girl and decide together on a wedding date. It might be wiser to wait until your return from New York to marry; but then again it might be pleasant for the two of you to make that concert tour together — a kind of paid honeymoon. Beulah could be your inspiration."

Myles stared into space until Buck gave him a shove. "Get on with you. She's waiting."

Beulah jabbed a clothespin into place, securing Samuel's overalls on the cord Papa had suspended across the kitchen. The laundry nearest the stove steamed. Beulah tested one of Daniel's diapers. It was still damp.

"You could at least try to talk to me," she accused the absent Myles. "How am I supposed to demonstrate unselfish love to a man I never see?" Her lips trembled. Clenching her jaw, she stabbed another clothespin at an undervest but missed. "No one tells me anything. For all I know, he's going back to New York without me."

Recalling Myles's singing in church, she brushed a tear away with the back of one hand. "He was so handsome. I hardly knew him without his beard. He looked like a stranger. And oh, his song made my soul ache." Pressing a hand to her breast, she allowed a quiet sob. "You have changed his heart, haven't You, God? Mama was so right. After all my accusations that Mama wouldn't give Myles a chance, *I'm* the one who quit on him at the crucial moment. Please let me try again, Lord."

Samuel's wool sock joined its mate on the line.

A whimper of sound escaped as Beulah's lips moved. "If you have changed your mind about me, the least you could do is come and tell me so. Oh Myles, I love you so much!"

A lid rattled. "Who are you talking to, Beulah?" Samuel slipped an oatmeal cookie from the crock and took an enormous bite. Watchful sat at his feet, tail waving, hopeful eyes fixed upon the cookie.

Startled to discover that she was not alone,

Beulah glared. "Myself."

"Finally found someone who wants to listen, hmm?" Samuel ducked when she threw a wet towel at his head. Laughing, he left the kitchen with Watchful at his heels.

"I thought you were too sick to go to school," Beulah yelled after him. "You'd better get in bed before Mama comes home."

She retrieved the towel, brushing off dust. Sighing, she decided it needed washing again. "My penalty for a temper tantrum."

Scraping damp hair from her face with water-shriveled fingers, she drifted to the window and stared outside. Movement drew her attention to her garden. A doe and two large fawns, dressed in their gray winter coats, nibbled at bolted cabbages. Resting her arms on the windowsill, Beulah felt her heart lighten. "Better not let anyone else see you," she warned the deer. "One of your former companions is hanging on the meat hook by the barn. We have plenty of venison for the winter, but you never know."

The animals' ears twitched. All three stared toward Beulah's window. After a tense moment, the doe flicked her tail and returned to her browsing. Then the three deer lifted their heads to stare toward the barn before springing away into the forest.

Watchful barked from the entryway, and Beulah heard a man's deep voice. Her hands flew to her messy hair, and her eyes widened.

"Al is here!" Samuel shouted. "He brought something in a basket."

"I'll be right there," she said, relaxing. It was only Al. "Why aren't you in bed, Sam?"

Samuel pounded upstairs, skipping steps on the way.

Myles lifted his hand to knock just as the door opened. Al waved an arm to usher him inside. "Enter, please. I'm on my way out. I'll take my mare back and leave the buggy for you. Want me to stable Bess before I go?"

Myles nodded as he limped inside. "Thanks, Al." He swallowed hard. "Where is Beulah?"

Al's grin widened. "In the parlor. Sitting on your bear."

"My bear?" Myles stopped, puzzled.

"It makes a nice rug."

"Oh, the bear."

Shaking his head, Al laughed. "Go on. Talking to you is useless." He clapped his hat on his head and slammed the door as he left.

Myles licked his lips and took a fortifying breath. *Lord, please help me.*

He stepped into the parlor. A shaggy brown rug lay before the stone hearth. Beulah sat Indian style in the middle of the bear's back, and in the hammock of her skirt lay Pushy and four tiny kittens. Firelight glowed in Beulah's eyes and hair. The cat purred with her eyes closed while her babies nursed.

"Myles!" Beulah's voice held all the encouragement Myles required. "You came."

Daniel lay on his back near the rug, waving a wooden rattle with one hand. At the sight of Myles, the baby rolled to his stomach and called a cheerful greeting. Myles bent to pick up the baby, enjoying the feel of his solid little body. Daniel crowed again and whacked Myles in the face with a slimy hand. Bouncing for joy, he dropped his rattle.

"I came. You like my kittens?" Favoring his left leg, he settled near her on the rug. Daniel wriggled out of his grasp and scooted toward the fallen toy. "I wanted you to see them before their eyes opened."

"They are adorable." Beulah lifted a black and white kitten. Its pink feet splayed, and its mouth opened in a silent meow. Pushy opened her eyes partway until Beulah returned her baby. "I love them, Myles."

Hearing a catch in her voice, he inspected her face. "What's wrong?"

"Does this mean you're leaving? You brought the kittens to me for safekeeping."

Myles noted the dots of perspiration on her pert nose, the quivering of her full lips. Tenderness seemed to swell his heart until he could scarcely draw breath. "No, my dearest. I simply wanted you to see them. I have just spoken to your stepfather, as your mother wisely advised."

Beulah's dark eyes held puzzlement. "You

spoke to Papa?"

"Have you changed your mind, Beulah? Do you still wish to marry me? Can you forgive me for swearing at you and threatening you?"

She clasped her hands at her breast. "Yes, Myles! More than anything I want to marry you!" She started to rise then remembered the burden in her lap.

Chuckling, Myles scrambled to his hands and knees, leaned over, and kissed her gently. Below his chest, Pushy's purring increased in volume.

When he pulled away, Beulah's eyelashes fluttered. Her lips were still parted. He returned to place a kiss on her nose. "We need to talk, honey."

"Your mustache tickles."

Just then, Daniel let out a squawk. Startled, Myles and Beulah turned. Only the baby's feet projected from beneath the davenport.

"Oh Daniel!" Beulah cried. "He rolled under there again. Would you get him, Myles?" She deposited kitten after kitten in the blanket-lined basket. Pushy hopped in and curled up with her brood.

After crawling across the room, Myles took hold of Daniel's feet and pulled him out from under the davenport. As soon as he saw Myles, Daniel grinned. "You're a pretty decent chaperone, fella," Myles said. "Better than Pushy is, at any rate."

Beulah hurried to scoop up her dusty

brother. "He moves so quickly. I got used to him staying in one place, but now he's into everything."

"Can I come in yet? Are you done kissing?" Poised in the parlor doorway, Samuel wore a pained expression.

"Don't count on it," Myles said.

Beulah shrugged. "You might as well join us. You're no more sick than I am, you scamp. But at least this way you get to be first to hear our news: Myles and I are getting married."

Samuel stretched out on the bearskin, combing its fur with his fingers. "I know. I heard you."

"You were listening? Samuel, how could you?"

"Easy enough. I was sitting on the stairs." He lifted a gray kitten from the basket and cradled it against his face.

While Beulah gasped with indignation, Myles began to chuckle. He sat on the davenport and patted the seat beside him. "Come on, honey. It doesn't matter. We've got important things to discuss." After depositing Daniel on the rug for Samuel to entertain, Beulah snuggled beneath Myles's arm and soon regained her good humor.

While Samuel played with kittens and Daniel rolled about on the floor, the lovers planned their future.

Epilogue

January 1882, New York City
Curled into the depths of a well-cushioned sofa, Beulah shut her book, smiling. Snow drifted upon the balcony outside her window, mounding on the railings like fine white sugar. Closing her eyes, she sighed in contentment. *Thank You, Lord. Married life is better than I ever imagined.*

The Van Huysens had opted to stay in one of the older hotels in the city. Its old-fashioned splendor was sufficient to please Beulah without overwhelming her. At times, especially around the holidays, she had suffered pangs of homesickness. But Myles's adoration, combined with the knowledge that this tour was temporary, soothed her occasional feelings of inadequacy and loneliness.

She slipped a letter from inside the book cover. There on the envelope her new name, "Mrs. Myles Van Huysen," was written in Mama's neat script. Beulah ran her finger over the words. She was eager to share family news with Myles that night after the concert. He was currently at the theater, practicing.

"Beulah?" A familiar voice called from outside the hotel door. Virginia did not believe in knocking. Beulah hurried to let in her new grandmother.

Virginia bustled into the room, her arms filled with packages. "I've been shopping. Wish you had come with me, but I still managed to spend a good deal. I want you to try this on." After dropping several boxes upon a table, she shoved the largest in Beulah's direction.

"What have you done, Gram?" Beulah chuckled. "What will Myles say?"

"I don't care what that boy might say. It's my money, and I'll spend it as I like." Spying the letter in Beulah's hand, she said, "So you've heard from your mother again? How is everyone back home?"

The crisp inquiry warmed Beulah's heart. She kissed Virginia's cheek. "I love you, Gram. Mama says to tell you 'hello.' They are all well. Daniel is pulling up to stand beside furniture now. Sheriff Boz and Miss Amelia have set February fourteenth as their wedding day, so we should be home in time for the wedding. Um, let's see . . . Eunice found homes for all four of Pushy's kittens. Mama and Papa are letting her keep the black one, Miss Amelia chose the black and white girl, and Mr. Thwaite picked the gray boy. Believe it or not, Al decided to take the black one with white feet! After all his teasing Myles about liking cats, he now has a pet cat of his own."

"That's so nice, dear." Virginia smiled fondly at the girl. "Only a few days now until we'll all be on the train headed for Wisconsin."

"Will you be sorry to leave New York? You must miss your old house. Didn't it hurt to see strangers take it over?"

Virginia pursed her lips and gazed through the window at blowing snow. "For many years now New York has not seemed like home. Ever since the boys left me, I've been a lonely soul. My friends are all gone, and sometimes when I walked around that old house, I missed my dear husband, Edwin, so much. . . . I could picture John and Gwendolyn chasing up and down the stairs — they were our only children, you know. John was killed in the war, and Gwen died of cholera at age fifteen."

Shaking her head, she said firmly, "Dwelling in the past is detrimental to one's mental and spiritual health. Now I have Myles, you, and many friends in Longtree." Her expression brightened. "My life is in the future now. First in Wisconsin, then in heaven!"

Seeing Beulah dab at a tear, she started back into action. "Now take these boxes and try on the gown. It's only a short time 'til we must leave for the theater. Don't want to be late! I had a note from Mr. Poole this morning — he will be at the concert tonight. The man seems to take personal pleasure in Myles's success, which is not too strange considering his role in the boy's return to the stage. I hear it's another sold-out house. Myles's agent has been begging him to reconsider and stay on permanently."

Arms loaded with boxes, Beulah turned back to grin. "Poor man! He hasn't a chance against Cyrus Thwaite's farm."

Beulah perched on the edge of her seat, absently fanning herself. Her emerald taffeta evening gown rustled with every movement, but it was impossible to keep entirely still.

"Hard to believe it's snowing outside, isn't it?" Virginia leaned over to ask. She smoothed a bit of lace on Beulah's shoulder and smiled approval.

Beulah nodded in reply. The old lady's whispers were sometimes louder than she intended. Myles was singing a heart-wrenching aria from *Aida,* and Beulah wanted to listen.

"Hard to believe this is the last week of Myles's tour," Virginia commented a few minutes later while Myles performed Schumann's A Minor Piano Concerto. Again, Beulah nodded briefly.

After weeks of attending her husband's concerts, she still had not tired of hearing him sing and play. Each night Myles varied his repertoire. Always he sang opera, usually Verdi or Mozart; often he performed a few ballads and popular songs; most nights he took requests from the audience. Beulah's favorite part of each performance was discovering which hymn he would choose for his finale.

Tonight he sang "Holy, Holy, Holy." Beulah closed her eyes to listen without distraction. No matter how cross, irritating, or obstinate Myles might have been during the day, each night she fell in love with him all over again. He was so handsome, charming, and irresistible up on that stage!

"I think I'll head home now, dear," Virginia said while Myles took his bow.

Beulah stopped clapping long enough to return the old lady's kiss. "Thank you so much for this marvelous dress, and the gloves, and the reticule, and everything! Your taste is exquisite. You are too good to me." Beulah smoothed the ruffles on her bouffant skirt.

"Child, it was my pleasure. I trust Myles will approve. I hope you know how thankful I am to have you for a granddaughter. Myles has excellent taste, too. Good night." She patted Beulah's cheek and bustled away. Although Myles often requested her to let him escort her home, Virginia maintained independence, insisting that she was perfectly capable of hailing a cab and returning alone to the hotel.

As soon as the red velvet curtain fell, Beulah gathered her things and hurried backstage. Myles waited for her in his dressing room, smiling in welcome.

"Do you like it?" Beulah twirled in place. "Gram bought it for me. Isn't she wonderful? Not that I'll find much use for an evening gown back in Longtree. Gram fixed my hair, too."

Myles's eyes glowed. "You are beautiful, my Beulah. More than any man deserves." His voice was slightly hoarse.

When he closed the door behind her, Beulah wrapped her arms around her husband's neck and kissed him. "Thank you, thank you for bringing me with you to New York. I wouldn't have missed this experience for the world," she murmured against his lips.

"You say that every night," he chuckled, pressing her slender form close.

"And every night I mean it," she insisted. Framing his face with her hands, she studied each feature. "Sometimes I miss your beard, but I do love how your face feels right after you shave."

"You're standing on my feet." He rubbed his smooth cheek against hers.

"That way I'm taller." She stood on tiptoe

to kiss him.

He took her by the waist and lifted her off his feet. "How about if I bend over instead? These shoes were expensive, and my toes are irreplaceable." Smiling, he kissed her pouting lips.

Consoled, Beulah snuggled against him. "Darling, sometimes I don't want this honeymoon to end; other times I want so much to be back in Longtree, setting up our new home. But it will be hard to return to ordinary life after all this glitter and glamour."

"This has been a marvelous honeymoon tour, but I think we would soon tire of such a hectic lifestyle. Think of snowball fights, ice-skating on the beaver pond, and toasting chestnuts. We need to hike up the stream and visit our waterfall while it's frozen."

"And I am looking forward to experiencing everyday things as your wife," Beulah added. "Cooking breakfast for you in our own kitchen, washing your laundry, collecting eggs from our own chickens."

Myles hugged her close and rocked her back and forth. Secure in his arms, Beulah felt entirely loved.

"Yes, each day offers its own pleasures," he mused aloud. "Be content with the joys of today, darling. This tour has been successful beyond my wildest dreams. I know God paved the way, and I'm sure we can trust Him to plan the rest of our future as well. We're

making memories right now that we'll treasure for the rest of our lives. God is very
good."

■ ■ ■ ■

LETTERS FROM
THE ENEMY

BY SUSAN MAY WARREN

■ ■ ■ ■

*To Pops and Grandma Niedringhaus.
In my fondest recollections, I can see you
sitting on the sofa, still holding hands after
three decades of marriage. I miss you.
To Curt and MaryAnn Lund.
It's your memories that make my
own so sweet.
To the Lord Jesus Christ, for loving me
first. Thank You for setting me free.*

CHAPTER 1

June 1918

"We're going to miss the train!" Lilly Clark dashed across the South Dakota prairie, trampling a clump of goldenrod with her dusty boots. The withering grass shimmered under the noonday sun. A humid wind skipped off the Missouri River, and clawed at her straw hat. She clamped a hand over the back of her head and pumped her legs faster toward the crumbling knoll that overlooked the town of Mobridge. Her heart beat out a race against her feet; she could already hear the train thundering through the valley.

Behind her, Marjorie Pratt strained to keep up. "Wait . . . for . . . me," she gasped.

Lilly forced herself up the hill, gulping deep breaths. At the crest, she yanked off her hat and wiped her brow. Squinting in the sunlight, she scanned the horizon and spotted the iron snake threading its way between bluffs and farmhouses toward the Mobridge depot.

"Is . . . it . . . here?" Marjorie staggered to the top.

"Almost," Lilly replied. "We have to hurry."

Marjorie shed her calico bonnet and patted her brow with it. "Just . . . let . . . me rest." Shielding her eyes, she searched for the train.

"It's over there," Lilly said, pointing. Her other hand clutched a lavender envelope, tinged with a thin layer of dust. She scowled and blew on the envelope, assigning the soil to the greedy wind. For a brief second she regretted the extra moments it had taken to saturate the precious letter in perfume and dry it, but the thought of Reggie's smile as he smelled the fresh lilac erased her doubts. She would just have to run faster.

She cast a look at her friend. Marjorie fanned herself, breathing heavily.

"Give me your letter, and I'll go on ahead," Lilly suggested.

Marjorie shook her head. "No . . . I'll make it."

Lilly nodded, then scrambled down the cliff, stepping on roots and boulders to slow her descent. There was an easier way into town, but taking that route would sacrifice valuable minutes and probably her delivery of this week's letter. She heard Marjorie hiss as she started down the cliff behind her, but Lilly knew her friend would make it. Marjorie came from sturdy English stock. She just didn't have the exercise of hoeing and weed-ing the kitchen garden in her favor. Instead, Marjorie devoted all her time to Red Cross work, assembling field kits.

"I'm going to fall!" Marjorie shrieked, sounding more angry than afraid. "It's your fault we're late! If we'd left on time, we wouldn't have had to scramble across the prairie like a couple of jackrabbits!"

Lilly laughed. "You're hardly a jackrabbit, Marj. Just be careful!" With Lilly's long brown hair quickly unfurling in the wind and her tanned face, she knew she was much more likely to be compared to a longhaired wild animal than her dainty friend. Thankfully, Reggie didn't seem to care that she didn't have Marjorie's sweetheart face, candy red lips, and blond hair.

Lilly reached flat land and sped toward town, picking up as much speed as her narrow gingham skirt would allow. At least it was wider than the dreadful hobble skirts that had been in fashion before the war. She'd ripped out two before her mother conceded defeat and allowed Lilly to sew her own styles.

The train's whistle let out an explosive shrill. Lilly glanced back at her friend, now a good fifty feet behind her.

"Lilly, hurry!" Marjorie waved her on.

Squinting into the sun, Lilly spotted the tiny depot, situated on the edge of town like a lighthouse to the outlying northern farms. As the train pulled in and belched black exhaust, Lilly ignored the fire in her lungs and forced her legs to move.

The exhaust settled, and Lilly caught sight of the doors of two livestock boxcars being opened and a ramp being propped up to each entry. Cowboys ascended the ramps, disappeared into the black hole of the boxcars, and emerged dragging angry bulls or frightened horses.

Suddenly, a scab of sagebrush caught the edge of her boot. Lilly screeched, stumbled, and directed her attention back to the jagged prairie.

The train whistle blared, emitting its first departure signal, and fear stabbed at Lilly's heart. She leaped over a railroad tie, used as a property divider, and, grinning between gasps, glued her eyes to the station's platform steps.

If she'd been one step closer, Lilly would have been crushed under the hooves of a mustang, dancing in a frenzied escape from his handler. He blew by her like a tornado, his whiplike tail lashing her face and neck. Lilly screamed, stumbled, and plowed headfirst into the dirt, swallowing a mouthful of prairie in her vanished grin.

She sprawled there dazed, hurt, and dirty.

"Are you all right, *Fraulein*?"

The words barely registered in her fog of confusion. Then a strong arm hooked her waist, pulling her to her feet. Lilly absently held on as she steadied herself. She ached everywhere, but nowhere more than in her pride.

"*Fraulein,* are you hurt?"

She looked up and gaped at a Nordic giant in a cream-colored ten-gallon cowboy hat. Dirt smudged his tanned face and dark sapphire eyes radiated concern under a furrowed brow.

"Sorry. That stallion is a rascal."

Lilly ran her trembling hand over her mouth, trying to gather in her scattered wits while she took in the man's apologetic smile. Her disobedient heart continued to gallop a rhythm of terror.

The cowboy squinted at her, as if assessing her ability to stand on her own, and Lilly realized she still clutched his muscled arm. She yanked her hand away, a blush streaming up her cheeks. When he bent over, she noticed how his curly blond hair scuffed the back of his red cotton shirt collar.

"This yours?" He held the lavender envelope, now dirty and crumpled, between two grimy fingers.

"Oh!" Lilly cried in dismay. She reached for it, but the cowboy untied his handkerchief from his neck and used it to clean the envelope before handing it over.

Tears pricked Lilly's eyes. Her letter to Reggie, ruined. "Thank you," she whispered.

"Sorry," the cowboy muttered.

The train whistle screamed again. Lilly jumped, remembering her mission. She turned toward the depot but pain bunched at her ankle and shot up her leg. She cried out and began to crumple.

The cowboy gripped her elbow, steadying her. "You are hurt."

"Well, I would think so, after being almost run over by your horse," Lilly snapped, unable to hide her irritation.

"Can I help you inside?"

Lilly shook her head. "I can make it. Just go get that beast before it kills somebody." She yanked her elbow from his grasp and turned on her heel, biting her lip against the pain.

"I really am sorry," he offered again.

Ignoring the last apology, Lilly hobbled to the platform stairs and gripped the railing. She paused, then glanced over her shoulder at him.

The cowboy had taken off his hat and was crunching it in his hands. He gazed at her with eyes steeped in remorse. Her anger melted slightly. "Just go get that horse, sir. I'll be fine."

He nodded and shoved his hat on his head. Lilly blew out a frustrated breath and climbed the stairs, wincing. Reaching the top, she swept up wisps of her tangled hair and tucked them under her straw hat. She felt flushed and grimy, but at that moment she didn't care who saw her. Her letter had to make the mail train.

Lilly limped across the platform and entered the depot. The screen door squealed on its hinges. Two men looked up and stared at her.

She ignored the first, a grizzled Native American perched on a lonely bench by the window, and approached the second, a tall, pinched man who eyed her sternly.

"Hello, Mr. Carlson," Lilly said, noting her shaky voice and smiling. He took in her appearance and flared an eyebrow.

"Do you have some mail to send to France?"

Lilly held out the lavender envelope. He grabbed it and dropped it in a bulging canvas bag.

"Just in time." He bent to tie the bag.

"Wait, please." Lilly peered out the window, searching for Marjorie, just now hauling herself up the platform steps.

Mr. Carlson scowled. "Hurry up."

Lilly gave the station manager a pleading smile. "Please, it's for true love's sake."

Mr. Carlson sighed and shook his head. "This war has generated more true love . . ."

He waited, however, until Marjorie trudged through the door and handed him her own bulging envelope, before closing the bag and dragging it out to the hissing train.

Marjorie and Lilly watched in silence as the

porters loaded the mailbag, hoping the letters would, indeed, find their recipients. Lilly realized it was a fragile link, this postal system across the Atlantic. She only hoped it was strong enough to sustain the covenant of love between her and Reggie Larsen.

Mr. Carlson returned, his brow dripping with perspiration. He leaned upon the tall stool behind his counter, glowering at the two girls. "So, what are ya waiting for?"

Lilly eyed him warily. "You don't suppose there is any chance you could look . . ."

"Be gone with ya!" Carlson bellowed, reaching for a glass of tepid water languishing next to his schedule book. "You'll get the mail in your boxes, like always."

Marjorie put a hand on Lilly's arm. "Let's go get a lemonade."

As they exited the depot, Marjorie noticed Lilly's limp. "What happened to you?" She stepped back and surveyed her friend. "Why, you're filthy!"

Lilly brushed herself off. "A wild mustang plowed me over."

Marjorie slid a hand around Lilly's waist. "Are you going to be all right?"

Lilly smiled wanly and nodded. Her ankle would be fine. What upset her more was the lingering image of a handsome young cowboy who had nearly derailed her well-laid plans.

CHAPTER 2

"Can we . . . rest . . . ?" Lilly braced her arm on Marjorie's shoulder and gritted her teeth against the pain spearing her leg.

"You're really hurt, Lilly," Marjorie said. "Maybe I should take you home. I could ask Willard if he would drive you in his Packard."

"No!" Lilly snapped, then regretted her tone. "I want to wait for Reggie's letter. I haven't heard from him in two weeks."

Marjorie gave her a sympathetic smile. "Don't worry. I'm sure he's fine."

Fine? Lilly stamped down her bitterness, but it sprang back like a hardy thistle. Fine would be him here, planning their wedding, preparing to be a pastor. Fine would be him riding roundup or walking her home from church on Sundays. Fine had nothing to do with war or Germans or the fear that boiled in her chest.

She knew the truth. She read the newspapers, despite her father's ministrations to hide them, and knew how "fine" the doughboys were in France. Some were coming home with limbs missing, others in pine boxes. She bit her lip to ward off tears. How fine would she be if Reggie returned home in a flag-draped coffin? Then whom would she marry? Lilly winced at her selfish thought and shook her head to dismiss it.

A heated wind snared a strand of hair from her bun and sent it dancing about her face. Lilly caught it and wiped it back. "Yes, he'll be fine," she agreed, needing to hear the affirmation.

"You should be happy Reggie proposed before he left." Marjorie untied her bonnet and wiped the back of her neck.

How did Marjorie always manage to look beautiful, even under the blistering prairie heat? Her buttery hair turned golden in the blinding sun, and her creamy face never burned. Try as she might, Lilly couldn't control the mass of freckles that overran her face each summer; and her hair, well, she'd seen a prettier mane on her father's worn-out plow horse.

"He didn't formally propose, Marj." Lilly rotated her throbbing ankle, longing to unlace her high boots. "He just kissed me and told me we'd be married when he returned."

Marj sighed. "But that's enough." Her eyes glistened. "Harley didn't even do that much. Just waved with his floppy army cap as the train rolled out of the station."

Lilly smirked. "That's just because he refused to stand in line with all the other boys saying good-bye to the town sweetheart."

Marjorie blushed and had the decency to look chagrined.

"If I had half as many suitors as you —"

"You didn't need them. You have the most eligible bachelor of them all." Marjorie's eyes twinkled, and Lilly was instantly grateful for a friend who didn't point out the stark reality. Even when Reggie had been away at seminary and the town teeming with cowboys and railroad brakemen, not one had taken a shine to the poor Clark girl from the farm up the road.

Then Reggie reappeared on her front porch. Fresh out of seminary, he told her that life with him would be heaven and that he'd been waiting for her since she was in pigtails. His wide smile was like honey to her heart. He'd changed, of course, become refined, serious, exacting of himself and others, but that only inspired her respect. He never stepped over the line with her and treated her as if she was his own cherished possession. Reggie was her future, her security, the man God had chosen for her. Her feelings felt more along the lines of gratefulness, but then again, who wouldn't be grateful for the security of a husband and a family? Wasn't gratefulness a part of love? Reggie would protect her and give her a home. Reggie was God's steadfast reminder He had not forgotten her. After all the years of obeying the church and her parents and striving to be a woman of God, the good Lord had finally noticed and sent her Reggie.

And, if she did everything right, he would be hers forever.

"Let's go," Lilly said, pointing her gaze toward town. "Please drag me to Miller's, Marjie. If I don't get a lemonade soon, I might perish."

Marjorie laughed and shouldered Lilly's weight. They hobbled down the dusty road toward Mobridge.

They passed the shanties the Milwaukee Road had built for their brakemen and engineers who worked this end of the line and turned the corner onto Main Street.

"Billy Harper, you watch it!" Marjorie cried as a large hoop rolled in their direction. The barefoot ten-year-old deftly turned it, and a wide grin shone on his dusty face. As they shuffled along the boardwalks that edged the handful of false-front buildings, they dodged women in wilted bonnets scurrying from shop to shop, baskets of produce in one hand and unruly toddlers in the other. The clop of horses' hooves echoed on the hard-packed street.

Lilly spied Clive Torgesen parked in front of the armory, propped against his gleaming

Model T, arms folded over his chest as he accepted the fawning of goggle-eyed teenage boys admiring his new toy. Clive spotted her and pulled a greeting on his black Stetson. Lilly turned away, not wanting to give the town troublemaker any encouragement.

The smell of baking bread drifted from Ernestine's Fresh Food Market, delicious enough to tempt Lilly to change her destination, but her parched throat won. She and Marjorie shuffled into Miller's Cafe.

Ed Miller had his hands full serving a row of thirsty cowboys and field hands who were downing lemonade or sipping coffee. Marjorie joined the line by the cashier as Lilly claimed a spot by the bookshelf near the windowsill. The shelf sported a yellowing pile of magazines from the East: *Vanity Fair, Ladies Home Journal,* and a thick stack of *American Railroad* journals. Lilly picked up a week-old *Milwaukee Journal,* flipped through it, and listened to the murmur of muddled conversation around her. Opinions of Wilson's latest political blunders, General Pershing's field maneuvers, skirmishes on the western front, and Hoover's wartime food regulations seemed to be the talk of the day.

"They're movin' the draft up ta age forty-five, I hear," said a weathered cowpoke.

"It don' matter, I'm gonna enlist anyway," replied his neighbor. "At least then we'll get ta eat some of the beef we've been tendin'.

These ration days are gonna whittle me down ta bones."

"Yeah, but it might be better than having to face those Germans with nothin' more than a spear at the enda your gun. I hear Pershing has 'em runnin' straight into gunfire with no more than a yelp and a prayer."

"That ain't true, Ollie. I know that our doughboys have themselves real live ma-chan-i-cal rifles. Spit out bullets faster than rain from a black sky. I do think I'd like to get my hands on one a those."

"Well, you're gonna have to live through the boat ride across the ocean first. I heard Ed Miller's boy left a trail from New York to Paris."

Lilly smiled as she heard the cowboys' guffaw and Ed's growl in their direction. She wondered what the war really looked like, up close.

Marjorie nudged her, holding a fresh glass of lemonade.

"Thanks." Lilly took the cold drink and held it to her face, letting the cool glass refresh her skin. Then, she gulped it half down. Marjorie's shocked face stopped her from tilting it bottoms up.

"Sorry." Lilly licked her lips. "I was thirsty."

Marjorie scowled. "So it seems."

Lilly cringed, but caught sight of Reverend Larsen emerging from the alley between Ernestine's and Morrie's Barbershop. Lilly shoved her almost-empty drink into her friend's hand. "I'll meet you at the postal." She hopped toward the door, ignoring Marjorie's cry of protest.

Lilly limped across the street, dodging shouts of outrage from two cowboys on horseback and upsetting Billy Harper's hoop. "Reverend Larsen, sir!"

Reverend Larsen halted two paces from Morrie's front entrance. His angular face held no humor as he surveyed her disheveled appearance. "Lilly, what happened to you?"

Startled, she stared down at her dress. Grime embedded its folds and the sudden image of a cowboy with jeweled blue eyes glinting apology scattered her thoughts. Her mouth hung open, wordless.

"You ought to take better care of your appearance." Reverend Larsen's voice snapped her back to reality. "Just because Reggie is halfway around the world doesn't mean he doesn't care how you look. You have his reputation to uphold now." He cocked a spiny eyebrow.

Lilly bit back defensiveness and instead extracted a respectful tone. "Have you heard from Reggie?"

"Of course not. He has a war to fight. You just do your part and keep writing to him. I am sure he will write back when he can." He stabbed a skeletal finger into the air. "We all have a job to do in this great war, Lilly, and yours is to make sure our Reggie remembers what he has to come home to."

Lilly blew out a trickle of frustrated breath. "I have been writing, sir."

Reverend Larsen laid his bony hand on her shoulder, his gray eyes softening. "I'm sure you have. Mail's often slow at the front. Be patient and trust him to the Lord's hands. He'll write soon."

Lilly nodded. Reverend Larsen stepped into the barbershop, but his parting words lingered. Reggie was in God's hands, and God wouldn't let her down. She, her family, even the entire town knew she would become Mrs. Reginald Larsen, and she would trust the Lord to make it so. The alternative was simply unthinkable. Besides, she'd been so faithful to God, done everything right. She deserved God's cooperation, didn't she?

"Have you lost your senses?"

Lilly whirled and met a frowning Marjorie. "You look like you've wrestled a tornado, and you run up to Reverend Larsen like a lost puppy? What's he going to think about his son's fiancée?" Marjorie scowled. "You've got to learn to curb your recklessness if you're going to be a pastor's wife."

Lilly grimaced. Impulsiveness was her worst trait, constantly running before her to embroil her in a stew of awkward situations. If she weren't careful, Reggie would choose someone else to mother his flock.

"C'mon, let's check the mail." Marjorie tugged on Lilly's arm.

At the post office, they crowded in behind anxious women waiting for the mail.

"Is it here?" Marjorie whispered.

Lilly shrugged, but her heart skipped wildly. A letter from Reggie — something to remind her she was still his. *Please, O Lord.* Then she glimpsed Mrs. Tucker as the thin woman pushed through the crowd. She held a letter in her hands, raised high as if a trophy. Lilly's heart gave a loud inward cry, and Marjorie breathed the answer, "It's here."

Although the line moved faster than expected, an eternity passed before Lilly finally stood at the counter, biting her lower lip as they checked the Donald Clark family box.

They brought her a letter, postmarked from France, with tightly scrawled handwriting that could only belong to Reggie. Lilly clutched it to her chest and pushed her way to the door.

On the dusty street, Lilly paused, fighting the impulse to tear open Reggie's letter and know in seconds whether he was all right, unhurt, and missing her. But then it would be over, the news spilled out like sand on the Missouri River shore. Lilly gulped a breath and calmed her heart. No, it was better to wait, to savor each word and hear his voice as she read the letter slowly under the oak tree behind her house. Or perhaps she would go

959

to the ridge, past the grove of maples that overlooked the river, and imagine him beside her as the sun slipped over to his side of the world. Lilly tucked the letter into her skirt pocket.

Marjorie's scream of delight preceded her from the post office. "It's from Harley!" She waved a wrinkled envelope at Lilly, her smile streaming across her face.

She ripped open her letter, and the envelope drifted to the ground. Lilly picked it up, watching Marjorie silently mouth Harley's words.

"He's okay," Marjorie mumbled absently.

Lilly breathed relief and gazed westward at the sun, now a jagged orange ball, low on the horizon. It had lost its fervor during the downward slide, and the air carried on it the cool scent of the Missouri. The field locusts began their twilight buzz, beckoning her homeward. Lilly limped away, leaving her friend standing in the street, a pebble among a beach of other women: sweethearts, mothers, and daughters who had paused to read the mail. But not just any mail . . . mail from France, Belgium, and all along the Western Allied front lines. Mail that gave them one more day to hope the madness and worry would soon end.

Reggie's letter burned a hole in Lilly's pocket, beseeching her to open it. She put her hand on the envelope, thankful for its presence. It was a shield against the unrelenting reminder of war and the horror that threatened to crash down upon her if Reggie never came home.

CHAPTER 3

The handwriting was bold and sturdy, the very essence of Reggie. Lilly clearly pictured him: his long fingers gripping a stubby pencil as he bent over the parchment, a shock of black hair flung over his chestnut brown eyes.

Lilly caught herself. Reggie's black hair had been shaved, kept short to ward off lice. And the paper was smudged. Reality stabbed at her. Reggie would never willingly send her anything less than perfect. Her brow knit in worry as she devoured his words.

My Dearest Lilly,

I would like to tell you it's quiet here, that Europe is beautiful and I'll return soon, but I know how you hate lies, and those would be falsehoods of great proportion. In truth, I sit now in a support trench, my back against a muddy dugout wall, hoping Harley and Chuck will help me stay warm tonight. It's not that it's cold; on the contrary, the blistering heat of June has been my greatest challenge yet. The urge to throw off my pack, my helmet, and this grating ammunition belt and scratch the sweat and slime from my body is nearly as great as my desire to gaze into your emerald eyes and see that you miss me, desperately, I hope. No, I'm not referring to the cold that comes with a gathering Dakota blizzard. I mean the cold fear that lurks in the silence between offensives. Alone, I cannot staunch the panic that floods my heart when I hear the command, "Over the top!" The charges are bloody and hopeless. We fling ourselves headlong toward the Germans, hoping to win their trench and thereby regain Europe, yard by yard. But I will never erase the sight of so many fellow soldiers, pale and lifeless in the mist at dawn, tangled in the lines of barbed wire that run through the no-man's-land between enemy lines. I stare at them and wonder if and when that will be me. It is then I shiver.

But Harley and Chuck help fend off the cold. Together we remember the things worth living for: you and Marjorie, little Christian and Olive and all the others we protect. We are our own fighting unit, and these brothers have become closer to me than blood. It is with them I hope to return to you, soon.

Our troops are spread throughout Europe, providing the gaps left by Allied casualties in the French and British lines. I cannot tell you where I am stationed, but I serve with men such as Frances, Marc-Luc, Kenneth, and Simon.

As I reread this letter, I realize it seems hopeless. But I am not hopeless. I have you and the vivid memory of your brown hair loosened and fingered by the wind as you waved me off that day, not quite a year ago, as our train pulled away from the platform. Your tears etched sorrow down your cheeks and spoke to me of your devotion to our plans. My thoughts are ever turned toward you, and if (I hate to write it, but I must) I should fall and perish on foreign soil, I pray you will remember me as yours, devoted until the end.

Faithfully,
Reggie

Lilly hugged the letter. Despite the horrors of war, the fear he fought by the hour, and the evident ache of loneliness, Reggie remained the perfect gentleman, honorable and devoted. Tears filled her eyes. Oh! God would just have to bring him back.

Lilly read the letter again, her tears blurring every word as night enfolded her. Lilly listened to the crickets hum and the melody of the grass as the breeze danced off the river. She wondered if Reggie was warm now. She ached to do something for him . . . but she could do nothing but pray. Reggie was in God's hands.

Wasn't that, however, what she feared the most? God was so unpredictable. What if Reggie wasn't a part of her future? What if he was to die in the war and she would never marry the boy she'd waited so long for?

But surely, God wouldn't do that to His faithful servant. Surely, she'd earned the right for Reggie to come home safely. She'd done everything right and proper, acting in perfect obedience. Wasn't that what religion was all about?

Lilly ground her nails into the palms of her hands as she looked past the dark fields toward the sparkling stars. She would not let panic leak into her letters. It would only spoil the pledge she and Reggie had made. Of course, God wanted them together. He was good and loving and blessed those who followed the church's teaching.

God could prove His love, however, by bringing Reggie safely home.

She picked a blade of grass and freed it to the wind. Reggie belonged to her. They had plans, a God-given future, and nothing, not even a war, could destroy it.

Grateful to be out of the house, Lilly tightened her grip on her grocery basket's handle and picked up her pace along the dirt road. The heat pushed everyone to the edge of composure. It slithered into the house from the fields, soiling cotton blouses and melting patience. With three wild younger siblings, her sister Olive and her baby Christian living under the Clark roof, Lilly jumped at the scorching two-mile trek into town, hoping to find reprieve for her frazzled nerves.

Now, only the drone of buzzing grasshoppers accompanied her on the journey into Mobridge.

Daughters sent on last-minute errands packed Ernestine's Fresh Food Market. Lilly weaved past barrels of dill pickles, jars of sauerkraut, and burlap bags of dried corn and buckwheat kernels. The heady scent of peppermint and coffee encircled her as she slid into line, greeting Marjorie's sister Evelyn.

"What do you need today, Lilly?" Ernestine sighed, the sheen of perspiration glistening on her wide brow.

"Two pounds of flour, please."

Willard, Ernestine's balding husband, winked at Lilly as Ernestine dipped out the flour and poured it into Lilly's canvas bag.

"Get any letters from the front?" Willard's voice stayed low, but laughter sang in his eyes.

"Maybe," she replied, blushing.

His gray eyes twinkled. He winked again and turned away. Ernestine handed her the flour, and Lilly dropped a nickel into the shopkeeper's sweaty palm.

The basket groaned as Lilly dropped the bag of flour into it. She tucked it into the crook of her arm and pushed toward the door, where the late afternoon sun flooded over the threshold. As Lilly stepped out of the shop, it blinded her, and she plowed straight into a pair of thick, muscled arms.

"Oh, excuse me!" Lilly stumbled backward.

Wide hands clamped on her upper arms to steady her. Her victim's tall frame blocked the sun, and Lilly stared unblinking at a Viking with a crooked smile, golden blond hair, and eyes blue like the sky an hour before a prairie rainstorm. Lilly's heart thumped like a war drum in her chest.

"You again!" She pulled her arms from his grasp.

He fingered the brim of his battered ten-gallon hat in apology and salutation. "I keep running you over, *Fraulein.*" His grin teased, but his eyes spoke apology. "Pardon me."

Lilly felt a blush. "It's my fault this time." Her gaze skimmed his scuffed brown boots, then returned to his angular face. An attractive layer of blond whiskers outlined his rueful smile.

The cowboy's grin evaporated. For a moment, his brilliant blue eyes kneaded her with an obscure emotion. Then it morphed into pure mischievousness. He stepped aside and doffed his hat, sweeping low and indicating, like an Arthurian knight, that she should pass.

"Thank you," Lilly stammered. She swept past him, feeling his gaze on her back as she took off in a rapid clip.

Lilly was passing Miller's when she heard the ruckus start. Angry voices and a string of curses punctuated the air. Lilly whirled, horrified, wondering who would use such vile language in the middle of Main Street.

Brad, Gordy, and Allen Craffey, three burly brakemen and recent imports from Milwaukee, surrounded the man Lilly had bumped into. They pushed him with their offensive words to the middle of the street.

"What's the matter, can't ya read?" Brad brandished a long stick, poking at his victim.

Lilly's stomach clenched. The cowboy had his hands outstretched, as if trying to explain. Gibberish spewed from his mouth.

"I said, can't ya read?" Brad taunted.

The cowboy stilled, but his words hung like a foul odor. A crowd began to gather. Lilly could smell suspicion in the sizzling breeze. Then she saw the foreigner ball his fists.

"See this . . . ?" Gordy dashed up the steps to Ernestine's. An assembly of speechless women, Ernestine included, watched as he ripped a sign from her door. Lilly knew it well and hated it: "No Indians allowed."

Gordy scrambled down the steps and flung it at the man's feet. "No Injuns allowed!"

The stunned onlookers stared at him, awaiting his reply. The cowboy spoke in tight, clipped English, enunciating each word. "I . . . am . . . not . . . an . . . Indian."

Obviously. His fair skin and white blond hair could hardly be compared to the crimson tan of the Oglala Sioux. But his accent alienated him. Lilly swallowed the hard lump in her throat. What was this young, strong foreigner doing here when the majority of Mobridge's male population was overseas fighting for their lives? An ugly murmur shifted through the crowd.

Lilly noticed Ed Miller, Roy Flanner, and Morrie from the barbershop clumped on the boardwalk, watching with stony eyes.

"Where ya from, blondie?" Brad said it, but it could have been anyone's voice.

"Deutschland." The cowboy lifted his chin slightly.

"Dutch land!" Gordy screamed. "Where's that?"

"I think it's near England!"

"It's next to Norway!"

"Isn't that where they make those wooden shoes?"

Lilly felt as if she'd been slugged. *No, it's our enemy, the people who are trying to kill your sons and husbands.* They had a German right here in their midst.

Brad took the confusion and turned it into violence. He cursed and shoved the German with his stick. Lilly held in a horrified scream as Gordy pounced on the German's back and Brad landed a blow into the man's chest. He sagged slightly, lost his hat. Brad trampled it and slammed his fist into the German's stomach. He grunted. Lilly winced. A broken bottle suddenly appeared in Allen's grip. The wiry Craffey sneered at the German and slashed wildly.

Lilly's breath caught when the German threw Gordy off his back, then caught Brad's stick above his head. He wrenched it from Brad's grasp, while dodging Allen's jagged weapon.

Why didn't the German attack? Throw a punch to defend himself? Lilly teetered at the edge of the boardwalk, horrified yet transfixed. Craffeys came at him time and again, yet he stood his ground, no quarter given, but none taken.

Allen hurled the bottle at the German, and it ripped a gash down the side of his face.

Lilly bit her trembling lip and fought with herself. She should help him. No one had moved to his defense. Shame tasted like bile in her throat. What kind of town had Mobridge turned into when a group of Christians let a man be beaten? What had he done but be a foreigner in a suffering town?

Then again, he wasn't any foreigner; he was German. He deserved to be beaten.

Her sense of justice grabbed her and

screamed logic. This German was not part of the Central Powers, the German/Austrian force that started the Great War. He might be an unwelcome presence in their town — but he hadn't caused the deaths of their South Dakota cowboys.

And Lilly could not let the Craffey boys cause his death.

She dropped the basket and ran headlong into the fight.

CHAPTER 4

Lilly didn't know what terrified her more, the venomous look on Gordy Craffey's face or her own bloodcurdling scream. The sound scattered the Craffey brothers with the effectiveness of three quick jabs.

Brad and Allen stared at her, eyes wide, backing away from her. Lilly halted in a strategic location between the Craffey brothers and the bleeding German. Balling her hands on her hips, she planted her feet and tried to appear fierce. Her pulse roared in her ears.

Gordy Craffey picked himself off the dirt. He stepped toward Lilly like a boxer, his fists high. "Get out of here, Lilly Clark."

Lilly shook her head, trying to summon her voice. She glanced at the German. His wide chest rose and fell in rapid rhythm; blood dripped off his chin.

"I said get, Lilly." Hatred animated Gordy's dark eyes.

Lilly held her breath. Would Gordy strike

her? With his whitened fists and neck muscles bunched, he resembled a mad bull. Lilly battled the impulse to flee. *There are at least fifty people watching,* she reasoned. *Gordy wouldn't dare hit me.* Judging by the angry scowls from the onlookers, Lilly wasn't so sure they wouldn't join ranks with the Craffeys and drag her, kicking and screaming, from the fight.

She crossed her hands over her chest and fought a violent tremble. "Leave him alone, Gordy. Save your anger for the real enemy."

Apprehension rode through Mobridge on a smoldering breeze. Lilly smelled the foul odor of perspiration as she met Gordy's black eyes. They narrowed, raising gooseflesh over Lilly.

"Get him outta here," he growled.

Lilly freed a shuddering breath and glanced at the German.

"Do you have a wagon?"

His gaze remained on Gordy as he jerked a nod.

"Good, you can drive me home."

Lilly dodged Gordy's searing gaze as she and the German back-stepped. When they reached a graying buckboard parked in front of Bud Graham's pharmacy, the German untied the rig while Lilly scanned the faces of the townspeople. It wouldn't take long for news to race across the prairie. She briefly considered bandages for the German's wound, but when she saw the cold abhorrence in Bud's eyes, she snared her broken basket and climbed into the wagon.

"Where to?" the man asked without looking at her.

"North out of town, about two miles."

The acrid stares of the townspeople burned Lilly's neck as she rode tall and eyes forward on the bench. But her mind wrung out her impulsive actions. How many understood the German's words? Lilly bit a quivering lip.

They churned the dust into a thick cloud as they galloped out of the valley and into the yellowing bluffs. Horror throbbed behind Lilly's every thought, and only her grip on the bench kept her from covering her face with her hands and weeping. What had she just done?

Aside from the obvious foolishness of riding alone with a stranger, she'd just stuck her neck out, in full glare view of the entire Mobridge population, for a virtual enemy, for someone her own Reggie was trying to kill — and avoid being killed by! *Traitor.* Lilly went cold.

A mile out of town, the German slowed the horses to a walk. The road rippled as waves of heat skimmed it. Overhead, a stealthy red-tailed hawk hunted jackrabbits in an erratic pursuit. The field locusts hissed, interrupted only by the roar of an intermittent breeze. Perspiration layered Lilly's forehead and began a slow slide down her cheek.

She glanced at the man she'd saved. Blood continued to drip onto his work pants, but he seemed mindless of it. His eyes were trained upon the horses, the endless prairie, perhaps even a land far away across the ocean.

"Are you okay?" Lilly ventured. *No, obviously not!* Lilly grimaced at her question. *He is bleeding and was attacked by three men!* Lilly recalled the confusion, perhaps even panic, that twisted his foreign words. It had horrified her; now she only felt sorry for him. Her own countrymen sickened her.

Bigotry always incensed her. It only took her history with the never-ending problem of the prairie dogs to see that injustice eclipsed all rational thinking on her part. Her father was always inventing new ways to extinguish the pests, and it wasn't without a measure of sympathy for the furry creatures from the women in his family. For a time, Lilly headed up a smuggling ring, teaching Bonnie, DJ, and Frankie how to sleuth out and uncover the dammed-up dens. Then her father discovered their scheme and employed the thin end of a willow switch to help them see the error of their ways. Nevertheless, pity swept over Lilly every time she saw one dart through their carrot patch, and although she shooed them away, she still couldn't bring herself to alert the local posse. Perhaps, as Lilly watched the Craffey brothers pummel the hapless blond German, she'd been reminded of a prairie dog — hated and stalked. Perhaps that was why she flew into the middle of a street brawl, abandoning her common sense.

She was going to regret that act as soon as her father found out. And what if Reggie heard about it? Aiding and abetting the enemy in his own backyard. Lilly shuddered.

The horses snorted. Their coats were spotted with sweat, darkening their chocolate hides. The German clucked twice to them, encouraging their labors.

Out of the corner of her eye, Lilly scrutinized the blond, German cowboy. His eyes were hooded, and they squinted in the light. He'd left his hat in the dust back in Mobridge, and Lilly couldn't help notice his golden hair had dried into a curly, askew mop. He had a strong jaw, now clenched, as if reliving the fight.

Lilly cleared her throat and asked again, louder, "Are you okay?"

The German shrugged, deflecting her concern. Lilly frowned, annoyed. Didn't he know what her actions might cost her?

"You could at least thank me! You know, I'll never be welcome in town again because of you."

"I didn't ask for your help." His toneless reply sent fury into her veins.

"But you needed it. They could have killed you!"

The German turned, pinned on her an eternal, impenetrable gaze. Lilly raised her chin against it. Then the corner of his mouth upturned in a teasing grin.

"You think so, *ja*?"

Lilly's mouth sagged open, and she bit back a flood of hurt. *What an ego.* Lilly focused on the sharpening outline of the Clark farm.

Beside her, the German chuckled. She glared at him. He drove, eyes ahead, a loose smile playing on his lips. His powerful sun-baked forearms rested on the patched knees of his work pants as he fingered the reins, and he was so tall sitting beside her, she could hide inside his massive shadow. The absurdity of her protective act hit Lilly like a fist. This man was no prairie dog. No wonder he had laughed.

Lilly hung her head as a blush crept up her face.

Who was this man? Why was he here? Frustration blurted out her question. "What's your name?"

The German peeked at her and hesitated slightly before answering. "They call me Henry. Henry Zook."

"Henry Zook." Lilly twisted the name over her tongue.

"But my friends call me by my given name, Heinrick." He said it in a tone that made it sound like a request.

Lilly bit her lip. Friends? She wasn't, couldn't be his friend. A knot tightened in her stomach.

"Stop please!"

Heinrick yanked on the reins, and the horses skittered to a stop. They were still a stone's throw from the Clark lane, but common sense screamed at her to leave, immediately.

"What is it?"

Lilly gathered her skirt and hauled herself over the side. Heinrick watched her without a word as she retrieved her basket. When Lilly glanced at him, however, his jaw hardened and he swallowed. Lilly stepped away and waited for him to drive off.

Heinrick made to slap the horses, then paused. He turned and looked at her, and a palpable sadness filled his eyes. Lilly felt a small place in her heart tear apart.

"Thank you," Heinrick said in a soft tone. Then he flicked the reins and trotted away.

CHAPTER 5

"Mother, I'm back." Lilly swiped off her straw hat as the screen door slammed behind her.

Mother Clark entered the mudroom, wiping her hands on her patchwork apron. She scowled as she took the smashed basket from Lilly's hands.

"What happened to this?"

Lilly hung her hat on one of the pegs fastened to the wall. She steadied her voice, hoping it sounded close to normal. "I'm sorry, Mother. I dropped it."

Her mother first examined the basket, then she scrutinized Lilly's flushed face. Lilly offered a rueful smile and saw concern seep into her mother's brown eyes.

"Well," her mother said at last, "go wash up. Dinner is almost prepared."

Lilly poured herself a bowl of water and washed off a sticky layer of prairie dust, as well as, she hoped, any indications of her outrageous behavior in town and the disturbing ride home. She freshly braided her hair and pronounced herself recovered, despite an odd soreness in her heart.

Dinner hour in the Clark home was as sacred as a church service. Lilly heard her father tramping about upstairs as he washed off the dirt from the fields and changed out of his grimy overalls. Her younger sister, Bonnie, hollered from the front door, and a moment later DJ and Frankie blew in from the yard like twisters. Lilly poured fresh milk into glasses while her mother removed a batch of biscuits from the wood-burning oven.

"Any news from town, Lilly?" Olive breezed in with a clean and chubby-faced Christian on her hip. Lilly's mouth went dry.

"Olive, could you please open a jar of pickles?" Mother Clark untied her headscarf and apron, hanging them on a hook near the mudroom door. Olive headed for the pantry, and Lilly licked her dry lips and felt her heartbeat restart. Maybe she could keep a lid on her latest reckless exploit.

Her father blew a feathery kiss across her mother's cheek, then took his position at the head of the table. The family gathered around him, leaving an opening where Olive's husband, Chuck, normally sat. Her mother set a bowl of gravy on the table and slid next to her husband on a long bench. Lilly noticed her father's face seemed drawn. After he asked the blessing, she discovered why.

"A drought is coming. I read it in the almanac, and I see it in the clear blue sky. No rain. The soil is drying up, and even the wheat I planted in last year's fallow field is withering."

Her mother slid a hand over her husband's clasped hands. Lilly noticed her father's green eyes seemed to age. "We need to find a way to lay up stores for the winter. I don't think we'll make enough on the wheat to hold us through."

Her father couldn't tend the crop alone, and without Chuck's help, the eighty acres he'd added two years ago would revert to the bank.

Despite the beckoning aroma of beef sauced in onion and dill gravy, dinner went nearly untouched. Only Frankie and DJ dove into their food. Lilly wished, just this once, she had their naive trust.

Olive adjusted Christian on her knee and handed him a biscuit scrap. "I volunteered to help out at the armory, with Red Cross packages, but maybe I can find a job, instead. I know they're advertising for cooks at Fannie's boardinghouse."

Her father, who had been examining his fork, glanced at her and smiled. But his eyes spoke regret.

Lilly played with the fraying edge of her cotton napkin. "Mrs. Torgesen asked me to make her something for the Independence

981

Day picnic," she said. "That will help." She peeked at her mother, who flashed a reassuring grin.

"We'll all work together and put it into the Lord's hands," her father quietly summed up. The matter was dropped, but apprehension lingered as the shadows stretched out in dusty patterns along the kitchen floor.

"Have you lost your senses, or are you *trying* to destroy your life?" Olive added a hiss to her furious whisper.

Lilly clasped her hands and sat still as stone on the straight-back chair. News traveled like a lightning bolt across the prairie and, as Olive marched out her fury on the clapboard floor of Lilly's second-story bedroom, Lilly knew her rash behavior in town had ignited.

Olive bounced little Christian over to her other hip. Christian giggled at the bumpy ride. The two-year-old loosened a strand of his mother's chestnut brown hair, unraveling the bun at the nape of her neck, to match Olive's demeanor. Her sister had stomped home an hour earlier, her after-dinner stroll with Elizabeth White destroyed by "a sordid tale that involved Lilly cavorting with a stranger in town."

"You have no idea who that man is, nor where he is from. He could have hurt you!" Olive's voice rose a pitch. Lilly winced. "You stepped into a fight that was none of your business! I heard the Craffeys caught him stealing — he had two apples in his coat pocket!"

"He wasn't wearing a coat, Olive."

"And he spoke a different language — like he was demon-possessed!"

Olive paused in her tirade to plunk Christian down on the double bed Lilly shared with Bonnie. Christian rolled across the quilt, drooling.

Lilly sucked a calming breath of air. "Olive, listen. I admit my foolishness." She held up her hands in surrender. "I won't do it again."

Olive bent down and glared into Lilly's face. "You bet you won't. Because if you do, I'll tell Chuck . . . and he'll tell Reggie!"

Lilly recoiled as if she'd been slapped. Her sister's threat hung in the air like an odor. Lilly willed her voice steady. "Don't worry, Olive. I don't even know who he is. I'll never talk to him again, I promise."

Olive clamped her hands onto her narrow hips. "You better not, or you'll be sorry." She scooped up Christian. "Reggie doesn't need distractions, Lilly. Do you want to get him killed?"

Lilly gasped. Olive stormed out, slamming the bedroom door behind her.

Lilly closed her eyes. "Please God, no." She hadn't considered that perhaps God would punish her for helping the German. Perhaps He, too, considered her a traitor. But would

He let Reggie die because she'd sinned?

Lilly fought the insidious idea and walked over to the window seat. The cushion in the alcove was one of her first sewing projects, a calico pillow in blue and yellow. Lilly climbed into the nook, pulled her knees to her chest, and rested her head on her crossed arms. The prairie stretched to the far horizon, forever past the hundred and twenty acres that belonged to the Clark family. The sun painted the wheat field hues of rose gold and the hay field to the north a jade green. Her father would begin haying soon, cutting the grass, letting it dry, and gathering it up into giant mounds for cattle feed during the winter.

Was it only two years ago she'd worked with Reggie, mowing the hay? She smiled at the image of his serious brown eyes, the sun baking his back and arms. Even then, he'd wanted to protect her. "Lilly-girl, you shouldn't be working here. This is men's work." She wanted to cry. After all he'd done for her, and she'd betrayed him.

Oh God, please send him home! If Reggie were here, perhaps he'd be working with Chuck, dragging in water from the Missouri to keep the crop alive.

The front door slammed, and she watched her father stride out to the barn, heading for the evening milking. The Clarks had two dozen Holstein her father used to run a fairly lucrative dairy route on the west side of the

Missouri to the ranchers who didn't raise milkers.

But if the prairie dried up, so would their Holsteins. Lilly's eyes burned. The threat of drought made her escapade in town seem all the worse.

"I'm sorry, Reggie, I'm sorry." Had she really betrayed him? Lilly pressed her fists into her eyes, but she couldn't erase the clear image of Heinrick, hands up in surrender, backing away from the Craffey boys, jabbering incoherently. Nor could she forget the tone of longing in his voice when he'd offered his name in friendship. No, she hadn't done anything wrong; she'd merely performed a Christian duty of kindness. At least she hoped that was true. She hoped she hadn't somehow stepped over the line of faithfulness to Reggie or to her country and summoned punishment from the Almighty for her misbehavior. Dread seeped into her bones.

"Please forgive me, God," she moaned feebly.

She would never see the German again. Lilly resolved it in her heart, to herself, to Reggie, and finally to God.

CHAPTER 6

"Please, Mrs. Torgesen, just two more pins." Lilly snatched a straight pin from the corner of her mouth while she struggled with the flimsy newspaper pattern.

Mrs. Torgesen, wiggling about as if she were a two-year-old, held the latest edition of the *Ladies Home Journal* and flipped from page to page as if window-shopping in Boston.

"Oh, this eggshell blue chiffon is just breathtaking! How long did you say it would take to order?"

Lilly stifled a groan as another page tore across Mrs. Torgesen's ample backside. Doggedly, she pinned it together. "Two weeks, earliest."

Mrs. Torgesen sighed, then glanced down at Lilly. "Well, how's it coming?"

Lilly managed a smile. "Do you want pleats or gathers?"

Mrs. Torgesen hopped off the tiny stool, and Lilly heard the remainder of her pattern rip to shreds. She sighed and conceded defeat. Mrs. Torgesen would change it three or four times before completion, anyway. Lilly stuck the pins into her wrist cushion and collected the scraps of paper.

"How about this one?" Mrs. Torgesen held out the magazine, pointing to a picture of a two-tiered gown in muted lavender. The skirt slid to just below the knees, with wide pleated rows running hip to hip. An underskirt, in the same shade, continued to the ankles. The bodice was a simple white cotton blouse with puffed sleeves and a boat-style neck. What made the piece stunning was the sheer lace lavender overcoat that covered the blouse and flared out over the hips. The ensemble was then secured with a wide satin belt, accentuated on the side with a six-inch satin rosebud.

"How exquisite." Lilly passed back the magazine.

"Make it for me, Lilly. I know you can." Mrs. Torgesen rained a toothy grin down on her. Lilly smiled as if she couldn't wait, but she wanted to grimace. The woman would be a giant purple poppy.

Lilly stood up. "Let's see what you have for fabric. Maybe I can do it from scraps."

"You know where the fabric is, dear." Mrs. Torgesen patted her glistening brow with a lace-edged handkerchief. "I need a glass of lemonade." She waddled off toward the kitchen.

Lilly always thought Mrs. Torgesen could

be described by one word: excessive. She was a woman who couldn't be contained — or contain anything, including her appetite for food and clothing. She lived with one foot dangling in the waters of lavishness and laughed away the criticism of brow-raising conservatives from the North Dakota border on down. Yet all tolerated Mrs. Torgesen, despite her fanciful ideas, and Lilly supposed it was for one very large reason — the breadth and strength of the Torgesen T cattle ranch.

Lilly slipped off her wrist cushion and tucked it inside her sewing box. She considered it a blessing to be employed by Mrs. Torgesen — not only did it allow her to work with feather-fine silk, transparent chambray, and filmy chiffon, but Mrs. Torgesen's dreams pushed Lilly's skills to new heights. And, despite Mrs. Torgesen's desire to dress like a French dame, her generosity had helped Lilly finance her wedding dress and prepare for the event she knew her father would struggle to provide. And now, the work could help keep the Clark family fed.

Lilly headed upstairs to the sewing room. Mrs. Torgesen couldn't even sew a straight stitch, but she owned a gleaming black Singer. Lilly preferred, however, to bring her work home and sew in the comfort of her bedroom, laying the pattern out on the hardwood floor or on the kitchen table. And, at home, her mother was always available for advice.

The high sun spilled through the yellow calico curtains, lighting the corner room in an array of cheery colors.

The remnant fabric was stuffed into a three-door oak wardrobe. The doors creaked as they opened, the wood split from years of dry prairie heat. Lilly wrinkled her nose against the pungent odor of mothballs and dove in, wading through a sea of jeweled fabrics from dyed wool in jade and mauve to calicos in every shade of blue.

Lilly finally unearthed five yards of plain, sea foam green cotton and a piece of white flowered lace large enough for the overcoat. Perhaps she could dye it. Tucked in the back, behind a piece of red calico, she pulled out a forest green satin, perhaps meant for a pillow edge. It would make a perfect sash. Mrs. Torgesen would be a flowing willow, drifting along Main Street on Independence Day. Lilly stifled a chuckle.

Lilly was piling the fabric pieces onto a small box table next to the Singer when movement in the yard below caught her eye.

The sight of a golden mustang, bucking and writhing beneath its rider in the sunbaked corral, made her step toward the window. The animal's black eyes bulged with terror as the cowboy atop the bronc whooped, grabbed the saddle horn, and spurred the horse. The mustang reared, then threw himself forward and bucked, flaying out his hind legs. Sweat flicked off his body. Lilly stood transfixed at the desperate wrestle.

Suddenly, the cowboy dropped one of the split reins. Lilly winced as she watched him grab for the saddle horn. His whooping had stopped and only her thundering heart filled the silence as the horse bucked and kicked, twisting under its mount. Then, with a violent snap, the mustang pitched the cowboy into the air. Lilly watched him climb the sky in an airborne sprawl. He flew a good ten feet and landed with a poof of prairie smoke.

The mustang continued to twist, jump, and kick in a hysterical dance. His wide hooves landed closer to the hapless cowboy with each furious snort. All at once, the animal reared, pawing the air above the terrified rider. The man wrapped his arms around his head, curled into a ball, and waited to be trampled.

Lilly covered her eyes and peeked through her fingers.

Suddenly, a figure erupted from the barn door. A blond whirlwind, he burst right up to the furious animal. Holding out both hands as if to embrace the beast, he closed quickly and in a lightning motion snared the dangling reins and planted his feet. The downed cowboy scrambled toward the barn.

The mustang reared and snorted. The man extended his hand to catch the horse's line of vision. The horse jerked his head and pawed at the ground, but with each snort, the terror dissipated, his feet calming their erratic dance until, in one long exhale, he stopped prancing altogether. The man brought a steady hand close to the horse's eye. The mustang bobbed his head twice, then let his captor touch his velvet nose. After a moment, the man stepped close and rubbed the bronc between his eyes and over his jaw.

Lilly exhaled and realized she'd been holding her breath. Whoever he was, the cowboy had a way with animals that tugged at her heart and stole her breath. As she watched, the man turned and looked toward the house. The sun glinted in his blue eyes, and he wore an unmistakable half-smile. Lilly jumped away from the window. Her heart did an erratic tumble in her chest, and her skin turned to gooseflesh. Despite her vow, she'd somehow found Heinrick.

Lilly heaped the fabric into a ball, scooped it into her arms, and scrambled downstairs. Her heart flopped like a freshly netted fish, dazed and horrified at the recent turn of events. The last thing she needed was a reminder of yesterday's scandalous incident. She would keep her head down and flee like a jackrabbit from the Torgesen T and its troublesome German.

"Ma, I don't think Buttercup is the right

name for that mustang!" Clive Torgesen slammed the screen door and dragged a trail of prairie dust into the kitchen. Lilly skidded to a halt in the doorway, clutching the fabric to her chest. She didn't realize it had been Clive, Mrs. Torgesen's uncouth son, who had ridden the terrorized animal. At best, Clive was a roadblock to a speedy, unsuspicious escape; at worst, he would smear her with one of his crude remarks and recount yesterday's embarrassing tale in embellished detail. Lilly gritted her teeth and sidled out of view.

The fair-haired Torgesen boy was one of the lucky — he'd been granted a bye in the enlistment lottery. Some thought it was because he was Ed Torgesen's only son. Others believed it had something to do with a wad of George Washingtons in the county registrar's back pocket. Nevertheless, Clive Torgesen was now one of the few, and of them the most, eligible bachelors in the state.

To Lilly's way of thinking, that wasn't saying much. Underneath the ruggedly handsome exterior — his curly, sandy-blond hair, his earth brown eyes, and his heavy-duty muscles — was a completely rotten core. As her father liked to say, "There was a foul smell to that bird's stuffin'." Lilly had the unfortunate experience of sitting next to Clive in school. She'd seen his pranks firsthand, from cutting off the braids of little girls to throwing youngsters into the Missouri

River in October. Now older, he was down-right dangerous. Lilly had heard the gossip, seen the faces of girls he'd "courted," and doubted the honor of the man in the wide-brimmed black Stetson.

Clive plopped down in a willow-backed chair next to his mother at the kitchen table. The housekeeper, Eleanor, served him a sweating glass of lemonade, and he guzzled it down.

Mrs. Torgesen dabbed at her forehead with her handkerchief. "Your father thinks the mustang will make a wonderful stallion. He is expecting two brood mares from Wyoming in a week or so."

"Well, he's impossible to ride. He ought to be hobbled."

"Hobbled!" Lilly cried and burst through the door. "What he needs is a gentle hand, Clive."

Clive sat back in his chair and tipped up his hat with one long, grimy finger. "Well, Lilly Clark. Since when are you the expert on wild horses?"

Lilly clamped her mouth shut. Her face burned, and she wanted to melt through the polished clapboard floor. Mrs. Torgesen leveled a curious frown at her. Lilly swallowed, and held out the fabric to Mrs. Torgesen. "I think I found something that might work," she croaked.

Mrs. Torgesen turned her attention back to

Clive. "Give him a week or so, dear. He'll settle down. Pick a different horse."

Clive snuffed. "I almost had him broke, too, Ma. Until that stupid German interfered."

Mrs. Torgesen peeked at Eleanor, then drilled a sharp look into Clive. "He's not German, Clive. He's from Norway, just like us."

Clive's eyes narrowed, squeezing out something unpleasant. An eerie silence embedded the room while Clive and Mrs. Torgesen sipped their lemonade and glowered at each other. Lilly glanced at Eleanor, but she busily stirred a pot of bubbling jam on the stove. The sharp, sweet smell of strawberries saturated the humid air.

Clive gulped the last of his drink. He examined the glass, turning it in his hand. "Well, whatever he is, he's a troublemaker, and I'd keep my eye on him if I was you, Ma."

Mrs. Torgesen slid a dimpled hand onto Clive's arm. "That's why you're the foreman."

Clive emitted a loud "humph." He set the glass on the table and ran a finger around the edge. "So that means I can do what I want with him, right?"

"It's your crew, dear."

Clive smiled, but evil prowled about his dark eyes. He stood and tipped his hat to Lilly. "See ya 'round." He winked at her as he turned away.

The bile rose in the back of Lilly's throat.

Mrs. Torgesen sighed. "Let me see the fabric, Lilly."

The next two hours crawled by as Lilly fashioned a makeshift pattern from a remnant piece of muslin. The costume would require a mile of fabric, it seemed, and Mrs. Torgesen would bake in it under the hot summer sun, but she obviously had no regard for such discomforts.

"I want it ready by the Fourth of July."

Lilly pushed a rebel strand of brown hair behind her ear. One week. "Yes, ma'am."

The low sun tinged the clouds with gold and amber as Lilly plodded home. Three miles to go and her arms screamed from the weight of the small mountain of fabric. But the wind was fresh on her face and not only had she avoided another perilous run-in with the German, but neither Mrs. Torgesen nor Clive hinted Lilly might know him. Either they hadn't heard or they were hoping she'd keep their secrets if they kept hers.

A hawk circled above, and Lilly heard Reggie's voice, strong and wise, in her head. *Watch the hawk, Lilly, it will lead you to dinner.* She didn't do much hunting, but somehow his words stuck in her memory. Just like his firm hand upon the small of her back, or nimble fingers playing with her hair. She could never forget his kiss — just one, on an eve such as this, as the sun slid behind the bluffs beyond the river. She and Reggie had strolled to her favorite refuge, a tiny retreat nestled in a grove of maples. There, he told her he would marry her. He didn't have anything to give her, he said, "but his promise." Then he cupped her face in his strong hands and kissed her.

He'd left for the war the next day, yet she could still feel his thumb caressing her cheek, feel his lips upon hers. *Oh Reggie, please come home soon.*

The creak of a buckboard scattered her memories. At a hot breath over her shoulder, Lilly gasped and sprang into the weeds lining the dirt road. Laughter, rich, deep, and unpretentious, filled the air. Lilly whirled, squinting into the sunlight.

"Hello. We meet again." Heinrick greeted her with a sweeping white smile and twinkling blue eyes.

Lilly's heart raced like a jackrabbit eluding prey.

"Want a ride?"

Lilly shook her head.

"C'mon. I can repay you for saving me." His grin seemed mischievous.

"I thought you said you didn't need saving." Lilly shut her impulsive mouth and squeezed the fabric to her chest.

He raised his eyebrows. "Did I say that?"

Lilly frowned. Had he? It didn't matter. She

wasn't getting into a buckboard with an enemy of the community. She'd vowed it to Reggie and to God, and she wasn't going to break her promise.

"I don't want a ride." Lilly stepped into the road and started walking, her legs moving in crisp, quick rhythm. "Thank you, anyway."

Heinrick followed her, the horses meandering down the road.

"Go away, Mr. Zook!" Lilly called over her shoulder, annoyance pricking her.

"My friends call me Heinrick!"

"I'm not your friend."

He did not immediately reply, and Lilly felt the sting of her words. The locusts hissed from the surrounding fields, their disapproval snared and carried to her by an unrelenting prairie wind. Lilly pounded out her steps in silence, her knuckles white as she clutched the fabric.

"Why not?"

Lilly stopped and whirled on her heels. "Because you are German! And if you haven't noticed, America is in a war against Germany! My fiancé, Reggie, is over there" — she flung her arm out eastward — "trying not to get killed by your countrymen. I can hardly accept a ride from a man who may have relatives shooting my future husband at this very moment!" She sucked a breath of dry, searing air and willed her heart to calm. "That, Mr. Zook, is why I can't be your friend."

She saw a glimmer of hope die in his eyes with her painful words, and Heinrick's misshapen grin slowly vanished. A shard of regret sliced through her. She wasn't a rude person, but she had no choice but to be brutally frank. They were at war, America and Germany, she and Heinrick. And war was ruthless.

"Please, just leave me alone," Lilly pleaded.

Heinrick nodded slowly. "I understand." His eyes hardened. "But that's going to be a bit hard, seeing we both work for the Torgesens."

"Try, please, or you're going to get us both into a mess of trouble."

He leveled an even, piercing gaze on her. "I am sorry, *Fraulein.* Trouble is the last thing I hope to bring you. I'd much prefer to bring you flowers." Then he slapped the horses and took off in a fast trot.

Lilly gaped as she watched him ride away, his muscular back strong and proud against a withering prairie backdrop. Then her throat began to burn, and by the time she neared her house, she was wiping away a sheet of tears.

CHAPTER 7

An early afternoon sun cast ringlets of light through Lilly's eyelet curtains and across her vanity. Her brown hair was swept up into a neat braided bun, and a slight breeze, tinged with the smell of fresh lily of the valley, played with the tendrils of hair curling around her ears. Lilly bent over her parchment, scribing her words.

June 28, 1918

My Dearest Reggie,
   My thoughts were with you this morning as we walked to church. DJ, who'd lingered behind us, startled a ring-necked pheasant into flight, and I recalled the year when you found an entire nest and gave us three for Thanksgiving dinner. I also remember Harley's envy that year when you brought in two bucks to his doe. I am counting on your aim to protect you and Chuck and can't help but shiver

with you when I think of you huddling in the foxholes. I haven't said a word to Olive, who, I fear, believes you all within the safety of a fortified Paris. Perhaps it's for the best; she and little Chris prefer the cheerful reports from the censored *Milwaukee Journal*.

On to glad news. The city fathers have agreed to preserve tradition and host the Mobridge rodeo on Independence Day. In the absence of many regular participants, they have extended an invitation to the children, allowing them to compete in the center ring. Frankie is hilarious with joy. He commandeered Father's plow and spent the last week practicing his steer roping. As Father won't let him near the cows, Sherlock became his unfortunate victim. Frank stood upon the plow, flung about him the lasso you constructed, and then wrestled the hapless spaniel to the dirt. After three days of tireless practice, Sherlock finally crawled behind the lattice under the back porch, and since Friday has refused to reappear. Twice I saw Mother slide a bowl of scraps under the steps; I believe she has more than an ounce of empathy for the old pup!

The prairie is already beginning to wilt; the black-eyed Susans and goldenrod, which were so vibrant only a month ago, have joined the fraying weeds. The heat this year is insufferable, and I know if you were here, I'd find you in the Missouri, fighting the catfish for space. Do you miss the river and the song of the crickets at dusk? I can't imagine what France must be like — does it have coyotes or prairie dogs or cottonwoods to remind you of home?

Marjorie is distraught over Harley's cold. I hope he is recovering and has rejoined you in the trenches, not that I wish any of you there; rather I would have you all here. But I know how you must miss him, and I can't bear to imagine you alone during an offensive. May God watch over you.

Mother and Father send their love. I talked to your father in town two weeks ago, and he looked fit and calm, as is his nature. His courageous, faithful prayers continually inspire me; my own petitions seem so feeble in comparison. Nevertheless, my thoughts are constantly upon you and the pledge we made in the shadow of the maples near the bluff. Please come home to me.

Faithfully,
Lillian

Lilly folded the page, slid it into a creamy white envelope, and propped it against her round mirror. She hadn't mentioned Heinrick, and a sliver of deceit pierced her heart. But why should she? She'd hardly mentioned the drought, either, for Reggie's own good. She didn't want him to worry, and neither did she want him to imagine a scenario that had never existed, would never exist, between her and Heinrick. Better to let the matter die in the dust. If he ever did ask, she would tell him she'd merely saved a man from a good pummeling.

She heard the screen door slam, then voices drift toward her room. Her heart skipped. The Larsens, and perhaps they had news from Reggie!

Or, and her smile fell at the thought, maybe they had news about her. So far, no one other than Olive had hinted a word about the event in Mobridge, already almost a week past. But, then again, her parents were busy people and didn't cotton to gossip. Unless, of course, it involved their daughter.

Lilly gulped a last bit of peaceful air, painted a smile on her face, and bounced down the stairs.

Reverend and Mrs. Larsen sat in two padded green Queen Anne chairs in the parlor, glasses of lemonade sweating in their hands. Reverend Larsen rose and greeted her. Lilly smoothed her white cotton dress, glad she hadn't changed after church, and sat next to her mother on a faded blue divan.

"So, news from Reggie?" she asked and

tried to ignore the tremor in her voice.

Mrs. Alice Larsen shook her head. "Simply a social call to our future daughter-in-law and her parents."

Lilly grinned. The coast was clear, no storms brewing on the horizon. Olive sauntered into the room, little Chris on her hip, still in his Buster Brown church uniform. She waggled his pudgy arm at the small crowd. "Going for a nap," she said in a baby voice, then backed out of the room. She glanced at Lilly, who caught the scorching look, as if in reprimand, from her older sister.

"Reggie wrote and told us that you're planning to join the Red Cross?" Reverend Larsen asked Lilly.

Lilly shrugged. "Oh, that was just talk. I'm not sure right now."

"Well, I heard they need volunteers. It sounds like the work is endless." It seemed Reverend Larsen knew everyone's needs, business, and talents. At least those of his congregation. "I am sure Reggie would be proud."

Lilly blushed.

"Lilly's been doing a lot of sewing, especially for the Torgesen family." Her mother winked at Lilly.

Mrs. Larsen dabbed a lace-trimmed kerchief on her neck. "It's so nice that you can help out your family, and sewing is such a needed talent in the church. It will serve you well as a pastor's wife."

"Lilly has much to offer to help Reggie get a firm hold on a nice flourishing congregation when he returns."

Lilly shot a glance at her father. She suddenly felt like a prize milking cow, up on the auction block.

"That is, until she starts filling the house with babies." Mrs. Larsen cocked her head and slathered Lilly with soupy eyes. "I can't wait to be a grandmother."

"So Reggie is going into the ministry after the war?" Lilly's mother rose to refill the half-empty glasses.

Reverend Larsen nodded. "He's all ready to follow in his father's footsteps." He held out his glass. "But I won't be handing over the pulpit too quickly. He'll have to tuck some experience under his belt first. Maybe take on a smaller church, perhaps up north in Eureka, or plant a missionary church over in Java, that new Russian community."

Lilly stared past them at the patterned floral wallpaper her mother had lugged west from her home in Illinois. Her mother had been a banker's daughter, brought up on fine linens and satin draperies. Life on the prairie had toughened her hands and character, but her refined, padded childhood still lingered in her choice of home decor. Lace curtains blew at the open window, and a portrait of Lilly's stately maternal grandparents hung on the wall over the rolltop desk. Lilly often wondered who her mother had been before she'd met Donald Clark, before he'd moved her to the prairie, and before life with blizzards, drought, and birthing five children etched crow's-feet into her creamy face.

"Lilly, are you listening?" Her mother's voice pierced her musings.

"What?"

"Mrs. Larsen asked you if you'd started your wedding dress yet."

Mrs. Larsen leaned forward in her chair. A thick silence swelled through the room. The tick of the clock chipped out eternal seconds.

"Uh, well, no, actually. I felt I should wait."

With her words, the fear about Reggie's future ignited. The questions, the fears, the unknowns. With one bullet, one misstep in the no-man's-land between battle lines, their hopes would die. Mrs. Larsen gasped, her eyes filled, and she held a shaking hand to her lips.

Lilly hung her head. "I'm sorry."

Maybe she should start on her wedding dress, as much for her own sake as Mrs. Larsen's. Maybe that was just what she needed to get her focus back on the plan and erase the memory of her traitorous encounter with Heinrick. The fact that she easily conjured up his crooked smile or those dancing blue eyes bothered her more than she wanted to admit.

"Thank you for the lovely sermon today, Reverend." Mrs. Clark filled the silence. Reverend Larsen leaned back into the molded chair. It creaked. "Thank you, Ruth. The passage about Abraham and Isaac is such a difficult one to interpret."

Her father threw in his chip as if to reassure the preacher. "You did well, helping us to remember it was Abraham's obedience that won Isaac back to him. He obeyed God, regardless of the cost; that's what is important."

Reverend Larsen nodded. "That's what I continue to tell our young people" — and he fastened steel eyes on Lilly, adopting his preaching tone — "obedience to God and to the church is the only sure path in this world. If they want to find peace, they will walk it without faltering."

Lilly smiled meekly and noticed he'd balled his free hand on his lap, most likely a reflex action. Unfortunately, the Clark parlor had no pulpit to pound.

"Take Ruth, for example," he continued, his voice adopting a singing quality. "She, without a husband, obeyed her vows, despite the fact that it would mean a life without children, and followed Naomi to a foreign land. And God gave her Boaz and blessed her for her obedience."

" 'Obedience is better than sacrifice,' Samuel told Saul," added Mrs. Larsen.

"That's right, dear." The reverend tightened his lips and nodded.

Bonnie entered the room with a plate of shortbread. Her mother took it from her and served the guests. "But what about faith? Wasn't it because of Abraham's faith that God counted him righteous?"

Lilly shot a quizzical look at her mother.

"Of course!" Reverend Larsen stabbed his finger in the air as if her mother had made his point. "Obedience is faith. It's faith in action. If we want to show God that we love Him, we will obey. And then, He will bless us — reward us for our faithfulness. Our obedience assures us of God's blessings and of His love."

Reverend Larsen shifted his gaze to Lilly's father. "That is why so many of our youth have problems today. They abandon the teachings of their church and parents. Without guidance, their lives simply run amok."

Her father nodded soberly.

"But not your Lilly, here." Every eye turned toward Lilly. "I always told Reggie that Lilly would make a fine wife. I've watched her since her childhood, especially while Reggie was at school, and decided she would have no problem being a submissive, obedient wife. I told Reggie so when he returned from college." He leaned forward, balancing his elbows on both knees, and pinned her with a sincere look. "I'm glad he listened to me."

Lilly forced a smile. Had Reggie chosen her because of his father? No, Reggie said he'd been chasing her since her bloomer days. She couldn't believe the look in Reggie's eyes was anything but true love. Besides, she *would* be a good wife. She would see to that herself. She had no intention of falling off the path of the straight and narrow and landing "amok," as Reverend Larsen so delicately stated it. She knew her path in life, and when God brought Reggie home, she would start walking down it.

Lilly saw Mrs. Larsen dab at her forehead. She suddenly became conscious of her own glistening brow and the oppressive heat that filtered through the lace from the prairie. It oozed into her pores, flowed under her skin, and bubbled in a place inside her body. The pictures of her grandparents spun at odd angles.

"Will you excuse me, please?" Lilly rose to her feet, reaching out her hand to grasp the back of her chair.

"Lilly, are you ill?" Her mother put down the tray.

Lilly shook her head. "I just feel a bit hot and dizzy."

"By all means, go lie down." Mrs. Larsen had also risen, concern on her pale face. Somehow, the woman managed to avoid the sun despite living in a virtual oven.

"Thank you for coming, Reverend Larsen,

Mrs. Larsen." Lilly fingered her temple, as if her head were throbbing. But as she exited the parlor and felt a cool breeze filter in from the kitchen, she realized it wasn't dizziness that had attacked her in the parlor . . . it felt more like the numbing grasp of suffocation.

CHAPTER 8

The week before Independence Day passed in a flurry of fabric, needles, and fittings. Lilly hiked out to the Torgesen ranch three times during the week to fit the skirt, then the bodice, and finally the end product.

She couldn't help but look for Heinrick. His presence at the Torgesen T was a magnet, and despite the warnings in her heart, Lilly couldn't stop herself from scanning the horizon as she left the ranch, certain she would see him and strangely disappointed when she didn't. Of course, if she had, she would have ignored him, but still, the fact that he seemed to be avoiding her registered an odd despondency in her heart.

Mrs. Torgesen did resemble a willow tree. Lilly's mother dug up a half bottle of Christmas dye, and Lilly colored the lace overcoat a rose leaf green. The three shades of green blended into a pleasing harmony, and Mrs. Torgesen bubbled with delight as she sashayed around the kitchen during the final fitting.

"Lilly, dear, fetch the millinery box from the parlor, will you? I want you to see the new hat I ordered from Chicago. It came on yesterday's train."

Yesterday's train! Lilly had been so busy, she'd forgotten about the mail train the day before. Her heart pounded as she retrieved the hatbox. There might be a letter from Reggie waiting in her mailbox right now.

Lilly set the box down on the kitchen table. Mrs. Torgesen opened it and wiggled out a wide-brimmed, purposely misshapen hat. It was long and oval, meant to be propped low and sideways on Mrs. Torgesen's head. The brim curled like an upturned lip in the back and sported three layers of transparent white lace wound around the bowl. A flurry of leftover lace dangled from the back like a tail. The crowning feature of Mrs. Torgesen's new hat was a molded bluebird, nestled in the lacey layers and snuggled up to the shallow bowl of the hat in the front. Lilly swallowed a laugh — a bird in the willow! Mrs. Torgesen plopped the hat on her blond head and tied the mauve satin sash under her chin.

"Well?"

Lilly shook her head slowly. "Amazing."

Mrs. Torgesen glowed. "Well, just because one lives in the middle of a wasteland doesn't mean one has to blend!" She let out a hearty laugh, as did Lilly. The one thing Erica Torgesen *didn't* do was "blend."

The sun was still a high brilliant orb as Lilly stepped out into the Torgesen yard. Mrs. Torgesen had paid her well, and Lilly headed for town to pick up more sugar for her mother's currant jam, also planning a quick stop at the post office.

Lilly tugged on the brim of her straw hat and tucked her basket into the crook of her arm. A hot breeze whipped past her and brought with it a horse's whinny. Lilly shot a glance toward the corral just in time to sight a cowboy riding in astride a magnificent bay. The man didn't notice her. His shoulders sagged as if from exhaustion, and dust layered him like a second skin. But, as he dismounted, Lilly plainly recognized Heinrick. She gasped and reined in her traitorous heart. Her feet seemed rooted to the ground. Heinrick looped the horse's reins over the fence and turned toward the house.

In a breathless moment, Heinrick's eyes fastened upon her, and a wave of shock washed over his face. It seemed as though, in that instant, some film fell away from him and she could see him clearly, unfettered by prejudice and stereotypes. He was a man etching out a life on the prairie, building simple hopes, maybe a home and a family, just like every pioneer before him. The sense of it overwhelmed her, shredding her resolve to turn a hard eye to him. Trembling, Lilly bit her lower lip and blinked back tears.

A smile nipped at the corners of Heinrick's mouth. She waited for it to materialize into fullness, but he abruptly extinguished it and offered a curt nod instead, tugging on the brim of his hat. He didn't move, however. They stood there, fifteen feet apart, staring at each other, and Lilly felt the gulf of an entire ocean between them. The desire to tell him she was sorry and ask how he was doing pulsed inside her. But she stayed mute.

Heinrick finally pulled off his leather gloves, tucked them into his chaps, and turned away from her. She watched him lumber toward the bunkhouse, feeling in his wake the weight of his loneliness.

She carried it all the way into Mobridge.

Independence Day preparations had sparked the town into activity. Westward, near the Missouri, Lilly spied the makings of the Fourth of July fair: unfamiliar rigs, buckboards, tents, and various prize livestock. On the other end of town, stood makeshift cattle pens and a large corral. In two days, cowboys from all over South Dakota would gather to duke it out with untamed beasts in the Mobridge rodeo. Lilly loved the exotic, recaptured display of bygone days from a now-tamed West. Reggie always participated as a hazer for his authentic cowboy buddies. A rugged memory hit her like a warm gust of wind. In his nut-brown leather cowboy hat, the one with the Indian braid dangling down the back, and his fringed sandy-colored chaps, Reggie easily passed for a ranch hand, and a dashing one, besides.

Despite the fresh ache of Reggie's absence, Lilly knew Mobridge desperately needed the rodeo and the mind-numbing gaiety of Independence Day. They needed to celebrate with gusto, to remind themselves why they sacrificed, all of them — mothers, sons, wives, and husbands. They were at war to make the world safe for freedom, for independence.

Lilly jumped at the *hee-haw* of a late model Packard. She skittered to the side of the street and watched a mustard yellow Roadster roll by, the *oohs* and *aahs* of admiring farmers rolling out like a red carpet before it. Lilly smirked. Clive's Model T wouldn't be the only attraction in town over the holiday.

Ernestine's burst with shoppers, most of whom had unfamiliar tanned faces. A handful of Russian women, their wide, red faces glistening under colorfully dyed headscarves, haggled with Willard over a batch of home-canned sauerkraut and pickles. Their jumbled words stirred a memory within Lilly, and at once, Heinrick's sharp, strange mother tongue filled her mind. She fought the image of his tired eyes and sagging shoulders.

"What do you want today, Lilly?" Ernestine barked.

"Two pounds of sugar, please?"

Ernestine pinched her lips and searched under the wooden countertop for an extra burlap bag. She filled it with sugar and passed it over to Lilly. "Bring the bag back."

Lilly paid Ernestine, turned, and plowed straight into Marjorie's mother, Jennifer Pratt.

"Be careful, girl!" Mrs. Pratt exclaimed.

Lilly blushed. "Excuse me, Mrs. Pratt."

Mrs. Pratt's voice softened. "How are you, Lilly?"

"Fine, thank you. How is Marjorie?"

"She's at the armory. Why don't you stop in and ask her yourself?"

Lilly tried not to notice the stares of three other women who had turned curious eyes upon her as soon as Mrs. Pratt announced her name. Shame swept through her bones.

"I'll do that," she mumbled. "Good day, ma'am."

Mrs. Pratt nodded and moved past her. Lilly made for the door.

She stopped next at the post office. Lilly's heart did a small skip when the clerk handed her not only a letter from Reggie, but also one for Olive, from Chuck. Her sister would be ecstatic. She tucked both into the pocket of her apron as she crossed the street and headed to the armory.

The former one-room tavern swam with the odor of mothballs, cotton fibers, and antiseptic. A handful of uniformed girls ripped long strips of cloth.

Marjorie appeared every inch a Red Cross volunteer as she cut and wound long sheets of muslin and assembled first aid kits to send to the front. Over her calico prairie dress, she wore a standard-issue Red Cross white cotton pinafore, with two enormous pockets sewn into the skirt. Pinned on her head was a fabric-covered pillbox hat emblazoned with a bright red cross on the upturned crown.

"Lilly!" Marjorie dropped her fabric onto a long table and embraced her friend. "Did you hear the news?"

"What news?"

Marjorie's eyes twinkled. "Harley proposed."

"What?"

Marjorie grinned. "His last letter said he couldn't keep fighting without knowing I was pledged to him and our future. We'll be married as soon as he returns."

"But Marj, what if he doesn't come back?" Lilly instantly clamped a hand over her mouth, wishing her words back.

Marjorie gaped at her. "How can you say that? Of course he'll be back."

"I'm so sorry. Please forgive me."

Marjorie's anger dissolved, and she gathered Lilly into a forgiving hug. "No harm done. I know you're worried, too."

Tears pooled like a flash flood, spilling from Lilly's eyes. "I keep telling myself Reggie will be all right," she whispered. "I just wish I knew for sure that he would come home."

Marjorie looped her arm through Lilly's. She led her away from curious ears. "Let's not think about it. There is nothing we can do anyway. We just have to wait."

Lilly wiped the tears with her fingertips, already feeling her composure returning. But they had left their mark. Obviously, she missed Reggie more than she realized. She hadn't cried over him since receiving his last letter.

The pair stared out of a grimy window onto the street, at women lugging loaded baskets and dirt-streaked children running with hoops. Morrie stood in his doorway, his apron stained with shaving cream and strands of hair. A pack of cowboys emerged from Flanner's café. Some straddled their horses while another group surrounded the Packard, wishing for a more sophisticated form of transportation.

"By the way, are you all right?"

"What?" Lilly glanced at Marjorie and frowned.

"You can tell me, Lilly. Did he force you to help him?"

Lilly peeled her arm from Marjorie's grasp. "What are you talking about?"

Marjorie's eyes darted away, then back to Lilly. She lowered her voice. "The foreigner. I heard all about it from my sister. She said he grabbed you and forced you to drive him home."

So that was the local story. Or, at least one version of it. She shook her head. "That's not how it happened, Marj."

Marjorie paled. "What do you mean, Lilly? Did something else happen?"

Lilly held her friend's hands. "Listen, I will only say this once because, frankly, I am trying to forget it happened. The Craffey boys attacked Heinrick. It was unprovoked, no matter what anyone says, and entirely mismatched. I felt sorry for him, so I butted in."

Marjorie's eyes widened. "Heinrick?"

Lilly's face heated. "Forget I told you. I've already forgotten it and him."

Marjorie peered at her friend, as if seeing into her soul. "You don't look like you've forgotten it, Lilly. You're blushing."

"Am I?" Lilly's mouth went dry, and she dropped Marjorie's hands as if they were ice. "I'm just embarrassed, that's all."

Marjorie stepped away from her, her eyes skimming her in one quick sweep. "Right."

Marjorie's mistrust felt like a slap. She winced and wanted to argue, but for a moment, in her friend's suspicious eyes, she saw the truth. Despite the fact she'd rejected the enemy and turned her back on Heinrick, his sapphire eyes glimmered steadily in her mind. He was far from forgotten.

CHAPTER 9

Lilly headed to a bluff overlooking the Missouri, a nook nestled in the shade of a few now withering maples, to read Reggie's letter. The sun, a salmon-colored ball, bled out along the horizon. As the wind loosened her unkempt braid, a meadowlark sang a tune from the fallow field nearby. The smell of dust and drying leaves urged feelings of fall, although the summer heat spilled perspiration down the back of her cotton dress.

This letter was longer, the writing blocked and smudged in places. Lilly determined to analyze each agonizing detail and truly know the cold he'd described in his last letter. More than that, she hoped to sense they were together somehow, that they could bridge this awful, growing chasm between them.

My Dearest Lilly,

I hope this letter finds you well. It's been two weeks since my last batch of mail, and I have concluded that the mail service has fallen into the hands of ineptitude, as has much of this man's army. Although I am proud to be serving the Red, White, and Blue and can say I know it my Christian duty to protect the ideals of democracy, I am sometimes weakened by the lack of supplies and the ever-worsening conditions. I know, in principle, this is not a result of Pershing's leadership or even of President Wilson. Rather, it is the result of too much war, too little sleep, too few supplies, and, worse yet, too many casualties.

I sit now in a reserve trench. Dawn approaches, long shadows licking the edges of the gully where I sleep, eat, and spend my off days. Others head for a nearby village, where they take refuge in French cafes, taverns, and, I fear, boardinghouses within the arms of French women. But of this I do not know firsthand, of course. I will sit here today and try and sleep on my helmet or on one of the many lice-covered bunks left in the shallow dugouts. Oh, how I loathe lice! I feel them move over me as if my skin is somehow unhappy on my bones and seeks to new habitation. I have been without a bath for so long, I have forgotten the sense of water upon my body. How I long for the Missouri.

I spent the last week on the front lines, in the firing trench, curled in a dugout while the cover trench lobbed shells over my sleepless head. We are awake at night, searching the darkness for foreign bodies that attempt to cut the barbed wire and murder us in our gopher holes. God has preserved me thus far so I know He must be hearing your prayers. One morning, as the dawn revealed the unlucky, I saw that two of my compatriots had been struck. One was a Brit named Martin and the other a fellow Dakotan from Yankton, who had received so much mail here we dubbed him Lucky Joe. I remembered then a moment of agonized cries and frenzied shelling, like lightning in the sky, and knew a firefight had been waged a mere hundred yards from me. And where was I in that desperate moment? Blinking through the darkness, holding at bay the erratic, armed shadows. I know, Lilly, if I blink too long, one of those shadows will emerge, and then I will be the one to sleep forever, slain in this muddy dugout.

Poor Lucky Joe. He often told me of his parents' small wheat plot and worried about their fate with their crops this year without him. He was their only son.

I will not think about it. I will come home to you and our future. It is for you I fight, you and our God-ordained dreams.

Mother, in her last letter, told me you

were among those to help house and feed a group of Wyoming doughboys, headed east in May. My heart was both envious to think of those boys having the advantage of seeing your lovely face and pleased my future bride is so faithful in her outpouring of love and concern. I am proud of you, Lilly-girl, and wrote my mother precisely that in a recent letter.

Is it warm there? Did your lilies bloom this year? I remember how tediously you tended them in years past. How are Bonnie and DJ? Chuck tells me all is well with Olive, and I am glad for him. He carries her picture in his helmet.

The sunlight is upon us, and I hear the clang of the kitchen bell. This morning, perhaps, I will get a hot meal. Please hold on to the promises we made and write to your soldier doing his part at the front.

Yours,
Reggie

Lilly smoothed the letter on her lap, and her throat burned. Fixing her eyes on the streak of orange that scraped against the far bluffs, she fought the image of Reggie lying in a dugout hole, a lone man holding back the German lines. On Sunday, she would say an extra-fervent prayer for his safety. Lilly closed her eyes and searched her heart for any sins that might somehow, through Divine justice, send a bullet into Reggie's hideout. She didn't have to dig far to unearth one. It was painfully clear she must fight every errant, impulsive thought of Heinrick, his jeweled eyes, and the way she felt embraced by his smile. She must purge the German from her mind and instead cling to the future Reggie had planned. She must do her part to help Reggie come home alive — tend to her letters and never think of anyone but Reggie again. Ever.

A hawk screamed and soared into the horizon, where it melted into the sunset. Behind her, the wind rustled the drying leaves of the maples. They seemed to sizzle as they shattered and fell. The prairie was drying up. The world was at war. And Lilly's future seemed as fragile as the maple leaves.

Lilly held the reins to a dozing Lucy and patted the horse's soft velvet nose. The Appaloosa's eyes were glassy mirrors, glinting the barely risen sun. She gazed at Lilly and seemed to ask, "What am I doing here?"

Lilly rubbed her hand along the forelock of the twenty-year-old mare. "I don't think this is a great idea, either, old girl. Just be careful and don't go too fast."

Not far off, Lilly caught a different set of instructions delivered by her father to his antsy ten-year-old son. "Ride like the wind, Frankie. Don't let those other cowboys nose in front of you. Keep your eyes straight ahead and remember you're a Clark!" He clamped the boy on the shoulder, and Lilly stifled a giggle as Frankie nearly landed in the dirt.

"I don't know, Donald. . . ." Mrs. Clark pinned her husband with a worried look.

"He'll be fine," he assured her.

Lilly tugged on Frankie's beat-up hat as swung into the saddle. "Behave yourself." She knew he had other plans in mind — another route for the race that might indeed place the youngster at the head of the pack. A piercing gunshot ripped through the morning air. Frankie urged Lucy to the starting line. From Lilly's point of view, Frankie would have a time just getting the horse up the hill out of Mobridge, let alone all the way to the Torgesen T and back. Frankie grinned like a hyena, oblivious to the fact he was the youngest contender. Lucy fought sleep. Then the next shot rang out and the pack exploded. Frankie kicked Lucy, wiggled in his saddle, and plowed his way through the dust churned up by the other horses. The horde had long vanished by the time Frankie disappeared behind the bluffs.

Lilly plopped down on the picnic blanket and watched the sun stretch golden fingers into the first hours of the Independence Day picnic. Two hours later, every rider had returned but Frankie. Mrs. Clark sent her husband furious glances as she squinted toward the north. Lilly fought the urge to betray Frankie's plan to cheat and cut a shortcut across the Clark farm to the Torgesen T. Just when she'd decided to turn him in, he and Lucy appeared on the horizon. As they plodded closer, she noticed two things: He and old Luce were covered to their hips in Missouri mud, and he wasn't alone.

Frankie rode in sporting a sheepish grin, bursting with an obvious story to tell. An exuberant crowd greeted him as if he were a doughboy returning from war. But Lilly's eyes were glued to the cowboy in the wide milky ten-gallon hat and muddy black chaps, who beamed like he'd caught the canary. His blue eyes twinkled, and he pinned them straight on Lilly.

Lilly crossed her arms against her chest, turned to Frankie, and ignored the man she couldn't seem to get rid of.

His father helped Frankie down from Lucy, and his mother wrapped him in a fierce hug. Ed Miller, the race official, pushed through the crowd. He glared at Frankie, and demanded an explanation.

Commanding the crowd like a well-seasoned preacher, Frankie spun a tale of adventure and peril. He glossed over the part where he cheated and focused on the usually free-flowing Missouri tributary he'd attempted to cross during his shortcut to win the race.

"Good Ole Luce fought like a rattler caught by the tail, but the mud sucked her down!" All grins, Frankie described Lucy's battle with the clay only the Missouri could produce. Lilly grimaced as she pictured Lucy slogging about in panic, gluing herself and Frankie to the riverbed.

"I tried to break her free, but finally gave up. There weren't anything I could do but holler," Frankie said. To illustrate, he bellowed loudly over the crowd, which elicited riotous laughter from the other competitors.

"I was just plain lucky this here cowboy was near enough to hear me." Frankie gestured to his hero and grinned in glowing admiration. Heinrick, who had moved with his mount to the fringes of the crowd, kept his head down and tugged on his hat. Lilly's heart moved in pity for him. Obviously, he didn't want to revive any previous memories of his appearance in town. But if any of the folks recognized him, they stayed mute. Frankie continued his saga by describing how Heinrick had wrestled Lucy and Frankie from the grip of the mud with an old bald cottonwood.

When Frankie finished his tale, Ed dressed him down, then clamped him on the shoulder. "I do believe, son, you win the award for most daring contestant." The crowd erupted in good-natured cheering. Even Lilly's father, who had listened with a frown and pursed lips, gave in to forgiveness and tugged on his son's grimy hat.

The crowd dispersed, and Frankie pulled his father over to meet his hero.

"Thank you," Mr. Clark said to Heinrick as he pumped the German's hand.

Heinrick shrugged. "Glad to help." Lilly noticed the proud, triumphant smile had vanished, and in his eyes lurked that lonely, desperate look she'd seen earlier.

"Would you like to stick around for some breakfast? My wife's fixed up some hotcakes and has some homemade peach preserves in her basket."

Lilly's heart jumped. She heard Olive's quick intake of breath behind her. Heinrick looked past her father to Lilly, reaching out to her with his blue eyes and holding her in their magical grip. His tanned face was clean-shaven this morning, although his hair was longer, curling around his ears and brushing the collar of his red cotton shirt. He shifted in his saddle, considering her father's request, all the time staring at Lilly, who felt herself blush. She forced herself to close her eyes and look away.

When she opened them, Heinrick was shaking his head and extending his hand again to her father.

"Thank you, sir. But I'm afraid I need to prepare for the rodeo this evening, and I don't have time."

Mr. Clark nodded. "I can understand that well enough, son. Maybe another time."

"Sounds good," Heinrick returned, a smile pushing at his mouth. He tossed a last glance at Lilly, one eyebrow cocked, and an inscrutable, almost teasing look pulsed in his eyes. Lilly gasped, and the blood simmered in her veins. The nerve of him, suggesting she was wrong and he could be accepted as a friend into their family! Well, her father didn't know he was shaking hands with a German in front of the entire town. Lilly shot Heinrick a halfhearted glare. To her chagrin, Heinrick only gave her a delighted smile. Then he pulled on his hat again, spurred his quarter horse, and trotted toward the Torgesen T.

"Who was that?" gasped Bonnie, her eyes saucers.

Lilly produced an exaggerated shrug, turned away, and pulled Chris from Olive's arms. Olive's dark eyes smoldered. Lilly offered an innocent smile. She'd done nothing to encourage their father's offer, and could she help it if Heinrick had been the only cowboy willing to lend a hand to a scared ten-year-old boy?

Heinrick's comment puzzled her, however. He couldn't possibly be riding in the rodeo, could he? Certainly, Mrs. Torgesen and Clive wouldn't allow him off the ranch to share their little secret. She still hadn't figured out how he'd come to work for them in the first place. But she would never know, because she would never ask.

The blistering sun was on its downward slide, and the heat was dissipating. Still, sheltered in a merciful trace of shade next to the Clark wagon, little Chris's downy curls were plastered to his head in a cap of sweat as he nestled against Lilly. She'd spent the last hour watching her nephew sleep and harnessing her relentless obsession with the mysterious German. Thankfully, thinking upon the events of the fair gave her some respite.

Practically overnight, their little town had become a metropolis, including a fine display of motorized vehicles and parasol-toting French prairie ladies. Their stylish outfits seemed outlandish, however, among the handful of sensible farm wives who wouldn't be caught dead at a picnic in spike-heeled boots and a suit coat. Even so, Lilly and her sisters wore their Sunday best: high-necked blouses, puffy sleeves with lace-trimmed cuffs, and empire-waist cotton skirts. Her mother had even dusted off her wide-brim fedora, saying, "It will keep my face out of the sun."

The picnic started shortly after the race with a weight-guessing contest. Someone suggested they guess the weight of Erica Torgesen, who wasn't there, fortunately, and the townspeople erupted in good-humored laughter. They resorted to guessing the weight of Hans Sheffield's prize burnt-red duroc, and Lilly cheered when Frankie nabbed the prize with a guess of 942 pounds.

Since no one had a scale, they took the word of Hans, who was delighted to hand over the city's prize — free lemonade at Miller's. Frankie and a flock of boys migrated into town and started a stampede that lasted most of the day, until Miller announced he'd run out of juice.

The rest of the picnic continued with an array of harmless amusements from prairie dog chasing to pie eating to rock skipping in the shallow, muddy Missouri. Lilly stayed glued to Olive, watching little Chris and avoiding curious looks from Mobridgites who, she supposed, toyed with the idea she might have been kidnapped. Gratefully, she heard not a scandalous word, and, by the end of the day, Lilly decided the entire event had succumbed to a quiet, merciful death.

"I'm going home now." Olive's lanky shadow loomed over Lilly. "Are you coming with me?"

Lilly considered Chris's sleeping form. His eyes were so gently closed they looked like film. Not a worry lined his face. A small spot of drool moistened her blouse where his lips were propped open and askew. Oh, to be so young, naïve, be gathered inside safe arms and believe the world was in control. "No,"

Lilly said. "I'm going to the rodeo."

Lilly ignored Olive's vicious glare. She climbed to her feet, eased Chris from her arms, and gently handed him to Olive. Olive marched away, his head bouncing against her bony shoulder.

Lilly beat back the hope of seeing Heinrick and ambled toward the rodeo grounds.

CHAPTER 10

The rodeo grounds teemed with spectators, animals, and anxious cowboys. A pungent brew of dust, animal sweat, hay, and manure hung in the air. The familiarity of it moved a memory in Lilly and she couldn't stop the twinge of guilt. Last year, it had been Reggie she'd come to watch.

Lilly spotted Erica Torgesen perched in all her green finery on the seat of her covered surrey and went to greet her.

"You're looking wonderful tonight, Mrs. Torgesen," Lilly said, grinning.

Mrs. Torgesen winked at her. "You're an angel, Lilly. Already Alpha Booth from Eureka and Eve Whiting have asked for your name. And I gave it to them!" She clasped her hands together, beaming as if she'd just published her best apple pie recipe.

"Thank you," Lilly replied before blending into the swelling crowd. Mrs. Torgesen's reference could mean more business for her, which would in turn help her family. Glancing over her shoulder, she giggled, deciding the eccentric Norwegian resembled a queen upon her throne, peering over her subjects with her little bird in a nest.

Lilly threaded through the crowd to the makeshift bleachers, constructed from dead cottonwood and oak trees dragged from the drying riverbed. Those who didn't want to sit on the skeletons of old trees found stumps or stood on the back of wagons.

Marjorie had commandeered for them a place on the upper branch of a wide peeled cottonwood at the south end of the corral. Lilly climbed aboard next to her friend just in time for the first event. Somehow, the town officials had rounded up more than a smattering of eager cowboys. A group of cowpunchers lined up at the animal pens, adjusting their spurs, straightening their fur chaps, and wiping the sweat from the lining of their Stetsons.

Ed Miller mounted the announcer's platform and yelled over the audience. He read the names of the contestants for the steer wrestling competition. Twenty brave cowboys lined up, and, one by one, young steers were loosed. Lilly's heart beat a race with the hazers as they kept the animals on course. She winced when the bulldoggers ran a steer down on horseback, tackled it, and wrestled the hapless animal to the ground. But the animals pounced to their feet, unscathed.

Occasionally, she broke her attention to search the stands for Heinrick. He was nowhere to be found.

The bulldoggers worked quickly, and a cowpoke named Lou out of Pierre took first prize. Calf roping was next, and another set of unlucky creatures ran through the gamut. Two cowboys from Rapid City won the ten-dollar prize. Sandwiched between events, a clown, Ernestine's Willard, entertained the crowd with cornball antics. His real job was to protect the cowboys from dangerous, enraged animals. Lilly decided he was the perfect clown.

Frankie claimed fifth place in the youth barrel racing event on an exhausted Lucy.

The grand finale was bronco riding, and Lilly was shocked to hear Clive Torgesen's name announced as a contender.

"I saw him bucked off a mustang just last week," she whispered into Marjorie's ear. Marjorie arched her brows in astonishment. Lilly knew Clive's bragging often left an entirely different impression, so she nodded and returned a grim look.

From Ed Miller's introduction, Lilly found out that Clive's bronc, dubbed Jester, had a habit of slamming his body into the fence, squashing his rider's legs. Lilly leaned forward on the branch and held her breath, suddenly thankful for Willard.

The bronc tore out of its pen like a frenzied

bee, furious and craving blood. Clive made a valiant show and stayed on for five entire seconds. When Jester finally threw him, he hung in the air, as if taking flight upon a hot gust of wind, and the crowd held their breath in a collective gasp. When he hit the ground, Lilly heard his breath whoosh out as clearly as if he'd landed in her lap. The stands quieted while Willard raced after the bronco and quickly succeeded in snaring his loose reins. He pulled the skittering beast through the exit gate, then rushed to Clive.

Clive rose feebly to his elbows, and it seemed all of South Dakota erupted in a massive cheer. Even Lilly clapped, wondering how he'd managed to stay on that bronco.

The prize went to a fresh young cowpoke from Minnesota, Patrick Hanson. A congregational murmur of appreciation ascended from the stands. The rodeo had managed a decent showing.

Disappointment flickered briefly in Lilly's heart. She doused it quickly, disgusted that she'd wanted to see Heinrick at all, let alone see him perform in a rodeo. But why had he lied to her father?

Ed Miller shot a rifle in the air, the sound creating a cascade of unhappy responses from nearby livestock, as well as mothers with sleeping babes. He held up his arms, and the crowd settled into expectant silence.

"Stick around, folks, we have a new event

this evening! Fresh from Wyoming, where cowboys know how to ride the wind, comes — bull riding! This Brahma bull will make your blood curdle! One look at this beast will remind you why cowboys don't ride bulls. We've even found three courageous cowpokes who will give it a go! Please welcome Lou Whitmore from Pierre, Arnie Black from the Double U, and Henry Zook from the Torgesen T!"

Lilly's heart went dead in her chest. It couldn't be. "Heinrick," she whispered.

Marjorie shot Lilly a quizzical look.

Lilly sought out Erica Torgesen's face in the crowd. The woman smiled and chatted with her neighbors, unaffected. Something wasn't quite right. Maybe it wasn't Heinrick. . . .

Then, there he was, on the platform, next to Lou and Arnie, waving his hand to the crowd, his crooked grin flavoring his face with amusement.

What was Heinrick thinking? Those bulls had horns — sharp ones!

"Is that *your* Heinrick?" Marjorie breathed into her ear.

"He's not my Heinrick," Lilly hissed.

"Of course he's not," Marjorie said indignantly. "You know what I mean."

Lilly bit her lip and nodded slowly.

"He's got spunk," said Marjorie in amazement.

"He's going to kill himself," Lilly replied, horrified.

Lou from Pierre sailed through the air. He landed with a grunt and scrambled to his feet. The bull raced after him like a dog to a bone. He swung his massive head, slashing the air, and missed skewering Lou by a hair as the bull rider dove under the fence. The Brahma's bulky frame thudded against the corral. The wood cracked, the sound like a whip, stinging the crowd and extracting a chorus of gasps from terrified women and children. Marjorie covered her mouth with her hands and went ashen. Lilly clenched her fists in her lap.

Having dispatched Lou, the bull turned and memorized the horror-struck crowd, as if searching for his next victim. His black eyes bulged, furious. He breathed in great hot gusts. Fear took control of Lilly's heartbeat. Heinrick was a greenhorn, a laborer from Europe, big but inexperienced. He would be, in a word, sausage. He was either a fool or the bravest man she'd ever met.

Arnie Black from the Double U fared worse than Lou. He escaped the bull's razor-sharp horns only because Willard the Clown rolled a tall rain barrel in his direction. Arnie dove in a second before the bull grazed the back-side of his britches. The Brahma rammed the barrel around the corral until it lodged under the bottom of a flimsy fence rail. Arnie scrambled out, breathing hard.

Willard, turning out to be a braver man than Lilly assumed, opened the exit gate and flagged the bull through where three cowpunchers herded him into the starting pen.

Heinrick straddled the pen, one leg on each side of the narrow stall. When ready, he would wind his hand under the rope that encircled the bull's massive body and jump aboard. Lilly held her breath. Heinrick rolled up his sleeve, worked his ten-gallon down on his head, and tugged on his leather glove. His face was grim, his mouth set, and he didn't spare a glance at the crowd. After an eternal moment, he slipped his hand under the belt and nodded. Lilly's heart skidded to a stop.

The bull shot out of the pen, snorting, heaving his body as if possessed. His powerful back legs kicked; he threw himself forward, jerked his head from side to side, whirled and twisted. The stunned crowd was so silent, Lilly could hear Heinrick grunt as the bull jolted him. But he hung on. Five seconds, six. The disbelieving crowd began to murmur. Then the Brahma started to spin, a frenzied cyclone of fury. Lilly covered her mouth to seal her horror. How would Heinrick stay on for the required eight seconds? He would whistle off like a piece of lint, and the bull's horns would spear him on takeoff. Lilly squeezed her eyes shut, then forced them open.

Willard grabbed a red handkerchief and readied himself to dash into the ring.

Suddenly, Heinrick freed a war whoop that sounded like a forgotten echo from the valley of the Little Bighorn. He flung his hand up over his head and rode the bull, melding into the whirlwind spin. Man and beast seemed to flow and dance as if they were one.

A nervous titter rippled through the audience.

Round and round the pair twirled. Lilly lost count of the turns and only watched, mesmerized. Heinrick's powerful legs gripped the sides of the bull and his hat flew off, his blond hair a tangled mass flopping about his head. Lilly could see the muscles ripple through his wide forearm, steady and taut as he clung to the belt. The violence of the event made her reel, yet the raw courage that it took to wrestle a two-ton beast awed her.

A shot fired, and Lilly nearly bolted from her skin. The eight-second mark! Heinrick spurred the bull, and the Brahma burst out of his erratic dance into a headlong stampede for the fence, bucking forward and back. A dusty hazer on a quarter horse shot up to the animal. Heinrick let go of the bull's belt, wrapped an arm around the waist of the cowboy, and slid off his perch. The bull snorted and bolted toward Heinrick. Heinrick hit the ground running and dove under the corral fence. The barrier stopped the Brahma, but as he pawed the dirt, his furious snorts pursued the escaping bulldogger. Willard whooped and sprang into the middle of the ring. The bull turned, considered, and then launched himself toward the next available prey. Willard's quick dash to the exit fence drew the animal like a magnet, and in a moment, he'd dispatched the bewildered bull into a safe holding paddock.

The crowd paused for a well-earned sigh of relief, then exploded in triumph. Henry Zook, whoever he was, was some sort of cowpuncher to last over eight agonizing seconds on a raging bull! Lilly's heart restarted in her chest. She trembled, blew out long breaths, and smoothed the wrinkles from her skirt. Heinrick was a strange brew of interesting surprises, at the very least.

Lilly watched the handsome blond German dust off his coal black chaps and climb the announcer's platform, embedded in riotous applause. Clive Torgesen followed him, waving to the crowd as if he himself had ridden the bull. Lilly's eyes narrowed. What was Clive up to?

Heinrick accepted the handshake and congratulations of a flabbergasted, but beaming Ed Miller. Clive Torgesen stood beside his hired hand, grinning like a Cheshire cat. Ed Miller raised his arms and calmed the crowd.

"Ladies and gentlemen, I am pleased to announce the winner of the first annual Mobridge bull riding contest — Henry Zook, from the Torgesen T!" The crowd burst into another chorus of applause that could have been mistaken for thunder roaring across the prairie. Then, as Ed handed the envelope containing the fifty-dollar prize money to Heinrick, Clive reached over and plucked it from Heinrick's grasp. The clapping died to a spattering.

"And, on behalf of Henry, who represented the Torgesen T in this momentous event, the Torgesen family accepts this award!" Clive waved the envelope above his head, and Lilly noticed Heinrick inhale deeply, his barrel chest rising. But the ever-present white smile never lost its brightness. The crowd offered a modicum of confused applause, which quickly died into a raucous murmuring as Clive thumped down the platform steps.

Lilly gaped in bewilderment. Why would Heinrick risk his life, then hand over the prize money — a half-year's salary for a cowhand? It didn't make sense at all. Heinrick Zook was a confusing tangle of secrets, and he intrigued her more than she wanted to admit.

CHAPTER 11

Long shadows crawled over the rodeo grounds. Lilly threaded through small clumps of townspeople absorbed in conversation. A sense of reluctance to abandon the illusive normalcy the rodeo, picnic, and fair provided hung heavy in the air.

Lilly was oblivious to the cheerful conversation. Heinrick and his perplexing behavior consumed her mind to the point of distraction. She meandered toward the cattle pens and stopped at the bullpen, where the Brahma raised its head and considered her. A thick rope was tightly knotted around his nose ring, and his wide sides moved in and out in largo rhythm. His eyes were fathomless black orbs, as if he, too, was trying to comprehend the evening's events.

Why did Heinrick give up his painfully earned prize money for a family who loathed him? She turned over the question in her head, examining it from every angle, discovering nothing.

Gooseflesh prickled her skin a second before clammy breath lathered the back of her neck. Lilly whirled. The pithy odor of whiskey hit her like a fist.

"Well, Miss Lilly. What are you doing over here, staring at the cattle?"

Lilly reeled as Clive Torgesen grabbed the rail behind her. His eyes were dark and swam with trouble.

Fear pounded an erratic beat in Lilly's heart. "Get away from me, Clive." She started to slide away.

Clive snaked out a hand and grabbed her by her slender arm. "Where are you going, Lilly?"

Lilly trembled, and her pulse roared like a waterfall in her ears. Her voice seemed but a trickle behind it. "Let go of me."

"You're such a pretty thing, Lilly. Don't think I haven't noticed over the years."

Lilly twisted and pulled her arm, but his grip tightened. A cold fist closed over her heart.

"Why, Lilly, it seems to me you should show your boss a little respect."

"You're not my boss," she bit out.

Clive laughed at her. "Sure I am, honey. You work for the Torgesen T." He leaned close, his unshaven chin scraping her cheek. "And that means you work for me."

Lilly bit her lip. Her knees went weak. "Let me go, Clive."

The smell of dust and sweat enclosed her, and dread pooled in Lilly's throat. She felt a scream gathering, but for some reason couldn't force it out.

Clive's whiskey breath was in her ear. "You know, Lilly, your boy Reggie ain't comin' back. Those Germans are going to kill him like a dog in the dirt, and then you'll need somebody to turn to." He loosed a savage chuckle. "I'm here for you, darling."

He raised his gloved hand, as if to stroke her cheek. Lilly glimpsed something odious prowling in his dark eyes. Fear shot through her; she lashed out, kicked him hard on the shin.

He swore, caught her other arm, and shook her. "Be nice!"

Lilly glanced over Clive's shoulder. *Please, God, anyone!* But the shadows had widened, and darkness layered the rodeo grounds. Along the bluff, campfires teased her with their safe glow.

"I'm going to scream, Clive."

"Go ahead, Lilly," Clive mocked her. "Who's gonna hear you?"

Lilly trembled as her courage fled. Tears blinded her.

"I will, Clive."

The voice came out of the darkness, with just enough accent for Lilly to recognize it at once.

"Let her go."

A smile curved up Clive's cheek. His eyes narrowed. "I'll be back," he promised as he shoved Lilly against the fence. He whirled. "Get outta here. This ain't none of your business." The curse that followed made Lilly sick. She shrank back, rubbing her arms, poised to bolt as soon as Clive was out of reach.

"What's wrong with you?" Heinrick's disgust thickened his voice, even through the haze of a German accent.

He stepped up to Lilly and held out his hand. "C'mon, miss." Clive slapped it down. "I said get outta here! Or you'll spend two more years hauling manure on the Torgesen T!"

Heinrick's voice was low, but Lilly detected a warning edge. "I paid you six months' worth tonight, Clive. Christmas, then I'm free. No longer than Christmas."

"We'll see about that." Clive shuffled closer and balled up his fist. The pungent odor of whiskey sauced the air.

Lilly knew she should run, but she couldn't move past the fear that had her rooted.

Heinrick sucked a deep breath, and his voice escaped with a sigh. "You're drunk, Clive. Go home."

"I'm going to skin you like a piece of Missouri driftwood," Clive sneered, undaunted.

A muscle tensed in Heinrick's jaw, but he blinked not an eye as he batted away Clive's fist. Clive roared and charged, throwing his arms around Heinrick's waist. The German stepped back and easily tossed Clive to the ground. Clive wobbled to his knees and wheezed.

Lilly's fingers bit into her arms as she waited for Heinrick to resign Clive, face-first, to the dirt. Instead, Heinrick swiped Clive's fallen Stetson from the ground and held it out. "Go home, Mr. Torgesen. It's late, and you're tired."

Clive cranked his head upward and glared at Heinrick, his brown hair matted, a line of drool dangling from his lips. He leaned back on his haunches and lunged for his hat, snaring, instead, Heinrick's forearm. He yanked hard and landed a blow on the German's cheek. It echoed like the snap of an old cottonwood.

Heinrick jerked back. He set his jaw, and his eyes hardened to ice. His fists balled, but he held them to his sides. "Okay, that's enough. Go home, Boss."

The exertion of that one punch had emptied Clive. He gaped at Heinrick, his mouth askew, confusion glazing his eyes.

Heinrick stepped toward Lilly and again extended his hand. She hesitated, then slid hers into it. His hand was warm and firm and held hers with gentleness. Lilly scooted around Clive like a jittery cat.

Lilly and Heinrick marched ten quick, solid

paces before he released her hand. It continued to tingle, and she felt the absence well. Heinrick had saved her. The significance of that hit her hard, and she squinted at the man she'd considered her enemy.

"I never did get your name," Heinrick said, his eyes ahead.

Lilly fought a war of emotions. He was still a foreigner, the enemy. But as she walked next to him, hearing only the crunch of prairie grass and the beating of her heart, she knew that wasn't a fair assessment. He deserved courtesy, if not her friendship. "Lillian," she whispered. "But my friends call me Lilly."

"Lilly it is, then." A smile tugged at his lips.

They walked through the velvet darkness, the field grass crunching under their steps, the crickets singing from the riverbed not far off, and a lazy ballad humming over the bluffs from distant campfires. The wind skimmed the aroma from a pot of stew and carried it across the prairie. Lilly's stomach flopped, but not from hunger.

"I guess I owe you." She peeked at Heinrick and saw his smile widen.

"How's that?"

"You're one up on me. You saved Frankie and now me."

Heinrick chuckled, and Lilly was oddly delighted.

"Well, let me see. How can you save me?"

Lilly walked along and pondered that question, wondering what she could offer a man who seemed to carry the world in his wide palms, wondering even if she should. Curiosity swelled inside her. Who was this man, and why did he risk everything for the Torgesen T? The confusion stopped her short.

Heinrick walked out before her.

"Heinrick?"

He turned. "I haven't heard anyone use my name for nearly five years. It sounds like a song coming from your lips."

Lilly's delight was like a strong gust of warm wind. She felt an impending blush and bit her lip. But the endearing twinkle in his eyes mustered her courage. "Why did you give Clive your prize money?"

His expression darkened.

"What is it?" Lilly's heart fell, afraid she'd offended him after he'd been so kind to her. "I'm sorry."

Heinrick held up a hand to stave off her apology. He gazed into the protective obscurity of night. "I gave Clive the money because" — he cleared his throat but couldn't dislodge a distinct hoarseness — "they own me."

"What? How can they own you?"

Heinrick freed a sigh of pure frustration. "It's a long story, Lilly."

She crossed her arms. "I like stories."

Heinrick winced as if his words brought

pain. "I don't think that is a good idea."

He turned away, running a hand through his thick, curly hair. "Don't you remember? I'm the enemy. Your fiancé, Reggie, is being killed by my relatives." He blew out another breath, then turned back to her. "I'm dangerous."

A melancholy smile flickered over his face, but his eyes betrayed ache. "Or did you forget?"

Shame poured over Lilly. He was right, and the truth of it distanced them as if he was a coyote and she a long-eared jackrabbit. They were enemies.

Somehow, however, Lilly just couldn't muster up the feelings of loathing one ought to feel for an enemy. Today had changed all that. He'd gone out of his way to save Frankie and had toed up to Clive for her. Heinrick was too kind, too forgiving, too, well, downright honorable to be the enemy. And therein lay the paradox. She didn't want him to be an enemy. She wanted him to be Heinrick, her friend. It would mean nothing. Reggie was still her fiancé. She wasn't stepping past the boundaries of their covenant.

Heinrick wasn't part of the massacre. He was, in fact, a casualty himself, imprisoned and wounded by Clive and the Torgesen T. And he needed a friend. If Reggie were caught behind German lines, hurt and friendless, wouldn't she want some kind German *fraulein* to watch over him? The answer sealed her decision.

"You're not my enemy, Heinrick. I was wrong to call you that. Please forgive me."

His radiant smile nearly knocked her off her feet. "You're forgiven." His reply lit a glow of peace in Lilly's heart.

"Please," she said softly, "tell me your story."

Heinrick's eyes crinkled with delight. They turned and began to stroll across a prairie lit only by the windows of heaven and an unblemished full moon.

"Well, the Lord sure does bless a man when he is patient. To think my first friend in this new country is a pretty little lady named after a flower."

Lilly caught her breath, ignored the trembling of her heart, and slowly relaxed into the gentle rhythm of his step.

CHAPTER 12

Heinrick unfurled his story as they strolled into the black expanse of prairie. With each step, Lilly sensed that the telling was a catharsis, a long healing sigh after years of silence. The soft strength of his voice soon erased her haunting encounter with Clive.

"I was born in Germany, but my mother, Anna, was Norwegian. She came to Germany to study and lived in Hullhorst. My father worked as a farm hand in Neidringhausen, a nearby village." Heinrick swiped off his hat and rubbed the rim as he walked.

"As love stories go, Papa met her at a church social and they were married a few months later. My best memory of Mama is watching her roll out the *kuchen* in our tiny kitchen. She always gave me the first piece, sprinkled with sugar." He hummed. "I love the taste of a freshly fried roll *kuchen*." He paused, and she felt memory in his tone. "Mama was laughter and sunshine, sugar, kisses, and the smell of fresh bread." He paused again, this time longer. "I was eight when she died of typhoid fever."

Lilly bowed her head. "I'm sorry."

"My father never recovered," he said hoarsely. "To an eight-year-old, a father's despair can be felt as your own. I suppose I was really a . . . what do you call a person without parents?"

"An orphan."

"*Ja,* an orphan. My mother had family in Norway and distant cousins in America. They arranged passage when I was seventeen, five years ago. I've spent one year working for each family, paying off my passage." Heinrick's voice turned hard. "And then some."

The wind fingered the disobedient strands of Lilly's hair, tickling her neck. "So, the Torgesens *do* own you."

Heinrick sighed. He stopped and turned, his face a defined shadow in the darkness. "No, I was wrong to say that. The Torgesens don't own me. I came to America of my own will, and I chose to honor my promise, or rather my family's promise, to them. Perhaps they consider me their servant, but I serve them because I serve my Lord."

"Your Lord?"

"God Almighty, the Maker of the heavens and the earth."

Lilly nodded. "Of course. I am a Christian."

Joy glittered in Heinrick's eyes. "So am I!"

Lilly frowned. "How can you be — ?"

"Just because I am German doesn't mean I don't love and worship the same Jesus you do. Not all German Christians agree with Kaiser Bill. But we do agree the Lord Jesus is God and our hope for eternal life."

Lilly frowned. She hadn't considered that a foreigner, especially a German, would know the same God she did. She felt a strange kinship with this foreigner. "What will you do when your debt is paid?"

They began to walk again, bumping now and then when the prairie knocked them off balance.

"I don't know. Whatever God tells me to do, I suppose."

"Don't you have a plan? A dream?"

The breeze juggled Heinrick's laughter. "I have many dreams, Lilly. A family, a home, a good job, but most of all I dream of serving the Lord, wherever He desires to put me."

"How will you know? Who will tell you where that is?"

"God will, of course." Heinrick stopped, turned to her. "Doesn't God tell you what He wants you to do?"

Lilly stared past him, out into the sky, into the eternity where her God lived. "He doesn't have to. I already know."

Heinrick arched his brows.

"I'm going to marry Reggie when he comes home and be a pastor's wife. We have it all planned out."

"Who has it planned?" Heinrick said softly.

Lilly shivered. He wasn't just looking at her, he looked *into* her, examining her soul. The prairie was suddenly small, the night sky enclosing, the breeze cold, his presence invasive, and their walk, reckless.

The whinny of a horse shot through Lilly like an arrow. She whirled, squinted through the darkness, and recognized her father astride old Lucy. Frankie snoozed on Lucy's neck.

"I have to go," Lilly said quietly.

Heinrick nodded. He crossed his hands over his chest. Lilly stepped away, a tentative, grateful smile pushing at the corners of her mouth.

"Thank you for saving me, Heinrick."

Something in his eyes made her hesitate and halt her dash to intercept Frankie and her father. Standing there, with his shoulders sagging and with the wind shifting his golden mass of hair, Heinrick appeared every inch the orphan he'd described earlier. His eyes reached out to her with an almost tangible longing.

"Lilly, wait." Heinrick cupped a hand behind his neck and examined his scuffed boots. "You *can* save me back."

Lilly's eyes widened. "How?" She could hear Lucy scuffing closer.

"Teach me to read."

"What?"

"Teach me to read English. I never learned, and I'd like to be able to read and write."

Lilly glanced at her father. He hadn't seen them yet. Teach Heinrick to read? That would mean spending time with him, getting to know him.

It was a bad idea. She knew it in her heart. Her father may have been friendly this morning, extending the hand of fellowship to Heinrick when he thought him a ranch hand and Frankie's hero. But eventually he would find out he was German . . . then what? And what about Reggie? He could never know.

But Heinrick had called her a blessing. And he'd risked his freedom for her, standing up to Clive Torgesen. She owed him.

"Okay, one lesson, to teach you the alphabet. Agreed?"

He resembled a schoolboy with his churlish grin. "When?"

Her father was nearly within earshot. "Tomorrow, in the maple grove on the bluff near our property. Do you know where?"

Heinrick nodded.

"After church."

"I'll be there."

Lilly slipped into the envelope of darkness, heading toward Frankie and her father. The wind stirred the prairie grass, and Lilly thought she heard Heinrick call after her, "*Auf Wiedersehen,* Lilly."

CHAPTER 13

The condemnation that simmered in her chest during the morning worship service, under the glare of Reverend Larsen's stern sermon, threatened to turn her away from her promise. Then her mother had to ask her where she was off to when she breezed past her on the way to the maple glen.

"Going down to the river," Lilly answered, but shame settled upon her and deceit felt like a scarlet letter around her neck, even if based on the best of intentions. If Reggie found out, he would be cut to the core. At best, it would be hard to explain. At worst, he would leave her at the altar, resigning her to spinsterhood. She could be annihilating her dreams by this one simple meeting.

But the mystery of her German friend was just too puzzling to ignore. Since the day his mustang had almost plowed over her, Heinrick had been chipping his way into her thoughts. Her mind kept returning to a moon-basked prairie and the memory of a tall, muscled German disappearing into the folds of darkness. Heinrick's low, gentle voice, the syllables of foreign words, and his heart-filling laughter dulled her pangs of guilt. Moreover, Heinrick was a walking contradiction. There was something about him that seemed peaceful, unencumbered, even free. Yet he wasn't free. He was, for all practical purposes, an indentured servant, paying off a bill that seemed way too high. And he counted it as serving the Lord. He seemed even joyous about the task, and Lilly couldn't unravel the paradox in that. Bondage was not joyous. It was suffocating.

In the end, this riddle drove her to the river.

The maple glade had skimmed an adequate supply of cool air from the morning, and goose-flesh rose on Lilly's arms as she entered the shaded glen. A ripe river scent, rich in catfish and mud, rode in on the breeze and threaded through the trees. Lilly shoved a few rebellious, damp strands of hair under her hat, rubbed her arms, and hunted for her pupil.

He wasn't there. Lilly listened to the wind hiss through the leaves, feeling uneasy. Maybe it was for the best. She half-turned, poised to fly back to the farm and blot Heinrick from her memory, when he emerged from the shadows.

He peered at her with curious eyes and a

crooked smile. *"Guten tag."*

He'd dressed for the occasion: a clean pair of black trousers, polished ebony cowboy boots, a fire-red cotton shirt, and a buckskin vest. His blond hair may have been neatly combed, but the wind had laughed at his efforts and mussed it into wild curls. A hint of blond stubble peeked from tanned cheeks.

"You're here." Lilly gulped.

"Of course," he said. "I wouldn't miss it."

"Ready for school?" Lilly's voice sounded steadier than she felt. She shuffled toward him, dead leaves crunching beneath her boots.

He cocked his head, and a hint of mischief glinted in his blue eyes. "I'm not a very good student."

Nervousness rippled up Lilly's spine and spread out in a tingle over her body. Then Heinrick grinned wide and white, and his smile encircled her like an embrace. She had to admit he was just plain charming. She bit her lip and looked away, lest he see something he ought not to in her eyes.

His smile dimmed. "What is it, Lilly? Do you still think I'm the enemy?"

Lilly hid her eyes, staring at her shoes. "No, it's not that." Her mind raced. "I just don't know if I can help you. . . ."

Heinrick slid a hand under her elbow, and Lilly almost flew out of her skin. "I think you can help me more than you know."

The soft tone of his voice brought her gaze to his face. His eyes pleaded with her, and the longing in them took her breath away. "Please?" he whispered.

Since her mouth was dry and wordless, Lilly nodded.

"Let's sit by the river."

Heinrick led her into the sunshine, down the bluff, and they sat on a piece of bald cottonwood. Lilly pulled out her Bible, and passed it to him.

He held it in his large, rough hands and caressed the smooth leather with his thumbs. "A Bible," he murmured.

"Do you have one?"

"Of course, although mine is in German."

She nodded, letting that information digest. Then she flipped the Bible to Genesis. and read the first verse. "Reading is just a matter of decoding the letters, sounding them out to form words your ear already knows."

"My ear doesn't know many words."

"Heinrick, I've heard enough to know that you will read just fine. You have a wonderful vocabulary. And what words you don't know, I'll explain."

He nodded, and she continued the lesson. "Our English alphabet is made up of twenty-six letters. From these letters, you form words, using a few basic rules, which I will teach you. First, let's learn the letters."

She pointed out each letter from the text in

Genesis. He was a good student, despite his warning, turning each one over his tongue with little accent. Recognition came more quickly than she expected, and by the time the bluff swathed them in shadow, he'd read all the words in the first and second verses.

Lilly beamed at him. "You're a good student."

"Thanks," he said, his gaze buried in the Bible. He was running his finger over the third verse when she pulled the book from his grasp and folded it on her lap.

"Enough school," she declared. "Tell me why I've never met you before. I've been working for Erica Torgesen for almost a year."

"I only just arrived to the Torgesens. I've lived many places in America: New York City, Ohio, Milwaukee, Iowa, and now Dakota."

He acted as if it was normal to live so many places, like a homeless stray.

"I see," Lilly said, realizing how lonely his life must be. "Do you miss your home?"

He was silent, and when he turned to her, a thousand images gathered in his eyes. He blinked as if trying to get a fix on just one. Then the images dissolved, leaving a residue of pain in their wake. "Yes."

Lilly noticed how his hands curled over his knees, completely encasing them.

"But Germany isn't home anymore."

Lilly's eyebrows gathered her confusion.

"Dakota is home now. I am home wherever

God puts me, because I am in God's hands."

Lilly shook her head. "Home is family. Home is friends. God gives us those, but you certainly can't say that Reggie, or Chuck, or Harley are home."

"Perhaps. But to spend your entire life yearning for something else, instead of surrendering to God's plans seems like a foreign land to me. Home is peace. And peace is being where God puts you."

"And God has put you here, in bondage to the Torgesens?"

"For now. But I know He has a plan, just like He had a plan for Joseph in the book of Genesis. I just have to trust Him and wait."

"But what if . . . ?" The words lodged in her throat. She looked downstream, away from Heinrick.

"What if what, Lilly?"

"What if things get messed up; what if life doesn't go according to plan?" Lilly felt Heinrick's gaze on her neck and bit her lip. She knew she'd just opened her heart for his scrutiny.

"Whose plan?" he asked softly. His knee bumped hers as he turned toward her.

Lilly swallowed her leaden heart. "Well, our plan, of course. The plan of life, the one we spend our entire lives creating."

"Whose plan is it, though? Don't you think Joseph struggled over the death of his dreams, while trudging behind a caravan of camels on his way to Egypt? But he trusted God's plans, even while sitting in a prison, accused of a crime he didn't commit. God delivered him and a nation. Shouldn't all our plans belong to God?"

Lilly studied her fingernails, acutely aware of his gaze on her. "But God's plans are what the church and your parents say they are, aren't they? Isn't that God's voice?"

"It could be. God does speak through our church and family." He nodded slowly. "That's one way."

"How else, then, do you know what God wants you to do?"

Heinrick tapped her Bible. "God's Word. You have to read. God's plans are revealed one day at a time, through His Word and the Holy Spirit working in our lives."

Lilly rubbed the leather. "Listen, Heinrick. This is all very interesting, and I am sure, where you come from, it is part of your religion. But here, God leads me through my pastor, through my parents, and through Reggie. I just have to obey them to do what God wants."

Heinrick stared out over the water and beyond. "Lilly, do you know the difference between faith and obedience?"

Lilly's eyes narrowed and she shook her head warily. Whose lesson was this, anyway?

"Why wasn't Cain's sacrifice acceptable to God?"

Lilly frowned, confused. Heinrick's eyes gleamed, so intent was he on his sermon. He tucked a hand over hers on the Bible.

"Because it was a fruit offering?" she stammered, her gaze on his warm hand.

"No. It wasn't about the offering; it was about his heart. God looked at Cain and Abel first, then upon their offerings. He looked at their hearts and their faith. Cain's offering was all about fulfilling the law, about serving himself, about doing what was necessary to secure his forgiveness. But Abel's heart belonged to God, and he offered his lamb out of worship and faith in God's salvation. Abel's sacrifice was accepted because of his faith.

"Lilly, faith is an action. Obedience is a reaction. We obey God because we love Him, not because we want God to love us or want to earn a place in heaven."

Lilly lifted her chin. "Show me your faith, and I will show you my faith with actions."

Heinrick pulled the Bible from her hands and flipped through it. Silently he scanned the pages, then, blowing out a breath, he handed it back to her. "Could you read Hebrews 11:1 for me, please?"

She scowled at him, but found it and read aloud, " 'Now faith is the substance of things hoped for, the evidence of things not seen.' " Lilly closed the Bible.

" 'If you love me you will obey my

commands,' " she countered. She hadn't spent years softening a pew for nothing.

Heinrick sighed and again pulled God's Word from her lap. He flipped, wearing his determination like a mask. But, in time, his resonant tenor voice stammered out the verse. " 'For by grace are ye saved through faith; and that not of yourselves: it is the gift of God: Not of works, lest any man should boast.' " He paused. Lilly listened to the hammering of her heart.

When he at last spoke, the words seemed to unroll from his very soul, passionate, authentic, and nearly desperate.

"Lilly, God loves us so much that when we were still sinners, before we obeyed even His slightest desire, He died for us. We don't have to earn His love or His salvation. He has good things waiting for us, even if sometimes it doesn't seem like it. We have to be like Joseph. He put his life into God's hands on a daily, moment-by-moment basis. But to put your life into God's hands and to surrender to His plans, you need to know Him. You have to read the Bible to know what He wants you to do."

"I know the Bible. It says that faith is obedience."

"Obedience is evidence of faith, Lilly. It isn't faith itself. Faith is unwavering trust in God to lead and to guide, wherever He wants. And it is knowing, in the pit of your soul, that He loves you and knows best."

His eyes glowed with their intensity. She wanted to flinch, but his gaze drew her in, like a warm fire on a cold night. Heinrick passed her the Bible. "Hebrews 11:6."

No one had ever spoken to her this way, not Revernad Larsen and certainly not Reggie. It seemed edging near impropriety to be talking about God so openly, so intimately with anyone, let alone Heinrick. Yet she was drawn to the mystery of his God, and when she read the words, something seemed to ignite deep inside her.

" 'But without faith it is impossible to please him: for he that cometh to God must believe that he is, and that he is a rewarder of them that diligently seek him.' "

Lilly closed the Bible and rubbed the smooth leather.

"Lilly," Heinrick whispered, "do you have faith in God? Do you trust Him to plan and manage your life on His terms? Do you know He loves you?"

Lilly bit the inside of her lip to keep tears at bay. "I'm confused. I don't know God that well, maybe."

Heinrick's voice was soft, like a caress on her skin, yet his words still bruised. "Lilly, perhaps you're afraid. Do you think that if you knew God and heard His voice, He might tell you something you don't want to hear?"

Lilly swiped away a tear.

The sun polished the surface of the river platinum. "I need to get home," Lilly mumbled.

"And I have chores," Heinrick agreed, but his voice betrayed disappointment. He pushed himself from the driftwood, then turned and offered her his hand. Lilly deliberated, then slipped her hand into his.

"Tomorrow?" he asked. "I promise I'll be a good student."

"You were a good student today," she replied, lifting her chin. She stood almost to his shoulder and noticed how the buttons to his shirt pulled slightly across his wide chest. He put an arm around her waist and hauled her to the top of the bluff. They stood there for a moment, the wake of their conversation shifting between them like a fragrance neither could acknowledge.

"Tomorrow, after supper," Lilly blurted. Then she yanked her hand from his and ran toward home.

CHAPTER 14

Lilly sat on the bald cottonwood by the river watching the amber sky melt into the mud, listening to the crickets scold her for her naiveté. Why had Heinrick stood her up? After four days, she'd learned to count on his punctuality. He read with remarkable precision, and although she hated to admit it, his accented voice made warm syrup run through her veins. Her heart began to long for that moment when he turned his blue eyes into hers and asked for another lesson.

Where was Heinrick? Tears bit her eyes. How rude! Didn't he know that she dodged suspicion every time she raced down to the river to meet him? It was becoming harder to weave tales that only skimmed the definition of lies.

But she ached to see him. Heinrick was no longer a mystery, an enigma, to her. He'd ended each lesson with a story, something from his childhood. He wanted to own land. To travel. To have a family. And he longed for, more than anything, to find a niche for himself in this new world. He'd left it unspoken, but Lilly guess that Heinrick's deepest fear was his harsh reality — being forever a foreigner in his adopted homeland. She couldn't help feel as if he had handed her the delicate pieces of his heart.

And now that she'd seen it, she was drawn even more to the mysterious German, to his gentle character, his passionate love for God, his simple yet noble dreams.

Was this the end? Was it the end of his infectious laughter, his enthralling stories of an unruly boyhood in the Black Forest? Lilly dug her nails into her bare arms and steeled herself against the ripple of sorrow. How could she expunge the flame that he had ignited in her heart? The warmth of their friendship drew her to the bluff every evening like the glow of a beckoning campfire on a brisk autumn night. Somehow, even the July twilight would seem cold without Heinrick's smile.

Was Heinrick playing games? Maybe all he really wanted from her was language lessons. Had she imagined the warmth in his eyes and the softness of his touch on the small of her back?

A sour brew of fury and hurt burned in her throat. She jumped to her feet and scrambled up the bluff. It was all for the best, anyway. Heinrick was nothing but trouble, and she should have seen that when his horse almost trampled her.

Lilly marched through the grove, her feet pounding out a rhythm with her heart. Tears dripped down her cheek, and she violently whisked them away. She'd been a fool to trust him, to let him into her heart. At least she would be free of his endless probing questions about her faith. His God was simply different from hers . . . closer somehow, but perhaps that wasn't a good thing. She hardly wanted to trust a God who might cast her into the hands of a person like Clive Torgesen. Heinrick must have fallen out of God's favor, somehow, although she questioned the idea of such an honorable man offending God. Still, surely, God blessed those more who obeyed Him best. It just made sense that God balanced things out, and if she managed her side correctly, He would keep things even.

Lilly skidded to a halt in the middle of a withered clump of goldenrod. Maybe this was God's way of punishing her! She'd betrayed Reggie and deserved to have her heart ripped out, even by another man. Shame wound into her soul.

She'd made a terrible mistake. The only thing left to do was to forget. Thankfully, Reggie would be home soon, and the entire horrid experience could be safely tucked inside a secret chapter of her life, never to be read.

Lilly tightened her jaw as she climbed up the porch steps. She tiptoed into the house, noting her mother knitting at the kitchen table, lost in conversation with her father. Lilly ducked her head, scampered up the stairs, and threw herself across the bed. There, in the privacy of her folded arms, she cried herself to sleep.

Her subconscious put a picture to her fears. She found herself on a battlefield, searching among wide-eyed, lifeless soldiers. Some clutched pictures of sweethearts; others embraced their weapons like teddy bears. Lilly whimpered as she peered into faces, finally uncovering the one she feared to find. She cried out when she saw him, his dark hair hanging over his closed eyes, lying upon a pile of erupted earth as if he was sleeping. She crawled to him, gasping, and removed his helmet. His face was covered in a layer of black stubble, and he seemed warm. But she knew, as she curled a hand under his filthy neck, Reggie was dead.

In the background, she heard the *rat-a-tat-tat* of machine gun fire. A voice, crisp and clean and accented in German, rose over the clatter. "Trust me."

Lilly shuddered, for in its wake came a knowledge that if she surrendered, it would cost her everything she held dear, her dreams,

her will, her very life.
Lilly woke herself up screaming.

CHAPTER 15

Five days crawled by, and the dream, instead of dissolving into the hazy folds of memory, invaded like a virus, multiplying in strength and repeating itself in crisp, horrifying detail every night. Lilly awoke each time gasping, tears rushing down her cheeks, hands clenching the snarled bedclothes. Twice she woke up Bonnie, who frowned with worry in the streams of dawn. Perhaps her sister had even mentioned it, because once, while Lilly and her mother gathered in the sun-dried laundry, her mother questioned Lilly about not sleeping well. Her mother hesitated when Lilly brushed off the matter, but didn't pursue the truth.

Lilly clawed through the days, trying to drown the German-accented voice in her ears. She pulled weeds, the only things that seemed to be thriving in the kitchen garden, canned cucumbers, and stirred jam on the potbellied stove. Not once did she wander down to the river after dinner hour.

On Thursday, Olive returned from Mobridge with two letters, one for herself and the other for Lilly. Olive tucked the letter from Reggie into Lilly's apron pocket while Lilly was wrist-deep in a bowl of bread dough. The kitchen smelled of dill weed and onions, and jars of pickles cooled on the washboard. Lilly, shocked at the addition to her apron pocket, glanced at Olive. Her sister returned a glower.

"Did you forget the mail train came today?" Olive balled her hands on her.

Lilly's mouth dropped open, not only at Olive's loaded accusation, but also at the knowledge that she did, indeed, forget about the train and for the briefest of moments, Reggie.

"What is wrong with you?" Olive's screeching voice summoned their mother to the kitchen. "You're stumbling around the house like a drunkard, not paying attention to anyone! Why, yesterday, Alice Larsen came by, and you didn't even come out of your room to greet her." Olive's lip curled and she nearly snarled. "What sort of daughter-in-law are you?"

"That's enough, Olive," her mother said sharply. "Please leave us."

Olive shot an exasperated scowl at her mother, then stormed out of the room.

As Mrs. Clark sat on a straight-backed chair, Lilly dove into her bread dough and kneaded with vigor.

"You *have* been acting strangely, Lilly. I'd call it snippy, and that's not you." She paused and touched Lilly's forearm. "Bonnie told me about the nightmares. Sit, child, and talk to me."

Dread multiplied through her bones as Lilly met her mother's gaze. But her eyes beheld a tenderness that reached out and enfolded her, and Lilly's fear ebbed. She wiped her hands on her apron and drew up a chair, wondering what to reveal, opting for the truth.

"I taught that cowboy who saved Frankie how to read."

The shock Lilly expected was strangely absent. The older woman folded her hands together on the table. "Hmm, so that's what you were doing."

"You knew?"

Her mother's eyes twinkled. "I know a lot more than you think, Lilly. I watched you every night clean up, fix your hair, and change your dress. I knew it wasn't for the prairie dogs. And, when you finally floated home, I knew something other than the sunset had touched your heart."

"Why didn't you stop me?"

Mrs. Clark studied her clasped hands. "Because I trust you. Obviously more than Olive does. And I know in your heart is a seed of goodness and wisdom."

Lilly blew out a ragged breath. "Does Father know?"

Her mother shook her head. "He's too worried about the wheat and the drought to be caught into the tangled mystery of his daughter's heart." She reached for Lilly's hand. "Darling, this nightmare. Does it have to do with the cowboy?"

Lilly closed her eyes, seeing Heinrick's heart-catching smile and his mesmerizing blue eyes. "Mother, do you pray?"

"Of course."

"No, I mean pray, when you aren't in church. By yourself, without Pastor Larsen leading you."

Her mother smiled. "I pray when I hang laundry, when I see the sunshine spray the grass with tiny gold sparkles. I pray when I kiss DJ and Frankie in their sleep and see the peace of innocence written upon their faces. I pray when I see your father, dozing in his rocking chair, his spectacles dripping down over his nose and the Bible open on his lap. I pray for Olive and Christian and especially Chuck every night when I read the paper. And I pray when I notice you, Lilly, standing at the edge of the yard, your long hair taken by a prairie gust. I thank God and pray for His protection and His will to be done in all our lives."

Her mother's speech enraptured her. For the first time, Lilly considered her mother had thoughts beyond cooking, and canning, and hanging laundry. She saw her mother young, dreaming of a family and a home, and most of all trusting in a God who reigned over her life. In that instant, Lilly was jealous. Jealous her mother knew where she was planted and was already reaping the harvest in the garden of life God had given her.

Somehow, during the past week, Lilly's own surety about the life she thought God had planted for her had been swept up like dry prairie soil into a whirlwind of doubt. Heinrick's suggestion that God would do what He wanted, regardless of her prayers and her sacrificial obedience to everyone's plans for her, scared her more than she would admit. Was Heinrick right? Were she and Reggie like Joseph, helpless and at the mercy of an unpredictable God?

"Mother, did you always know it was God's plan for you to marry Father?"

Mrs. Clark gave a slight frown. "Have I never told you how I met your father?"

"You met him at a social at your church."

Her mother shook her head. "It wasn't at my church. Your father was from a church in the country, a different denomination. And, Lilly, I had promised to marry another man."

Lilly froze.

Her mother nodded. "He was a rich man, had been married before, and his wife died giving birth to their son. But he was still young and a friend of your grandfather's. He wanted a wife, and my father wanted a secure future for his only daughter. So Timothy began to court me. He was a very nice man. Good humored and kind. He treated me with respect, and my family and friends told me it was a good match. And I agreed. So he proposed to Father, then to me, and the plans were laid."

Lilly's chin drifted downward.

"Then I met your father." A playful smile lit on her mother's face. "He was a hired hand on a farm outside town. I went to the social with my friend, Marcie, whom I was visiting for the weekend. We were studying together at a finishing school in Chicago. Donald was at the social, and the day I met him, I knew."

"You knew?" Lilly breathed.

Her mother's eyes sparkled with an unfamiliar passion. "I knew I couldn't do what was expected, that I couldn't live a life committed to a man I did not wildly love."

"Mother!"

Mrs. Clark sat back in her chair, folding her hands across her chest. "It's true, Lilly. Marriage is difficult and not a place for lukewarm commitment. I knew if I married Timothy, it would be for many good reasons, but not the one that mattered."

"But what about your family, your parents?"

"Your father was patient. He courted me

for three years and proved to my parents that he was committed and a hard worker. Finally your grandfather relented."

"But weren't you afraid?"

"I was more afraid of not surrendering to God's plans for my life and missing out, perhaps, on the fullness of joy He wanted for me."

"How did you know that was what God wanted . . . I mean, your father and all your friends said you should marry Timothy. Why wasn't that God's plan?"

"Because I never felt it was right. I knew I didn't truly love Timothy, although he would have been a wonderful husband, I am sure. When I prayed, it seemed as though God wrote your father into my heart. He was the answer.

"So, in answer to your question, yes, marrying your father was always the plan. But I didn't know it until I asked, then listened to God."

Lilly blew out a troubled breath. "Well, I know it is God's plan for me to marry Reggie."

Her mother's chair creaked as she leaned forward. "God always has a plan for our lives, Lilly. But it may not be the one we think it is. We have to ask Him, then listen."

Lilly sloped back in her chair and crossed her arms, not sure she'd recognize God's voice if she heard it.

Dinner was a quiet, contemplative event. Lilly's father informed the family that haying season had arrived, and Olive read portions of Chuck's letter aloud.

We rotate through the line of trenches by week; next week Harley and Reggie and I will move forward to the supply trench, running ammunition to the support trench. I feel most sorry for the Sammies stuck in their bunkers on the front, knowing it's wet and cold and they are eating out of tin cans. But, in two weeks, I will be there, and they will feel sorry for me. Don't worry, Olive, for our good Lord protects us, and in a few short months I'll return, victory in hand. Kiss my Christian for me.

Corporal Charles Wyse

Reggie's letter burned a hole in Lilly's pocket and suddenly she wanted to tear it open, clutch it to her chest, and remind herself of the sanity of their commitment.

Olive's tears streaked down her cheeks, and next to Lilly, Bonnie hiccupped a sob. Melancholy bound them together in silent meditation.

"He'll be back, Olive," Lilly reassured in a solemn tone. Olive lifted red-rimmed eyes, attempting an acquiescing grin. It dissolved into the trembling of her chin. She buried her face in Christian's neck.

Guilt pierced Lilly's heart and twisted. How could she have forgotten Reggie?

Olive wiped her stained cheeks with a free hand. "Lilly, I saw Erica Torgesen at Ernestine's. She asked if you could come to the ranch tomorrow."

Despite the wild dance of her disobedient heart, Lilly bit her lip and nonchalantly nodded.

Lilly stretched across her bed and read Reggie's letter.

Dear Lilly,

I gladly received your letter of June 23, and your tender words greatly encouraged me. I cannot express to you adequately the happiness your promise brings me; it is a beacon of hope during this chaotic and unforgiving war. When the enemy is upon us, shells exploding in our bunkers, I clutch my helmet and think only of you, your emerald eyes, and the future we have laid out. I am not the only doughboy to cling to dreams of home; this hope is the veritable fuel that drives all us good Sammies over the top in a desperate attempt to chase those Germans back into the hole from which they crawled and thereby return to our shores that much sooner.

I am sure you have heard of Harley's proposal to Marjorie. I advised him toward it, he being the shy one. I assured him that Marjorie's promise would give him the courage he needs to survive this horrendous war. Just as you give to me. He is happy, and, although he has not received her reply, he is assured in his heart of her affirmation.

As I write this, the sun is disappearing behind our lines, giving relief to the relentless view of the unburied dead, destroyed machinery, and shattered earth. Tonight I am in a cover trench, my job to fire over the heads of those in the firing trench as they move along the front. Hopefully we will not hear, "Over the top!" this evening, as most of us are tired and ready for a night to merely avoid the German star shells and lob an occasional barrage over to their side. Last night, the Germans decided to focus on our sector and shelled us for three solid hours. I spent much of the night in cover, wearing my gas mask and dodging the bombs, but we did manage to pitch a few shells and, I think, send a few Germans to their unholy eternity. We are fighting like the coyote, desperate and unrelenting and hopeful that soon, very soon, we will save the world for democracy.

I am hesitant to address this next topic, but, as your future husband, it is my duty to direct you toward righteousness. My mother wrote me about a rather unpleasant altercation in town where she mentioned you had placed yourself in grave danger between two fighting men. Then she suggested, and I pray in error, you may have ridden off with one of them! I am grieved by these words, Lilly. I hope it is either an erroneous report by my mother or a miscalculation in judgment on your part. Whatever the case, I admonish you to choose carefully your behavior. As my wife, you must set an example for the community on proper and modest behavior and not be fodder for gossip.

Of course, I know you are aware of this, and I trust you to conduct yourself as the Christian lady I know you to be.

One other thing, Lilly. Mother mentioned your employment by the Torgesens as a dressmaker. Please, I beg of you, be ready to cease this activity. It is not befitting a Christian wife and mother to have an occupation. You will be busy enough taking care of our children and home. I know perhaps this is a hobby for now, while you wait for my return, and because of this, I will permit it. But when we are married, and I pray soon, you will have enough to occupy yourself — taking care of me!

I think of you always and commit you in good faith to our God in heaven to honor our plans and reunite us once again.

Love,
Reggie

CHAPTER 16

Perhaps it was exhaustion from the sun sucking every ounce of energy as she trudged toward the Torgesen T. Maybe it was fresh guilt, churned up at the reading of Reggie's letter. Or, it could have been the hope of seeing Heinrick. Lilly couldn't put her hands around the exact reason, but regardless, knots twisted her stomach by the time she reached the Torgesen ranch.

"I need a new dress!" Mrs. Torgesen exclaimed after she'd piled Lilly's lap full of new editions of *Ladies Home Journal* and *Butterick Fashions.*

Something *nouveau* and fabulous." Mrs. Torgesen's eyes twinkled as she wiggled her pudgy fingers at her. "Get to work."

Lilly flipped through the pages, determined to make Mrs. Torgesen look better than a willow tree this time around. Mrs. Torgesen headed for the kitchen.

After examining fashions from velvet empire skirts to long-neck prairie blouses with poet sleeves and French cuffs, she decided upon a two-piece suit, ankle length, with a double-breasted jacket. She showed it to Mrs. Torgesen, who drooled on the page, then Lilly buried herself in the fabric wardrobe for over an hour measuring scraps. She finally settled on brown and beige twill for the jacket and a skirt of brown wool.

She spent the rest of the morning piecing together a muslin pattern from scraps until she'd produced a pinned-together likeness of the skirt and jacket.

"When will I have my first fitting, Lilly?"

"Next week, perhaps. I think I can have the skirt ready to fit by then."

Mrs. Torgesen sat at the kitchen table, eating a fresh peach like an apple. Juice pooled at the corners of her mouth and dripped off her wrist. The humid kitchen absorbed the rich aroma and spiced the air. At the stove, Eleanor was steaming jars and parboiling a pot of peaches for canning. Stacked near the door were three wooden crates of fresh peaches, wrapped in green paper. Lilly couldn't help but to stare longingly at Mrs. Torgesen's peach. The Clark family would have no peach preserves this winter.

"Would you like a peach, Lilly?" Mrs. Torgesen gestured toward the crates.

Lilly shook her head. "Oh, no thank you, Mrs. Torgesen." She didn't know why, but suddenly she felt as if accepting the peach would be traitorous to the entire Clark family. She already felt like Benedict Arnold.

Mrs. Torgesen shrugged. Lilly gathered up the fabric and folded it into a canvas bag.

The noon sun burned the prairie until even the crickets hissed in protest. Lilly noticed a clump of Holstein on the horizon as she left the Torgesen T. She hadn't seen Heinrick, and an errant thought escaped, *Where is he?* Seeing Heinrick would only open the crusty scar upon her heart. Yet, she couldn't ignore the shard of disappointment that seemed to wedge deeper with each step away from the ranch.

A sharp whinny caught her ears. Lilly stiffened. She hadn't seen Clive at the Torgesen T either, but he was never far off. She quickened her pace, not looking back, but the thunder of hoofbeats beat down upon her. Lilly gritted her teeth and whirled, intending to meet the brute head-on.

"You look angry, Lilly." Heinrick reined his mount, pushed up his hat, and leaned on his saddle horn.

Lilly gaped, then clamped her mouth closed. A thousand words rushed to mind, but not one could be formed upon her lips. Instead, Lilly balled her fists, fixed them onto her hips.

"You *are* mad." Heinrick's crooked white grin faded. "I'm sorry I didn't show up, I . . ." He glanced away, across the golden-brown prairie. "I just couldn't make it, that's all."

Lilly's bottled fury erupted. "I guess it didn't matter that I put my reputation, not to mention my future, on the line for you! You don't feel like it, so you don't show up? Do you think I'm bored and needed some cheering up? Or did you just determine to pester me with all that talk about God and my religion?" Lilly crossed her arms across her chest, squeezing hard to smother her anger. "Well, it just so happens, Mr. Zook, that I was planning on telling you that you know enough English and you can learn to read just fine on your own." Lilly turned on her heel, shaking. He would have to ride away now, and she wouldn't have to worry about him one day longer, him or his probing spiritual questions.

Her knees shook when she heard him dismount and felt his presence edge in on her, ushered in by the smell of soap and a tinge of masculine perspiration. He placed a hand on her shoulder and gently turned her around. She glued her eyes to his scuffed boots, refusing to betray what might be hidden in her eyes.

"I'm sorry, Lilly. I *am* grateful for all you did for me. Please forgive me."

Lilly squinted at him. He looked stricken.

His pitiful posture turned Lilly's heart. "Okay. I forgive you."

His crooked grin reappeared. "Thank you.

Now, come riding with me."

"When, right now?"

Heinrick nodded. "I have to ride fence this afternoon down near your place. Come with me."

Lilly's jaw dropped. "Are you sick, Heinrick? Have you heard one thing I've said to you? I can't be seen with you anymore. I'm going to marry another man!"

Heinrick raised his blond eyebrows and peered at her as if she was the one with the sickness. "I'm not courting you, Lilly. I just miss your company." His mouth flattened into a line. "But, of course, I understand. I don't want to force you into anything; I just thought it might be, well, fun." Heinrick pulled on the brim of his hat. "It sure was good seeing you again, though."

Regret boiled in her chest as she watched him ride away. She felt as if she'd been offered the priceless pearl, turned it down, and would never be the same for it. A compelling urge told her to call him back, to ride with him under the full view of the sun, and not be afraid.

"Heinrick!"

He reined his horse, turned, and smiled.

CHAPTER 17

Heinrick didn't allow Lilly time to change her mind. "Stay here, I'll be right back." With a whoop, he galloped back to the Torgesen T to saddle another mount. Lilly shrank into the shade of an aging ash and fought her swelling emotions. She kept telling herself he was just a friend, her student, and they were only taking a ride through the fields on a sunny day. But her stomach fluttered, and she couldn't deny the music in her heart.

Heinrick returned with a gray speckled mare tethered by her reins to his saddle horn.

"Do you know how to ride?"

"I've ridden Lucy a few times." She tied her bag to the mare's saddle.

Heinrick helped her place her foot in the stirrup, and she slid on, sidesaddle.

"We won't go fast."

It felt awkward and unsteady to be halfway on a horse, and Lilly struggled to find the rhythm. "I wish I was wearing my riding skirt," she muttered. Beside her, Heinrick erupted in honeyed laughter.

They meandered through Torgesen grazing land, which rolled like giant waves toward the Missouri riverbed.

"Someone once told me the Dakota prairie was like the ocean, endless and constantly moving," Lilly commented. The sun overhead winked at her. Prairie grass crunched under the horses' sturdy hooves, and a lonely meadowlark called to them, hidden in a clump of goldenrod. Lilly pushed her straw hat off her head, letting it dangle down her back by a long loop of ribbon. The wind fingered her braided hair. Beside her, Heinrick hummed softly.

"Perhaps," he finally agreed. "The prairie does seem to be constantly moving, and the wind is louder here than on the ocean, more fierce. It roars." Heinrick followed the movement of a circling hawk. "Look, Lilly," he said, "watch the hawk. Where it is, you will always find food."

Lilly's mouth went dry. "What did you say?"

Heinrick's voice was an ocean away. "My father and I used to hunt in Germany when I was young. He told me that, and I've never forgotten it."

Lilly nodded slowly, her heart thundering. The sun began to glare. The hot wind stung her face. "It's not a thing you forget, I suppose," she said weakly.

Heinrick continued, as if lost in a memory.

"The hawk reminds me of the seagulls, soaring above the seascape. The sea seemed endless, like the prairie, but much more unforgiving. I was sick for fourteen days."

Heinrick reined his horse to a stop on a small bluff. Lilly took in an unmarred view of the Clark homestead and, farther on, the Pratt farm. Heinrick pointed to a V in the horizon. "That's the end of Torgesen land, and the little black line running along the hills is the railroad. See how it disappears behind that bluff?"

Shading her eyes, Lilly nodded. She hardened herself to the guilt that nipped at her, reborn by Heinrick's words — Reggie's words! — and focused on Heinrick's voice.

Heinrick now pointed past her own home. "The train reappears there and runs all the way into Mobridge." He shook his head. "I hear the railroad connects one end of the country to the other. Amazing."

Lilly wasn't examining the railroad tracks. She saw only Heinrick and his blue eyes. They were almost transparent, as if she could see inside him to his optimist's heart. He wore a faded bronze shirt, untied at the neck, and had pushed his brown bandana around so that the knot seemed a little bow tie at the base of his thick, tanned neck. He wore leather gloves, but his sleeves were rolled past the elbow to reveal muscled forearms. Weathered tan chaps covered his strong legs, and he seemed to be almost one with his mount. But Lilly was especially drawn in by his voice and an accent that betrayed a man who had surmounted fear, climbed aboard a ship, ridden over an angry sea, and was forging out a life in a hostile land.

"I want to work on the railroad someday, Lilly," he said softly. "I want to ride those black rails from shore to shore and see America. Discover why my relatives left Norway for America."

"Heinrick, why did you stand me up?"

Heinrick's gaze fell away from her, and a shadow crossed his face. "Clive needed the barn mucked out."

Lilly's heart twisted and shame eclipsed the anger she'd felt. "I'm sorry."

He lifted his gaze to hers, and she saw in his eyes a passionate blaze that betrayed his frustration. "Christmas, Lilly," he said. "By Christmas, I'll be free!" He suddenly whooped and spurred his horse, which shot off into a gallop along the ridgeline. Lilly clucked to her mare, and the horse cantered after him. She clutched the saddle horn and tried to swallow her terror.

"Move with her, Lilly. Don't be afraid." The wind brought his voice to her. "Give her some rein!"

"That's easy for you to say, you're not riding in a dress!"

Heinrick's laughter formed a vivid trail, one

she could have followed with her eyes closed. He slowed his mount to a walk.

"Give your horse some freedom to move, Lilly. She wants to obey you, but if you choke her, she has no choice but to fight. Your horse has to be controlled by you, but you have to give her room to trust you. A horse that is afraid and choking on the bit is a horse that can't be ridden."

Lilly fingered the leather reins, loosening her hold. Her mare fell into a graceful walk next to Heinrick.

"It's like faith in God, Lilly. You are like that horse. You have to trust God, who loves you. No matter what He does, it is for your eternal good. You can't make God do what you want, just like your horse can't make you obey. The rider is the master of the horse, but the horse can make things a lot harder by grabbing the bit in her mouth and running off with it. A horse that won't surrender freely can't be used and is no good." Heinrick leaned over and put a hand on her reins. A crooked smile creased his face. "We shoot horses like that."

Lilly grimaced. Heinrick winked at her, his eyes twinkling in the sunlight. Then his smile vanished.

"You have to trust in God's love to fully surrender to His leading. Without that trust, you'll constantly be trying to grab the bit."

Lilly ran her eyes along the horizon. The

fence line hurtled the next ridge and ran beyond that to the Clark farm. The joy had evaporated from the afternoon ride. First the reminder of Reggie and now Heinrick's spiritual invasion. Couldn't he just leave her religion alone? Why did he have to rattle her beliefs every time they were together?

"Lilly, do you trust that God loves you?"

Lilly shrugged and turned away. Tears edged her eyes.

"What's wrong?" His soft voice caressed her fraying emotions.

His saddle creaked as he dismounted. He stood next to her, holding her reins, searching her eyes. Lilly bit her lip and turned her face away. Heinrick pulled off his glove and took her hand.

"Did I say something wrong?"

She shook her head but couldn't form words. How could she explain something she couldn't even understand herself? Of course, God loved her; the Bible said so, right? And Reverend Larsen had spelled it out so many times, she didn't have room for doubt. Believe and obey. She did both.

Then why did Heinrick's religion seem so different from hers? She was envious of Heinrick's absolute confidence of God's love. God's love to her had always meant tangible blessings, life in control. If Reggie died, did that mean God didn't love her? Lilly frowned at the turquoise, cloudless sky.

Why did Heinrick have to challenge everything? He'd practically accused her of not being a Christian! He'd ripped apart her religion until it was shredded. Now she didn't know what she believed.

Two betraying tears sneaked down her cheeks. Heinrick wiped one away with his wide thumb. "What is it, Lilly?"

Lilly grabbed his wrist and pulled his hand away. She shook her head, until, abruptly, the fear shuddered out of her. "No, I don't know God loves me, and I'm afraid! I'm afraid I can't be everything He wants me to be, that I will somehow destroy my chance at happiness, maybe even my salvation! And I'm afraid He's going to let something bad happen, maybe even because of something I've done, and it'll ruin everything." The truth thinned her voice to sobs.

Heinrick's brows puckered. "Lilly, God does love you. He wants to give you salvation *and* a happy future. You just have to trust Him."

Lilly shook her head. "How do I trust Him if I don't know what He's going to do?"

"You trust Him because He's already shown you His love. And you can count on that."

Lilly frowned and bit her lip. How had God shown her His love? She dared to look at Heinrick. Compassion swam in his blue eyes, and, in that moment, all she wanted to do was slide off the mare and into his strong arms. And that frightened her almost as much as surrendering to an uncontrollable God.

"Heinrick, I have to go home. This is no good. I can't be here with you. I'm going to ruin everything."

Lilly leaned on his shoulders and slid off the horse. Then she stepped away. "Thank you for the ride."

"Lilly, you aren't going to cause Reggie to be killed by going for a ride with me."

Lilly's heart lodged in her chest. She stared at him, horrified. He'd summed up, in his statement, every nightmare she'd ever imagined.

"Do you think you can earn God's favor or His love by following all the rules? By doing all Reggie, your parents, and your church tell you to?"

Heinrick pulled off his hat. The wind picked through his matted hair. "Your salvation is not based on anything you do, Lilly. No one can be good enough to be saved. That's why Jesus came and allowed Himself to be crucified. No one can live up to the Jewish law. It only serves to point out our sins. But Jesus sets us free from death by paying the price for our sins. All we can do is ask for forgiveness and receive salvation! We cannot earn it. Salvation isn't a bargain with God, it's a gift from Him."

Lilly saw him through watery eyes.

Heinrick wrapped his massive hands around her upper arms. "I don't know much, Lilly, but I know this. It is by grace you are saved through faith. Grace, Lilly. Something unearned, undeserved, and without rules." His voice was like the wind, refreshing and tugging at the bonds of her soul. "If you truly want to follow God and to know Him, then you have to understand this. If there is nothing we can do to earn salvation, if Jesus paid for our sins before we knew Him, when we were the *worst* of sinners, then there is also nothing we can do to lose it. His sacrifice is enough to pay for *all* of our sins. You cannot ruin your salvation because it is not in your power to ruin it! He loves you, and there is nothing you can do about it."

Lilly gasped as the truth hit her heart. She felt the first inklings of a freedom she'd been searching for all her life. "Not in my power to ruin it?"

Heinrick lifted her chin with his forefinger, and his gaze held hers. "God loves you, Lilly. You can trust His plans; for you, for Reggie, for your life."

She nodded, then slipped under his arms and started toward home. Halfway across the Clark hayfield, she began to laugh, joy bubbling from some broken vault in her soul. Lilly opened her arms, embracing the sky, twirled twice, and broke into a run. The canvas bag bumped against her back as she went leaping across the fallow field, laughing, crying, and most of all singing, as her soul, for the first time, found freedom.

That night, after Bonnie's breath deepened in sleep beside her, Lilly slipped out of her bed and onto her knees. Embedded in the glow of moonlight, Lilly prayed and, for the first time in her life, fully surrendered to the One who loved her.

CHAPTER 18

The melody of an early rising bluebird floated in on a cool dawn breeze. Lilly awakened slowly, bathed in the peace of a new morning, and realized she'd slept straight through. No nightmare. The terrifying dream had vanished, as had the fear that seemed to dog her since Reggie's departure. Worry still throbbed on one side of her heart, but it wasn't the same frantic panic that had boiled in her soul.

The second thing that impressed her as she sat up and gazed at her light-dappled walls, was the unfamiliar, remarkable lightness of soul, as if the day was hers and nothing could pin her down. It was the intoxicating breath of unconditional love, giving her hope wings. It made her gasp.

Bonnie sat up next to her, rubbing her eyes. "What?"

Lilly whirled and embraced her sister. They fell together on the stuffed mattress and giggled.

Lilly threw off the sheet, skipped to the window, and pulled back the curtains. The shadow of the house loomed long across the yard, but the sun lit the field rose gold. "With each sunrise, there is new hope."

Bonnie stared at her as if she'd grown another leg.

Lilly pulled off her cotton nightgown. She needed something refreshing, something sunny. She chose a one-piece cornflower blue calico with minute yellow daisies. It had a fitted bodice, with a lace-trimmed boat neck and turned-up cap sleeves. Lilly slid it over her head, then loosely braided her hair down her back.

"You going somewhere?" Bonnie asked, her knees drawn up to her chest under the sheet.

"Going out to greet the dawn."

Lilly reckoned, from Bonnie's look, she must have turned purple. But she didn't care. On impulse, she grabbed her Bible and tucked it under her arm. Then she left her bewildered sister to flop back onto the feather pillow and tiptoed down the stairs.

Lilly's mother was in the kitchen whipping pancake batter. She glanced up, spied Lilly, and her brow knit into a frown. Lilly shot her a wide smile and stepped out onto the porch. Across the yard, the barn doors were open, her father inside, milking. Lilly headed toward her maple grove.

The wind whispered in the branches, and

the glade was cool and shadowed. Lilly strolled to the bluff and stared out at the endless prairie. A hazy residue of platinum, rose, and lavender simmered along the eastern horizon. From the opposing shore, a startled pheasant took flight from a clump of sage. Hope rode the air, tinged in the fragrance of columbine and jasmine, which continued to bloom in hardy defiance of the drought.

Lilly sat on a piece of driftwood to read her Bible. She had no idea what she was doing, but it seemed the right thing to do. Like Heinrick said, if she was to trust God, she ought to know Him. And Heinrick seemed to think knowing God meant more than just attending services. She randomly flipped open the thick Bible and determined to give it a try.

She landed somewhere in the Old Testament. Jeremiah. She hardly recalled the book, but ran her finger down the page. Then, to her profound surprise, she noticed someone had marked a verse. Verse eleven of chapter twenty-nine was underlined ever so slightly in pencil, and she heard her heart thump as she read. "For I know the thoughts that I think toward you, saith the LORD, thoughts of peace, and not of evil, to give you an expected end. Then shall ye call upon me, and ye shall go and pray unto me, and I will hearken unto you. And ye shall seek me, and find me, when ye shall search for me with all your heart."

A shiver rippled up Lilly's spine. *"Ye shall seek me, and find me, when ye shall search for me with all your heart."* Lilly bit her lip and looked up at the pale, jeweled sky. Could the Maker of the heavens really be talking to her, calling out to her? "The Living Word," Heinrick had said. God talking through the Bible. The thought was terrifying and exhilarating and beyond her comprehension.

Lilly bowed her head. *Yes, God. I want to seek You. I want to find You. I know You love me, and I want to surrender to You and Your plans for me.*

As she lifted her eyes, the fragrance of peace swept through her heart. She drew in a long breath, and the feeling seeped into her bones. But would it linger when the heat of day battered it, when fear reared its head in the form of news from Europe? Would she be able to trust?

This surrender would have to be a daily, moment-by-moment thing. *God, please, help me to know You so I am not afraid, so I see Your love. Help me to trust You.*

It was the briefest of moments after the prayer left her lips that she realized she must tell Reggie. Everything. The half truths of her letters were, simply put, sin. She had to be honest. Most of all, she had to share with him the joy of grace. Maybe it would give him the one thing he so desperately needed

— release from the cold knot of fear.

She would write to him on lavender paper, send a pressed lily, and hope he would truly understand her newfound joy.

Most of all, she would pray somehow the news of her spiritual awakening would cushion the tale about Heinrick. To tell Reggie the truth, she would have to tell him about her German friend. She would put her surrender, that peace, to the test and trust the Lord for the outcome.

Lilly stood, flung out her arms as if to welcome the day, and then picked her way through the grove of maples and back to the Clark farm for breakfast.

Lilly spent the morning laying out and cutting the skirt for Mrs. Torgesen's suit on the kitchen table. Lilly's mother peeked over her shoulder, offered a few hints, and finally admitted to Lilly that she'd surpassed her mother as a seamstress.

"I don't know how you can just look at a picture and make it come alive." Her mother shook her head in parental admiration.

After a lunch of warm milk, bread, and jam, Lilly escaped to her room and wrote to Reggie. The story was more difficult in the telling than she'd anticipated, and it took her two full hours to fill two evenly scrawled pages. She started over twice and finally resigned herself to the reality that regardless how she wrote it, she'd betrayed him. She'd spent a week in the company of a man not her fiancé, despite its innocence, and she would have to hope Reggie trusted her. She slipped a sprig of lily of the valley into the envelope. Its tiny white bells were withering, but the fragrance lingered. She hoped Reggie would be encouraged by it. She sealed the letter and propped it on her vanity. She couldn't mail it until Monday's train, but she felt that much the cleaner for having revealed the truth.

"Lilly, could you run into Ernestine's for flour and molasses?" her mother called from the bottom steps. Lilly grabbed her basket and her straw hat and set off for Mobridge.

A buzz of tension, beyond the hum of the riverbed grasshoppers, drifted through the town. Horses were packed into tight rows, tethered to hitching posts. Buckboards stood at a standstill, filled with goods. Women in bonnets and men chewing on straw milled about on the clapboard sidewalk. Curious, Lilly quickened her pace toward Ernestine's.

The news met her there.

"Did you hear about the battle?" Ernestine's fat sweaty hands worked quickly, filling the flour sacks. Lilly handed her the empty burlap bag she'd borrowed. Ernestine took it and continued her monologue. "We just got the news in the *Milwaukee Journal.* A big battle over a river in France someplace." She gave Lilly the flour. Her probing eyes seemed to soften. "They say our boys are in the fray."

Lilly bit her lip and nodded. "Can I have some molasses, also?"

Ernestine turned and searched the shelves for a bottle. Lilly was glad for the moment to compose herself. Her heartbeat throbbed in her ears, and she fought a tremble. Ernestine returned with the molasses. Lilly dropped it into her basket and paid her.

"God be with you and Reggie." Ernestine offered a smile that felt too much like a condolence.

"Thank you," Lilly managed. She darted for the door.

At Miller's, Ed shrugged. "Sorry, Lilly, we're out of fresh newspapers. Try the postal."

Lilly hustled to the post office and discovered they, too, were sold out. Heart sinking, she headed for the door.

"Lilly, you have a letter." Mildred Baxter, the postmistress, handed her a small envelope.

Lilly frowned. "Did I miss the train?"

Mildred shook her head. "I don't know who it's from."

Lilly stepped out into the sunshine, confusion distracting her disappointment over the shortage of newspapers. The letter *was* for her. Her name was spelled out in small, bold capitals on the bleached parchment envelope. And there was no postage.

Lilly examined it for a moment, then decided to open it on the road home, away from any prying eyes on the street. She slipped the letter into her basket.

Her last stop was the armory. She found Marjorie red-eyed and folding bandages with unequalled passion. Lilly pulled her friend into an embrace.

"Don't worry, Marj. God will watch over them."

Tears flooded Marjorie's eyes. "That doesn't mean Harley will come back home. It doesn't mean everything will be okay."

Lilly peered into her friend's anguished face, her heart reciting everything she'd embraced over the past day. "Yes, it does. God loves us, and because of that, everything will be okay."

Marjorie studied her a long moment, as if absorbing her words. Then she laid her head on Lilly's shoulder. Lilly held her, briefly bearing her friend's burden. Then Lilly left Marjorie to assemble soon-to-be needed action kits and headed home.

A half mile out of Mobridge, Lilly remembered the letter. She retrieved it from the basket and worked the envelope open.

It was from Heinrick.

Dear Lilly,
I never thanked you for the lessons.

Please meet me at our "school" tomorrow
night at sunset.

Your friend,

Heinrick

Lilly's mouth dried, and she nearly allowed
the wind to snatch the letter from her grip.
In some strange, awkward way, his invitation
was a soothing balm on the worry tearing at
her heart; as if time with Heinrick could actually help her believe the words she'd so
confidently spoken to Marjorie — that God
would make everything okay.

She ambled home, attempting to unsnarl
the paradox in her heart.

CHAPTER 19

With the news of the ongoing battle in France, worry moved into the Clark home. It brought with it a foul mood. Olive did nothing but clutch Christian and sit on the porch in the wide willow rocker, staring with glassy eyes out over the dead wheat field. Her father and Frankie rose long before dawn to cut prairie grass. Her mother canned three dozen jars of gooseberry jam, her lips moving in constant prayer. Lilly basted together, in wide stitches, Erica Torgesen's skirt and hoped she would have a happy occasion to wear it to, instead of a funeral.

Lilly had greeted the dawn by the river, praying and watching the sun creep over the horizon from Reggie's side of the world. Her morning reading, from Psalm 56, seemed a shield against the barrage of the day. "What time I am afraid, I will trust in thee. In God I will praise his word, in God I have put my trust; I will not fear what flesh can do unto me." God certainly knew how to meet the need of the moment. Lilly memorized the verse and recited it often, especially when worry curled around her heart like a stinging nettle.

The day drew out like old honey. Although anxiety strummed in her heart, Lilly couldn't deny that time crawled in response to the anticipation of seeing Heinrick. Curiosity ran like wildfire through her thoughts. More than that, however, she longed for his calming presence to remind her of God's love. Somehow, Heinrick could see into her soul, unearth her deepest fears, and scatter them with a word of wisdom.

Dinner was sober and simple: new potatoes, hot bread, and gravy. Lilly made a salad from carrots and dandelion greens. Olive excused herself to her room, and Bonnie cleared the table. Lilly washed the dishes in silence, but her heart thundered with the ticks of the mantle clock. Finally, the last dish sparkled, and she dashed upstairs. She changed into a jade green skirt and white blouse with a Buster Brown collar and puffy short sleeves.

Lilly noticed her mother glance up from her knitting and raise her thin brows as Lilly flew past her on the porch.

Heinrick was waiting, embedded in the shadows of a great maple. He'd spiffed up for the occasion, a pair of clean black trousers, polished boots, a brown cotton button-down shirt, albeit frayed at the elbows, and a fringed dark chocolate leather vest. He'd even slicked back his golden hair. He gave her a wide grin and stepped from the arms of the tree.

"*Guten Abend,* Lilly." His voice was warm, and he offered her his arm.

"Hello, Heinrick," Lilly returned, suddenly gripped with shyness. She lowered her eyes, but wrapped her arm around the crook of his elbow. He led her out onto the bluff, then down to their cottonwood bench. The sun melted along the horizon, and the air smelled faintly of drying hay.

He didn't look at her, but instead chose a family of prairie dogs, darting along the other shore, for his attention. "I wanted to thank you, Lilly," he started in a halting voice. "You've given me my future. If I can read, I can do anything. I know it cost you to meet me, and I will never forget your sacrifice."

Lilly considered him, her gaze running along his wide-set jaw and his blond hair curling behind his ears. His shirtsleeves tightened around the base of his muscled arms, and he had his hands folded in his lap. She remembered the way those hands had caught the blows of the Craffey brothers, tamed a wild stallion, batted away Clive's anger, and tenderly wiped a tear from her cheek. So powerful, yet profoundly gentle. She may have taught him how to read, but he'd taught her how to live.

"I have to thank you, also." Lilly gazed toward the melting sunset. "I did it, Heinrick. I prayed and surrendered to God's love." She glanced at him. His eyes drew her in and held her. They were filled with a vivid, tangible joy, and in that moment, she saw herself as he saw her. Not as Reggie's fiancée, or as a farm girl, or even as his teacher, but as a lady he admired. She knew, as long as she lived, she would never forget the way Heinrick made her believe she was special . . . and loved. Then he smiled, and she could have danced in the music of it. Heinrick reached into his vest pocket. "I have a gift for you." He pulled out a wad of cotton and held it out to her.

Lilly unwrapped it carefully and gasped. Inside lay a long-toothed, hand-painted, brass butterfly comb, with an emerald-colored glass stone in the center. Wide wings, painted a ginger brown, flared from the center stone body. At the bottom, a brass tail was fashioned into a row of delicate loops. It was antique, exquisite, and doubtlessly expensive.

"It's breathtaking," Lilly whispered.

"It belonged to my mother."

Lilly's eyes teared. "I don't know what to say. I can't accept it."

Heinrick frowned. "Why not?"

Lilly bit her lip. Why not? It was just a gift from a friend, a sort of payment for her kind deed. She felt herself shrugging. "I . . . I don't know."

"Please take it, Lilly. I want you to have it."

With trembling hands, she folded the comb carefully back into the cotton. "Thank you. I'll treasure it."

Heinrick smiled, delight in his blue eyes. "Now, tell me about the dress you are making Erica Torgesen that has her waltzing around the ranch."

Lilly laughed, and together they sat on the cottonwood bench, knees touching, while she told him about Mrs. Torgesen, the willow tree dress, and her fashion dreams. Heinrick laughed and listened, resting his head on his hands as he watched her.

Twilight hued the Missouri copper. Lilly heard a voice threading through the maple grove, calling her name. A voice edged in panic.

Lilly jumped to her feet. "Over here, Bonnie." She cast a frown at Heinrick. "I have to go."

He nodded and scrambled up the bluff, then reached down for Lilly. Lilly climbed over the ridge just as Bonnie burst from the shadows. She skidded to a halt and stared at the pair, eyes bulging, mouth agape. She found her senses quickly, however, and turned her attention to Lilly. Her eyes were troubled and her voice shook. "Come home, Lilly."

"Bonnie, you're scaring me." Lilly wound her arms around herself.

Bonnie's eyes flooded and her chin quivered, but she managed an explanation. "Olive got a telegram. Chuck's been killed."

Lilly covered her mouth with her hand, stifling a cry of anguish. She felt Heinrick's arm wind around her waist.

"Lilly, that's not all." Bonnie paused and took a step toward Lilly, a hand extended as if to steady the news. "Reverend and Mrs. Larsen are up at the house."

The blood drained from Lilly's face.

"Reggie's missing."

CHAPTER 20

Lilly leaned back on her heels and rubbed a grimy wrist across her sweaty brow. Her body felt dry and dusty, and her hands were cracked and sore from pulling weeds. But the sting in her palms felt easier to bear than the searing wounds in her heart. Each member of her family dodged the specter of grief in their own way. While Lilly tediously weeded the dying garden, her father worked from dawn 'til dusk in the hay field, dragging an exhausted Frankie with him. Her mother canned thirty-six jars of dills and twelve of relish, DJ chased the kittens around the dry yellowing yard and played with Christian, and Olive stopped living. She was a wasteland, crushed in spirit and hope, withering by the hour. She ceased eating and, after the first day, stopped dressing. By Sunday, she wouldn't even rise from her double bed. Lilly brought her meals, stroked her sister's waist-long chestnut hair, and tried to comfort her. But for Olive, there was no solace. To Lilly, she was a frightening prophecy of what might come if Reggie was confirmed dead. Lilly clung to the hope, should that dark hour transpire, her newfound peace would carry her above the grave and keep her from being, in essence, Olive, a woman who believed she had no tomorrows.

Lilly buried herself in the Psalms. It seemed a desperate escape at first, and Lilly doubted that the Bible would offer her any sort of encouragement. She was infinitely mistaken. The never-before-read passages became nearly tangible in their spiritual embrace and, as she wound herself inside the sorrows and joys of the Jewish king, David, she reaped the one thing Olive lacked — faith. David praised God in the midst of sorrow, and she would as well, clutching the belief that God loved her.

"It's addressed to Lillian Clark." Bonnie's face was ashen as she handed Lilly the telegram. Lilly took the envelope with shaking hands. Two weeks without a word and finally the army had sent news. It must have taken them that long to sift through the bodies.

Her mother crept up beside Lilly and wound an arm around her waist. "Open it, honey."

As the last embers of hope died within her, Lilly worked the telegram open. Brutally

1116

short, it was from the person she least expected to hear from.

Dear Lilly,
   Alive. In Paris hospital. Harley KIA.
Chuck KIA. Coming home.

                              Reggie

Lilly gasped, covered her mouth, and sank into a kitchen chair. She handed the telegram to her mother, who read it aloud and wept.
Hot tears ran down Lilly's cheeks. God had saved Reggie. He was coming home. She wrapped her arms around herself and pushed back a tremble.

"Oh Lilly! It's so wonderful!" Bonnie squealed and embraced her, and Lilly's father squeezed Lilly's shoulder as he passed by. Only Olive was speechless. She stood at the end of the table, looking brutal in her bathrobe and wadded, greasy hair. Lilly glanced at her and, in that instant, felt her sister's jealousy as if it were a right-handed blow.

Lilly offered a sympathetic smile, but Olive's disbelieving eyes tightened into a glare. She whirled and ran to her room.

The only thing left to do was to tell Marjorie. Dread weighted Lilly's footsteps all the way to the Pratt farm. When she rapped on the peeling screen door, Mrs. Pratt opened it and greeted her cheerfully. When she saw Lilly's face, however, she ushered her to the

1117

kitchen, then sent Evelyn into town to fetch Marjorie.

Why it had been ordained for Lilly to inform her best friend her fiancé had been killed, she would never understand. It seemed utterly unfair to be shouldered with the job. And yet, she knew the hope she'd just discovered and so desperately clung to was the only hope she could offer her friend. She longed to tell Marjorie that God could not only comfort her, He could create a future for her despite the destruction of her well-laid plans.

Marjorie read the telegram twice and handed it back to Lilly. Her hands shook. "Maybe he's mistaken."

"Maybe." But doubt filled Lilly's reply. Marjorie heard it, and her mourning wail shredded Lilly's heart. Marjorie crumpled into Lilly's arms and sobs shuddered through her. Lilly rubbed her hair and mourned with her as the horror of war shattered their hearts.

Lilly finally tucked a spent Marjorie into bed. Wandering home under a starlit sky, she listened to the breeze moan in her ears and wondered what tomorrow would bring.

Chuck and Harley were gone, but Reggie was coming home. It was a sign. God wanted them together. She would obey, even though she only saw Heinrick each night in her dreams.

Alice Larsen visited a few days later, recovered from her grief and unfurling dramatic plans for Lilly's wedding. She was aghast to discover Lilly hadn't started on her wedding dress.

"I would think, with your love of sewing, you would have it cut out and basted, at least."

Lilly smiled and mentioned she was helping Erica Torgesen with a dress. Mrs. Larsen waved the thought away with the back of her hand. "You'll just have to tell Erica Torgesen you are much too busy now to dress her up like a doll. She's too concerned with frills, anyway." Mrs. Larsen laid a hand on Mrs. Clark's arm and, looking at Lilly, breathed into her mother's corner of the table, "It's as if she thinks life is a fashion show!"

Lilly and her mother exchanged looks and smiled. That was exactly what Erica Torgesen thought.

"Even so, Mrs. Larsen, I promised her an outfit, and I intend to finish it," Lilly said.

Mrs. Larsen recoiled as if Lilly had slapped her. "Well, I know you like to sew, Lilly, but really, your priorities are with Reggie, now that he is coming home. I thought he'd written to you as much."

Lilly gaped. Was Reggie duplicating his letters to her to his mother? She quickly clamped her mouth shut and folded her hands on the table. "Reggie and I will discuss it when he returns."

Mrs. Larsen gave her a disapproving look. "You shouldn't have to *discuss* anything with Reggie. He's your husband, and your job is to obey."

"He's not my husband yet, Mrs. Larsen."

Mrs. Larsen gasped, but recovered in lightning speed. "And he may not be with that attitude!" She shot a glance at Lilly's mother, who'd planted a smile on her face.

"Well." Mrs. Larsen pounced to her feet. She seemed to search for words. "Good day, then."

Lilly stood. "Good day, Mrs. Larsen." She smiled, but Mrs. Larsen did not.

"I hope to see some progress on that dress and the wedding plans when I return."

Lilly nodded as if that was exactly what Mrs. Larsen could expect. The woman let the screen door bang behind her.

Mother Clark's smile faded as she eyed her daughter. "Is there something you want to tell me?"

"Of course not, Mother," Lilly replied in a thin voice.

She was just confused. Things were happening too fast — Reggie's telegram, Chuck's death, the elaborate Alice Larsen–created wedding plans. Lilly lay on her bed, staring at the ceiling. Confusion was the only reasonable explanation for the heaviness that settled over her when she thought about life with

Reggie. She was just feeling rushed, all her dreams cascading upon her. Even her prayers seemed to be hitting the ceiling and bouncing back.

She determined to count her blessings and make Reggie's homecoming everything he and Mrs. Larsen hoped it would be.

August slid by without a word from Reggie, or Heinrick, for that matter. The cessation of Reggie's letters lit worry in Lilly's heart. She wondered if perhaps Reggie had been mistaken about his homeward destination. September rode in, carrying with it the crisp, expectant fall air. Lilly finished Erica Torgesen's suit, but turned her down when Mrs. Torgesen asked for a Thanksgiving outfit.

Mrs. Torgesen frowned her disappointment. "Why, dear?"

Lilly forced a smile. "Because I plan to be getting married right about then."

A delighted Mrs. Torgesen clasped both hands to her mouth, then embraced Lilly.

Lilly tarried as she left the Torgesen T the final time. She leaned on the corral and watched Buttercup run among the group of stock horses, obviously the master of the herd. The mustang trotted near, stopping five feet away to examine her. His glassy brown eyes seemed to search hers, and she extended a hand to him. He sputtered and backed away.

Lilly withdrew her hand. Well, she understood. Her heart seemed just as skittish, afraid to step forward and be caught.

And yet, that was what she'd been waiting for her entire life.

She dragged home. The prairie grass had turned golden. The leaves were tarnished, the maples blushing red and orange. The smell of wood fires spiced the air. A skein of Canadian geese overhead honked their way south. Winter would soon shroud the prairie, with its endless whiteness and wind that seemed to scream in one eternal blast. Winter was for family, and quiet times, and embracing all hibernation had to offer. By then, she hoped, Reggie would be home, they would be married, and she would finally again know the sweet fragrance of peace.

CHAPTER 21

"May I walk home alone?" Lilly gathered her shawl over her shoulders and glanced up at her mother, who was tucking DJ into his woolen coat. Her mother met her gaze, compassion written on her face. She nodded.

Lilly let a sigh of relief escape her lips. The cool starlit night would be a refreshing change to Reverend Larsen's heated sermon.

The reverend's territory-wide announcement for all members of the congregation to meet and pray for the safety of their soldiers was a gathering meant to heal and extend hope to the hurting. The entire community, tired of harvesting a dying crop and weary of leaning on faith, mustered to the call, and the little church nearly burst to overflowing, yearning for fresh hope. Reverend Larsen, recognizing an opportune moment, preached a pointed sermon about obedience. It seemed to Lilly every word was meant for her ears.

Over the past month, Alice Larsen had been dutiful in her visits, inspecting Lilly's progress on her wedding dress, as if Lilly were sewing together the older woman's hopes and dreams.

Lilly exited the church cloakroom. The cool autumn breeze nipped at her ears as she watched Dakotans scatter in all directions, walking or riding buckboards. Her parents, Frankie, DJ, and Bonnie in tow, hustled past her.

"Don't tarry too long," her mother whispered.

Main Street was lonely and deeply shadowed. As she meandered down the dirt street, early stars winked at her. Dying leaves hissed, stirred by the breeze. Lilly stared into the night sky, and emptiness panged in her heart. Despite her prayers and growing faith in God's love, her spirit seemed to be dying within her, and she'd never felt so despondent. "God, what's wrong with me? Why do I feel as though I am walking through a tunnel that's only getting darker? Why am I not rejoicing? Reggie is coming home. This is a gift from You!" She wrapped her arms around her waist and moaned. The sound was snagged by the wind and amplified. "Help me, Lord." The words seemed a catharsis, and, with them, she realized she needed God more than she ever had before. She needed Him to remind her He had it all worked out, that He was still in charge — that marrying Reggie was right and His ordained will.

"Please, God, give me peace in my heart." Her words ended in muffled sobs as she buried her face in her hands.

"Lilly?"

Heinrick approached her dressed in a muddy ankle-length duster, and holding the reins to his stomping bay. He smiled, but his eyes betrayed worry.

"Where have you been?" She clamped a hand over her mouth, ashamed at the desperation in her voice.

"Roundup."

Lilly felt like a fool. All this time she thought he'd been ignoring her, hiding somewhere in a clump of Holsteins.

"I'm sorry, Heinrick. I just, well, missed you." There, she'd said it. And it was the truth. She could have used his kind words, his wisdom, and his nudges to trust in the Lord.

Heinrick looked stricken. He grabbed her by the arm. "I need to talk to you." Flinging his reins over a hitching post, he led her to the alley between Graham's Pharmacy and the armory. Lilly frowned as he stepped into the shadows, but followed. Camouflaged in the scmidarkness, Heinrick blew out a heavy breath, turning her to face him. His hat was pushed back on his head, and his hair was an inch longer, caught in the collar of his coat. Thick, white-blond stubble layered his cheeks, and something disturbing darkened his eyes.

"Lilly, I'm sorry. I didn't tell you the whole truth."

Her brow knotted in confusion.

"I saw you when you came out to the Torgesen T the last time. But . . . well, I didn't want to see you, so I rode out, away from you."

Lilly's frown deepened, and she crossed her arms under her wool cape.

"I didn't want to hurt you, Lilly, or confuse us."

Us? "What are you talking about, Heinrick?"

He swept off his hat, rubbed the brim with his hands, and stared at the ground.

"I'm talking about you belonging to another man, Lilly. I'm talking about the fact you are pledged to marry someone else, and . . . I'm in love with you."

Her jaw dropped and a tremor rippled up her spine.

"But I can't have you." Heinrick's voice was hoarse, and he avoided her eyes. "And every time I see you, it feels like a knife turning in my chest."

Shock rocked Lilly to her toes. Then, like a fragrant breeze, the joy swept through her heart. Heinrick *loved* her. That was why his eyes twinkled with delight when she was with him, why his voice always turned tender, and why he now looked more afraid than she'd ever seen him, even when facing the Craffey brothers. And she knew why her own heart now felt suddenly, wonderfully, alive.

"Oh Heinrick," Lilly blurted, unable to stop herself. "I love you, too."

Heinrick's blue eyes probed hers, searching for the truth.

Lilly smiled broadly, love coursing through her veins with every beat of her heart. "Ya, Heinrick, I do!"

His eyes shone as a lopsided grin appeared on his face. He closed the gap between them in one smooth step. Then he slid a gloved hand around her neck. She jumped, then leaned into his strong grip.

Heinrick studied her for a moment, as if imprinting her face on his memory, examining her eyes, her hair, her nose, finally her lips. The expression in his eyes betrayed his intentions.

He wanted to kiss her.

Lilly's breath caught in her throat and she tingled from head to toe. She felt frightened and hopeful all at once. She wanted to be inside his powerful arms, to feel the tenderness of his touch. But it was wrong. Despite her feelings and his, so vividly written on his face, she couldn't allow him to kiss her. Lilly touched his chest, intending to push him away.

"Lillian Clark, what are you doing?"

The voice ripped them apart. Heinrick

stepped away from her as Lilly whirled. Marjorie Pratt stood on the street, next to the armory, staring at them as if they had planted a bomb on Main Street. "What are you doing?" she repeated, her voice rising in horror.

Lilly felt sick. "Marjorie, please."

"You are engaged to Reggie! And this man" — Marjorie pointed wildly at Heinrick — "is a *German*! His kind *murdered* Harley and *Chuck* and almost killed Reggie, and you are *kissing* him?" Her voice reached a shrill pitch, and Lilly stepped toward her.

"Marjorie, I'm not kissing him. We're just talking."

"That's not what it looked like to me!"

Lilly shook her head, "Marj, please listen. . . ."

"I will *not* listen, you . . . you . . . *traitor*!" Marjorie glared at her, shaking with fury. Lilly saw Marjorie's rage and realized her friend was beyond reason. Then Marjorie bolted, plunging into the darkness. Lilly started after her, groaned, and let her go.

She turned and shot a helpless look at Heinrick. His defeated expression terrified her more than Marjorie's fury. Heinrick replaced his hat, his mouth set in a muted line. His eyes were distant. "I'll take you home."

Lilly wanted to scream, weep, throw herself into his arms, and make him affirm his love for her. But his emotions were locked safely

1128

behind the same tortured, lonely expression she'd seen back at the Torgesen T. This time, however, instead of reaching out to her, pulling her into his world, he pushed her away. Her eyes filled.

Heinrick helped her into the saddle, then mounted his horse behind her. His arms wrapped around her, and she let herself enjoy the strong, safe place inside his forced embrace. He said nothing the entire ride home, but Lilly felt his chest move in heavy sighs as she leaned against him. When she glanced up into his shadowed face, hoping to find a glimmer of the love he'd unveiled in the alley, she saw only stone blue eyes peering into the darkness.

The wind moaned, along with her heart. The smell of wood fires lingered in the air, and perhaps the smoke singed her eyes, for tears edged down her cheeks.

When they reached her road, Heinrick reined the bay. "Should I take you to the house?" His voice seemed pinched, as if pushed through a vise.

Lilly's throat burned. "No. I'd better get off here."

Heinrick nodded and dismounted. Lilly let herself slide into his arms. He held her one moment longer than necessary, or maybe she imagined it. Then he released her, and she stepped away. She lifted her chin, waiting for him to remount his horse. A thousand words formed, but she couldn't get them past the sorrow flooding her heart.

Heinrick grabbed his saddle horn and stared out across the prairie. "You were right, Lilly. I should have listened to you from the beginning. I seem to bring you nothing but trouble. I'm sorry."

Lilly longed to refute his words. *Oh no, Heinrick, you've brought me nothing but joy.* But she saw in his eyes the futility of argument.

"I think, for your sake" — Heinrick's voice turned stiff — "and for mine, this is good-bye."

Lilly bit her lip and nodded woodenly.

"Lilly, don't forget God loves you." He kept the rest unspoken, but oh, how she wanted to hear it: *and so do I.*

She shivered as she watched him climb into the saddle. He spurred his horse and, in violent abruptness, was gone in a full gallop toward the Torgesen T.

Then there was just the terrible roaring of emptiness in her heart.

By Lilly's estimation, the shelling started shortly after midnight. The first rock shattered one of the glass windows on the front of the house and landed in the living room, next to her mother's willow rocker. The second volley destroyed the other window and smashed a stack of fine china her mother had carted west from Chicago.

By the time the third rock hurtled through the parlor window and crushed the mantle clock, her father was in the living room, pulling on his cotton workpants and flipping suspenders over his shoulders. Lilly watched from the doorway of her bedroom as her mother flew down the stairs, despite orders to stay put. Lilly realized her mother's intentions were not to save her collection of gel teacups from the old country nor the freshly caned straightback chairs. No, she headed straight for Olive and Christian's room, located in the lean-to on the main floor.

Olive appeared, clutching a screaming Christian, her face the color of chalk. "What's going on?" she shrieked.

Mother Clark slung her arm around them. "Upstairs!" she commanded.

From the landing, Lilly clutched Bonnie's hand and watched them race for the stairway. A rock blew through the kitchen window, scattering glass at their heels. Olive's terrified scream shook the house.

"Hurry!" Lilly yelled.

Olive and her mother scampered up the stairs two at a time. Her older sister dove past Lilly and flew into her parents' room. Lilly saw her throw Christian on the bed and cover him with her body. Mrs. Clark grabbed Bonnie by the arm, meaning to pull both her girls along with her, but Lilly broke away from Bonnie's grasp and scrambled down the stairs.

"Lilly, come back here!" her mother called, racing down the hall to retrieve the boys.

Lilly skidded to a halt in the parlor. Her father was crouched below a window. He shot her a frown. "Get down."

She dropped to all fours and crawled across the floor. "Who's doing this?"

He put a finger to his lips.

Outside, Lilly heard slurred, enraged voices.

"That's Clive Torgesen!" Her chest tightened. A rock ripped through an unbroken pane and glass sprayed the room. Lilly cried out as her father shielded her with his body. The rock thudded into a Queen Anne armchair.

"I'm going out there," he said.

Lilly grabbed his arm. "No, Father, they'll kill you!"

He jerked his arm away. "I've got to stop them before they do real damage, like set fire to the house."

Lilly's heart froze in her chest.

Jumping up, she scuttled behind her father.

"Lilly, get upstairs!" He opened the front door.

She backed away and hid behind the parlor door frame.

Her father stepped onto the porch. Lilly tiptoed to the front door, sidled to one side, and peeked out. In the moonlight, she could make out four men: Clive Torgesen, two of his cattle hands, and an older man. Lilly gasped. The last was Harry Bishop, Marjorie's cousin, and from latest accounts, an outlaw. Marjorie had obviously raced straight home and informed her family what she'd seen in Mobridge.

Mr. Clark held up a steady hand and spoke in a loud voice. "Howdy, boys. What seems to be the problem?"

Guilt edged Lilly onto the porch. This was her doing, and she had to face it.

Clive balled his hands on his hips and swayed. "Your daughter's a Benedict Arnold, Clark!"

"I have three daughters, boys, and all of them are loyal to the Red, White, and Blue." Her father's calm voice mustered Lilly's courage.

Harry pointed a quivering finger at him. "That ain't true! Marjorie caught her kissing a German right here in this very town!"

Lilly's breath caught, but she propelled her legs forward and darted behind her father, clutching his arm. The wind whipped through her cotton nightgown and even from five feet away, the pungent odor of whiskey hit her with a stinging force. Lilly's eyes watered from the stench. Her father didn't spare her a glance.

"My daughter is engaged to Reggie Larsen, boys. She wouldn't go near another man."

His voice sounded so sure, Lilly was sickened to think he was about to be made a fool.

"You need to keep a shorter leash on her!" Clive stumbled forward and threw a bottle onto the porch. It smashed at her father's feet. He didn't even flinch.

"This here is a warnin' — you keep that girl of yours under lock and key and away from the enemy, or we'll teach her and your whole family a lesson in patriotism!" Clive curled his lip and spat on the ground. He waved at Lilly, who shrank behind her father. "I see you there, missy. And I know what ya done. Your friend Henry is gonna git a reminder about keepin' his paws off American girls!"

Lilly went cold. Heinrick against Clive and three drunken brutes? She closed her eyes and buried her face in her father's back.

"Get outta here, boys." Her father's voice carried on the wind and must have seemed like thunder to the inebriated men because they spooked and backed up.

"You remember what we said, missy! You stay home!"

As her father stood there, Lilly saw him as a lone wall of protection between a prejudiced world and his family. She was horrified to know she'd brought it on, but profoundly thankful for her father's courage. He was stoic as the four men rode off. Then he whirled, grabbed Lilly by her thin cotton-clothed arm, and marched her back into the house.

That's when she began to tremble.

CHAPTER 22

"We'll clean up, then we'll talk." Her father's voice was tight.

Lilly instantly discovered untapped energy. She swept the broken glass and fastened the shutters. Her mother, Olive, and Bonnie worked silently beside her. Lilly shed noiseless tears as she watched her mother pile the broken china on the kitchen table. Bonnie occasionally frowned in her direction, but it was Olive's unmasked glare that made Lilly want to crawl under her bed and hide.

Finally, the house was put in order. Their mother sent Bonnie, DJ, and Frankie to their rooms. Olive stomped upstairs and slammed the door to her parents' bedroom. Lilly's mother sank into the willow rocker and folded her hands on her lap, her mouth a muted line. Her father ran his hand through his brown hair and paced in a circle near the sofa. Lilly knew he fought a swelling anger.

"What's this all about, Lilly?"

"I know what it's about!" Olive snarled

from the top landing. A scarecrow in her white nightgown, fury blazed in Olive's dark eyes, and her face twisted in rage. She stormed down the stairs, waving a parchment envelope.

Lilly went numb. "Where did you get that?"

Olive ignored her. "It's a letter from him. From that German spy she met in town!"

Lilly clenched her teeth and glanced at her father. A muscle tensed in his jaw as he looked between his two daughters. He frowned at Lilly, and she shrank into a hard-backed chair.

Olive wore a crazed look. "You've been getting letters from him, haven't you? Letters from the enemy! You're a traitor! You've betrayed us all." She threw the letter at Lilly. It spiraled to the floor. Lilly ducked her head.

"Go to bed, Olive."

Olive recoiled from her father's command as if she'd been slapped. She stabbed a finger at Lilly. "She doesn't deserve Reggie."

Silence threw a thousand accusing jabs as Lilly weighed those words. Then Olive's wretched sobs broke the stunned quiet. She covered her face with her hands, and her body shook. Her father held her.

Lilly's heart twisted and tears flowed as she watched her sister suffer. She'd never meant to bring this kind of grief to her family.

Olive finally disentangled herself from her father's grasp. Without a glance at Lilly, she turned and climbed the stairs, every thump echoing through the house. Lilly heard her parents' bedroom door close.

Her father turned to her. His lips were pinched in suppressed fury. She sucked a deep breath and glanced at her mother, who offered her a slightly pitying look. Mr. Clark sat on the edge of the sofa, clasped his hands together, and raised his brows.

Lilly gulped. Then, working her fingers into knots, she spilled out the story. She started with the fight on the street, included the English lessons, the horseback ride, the butterfly comb, and her confrontation with Marjorie.

"But I didn't kiss him," Lilly insisted.

Her father shook his head. "You didn't have to — you already gave him your heart. That's betrayal enough."

Lilly caught her breath. He was right. She *had* given Heinrick her heart. And in doing so, she'd been unfaithful to Reggie. But they were all missing the most important part of her story.

"Father, Heinrick opened a door to God. Somehow, through his words, I saw that I feared God, as if He were a wolf waiting to eat me if I did something wrong. But Heinrick showed me that isn't true. God loves me and has a good plan for my life. And when I make mistakes or don't do everything right, I am still loved. Heinrick taught me how to trust God, no matter what happens. He showed me the keys to freedom, to joy, and God unlocked my prison."

Her father's face softened, and Lilly was relieved to see his anger dissolve. "Lilly," he said in his controlled bass, "you've cost this family a great deal this evening by your impulsiveness. You've shown bad judgment —"

"But what about —"

He held up a hand and silenced his daughter with a piercing look. "You're engaged to another man, Lilly. You've made a commitment to him, and you owe him your promise."

Lilly glanced at her mother. Her mother's eyes were wide, and she leaned forward in the rocker.

"I forbid you ever to see this Heinrick again, Lilly. You will stay home, and if you leave the house, you will be with Bonnie, Olive, or your parents." Her father lowered his voice. "When Reggie gets home, you will plead his forgiveness. And we will all hope and pray he forgives you and decides to marry you anyway."

Lilly felt as if he had slugged her. "Father, you can't want me to marry someone I don't love!"

He leaned back into the fraying sofa and put his wide weathered hands on his knees. "You do love Reggie, Lilly. You haven't seen him for over a year. You were lonely, and we can understand your vulnerability. But that's over. Reggie is coming home, and you'll see I'm right." His eyes kneaded her with a sudden tenderness, and Lilly's eyes filled with new tears. "Honey, I am doing this for you. For your own good." He glanced at his wife. "She'll thank me later."

Lilly couldn't look at her mother. Tears dripped off her chin, and she felt as if she'd just been dressed down like a six-year-old. She had less freedom than Frankie did. And her father was going to give her to a man she didn't love.

The realization hit her like a winter blast. She didn't love Reggie. How could that be? She'd grown up with him, practically worshiped him from the day he started teasing her at school. She thought he'd made her dreams come true when he asked her to marry him. Reggie was her life. How could she think she didn't love him?

But it was true. Somehow, she'd denied it, for how long she couldn't guess. Her feelings for Reggie were wrapped in a package of expectations, respect, and gratefulness. But Reggie couldn't make her heart soar. Only Heinrick could do that. Only Heinrick knew the real, unmasked Lilly, the afraid Lilly, the impulsive and even brave Lilly. He unearthed her innermost thoughts and embraced them with a touch of unconditional and breathtaking love. Lilly choked, feeling as if her father had tightened a noose around her neck. She had no choices. Trusting God, consulting Him, surrendering to His plans, whatever they were, were not a part of the equation. She had others to obey — her parents, Reggie.

Despair snuffed out the ember of hope that had burst into flame only earlier that evening.

Lilly hung her head. "Yes, Father."

Darkness hovered like a fog over the wheat field. Lilly sat in the window seat, her head in her folded arms, her eyes swollen. Her father had dismissed her to her room an hour prior, but sleep was forgotten in the mourning of her heart. She slouched in the windowsill and felt a numbing cold creep over her.

Lilly rose and tiptoed toward her closet. Maybe her father would allow her a brief trip to the river to watch the sunrise. She needed the fingers of light to weave into her soul; and the maple grove, despite the memories it stored of Heinrick, was also the place God had spoken to her and reminded her to seek Him. He promised she would find Him when she looked for Him. Even when she'd been bereft over the loss of Reggie, God had carried her. He could carry her now.

She changed into a brown wool dress and long stockings and grabbed her knit gray shawl as she padded from her room.

Lilly approached the landing and heard her

parents' muffled voices from the family room below. They had not gone to bed, either. Guilt burned in her chest, but she couldn't keep her curiosity from planting herself on the top step. Their conversation became distinct as she held her breath and ignored her pounding heart.

"My father felt the same way," her mother was saying. "Don't you remember the night you asked him for my hand? He nearly broke his arm throwing you out of the house."

Lilly's heart lightened to hear her father's soft chuckle. Then his voice turned solemn. "This is different, Ruth. I wasn't a foreigner. The world wasn't at war."

"No, you were from a different church. And you were poor. To my parents, that was worse."

Lilly wrapped her arms around her knees and concentrated to catch every word.

"And what about her new faith, Donald? You can't say Reggie brought her that."

"Reggie is a good man. He loves God and will guide her spiritually."

Her mother's harrumph ricocheted up the stairs. "If Reggie's belief in God is anything like Pastor Larsen's, I think it is Lilly who will teach him."

"Now Ruth, Pastor Larsen is a wise man."

"Wise and firm. But is he kind? And what about Reggie? Will he treat Lilly with gentleness and love?"

"Of course he will. And he has a sound future in front of him. What kind of life can some German immigrant give her? Is that what we want for Lilly?"

"I don't think it's up to us, Donald. Lilly trusts us, but we need to let her make her own decisions."

"I'm her father. I have to look out for her."

Lilly sensed the texture of her mother's voice soften. She imagined her touching her husband softly on the arm, as was her habit. "Just like my father looked out for me and gave you a chance to prove your love. He knew I loved you, and he knew I thought God wanted me to marry you. So he waited in giving my hand until he was sure of the one God had chosen. God's given me a good life with you, dear. It may not have been an easy life, but it's been a joyful one."

Tears edged Lilly's eyes. She shouldn't be listening to their intimate conversation. She gathered herself to creep back to her room. But her father's last words burned in her ears.

"Ruth, you're a persuasive woman. If this fella can prove to me he loves her more than Reggie, I'll give him a chance."

Lilly stumbled to her room, stifling a cry. Her father would have let Heinrick prove himself! But it was too late. Heinrick had told her good-bye, and right now, he was probably lying in a pool of his own blood. Lilly

1143

threw herself on the bed next to Bonnie, curled into a ball, and wept.

CHAPTER 23

"Get your paws off Christian," Olive snarled and turned her dark eyes on Lilly. Lilly slowly put the toddler back on the floor, where he'd been playing with a wooden spoon, and backed away from him. She avoided Olive's glare, but shuddered as she heard Olive slam a plate down at her place on the table. Olive acted as if Lilly's betrayal had singularly led to Chuck's death. It was more than a cold, aloof snubbing. Olive sizzled with hatred and was directing the blaze at Lilly.

Lilly felt like the apostle Paul, under Roman house arrest. She even envied the birds, the lark and crow, who scolded her, then lifted in flight over the prairie. What did their eyes see when they flew over the Torgesen T? Did they see Heinrick, well and hustling cattle? Or was he lying in a bunkhouse, bleeding, broken, near death? The horror of it assaulted her at odd times; while she hung laundry, when she dipped out water from the rain barrel, once when she milked the cows.

And, despite her attempts to push the memory aside, she couldn't seem to escape the look of joy in his eyes when she told him she loved him.

Lilly mourned Heinrick in private, pouring out her tears late at night under cover of her quilt and praying for release from the grip of heartache. His magnetic blue eyes and tireless smile pressed against her, and there were times she felt crushed and thought she would break from the pain. Other times, the load seemed to lighten, as if some hand had lifted it from her heart. Lilly fought to put him out of her mind. From dawn to dusk, she buried herself in her chores, read her Bible, and hoped for dreamless, exhausted sleep. She relentlessly tried to believe her father's words — she'd simply been lonely and her feelings for Heinrick were built upon boredom. But, as the days turned over into weeks and October blew the fire-lit leaves of ash and maples into the yard, she realized a part of Heinrick would always be hers. He'd left her his legacy, the imprint of the force that defined his life — a personal relationship with the Lord of the universe. The key to joy incarnate was Heinrick's gift to her. For that freedom, she would always be grateful she'd met him.

Lilly altered her wedding dress, finishing it the first week of November. She embroidered, white upon the white satin, a floral pattern designed from her own drying lilies of the valley, with oversized bells that cascaded down the skirt from the sculptured empire waistline. She removed the sheer lace over-skirt and added the lace instead to the elbow-length sleeves. The wide, wispy cuffs were contrary to popular styles, but they were exactly what she wanted. She hung the dress over the door of her wardrobe.

"Lilly, it's breathtaking." Her mother folded her arms and leaned against the door frame.

Grateful, Lilly smiled.

Her mother drew Lilly into her arms. "You'll be a beautiful bride."

Lilly nodded into her mother's shoulder.

Her mother pulled away and held her at arm's length. "I know you had hoped for something different. . . ."

She forced a smile. "No, Mother. I'm ready to marry Reggie."

Mother Clark's brows arched.

"I know it's the right thing to do."

Her mother flattened her smile and nodded, as if understanding. She laid a hand on Lilly's shoulder and squeezed gently, and Lilly wished she'd spoken the truth.

Lilly tucked her hair into a knit bonnet, pulled on a wool duster, and hustled out the door. Her family, minus Olive and Christian, were already headed into town.

Minutes ago, a rider on horseback had galloped through their yard, leaving in his wake the triumphant announcement — the Germans had surrendered to the Allied Forces somewhere in the middle of the French wilds. The war was over. Lilly watched the messenger tear north, toward the Torgesen T, and wondered how the news would greet Heinrick. He was no longer the enemy. She shoved the thought aside and caught up to her family. It didn't matter, anyway. Reggie would surely be home soon.

In town, forgiveness drifted on the crisp winter air. Mrs. Larsen, who had heretofore regarded Lilly with frigid eyes and an acid tongue, wrapped her in a two-armed hug and squeezed. "Now we can all get back to our lives," she whispered.

Main Street was packed, and Miller's did a thriving coffee and tea business while selling copies of the Armistice telegram that had sped across the country. Bonnie skipped down the steps of the pharmacy, waving the surrender details. Huddling next to her mother and listening as her father read the account, Lilly spied Marjorie standing in a clump of ecstatic women. Lilly tightened her jaw and ignored the stab in her heart.

The train whistle blew. Lilly took a deep breath and wondered if today, finally, she would receive word from Reggie. She had no address for him, had no idea where to send her own half-written scripts. But she didn't know what to say, either. They would have to sort it out when he came home, if he came home.

The train pulled into the station and coughed. The echo of it carried across town. Lilly made a mental note to check her box later.

She leaned forward and listened to her father finish the newspaper story. Her mother patted her hand. "Praise God, it's over."

Lilly could only nod. Finally, Mobridge could regroup, collectively mourn its losses, and rebuild. The community could patch the wounds, lay to rest the fears and the horror, and stumble forward into the future. Lilly knew they would find a way to hold on to the land, their legacies, and their love. They would survive.

A gasp washed like a wave through the clusters of gossiping townspeople. Lilly bristled, and an odd sensation rippled up her spine. She looked up and went weak.

"Hello, Lilly." Reggie stood in the middle of the street, his khaki uniform wrinkled under an open overcoat, his dress cap tilted crazily over his hand, and a sprig of short black hair sticking out like a flagpole over his eyes. He smiled a smooth milky grin. He leaned forward, as if she hadn't heard him, and repeated himself. "Lilly?"

1149

Lilly cried out and rushed toward his open arms.

Mrs. Larsen beat her to him. She clung to her son and wept. Reggie buried his head in his mother's neck and held her.

Lilly stood paralyzed. She waited, watching the wind toy with his hat, then knock it aloft. It fingered his short hair, lifted the collar of his coat, and carried to her the smell of wool and perspiration, confidence and strength. The smell of Reggie. She breathed in deeply.

Reggie finally extracted himself from his sobbing mother and stepped toward Lilly. She met his eyes and saw buried in them a thousand battles, not all with guns and bombs. Reggie reached out and slipped his hand around her neck. He paused, then in a desperate moment, drew her against him, burying his face in her hair. "Lilly," he groaned. "I feared I would never see you again."

She encircled his waist with her arms and pulled him close. They embraced while a hundred eyes watched them, measuring, considering. Lilly knew this was probably their last untarnished moment. Once his mother had him alone, she could reveal to him the indiscretions of his disobedient fiancée. If not her, then Marjorie, Ernestine, or even Olive. Somehow, the tale would emerge, and the unwavering trust between them that had been theirs before the war and now, in this magical moment, would be forever scarred. She clutched him tighter.

"You missed me," he said, his voice husky.

Lilly pulled back and stared into his wounded brown eyes. She felt the pricking of tears and nodded. A grin tugged at his mouth. "And I missed you."

Then he lowered his face and kissed her. It felt familiar and warm.

Reggie finally released her, pinned on her one last meaningful look, and then stepped into the multitude. Lilly let free a shuddering, cleansing breath. Hope had returned to the prairie in vivid intensity.

Mrs. Larsen pulled at Lilly's arm, her face close. "We'll be up tomorrow to discuss wedding plans."

Lilly nodded and saw Reggie disappear into the crowd.

That night, as she and Bonnie were undressing for bed, Bonnie stole up behind her and placed a small parchment envelope on her vanity. Lilly stared at it and blanched. "Where did you get it?"

Bonnie looked at her, curiosity in her youthful eyes. "I picked it up at the post office today."

Lilly fingered the envelope and examined the bold, block letters. Her skin prickled.

"Is it from him?"

Lilly shot her sister a glance.

Bonnie shrugged and smiled mysteriously. "Sometimes you talk in your sleep."

Lilly swallowed hard.

Bonnie giggled. "Don't worry. Your secret is safe with me."

What secret? Lilly turned over the envelope in her hands and cautiously worked it open.

Short and dated the first week of October, the note made her tremble.

Dear Lilly,

I heard about your home, and I am sorry for the trouble I caused you. The Torgesens have released me from my contract, and I am leaving Mobridge. Thank you for your friendship; you are written upon my heart. The words from Ruth 2:12 speak my hope for you. May the good Lord repay you for your kindness. May He protect you and reward you. Go with God, Lilly.

Yours,
Heinrick

Lilly moaned and clutched the letter to her chest. He was gone, and somehow, with him, went the last shred of a love that had seemed so intoxicating, so breathtaking, so encompassing. And so right.

Lilly fell to her knees, buried her head into the crazy quilt, and sobbed. Bonnie knelt beside her and rubbed her back.

Why, on the day of Reggie's return, when peace should finally be hers, did she feel as though she were back in battle?

CHAPTER 24

"I think we'll have a Thanksgiving wedding." Reggie tucked his hands in the pocket of his woolen gray duster and peered into Lilly's eyes. Sheltered in the grove of maples, the howl of the unrelenting wind didn't seem as loud and menacing. Lilly folded her mittened hands together and nodded, an acquiescing smile on her face. Two weeks seemed a mere blink away, but she'd been waiting for two years. The sooner it happened, the better.

Reggie studied her. "You've changed, Lilly. You seem, oh, I don't know, more serious. I expected my bubbly, carefree Lilly." His eyes clouded. "You seem pensive."

Lilly bit her lip.

Reggie turned away and propped up his collar. "You aren't even happy to see me."

Lilly's heart twisted. She put a hand on his arm. "Of course I am."

He turned and considered her a long moment. It seemed to Lilly he seemed shorter, not quite as towering as he'd been. And his dark eyes were sharper, older. His face was lean, his angled jaw cleanly shaven. She'd observed him all week, especially today at morning service, and noted he carried an unfamiliar air of wariness that could only be reaped by war. And once, when she'd slid her hand onto his arm while he gazed across the frost-covered fields, he'd nearly jumped out of his skin. His eyes brimmed with anger, and it took him a full painful five seconds to tuck some horrific moment into the folds of memory. But the residue of hatred frightened her.

Reggie pulled away from her touch and stalked out to the bluff. The breeze blew through his short hair. He stared across the river. "In France, this view was all I could think of. Home. Being with you. It seemed the only reason worth fighting. Whenever the commander yelled for us to attack and the blood froze in my veins, the thought of you waiting for me gave me the courage to climb over the barricades. One step at time, one shot at a time, I figured I was headed home."

Tears welled in Lilly's eyes. She edged toward him. "Why didn't you write? It's been three months since your telegram." Her voice cracked. "What happened?"

Reggie's voice hardened. "I couldn't write because I couldn't see. Some nurse sent the telegram for me." Rawness, as though the incident had happened yesterday, entered his tone. "I was hit by mustard gas the day Harley and Chuck were killed." He paused and drew in a deep breath. "Luckily, I shoved on my mask right after it hit, so I didn't get the worst of it. Instead, I saw my best buddies killed." Grief twisted his face. Lilly tugged on his arm and led him to a bleached cottonwood. He sat and hung his head in his hands.

Lilly tucked herself beside him.

"It was horrible. I couldn't breathe. After the fighting stopped, we crawled out of our bunkers and took off our masks. Then the torture began. My eyes felt as if they had been seared with a branding torch. They glued together, and my throat closed. It swelled up, and I couldn't swallow. I was choking."

Tears chilled Lilly's cheeks.

Reggie's voice dropped. "They had to strap me down."

Lilly gazed across the ice-edged river and conjured up a ghastly image of Reggie tied to a hospital bed. She felt ill and longed to close her ears to his words.

"All I could think of the entire time was you, Lilly. You and our future."

Lilly wrapped her arms around herself, pushing against physical pain.

Reggie turned to her. "I don't want to wait until Thanksgiving. I would marry you tomorrow if I could. I just want to get back to some kind of normalcy, the life I always dreamed of." He wrapped her upper arms in an iron grip and turned her to face him. "Please, say you will marry me, Lilly."

His brown eyes probed hers, and Lilly saw in them desperation and longing so intense, she knew she couldn't deny him. She couldn't cause him more pain. "Of course I will, Reggie."

He pulled her to himself and kissed her, powerfully, winding his arm around her neck and holding her tight.

Lilly fled into her wedding plans. Somehow, tucked inside Reggie's grins and Mrs. Larsen's babbling, Lilly felt a measure of calm, as if she'd negotiated a cease-fire in her heart. She marched forward, toward the inevitable conclusion, and told herself this was right.

But tiny sputters of doubt began to explode deep inside her heart.

"I saw Erica Torgesen in town today," commented Reggie as they sat together on the porch steps, bundled and staring at the hazy sputter of the sun.

Lilly peered at him sideways.

"She asked if you had time to sew her something for the New Year's social." He gave her a stern eye, his mouth a firm line. "I took the liberty of telling her you wouldn't be doing that sort of thing anymore."

Lilly looked past him, north toward the

Torgesen T, and said nothing.

Sunday, after church, Reggie closed in during the walk home. "Mother told me you haven't been attending the Ladies Aid meetings." His hand seemed rough on her arm. "I thought we agreed you would help with tea, Lilly."

She shot him a frown. Did she agree to help? Or had Reggie and Mrs. Larsen consented for her?

Lilly beat back the flames of doubt, however, with prayer and a patient spirit. She was just nervous, as any bride would be. She clung to the faith that God had her future in His hands and would lead her to a lifetime of joy. God would give her peace as she walked forward in faith. She just had to be patient.

Snow peeled from the clouds in soft translucent layers and melted on the hard-packed road. Lilly meandered toward Mobridge, her hands tucked in a beaver skin muff, occasionally catching a few flakes on her tongue and nose. The sun was a glittering pumpkin, brilliant against a silver gray sky and frosting the bluffs orange.

Lilly sighed and picked up her pace. She was already late, expected by Mrs. Larsen and the others on the Ladies Aid committee to help decorate the church. Her family would join her in an hour or so, Olive and her mother each toting the Clark family's

1158

contribution to the Thanksgiving pie social — pumpkin and apple pies.

Next year she would be appearing with Mrs. Larsen, toting her own pie, as Reggie's wife. Reggie had already prepared a room for them at the Larsen home while he readied himself to take on a congregation of his own. He mentioned a year of preparation while he worked with his father and learned the "trade." Lilly had considered, with the anger that bubbled out occasionally when he mentioned Chuck, Harley, the Germans, or anything that had to do with the Great War, it might take him longer to find the peace to minister to others. But she'd clamped her mouth shut after he told her it was none of her business and asked how she could possibly understand his nightmares. So, she determined to find a way to live in the Larsen household until she could create one of her own.

Mrs. Larsen was thrilled to have another helping hand around the house and told her so.

The town was barren; the shops closed, customary on the day before Thanksgiving. Lilly heard the train whistle skip along the frozen prairie in the distance and recalled the days when she would race the wind to greet the mail train with a letter. It was a time of innocence and naive hopes, a lifetime apart from what she knew now — the reality, and cost, of love.

She rounded the armory and was passing Miller's when she spotted him. She almost didn't recognize the man, dressed in a pair of forest green woolen pants and a knee-length matching wool coat — standard issue brakeman's uniform for the Milwaukee Road. He could have been any other railroad man, toting a lead lantern, headed for work. But he wasn't. She knew him the minute her gaze traveled upward and took in the long blond hair trickling out in curls from his wool railroad cap.

"Heinrick," she breathed into the wind. He whirled and saw her.

He paused, as if determining the distance between them, in so many ways, then turned and strode toward her. As he drew closer, she reached out her hand. He caught it in his and purposefully led her to the small alley between Bud's and the armory, where they had nearly kissed and been discovered. Where her heart had entwined hopelessly and forever with his.

Heinrick set down his lantern and glanced into the empty street. He released her hand, gripped her upper arms, and pinned his eyes to hers. "Lilly."

Lilly's breath caught. She heard in his raw tone and saw in his eyes what she hoped for — a longing for her, a missing so intense it was etched into his heart.

"Are you all right?" she whispered.

He cracked a crooked grin, and Lilly's heart thumped.

"I'm all right."

Three words, and yet with them, fear broke free and relief crested over her. Her voice shook. "I've been so worried, Heinrick. Clive said he was going to hurt you, teach you a lesson."

Heinrick closed his eyes and nodded. "Well, he tried, that's for sure." Then he opened his eyes and they twinkled with a familiar mischief. "But those boys never fought a man who worked shoveling sand ten hours a day. Besides, Erica Torgesen doesn't like roughhousing, and she put it to Clive to either let me go or leave me be."

Lilly squinted at him, noting an unfamiliar scar above his left eye. She wondered what he wasn't telling her. Lilly arched her brows. "So Clive let you go?"

"*Ja.* Did you get my note?"

Lilly nodded.

"I wrote it after I got my job on the line. I was passing through here and dropped it off."

Heinrick looked away. "I have bad timing."

Lilly frowned, then remembered the day she'd received his letter. The day Reggie came home.

"You saw Reggie."

Heinrick's mouth was pinched, and when he looked at her, hurt ringed his eyes. "I'm

1161

very happy for you, Lilly."

Lilly's eyes misted.

"I'm stationed in Sioux Falls now. I just stopped in today to pick up some gear I had in storage." He nodded to a rucksack on his back.

He bent to grab his lantern, as if intending to say good-bye and walk out of her life forever.

"Heinrick, wait." Lilly stepped toward him, not really knowing what she wanted to say, but realizing she had to say something, anything to keep him there long enough for her to know. . . .

Heinrick paused and looked down at her, almost wincing. He reached for a rebellious strand of hair that had loosened from her bonnet and rubbed its softness between his fingers.

"Lilly, I can't take you away from Reggie. You have to choose, on your own. You have to come to me freely. Because if you don't, you'll be exchanging one prison for another."

He dropped her hair, ran his finger along her jaw, then lifted her chin. "More than that, you must do what God wants you to do."

Lilly opened her mouth, and her thoughts spilled out. "But I don't know what that is."

Heinrick considered her a long moment. "Have you asked Him and really listened for the answer?"

Lilly gave him a blank look while her mind

sifted through his question. He was right. She'd never seriously listened to God's answer, never considered any reply but the one she already knew.

But it was too late to change course. Her wedding was two days away. She shook her head.

Heinrick's jaw stiffened. "Then I can't make your decision for you." The train whistle screamed as it pulled into the station. "I have to go, Lilly. May God bless your marriage." He turned away.

Lilly put a hand on his arm and folded her fingers into the wool. "I have to know, Heinrick." Her tone betrayed her heart.

He frowned.

"Do you love me?"

His mouth curved wryly, and she thought she saw a flicker of sadness in his stormy blue eyes. He covered her hand with his own. "I've loved you since the day you saved me on the street."

"I thought you said you didn't need any help."

His voice turned raw. "I needed help, Lilly. I needed, more than anything, for someone to walk beside me, to be my friend and encourage me to fight for a place in this country." He touched her cheek. "God sent you to do that for me. And now, because of you, I have a future here." His gaze lingered on her, and she felt the strength of his feelings sweep through her.

Then, he snatched the lantern and strode away. And, with each long step, Lilly knew he was taking with him her heart.

CHAPTER 25

Lilly headed for the cloakroom and pulled off her coat. Mechanical. Steadfast. Resolute. She walked into the sanctuary and presented herself for service. Alice Larsen shot her a scowl. Lilly ignored it.

The pews in the small sanctuary were pushed back against the walls, creating a large square gap in the center. Two cloth-covered tables lined the center of the room, a throne for the pies.

Ernestine put her to work lighting candles. Lilly glanced out a window. Pellet-sized snowflakes fell from the darkening sky and covered the fields in a thick blanket. Families began to stream in, pies gathering on the two tables. Lilly smiled, nodded, and greeted.

Her mother and Olive arrived and added their pies to the table. Bonnie peeled layers of wraps off DJ and Frankie. Her father came in, a film of crystalline snow on his wool jacket. "We're in for it, folks," he commented wryly.

Reverend Larsen offered Mr. Clark his hand. "Nothing like the winter of 1910, though. It started snowing in June that year and didn't let up 'til the following July!"

Lilly's father guffawed and pumped the preacher's arm.

Lilly slid up to the two men. "Excuse me, Reverend. Do you know where Reggie is?"

Reverend Larsen raised his eyebrows. "Lost track of him already, Lilly? And you aren't even married yet!" He eyed her father, who smirked.

Lilly blushed. Reverend Larsen put a hand on her shoulder. "He rode out earlier with Clive Torgesen and some of the other boys, hunting pheasants. He'll be here."

The crowd thickened quickly. The Thanksgiving pie feast was akin to the fair in terms of pie competition. Everyone had a favorite. Lilly favored Jennifer Pratt's vanilla crème. She surveyed the crowd but didn't find either Marjorie or the Pratt family.

Reverend Larsen led them in a time of Thanks-sharing, then the pies were attacked. DJ and Frankie grabbed their favorites, a tart crabapple from the Ed Miller family and a fresh peach from Ernestine's, which Willard admitted he'd made. Lilly accepted a bite of each, but wasn't hungry for her own. Her thoughts were occupied with a still missing Reggie, and Heinrick.

The crowd began to scatter, the adults

bundling up the children for the ride home.

"Coming with us, Lilly?" Her mother's voice carried over the room as she tugged DJ's cap over his ears.

Lilly shook her head. "No. I'll wait for Reggie."

Her father looked worried. "Don't stay out too long, Lilly. That storm is whippin' up."

Lilly helped clear tables with the Ladies Aid, but avoided the women when they clumped in gossip. The wind outside began to moan, but it drew her to the church entrance. Perhaps a blast of cold air could untangle the knot in her heart. Pulling on her coat, she cracked the door open and slipped outside. The wind encircled her, groaning in her ears, and pawing at her coat. She stuck her hands in the pockets and wrapped it around her.

Instinctively, her hand closed around an object in the well of her pocket. She pulled it out and her heart tumbled. Heinrick's butterfly comb. She turned over the exquisite gift, and the dull, throbbing wound in her heart ripped open.

How had it landed in her pocket? She shifted through memory and found the day when she'd pulled it from her drawer and tried it on. The ginger-colored wings illuminated the few gold threads in her hair, and Lilly had left it in as she read her Bible that morning. She'd lost herself in the Beatitudes and completely forgotten the butterfly comb until she made ready to run into town with Bonnie for supplies. The comb had tangled in her wool bonnet. She'd pulled it off and slipped it into her coat pocket.

Tears welled in her eyes. Heinrick had given her a gift of his heritage. To complement her gift to him — his future.

"What are you doing out here, Lillian?" Mrs. Larsen's crisp tone scattered Lilly's thoughts. Mrs. Larsen yanked Lilly inside and shut the door behind her. "What's the matter with you, are you trying to make yourself sick?" The older woman pushed her toward the sanctuary.

Lilly bit the inside of her mouth and tried in vain to conceal her tears. But they spilled out. Mrs. Larsen looked at her, her brow puckered. "Reggie will be fine, dear."

Lilly watched her pinched, soon-to-be mother-in-law join a group of cackling women and suddenly knew only one thing: She couldn't marry Reggie. She couldn't spend the rest of her life living a halfhearted love. She whirled and made for the door.

The door shuddered open just as she laid a hand on the latch. Reggie caught her as she stumbled forward.

"Where're you goin'?"

Her breath left her, and words locked in her mouth.

"You weren't going to wait for me?" Reggie's dark brows folded together. "What's this?" He snatched the comb from her hand. Turning it over, he examined it. His face darkened. "Where did you get this?"

Lilly balled her hands in her coat pockets. He looked at her, read her face. Then gave a sharp intake of breath, as if he'd been stabbed. He stared at her, shaking. "So it's true, then."

Her eyes widened.

"I know all about it, Lilly." His face tightened into a glare. "I know all about how you disgraced me, how you *kissed* another man, a German."

She saw the hate pulsing in his eyes, and her mouth went dry. She shuffled back into the church foyer. *Help me, Lord.*

"No, Reggie. You don't understand —"

Reggie hurled the comb out into the darkness. Then he stepped inside and pulled the door shut. The world seemed suddenly, intensely, still.

Lilly's pulse roared in her ears.

Reggie sucked a deep breath. He spoke quietly, through clenched teeth. "I can't believe you betrayed me with a German! If you were going to be unfaithful, couldn't you have chosen an American?"

Lilly's knees shook. "I'm sorry, Reggie."

Reggie must have detected her fear, for his glower softened, leaving only cool, stony eyes. He backed Lilly into the wall, put a hand over her shoulder, and leaned close. She felt his hot breath on her face and couldn't move. He seemed to be making an effort to keep his voice calm. "Listen, Lilly, I'm willing to marry you anyway. Because you're mine and all I've ever wanted."

She fixed her eyes at the snow melting on his shoes, not wanting to speak the truth. But she owed him honesty. She'd never sent the letter she'd written explaining everything, so he didn't know. Didn't know the painful news about Heinrick, yes, but he also didn't know about the joy and life she'd found. He didn't know that God could change the plans, and everything could still turn out all right, even better, for both of them.

She summoned her courage. "But I don't know if that's what God wants," she said softly.

He took it like a blow and recoiled. "What?"

"I don't know if I am supposed to marry you, Reggie. I don't know if that is what God wants. I, we've, never really asked Him."

Reggie frowned at her. "Of course not! We don't have to ask God whom we're to marry. We just decide what we want, and if we do it right, He blesses us. God doesn't care whom we marry. He just wants us to go to church, to obey His commandments, to do what is right."

"I think He does care. I think He cares so much that if we don't ask Him, it's a sin."

1170

Reggie blew out an exasperated breath. "Lilly, what do you know? I'm the one who is going to be a pastor." He looked at her steadily. "I want you. That's enough for me. Even though you betrayed me. Doesn't that prove my love for you?"

Confusion rocked her. Reggie's love felt constricting, suffocating — so different from Heinrick's.

"I don't need God's blessing to marry you."

Lilly raised wide eyes, thunderstruck. Embedded in Reggie's words, she discovered what was missing from their future, their plans, and her heart. She realized why her soul had never been, could never be, at peace about her marriage to Reggie. She didn't feel God's blessing.

"I . . . I can't marry you right now," Lilly stated in a faltering voice. "I have to wait on God. I have to know what He wants. Because I know He loves me, I want His plans for my life."

Reggie pounded his chest and stared at her, desperation punctuating his voice. "*I'm* His plan for your life!" He raked a hand through his snow-crusted hair. "Maybe Mother was right. I should have picked Marjorie." His expression darkened. "At least she would have been faithful."

Lilly felt a cold fist squeeze her heart.

Reggie's voice turned wretched. "But I chose you. You were the one I wanted. I've been planning this for years." He punched the wall behind her. Lilly trembled. "It isn't fair, Lilly. I've been through hell itself, and I return to find that someone's stolen my girl?"

Reggie's voice curdled in pain. Lilly closed her eyes and felt ill. He was right. This wasn't what he deserved. But they couldn't base their marriage, the rest of their lives, on pity.

"It wasn't like that," Lilly said evenly. She opened her eyes. "Heinrick didn't steal me. But you're right. It isn't fair. Not to you — or me!" She thumped her own chest. "I found something, Reggie. I found God. I found freedom and joy." Her voice slowed. "And maybe that's how God wanted it. Maybe He wanted to give us some distance so we could see He had something better for us. That's how it's supposed to be, I think. His will and not ours, and that's better, even when it doesn't make sense."

Reggie buried his head in his forearm. "This can't be God's will. God wouldn't take you away from me. Don't throw our lives, my life, away."

He drew back and fixed her with a desperate intensity, as if, by his gaze, he could control her bizarre thinking. "Lilly, listen, you belong to me. You don't have a choice."

Lilly put a hand on her chest and pushed back an odd panic. "I do have a choice. You can't force me to love you. If you make me marry you, it still doesn't mean I'll love you.

Love can't be forced or, for that matter, earned. It has to be a free gift. Like God's love for us, and ours for Him."

Reggie looked away. "He doesn't deserve our love."

Lilly winced at his words. She understood all too well. He believed God had let him down in leading him somewhere dark and painful.

"He *does* deserve our love, Reg, because He loved us first. He saved us when we didn't deserve it — still don't! But He loves us anyway. And we have to trust Him. We count on His love and His strength, and we surrender to His will. Because if we don't, I think we can never have peace."

"We get peace by obeying. By doing what we know is right. We don't have to ask; it's all written out for us."

Lilly leaned her head against the wall and sighed.

Reggie looked at her, his eyes narrowing. "I don't know what you think God wants, but I know this, Lilly. If you don't tell me right now you will marry me, then I don't want you."

She gaped at him and saw years of careful planning melt in the heat of his fury.

"I can't say yes," she whispered. "Not until I'm sure we have God's blessing, and right now, I don't know."

Reggie crossed his arms over his chest and

stepped back. His face was granite, and he said nothing.

Lilly muffled a small cry as the reality of her words hit her. She ran past him, threw open the door, and flung herself into the swelling blizzard. Scrambling away from the church, she ran everywhere and nowhere and straight into the blindness and pain of her surrender. Though faint and swallowed by the moan of the wind, Lilly thought she heard a voice trail her. "Lilllyyyy!"

CHAPTER 26

Lilly hugged her body and ducked her head against the snarling wind. Under the coal black sky, Lilly couldn't even discern her feet. She shivered as snow gathered on her neck.

She had no idea how far she'd run. But her feet were numb, and she shivered violently. She felt the fool. She'd plunged not only into the blizzard, but also into a life without Reggie, without the plans of her family or her church.

"What am I doing, Lord?"

The wind roared and spun her. She stumbled, then pitched forward. The snow climbed into her sleeves, layered her chin. She realized over a foot had accumulated. Lost and in the middle of a Dakota blizzard, she felt panic crest over her. "O God, help me!"

Climbing to her feet, she whacked the snow out of her sleeves. She tucked her hands into her pockets, wiggled her chin into her coat, and struggled forward. Her hair felt crusty and the wind whined in her ears. Lilly heaved one foot in front of the other, no longer able to feel the swells and ruts of the prairie landscape.

The bodily struggle felt easier than the war she waged against the angry voices in her head. She fought to filter through them, to hear only one. *What is Your will, Lord?*

If she'd asked earlier and had the courage to listen and obey, maybe she wouldn't be stumbling in the cold darkness.

She could no longer feel her legs. They seemed like sticks, and, at times, she wondered if she were truly moving or merely standing still. She was so tired; she just wanted to close her eyes. Couldn't she just rest a moment? Her ears burned, her hair was frozen, and her head throbbed.

She hit something head-on, and it knocked her on her backside. *Lord, is this it? Will I die because of my impulsiveness?* She rolled to all fours, gritted her teeth, and reached through the darkness. Her hand banged against something solid. She traced it upward and discovered metal at head height. A handle. Sliding her wrist around it, she heaved it open.

The smell of hay and manure had never been so sweet. Lilly crawled inside, feeling the heat of barn animals warm her face and filter through her clothing. She heard the snuffing of hay, the low of a cow. Fumbling forward, she bumped into a bucket of water, tipping it over. The water doused her hands and knees and felt like fire against her skin. Lilly pulled herself to her feet, knees quaking. Her head spun multi-colors. Groaning, she shuffled the length of the barn, clasping the stalls with her stinging hands until she discovered a mound of hay stacked in an empty paddock. Collapsing into it, she clawed out a hole. Then she climbed inside and curled into a ball. She knew she shouldn't sleep, but, oh, how sleep called her name, moving over her slowly, laying like a blanket upon her eyelids.

Lilly blew on her hands. *Thank You, Lord, for this place.* She tucked her legs under her coat. She must stay awake. She recalled stories of victims who had succumbed to sleep and frozen under a mound of crusted snow. Sleep was her enemy.

If she could stay awake, she was safe for the moment. But a much larger storm lurked outside the barn doors. Eventually they would find her, discover what she'd done, how she'd hurt Reggie. Then what? Heinrick was gone. Even if she could somehow find him and declare her love, what kind of life would that be? Outcasts, shunned by her family, her community. Living life as strangers in some foreign town. Lilly shook her head as if to exorcise the images. Besides, was Heinrick God's choice for her?

She kept returning to the lack of the blessing for which her soul seemed to scream. And what had her mother said so long ago? Marriage was too difficult for halfhearted commitment. And something else about missing out on the fullness of joy God had planned for her.

Lilly buried her face in her hands. *Lord, what should I do? What do You want for me?* She closed her eyes and listened, aching to discern an audible voice. But the only things she heard were echoes, impressions from things she'd read, illustrations from Matthew about Jesus, the way He reached out in love, extreme in His pursuing of the people who rejected Him. They clung instead to the law, to an old way that would lead to death, most certainly beyond the grave, but in large part to death in life, also. A death of joy, a death of an exhilarating relationship with Christ.

Reggie was that death. That thought became the one clear beacon in her sleep-fogged mind. Reggie was the law. He clung to a religion that created laws that led to salvation rather than a salvation that led to obedience. It was a stagnant, suffocating, demoralizing religion. And it had been hers as well.

Until Heinrick introduced her to a God who loved her enough to die for her, when she was the most wretched of sinners, then gave her the choice to respond to Him in love. It was the ultimate love affair. Love given, not demanded. Love offered unconditionally.

Suddenly she knew she could never be trapped inside the circle of suffocation again. Better to fling herself out into an unknown dark blizzard and into the arms of her Savior than cling to a life that threatened to choke her.

Even if she could never see Heinrick again, even if he wasn't God's choice for her, she knew she could never return to the law, to Reggie. The resolve deepened with every warming heartbeat.

The straw crunched as she settled deeper into her well. She took a cleansing breath. She'd asked God and listened, and the Almighty had answered clearly.

She would wait for His choice, His blessing. One day at a time, she would surrender to His plans. She would ask, seek, and find. And she would live in the fullness of joy.

The door at the end of the barn rattled, groaned, and then pushed inward. The snow screamed as it entered, rolled around the startled animals, and ushered in a figure wrapped in wool. Lilly bolted upright. Her heart hammered as she peered through the padding of darkness.

The hooded figure raised a massive lead lantern, glowing blue from one of its brilliant orbs. It cast eerie gray shadows off the haystacks and caught the cows wide-eyed. "Lilly?"

Perhaps she was already asleep, and this was a dream. "Heinrick?"

He swung the lamp toward her voice, his feet crunching cold, stiff hay. From his muffler dripped a layer of snowy diamonds, and his eyebrows stuck out in frosty spikes. His blue eyes, however, blazed.

"Over here." Lilly's heart thundered as she fought to believe her eyes.

Heinrick closed the gap in two giant steps. "Oh, thank You, Lord." He set the lantern down, dropped to his knees, and reached out his frosted arms. He pulled her to his chest and tucked her head under his chin. His heart banged in his strong chest, and she felt relief shudder out of him. He held her long enough to betray the depth of his worry.

When he released her, he pulled off his gloves and clutched her face with his icy hands. "Are you all right?" He looked her over, head to toe.

Lilly closed her eyes and nodded.

"*Ja,* but you are freezing!" Heinrick peeled off his coat.

"How did you find me?"

He tucked the coat around her. "By the grace of God, Lilly." He dusted the last snow off the collar and avoided her eyes.

Lilly squinted at him. "I thought you left town. What happened?"

"The train got snowed in." He began to knock down hay. "I was headed toward Fannie's when I saw you run out into the storm." The hay fell in quiet rustles around her. He worked steadily, mutely, and she knew something was amiss. Had he heard her fight with Reggie? Heinrick didn't stay quiet unless he was fighting a battle. Then he was a man of few words and a set jaw.

She watched him build a tiny castle of insulation. The heat from Heinrick's coat was warming her with the effect of a roaring fire. But the fact he'd found her in the middle of a whiteout heated her from the inside out. This had to be her answer, her audible voice. Just like the voice calling through the mists of the battlefield in her dream, Heinrick had searched through a blizzard for her. Loving him would cost her everything, but as she embraced the idea, the fragrance of peace was so intense, she gasped.

Heinrick was God's answer. He'd been trying to tell her for months. From the moment Heinrick had nearly run her over with a mustang, to the day he sent her the note committing her to the Lord, God had written Heinrick on her heart and filled her mind with his voice. Only Heinrick loved her the way God wanted a husband to love — unconditionally, fully, and sacrificially. Only Heinrick pointed her to the Savior.

Heinrick crawled inside his fortress, then

threaded an arm around her and pulled her against his muscled chest. "We'll stay here until the storm breaks. Then I'll take you home."

"I am home." Lilly tilted her head to look at him.

Heinrick considered her, his arched brows like a drift of fine snow. "Lilly, you're cold and confused. I saw you run from the church, and I saw Reggie standing in the door. You had a fight, that's all. Things will look better after the storm blows over."

"I am home, Heinrick," Lilly repeated emphatically. "Home is where God puts you. It's being with those you love. It's where you have peace, remember?"

Heinrick gave her a slow nod.

"I have peace with you. I think *you* are my home."

A rueful grin slid onto Heinrick's face. "But I am the enemy, Lilly. A foreigner."

Lilly put a hand on his cold, whiskered face. "Do you remember your last note? You quoted Ruth, when she made the ultimate act of commitment. Let me finish it for us." Lilly closed her eyes and paraphrased, "Don't urge me to leave you or turn back from you. Your people will be my people, and your God my God."

Heinrick placed his hand over hers. It belonged there. "And you will be blessed because you left your home and traveled to a

1182

foreign land."

"Ya," Lilly said.

Heinrick winced at her terrible German impression. Then, growing serious, his intentions pooled in his eyes for a second time. He ran a finger under her chin; she lifted her face to his and let him kiss her. It was gentle, lingering, and full of promise.

Lilly pulled away, her eyes wide, and saw that his own were dancing. "You do love me."

"*Ja*, my Lilly, I love you." He kissed her again, and she knew she had never loved Reggie like she loved this man.

Suddenly, she pulled away and groaned. "Heinrick, what about my parents? I told Reggie I didn't want to marry him. I told him I had to wait until I knew what God wanted, until I had His blessing. But I can't get married without my parents' blessing, either."

Heinrick caressed her face. "And do you know what God wants? Do you have His blessing?"

"Yes."

His eyes glowed with an unmistakable passion. "Jacob worked fourteen years for the woman he loved, and it seemed to him but a moment for his love for her. I am a patient man. I will wait until I am no longer the enemy."

Then he leaned back, the straw protesting, and nestled her against his chest. She warmed and eventually slept. He held her until the sun rose and chased away the irate wind and kissed the fields with tiny golden sparkles.

"See, the prairie is the ocean," said Lilly as Heinrick helped her through the crested snow.

Heinrick laughed. "I crossed it, my sweet Lilly, to find you."

EPILOGUE

They had planned a Thanksgiving Day wedding, and when Lilly awoke that morning and saw the pink beads of dawn glinting off the snow-blanketed fields in heavenly magnificence, she knew Heinrick was right. Thanksgiving was the perfect day to commit their lives to one another; after all, it was a celebration of God's grace and salvation after a season of struggle. Lilly counted it as a miracle that it had taken only a year for her father to consent to their marriage.

"Are you ready?" Bonnie asked. Lilly glanced at her sister, whose joy was evident in her teenage smile and dancing eyes. Lilly nodded. She cast one last look at the prairie from the window seat in her bedroom. Giant waves of snow, halted in mid-crest, leaped across the fields, the sun's rays glancing off them like a golden mist. It was glorious, the aftermath of a Dakotan blizzard. The contrast between the fury and the calm never ceased to amaze her, just like peace that filled her heart after a difficult surrender.

Lilly felt a warm hand on her shoulder. She turned, and her mother's gentle eyes were on her. "He's waiting," she said softly, a smile tugging at her lips.

Lilly stood, brushed off her slip, and stepped into the wedding gown her sister held. A twinge of regret stabbed her; she wished Marjorie were here. But her friend's wounds were deep, and Lilly knew healing would be long in coming. Lilly's prayers for Marjorie were constant, as were her prayers for Reggie. She hadn't seen him since the night of the fateful blizzard a year ago and heard he'd left to find his fortune in the Black Hills gold mines. It hurt her to know she'd caused his flight, and she prayed he would find peace, as would her sister Olive. Olive continued to live in the shadow of grief, crawling through each day without words or hope. Although her sister's form was present downstairs, her spirit was still locked inside a prison of despair. Lilly knew only Christ held the keys to her freedom.

Bonnie buttoned up the dress in back while Lilly fiddled with the veil.

"You're beautiful," her mother said, and Lilly caught a glistening in her eye. "I'm so glad you waited for the Lord's choice."

Lilly nodded and bit her lip to keep her own eyes from filling.

Her sister and mother left her alone, then,

to sort out her last moments. Lilly listened to shuffling below, then the sound of Willard, plunking out a hymn on the piano. The stairs creaked, and Lilly recognized the footfalls of her father. She pulled a calming breath and felt a wave of peace fill her just as a rap sounded on the door.

Lilly opened the door. Her father looked dapper in a black woolen suit. A smile creased his face, but tears in his eyes choked his voice. "This would be more difficult if Heinrick wasn't such a good man."

His words left her speechless, so she wound her arm through his and nodded.

Her father patted her hand and escorted her down the stairs. The parlor overflowed with guests, a smaller crowd than would have been at the church, but even so, a solid, well-wishing crew. At the end of the room, next to the fireplace, which glowed, waited Heinrick. He appeared every inch the hero she knew him to be. His blond hair was clipped short, but the curly locks refused to lie flat. She noticed his clean-shaven chin and the outline of thick muscles over his tailored navy blue suit. His job as brakeman on the Milwaukee Road and part-time hand on the Clark farm kept him in good shape and had cultivated in him an aura of confidence. He'd become a man who made others feel safe and comfortable.

Lilly's heart fluttered as Heinrick's blue

eyes locked on hers. Then his mouth gaped in an open smile, and written on his face was a tangible delight. She wanted to sing. He was a hard man to unsettle, but obviously the sight of his bride had unraveled his stalwart composure. She floated toward Heinrick and the new preacher from Java, noting the happiness glinting in her mother's eyes and others who thought, a year earlier, Heinrick was the enemy.

Even Erica Torgesen was radiant, grinning uncontrollably in her new sky blue wool suit. Lilly slid her hand into Heinrick's gentle grip and felt embraced by the love shimmering in his eyes. In a trembling voice, Heinrick pledged to love and care for her as long as they lived. Then, he cradled her face between his wide hands and kissed her. At that moment, Lilly knew she would be forever thankful to God for bringing the enemy into her midst.

Rose gold sunshine flooded the room as they marched down the aisle. And, as Lilly glanced up at her young, handsome husband, she knew, one step at a time, she was walking in the fullness of joy.

ABOUT THE AUTHORS

Mary Davis is a full-time fiction writer who enjoys going into schools and talking to kids about writing. Mary lives near Colorado's Rocky Mountains with her husband, three children, and six pets.

Kelly Eileen Hake received her first writing contract at the tender age of seventeen and arranged to wait three months until she was able to legally sign it. Writing for Barbour combines two of Kelly's great loves — history and reading. A CBA bestselling author and member of American Christian Fiction Writers, she's been privileged to earn numerous Heartsong Presents Reader's Choice Awards and is known for her witty, heartwarming historical romances. A newlywed, she and her gourmet-chef husband live in Southern California with their golden lab mix, Midas!

Tracie Peterson, bestselling, award-winning

author of over ninety fiction titles and three non-fiction books, lives and writes in Belgrade, Montana. As a Christian, wife, mother, writer, editor, and speaker (in that order), Tracie finds her slate quite full. Published in magazines and Sunday school take home papers, as well as a columnist for a Christian newspaper, Tracie now focuses her attention on novels.

Jill Stengl was born and raised in Southern California, the youngest of four children. She met her husband, Dean, in 1982 at Green Oak Ranch children's camp, where she was a counselor and he was a lifeguard. Dean and Jill married the next summer. Dean was an air force pilot for fifteen years, so Jill traveled with him all over the country and to England, having children at various military bases. Now Dean is out of the military and working as a commercial pilot, so the family has settled in Wisconsin. Her greatest hope is that her readers will learn to love God and their spouses more because of reading her romantic books.

Susan May Warren, former missionary to Russia, lives in Minnesota with her husband and four children. She is a bestselling, award-winning author who loves to share her craft with other authors.

The employees of Thorndike Press hope you have enjoyed this Large Print book. All our Thorndike, Wheeler, and Kennebec Large Print titles are designed for easy reading, and all our books are made to last. Other Thorndike Press Large Print books are available at your library, through selected bookstores, or directly from us.

For information about titles, please call:
(800) 223-1244

or visit our website at:
gale.com/thorndike

To share your comments, please write:

Publisher
Thorndike Press
10 Water St., Suite 310
Waterville, ME 04901